TABBY SWAIN

a Monster-Boy Bromance

SITHIA QUEEN

BLADENBORO

BEAST BOOKS

BBB

Bladenboro Beast Books
504 Emily Drive #1007
Clarksburg, WV 26301
United States
https://bladenborobeastbooks.com

First paperback edition March 2024

ISBN 9781962462006 (hardback)
ISBN 9781962462013 (paperback)
ISBN 9781962462020 (ebook)

Library of Congress Control Number: 2023916577

Book design by Asya Blue Design
Illustrations by Daniel Mendes Matui

WARNING

The following novel is intended for mature audiences.

Reader discretion is advised.

For a list of content warnings, visit https://sithiaqueen.com.

To all the lonely people.

CHAPTER 1

Birds of a Feather

Matthew

A cracked sidewalk stretches ahead of me, lit by the early morning sun and the mocking glow of the waxing gibbous moon; I grimace and focus on the upcoming intersection. Walking languidly on my left, Mark yawns, baring razor-sharp teeth and a split tongue he passes as major body modifications to the world at large; after four long seconds, his teeth clamp together into a wicked grin that means he's thought of something stupid to talk about on the short walk to school. "Hey, Matthew."

"What?" I adjust my baseball cap as we walk out of the shade.

Mark steps up to the traffic signal at the corner and presses the crosswalk button; under the bright morning sun, his deep-red hair matches the shade of a cherry. He turns around, all smiles, but the scar etched across the left side of his face steals my attention; his chin-length hair fails to hide the five pale lines running from his upper lip, over his eye, and into his hairline.

I stare instead at the purple frames hanging from the collar of his shirt. Last year, his astigmatism got bad enough that his mom bought him some reading glasses, though he rarely uses them. I know he inherited it from his dad, but I often worry the injury made it worse.

Mark notices my sour mood and returns to my left side. "Okay, so, I was staying up late again last night, thinking about stuff, you know how it is, and I gotta ask, if you could marry any monster girl, what kind would you pick?"

"Hmm . . ." I let my mind wander until someone special comes to mind; before I can run off fantasizing, a robotic voice notifies us that we can "safely" cross the road—the reckless drivers around north Raleigh beg to differ. As we walk across the faded crosswalk, I say, "I'd honestly marry a human."

"*Boring~*" Mark draws it out as long as humanly possible, and as soon as we hit the sidewalk, he says, "C'mon, bro! Give a real answer!"

I roll my eyes but try to give the question some serious thought; I'm not picky, but there has to be something that suits her best. "*Fine*. I'd marry a dog girl."

"Just a dog? Not a wolf?"

"Mm-hmm. Wolves are too intense."

Mark glances up, holding his hands behind his head, and another grin splits his lips; he looks at me out of the corner of his yellow eyes, his vertical slit pupils mere lines in the intense sunlight. "Got a breed in mind? A Lab, maybe?"

I scowl; he definitely knows who I was thinking about. After he grins forever, I sigh and ask, "What about you?"

"Oh, I thought you'd never ask~" He crosses his arms in front of his chest. "You know, I've been thinking about bunny girls lately."

"Bunny girls? Really?" We turn the corner onto the shaded street of our school, easing the sun out of our eyes.

"Mm-hmm~" Mark sighs dreamily, cupping his cheeks in his hands. "They have adorable ears . . . a cute little tail . . . and their fur would be so fluffy . . ." Suddenly, he frowns. "The only hard negative is no paw pads."

I roll my eyes. "Of course you'd miss the paw pads."

Mark drops his arms. "Can you blame me?!"

"I think you have an obsession."

"I do not!"

I lift an eyebrow.

Mark huffs. "You wouldn't get it, bro."

"I think I get it on a personal level. Uncomfortably so."

Mark opens his big mouth to retort, but shuts up when he notices we've reached the end of the street; along the curb, a long car pool line parades into the packed parking lot of our school. Many of the cars are decorated with washable paints on their rear windshields and side windows celebrating the start of their senior's final year. Mark sighs as we join the leagues of students on their way to the front entrance.

I remove my baseball cap. "Is my hair okay?" I tilt my head in Mark's direction.

Mark gazes at the top of my head and gives me a thumbs-up with an absolutely unnecessary wink. "You're good, bro." Then he slings an arm around my shoulders. "Excited for your first day of sophomore year? I'm sure you can't wait for first-period gym class."

"Rub it in, why don't you." I shuffle toward the staircase, dragging Mark along with me. Unlike him, I decided to wait the only year I could to take the one required gym course in our high school curriculum.

Mark lets go of me as we walk up the steps that curve up to the front entrance of Gibson High School; we walk inside, and all it takes is a left turn down the first hall for us to part. Before he goes up to the second floor, Mark turns around and pats my shoulder. "Don't worry too much about the locker room; most guys are too busy talking about their own dicks to pay any attention to you."

I glance aside with a small smile. "Thanks, Mark. See you at lunch?"

He grins again. "You know it!" Then he dashes up the stairs.

I turn away from the staircase and head down two long hallways until I reach a wider hall with two gyms on the left and a small courtyard on the right; between the gyms is a double door that leads down to the locker rooms. I adjust my book bag's straps over my shoulders, take a deep breath, and walk down the long flight of stairs to the basement floor; at the bottom, I turn left, pass the outdoor exits, and lean against the wall next to the boys' locker room. A couple of guys chat about football in front of the door, while another guy, tall with long, wavy black hair, stands about two yards off to the side. Not knowing how long we'll have to wait, I take my book bag off and lay it at my feet.

Within a minute, a PE teacher comes by and unlocks the door for us, effectively wasting my effort to relieve my back. I sigh internally and heft my book bag back onto my shoulder.

The tall guy slips in behind the other guys, followed shortly by me; the tall guy disappears behind the rows of lockers, while the other three stay to change in the front. I follow in the tall guy's footsteps and find a blessed corner where I can quickly change into my gym clothes without any peering eyes on my back. With the locker room as empty as it is, I avoid giving myself a heart attack, but that'll change at the end of the period.

Unnerved, I wait in front of a rusty locker as more and more boys file into the room; fortunately, no one comes to change within sight. The din of the boys' locker room increases in volume with every passing moment, and I take a few minutes to look over my schedule for the day again. Once I've stared at the paper long enough, I put it away and stuff my book bag into the long-neglected locker; our teacher calls us out of the room, and I slam the locker door shut.

I stand with my class in an uncoordinated row in front of our teacher; another cluster of students stands on the other side of the gym with a different teacher, whom we'll have to share the limited space with. Like a lot of schools in the area, there are far too many students and not enough seats to accommodate them, so they've had to squeeze as many kids as they can into one block of time. Our teacher, a surprisingly muscular man, though not particularly tall, calls out roll. I make a poor attempt to pay some amount of attention, but my mind drifts as soon as he reaches *C*.

"Matthew Stroud?"

I raise my hand up to my chest. "Here."

"Rebecca Turnpike?"

A girl with fluffy auburn hair raises her hand.

"Andrew Vance?"

A blond boy wearing expensive athletic clothes says, "Here."

"John Woodcock?"

The tall guy that disappeared into the locker room earlier raises his hand with a suave "Here." Despite the unfortunate last name, John looks like the epitome of tall, dark, and handsome. Standing around six feet, he has a chiseled face, dark-brown eyes, a tan complexion, and that long black hair pooling just past his shoulders; if not for his grumpy expression, I imagine girls would fawn all over him.

Roll call ends and both teachers lead us through a set of warm-ups, which I perform easily enough without being spectacular; my stamina is better than Mark's, but my personal exercising activities start and end with walking to and from school. After completing the warm-ups, the teachers inform us that we'll be running the mile.

Everyone in the room groans; sapped of what meager energy we had, both classes file outside and walk together down a stretch of sidewalk to the track.

I carefully drag behind to the back of the pack of students until I'm near John; he shuffles along, squinting against the sun, but there's something rigid about his gait. Before I can get a better read on him, the teachers open the rusty gate at the end of the path; they line us up and tell us how many laps we need to run and the expected time we're supposed to take. There are always a few guys who can run the whole thing in as little as five minutes—and those who walk it all and take more like twenty. I'll be going for a time between the extremes: fast enough to get it over with but not so slow I embarrass myself.

Our teacher blows his whistle, and we start running. I settle into the second innermost track and pace myself for the jog ahead, only to finish my first lap so fast I get a cramp in my side; I slow down and catch my breath for the next. A light breeze cooling my face, I round the bend in the track for the third time.

Not too far ahead, John bounds down the straight, his loose gray shirt flapping in tandem with his footfalls; when he makes an abrupt sidestep around a group of three walking girls, the hem catches on something black and fuzzy.

Curious, I pick up my pace until I'm close enough to make it out but far enough he doesn't notice me; my stomach drops the moment I realize what it is.

In a normal world, John would have a tattoo or a large birthmark too embarrassing to reveal, but instead, he has something far worse: peeking out directly above the waistband of his shorts and conveniently holding his shirt up like a hook is a small, furry tail—a bunny tail. And John has no clue that anyone behind him can see it clear as day.

Without a second thought, I charge up, slap him on the back, and shout, "Watch your tail!"

John immediately startles and looks at me with a pale face. He thrusts his hands over his twitching tail, hastily pulls his shirt up and over the appendage, then speeds up, his long legs easily carrying him beyond a pace I could match. As he runs farther and farther away, I study his long hair again: It's let down except for a small ponytail near the nape of his neck, right above where I imagine he's hiding the bulk of his bunny ears; it must be a pain in the ass to keep his hair that long just to hide them.

John stays far away from me for the rest of our gym class, but I don't take any offense; I know better than anyone how scared I'd be if someone knew my secret.

As soon as we're released into the locker rooms at the end of class, I disappear into the little corner that none of the other guys managed to find earlier.

Just as I grab the hem of my shirt, John throws his book bag on the ground in front of me and collapses onto the bench; he grips his knees hard, unable to meet my gaze. "Hey, um . . ." His voice warbles at an impossibly high pitch.

"Matthew."

"Uh, okay, um . . ." He screws his eyes shut and whispers, "Please don't tell anyone what you saw!" Tears threaten to fall.

I almost smile because I know exactly where he's coming from. "I'd never tell anyone"—I take off my shirt—"because we're not so different."

John looks at my bare upper body and sucks in a breath; the fear leaves him, and he stares at his white-knuckled hands.

I calmly put my casual T-shirt on, covering the cat tail wrapped around my torso.

We sit there silently, the rest of the guys in the room talking and laughing loudly at jokes we can't make out.

I pull my book bag out of the locker and stuff my gym clothes inside. "Hey, John."

He turns his head, wide-eyed.

"What lunch do you have?"

John looks away and wipes his hands on his jeans. "Um, *A*, I think."

"Do you pack a lunch?"

He shakes his head, inadvertently pulling more hair over his shoulders. "I eat in the cafeteria."

That makes things complicated, but—

The bell rings, and John jumps to his feet.

Before he can dart away, I yell, "Look for a guy with red hair when you go to lunch; you can't miss him."

I catch his eye for a fleeting moment; with a silent acknowledgement, he escapes around the corner.

CHAPTER 2

Getting to Know You

John

A long line stretches out ahead of me, student after student slowly working through the cafeteria line to fill their foam trays and pay before finding an open seat in the overpacked room. As I shuffle forward, I scan the cafeteria for Matthew and his friend, only to come up short; natural redheads are rare enough to begin with, and the few I spot aren't next to a short boy with curly brown hair. I hope I didn't mishear him.

After losing a few minutes to my fruitless search, I finally reach the beginning of the cafeteria line and divert my attention to gathering my subpar lunch for the day. When I get to the cash register, I pay the lunch lady for the food and go back to looking around. Since they weren't in view earlier, I assume that Matthew and his friend must be sitting in the half of the room past the cafeteria line. The moment I turn my head to the right, I spot a skinny guy with dyed red hair next to Matthew in the corner of the room.

I stride as confidently as I can over to their table, though I'm nervous about talking to two people I barely know, especially after one of them saw my tail. Hoping to call as little attention to myself as possible, I sit down across the table from Matthew.

The moment my tray hits the table, Matthew's lively conversation with his friend grinds to a halt. "Hey, you came." He smiles gently.

Matthew's friend evaluates me with a cool gaze. "So this is the one you were telling me about?" He rests his right cheek in his palm, his elbow on the table. "Should've known it was gonna be a guy."

"What's that supposed to mean?" Why would this guy think I could be a girl? It's not like my name is unisex, and I don't look nearly as androgynous as I used to.

"Ah, sorry; ignore him." Matthew holds up his hand. "He was fantasizing about bunny girls this morning, so I thought I'd mess with him by omitting that little detail."

His friend sighs. "I'm beginning to think monster girls don't exist at this point. Five years later and we've only met one other guy."

I'm missing a ton of context, but I try not to let my confusion get the best of me. "So you guys already came up with terms for this stuff?"

Matthew's friend raises one red eyebrow. "And you didn't?"

I shake my head, embarrassed I never thought that far over the past two years.

Matthew furrows his brow. "We can catch you up on all that later; anyway, you should introduce yourselves."

"Oh, right!" Matthew's friend grins, revealing a gnarly set of serrated teeth. "My name's Mark. Nice to meet you."

"I'm John," I say, "and likewise."

We stare at each other awkwardly; completely at a loss of where to take the conversation, I scrutinize Mark. He has an awfully boyish face, an asymmetrical bob hairstyle that's cropped on the right and down to his chin on the left, pointed ears, and . . . there's a striking, scratch-like scar on his face, so pale against his lightly tanned skin that it must be years old. The scar runs through his left eyebrow and eye, leaving noticeable gaps where hair no longer grows in the scar tissue—he's even missing a few red eyelashes. It's not unheard of for someone to dye their eyebrows, but the eyelashes are a bit much.

"Mark, right?" I say.

"Yeah?"

"Your hair is natural, isn't it?"

Mark grins again. "Yep. Pretty cool, huh?"

I smile. "Beats having to redye your hair all the time." One of my sisters gets hers done every two months without fail.

Mark leans over the table and whispers, "It only sucks when people start wondering why my roots never show."

"That makes me glad my hair stayed black."

"Sometimes I wish my hair stayed black. And the eyes are a whole 'nother story." Mark pulls a grape out of his lunch box and pops it in his mouth. "So are you from around here? I'm surprised we never noticed you before."

I rub the back of my neck. "We must have gone to different middle schools. Pretty much everyone from mine went to Workbourne High, not Gibson."

Mark grabs another grape. "The school districts are weird like that. I'm guessing you're from Workbourne Middle?"

I nod. Given Mark's inadvertent reminder, I pick up and take a bite out of my unfortunately whole-grain chicken sandwich.

Matthew says, "We went to Barrett. Almost everyone from there gets tracked here."

"It kinda sucks since my only friend doesn't go here." I take another bite. "He's actually like us, so I hope he's okay without me."

Mark gapes. "Whoa, really? What is he?"

"A bear. Funnily enough, everyone calls him Teddy."

"That *is* pretty funny." Mark nudges Matthew with his elbow. "Isn't it, Matthew? Or should I say . . . Tabby~"

Matthew frowns so deep I'm afraid he might growl. "Are you ever going to shut up about that?!" He bares his teeth, his long, sharp canines poking out over his lower lip.

"I'm guessing there's a story behind that one, huh?" I say.

"Please don't ask." Matthew slumps into his seat.

"Please do ask. I love telling people things." Mark grins.

"I can tell." I decide to save Matthew the trouble of a likely embarrassing story, especially after he did me such a big favor during gym class, and instead home in on Mark's scar; furrowing my brow, I think carefully about my next words, but my curiosity trumps my general politeness. "I'm sorry if it's rude to ask, but how did you get that scar?" I gesture toward the left side of his face, careful not to point at him.

Matthew's annoyance morphs into unease, but Mark's languid smile steals my attention; he pulls out two gold hair clips and slides them in his hair, showing off the entirety of his scar. It spans the upper left quarter of his face, trailing down from his temple all the way to his upper lip: the line farthest to my left curves down from the middle of his forehead all the way to the edge of his left nostril; the second line from the left curves down from the edge of his hairline, meeting the end of the farthest left; the middle line passes straight through the center of his snakelike eye; and the two on the farthest right curve down together from his temple and over his cheek. The lines span wide apart on his forehead and grow close together at the region of his cheek directly left of his nose, and all but the farthest to my left curve to the right on his face;

it looks like a giant cat scratch, but I doubt he would've survived with such a clean scar if he actually got mauled by an animal.

"I was wondering when you'd ask." Mark flourishes his hand. "It all started a few years ago, when I went on a missionary trip to Africa, and in my childish curiosity, I wandered off into—"

"Don't bother asking Mark where he got that crazy scar. He tells a different story every time." A bottom-heavy girl wearing a dirty-blond ponytail drops her hands on Matthew's shoulders.

He flinches, his pupils blown out into huge circles.

The girl grins, scanning me with light-brown eyes devoid of makeup. "And who's the new guy, anyway?"

"Emily . . ." Mark pouts, drooping as he removes his hair clips. "You're no fun."

Emily rests her forearms over Matthew's shoulders and presses her small chest against the back of his head. "Somebody has to protect the innocent minds of your victims! You always make those stories of yours needlessly gory."

"C'mon, you don't want to hear about my missionary trip to Africa? I was going to fight a lion this time."

"I think the story about the jaguar in the Amazon rainforest, the puma in the Grand Canyon, and the tiger in India are good enough."

"I guess I should've known better than to ask something so personal." I rub the back of my neck.

Emily fans the air. "Don't feel too bad! This idiot actually wants people to ask with how detailed his stories get. You plan them in advance, don't you, Mark?"

"Nah, nah, nah. It's all improv, for real."

Emily puts one hand on her hip. "I seriously doubt that."

Mark opens his mouth, one finger pointed in the air, and—

"Emily . . ." Matthew taps her hand with his fingertips. "Sorry we forgot to tell you our change of plans before lunch started."

Emily smiles. "It's no big deal; we barely started eating together before school ended, anyway." She rubs Matthew's shoulder absently, then perks up. "Oh, I should introduce myself! My name's Emily, and I've been friends with these knuckleheads since the beginning of the year. And you are?"

"John." I'm unsure how to approach this girl; how much does she know? "I met Matthew this morning."

"Oh, really?" Emily's eyebrows lift. "Mister doom and gloom is the befriender?"

"C'mon, Emily." Matthew pouts. "I'm not that bad."

"You do have some major RBF." Mark nudges him with his shoulder.

Matthew mutters, "God . . ."

Since I'm basically out of this equation, I try to finish the food I have left on my tray; the taste of whole-grain wheat and overbaked chicken never gets any better.

"Anyway, do you think you'll be online tonight?" Matthew glances at Emily.

She brings a finger next to her lips in mock thought. "I might be able to figure something out; it *is* only the first day of school. I'll text you if I decide to get on."

"Cool."

Emily lounges against Matthew with a grave expression on her face, like she's contemplating something difficult.

Each additional second of contact adds a darker shade of pink to Matthew's pale cheeks.

After the beat of silence lingers too long, Emily says, "I think I'll leave you three to your guy talk or whatever." She extracts herself from Matthew's back and waves. "Bye, guys! Bye, John!"

I'm surprised she bothered to address me. "Bye."

"Bye, Emily." Matthew hardly looks over his shoulder.

"Bye!" Mark says.

Emily waltzes off as if she never came.

Matthew sighs heavily.

Mark thrusts his right arm over Matthew's shoulders. "Emily's gotten really touchy with you, huh?"

"C'mon, lay off." The beginnings of a purr drift from Matthew's direction, but it's gone as soon as he clears his throat. He puts his face in his hands. "It's so hard not to mess up around her."

"So she doesn't know?" I say.

Matthew drags his fingers over his eyes, exaggerating a groan. "No, and I'd like to keep it that way."

"There, there." Mark rubs Matthew's shoulder.

Matthew closes his eyes and huffs out a long, shaky breath, then nudges Mark's hand off.

Smiling fondly, Mark shakes his head and looks at his phone. "Goodness, where has the time gone!" he exclaims in a silly posh accent, then looks at me. "Sorry about that interruption back there. So much for telling you about my scar!" He pretends to be upset about it.

"It's fine, really," I say.

Mark waves me off. "You're so polite, dude. Relax . . . Anyway, you got a phone? We should trade numbers."

"Oh, sure." I fumble around in my jeans pocket and pull out my ancient smartphone; I unlock it, create a new contact, and pass it over to Mark.

He types in his information, presumably creates another new contact, and passes it to Matthew.

His pupils contract into wide slits as his eyes adjust to the bright light of the screen; he records his information and promptly returns it to me.

Mark says, "The bell's gonna ring in, like, one second, so—"

A shrill ring echoes around the room, though it's not as sharp with my ears folded down over my head.

"Ah! Just text us and we'll know it's you. We don't have many friends!" He rushes off to his next class.

Matthew lingers, smiling fondly; after he blinks, his pupils dilate back to a round shape. "Sorry. Mark can be a bit much, but he means well."

"That's alright. I think he's interesting," I say.

Matthew chuckles. "That's one way to put it! Anyway . . ." He gets up, knocking his knuckles against the table. "Thanks for coming by. It's not every day we meet other people like us."

"Yeah, no problem."

"See you at gym tomorrow."

"See you."

He slips into the waves of students filing out of the cafeteria.

I get up and put my empty tray where it belongs.

A dull basketball bounces off the rim of the hoop on the far side of the gym. Matthew grumbles as he jogs over to the ball, grabbing it before it can hit the girls playing tetherball in the corner. He turns around and tosses it toward me.

The ball bounces twice before I scoop it into my arms and make another shot; it bounces off the backboard and ricochets off the rim, landing on the shiny gym floor. With a bored huff, I pick the ball up before it rolls against the bleachers.

Matthew and I keep shooting hoops, sighing and grumbling our frustrations, but all I can think about is Mark's scar. It's only been one day, yet I'm positive I know the answer to his poorly veiled riddle: a cat boy plus a guy who tells tall tales about fighting big cats plus a five-line scar that looks suspiciously like it was made by a human hand tipped with claws can only equal one truth. The only question remaining is why.

Matthew, huffing from the constant back and forth chasing after the wayward basketball, prepares to throw the ball my way once again. He supports it with his right hand—his dominant hand—and, putting the perfect amount of power behind it, tosses it toward me.

I catch it effortlessly, thinking it's not my business to ask Matthew about Mark's scar, and shoot the ball in one fluid motion; it hits the backboard and lands on the rim, rolls around like a dirty tease, and drops into the hoop. The resounding thump of leather on wood seals my decision.

As soon as I retrieve the ball, our teacher blows his whistle and tells us to gather our things and head to the locker room. I throw the basketball into the overloaded storage box and follow Matthew downstairs to the boys' locker room. Once we get to our little corner, we change as fast as humanly possible, Matthew outpacing me as usual; he can't simply turn his back to the wall like I could if someone walked by.

Dressed in the usual jeans and T-shirt, I sit down next to him and say, "Matthew."

Eyes closed and hunched over, he hums his acknowledgment.

My heart beats a little faster. "Can I . . . ask you something personal?"

He opens his eyes and stares at the book bag at his feet. "Sure. Go ahead."

"Mark's scar . . . Did you . . . ?" I already feel stupid for opening my mouth.

Matthew furrows his brow and parts his lips, staring at his hands lying limp between his legs. He turns his right hand palm up, clenches his fist and unclenches it. He ponders his palm like it's an alien thing infecting his skin. "I was hoping you wouldn't ask."

I swallow. "I'm so—"

"But it must be obvious to you." He covers his face, and without a sound, wipes his fingers over his eyes and down his cheeks, lifting his chin up toward the locker in front of him. After a deep breath, he steals a glance. "There's a stone bench right outside the door near Student Services. Meet me there during lunch. I'll wait." The bell rings; he grabs his things and disappears around the corner.

Guilt gnawing at my chest, I sling my book bag over my shoulder and leave the room.

CHAPTER 3

Fight or Flight

Matthew

The sun warms my back, and part of me wants to take off my shirt and bask in its rays on the grass of the steep hill in front of me—to stretch out and dig my claws into the dirt—but I remain seated on a hot stone bench made bearable by the cloth of my cargo shorts, the moderate shade from the brim of my baseball cap shielding my eyes from the bright light of day. I bring a sandwich to my lips, a mixture of white bread, salami, and Gouda coating my rough tongue. I chew and swallow and take another bite. I expect John will be a few minutes, considering he gets his lunch from the cafeteria, and I wouldn't want him skipping a meal over a shitty story of mine.

I don't want to talk about it, but neither do I want his imagination to take him places that are far worse than the truth. What happened between me and Mark isn't that big a deal, yet I feel terrible every time I see the consequences of my actions. I ruminate on the pit in my stomach, finishing off my sandwich and starting on a small bag of cheese crackers; it's not the healthiest thing in the world, but food that I can prepare fast is food I prefer.

About halfway through my crackers, John sits next to me; he holds a foam tray full of slop and uses his free hand to lay his book bag on the ground next to the bench. John stares at his tray for a moment, then glances at me with normal, human eyes. "You don't have to tell me if you don't want to."

I squint up at the sky; soft cotton clouds float over the moon. I eat another cracker, the taste of sharp cheddar clouding my misgivings. "I've never been able to tell someone before. Mark knows, of course; his mom, too, but not from me."

"So I'll be the first."

"Yeah." I look into my bag of crackers; it's nearly empty. "It's not a story I can tell to someone who doesn't know. I'm not the best at telling stories anyway. It might be all over the place, but . . ." I glance at John. "Do you still want to hear it?"

"I've got time." He picks up a sad excuse for a soft taco and bites into it with perfectly human teeth.

I finish my last cracker, crumple up the bag, and put it aside for disposal. I breathe in the late summer air and remember a day almost five years ago.

It was a cool, fall day in October, but as the morning dragged on into afternoon, I started to feel warm, almost hot, and eventually, my fingertips began to burn. It was uncomfortable and painful, and somewhere deep within my young mind I knew it was something so bad no one could know about it. Right before recess, I noticed that my nails were unusually long and growing sharper, so I shoved my hands into my jacket pockets and started counting the seconds.

When class finally ended, I filed outside with the rest of the class, and once I thought I had my chance, I drifted away from the playground. There was a grassy hill covered in wild garlic and clover, and toward the bottom was a rickety white bridge that led into the woods. We were constantly reminded not to cross that bridge, so I thought it was the best place I could go to hide from my teachers and classmates. I stumbled down that hill, the mounting pain in my extremities clouding my situational awareness.

Panting, I crossed the old bridge and limped into the forest; I was terrified, and wondered if there might be big, scary animals inside, but that fear wasn't enough to stop me in my path. It was eerily quiet; I could hear every excruciating crunch of the fallen leaves I treaded over. The scalding heat in my feet only got worse with each step, but I didn't want to stop until I was sure I was safe; eventually, I came across a large oak and collapsed.

Shivering and sick, I kicked off my oddly uncomfortable shoes and unzipped my jacket, though I couldn't muster the strength to take it off. Suddenly, a wave of pins and needles invaded my arms, legs, ears, and spine, and I dug my claws into the tree trunk like it was some fucked-up scratching post. Within seconds, my arm and leg hair grew into a thick layer of striped brown fur, and a long tail burst out of my lower back, contorting painfully at awkward angles under my shirt—all the while my ears shifted to the top of my head, leaving an aching headache in their wake. That first transformation was so bad I nearly passed out.

My mind numb and limbs sore, I wondered what had happened to me. My worst thought was that I'd become a hideous monster fit for the big screen, like in the slasher movies Dad loved to watch; I sobbed hysterically, convinced I was doomed to kill and eat people.

Ashamed and hurt and confused, I tried to softly bite my lip to stifle my wailing, only to accidentally cut it with an insanely sharp canine tooth. I flinched and opened my eyes, witnessing the damage to my body; I couldn't recognize my own hand, and was too afraid to look at anything else. I stared at my alien hand with webbing stretched between each digit. I counted the fingers and the thumb: four and one, each the right shape and length, but where there should've been skin and nails was fur and claws. Hooked claws, pale and sharp, sliding out from the tips of my fingers into the rough bark of the tree. Cat claws.

I dared not move. I thought it wasn't real. It couldn't be real. I was dreaming. I got really sick overnight and dreamed the whole thing up, and once the nightmare was over, I'd wake up in the morning with a high fever and a bad headache and horrible chills, and there wouldn't be webbing between my fingers or fur all over my arms and legs or claws digging into the bark or tail bent awkwardly under my shirt or cat ears plastered against my skull.

But a branch snapped behind me.

I whipped my head around, my whole body turning along with me, and scrambled back against the tree, digging my claws in near the roots.

A scrawny kid stood near me, his brown eyes blown wide and face scrunched up in a twisted expression of pure horror. He stared at me, eyes flicking over my entire body, and held his arms up near his chest; I was surprised he didn't scream. After many agonizing seconds, he said, "M-Matthew . . . ," and stepped closer to me, the crunch of the leaves under his shoes muffled.

I trembled, the heat of change having long left me, and gripped the tree desperately. "N-No . . . Go away . . ." I growled softly, my tail puffing up against my will.

Mark stepped closer. "Wait, I can help you."

I screwed my eyes shut and shook my head, trying in vain to make him go away. "Please, leave me alone . . ."

He kept creeping closer.

My breathing became ragged, my overworked brain scrambling to find an escape. I felt trapped: there was a tree against my back and Mark closing in; I was exhausted and sore and burning and he kept getting closer and I was afraid and I was scared; I was terrified he would hurt me, chain me up and turn me into a circus freak, and—

He got too close. He reached out his hand and kept saying things I couldn't hear and caging me in. So I scratched him. I threw out my fucked-up hand and swiped his face, leaving five bloody streaks from his forehead down to his cheek.

Mark wailed and clutched his face with his left hand. Tears gathered in his uncovered eye, but he put his right hand on my shoulder anyway.

I stared at the blood glistening between his fingers, felt the remains of his skin under my claws, and watched Mark point at the hand over his left eye. It was red, but not from blood.

"I'm like you!" His hands, both of them, were covered in smooth red scales and adorned with freakishly long, curved black claws. His dark-brown eyes had turned yellow. And despite what I'd done, I had the gall to feel relieved I wasn't alone.

"Anyway," I say, "that's how Mark got his scar. I still feel awful about it even though I know I was young and it was pretty dumb of him to approach me while I was so scared, but you know what he always says whenever I try to apologize about it?"

"What's that?" John asks.

I manage to smile. "He always says, 'Chicks dig scars.' Pretty stupid, right?"

John leans forward, having long placed his empty tray aside. "I can't say I'm surprised. He seems proud of it."

I bring a knee up to my chest and wrap my arms around it. "I just wish I could get over it. I feel awful every time I see it."

John looks at his hands clasped in his lap. "I can't say I understand it perfectly, but . . ." He gazes at the sparse clouds in the sky, memories in his eyes. "I have a lot of sisters, and we don't always get along. My little sister especially. We share a room, so there're more opportunities to fight. We get along fine now, but we were at each other's throats when we were little; I got so fed up with her once that I slapped her clean across the face. Left a big red handprint and everything. I didn't hold back at all, not that I understood how to when we were seven.

"She bawled her eyes out and my parents got so angry at me. I'm the only son, so they like to be especially hard on me sometimes, but I really was in the wrong back then. I told myself I'd never hit any of my sisters again. I was younger than you were, but I still feel bad about it from time to time. Jenny—that's my little sister—sometimes she'll bring it up just to guilt me into doing something, though it doesn't work most of the time because I have my own ammo against her and the rest of my sisters."

"You were both seven?"

"We're twins. I'm older by, like, eight minutes."

"How many sisters do you have?"

John smiles funny. "I have six older sisters. So seven including Jenny."

I gape. "Seven?!"

John grins. "Yup. It sucks ass."

I gaze into the woods down the hill. "Damn. I don't even have one sibling."

"What about Mark?"

"He's also an only child." I sigh wistfully. "I used to want a sibling when I was little."

John claps a hand on my shoulder. "Trust me, you're better off without one."

I have my doubts, but I say, "I'll take your word for it."

After a beat, the bell rings.

John groans and stands back up to his towering height. "I feel like lunch is way too short."

"Tell me about it." I get up, take off my baseball cap, and place it in my book bag.

John throws his book bag over his shoulder. "Thanks for telling me that story. It wasn't that bad, honestly."

I nod, the sun bathing my face. "Thanks for listening. I guess it was a story I needed to tell." I walk back inside, feeling like those clouds drifting in the ocean of that blue sky.

"Mat . . ."

"Matth . . ."

"Matthew?"

Emily peers at me with a sweet smile, the early afternoon sun enhancing the green in her beautiful hazel eyes. "What's got your head in the clouds?"

I pull the brim of my cap lower, hoping my pupils aren't noticeably slit. "Nothing special. I was thinking about when I met Mark."

She gazes at the boy in question; he glances back and lifts a brow. "Did he always have that scar?"

No. I gave it to him. "He's had it since we became friends."

With a big grin, Mark shouts, "Stop asking about my scar, Emily!"

"I'd stop asking if you gave me a straight answer!"

"I personally prefer giving gay answers!"

Emily's expression falls flat.

Mark snickers.

"He is so . . ." Emily scrunches up her nose; it's absolutely adorable.

"Insufferable?" I say.

She crosses her arms and nods. "Insufferable."

A dated burgundy Honda Odyssey rolls into the car pool lane.

"Oh, that's my ride." Her smile returns. "Talk to you later!"

We wave goodbye, and she gets into the passenger seat of her mom's car.

With Emily on her way home, Mark and I walk down the sidewalk and leave school property. We turn down familiar streets and pass through blessed shade, the trees planted along the road completely still. After ten minutes of silence, we stop at the intersection and wait to cross.

"So," Mark says, "you told him?"

"Yeah," I say.

Frowning, Mark nods.

"I'm sorry again. Emily wouldn't be in your business if—"

Mark holds his hand up in front of my face. "Matthew, you don't need to apologize for defending yourself. And Emily would be in my business about everything else whether I had a scar or not."

I watch vehicles speed by in front of us. "Doesn't it annoy you?"

Mark crosses his arms, squinting against the sun. "What specifically?"

"People asking about it all the time."

Mark puts his glasses on and flattens his lips. "Honestly, it does get annoying after a while, but that doesn't mean I hate it. I don't regret trying to help you, and I don't hold what happened against you. It's not like we can take it back; I don't even want to." Smiling, he cocks his head. "And it's fun to tease Emily every time she asks."

I sigh, but smile, too. "Do you think she'll ever drop it?"

"She's way too stubborn for that!" He grins. "She didn't even let your cold shoulder push her away last year."

The white walking man–shaped light flickers on; as we cross, I think about all the times she bothered me in Honors Biology. She sat next to me and constantly tried to start conversations or study with me, and I eventually felt too bad to keep brushing her off; it's hard to ignore a pretty girl desperately demanding your attention. But we weren't really friends until she met Mark in their gym class last semester. "I hate lying to her all the time."

"Me too, bro," Mark says, his gaze far away, "but it can't be helped. And it's our personal business, anyway; we don't owe her an explanation for every little thing about us."

"That doesn't make it feel any better."

He shakes his head. "No, it doesn't."

Ten minutes later, we reach Mark's humble two-story house.

"Do you want to stay for dinner?" he asks.

I shake my head. "I need to keep up with my chores. But I'll be staying over this weekend."

Mark nods, a thoughtful frown pursing his lips. "I was thinking about inviting John over."

If my ears were out, they'd be perked. "But I'll be . . ."

Mark grins. "Exactly. He might not deal with all that moon stuff; it'll be easier to explain if he sees it for himself." He gets close and whispers, "And not gonna lie, I really gotta see those bunny ears."

I screw my face up. "Cut the guy some slack."

Mark shrugs, lifting his hands without a care. "I'll give him an out!"

I shake my head. "Keep your fetish to yourself, bro."

I wave goodbye and walk the additional ten minutes to my house down the street; the white, perfectly paved driveway is car-less as usual. I enter the house with my keys, take off my shoes, and go upstairs to my room. After placing my book bag at the foot of my computer desk, I push the keyboard aside, take out the meager amount of homework that's due tomorrow, and get to work.

By the time I finish my homework, it's a little after four. I put my work away and go downstairs into the empty kitchen; the clocks tick audibly in the quiet space. I open the fridge and pull out the raw chicken breast tenderloins I requested the other day. I put the package on the counter next to the stove; pull out a frying pan, some olive oil, and some seasoning; and prep the chicken to fry. It takes me forty minutes to cook all ten tenders.

While the chicken cools, I microwave some mashed potatoes and steamed broccoli—I'm not the biggest fan of vegetables, but I'd rather have something green in my diet every day than nothing at all. About ten minutes later, everything cools enough to serve; I fill a plate and eat in the dining room alone. Sometimes I miss the days my parents made enough time to eat dinner with me, but I don't miss the copious amounts of takeout.

Part of me feels neglected, but another part of me recognizes all the things I get to enjoy because my parents work so hard. But there's no life in a house you don't share. I'm not much more than a tenant. I pay my dues in chores and they leave me alone. Maybe that's for the better, so they never find out their son is a freak of nature.

I take my cleaned plate to the sink, rinse each dish piled inside—some of them smeared with day-old ketchup, ranch, or soy sauce—and load them into the dishwasher. I take the frying pan off the stove, pour its dirty oil into the trash can, wash it off, and place it in the dish rack to dry. I put the leftovers away, clean the counters, and take out the trash.

After I lock up the back door, I go upstairs and prepare to shower, taking a fresh pair of pajamas out of my dresser and crossing the foyer to my bathroom—the smallest of the three in the house, it holds a sink embedded in a large countertop, a towel cabinet, a toilet, and a tub and shower combo; in an unused corner, I keep a hamper for my dirty clothes. I put my pajamas on the counter, take off my shirt, let my tail unwind from my body, and lift my ears up out of my hair. The muscles in my cat appendages loosen from another long day of exertion, leaving them tense and sore— it's probably unhealthy to keep them tightly wound all day, but I have no choice when I'm out in public.

I remove the rest of my clothes and start the shower, adjusting the temperature until it's perfectly warm, then step under the spray.

With a content sigh, my aching muscles melt into bliss; despite awakening into a cat boy, I still love bathing and showering—hell, I love it even more because the cat in me constantly demands to be clean—though the feeling of wet fur isn't fun, so I always shower in dormant form if I'm well enough. Thoroughly soaked, I work shampoo into my hair and the fur that covers the back of my ears; afterward, I carefully massage another squirt of shampoo down the entire length of my tail. I duck my head under the shower spray and rinse the soap out, keeping my ears back so the water doesn't clog my ear canals, and card my fingers through my tangled hair. Once I get all the shampoo out of my hair and ear fur, I run my hands down my tail until it's clear of any stubborn suds.

I do it all over again with conditioner, then lather my body, excluding my ears and tail, with bodywash. I rinse again, turn off the stream of water, grab the clump of hair and fur off the drain cover, and step out of the tub. I toss the clump into the trash bin near the toilet, dripping sparsely onto the tile, and grab a raggedy white towel from the towel cabinet. I rub my face and hair dry, then work on the rest of my body, saving my tail for last; I wrap the towel around the base and slowly rub up and around it's length half a foot at a time, carefully ignoring the powerful urge to lick dry the parts I can reach with my tongue. After all that effort, my tail remains damp.

Bitter, I toss the used towel into the hamper, put on my pajamas, and face the mirror. I stare into my sapphire-blue eyes, frustrated that even the dim bathroom lights cause my pupils to contract into slits. I avert my gaze to the lone toothbrush holder, grab the manual toothbrush inside, put toothpaste on the head, and brush my teeth, giving special attention to my elongated canines. I usually brush my tongue, but it irks me to run the bristles against the papillae that litter its surface; despite the bad taste in my mouth, I don't have the heart to do it today.

I rinse off my toothbrush and rinse out my mouth, watching the frothy mint-green paste drain away in swirls. I suck up and spit out my errant saliva, suddenly dizzy and tired; maybe it's the moon staring at me through the walls.

With one final glance at my pale face, I stumble out of the bathroom. I don't bother putting my tail away or flattening my ears because there's no one home to see them. Dazed, I enter my bedroom, fail to close the door all the way, and collapse into bed. I'm so tired. Tired of being tired. Tired of being an inhuman freak.

I close my eyes and take a deep breath; I shouldn't think like that. What would Mark say? What would John?

If she knew, what would Emily think of me? Something like me . . .

Full of uneasy thoughts, I pass out.

The front door slams shut—surely Mom's doing—startling me awake. I stretch out, get up, and close my door. With my privacy preserved, I check my phone; a text from Emily sent thirty minutes ago says, *I'm on.* I smile, my tail rising and curling at the tip, and turn on both my TV and my Xbox One. I pick up my controller, sling my headset around my neck, and sit down in my ancient office chair; the moment I log on, Emily invites me to a party.

"What took you so long?" she asks, her voice distorted by my cheap headset.

"I took a power nap right after my shower," I say. "I must have missed your text."

"You and your naps . . . I'd swear you're part cat."

"Yeah, yeah . . . You say that every time."

"It's not good for you to sleep so much!"

I chuckle mirthlessly. "I've gotta make up for all the time I lose playing games somehow."

"Then maybe you shouldn't stay up so late." She snorts.

"I'll think about it." I wouldn't nap so much if my shitty instincts stopped waking me up at twilight.

"You better," she says, "or I'll—"

A notification pops up; our intruder says, "Hello, Emily, Matthew. Nice of you to invite me."

"We leave the party open on purpose, you know," I say.

"The least you can do is give me a text," Mark says.

"Sorry! I always forget to!" Emily says.

Mark hums static. "I don't know~ I feel like you 'forget' on purpose."

"Nonsense! I would never!"

"If you say so~"

Smiling faintly, I launch *Smite*—the latest free-to-play game we're giving a whirl—knowing we'll be up until midnight once again.

CHAPTER 4

Blood and Water

John

Dragging a duffel bag over my shoulder, I get out of the car; immediately, my sister Hope drives away. Nervous, I walk up to Mark's front door and press the doorbell.

A woman yells, "One moment, please!"

A door slams. "Wait! I'll answer it!" Mark opens the door and grins at me, dressed in nothing but his purple glasses and a pair of pajama shorts. "Come in, come in."

I reluctantly step inside; as soon as I breach the doorway, Mark locks up behind me, shutting out the meager sunlight. I survey the small living space furnished with a couch, a coffee table, and an average flat-screen TV sitting on its stand; beyond the living space lies a dining room table fit for up to four people, and beyond that is an open kitchen behind a pony wall. A shoe rack lies against the wall beside the doorway; I kick off my flip-flops and place them next to Mark's tennis shoes.

A woman wearing her black hair in a bun walks out of the kitchen. "You must be John. It's nice to meet you. It's not too often Mark invites a new friend over."

I take off my cowboy hat and smooth my hair with my left hand. "Thank you for having me. You must be . . ." I study the woman's features: her upper eyelids have a tapering crease, and her eyes are a rich dark brown; she has small, plush lips, and wears a modest amount of makeup, enough to add some warmth to her skin and depth to her eyes; and she appears thin, her collar and cheeks sunken, but excess skin striped by silver stretch marks hangs around her upper arms. Her upturned nose is the only feature she shares with Mark.

She smiles. "Mrs. Koenigsegg, but please feel free to call me Miss Ashley." Mark's last name is such a mouthful, so I'm grateful she doesn't mind being called by her first name. "Please, make yourself at home."

I glance aside, wondering where Mark wandered off to while I met his mom. "Thank you for having me, Miss Ash—" I choke on my words, gaping like a fish out of water.

Mark slinks out of the hallway on reptilian paws, his arms and legs covered in a plating of smooth red scales; smaller scales back his elf-like ears, and a long, snakelike tail trails behind him. Each paw has four long toes, all of them tipped by curved black claws.

"Mark! Your mom is literally right there!" My heart threatens to pump straight out of my chest.

Miss Ashley jumps, looks at Mark, and frowns thoughtfully.

Mark has the gall to cock his head and say, "Yeah, I know. What about it?"

Holding a wedding band–clad hand over her heart, Miss Ashley sighs. "Mark, baby, you didn't tell him that I already know?"

Mark holds his scaly hands up and grins awkwardly. "Oh, uh, my bad."

"Oh my God . . ." I close my eyes, holding a hand against my chest; one strap of the duffel across my shoulder slides down, so I pull it back up, my booming heart slowly calming.

"Sorry for the scare, hon," Miss Ashley says. "I'm aware of what you are, too, but you don't have to show me anything if you don't want to. Matthew is still shy about it, and I've known him for years."

I glance at her gentle smile, uneasy that she knows I'm hiding bunny ears under my hair; my face burns, my hands clammy with sweat.

"Jeez, now I feel bad." Mark sighs, at least looking remorseful for scaring me half to death. He walks behind me, his claws clicking on the floor, and grabs my shoulders. "C'mon, let's go to my room! Bye, Mom!" Before I can protest, he pushes me forward, and I'm not about to resist with his claws over my bare shoulders; I reluctantly let him guide me down the hall and into a room on the right.

His bedroom looks like it was supposed to be a recreation room; it's at least double the size of mine, and I have to share with Jenny. The area on the left holds the essentials of a modern boy's room: a single twin-size bed fit with a red, orange, and yellow comforter; a TV stand littered with DVD cases, old cartridges, controllers, consoles, a criminal amount of wires, and a smaller flat-screen TV than the one in the living room; a large wooden dresser; a pedestal fan; and a small, freestanding electric fireplace. The right side of the room is far more cluttered, holding a messy desk next to a busted-up cat tree, eclectic storage bins stacked on top of each other, a freestanding clothing rack in lieu of a closet, and an occupied old leather couch against the wall right next to the door.

Mark closes the door behind me and plops into the chair in front of the TV. He picks up his controller and puts his muted headset on. "Sit wherever. We'll talk after I let Emily know you're here and get offline." He pulls the mic down, unmuting himself. "Hey, Emily, sorry about that . . ."

With Mark temporarily occupied, I cross the room, place my hat on his desk, drop my bag next to the desk chair, and look for somewhere comfortable to sit. I'd use the couch, but it's currently occupied by a cat-eared boy curled up under a blue blanket—I knew Matthew was going to be here today, but I wasn't expecting him to be sleeping in after two o'clock.

With no options other than the small, unappealing desk chair, I settle over the pale-yellow third of Mark's comforter and slump against the wall. After a few moments of listening to Mark finish his conversation, I get wise, take his bright-red pillow, and put it behind my back. Hopefully, he won't mind; he did say to sit wherever.

"Mm. Yeah, I'll let him know. See you later." Given another moment, Mark leaves the party and places his controller and headset on his TV stand but forgets to turn off his console. He swivels his chair toward me. "Sorry I went active on you earlier. I assumed Matthew had told you about my mom knowing when he told you about my scar."

I rub the back of my neck. "It's alright. He mentioned your mom, but I didn't put two and two together. Is there anyone else I should know about?"

He shakes his head. "My mom is the only human who knows anything. What about you?"

I flatten my lips. "My parents don't know about me, but all of my sisters do." I'm still embarrassed I let that happen.

Mark grins. "Matthew mentioned something about you having a ton of sisters!" His expression turns lascivious. "Are any of them bunny girls?"

"Dude."

Mark lifts his hands placatingly. "Hey, just asking."

I sigh, shaking my head. "They're all human."

Mark rolls his eyes. "Figures."

Before I seriously consider strangling him, I glance at Matthew dozing on the couch. "Does Matthew usually sleep this late?"

Mark crosses his arms, expression sobering. "No, he doesn't normally sleep this late." He frowns, lips parted. "I figure I have a lot to explain to you; I got the impression we don't see eye to eye."

My brow furrows, surprised by Mark's suddenly serious attitude. "I figured out some of the terms you use through context clues, but an explanation would be appreciated."

He nods. "I'll start with the simple stuff. We consider ourselves to be monster people, for lack of a better term, with a few subcategories. You and Matthew are specifically animal people: bunny boy and cat boy, respectively."

I study Mark's bizarre features. "And what would you consider yourself?"

He strokes his chin. "We aren't all that sure, but our best guess is a dragon boy."

How the hell . . . ? I can see how the arms, legs, tail, and facial features could be indicative of a dragon, but aren't they supposed to have wings and horns?

Mark grins. "Don't believe me? I don't blame you, honestly, but it's not like we have a better guess; there sure as hell aren't any real lizards with features like mine." He schools his expression back in, leaning back in his chair with his eyes closed. "Anyway, back to the point. Outside of monster and animal classes, we've also theorized a demon class just because of their prevalence in mythology."

I can guess what'd fall under their hypothetical demon class, but . . . "What exactly falls under the monster class?"

"Any mythological creature. So stuff like mermaids, harpies, dragons, and such."

"You really think those exist?"

"I'm pretty sure I exist, so probably."

"Probably . . ." I taste the possibility of something as ridiculous as a mermaid being out there; but do I really have room to talk when my own existence is beyond nature?

Bright-eyed, Mark leans forward so fast his chair groans. "Anyway, could you show me your ears? You don't have to go active or anything, I'm just super curious! Oh! I should explain that too, shouldn't I?"

I nod carefully, shocked by his sudden energy.

"Okay, so this"—Mark changes into his mostly human visage; no matter how many times I've seen transformations, it's still creepy to watch scales morph to flesh, claws shorten to blunt nails, and draconic paws shift to human feet—"is what we call dormant form. It's as human as we can look. And this"—he changes back into his dragon-boy visage—"is what we call active form. It's mostly so we have a name for things, and for instances we need to communicate about it in public. Saying 'I'm going active' isn't going to turn heads, you know?"

"Makes sense . . ." Remembering everything is going to give me a headache.

He nods and smiles, staring intently at the top of my head. "Anyway, back to the *real* point. Can I see them? Your ears?" He locks his hands together and begs. "Please?"

Feeling cornered, I grit my teeth. "You don't have to make it weird."

Sighing pitifully, Mark slumps in his chair. "Sorry . . . My bad . . ."

Grappling with Mark's moods in my head, I also sigh. "Honestly, I don't mind." It's just us three in here, anyway.

He immediately pumps his fist. "Yes!"

"You're a weird one, Mark." I reach behind my head and grab the black hair tie keeping my small ponytail in place; I pull it out, then slide multiple hairpins away from my bunny ears, carefully keeping them locked in my hair because I really don't want to go on another hairpin hunt. With everything out of their way, my long ears spring up to their proper position above my head.

Mark covers his mouth with his scaly hands, but the crinkles in his eyes fail to hide his interest.

Knowing he'll eventually beg to see it, I go active; in one painless second, my nails lengthen into blunt claws, my arms and legs grow a thick layer of black fur, and my feet shift into paws befitting a human-size bunny. I'm glad it doesn't hurt to transform anymore; my first year was a struggle between resisting the change as long as possible—often to disastrous results involving my sisters—and fruitlessly attempting to maintain a full dormant form without the bunny ears and tail; although I can enter that form with extreme amounts of willpower, it only lasts around two hours and leads to a violent recoil into active form, so I save it for situations I have to be naked around someone, such as doctor's appointments.

Embarrassed by my overly girlish appearance, I stare at the fuzzy fur sticking out of the hole in the right knee of my jeans.

"Oh, gosh." Mark squirms. "I knew a bunny person would be fluffy, but this is next-level!" He looks like he wants to squeal with fangirl admiration; he wiggles in place, his dilated eyes roaming across my fuzzy arms.

"What?" I hate his attention.

"Can I look at your hands?"

I lean against my propped-up leg and reach out my left hand.

Mark smiles and goes dormant; with nails that pose no danger, he takes my left hand into his two and studies the dark-gray fur covering my palm so densely that my hands look like mittens when my fingers are held together. He admires it, digging his thumbs into my fluff all the way down to the skin. He migrates to my fingertips and pushes back my fur to reveal a clear white claw. He smooths the fur back to the proper direction, and just . . . looks at it for a while, analyzing my separated fingers, my palm, and the abrupt border of black and gray at my wrist; I expect him to pet my arm, but he lets go of my hand.

"It's so cool that you don't have any paw pads." He goes active again.

I stare at my hand, flex my fingers, and rest it on my thigh; having a rabbit-obsessed sister, I've always known they don't have paw pads. But there's someone here who should have pads on his hands.

I glance at the couch on the other side of the room, where a lump of Matthew continues to lie. With my ears perked in his direction, I catch the unsteady breaths of an uncomfortable rest.

As if the time is just right, he grunts and pushes his blanket onto the floor, revealing his active form: striped brown fur covers his arms and legs, and cat paws have replaced his feet; his stripes and the fur on the bottoms of his paws are both black, his paw pads a dark gray.

Mark stares at him, a frown setting in. He blinks slowly and takes off his glasses. "It's about time I tell you why Matthew's out of commission."

Out of the corner of my eye, Matthew's right ear tilts toward us.

Twirling his glasses around by the temple, Mark says, "For whatever reason, he gets like this during the full moon: he struggles to stay dormant and feels so sick he sleeps all day."

That sounds like something out of a fairy tale, but the evidence lies before me. "If he knew he was going to be sick, then why invite me over?"

Mark's lips twist into a wry smile. "It's unbelievable, isn't it? We're already so strange to begin with, and we get to deal with some stupid moon curse, too."

"We?"

"Oh, I have my own problems on the new moon, but it's not as bad. I get all cold-blooded and fatigued and stuff." He glances at me. "What about you?"

I stare at my furry hands. "Nothing like that."

"Just us, then." He sighs, his eyes wandering over the couch and its occupant. "Sorry, I . . . It's stressful sometimes, dealing with all of this. We . . . wanted to invite you over because it happened to fall on a Saturday this time, and it's easier just to show you. All we've ever had is each other to watch our own backs, so . . . It's nice to have another person who knows where we're coming from."

My eyebrows furrow and I clench my fist. I think about what it would be like to be forced into active form every single month, to have to suppress that transformation for a good chunk of the day, to fool people while feeling like shit, only to come home and violently transform as a consequence. "Yeah."

"Yeah." Mark places his glasses on the TV stand and gets out of his chair, stretching his arms out above his head, his ribs sticking out as he breathes in deep. He huffs and winds back down, putting his hands on his hips and drumming his fingers. "I know it's not the definition of fun, but could you help me out with Matthew today?"

Hoarse, Matthew says, "I'm not helpless, Mark . . ."

A fuzzy black mass next to Matthew's belly trills.

Matthew starts to sit up but gives up nearly instantly; he rests his chin on the armrest and gazes at us. "See, Glenn agrees . . ." His eyes droop.

A black cat hops onto the back of the couch and stretches, butt up and forelegs out, its tail curled at the tip. It sits down, yawns, and licks its paw. That must be Glenn.

"God, it's hot . . ." Matthew closes his eyes.

Mark says, "You should probably drink some water. You've been asleep since breakfast."

All labored breath, Matthew asks, "Where did I put my water?"

"It's on my desk."

"Could you get it for me?"

Mark smirks. "Didn't you just say you aren't helpless?"

Matthew shoots him the meanest glare I've ever seen, his ears plastered against his head. "Fine. I'll . . ." He shifts into a sitting position on the couch, already panting. "I'll get it myself . . ." He grips the arm of the couch so hard his claws come out, then stands on unsteady paws. He stumbles forward, takes two shaky steps, and snags one claw in the carpet.

Before he face-plants, Mark catches him by his arms. "Hey, you good?" He holds Matthew's elbows so he stays afloat.

Matthew trembles, holding onto Mark's biceps with a death grip, his sharp claws dangerously close to Mark's fleshy shoulders.

"The . . . The moon . . ." He sucks in a shaky breath.

Mark looks at the alarm clock sitting on his dresser; it reads 2:35 p.m. "It just peaked, huh?" He guides Matthew onto his knees. "Take a break, then we'll get you back on the couch, okay?"

Matthew pants like he ran a marathon. "Yeah . . . okay . . ." He relaxes his grip on Mark but doesn't let go.

When Mark thinks he's ready, he wordlessly helps Matthew back to his feet, keeping their arms locked together, and helps him stumble back over to the couch.

Matthew sits down next to the armrest and immediately rests his head on it. "God . . . I hate this . . ."

"I know, bro." Mark steps back, grabs Matthew's water bottle off his desk, and brings it back to him.

Matthew takes it in his shaky hands and holds it with a death grip.

His eyebrows drawn up, Mark looks at him with a tender expression. "Want me to make you something for lunch?"

"If . . . If you don't mind . . ." Matthew unscrews the lid on his bottle, holding it between his thighs so he can put all his strength into it.

Mark smiles lightly. "Any special requests?"

Matthew brings the open bottle under his lips. "Fi- . . . Fish sticks . . . ," he says into the neck, warping his voice. He takes a sip.

Mark stretches up to his full height. "Alright, no problem." He glances at me, nodding his head in the direction of the door. "Let's go have lunch, then."

"Alright." I slip off his bed and go dormant. Although I'm not perfectly comfortable with Miss Ashley seeing them yet, I keep my ears out of the confines of my hair.

Mark gestures for me to walk ahead of him, but just as I reach the cracked-open door, Matthew clears his throat. "Mark," he says with a firm voice.

Mark stops midstep. "What?"

Matthew's lips flatten. "Put a shirt on. You have a guest over."

"Ah . . . ha ha . . ." Mark hunches over, a hand on the back of his head. "Do you mind waiting a moment, John?"

I take my hand away from the doorknob and turn around. "Take your time." It's not like I'm starving.

Holding a finger up, he says, "I'll be just a second." He trots to his dresser, stripping his pajama shorts along the way; the moment I glimpse a sliver of butt cheek, I turn around and stare at the door. This guy has no shame . . .

Wearing cargo shorts and an oversize DragonForce T-shirt, Mark opens the freezer door and pulls out a big bag of frozen fish sticks.

As he lays out fish sticks on a baking sheet, Glenn sniffs my feet. I let the cat do its thing and glance around the kitchen. Family photos line the walls, some glossy and professional-looking, others with red, glaring eyes typical of digital camera flash. There's one photo, old enough to be in black and white, of a young East Asian man in a Southwestern town; he smiles broadly, as if there's no better day than the day that photo was taken. Another one depicts a father, a mother, and their child; although she's overweight in the photo, I recognize the mother as Miss Ashley, so I assume the boy is Mark; he looks painfully average, sporting a short black mushroom cut, dark-brown eyes, and a big grin full of human teeth.

Mark lays the baking sheet on the middle rack of the preheated oven, then sets the timer on the electric stovetop. Turning his back to the corner counter space and resting his elbows against the edge, he cracks a smile at Glenn sniffing my hair and mewing. "He might let you pet him if you hold out your hand; he's pretty friendly for a cat."

I glance back at Glenn—he's standing on the counter next to the fridge—and hover my right hand at the height of his head; naturally, he sniffs it, then bumps his forehead against my palm. I rub his head, and he enjoys it so much that he walks his back under my palm and turns around for more. Stroking Glenn's chin, I say, "My little sister always wanted a pet."

"I'm guessing she never got her wish?"

"Nope."

"What did she want?"

I smile wistfully. "Ironically, she wanted a bunny. Did all this research on how to take care of them and everything, but Mom said we have enough mouths to feed as it is; I think she was worried it would poop everywhere." I cross my unoccupied arm over my stomach. "Jenny got her bunny anyway, even if it was the worst way possible."

Mark watches Glenn; his soft purrs fill the quiet kitchen. "I was wondering . . . how your sisters found out about it and all. Were you too young, or . . . ?"

I shake my head. "I was twelve when I changed for the first time. Jenny was with me in our room when I first transformed. I . . . wasn't careful enough with the rest."

"At least they took it well, right?"

I nod, taking my hand away from Glenn; he hops off the counter and slinks into the dining room. "It could've been a lot worse. All they do is tease me about it now. Of course I was upset about it at the time, but it's been two years, so—"

"Whoa, whoa, whoa!" Mark says, "You're only fourteen?!"

"Huh?" I gape. "Well, yeah."

Mark looks up at my face and my ears—they don't help me appear any smaller—muttering something about me being rather tall, and caresses his forehead. "Jeez, I really gotta stop assuming things."

"How old did you think I was?" I'd be lying if I said this was the first time someone's misjudged my age.

"Fifteen, maybe sixteen. Then again, it's mostly freshmen in that gym class, so I'm not sure what I was thinking."

He probably wasn't thinking. But before I can say as much, the timer goes off. Mark turns it off, pulls the oven door down, and flips all the fish sticks over with a pair of tongs. He closes the door again and sets the timer for the same amount of time as before. Our conversation lost, I gaze beyond the dining room into the living room. Miss Ashley sits on the couch watching TV, an empty plate and a half-empty glass of water on the coffee table in front of her. I wonder where Mark's dad is; even though it's a Saturday, I know plenty of adults who work twelve hours a day, seven days a week. But I also have a bad feeling.

Mark stares at the photos on the wall. At the family photo.

"Mark."

He looks at me, his mouth set in a deep frown.

"I have a question, but I'm not sure if I should ask."

He crosses his arms but doesn't seem angry. "Just ask."

"Is your dad at work or something?"

His expression hardens; after checking on Miss Ashley across the room, he says, "He's dead."

I look at my feet. "I'm sorry."

"Don't be hard on yourself." He smiles, though it's pained. "I knew you were going to ask eventually, and it's been a long time now."

"Still, I . . ."

He looks at that photo, the one with his parents and himself when he was still normal. "I spent a long time being depressed about it, but I think three years is enough. Dad wouldn't want me to grieve him forever."

I also look at the family photo; behind his father's fat face, I recognize Mark's round eyes and thin lips. I wonder how he passed, but I've imposed myself enough already. "I can't imagine . . ." I stare into his dad's photographed eyes.

"I wouldn't want you to." Mark glances at me, and I'm not sure what he sees in my expression, but he crosses the distance between us, opens the refrigerator, and pulls out a bunch of green grapes; as he eats straight from the bunch, not even bothering to use so much as a paper towel, he says, "Make yourself at home. You can eat whatever you want, just tell me or Mom if anything runs out."

I breathe out slowly, grateful he's given me an out for that awkward conversation. I wait for him to grab whatever else he wants from the fridge—that being a block of fancy-looking cheese—and make myself at home.

Matthew fell asleep sitting up while we were gone. His water bottle lies wedged in the crook of his elbow, while Glenn drapes his long, lithe body over Matthew's thighs; both of them have their ears slack and pointing outward, creating a scene that's two parts comical and uncanny.

Mark hands me the plate of fish sticks, puts his index finger in front of his lips, and mouths a shh with a wink. Quiet as a cat, he approaches Matthew and gently pinches the tip of his ear between his finger and thumb; somehow, Matthew remains dead to the world. Grinning wildly, Mark flips Matthew's ear inside out, then hops back just in case his victim retaliates; Matthew continues to sleep.

"Dude," I say, exasperated.

"Shush!" Mark says.

Matthew's unflipped ear flicks. He cracks an eye open and looks at us standing awkwardly near the doorway. He homes in on Mark's grin, then brings his hand up to his left ear; he flips it back up so fluidly I get the impression this is far from the first time Mark has pulled that on him. He puts his cheek in his hand, resting his elbow on the armrest, and thrusts his other hand out palm up; he has round, dark-gray pads on the tips of his fingers and thumb, one smaller pad on the ulnar side of his wrist, and a long strip of padding where his palm connects to his fingers. "Just give me the food," he says, obviously irritated.

I hand the plate back to Mark, who carefully puts it in Matthew's open hand; he lets go when he's sure Matthew has it gripped well enough that he won't drop it. When Matthew sits up properly, Glenn hops off of him, sprints across the room, and scales the cat tree.

Matthew puts the plate in his lap and stares at his fish sticks; blushing, he says, "Thank you." He picks one up and bites into it.

Mark says, "You're welcome," and drifts into his chair.

I settle down on his bed again.

Mark hums, using his foot to twist his chair back and forth. He notices he left his TV on, his console having long turned itself off to save energy, and snaps his fingers. "Oh, that's right." He spins his chair around to face me. "Do you play?"

I look at his hooked-up Xbox One. "I do, but we're still on the 360. I'll be honest, Jenny plays a lot more than I do."

"You share?"

I nod.

He makes a grave face. "Yet another perk of being an only child . . ." He shakes his head. "I can't blame you for not upgrading. The One had a terrible launch! I don't know what they were thinking, bundling it with the Kinect. I didn't upgrade until my birthday last year."

"When's your birthday?" I ask.

He smiles big. "Christmas."

"Christmas," I say, deadpan. "Doesn't that suck?"

He shrugs. "Maybe, but I wouldn't know. It's easier for Mom if it's one day a year. And I get bigger presents, too."

I cock my head and massage my chin. "You've got a point there."

"Well, anyway"—he leans down and presses the console's power button—"I think we can still play together as long as we're both on 360 games, so let's trade gamertags."

"Oh, uh, sure," I say, a little apprehensive.

Mark grins knowingly. The console boots up and his profile appears, revealing the most ridiculous gamertag I've seen in a while: XxF1reL0rdT4oxX. It takes my brain a moment to comprehend how to read that awful series of letters and numbers.

"Fire Lord Tao? Seriously?" I ask.

Pouting, Mark pulls up his friends list. "C'mon, I made it when I was ten. Cut me some slack." He presses *A* over the search bar.

Unfortunately, I can't say mine is any better. "Here, let me." I hold my hand out, and he hands me his controller; I type in my cringey gamertag—it's a pain in the ass without a keyboard—

BunC0k69. My poor decision-making skills on full display, I hand his controller back.

He reads it and giggles under his breath. "You're shitting me." He wheezes. "Buncock Sixty-Nine? Really?"

I blush, embarrassed I let Jenny convince me to go through with it, but I also find it funny despite how stupid it is. "I guess we all make bad decisions from time to time."

"Yeah!" He laughs. "You could say that!" He schools himself in enough to add me to his friends list. "But of all the stupid things you could come up with, why Buncock Sixty-Nine specifically?"

I rub my hands together nervously. "Well, I couldn't come up with anything when I made my account a few years ago, so my little sister offered it. I guess I thought it was funny enough at the time that I went through with it. It's a combination of bunny, my last name, and my birthday numbers."

"Your birthday numbers are six and nine?" he says incredulously.

I lean back against the wall, stretching my arms up. "Yup. June 9, 2001."

"Wow."

"What about you?" I ask.

"What about me?"

"How'd you come up with your gamertag?"

"Oh." He smiles wistfully. "I thought fire was the coolest element, thought the word *lord* sounded epic, smashed my middle name at the end, and added in some leet and *X*s because that was also cool, so, you know, stuff a ten-year-old would do."

"Your middle name is Tao?" It's unusual for such a White-looking guy to have a clearly non-White name. I can only think of two possibilities, one of them being that Miss Ashley wanted to be unique, but I have a feeling that's not the case.

He grins. "Mom named me after her great-grandfather. I never met him, but Mom really loved him. He was the man in that black-and-white photo in the kitchen. I can tell you a little bit about him if you'd like."

I'll bite. "Go ahead. I feel like I've been rather nosy between you two, though."

He waves me off. "Don't worry about it, bro! We're friends now, anyway, so it's no biggie. We're just getting to know each other, that's all."

I smile; it's been a long time since I've made friends. "You're right. I'm listening."

Mark leans back in his chair and rests his controller on his thigh. "Chen Tao, my great-great-grandfather, came to the United States sometime in the early 1900s." He leans forward with a sly grin. "Of course, he came by less than legal means, considering the law of the land at the time; Americans didn't like the Chinese all too much back then, and, well, we're always having beef with China even now, so no surprise there." He glances aside and leans back again. "Anyway, he smuggled himself in with a merchant family, got hitched, and had a kid so he could legally own land in his daughter's name. From there, I think he owned a shop or something; I honestly can't remember the exact details."

"I see . . ." I readjust myself against his pillow. It amazes me what he chooses not to remember.

Mark puts his hands behind his head and uses one foot to spin his chair back and forth. "I'm told that Chen Tao was a pretty laid-back guy, but his wife was a total bitch." Mark freezes, his grin contorting. "Maybe I shouldn't talk about my great-great-grandma like that . . ."

I shrug; I know my fair share of bitch-ass relatives, too.

Mark smiles awkwardly. "Anyway, Mom's great-grandma was the start of our family troubles; I think it's amazing it goes that far back." He stares at the ceiling. "You see, her daughter—my great-grandma—decided she wanted to marry a White man. Both families weren't particularly happy, and the two eloped to the East Coast, but the daughter kept in touch with her father, then had a daughter of her own. Just like the woman before her, my grandmother chose to marry another White man, but she happened to look White enough it didn't cause many problems for her." He glances at me. "I have quite the, ah, prejudiced family, as you can tell."

"Tell me about it . . ." I prop my elbow up on my knee and rest my cheek in my hand.

"It ended up being a whole thing when Mom was born. You might not have noticed, but it's obvious she has some Chinese in her. The White grandparents weren't all too happy about that, and her parents became estranged from the family. Both of them were fairly distant from her while she grew up, but she came into contact with her great-grandfather sometime down the line. He became a father figure for her, far more than her own father ever was. I'm told she'd often visit him in the summer, since he still lived out west in that old shop of his. Really says something they'd let her go out there on her own as a kid, but, hell, it was a different time."

Sloppy as it is, I feel like Mark's given me the most pertinent information, but one thing doesn't add up. "For someone who loved a first-generation Chinese man so much, you two don't seem to have much Chinese stuff in the house."

Mark taps his chin. "Well, we've got a few knickknacks here and there, but we just live like Americans for the most part. I mean, I don't look Chinese at all, and I certainly don't speak the language. It's so far off at this point that I couldn't tell you the first thing about being Chinese. God, imagine putting me at the Asian kids' table! I'd be lost."

How blunt. "How much are you?"

"One-eighth. I'm basically White."

He certainly acts like it. "I never would've guessed."

"Yup." He returns to his minute spinning. "I treat it more like a fun fact than anything else." He looks me over so quickly I almost miss it. "Oh! Since we're sharing, what are you?"

"I'm White."

He looks at me funny. "I can tell that much. What kind of White?"

"Uh . . ." I rack my brain for whatever the hell my mom has said in the past. "Italian, Spanish, and . . . French?" I'm not totally sure about that last one, and . . . "Probably some British in there, too."

He faces the couch. "Why don't you share, too, Matthew!"

"British . . ." Matthew mumbles groggily. "German . . . Irish . . . somethin' . . . I don't know, bro . . ."

"Good enough." Mark swings back to face me, his arms crossed. "As for me, I think there's some Swedish, maybe Russian . . . Definitely British . . ." He squints, then shakes his head. "Honestly, I couldn't really tell ya."

Personally, I think it's best not to think about it, and we've gotten way off track; his console is falling asleep again. When I'm sure his attention is back on me, I point at the screen, and he turns his controller back on so he can wake up his console.

Mark smiles lopsidedly. "I guess we should get back to the point." He returns to his friends list, which is full of people who haven't been online in years. He has three starred as favorites; he hovers over Tabby Swain—"That's Matthew's gamertag"— then hovers over emmie9lives—"and that's Emily's gamertag."

Suddenly, a sly grin dominates Mark's face. "Oh, Tabby~"

Matthew glares at him from the couch.

"Emmie hopes you feel better~"

"Shut up, Mark," Matthew says, "and tell her I appreciate it."

Mark salutes. "Aye, aye, captain!" He whips back around to send a message to Emily; she's still online playing *Minecraft*. He types absurdly fast for someone using a controller, and as soon as he sends his obnoxious message, he slumps back in his chair.

Out of the corner of my eye, Matthew slinks off the couch; the combination of carpet and soft paw pads makes his approach absolutely silent.

I raise an eyebrow.

Matthew holds a finger over his lips, grinning over contained laughter; the second Emily's reply pops up, Matthew grabs Mark's waist from behind his chair.

"Gah!" Mark jolts, so surprised he goes active, his tail bursting from his back and pushing him off his chair; he lands on his knees and elbows, carefully holding his controller out of harm's way.

Matthew plucks the controller out of his grasp and opens Emily's message; he reads it and smiles, even though all it says is *I'm glad :)*.

CHAPTER 5

The Unknown

Matthew

My stomach grumbles, rousing me from a dreamless sleep; I sit up on the couch and place my paws on the carpet. Mark sleeps in his bed, his comforter falling off the side because he always throws it off in the summer. John sleeps on the floor in a sleeping bag, his long ears lying back against the crown of his head.

The full moon waning, I feel well enough to stand without gripping the armrest. I tiptoe out of the room, leaving the door cracked open for Glenn.

I walk through the dining room to the kitchen, open the fridge, peruse my options, and pull out a plastic container of last night's leftover chicken noodle soup. I pull a ceramic bowl out of the cabinet and use a ladle to pour a few scoops into the bowl; once it's full, I put the ladle in the sink, the leftovers back in the fridge, and the bowl in the microwave; I set it for one minute and watch the bowl spin around and around until it beeps. I pull the bowl out, stick my tongue into the soup to check the temperature, and decide it's not hot enough; I give it another thirty seconds, and when I open the door, steam rises out of the broth.

I pour a cup of water and stick a stainless steel spoon in the bowl. Behind me, a page flips; Miss Ashley sits under the light of the lamp next to the couch, Glenn loafing halfway over her hip.

I turn away, embarrassed I failed to notice her reading in the living room; I can't help being out of it during the full moon, but I still hate my body's weakness.

I take the bowl and cup into my hands, wondering if it would be rude to sit in the dining room; even though Miss Ashley wouldn't mind, it feels wrong to distance myself. My heart thumping, I cross the dining room to the living room, hover near the coffee table, and place down my bowl and cup; I sit on the left end of the couch, curling my tail against my right thigh.

Miss Ashley glances at me, a gentle smile gracing her lips; even with grief weighing her down, she has the energy to be kind.

I stare at my hands firmly fisted in my lap. "You're still awake?"

Miss Ashley sighs, a short and wispy thing; her book closes with a muffled thump. "I know I shouldn't be, hon." She places her book on the coffee table. "It's just one of those nights."

I put my bowl in my lap. "I understand." My crepuscular instincts energize me at the most inconvenient times, but Miss Ashley's bouts of insomnia are for a completely different reason. I swirl my spoon in the soup, disturbing the shredded chicken and diced carrots.

"How are you feeling, hon?"

"Better." I bring a spoonful to my lips. "Mark and John kept me distracted."

"I'm glad you've found another friend. He reminds me of you."

I swallow and stare deep into the broth; the savory surface reflects my face. "How so?"

"He's very shy. He kept his ears folded back at dinner like you used to do way back when." She chuckles. "But I'd say he's much more polite."

"My bad." I pout, playing with my food again.

She grins a familiar grin, her eyes crinkling.

I flatten my lips and my ears; it's hard to gather enough courage, but I ask, "Miss Ashley, why have you always been so . . . okay with us?"

She falters.

I stop twirling my spoon around, ashamed I ruined the mood.

Miss Ashley repositions herself—Glenn catapults off her lap, totally offended she had the audacity to move at all—her nightgown rustling against the couch. "You asked me that a long time ago, didn't you?"

I nod. I couldn't believe someone could accept a monster child with open arms, much less with honesty and kindness. Hyperaware, I work on eating my soup before it gets cold.

"I'm sorry I didn't tell you back then. I thought the story was too inappropriate for someone your age." She clears her throat and folds her hands in her lap.

"Why did you think that?"

She smiles mischievously. "I may have had . . . intimate relations with an animal person."

My soup hits the wrong pipe; I cough uncontrollably.

Miss Ashley gives me time to settle. "Too much, hon?"

I pout, my ears drooping. "Just . . . leave those details out."

"I'll try my best." She giggles. "But I must warn you: it's a long story." She winks. "I wouldn't want you missing any sleep."

"Very funny, Miss Ashley . . ."

She reclines her head against the back of the couch and rests her arms in her lap. "It all started twenty-seven years ago in 1988, the year Grandpa Tao died. I remember waking up at the end of summer, depressed I'd have to leave him to go to college in a few days. But when I went to wake him that morning, he was cold; he died in his sleep at the ripe old age of ninety-two having lived a fruitful life, but I wasn't ready for him to go. I was never going to be ready to lose the only family I ever had.

"I mourned him every day until I had to leave, feverishly collecting memorabilia because I knew I'd never see his home again. Those were the most awful days of my life, especially because my great-grandmother did everything she could to make every minute as miserable as possible; at least she was too busy handling the funeral to take everything away from me.

"With what little I cared about, I went to college, stayed and studied in a tiny dorm room, and went to every party I was invited to so I could drink my grief away; it was reckless and awful and I regret it immensely, but it was at those parties that I met a man named Alex.

"Alex was mysterious, handsome, and flirtatious, so much so the frat boys liked to use him as bait to get as many girls as possible to come to their houses. We had a game between us to see who could bed him, but he never went past light petting; he would dance with you and brush against you, but the moment a girl tried to take it further, he found a way to leave.

"On the night of the full moon in September, Alex, who was always a hearty drinker, binged until he was so drunk he could barely walk straight. Despite being tipsy myself, I realized how weird it was for him to drink like that, and worried someone might end up on the wrong side of the bed later that night. But Alex must have known exactly how vulnerable he was; as soon as everybody else was drunk and distracted, he stumbled outside alone.

"Somewhere in my hazy mind, I thought it would be a great idea to follow him; I convinced myself I only wanted to make sure he'd be okay, and conveniently forgot how dangerous it is for a drunk woman to follow a man anywhere. I followed him into the woods, carefully keeping my distance so he wouldn't notice me.

"Eventually, Alex kneeled next to a tree and went active. I watched in dumbfounded awe as his ears grew fur and shifted to the top of his head, his claws formed and dug into the bark of the tree next to him, and his tail fell out from under his shirt; he was a wolf man, and he had no idea I'd witnessed the whole thing." Miss Ashley goes silent, seeing that moment again, the moment a man became a monster.

I wonder if she was scared. If she was disgusted. If she wished . . . "What did you do?"

She smiles so, so gently. "I turned around and walked back to my dorm room; I thought I was so wasted I was seeing things. But when I sobered up and continued life as usual, I started to notice things about Alex's appearance; his teeth, and his ears, and that sometimes, when he brushed up against girls, his nails seemed a little long. In hindsight, it's incredible how much self-control he had over his transformation to be able to flirt so shamelessly.

"Anyway, Alex got wasted again a month later, and stumbled out again, and I followed him. I didn't drink much that time, so when I saw him change against the tree for the second time, I knew it was real. I watched him, my brain hopelessly processing the fact that wolf men were real and I was dangerously close to one; I was frozen there with no idea what to do." She goes quiet again.

I stare at my reflection in the bottom of my empty bowl, wondering how her words might change how I see her. How I see myself.

"In the end, I waited too long. Alex turned his head and saw that I'd seen him. I was worried he was going to become aggressive—that he would eat me alive like a rabid beast—but all he did was look away. His ears drooped and his tail hung straight down, and I knew enough about dogs to realize he was scared, just like you were when we first met. I know there are people out there, animal or otherwise, who would've hurt me in his shoes, but Alex was no criminal.

"He kneeled there awhile, waiting for me to do something, but when he realized I was only going to keep standing there forever, he asked me what I wanted from him. He wanted me to stay silent about it but knew better than to expect someone to keep quiet without something in return; selfishly, I told him I wanted to know everything about him, and he agreed.

"I didn't interrogate him that night, but the next time there was a party, I took him aside to a room where we could lock the door for some privacy. Between the moaning and the music, no one was able to hear us; party after party, we would drink and talk in dark rooms, and before long, I felt like I could call him a friend.

"Alex also had a hard lot in life. Born to a White mother and a Mexican American father, he struggled to define himself in a world where he couldn't be enough for either side. He could never be White enough, or Latino enough, or human enough to fit in with anyone, not even his close-knit family. He told me, after he'd awakened at the age of twelve, he became disillusioned with the Catholic faith his relatives held dear, knowing they could never accept a wolf child without betraying their beliefs. People like you are absent from most religions, including Christianity; in some places you'd be worshipped as divine beings, but in this country, you'd surely be persecuted as demonic creatures.

"Besides his relationship problems, Alex also suffered from a moon curse, though it was different than yours. He was also forced to go active, but only at night, and his impulse control became so weak he wouldn't think twice before doing anything that came to mind. He could be a real handful on those nights, but I'll admit I didn't mind indulging him; I enjoyed petting him, and eventually, pleasuring him.

"Sometimes, when I look back on those nights, I wonder if I took it too far, if I treated him more like a pet than a person. Even though he wanted the attention—would even beg me for it—I think I was taking advantage of him. But even with my reservations, I did what I did; I can never take back how I treated him. So that's why I try to be more mindful around you all. I know all you want is to be treated with dignity and respect, just like every other person on this planet."

I put my empty bowl on the coffee table and take a sip of water, reflecting on her story; it's no wonder she always keeps her distance. I glance at her closed eyes and creased brow, then bring my knees up to my chest. "What happened to him?"

She barely opens her eyes. "He disappeared after winter break without so much as a word to anyone. He probably transferred or dropped out—all that partying wasn't great for our grades—but I felt like I'd been abandoned again. I tried my hardest to forget him, but I could never keep those nights in the depths of memory until I met George. I never told George the dirty details about my encounters with Alex, not until Mark came along and shattered what little sense of normal I'd pieced together."

I look away, forlorn. "Do you hate it?"

She doesn't answer right away, but out of the corner of my eye, she smiles. "There are many things I regret in my life. I regret all the lonely days I spent being sorry for myself; I regret drinking at pointless parties and taking advantage of Alex; I regret eating my emotions; and I regret every pound I gained as a consequence. I'd destroyed my relationship with my body so much that, by the time I became pregnant with Mark, I did nothing to stop myself from gaining far more weight than recommended. I developed preeclampsia and had to have an emergency C-section; it's a miracle Mark survived without major health consequences.

"But I can tell you with every fiber of my being that I've never once regretted my son, and by meeting Alex all those years ago, I was given the wisdom I needed to take care of him. I can still remember that day he broke his left wrist and his right forearm falling off the monkey bars at the playground. He was only five and getting ready to start school in a few months. We got him fixed up at the doctor with these little casts on each arm, and although there was a lot of crying, I knew it was normal for rambunctious little boys to get themselves hurt every now and then; he would heal before long and would probably forget it ever happened, but I was wrong once again.

"Mark came to our bedroom that night a few hours after I'd tucked him into bed. I thought he'd been having a nightmare and needed comfort, until I felt little claws poking my arm. George's old cat had died just a year before, so I knew they belonged to my son. Mark asked me if growing scales and claws was part of the healing process, bless him, but I knew better—I knew he was like Alex.

"In my partying days, Alex had told me a long list of triggers for going active, among them the night of the full moon, arousal, extreme emotions, and pain. I guessed Mark wasn't supposed to awaken until sometime during puberty, as was the case for you, Alex, and your new friend, but his injuries were severe enough his body chose to partially awaken his arms to help them heal.

"When I felt those claws, I was so scared; I didn't know how I could explain it to George or how I could tell Mark that he'd never be accepted in this world if people knew what he was. I hated that I had to do that to him, especially because I could already tell he was extroverted. My little boy would always have to isolate himself from his peers and the people around him, and I couldn't bear it if he felt isolated from his own parents, too. I wish George had taken the news well right away, but he came around after he realized how much he'd hurt Mark with his words." She glances at me, eyes crinkling. "You helped a lot with that, Matthew.

"What I want you to understand is that I could never hate any of you for what you are; it'd be better to say that I hate how you all have to treat yourselves, and I hate that it'd be dangerous to reveal that part of yourselves to the world. I love all of you, and I appreciate that you've been a great friend to Mark all these years; he cherishes your friendship more than you could possibly know."

I close my eyes and bury my head in my knees so she can't see my face. "I cherish him, too." If I had to be alone forever, I don't think I could take it.

Miss Ashley sighs wistfully, and her nightgown rustles again. Her hand lands on top of my head, and she rubs back and forth between my ears; I pout even though it feels nice. Her brief petting ends before it gets uncomfortable, and I peek between my knees to watch her take my bowl to the kitchen. She turns the sink on and washes it for me, then carefully puts it in the dish rack so it doesn't clink too loud. She pours a glass of water and returns to the couch. "Do you care if I turn off the lamp?"

"Go ahead," I say.

She turns the knob twice. "Good night, hon. Try not to stay up too late."

I lift my head. "Good night."

She walks upstairs to her room, leaving me alone in the dark; my eyes adjust until I can see in muted colors.

I shuffle to the other side of the couch, open the book Miss Ashley was reading, and skim the bookmarked pages, pausing at 1 Corinthians 7:8–9.

CHAPTER 6

A Woman's Intuition

Emily

Sunlight streams through the windows and directly onto Mark's desk. Despite the cool October morning, beads of sweat trickle down his flushed face. He pulls an old folding fan out of his book bag, carefully opens it—displaying a meticulously painted image of a bird and flowery branches—and fans himself from the left; his long red hair strikes his chin with each gust of wind.

"Is it really that hot?" I whisper, cupping the right side of my face so the teacher won't hear.

Mark doesn't bother opening his eyes. "The sun is shining directly on me." His lips part, revealing his sharp teeth.

This is far from the first time Mark has acted unusually sensitive to direct sunlight; I don't keep a record, but I've noticed he acts cold-blooded about once a month—it's yet another clue that he isn't as normal as he claims.

Slowly, Mark licks his chapped lips, the two prongs of his tongue out of sync. His bifurcated tongue isn't the only body mod he has: his sharpened teeth and pointed ears combine into a lizard-like visage, only further exacerbated by the yellow snake-eye contacts he wears every day. What gets to me is that he's apparently had these modifications since he was eleven, and what sane parent would consent to such complicated cosmetic procedures on their child? Not to mention the questionable legality in the first place.

His dyed hair is harder to question but isn't immune to scrutiny; it's one thing to dye the hair on your head, but another to dye your eyebrows, eyelashes, and body hair. And I've never once seen his roots grow out; supposedly, his hair is naturally black, which Matthew has corroborated, but Matthew has plenty of suspicious features himself. They're definitely covering for each other.

Mark glances at me. "Jeez, Emily; I know I'm handsome, but you don't need to stare." He smirks despite his apparent discomfort.

I stubbornly stare on through my embarrassment, watching his slit pupils contract a smidgen. I huff and look forward at the crude cube drawn on the whiteboard in green marker. "You wish I thought you were handsome." I do think he's handsome, but that doesn't mean I'm into him. There are tons of pretty guys I'd never go on a single date with, Mark included; he's way too immature for my tastes.

"You do have your eyes on a certain tabby cat." He fans away, the little gusts of wind hardly making a sound.

"Shut up, Mark." I nearly break the lead of my pencil on my math worksheet.

Mark shuts up but won't wipe that smirk off his face. He glances at me with those reptile eyes, and I swear his pupils dilate because they're real. I know, deep down, every modified inch of his body is entirely natural. His snake eyes, and his cherry-red hair, and his pointed ears, and his forked tongue. I know they're all real, but that's absolutely insane. It makes me feel deluded, like my weird personal interests are clouding my judgement.

I'll admit, I have a thing for monster boys: We're talking cat boys, incubi, werewolves, and any other mash between man and monster you can think of. There's just something especially appealing about the thought of petting a hot guy's fluffy ears and hearing him purr . . . And in my defense, I'm not the only one; after *Monster Musume* ended this past anime season, I had the displeasure of listening to Mark go on a very long rant about how much he likes lamias and arachnes. Sometimes, I feel like I know too much about Mark.

Of course, Matthew and John were in the party at the time, too, and as far as I can tell, they're not nearly as passionate as Mark is on the matter: John was mostly weirded out by the idea, while Matthew is more interested in tamer monster girls. I have to agree with Matthew on that one; I don't think I could deal with a centaur, but I can get behind a satyr.

"Emily, can you answer number ten for the class?" Our teacher glares down at me from above the rims of his glasses.

Oops; I got distracted again. "Right, um . . ." I look for number ten on the worksheet; fortunately, it's just the circumference of a circle. I recite the answer, and the teacher turns away to bother someone else.

"I'm cold . . ." Mark whines. "Matthew . . . share your body heat with me . . ."

Matthew sighs, holding the same sandwich he eats for lunch every day in his hand. "Come here." He shifts closer to the left edge of his stool.

"Thank you, bro . . ." Mark dramatically drops his upper body against Matthew and wraps his arms around him; he rests his head in the crook of Matthew's neck, goose bumps dotting his exposed skin.

"Weren't you complaining about being hot just this morning?" I ask, exasperated and not at all jealous.

"That was two periods ago, when I was being roasted alive by the sun," he says, "and now we're in the air-conditioned cafeteria with no direct sunlight, so I'm cold."

"Uh-huh." I take a bite out of my PB&J.

Matthew continues to eat despite Mark hanging off him like a loose robe; he acts like it's perfectly normal for his best friend to use him as a personal heater whenever he feels like it. Before long, a nearly inaudible purr wafts from Matthew's direction, but the rumbling dissipates as soon as he clears his throat. "Don't forget about your lunch, Mark." He bites into his sandwich again, his unnaturally long canines quickly piercing through the soft bread.

Mark sluggishly grabs a chunk of pineapple out of his lunch box.

I try not to watch Matthew eat. Mark isn't the only one that's given me signs of being something not quite human; as maddening as it sounds, I've long begun to think Matthew might be a real cat boy. He purrs whenever he's happy, his pupils contract into slits outside, all four of his canines are long and sharp, and he has the uncanny ability to nap at the drop of a hat. No matter how many things I've looked up about birth defects and genetic abnormalities, I can't excuse the purring. People don't purr, period, and no amount of "oh, Emily, it's just a cat right outside" is going to convince me otherwise. I've never once seen a single cat near the cafeteria, much less wandering around anywhere else on campus. I've heard there's a colony in the woods nearby, but those cats aren't around most of the time, and I sure as heck don't think they're conveniently there every time Matthew purrs. I know he doesn't mean to purr, and I'm certain he really doesn't want me to know he's a cat boy, but it's so obvious it hurts! But I can't deny the possibility I'm just hearing things, that I'm projecting my embarrassing desires onto the boy I have a crush on.

"Emily, is something wrong?" Matthew asks.

I twiddle my thumbs in my lap, glancing back and forth between his cute face and the ugly table. "Oh, um, just thinking about a really hard, uh, math problem." More like connect the dots, but I'm not about to say something that stupid.

Matthew frowns, obviously skeptical. "Do you . . . need help with it?"

I vigorously shake my head. "Uh, no, I can just look it up later!"

"If that's what you want." Matthew's gaze lingers on my face; in the dim lighting of the cafeteria, his pupils are round and normal, making it easier to convince myself I'm wrong.

Before I can ruminate on Matthew's adorable pout any longer, John saunters into our little corner of the cafeteria. He sits down on my right, shoves his book bag onto the stool to his right, and places his tray on the table. He glances between us, says, "Did I miss something?" and starts to eat.

"Nothing much. Mark's just being dramatic again." I grin.

"I'm not dramatic." Mark sulks and hides his face against Matthew's neck.

"I beg to differ," John says.

"Oh~" Mark dramatically brings the back of his free hand to his brow. "How could you side with her, bro?!"

"You're only proving her point, you know?"

Mark deflates and chews solemnly on another chunk of pineapple.

Their diets are another reason I think I'm wrong; neither Mark nor Matthew are pure carnivores, and Mark is particularly fond of fruit and other sweets. With that thought, I say, "Actually, I just remembered I was going to ask you guys something."

All three of them look at me nervously; does John have something to hide, too? That *would* explain why Matthew and Mark suddenly took him under their wing.

"I was wondering if you'd all like to go to the mall together for Halloween. My little brother wants to go trick-or-treating, and I thought it would be more fun with more people."

Mark perks up. "You have a brother?"

"Two, actually; they're both younger than me."

"How old?"

"One is ten and the other is thirteen."

"I don't mind going!" Mark grins and pats Matthew's chest. "What do you think, bro?"

Matthew closes his eyes and crosses his arms. "Mm . . . Let me check my calendar real quick." He takes his phone out and turns it on, the light of the screen making his pupils contract into slits; after he's done checking his totally made-up calendar, he puts his phone back in his pocket. "I can go."

I turn to my seat neighbor. "What about you, John?"

"I'll have to pass." John rests his hand on the back of his neck. "I already promised to hang out with Teddy that day."

I cock my head. "Teddy?"

John smiles with his brow furrowed. "He's my friend from middle school. I haven't seen him in a while since we've both been so busy lately."

I smile, too. "I hope you have fun with him."

"I'll try my best," he says, modest as ever.

John scrutinizes his shoe, drawing another arcing line on the piece of paper in front of him. He leans over the table, his long hair hanging in front of his shoulders; his hair is so beautiful I briefly wish I could draw a portrait of him rather than my tennis shoe, but that would probably weird him out.

I try hard to focus on our current Art I assignment, but I've been so preoccupied this whole day with everything off about my friends that I can't help but be hyperaware of John. I've only known him for all of a month and a half, and even after all that time, he's still an enigma; I keep wondering what exactly caught Matthew's attention enough to pull him into our group. Honestly, even Mark has been hesitant to befriend anyone despite how social he is—he usually leaves relationships in the classroom, never going beyond strong acquaintanceships. It's possible John might also be an animal person, but I haven't noticed anything spectacularly out of the ordinary with him.

John's hair shakes vigorously as he erases a lead curve with a rubber eraser. He wipes away the shavings with the side of his hand, then slowly redraws a part of the outline of the sole. He's surprisingly good at drawing, though he typically draws female figures more than anything else, often with elaborate outfits and detailed makeup—he's better at drawing the makeup than he is at drawing the outfits, though it's not like I have room to judge.

I return to drawing my shoe, but it looks so wonky already I want to erase the whole thing. I tap my pencil against the edge of my paper, wondering whether to start on the laces or just draw the sole next.

Another overplayed pop song comes on the radio, and John starts tapping his foot. I don't know if he actually enjoys the mainstream music the art teacher likes to play for the class, but he's good at finding the beat—another curiosity, but nothing to write home about.

As far as I can tell, John is a perfectly normal—if excessively tall—freshman: he has dark-brown eyes with round pupils; barely crooked teeth set with metal braces; and not an odd behavior in sight, except for his general shyness, which can be written off as typical social awkwardness. He's as normal as can be, so maybe I *am* wrong.

Suddenly, John whispers, "You're awfully quiet today."

I glance at his half-finished work, mine lying only half as full. "Do I really talk that much?"

"You've been asking me things almost every day."

"Have I?" I tap my page again. Over the past month, I asked him about himself, how he felt about Matthew and Mark, and about all seven of his sisters, one of whom is also a sophomore. But what I really want to ask him is what he knows that I don't. Part of me is frustrated that he's already so close with them, that he isn't confused about Mark's monthly bouts of cold-bloodedness or Matthew's strange episodes of weakness that make him go home early or not show up to school at all. But it'd be rude to ask that, wouldn't it? It'd be rude to imply he's getting special treatment just because he's a guy.

John smiles sweetly, sketching another line of lace. "Did you run out of things to ask?"

"Well," I say, finally blocking out another portion of the sole, "I was wondering if you do anything special with your hair. It's very pretty."

"That's a new one." He leans so far forward that his lengthy waves mask his face. "I don't do anything in particular, just wash it and brush it every day."

"Are you trying to grow it out more?"

"Hell no; I think it's long enough as it is."

"That's fair." John's comment reminds me of Matthew's complaints about his curly hair; he constantly calls it a pain in the ass, yet he says he'll never cut it shorter than he keeps it now. Maybe he deals with it because he likes how it looks on him, but nothing is ever that simple with him. He apparently cuts it himself, too, and still complains about the process as if he couldn't just pay a barber to do it for him. I shake my head; these boys are so confusing.

I focus on my sloppy sketch despite John's tapping foot demanding my attention; when I can't take it anymore and glance at his paper, it's become a smoky gray from his hand rubbing against the lead. I tear my gaze away and furiously finish my sketch; it's not as good as John's, but I never claimed to be an artist.

CHAPTER 7

The Sincerest Form of Flattery

Matthew

Glenn lies sprawled out on Mark's bedroom floor, his paws curled up and fuzzy belly exposed. He yawns and stretches, then effortlessly curves his back into a C-shape that would snap my spine in two.

Mark sneaks forward, his hands covered in a protective plating of red scales; when the time is right, he thrusts his palm onto Glenn's stomach.

Glenn grabs his hand, bites his fingers, and kicks his wrist repeatedly.

Mark pulls his hand out of the cat's needle-sharp grasp. "Glenn! Why are you showing me your belly if you don't want me to pet it?" He goes dormant and pokes Glenn's flank.

Glenn meows and flips over so he can attack the offending finger. Mark pokes whichever flank is showing, and Glenn keeps flipping over, trying his kitty best to bite and scratch Mark's hand.

"Maybe he wants to play," I say, taking a shot in the dark—cat boy or not, I can't read a real cat's mind.

"Maybe . . ." Mark crawls on hands and knees over to the edge of his bed, plops onto his side, and reaches deep underneath for the stick toy Glenn dragged under there the other day. When Mark successfully pulls it out by the fabric end, Glenn immediately flips onto his stomach, preparing for the hunt; he watches the toy with rapt attention as Mark backs away from his bed, wand in hand.

Mark casts the line out onto the carpet and waves it back and forth. Glenn follows the feathered end with swift snaps of his head, wiggles his butt, and pounces.

"Ah—" Pulled by the force of the black blur, Mark completely loses his grip on the wand; it goes flying across the room, landing next to Glenn feverishly biting and kicking his pretend prey.

While Mark retrieves the wand, I scroll through images on my phone, trying and failing to find inspiration for a Halloween costume. We might be too old for dressing up and going trick-or-treating, but free candy is free candy, and I wasn't about to turn Emily down if I could help it. The tip of my tail curls back and forth at the thought of her; I hope she wears something cute.

"What're you thinking about?" Mark asks.

"Nothing much," I say, "though I'm struggling to come up with a costume to wear."

Mark grins, a devious glint in his eye. "Need some help?"

I turn my phone off, slide it into my pocket, and lounge sidelong on the couch. "Shoot."

Mark lies down on the floor, the stick toy held firmly in hand; he flicks it around lazily. "How about . . . a pirate."

"No."

"Zombie."

"Too much makeup."

"Cowboy."

"Definitely not."

"Incubus."

"Really?"

"Mm . . ." Mark closes his eyes and rubs his chin until a smirk stretches his lips. "How about a bunny suit?"

"Now you're making no sense." Agitated, my tail thumps against the couch.

"You're no fun." Mark throws his arms out spread-eagle and drops the toy Glenn already lost interest in.

I sigh, knowing Mark's not likely to come up with something I'd be okay with; I may as well throw him a bone. "What are you going to wear?"

"Oh, I'm sure you'll love this one." With a goofy smile, he flips over on hands and knees and crawls to his dresser; he pulls open the bottom drawer and takes out some familiar accessories covered in fuzzy black fabric. "I'm gonna be a cat!" He puts a cat-ear headband on, then picks up two giant furry mitts shaped like cartoony cat paws. "I even found these really stupid gloves online." He puts them on and holds them up palms out, revealing pink fabric in the shape of paw pads. "Aren't they great?"

Only Mark has the utter disregard for social stigma to wear something so flamboyant; the ears even have pink ribbons and gold bells attached. "Emily will probably get a kick out of it." I smile, holding back a chuckle. "But her brothers might make fun of you."

"Pish." Mark waves his fake right paw forward. "Like I care about that. They can make fun of me all they want! I'm far beyond something as trivial as embarrassment!"

"You do you, bro." I turn onto my back and put my hands behind my head, moving my tail between my ass cheeks and legs so I don't crush it. As far as costumes go, I'm not as self-confident as Mark, so I'd prefer something that looks like normal clothes. Maybe a job-based costume would do the trick?

Suddenly, Glenn jumps onto the couch and crawls on my chest. He gets close to my face, sniffs loudly, and rubs his cheek against my nose; I gently push him away so I don't get cat hair in my eyes, then rub his cheek with the tips of my fingers. Glenn indulges my affections, slowly shoving his face all over my hand until he's left lounging across my torso and purring against my chest. I smile softly; it's amazing how animals can be so intuitive about the feelings of the people around them—though it's entirely possible Glenn just wanted attention.

A different black cat looms over my head; he holds his paws up and wiggles his oversize fabric fingers. "Wanna ask Mom to take us shopping? I need to get the rest of my outfit, and you could look for inspiration at the store." Mark mimics kneading near my face, his hair nearly hanging into my left eye.

"It's worth a shot." I sit up, trusting Mark to back away so I don't bonk his head. Glenn resists at first, but quickly gives up keeping me as a throne; totally offended, he springs off my stomach and charges to his ratty old cat tree. With Glenn out of the way, I stand and follow Mark to the living room.

Miss Ashley sits on the couch, enamored by the latest ridiculous plotline in today's episode of *General Hospital*; it still amazes me that she manages to keep up with a show that's been running longer than I've been alive. She spots us coming out of the hallway and pauses her show. "Do you two need something?"

Mark curls his gloves and rests his head over his knuckles. "Can you take us to the store?"

She checks the time on her phone. "It looks like it's not too late, but you'll have to drive. And let me finish my show first."

"We'll wait." Mark trots back to his room to put the cat ears and paws away.

I sit on the couch, and Miss Ashley resumes the episode.

⁀

I climb into the back seat of the late Mr. Koenigsegg's truck—a white 2011 Chevy Silverado 1500 he purchased only a month before his untimely death—and pull the heavy door closed. In the driver's seat ahead of me, Mark clicks his seat belt on; Miss Ashley and I follow suit. He does his due diligence, adjusting the mirrors and the position of his seat since he's taller than Miss Ashley, then turns the ignition, bringing the truck to life; he puts it in reverse and pulls out of the driveway.

For a guy who's only had his learner's permit a grand total of four months, Mark is a remarkably stable driver; he has his hiccups every now and then, such as stopping or accelerating too rapidly, but it's otherwise a smooth ride. Miss Ashley wants him to get his provisional license as soon as possible so she can buy herself something more compact.

I look out the window as Mark pulls onto the highway, the high ride height of his truck providing a decent view above the other cars speeding down the road—almost everyone speeds around here, adding to my hesitance to work on my driving skills; to be fair, my parents don't have the time to supervise my practice anyway.

We slog through after-dinner traffic, eventually reaching a three-district outdoor shopping center; Mark drives into the underground parking area and manages to squeeze the truck into the tight parking on ground level. After he parks, we hop out and walk into the shiny white-and-red interior of the nearby Target.

"I need to pick up a few toiletries while we're here." Miss Ashley pulls out a cart. "Try not to wander too far from the clothing section."

"I'll keep him from getting too adventurous," I say.

"I'm not that impulsive . . ." Mark says, "but if you can't find us, just go to electronics."

"Alright, hon." Miss Ashley pushes her cart away, making a right toward the portion of the store dedicated to cleaning and bathroom supplies.

Mark and I head straight forward to the opposite corner of the store.

The men's clothing section is woefully small compared to the women's, so almost everything available is immediately within view. I look around randomly while Mark parses through pants. A nearby rack of flannel shirts catches my eye, giving me a brilliant idea; I take a red plaid shirt off the rack.

Mark walks up holding multiple pairs of near-identical black pants. "Finally thought of something?"

"Yeah," I say, "I think I'll be a lumberjack."

"Always a simple one, you are."

"No need to make it complicated." And I'll still be able to wear the whole outfit throughout fall and winter, too. "Anyway, why so many pants?"

He frowns at his haul. "I'm not sure what cut I should go for. I'm not a big fan of jeans, but looser pants wouldn't look as good." We typically don't wear formfitting pants for the sake of comfort, and neither of us have ever cared about being fashionable. Skinny cuts are absolutely out of the question for me—my legs and waist simply aren't slim enough, and I'd rather not try to squeeze my balls into such a meager crotch area—but Mark has always been on the slender side, so he might be able to get away with wearing something with a tighter fit.

"Just try them on and see what you like," I say, pointing out the fitting rooms conveniently placed at the corner intersection of the men's and women's clothing sections.

He follows my finger to the sign overhead. "Oh." He smiles awkwardly. "I'll be right back."

I watch him walk away, idling until he enters the men's fitting room; in the time it takes for him to retrieve a plastic number card from the employee stationed there, I figure out the rest of what I'll need to complete my covert costume. Mark disappears into the corridor, and I turn around to look for pants. A rack holding suitable cargo pants stands a few feet away, though the color options are somewhat lacking; between dark gray, tan, and brown, I decide dark gray will fit the best; as for a belt, I already have one at home, so no need to buy another. Now all I have to find are boots and a hat.

I almost always wear a baseball cap in public, as it both hides and gives my ears a break from relentlessly folding back, but that wouldn't suit a lumberjack all too well. I wander over to the small hat display but can't recall what type of hat would work best, and this building has reception bad enough that I can't look it up. I squint, racking my brain for an answer. Definitely not a cowboy hat or a fedora . . . Bucket hats are out, too . . . I have no idea what *that* is, so it's definitely out . . . "Ah hah!" I say after spotting the beanies; they fit uncomfortably close to the skull, but I doubt anyone will notice I'm missing human ears since my hair covers the flat skin where they should be.

"Oh, there you are!" Mark slides next to me in the tiny aisle; when I turn to him, he shows me the one pair he kept, and I don't miss the light-pink fabric resting underneath it. "The slim fit wasn't too bad, and I got a pink shirt to match the paw pads."

"Going full flamboyant, aren't you." I grab a black beanie off the display.

"Guys can wear pink if they want!" He huffs, playing along with my jest.

I'm actually grateful Mark is so outrageous when he wants to be; people pay attention to him, which means they don't notice me. I know I should work on being more confident, but it's hard not to be self-conscious when I constantly have to hide my glaring inhumanity. "Are you going to add heels, too?"

He brings a finger to his lips, mocking thought. "Maybe an inch or two; I was thinking some lace-up boots." He smirks. "Of course, I'll have to work on my catwalk for the occasion."

An image of Mark walking across the mall like a model appears in my mind's eye, fit with the pink ribbons and the cat ears and the ridiculously big paws; I shake my head and snort. "You'll definitely be made fun of."

He struts toward the shoe section, one foot crossing over the other with each step. "So be it. Sacrifices must be made."

I follow him, smiling at his unflinching attitude. We enter the row of men's shoes, and it doesn't take long for him to find a pair of black lace-ups and for me to find some tan winter boots; I usually wear tennis shoes year-round, but there's no harm in trying something new for once.

The moment we step into the main walkway, Miss Ashley rolls up with her cart. "Did you both find everything?"

"We did." Mark puts his stuff in the cart.

I keep my items in my arms.

Without another word, we stroll toward the checkout at the front of the store. Before I can veer off to self-checkout, Miss Ashley catches my attention. "Matthew, I'll pay for your things." She smiles kindly, as she always does.

"You really don't have to. I have more than enough allowance." Dad pays me a small salary for chores in an attempt to make up for all the time he spends working.

"Oh, shush," she says with a wave of her hand. "Boys your age shouldn't have to worry about paying for these sorts of things."

I sigh, quickly giving up on trying to convince her otherwise; this is far from the first time she's insisted on paying for me. I put my clothes in her cart and follow her to a cashier-operated checkout aisle. While we wait behind a woman who's gathered an entire kitchen worth of products, I look at the assortment of snack foods on display. I used to always get a candy bar whenever I went to the grocery store with my parents, but I don't go as often now. I catch Mark perusing as well, his gaze lingering on a few of his favorites, but he holds off.

I stare ahead, catching the wary glances of the woman in front of us, her kid staring dead-eyed at Mark. She looks like she wants to chastise her kid for staring, but all Mark does is smile and wave. It's not unusual for children to stare at the people around them, but Mark's a special target considering his colorful appearance; I've also heard that kids tend to be more in tune with the super-natural, so it's possible the ones that stare can tell something is up with us. Either way, the woman gets her kid to stop staring once it's her turn at the register.

After a good five minutes, we finally roll up to the conveyor belt and load it with everything. The cashier scans our haul, and I adamantly avoid looking at the total price; as far as I'm aware,

Miss Ashley has a good job and little debt, but that doesn't mean I want to be another sink on her finances. Despite averting my eyes, the cashier states the total aloud; I nearly wince.

Miss Ashley happily pays with her debit card, then we roll the cart all the way to the truck; we load up the trunk, put the cart in its corral, and go home.

⌒

Mark parks the truck at an outdoor offshoot of the mall; we step out and close the doors with a resounding thump.

Miss Ashley takes the keys and puts them in her leather designer handbag—a long-ago gift from Mr. Koenigsegg. She smiles, her tired eyes crinkling. "Have fun, you two. I'll be doing some shopping at the bookstore, so just call or text when you're ready to go home."

"Will do." Mark proudly wears his flamboyant cat costume with a black jacket to stave off the mild cold; hyped for candy, he holds a black cat–themed Halloween bucket in the crook of his elbow.

I personally went without a jacket; I run warm on my best days, not to mention the added body heat generated by my tail—all the fur is nice when it's cold, but God help me when it's hot outside.

We walk together until Miss Ashley enters the Barnes & Noble. Mark and I cross the street, stroll through the bottom level of the parking deck, and reach the Belk entrance to the mall; since Mark is wearing those ridiculous cat-paw gloves, I open the doors for him.

I steel my breath while we walk through Belk, absolutely nervous about meeting up with Emily outside of school, but her brothers and Mark will be there, so hopefully my composure won't be completely shot.

We pass by the purses and a makeup booth I've never once seen in use, and straight outside the store stands the trio of Thompson siblings. When the tallest one, a brunette and likely the older of the two brothers, sees us, he leans down and whispers something in Emily's ear, obviously eyeing Mark, who bounds over like an overexcited puppy, and the younger blond brother stares bewildered at Mark in his cat costume coming at him, and all the while I take in Emily's adorable witch costume, my eyes roaming her thick thighs.

Oh my God, she's wearing thigh-highs! my mind screams, the black-and-purple striped fabric lightly squeezing her legs irresistible. I'm so immediately entranced by her totally unexpected costume that I go active; I stop in my tracks, infinitely grateful my hands are in my pockets and everything but my face is covered, because right now is the absolute worst time to be fighting my body. I try not to visibly freak out while Mark greets the group, gripping my thigh from inside my pocket. *Just breathe in and out, Matthew. In . . . and out . . .*

I rein it in and go dormant right as Emily waves me over, then carefully avoid glancing at her thighs as I join the group. "Hey. Hope we didn't keep you waiting."

The brunette brother eyes me down, his arms crossed over his scrawny chest; despite being two years my junior, he's about an inch taller than me.

Peeved by his height advantage, I lift my chin so he knows I'm not about to be intimidated by some middle schooler who doesn't even have the guts to dress up for Halloween—not that I have much ground to stand on, but at least I did something.

Emily smiles at me. "We just got here not too long ago, so no worries." She forcefully grips the brunette brother's shoulder—"Anyway, this is Connor"—then gestures to the blond brother hiding behind her in his simple pirate costume—"and this is Noah. Let's be nice to my friends, alright?" She mostly means it for Connor.

"Yeah, yeah. We get it, Emily," Connor says, obviously glaring at me.

Noah shuffles farther behind her back. "Your friends are weird."

"Noah!" Emily removes her hand from Connor's shoulder and holds it up in apology. "Oh my gosh, I'm so sorry . . ."

Mark laughs. "It's no biggie! We know we're weird! Anyway . . ." Mark walks behind the trio and corrals the brothers with his cat paws behind their waists; Emily steps aside, both brothers bewildered by the sudden loss of control. Mark rests his arms around their shoulders and says, "Let's go trick-or-treating!" He pushes them away, approaching the first of many stores giving out candy for the next two hours.

Connor looks back at me and Emily with an expression that screams, *Save me!*

Emily smiles and waves.

I realize Mark effectively left us alone together. Just little old me and Emily in her way-too-cute witch costume. I might combust. "We should . . . probably follow them." I'm not sure how long I can remain calm without a distraction.

"That's . . . not a bad idea," she says.

We walk side by side down the crowded mall, forced to stand nearly shoulder to shoulder so we don't run into anyone going any number of directions down the same walkway. I keep my eyes trained on Mark and company because I don't trust myself not to roam over Emily's outfit.

"I'm sorry my brothers were being so rude," she says, slouching.

I smile. "Like Mark said, it's no big deal. I'm well aware kids can be unfiltered." As for Connor, he was merely being protective of his sister. John's said a thing or two about how he feels about the various boys his sisters bring home; according to him, most don't last more than a month, so he doesn't bother playing nice. It'll be annoying later down the line, but I don't care if Emily's brothers like me or not; what matters is if she likes me. It'd be nice if her parents like me, too, but bad in-laws are unavoidable sometimes. Not that I'd ever get that far with her; I'm happy just being friends, because there's no way I could ever admit I'm a freak to her.

"Were you like that as a kid? Unfiltered?" Emily looks up at me sweetly from her slouched posture.

I glance up. "Not really. I was always a quiet kid." I narrowly guide Emily to the left so I don't shoulder check some guy and promptly ignore our arms touching; instead, I focus on Mark making catlike gestures with the express purpose of giving Emily's brothers second-hand embarrassment. "Mark pulls me out of my shell a lot, though." I wouldn't be talking to Emily right now if not for him.

"Sometimes I wonder why you two are so close. You're so different." She also watches Mark's antics; her lips keep quirking up and down, barely holding back laughter.

Without thinking, I say, "They do say opposites attract."

Emily gapes silently, nearly tripping over the short heels of her black boots; she bumps into me, a tiny apology tumbling from her pink lips. "U-Um, Matthew, you wouldn't happen to, uh, swing that way, right?"

Swing that way? The phrase dawns on me, and my mouth gapes open; now I'm the one nearly tripping over my boots. "No, no! I meant that platonically. Even if I did swing that way, Mark is more like a brother to me, so it'd be plain weird." We're physically comfortable with each other to an unusual degree, but that doesn't mean either of us want to have a sexual or romantic relationship with another man.

"Oh, thank God!" Emily holds her hand over her heart, her witchy minidress thankfully covering her entire chest; her boobs are on the small side, but it wouldn't take much from her to get me going—I'm more of an ass man anyway, which she has plenty of, but I promise I'm not looking! Right now, that is.

I quirk a brow, interested but not surprised she's relieved I'm not gay. "Would there be a problem if I was?"

"N-Not at all." She flattens her lips, watching her brothers with rapt attention. "Um, actually, I was wondering why you aren't trick-or-treating, too." The awkward look on her face makes it clear she wants to change the subject.

What do I even say to her question, though? I'm honestly way too shy to ask for Halloween candy at my age, but it's not like I love overindulging in sweets either. "I . . . don't like candy much." It's not a total lie, but it *is* a little dishonest; I don't hate candy, but I'd rather have other desserts if I had the choice.

"What? Everybody likes at least *one* type of candy." She smiles mischievously, totally recovered from her earlier blunder. She playfully tilts her head from side to side, then asks, "Are you trying to watch your weight?"

Watch my weight?! I gape once again, this time because she hit a sore spot. I'm sure she doesn't mean anything by it, but I glumly mutter, "Do I look like I need to?" I'll be mortified if she thinks I look fat.

"Oh my gosh, no!" She giggles. "It was just a joke."

A bad one, if you ask me.

"And I can't even tell because you're always wearing oversize shirts."

I'd actually wear my size if I didn't have a tail to hide, but Emily doesn't need to know that.

She picks up her pace and leans forward to look at my glum expression. "You look fine, I promise."

"Thanks." I avert my eyes, embarrassed for feeling sensitive about my appearance; although I'm within a healthy weight range last I checked, I carry more fat in my middle than I'd like. I pretend it's because I'm a cat person, but it's really just an unfortunate genetic trait I inherited from both of my parents.

Emily returns to walking by my side, fiddling with her witch hat. We stop a few feet away from Mark and her brothers as they gather more candy, and she adjusts her thigh-highs, pulling the elastic over the generous curvature that had forced the fabric down with every step; they pinch into her thighs, creating a minor muffin top.

It's kind of hot, so much so I say, "You look nice tonight." Immediately, my ears burn.

"Oh, really?" She pushes some stray hair behind her ear, a blush blooming over her cheeks. "I almost had an argument with my mom because of my costume. She thought it was, um, inappropriate."

I can imagine; I've gotten the impression that Emily's family is on the conservative side, the sort to have a heart attack if a girl wears spaghetti straps and normal shorts; God forbid she shows her shoulders, much less her upper thighs. How lucky for me that she got away with it. "How'd you get her to cave?"

"I got my dad involved." She laughs. "He can never say no to me, but I try not to take too much advantage of that."

Daddy's little girl, huh? If it ever happens, meeting her father will be hell.

"Um, anyway, I think you look nice, too. I don't think I've ever seen you wear a belt."

I'm surprised she noticed; then again, Emily's always been perceptive. "I thought I'd go the extra mile. Halloween only comes once a year, after all." And I definitely wasn't trying to be as impressive as possible for her; trying to forget my weakness, I smile. "Thank you for the compliment, by the way."

She shakes her head, a sweet little grin on her face. "You're welcome. And thank you, too."

"No problem." I feel utterly uncool yet confident at the same time. Before either of us can dig ourselves out of the ensuing awkwardness, Mark and company charge off in search of more treasure, forcing us to follow along. We walk together in silence, the noise of hundreds of strangers and the thumping of our boots filling my hidden ears.

We go from store to store, Mark pulling out his inner cat boy to either entertain or embarrass the people around him, all the while at least Noah seems to be having a good time; Connor, on the other hand, looks like he's given up on living with even a single shred of dignity left.

Emily smiles at the sight.

"Yo, Matthew! Emily!" Mark calls, cupping his cat paws around his mouth. "Let's take a picture!" They have a photo booth set up in the middle of the center court for the Halloween festivities.

"I don't see why not." Emily looks at me. "What do you think?"

As much as I hate taking pictures, I say, "Sure. Why not?" shrugging like it's no sweat; I'm definitely not paranoid about someone scrutinizing every little thing wrong with my body. Not at all.

Decision made, we get in line for a picture, largely surrounded by parents and their kids, with a few teenagers here and there. Connor glares at me a couple times, and once we reach the end of the line, Mark looks back and winks. "You two take your own picture." When the photographer calls for the next group, he rushes ahead, pushing the Thompson brothers along with him. Connor stands sour-faced, Noah with a childish smile, while Mark holds his cat-paw gloves behind their heads, two "fingers" held up with the others curled; he puts his head in the space between theirs, hovering dangerously close to Connor's shoulder. The photographer takes their picture, then calls me and Emily up.

With far more confidence than I'd ever have, Emily pulls me in front of the Halloween-themed background; standing hip-to-hip, she wraps her arms around mine with a big grin, and I muster the strength to smile. The digital sound of the shutter goes off, and she lets go of me to get our free photo; we rejoin Mark and the brothers away from the crowd, Emily smiling at our picture the whole way.

Mark drags everyone along for our remaining time, collecting as many treats as possible; after their final spree, we return to the first-floor Belk entrance.

"Thanks for coming, you guys," Emily says, her brothers at her side.

"It was no problem. We all had fun, right?" Mark grins directly at Connor.

Connor's lips stretch into a strained smile. "Sure. We had a great time."

Emily smiles awkwardly at Connor, then steps in front of me and holds out the photo we took together. "You should keep it; my parents will kill me if they see it."

I remember her complaining last semester that her parents didn't want her dating until she turned eighteen; a picture of her and some boy wouldn't look good on that front. I take the photo, the only evidence of our excursion with Emily the witch, and even though I can't see the outer ring of green in her hazel eyes, I'm secretly happy I get to keep it. Maybe I'll be able to give it back to her one day, but I know that's wishful thinking.

We wave our goodbyes, and the Thompson trio walks up the nearby staircase to meet their parents at the upper parking deck; when they leave our sight, we turn around, reenter Belk, and exit the mall proper.

CHAPTER 8

Speak of the Devil

Ashley

Warmth washes over my exposed skin as I walk through the doors of Barnes & Noble; I shiver, my body eager to heat up after the short time spent outside. It's no colder than high fifties tonight, but even high sixties gives me goose bumps.

I travel past the aisles upon aisles of various genres and formats of literature until I reach the reference section. There are all kinds of books full of random information the average person has no need to know, but that's part of the fun of learning. There are the dictionaries and the encyclopedias, the indexes and the almanacs, and all the specific subject books full of a vast array of general information; I scan the shelves until I find books specifically on animals, then parse the shelf for books about bunnies.

I've collected many books throughout the years I've known about animal people; it started with wolves, then Mark came along and brought a completely new mystery. After he fully awakened, I scoured books on snakes, iguanas, monitor lizards, Komodo dragons, crocodiles, and alligators—books on any and all reptiles commonly connected to dragons entered my growing shelf. I bought books about dragons too, both ancient and modern, eastern and western. Out of all my research, depictions of medieval European dragons slain by Saint Margaret of Antioch are the closest I could find; although highly inconsistent and extremely diverse, they often lacked horns, had paw-like feet, and sometimes had elf-like ears. Even if Mark's exact species remains a mystery forever, the knowledge on lizards became invaluable for helping him shed his skin, trim his claws, and manage his cold-blooded curse.

After Mark brought Matthew home, I bought a book about domestic cats; now he's added bunny-eared John to the mix. I'm not familiar with rabbits, and I haven't seen his active form yet, so I have no clue what breed he might be; at a loss on where to start, I pull a guide on pet bunnies, another on rabbits as farm animals, and one all about their wild cousins.

With those three books in tow, I peruse the other aisles to kill time; I could sit in the café, but I'd feel bad if I didn't buy something to eat or drink as penance for the space taken. I wander into the cookbook section, my eyes immediately drawn to the tall man standing in the middle. Out of habit, I make note of his general physicality: he wears his long golden-brown hair in a low ponytail; weary wrinkles make their mark around his peridot-green eyes and full lips; and his fitted purple sweater accentuates a prominent gut, tapering down to sharp chinos that can't mask the sizeable thighs underneath. I stand at a distance, just out of his line of sight, wishing I didn't recognize him. I wish he's just a crazy coincidence, that I could convince myself he's simply a doppelgänger, but his ears are pointed at their tips. He's changed so much with the weight of time, but I know this man is Alex.

I sidle up next to him and pretend to search for a cookbook, wondering whether I should talk to him or not. We knew each other in ways I only ever knew again with George, but he might not want to dig up that hedonistic past. My wedding band constricts my ring finger, a reminder of three lonesome years and the decades preceding them—a reminder that my promise to George has long been fulfilled. The ring slips from my finger and falls into my cardigan's breast pocket.

Alex sighs, his brow deeply furrowed, and puts the book he was evaluating back on the shelf; he scans the selection and pulls out another.

I peruse the books occupying the shelf next to his and notice the first cookbook I ever bought when I first tried to turn my poor diet around some five years ago; I pull the nostalgic book from the shelf, mull over the picture of a casserole, and glance at Alex. I shuffle closer and hold the book out toward him. "This one is good if you're just starting to learn," I say, guessing his beer belly isn't the product of a healthy diet.

The book in his hand thumps closed and he returns it to the shelf, his gaze lingering on my face; he reaches out, says, "Thank you," and accepts my offering. He pretends to look at the cover and read the table of contents, all the while assessing me out of the corner of his eye; and I stand there, letting him take me in, wondering if he can recognize the sodden woman before him. He turns the book over to the back cover and loudly clears his throat. "Excuse me if I'm wrong, but you wouldn't happen to be Ashley Sancur, would you?"

I smile. "That's right, though I go by Koenigsegg now."

He beams so brightly I envision his tail wagging. "Oh, you got married?"

My smile wanes, but I know it's better to rip off the bandage rather than let it stick to my skin. "Yes, but . . ." I hate the burn invading my eyes. "He passed three years ago."

His eyebrows furrow. "Oh, I'm sorry."

"It's alright." The words barely escape, a whisp of a thing because I have too much to hold inside. "How have you been, Alex? It's been a long time."

He smiles awkwardly. "Still single as ever, but I finally moved out of my dad's house, so that's something."

I laugh. "You'd be a wizard if not for me, huh?"

"Oh, don't say that." He rubs his cheek, clearly embarrassed; his hand travels to the back of his neck, right under his ponytail. "It's just hard to reveal, you know . . . especially in this day and age." He taps his ear.

"I understand." Back when we were in college, smartphones and the internet weren't so developed; nowadays, all it'd take is one picture to ruin his entire life. "I'm just . . . so happy to see you. You disappeared on me, and I wasn't sure what happened to you."

"I'm sorry. I really should've said something to you." He huffs, staring at the shelf before him. "That winter . . . I went home to see my folks, and we found out my mom developed stage III breast cancer."

I stifle a gasp.

He scratches his neck. "I transferred immediately and had my roommate send all my stuff back home so I could be there for her while she lived."

"I'm sure she really appreciated that. Is she . . . ?"

Smiling sadly, he shakes his head. "She made it seven years. They caught it so late it's a miracle she made it that long at all."

I smile sadly, too. "Here we are feeling sorry for ourselves all over again."

Alex snorts. "Old habits die hard."

I cup my cheek. "I would know."

Alex breathes long and slow out of his nose, and he looks at me, his eyes half-lidded; his gaze glides down my face, lingering on my lips, my neck, the skin tight over my collarbones.

"Alex?"

He looks away, canine tugging on his lip, and wraps me in his arms. He holds me close to his taut stomach, his book digging into my hip, and I wrap my free arm around his back, tracing my hand down its broad length. "God, I missed you." His warm breath tickles my ear. "I feel like I've missed you forever."

I run my hand up his back, his sweater soft beneath my fingers. "I missed you, too."

He pulls away, a blush coloring his tawny skin; he smiles all puppylike and rubs his cheek. "Would you like to catch up? I'll treat you to something at the café."

I think about it for a brief moment, think about running away and never seeing him again because it's only been three years and what would Mark think? But I say, "I'd love to," and hold my three books over my chest. "But we should check out first."

"Oh, right." He glances at the book I gave him. "I think I'll get this one, since you recommended it and all."

I smile. "I hope it works out for you."

We walk to the front of the store and stand in the nonexistent line; unsurprisingly, there's no associate at the register. We wait quietly for someone to come by, practically strangers despite our history.

Alex stands incredibly close to my back; slowly, he leans down and sniffs my hair, then backs away. As off-putting as that was, I decide to give him the benefit of the doubt—there must be a scent he's picking up that I'm not aware of.

One tired teenager steps behind the register and we take our turns checking out; the cashier pushes their membership a tad too hard, but I get a coupon for a cookie at the café with the receipt. Bags in hand, we walk over to the café counter. I linger behind Alex, contemplating the menus on display. He orders a coffee and steps back, forcing me to make up my mind. I order an iced tea and take advantage of the coupon because I had a light dinner.

We find a secluded corner, the people around us paying attention to their laptops or magazines, and set aside our purchases on a tiny round table. Alex sits down and adds some cream and sugar to his coffee, idly mixing it in with a small plastic spoon.

I settle in my chair and stare at the chocolate chunk cookie in its wrapper. I haven't eaten one in years. My mind wanders to a difficult place, so I ask, "What brings you out here, Alex? Did you move recently?"

He looks up from his coffee, the harsh overhead lights illuminating the bags under his eyes. "I moved just this Monday, actually. I got an apartment near where I'll be working. Just a one-bedroom, one-bathroom joint."

"What do you do for a living?"

"I'm an ob-gyn, but I'm not doing as many deliveries as I used to; I've always preferred the gynecological side more."

Dr. Alexander Delgado, huh? "I'm surprised you can manage a job with such an unpredictable schedule. What do you do . . . on those nights?"

He takes a long drag of coffee. "Sometimes I work through it, sometimes I call backup; it depends on the timing and how I'm feeling. Most of the time, it's not much of an issue."

"You can work like that? Wouldn't you . . . need to turn?"

He casts his gaze aside. "On my good nights, I'm so distracted by work I forget I have the urge at all. There are far more important things to be worried about."

"You were always good at that. Holding back even hours in."

He sighs. "Doesn't mean I like to." Even with caffeine in his system, he looks so tired.

I flatten my lips and worry the current subject might be too heavy; most times, my boys don't like talking about their animal-person problems, so Alex may feel the same. I look at the cookie lying on the table and open the wrapper; the rich scent of warm chocolate wafts out. "You were . . . sniffing me earlier. Do I smell strange?" Watching his face, I tear a small portion off the oversize pastry; it hovers near my lips, my throat dry and gut tight.

Alex splutters, that blush returning to his cheeks; he places his coffee down and clears his throat. "You smell fine, it's just . . ." He leans forward, cupping one hand around his mouth. "I caught two other scents on you, something like . . . pine, and charcoal, and I was wondering . . ." He checks for eager ears. "Do you happen to know any other guys like me? Those scents are too strong on you for it to be a coincidence, and it's not the kind of artificial scent you'd get from perfume; it's too musky for that."

I place the wedge of cookie on my tongue and chew on his question.

Alex leans back, his eyebrows furrowed.

By the time I swallow, I realize he's smelling Mark and Matthew. It might be dangerous to give too much away, but Alex can already tell they're fellow animal people, and I'd rather him not assume they're grown men. "Why, yes, I do. The charcoal is probably my son, and the pine, his friend. They're both in my house all the time, so that's probably why I smell so strongly of them."

"Your son. Then, your husband was . . ."

I shake my head. "No. We were like your parents. I never would've guessed our child could be like you until . . . My son broke his arm when he was five, and he . . . turned . . . prematurely. He could hide it back then, but when he turned eleven and finished the process, he wouldn't have been able to keep it a secret from me even if he tried."

"It's not just . . . ?" Alex taps his ear.

"It may be better if I show you." I take my phone out of my handbag. "Let me pull up a picture of him." I don't have many photos of Mark because he's hardly ever in a state appropriate for them—and the less permanent, digital evidence, the better—but he loves taking pictures with Glenn, so it doesn't take me long to find a selfie he sent me recently; he sticks his forked tongue out, Glenn pushing a black paw against his cheek while he drapes over Mark's shoulder. "Here." I hold my phone out across the table.

Alex unabashedly gapes, glancing between me and the damning pixels rapidly; without my black hair and brown eyes, Mark hardly looks like mine at all. "How do you manage to get away with him looking like this?"

I massage my forehead with my left hand. "It was an absolute headache; I'll just say I had to be *that* mom: lots of angry phone calls, some convincing-enough doctor's notes, and many, many parent-teacher meetings." I sigh; talking about it makes me pissed off all over again. "Most of his teachers gave up on it since he's a good student, so it's not like they could call him out for being disruptive; sure, his appearance is a little 'distracting,' but most people stop caring once they get used to it."

"Well, I meant . . . Isn't it beyond obvious he's . . ."

I smile, moving my hand from my forehead to my cheek. "You'd be surprised how oblivious people are. It even took me two tries to convince myself about you."

Alex gapes again. "You saw me twice?!"

"Did I never tell you?" I lock my phone and place it on the table. "I thought I was drunk that first time, and you were so inebriated you didn't notice me until the second time."

"Jesus . . . I gotta stop drinking so much . . ." He sinks so low in his chair he could rest his chin on the table.

My eyebrows draw up, and I hate that I'm not surprised; the way he drank back then . . . But there's no nice way to ask if he's an alcoholic. "I remember . . . you were a heavy drinker, even at eighteen. Are you still . . . ?"

He sighs and nods, sitting up with a hunched posture. "I've tried so many times to stop. There's just . . . I get stressed, and the moon . . ." He shakes his head, face contorting with shame and frustration. "Nothing helps." His lip curls up and his nose scrunches, like he wants to growl. "That's part of why I moved. I've always had . . . enablers . . . in my life."

Addiction is a difficult thing, compounded by yourself and the people around you; I did my time with food, and George hardly helped. Pleasant conversations were never our style, were they? "Would you like to talk about it?"

"There's not much to say." Alex takes another swig of coffee, his expression forlorn. "I told you way back when . . . that my dad got me into drinking, right?"

I nod. His father had an entire home bar and frequently allowed Alex to sample at a young age; while those activities can be harmless—I had, on occasion, taken a daring sip of my parents' drinks— Alex's addictive personality pushed him over the edge.

"That habit of his . . . it only got worse when Mom got sick, and when she died . . . we were a mess. We wouldn't go a day without drinking something. And I have a pretty good tolerance, so I never thought much of it. So I just let it be. It wasn't until I started blacking out every one of *those* nights that I thought I had a problem. And Dad didn't care. He wasn't even worried. The men in our family have always been prone to excess, so I was just fitting in with everybody else. And to make matters worse, I could afford it."

I'd imagine, even with the college and medical school debt, he must make a lavish salary. And without a family to care for, that's more money in his pocket.

"Once I started experiencing withdrawal symptoms, I tried to quit. But it was impossible. There was always something in the fridge, always something stressing me out at work, Dad bringing another damn woman home, so I just . . . I relapsed, over and over again."

I wish I could comfort him, that a problem like his could be magically whisked away, but nothing's that simple; sometimes, you trade one beast for another.

Alex grins sardonically. "I knew it was bad for me, that I could afford to go wherever the hell I wanted on this godforsaken planet, but I didn't want to abandon my dad. I was never really home and worked until I dropped, but that wasn't enough to stop me. I always came back to the bottle. And when the moon is full, I . . ." He clenches his teeth. "It's embarrassing, how much I drink and eat."

The consequences are plain to see. I remember how he drank as a teenager, but that probably pales in comparison to what he does now. "You don't have to get specific if you don't want to. Maybe I can't fully understand, but I can empathize; there was a time not too many years ago that I weighed more than you do now."

Alex stares at my gaunt face. "I sincerely doubt that, Ashley. I'm over two hundred pounds."

I smile and stare at my cookie; it's probably cold now. "I gained a lot of weight after you left. You wouldn't have recognized me at my largest." Even if I had a photo on hand, I couldn't bring myself to show him.

His gaze falls toward my chest and stomach hidden below the table. "How did you lose it?"

I cradle my elbow, unable to look at him. "I starved myself." My eyes burn anew.

"Ash, I . . ." He tries to look into my eyes; gently, he asks, "Do you want to talk about it?"

I sigh, holding my hands tight in my lap. "My husband . . . was a large man, much larger than myself. We had our share of health problems, which only grew worse throughout our marriage. I had to take medication for high blood pressure for a long time.

"After my son met his friend, I started to take my health more seriously, if only for their sake. I was able to drop some weight, but not as much as I would've liked; George, my husband, wasn't terribly supportive of my endeavors, which made it difficult for me to commit to better eating habits.

"Even so, my health markers gradually improved, while George's remained poor, if not worse as the years passed. It all came to a head a little over three years ago, when he . . . suddenly went into cardiac arrest." I pause, my throat tight.

Alex sucks in a breath.

I remember how he dropped like a sack of bricks in the middle of the kitchen. How I stood there, uncomprehending, staring at his motionless body. How Mark asked me if we needed to call an ambulance, and I ushered him to his room because he was too scared to stay dormant. And how I pressed into George's sternum with my fists, far too weak to penetrate his girth. For ten minutes I tried to restart his heart, sobbing and gasping and knowing it might be too late for him.

"They tried to do a bypass, but . . . he didn't make it. And I . . ." My mouth dry, a single tear slips down my cheek. Those phone calls I had to make late into the night. The call I made to Mark. "After he died, I couldn't bear to eat anymore, to so much as look at the thing that slowly killed him, that was slowly killing me. I lost a lot of weight that year. Too much. And now . . ." Another tear, and a third; I can't be crying like this, not in front of a man I barely know. I grab a napkin and dab my eyes, careful not to ruin my mascara. "I'm sorry. This isn't appropriate." I sniffle, struggling to contain my sorrow.

"Hey." Alex smiles softly, holding his hand out across the table. "Take my hand."

After I fail to move, staring too long at the old nicks decorating his fingers, he curls them up together twice, beckoning me; I place my right hand in his left.

"There you go." He rubs my knuckles with his thumb, slowly cresting each knobby bone. "You can tell me anything, Ash. No need to feel embarrassed."

"Ash again, huh?" I whisper, though it comes out more like a warble. "You've always been too sweet on me, Alex."

"You think so?" He squeezes my hand lightly, his head tilted down, gazing up at me.

I squeeze his hand back. "Maybe." As that old longing clutches my heart, my phone vibrates, and a notification pops up on the screen. I let go of Alex's hand and read the text message; it's already been two hours, so long yet not enough.

"Time to go?" Alex asks, smiling sweetly.

"Looks like it." I reply to Mark and slide my phone into my hand-bag. "Does my makeup look okay?"

He smiles wider, taking his time to roam my face; he lingers on my cheek, reaches out, and brushes it with his thumb. His calloused fingers glide across my skin and pull away, a tiny droplet shining under his blunt nail; he wipes it off on his thigh. "That should do it."

"Oh, thank you." My ears warm.

Alex leans back and reaches into his pants pocket, pulling out his wallet. "Do you have a pen?"

I fumble one out of my purse and hand it over.

He loops black ink onto the back of a small piece of cardstock, then holds it out to me between two fingers. "Here's my number."

I take the card.

"If you ever need to talk, just give me a call."

I put the card in my handbag.

We rise, and Alex wraps me in another hug.

"It was nice to see you again," I say. "I'm sorry for unloading on you like that."

"Don't apologize. I'd say we're even there."

We part and I gather my things, leaving Alex behind; right as I step foot outside, I spot a flash of red in the corner of my left eye. Mark joins me with a bucketful of candy and a dopey Matthew staring stupidly at a small photo. I pass the truck keys, eager to be on our way home.

We enter the highway, the headlights of dozens of cars shining nearby, and I turn my head to check on Matthew in the back seat; his round pupils turn green when the lights shine in them just right. "Matthew, is something on your mind?"

He stiffens, holding the little photo close to his chest. "Nothing much."

"Uh-huh." Mark glances at Matthew through the rearview mirror. "I so generously helped him get a picture with Emily."

Matthew huffs, narrowing his eyes at the back of Mark's head.

"May I see it?" I ask.

Matthew stares at it for an extra moment, mutters, "Sure," and holds it out to me; when I take it from him, he faces the window, crossing his arms and leaning back as if he's all cool and collected—I've always found it cute how hard he tries to act like he doesn't care, but if his ears were out he'd surely have one pointed toward me.

I look at the little photograph depicting Matthew and a girl in a cute costume; his lips are quirked up in an awkward smile, while the girl holds his arm close to her hip. She wears a frilly black minidress, a crooked witch hat, and striped stockings; I can imagine exactly what she was thinking when she decided on her outfit. "She's cute."

Matthew makes a noncommittal noise, holding his head in one hand while he stares out at nothing in particular.

Ah, young love . . . I feel melancholy, knowing the struggle my boys will face pursuing whoever catches their eyes; will they be forever bachelors like Alex, or will they take a chance on the one they love? I wish I could do more for them, reassure them that there are good people out there who won't take advantage of them, but I can't know that any better than they can. It's all I can do to be a mother and a guardian for them; I want wherever I am to be a place they can call home.

I crash on my bed, phone in hand and card on my chest; I lift it up, and Alex's youthful face smiles back. Scrawled in doctor's chicken scratch, I read his cell number again and again. It's an old business card for a gynecology practice in Atlanta, Georgia. His jawline is sharp, his hair cropped above his ears, and his wrinkles nonexistent; his skin is a beautiful bronze, his mouth stretched in a white-toothed grin—an Alex I never knew and will never know.

I place the card on my sagging breast, balancing it over my nipple. I open my phone and add a new contact, type in his number, his name, agonize, delete it, and add it all over again. I turn my head to the mirror attached to my closet door; my old face stares back, plain and tired, my hair a shadowy puddle around my head. I'm not the looker I used to be, but neither is Alex. We're both old and marred and lonely. So there's no harm in it. I can contact him, and it won't kill anybody.

I type out a long, drawn-out text, bite my lip, and delete every word, then sigh because I'm being ridiculous. *Alex. This is Ashley. I didn't want to call because it's late. I hope you made it home safe. And thank you for treating me.* Without a second thought, I send the text and wait.

Not ten minutes later, my phone buzzes in my hand. *It was no trouble! And it was great to see you!*

You're still awake?

My sleep schedule is messed up these days.

I purse my lips. *Is it from the move?*

Kinda . . . And you're still awake, too.

I am. I have a lot on my mind.

Want to share?

I smile, but I shouldn't indulge. *Another time. We should sleep. Good night.*

Good night.

I don't sleep for a long time.

CHAPTER 9

Monotonous Maintenance
Matthew

I push my bangs out of my eyes with my left hand so I don't have to look at my worksheet through my hair; it's getting too long again, but I never feel like cutting it. Unfortunately, it's important that I maintain it's form, or else it'd get too heavy, the crown would get weighed down, and my ears would become too obvious. The sheer amount of layering and precision needed to get my curls to frame my face *just right* is abysmal. I'll get around to it eventually, but, *man*, what I would pay to have someone trim it for me.

"You good there, bro?" Mark nudges my shoulder. "You look like you're about to burn a hole through that homework."

Do I look that angry? After I finish writing a sentence, I say, "Just thinking about my hair is all."

"Your hair?" John sticks his plastic fork into some sloppy excuse for lasagna. I'm always in terrified awe at what this school manages to serve in the cafeteria every day, and that John actually eats it; his stomach must be made of steel.

"Yeah." I read the next question on my worksheet. "It's too long again and needs to be trimmed, but it always takes me about two hours to get it done."

"Two hours?!" John gapes. "Isn't that a bit much?"

"I never said I was good at cutting hair!" I press so hard against the paper that the tip of my pencil chips. "And it's hard to get it shaped right, especially in the back." I take my hand out from under my bangs and jerk my thumb at Mark. "It was much easier to cut his the one time I did it, and that's mostly because his hair's straight."

Mark says, "Oh, I almost forgot you cut my hair that one time. I was deep in my emo phase. Good times."

"*You* had an emo phase?" John scrunches his face and points the end of his fork at Mark.

"Didn't we all?" Mark flips the long side of his hair up.

I say, "I'd like to think *I* didn't have one."

Mark grins. "That's because it's not a phase for you, Matthew."

If I wasn't annoyed enough . . . "Nice one, Mark." I'm glad Emily happens to be busy working on a group project right now; she would've laughed at me for that one.

Mark chuckles and returns to his lunch. I should start eating mine, but I want to get this worksheet done since I already got through half of it last period; I have one last question to answer, then—

"Hey, Matthew."

I look up from my worksheet to see John staring at his half-eaten government-approved meal. "What's up?" I wonder what's got him all nervous.

He briefly glances at me, stabbing his plastic fork back into what's left of his lasagna. "I was thinking that, uh . . ." He purses his lips, takes a deep breath, and lifts his head to face me properly. "If you'd like, I could cut your hair for you."

"Shit, that's right!" Mark says, "You'd have to know how to cut your own hair, too!"

Smiling faintly, John nods. "I've been trimming it myself ever since I was old enough to learn. I even cut my sisters' hair sometimes, so I have some experience with different styles, though I'll have to do some research for your hair type."

I stick my hand in my bangs again, playing with the springy strands. "Gosh, I . . . really appreciate your offer, John. Seriously." I smile. "Do you think you could come over this Saturday? As long as that's not too much trouble, of course."

"Sure, I don't mind. I'm guessing Mark's place again?"

"You know it, bro!" Mark says, "Come whenever you feel like. You can stay the night if you want, too; we always like to have company, right?" He smiles at me, slinging his arm across my shoulders.

"Of course." I feel almost giddy; I haven't had someone cut my hair since I was ten—I didn't realize I'd miss it so much until I was forced to do it myself. I can't wipe the smile off my face as I finally finish my worksheet, which I promptly put into the folder in my book bag; after tossing my pencil in its pouch, I finally take my lunch out and start to eat.

⁓

The doorbell rings right as I place the stool in front of the long mirror hanging between the dining and living rooms of Mark's house. I swiftly tuck my tail under my shirt, put a hat on my head, and open the front door.

John waves from the other side of the doorway, carrying his usual overnight bag plus a tool bag strapped with a blow-dryer in its holster. "I hope it's not a bad time." He glances at the empty driveway. "I saw the truck isn't here."

I step back so John can walk in. "Not at all, though it's just you and me for now. Miss Ashley and Mark went shopping for Thanksgiving; you know how they clear out the grocery stores this time of year."

"Oh, that's right." John sets his stuff down in the entryway and takes off his boots. "My family usually drives out to see my mom's folks for some ridiculous party." He places his intricately designed cowboy boots on the shoe rack, then picks his bags back up.

I close the front door, take my tail back out, put my hat back on the coatrack, and lead John to Mark's room. "I usually come here for Thanksgiving, and my parents come by for dinner if they aren't busy."

"Your parents work on Thanksgiving?" John asks as we enter the bedroom.

"Yeah. My dad works in the ER, while my mom is a news reporter; days off are pretty rare for them, and their schedules are all over the place, too." Ever since that horrible day I awakened, I've spent every holiday I can in this house because I don't like being home alone.

"Do your parents get along with Miss Ashley?" John drops his overnight bag next to Mark's desk, then places his tool bag on top; his hands free, he removes the ties and pins keeping his ears confined to his head.

I turn his question over in my head, trying to recall the last time they communicated with each other. "I'd say they get along fine, but they're not particularly close; it's kind of a let's-get-along-because-our-kids-are-friends sort of thing."

"Makes sense." He combs his fingers through his hair, his ears standing at a neutral forty-five-degree angle. Once he has his wavy black locks how he wants them, he picks his tool bag back up. "So where are we doing this? The bathroom?"

"Nah. There's a body-length mirror at the edge of the dining room I always use. I already put a stool down before you got here."

"Good, because I just remembered how tiny that bathroom is."

"You got that right." I lead John back out to the living area and seat myself on the stool, resting my feet on the bar between its legs.

John sets up on the dining room table, placing down two shears, a bunch of sectioning clips, and a cutting comb with both wide and narrow teeth; he fiddles with everything for a while, getting it into whatever perfect position will satisfy him. Through the mirror, John steps behind me with the comb and a spray bottle in hand. "Alright, I'm gonna ask a few questions before I start."

"Shoot."

"I'm guessing you're fine with your current style but looking for a trim. How short do you want me to cut it?"

"Yeah, the style's fine. I usually try to get it as short as I can." I point at the side of my head, placing my finger around where my human ear would end if I still had them. "Basically long enough no one would notice I don't have the ears I'm supposed to have, but no longer than that."

He grins. "You're lucky I know enough about anatomy that I can pull that off." He scans my head, his long ears held erect. "My only other question is whether you want me to cut wet or dry. I looked up what I could, but people with curly hair are divided on what works best."

Back when I was teaching myself, it was frustrating that some professionals swore by dry cutting while others swore by wet—dry bears the risk of breakage while wet bears the risk of excessive shrinkage; at least my hair isn't coily, so it *can* be cut wet in the right hands. Even wavy hair experiences some amount of shrinkage, so John shouldn't be completely clueless. "I don't care either way, so whatever works best for you. I usually cut it wet and finish fixing it up dry."

John smiles. "That's all I needed to know. Ready to start?"

I nod.

John starts spraying my hair with water, and the moment he gets my bangs wet, I close my eyes. He sprays until my thick hair is damp enough to detangle, then runs the wide-toothed half of the comb through my unruly curls. He combs from root to tip in increments, carefully skirting around my delicate ears, until he gets the entire daily cropping of knots out of my hair; he's perfectly gentle, not yanking through a single snag. Once he's done, he touches my forehead with the tip of his middle finger and says, "Look up."

I crane my neck back.

John sections my bangs out from the rest of my hair, his comb raking all the way down my nose. "Jeez, you've got a good couple of inches shrinkage." John grasps my bangs between his pointer and middle fingers; using them as a guide, he cuts the first quarter inch off my locks.

"I know. It's always made me paranoid I'd cut too much off."

He keeps combing and cutting. "I'll try not to ruin your bangs. My oldest sister likes to curl her hair, but she always goes to a professional hairstylist."

"I've never understood why people like to change their hair like that."

John finishes working on my bangs and shifts over to the right side of my head. "Tilt your head to the left." He pushes my head in the proper direction with the tips of his fingers, then sections off the front from the back. "Hair is a form of self-expression; I'd even go so far as to say it's an art." He snips off bits and pieces, the meager ends of my hair drifting onto my shoulders. "Everyone in my family looks the same—all of us have brown eyes and dark hair—so the best thing we can do to stand out without doing anything drastic is to play around with our hair." John's face is hard and unforgiving, like he has a bitter taste in his mouth. He's hardly sectioned my hair at all, freely point cutting into my layers as if he's done this exact trim thousands of times before.

"I never thought about it that way; it's always just been another hassle." I haven't been able to openly express myself because of the ears on my head, so I'd forgotten something so simple. "If I had the choice, I think I'd give myself a fade."

John smirks, glancing at me through the mirror with one ear turned toward it. "Really? I'll be honest, I'm so used to your bob that I can hardly imagine that." He takes the back side of my hair out of the sectioning clip, then uses the front part to guide his next cut.

I stare at myself, at my damp, half-cut curls, and imagine how different I'd look if I were human. "What about you? Would you change your hair?"

John rakes the comb through my hair, still working just as gently as he started. "I don't hate my hair, but I wish I could experiment more. I was actually growing it out before I awakened; good thing, too, because I would've been screwed if I couldn't cover my ears."

"Was there a particular reason? Or was it just on a whim?"

John slows his combing, stopping just as he slots my hair between his fingers. "I'd say . . . a little bit of both. I just felt like it, but I also wanted to make my parents mad. I'm the only boy, so they've always hovered over me on every little thing. I was tired of being some perfect little heir to the family name, so I stopped styling my hair the way they wanted me to.

"And they always say the most passive-aggressive shit about it! Like, 'Oh, John, doesn't this actor have such nice hair?' or, 'Doesn't your cousin look so nice in this photo?' I know they want me to be able to fit in or whatever, and they worry about me getting a job one day, but it's not like I want to work at a place that would force me to keep my hair short anyway. My parents aren't all that happy about my career aspirations, either."

I don't think I've ever seen John so worked up before, gritting his teeth and raising his voice only to return to a more familiar downtrodden expression. Done with his short rant, he huffs and returns to combing and cutting away at my hair; after he finishes the right side of my head, he tells me to look down, pushing lightly at the back of my skull.

Hoping to lighten the mood, I ask, "What do you want to do after high school?"

He slows his combing again, glancing up at the mirror with his eyebrows drawn up; he returns to staring at my hair, looking all shy and embarrassed. "I . . . want to go to beauty school and learn to be a hairstylist. I know it's kinda girly, but it's what I want to do, and I like to think I'm good at it." Sullen, he continues working on the back of my head.

I can understand that feeling of girlishness, that desire to always seem as manly as possible so people don't emasculate you more than you already do yourself. Being short and a cat boy doesn't help me feel like much of a man; I'm hardly taller than half the girls I meet and dwarfed by the vast majority of the boys around me, John included. "I don't think there's any shame in that." There's nothing girly about giving haircuts—as far as I know, most barbers are men, so what's the big difference if John wants to be a hairstylist instead?

John smiles faintly, his ears relaxing back into a neutral position. "You think so?" He keeps snipping at my hair, running his fingers and his comb and his shears through it so expertly I'm surprised I haven't purred. Once John finishes working on the back, he tilts my head to the right so he can work on the final large section of my unruly hair. He does what he did before, sectioning off what little is necessary for him, creating a guiding cut for the longest layer, and shaping up the rest. It seems almost effortless compared to the work I have to do to get similar results.

After he finishes, I bring my head level again.

In true hairstylist fashion, John starts playing with my hair.

"I think it'd be a shame for you to give up just because some people think it's girly. You have some real skill from what I can tell, and you're only fourteen! Imagine what you'll be able to do after beauty school, right?"

John smiles wide, drifting around and checking for crooked layers and wiping the remaining clumps of hair off my shoulders. "I had a good base to work with; you're not bad for someone who hates cutting his own hair."

"That's because I agonize over it forever. I'd be much worse if I tried to do it as fast as you can."

"Maybe." He makes tiny corrections as my hair air-dries—he hasn't bothered to use the blow-dryer because he did his homework and knows they're hell on my hair type. "Thanks, though, for saying that. I used to get made fun of a lot, so it can be hard to believe it."

My hair dries enough for my eyebrows to appear. "Is that why you were hesitant to offer me a haircut?"

"A little." He shapes up the bottom of my hair while his eyes stare through to the floor. "Like, I know you cut your own, and that it was pretty obvious I had to cut my own, but people have always given me shit for it. I've been called a girl because of my long hair and called gay because I like to cut it for myself and my sisters. So I don't know. It can be hard to open up, but then I feel all stupid for being insecure. And being a bunny person doesn't help. I feel too cutesy and effeminate for a guy, and I know it doesn't matter, but I can't help but care."

"That sucks. And I know what you mean with the bunny thing. Cats aren't exactly considered manly either, so I guess we're in the same boat there."

He looks up, sees my face, and chuckles. "I can actually see your eyebrows now."

"That you can."

He keeps laughing under his breath.

"What's so funny?"

"Oh, sorry." He grins. "I was thinking you look less bitchy."

I grin, too. "C'mon . . . And I was just trying to empathize with you . . ."

"Sorry, sorry." He giggles, waving his shear hand in the air as he bends away.

While he can hardly contain himself, I pull my shirt and shake out the hair stuck under it.

John settles down enough to put his shears and comb back on the dining room table, then turns around to give my hair one last inspection. "Anyway, looks like I didn't mess up too bad; you should be good to go for another month or two."

"You're too hard on yourself—it looks better than ever if you ask me! And actually, while I'm thinking about it . . ." I pull my wallet out of my pocket and take out a twenty-dollar bill. "Here: for your services."

John gawks, his ears perking straight up. "You don't have to pay me!"

"I want to pay you."

John doesn't make any move to accept the cash.

Smiling, I roll my eyes, get up off the stool, take his hand, and press the bill into his palm. "I'm guessing your sisters don't pay you, but you gotta remember I'm not your sisters; I'd rather not take advantage of you, even for something like this."

"Well, if you insist . . ." He folds it carefully and shoves it into his jeans pocket, placing his free hand on his neck. "I guess I'm just not used to people paying me for things like this. And to be fair, my sisters *do* pay me in their own way; I always get free rides from the ones that can drive when I ask."

"Favors for favors, huh . . ." Now that I think of it, John might not get much of an allowance since he comes from a ten-person household; it'd be hard to use money as payment if you don't have any to begin with. And there are plenty of times Mark and I have done each other favors without expecting anything in return; even so, a haircut is a haircut, and I certainly would've paid a professional had I gone to one, so I have no intention of taking my money back.

John drops his hand and glances around. "Anyway, where's the broom closet? We should clean up before Mark and Miss Ashley get home."

I survey the mess of hair on the floor all around the stool, then nod my head toward the hall. "It's right next to the bathroom." I show him where we keep the majority of our cleaning supplies, take out the broom and the mop, and walk back over to the mess we made. "I'll clean the floor and you take care of your tools?"

John shrugs. "Works fine by me."

"We're home~" Mark says, rudely interrupting my explanation of a math problem John asked me for help with. He's holding a ridiculous amount of grocery bags, Miss Ashley not far behind with a more reasonable amount in tow. As he walks past, he says, "There's more in the truck."

"That's our cue to help out." I get out of my chair.

John trains his ears on me, reminding me how much of a pain in the ass it is for him to hide them.

"Scratch that: it's *my* cue to help out. I'll be back in a second." I quickly conceal my ears and tail, then help bring the remaining groceries inside; while we put them away, Miss Ashley requests that we leave out a box of instant mashed potatoes, a packet of brown gravy mix, a bag of brussels sprouts, and a package of raw sirloin steak. Steak is a bit unusual in this house, so I ask, "What's the occasion?"

Miss Ashley smiles. "It was on sale, so I bought it on a whim."

"You probably forgot, but it's also Mom's birthday today." Mark pulls out a pot, a frying pan, and a baking pan.

"Oh, jeez." I scratch my cheek. "Happy birthday."

"Thanks, hon." Miss Ashley grabs salt, pepper, and olive oil. "I don't blame you for forgetting; once you get to be my age, you have to celebrate for yourself!"

I can't remember the last time we celebrated her birthday; it was probably more than three years ago, before Mr. Koenigsegg died.

"Anyway, Mark and I will get started on dinner in a moment. You and John can go back to working on that homework if you'd like."

"Sure you don't need any help with anything?"

Miss Ashley waves me off. "We have it handled. But if you don't mind, could you put the cake on the table?"

"Oh, sure." I take the container of sliced marble cake and place it in the middle of the dining room table. I return to helping John, hovering behind his seat; he's not much of a math guy, but I have a lot of patience to go around.

As we work, Miss Ashley and Mark busy themselves in the kitchen. Mark preps the brussels sprouts for the oven, while Miss Ashley lays the steak in sizzling hot oil; she has a massive smile on her face, humming to herself without a care in the world.

She's been different lately. Eating more. Experimenting with new recipes. Always waiting for someone to text her back only to agonize over her reply. It's like she's in love with life again.

By the time John's able to connect enough brain cells to understand the gist of his homework, the oven timer goes off. John takes his completed worksheet to Mark's room, and once he returns, we all serve ourselves and sit together at the table. Miss Ashley bows her head in prayer, hands in her lap and eyes closed; she never says the blessing aloud when John is over because none of us know his particular beliefs.

Although I'm not particularly devout, I send my own prayer; I hope that whatever happened to make Miss Ashley happier continues to help her, and I thank God for the peace I've managed to gather in my life. I wish that peace could last forever, but I know, someday, it could all be ripped away; I pray, too, that that day comes when I'm ready for it.

Everyone having taken their time to contemplate, we begin to eat the meal so kindly prepared for us. Over the course of dinner, we talk about all the little things; Miss Ashley asks us about school, Mark talks about their hectic trip to the grocery store, and, inevitably, we wander into holiday plans.

"Actually, I've been meaning to ask," John says, scraping bits of mashed potatoes and gravy with the side of his fork, "would you all happen to be free the Saturday before Christmas?"

Miss Ashley opens the cake container and pulls a slice out with her bare hands; she holds it up to her mouth, says, "We usually don't do anything until Christmas day, so we should be," and bites into the slice like it's a piece of toast.

Marks reaches across the table and pulls the container toward himself; he takes one slice out, puts it on his plate, stares at it for a moment, and takes a second. "We don't travel much or anything." He bites into one slice, leaving behind a jagged corner. "Got something going on?"

"Ah, yeah." John places his hand on the back of his neck. "My parents host a party every year the Saturday before Christmas. It's mostly just to show off, but my mom's been hounding me about meeting all of you sometime."

Smiling heartily, Miss Ashley places her half-eaten slice on her plate. "I'm sure she wants to make sure you're in good hands. Mothers worry like that."

"Sure." John grins awkwardly. He, too, reaches for a slice of cake, easily taking one from the container in front of Mark's plate with his long arms. "You can feel free to come by, but my only concern is my sisters; one look at you two and they'll immediately know you're like me. But Teddy will definitely be there, so if you want to take the risk, you'll get to meet him."

I consider John's offer; on the one hand, I'm incredibly nervous about his sisters, but on the other, an opportunity to meet another monster person is hard to pass up. And even if his sisters figure us out, it's not like they've done anything to John after the two years they've known about him; maybe . . .

"I'd love to come!" Mark says without a hint of hesitation; shameless as he is, I'm sure he's eager to see a bear boy in person. "What about you, Matthew?" Mark says it so gently, I . . .

"I'll . . . I'll come." I'm nervous, but this is a good opportunity to get over my fear. If I'm ever going to tell Emily the truth, I'll need a little exposure; who knows: maybe I'll get over it?

"If you guys are sure . . ." John's ears lie back, betraying his nerves. "Do you have something to write on? There's a lot of little stuff my mom is specific about."

"Oh, sure, hon." Miss Ashley gets out of her seat. "Let me grab a notepad and a pen for you."

As she walks upstairs to her room, I gesture for Mark to push the container of cake my way; it takes him a second, but he gets the idea and slides it in front of my plate. I grab a slice and bite into it; it's soft and sweet and sits heavy in my stomach.

CHAPTER 10

Go Big or Go Home

Mark

park the truck on the side of the street in one of the fancier parts of town, get out, toss Mom the keys, and stare at John's house. It's huge as hell! Maybe not quite a mansion, but the elaborate exterior and pristine white outlines scream excessive opulence.

Mom says, "Wow . . . I wonder how much they pay in property taxes . . ."

"Probably a lot," Matthew says, toting along our two gifts for the "kids" white elephant exchange toward the end of the party. Mom has a nicer gift for the adults version, and I carry an additional present with a personal recipient.

Mom smiles awkwardly. "I suppose we should head to the door. No need to stand out in the cold any longer!"

Eager to get out of the freezing cold, I rush up to the front door and ring the bell. I've only been outside for a few minutes and my bones are already rattling; I started brumating a few weeks ago, so my body's running colder than usual.

Mom and Matthew join me on the fancy patio and kindly stand at my sides, helping stave off the cold a smidgen.

The door opens, and a tall, flat-chested girl with bleached blond hair and black roots peeks outside; noticing our presents, she ushers us inside.

Mom removes her coat and hangs it on the messy rack in the massive two-story foyer; I elect to keep mine on.

The girl, likely one of John's seven sisters, looks me up and down with obvious scrutiny, raising one eyebrow dramatically, then turns her head toward the hall straight in front of us. "Yo, Jack! Your friends are here!"

John bounds down the hall, his hair hiding his ears as usual, though he's wearing black sweatpants instead of his typical jeans. "Thanks, Esther."

She shrugs and saunters down a different hall to who knows where, but before she disappears from my sight, she takes her phone out and rapidly types something.

"Jack, huh?" I grin, looking up and around the entire foyer—there's an extravagant chandelier hanging from the ceiling, fit with dozens of sparkling crystals. "Nice house."

"Yeah, don't wear it out." Face sour, he crosses his arms.

We kick off our shoes and John leads us down the hall ahead; it's moderately furnished with elegant accent tables, all topped with fancy vases holding fresh live flowers, and along one side hang portraits of similar-looking men, each frame above a small plaque with a name and year—they're all professional paintings, ultimately ending with a portrait of a much younger, short-haired John; judging by his face, he must've been no older than ten when it was painted, though he's still got the same grimace he sports whenever he gets particularly fed up with me. We walk too fast for me to read any of the plaques and turn the left corner into an insanely fitted kitchen and dining room: more chandeliers, lots of marble, and very shiny knobs. Despite the immaculate condition of everything else, scuff marks cover the wooden flooring—even the rich have repair limits.

A tall, black-haired woman and a short, black-haired man round the pony wall separating the kitchen from the dining area. "Oh, you must be Ashley!" The woman holds her hand out to Mom with an awfully stretched-out smile.

The two shake hands.

"I'm John's mother, Delilah."

Mom plasters a more convincing fake smile on her face. "It's wonderful to meet you." She starts to sing John's praises, and I tune out before John's father gets a chance to say anything.

I scrutinize the room. The table in the middle of the dining space is big enough for twelve people and made out of what appears to be wood, along with twelve side chairs with fancy patterns on the upholstered seats; the table's been completely cleared off aside from four small, wrapped gifts in the middle. I'm too far from the kitchen to see anything in great detail—my vision gets blurry the farther things are from me—but I don't miss the multitude of catering trays set out on the island; I wish I had the appetite to appreciate everything.

John smacks my shoulder lightly, then whispers, "You two can put those presents on the table."

I snap my fingers near the top of Matthew's head; he looks up at me, then I point at the presents he's holding and the table. His mouth opens in a nonverbal *oh*, and he puts the two wrapped presents next to the other four. When he turns around to return to my side, he freezes, staring stupidly at something on the wall; I turn around and meet face-to-face with a giant replica of Leonardo's *The Last Supper*. I'm beginning to understand why John never talks about religion.

"It's a bit obnoxious, don't you think?" he says under his breath.

"More than a bit." I may be a religious person, but I've always thought it's better to be modest about these sorts of things. Leonardo's art may have nonreligious merit, but I don't think I'd want this one in my peripheral every time I ate at the table.

Matthew returns to my side, and we face the three conversing parents.

Mrs. Woodcock leers at me. "Your son's hair is very . . . red. And his eyes . . . ," she oh so gracefully points out.

Mom's smile turns awkward. "Oh, well . . . he's always been a colorful boy." I've always felt bad ever since my body changed so drastically, because not only does it reflect on me, but on her ability as a mother. People are so damn judgmental about every little thing. "I don't see any problem in letting him express himself as long as he's doing well in school."

"I *suppose* that's fair." Mrs. Woodcock's gross gaze shifts to John's face. He looks about as pleased as I would getting unwanted comments about my appearance, and I know for a fact that John's grades are average at best—not that I judge him for it: not everyone has the will to waste time studying shit they'll soon forget. And I'm not even the smartest one here; Matthew, as lazy as he is, happens to have excellent academic instincts—I still ask him for help from time to time on stuff that isn't clicking in my head.

Wearing a stone-cold expression, John asks, "May we be excused?"

Mrs. Woodcock frowns, the wrinkles around her mouth deeply set, and—

The doorbell rings.

Mr. Woodcock clears his throat. "Son, why don't you and your friends go get the door?"

Mrs. Woodcock glares at him.

"Thanks, Dad." John places his hands behind our backs and leads us out of the room before Mrs. Woodcock can give us a deadly glare, too. Once we get into the hall, out of sight and out of earshot, he lets us go and walks ahead, massaging his forehead as he makes his way back into the foyer. He takes a deep breath and places his hand on the front doorknob.

A girl with curly copper hair wearing a Santa dress peeks out from the other hallway.

John notices her and shoos her off with a wave of his hand.

She giggles and turns around, making brief eye contact with me, a mischievous grin splitting her lips as she trots off—I swear, these sisters are giving me the strangest looks.

John sighs, shakes his head, and opens the front door; two towering figures clad in heavy coats walk inside.

The older man takes off a classy trilby hat, revealing short, silver-streaked blond hair; he places the hat and his coat on the overloaded rack. "Y'all care if I head back?" He jerks his thumb toward the main hallway.

"Go ahead, Mr. Brown," John says. "Mom and Dad should be in the kitchen."

Mr. Brown nods, then holds out his hand to the younger blond. "I'll take the presents where they go."

The younger blond hands his gift bag over.

Mr. Brown saunters away, giving me an ominous side-eye as he passes.

I shiver.

The younger blond smiles awkwardly, gaze following Mr. Brown's back before landing on me; his eyes widen, regarding me. He has a black guitar case on his back, a massive build, and a clean fade. I linger on his pointed ears; he must be Teddy.

"Are you just gonna stand there or what?" John crosses his arms, tapping his foot with all the patience of a squirrel.

Teddy gives him a lazy smile. "Sorry, Jack." Without another word, he sweeps John into a tight hug. "How've you been?"

Jack melts into Teddy's massive torso. "I could be better. You know how it is." He hums, departing from the hug before it becomes awkwardly long.

Teddy slips the guitar case off his back and takes off his coat, revealing an awfully tight black T-shirt, his gaze lingering on me and Matthew. "Are y'all the guys Jack's been telling me about?"

I nod, but before I can reply, I catch another girl squinting at us from the side hall; she wears her black hair in a ponytail and looks a little too much like her mother, including the evil glare and haughty posture.

Teddy leers at her, then lowers his voice. "Why don't we talk in his room, yeah?"

John frowns, glaring at his sister. "Yeah."

Teddy grabs his guitar and John leads us up the stairs on the left side of the foyer.

The girl watches us ascend and slips away.

We go down a few more halls, taking this left and that right, until we reach a door with an old No Girls Allowed sign, fit with a myriad of rebuttals in permanent marker; John opens the door and we file inside.

I close the door behind me. The room is cramped, all the furniture covered with clutter, except for a small amount of empty space available on the desk against the left wall. I place the special present I've been lugging around in the corner made by the TV stand and a bookcase filled with random trinkets.

John sits down on the bottom bunk of the bed against the right wall, Matthew takes the tiny wooden desk chair, and Teddy pulls a stool and a guitar stand out of the top right corner of the room.

I roll the hand-me-down office chair—it's more foam than leather in some places—between Matthew and Teddy, then sit down, lean back, and cross my ankle over my knee.

John slumps forward and rubs his hand down his face. "Sorry about my mom earlier. And my sisters. I told them not to bother you guys, but they never listen."

"You shouldn't be surprised." Teddy places his guitar case on the stand. "I can count on one hand how many times my sister has listened to me."

John rests his chin in his palm. "I always forget you have a sister."

"Me too!" Teddy laughs.

"How do you forget you have a sister?" I ask.

"It's pretty easy when you don't live together for a few years. I live with my dad and she lives with my mom."

"Divorce?"

Teddy nods. "We don't see each other much. She's coming over for Christmas, though. Then I'll be at Mom's for New Year's."

"What's her name?"

"Heather, right?" John says. "Oddly enough, she's also Teddy's twin."

I feel like I've heard of a Heather before. "You both have twin sisters? That's a weird coincidence."

John groans. "You're telling me . . ."

The doorbell rings again; I bet we'll be hearing that telltale ding-dong many more times tonight.

Teddy leans forward, propping his legs up on the bottom rung of the stool and clasping his hands together over his thighs. "So, y'all are both, how should I say . . ."

"Monster people?" I mimic Teddy's posture, except I let my hands hang between my legs. "Yeah. We heard you are, too."

John stares at his hands, rubbing his right thumb over his left, his fingers loosely held together.

Teddy glances at him, brow furrowed, and meets my gaze. "It's . . . pretty new to me. Less than a year. Jack told me y'all have dealt with it a lot longer than us."

I nod. "I've been aware for almost eleven years but didn't actually awaken until around four years ago."

Matthew says, "I awakened when I was ten, so over five years now."

"That young?" Teddy shuffles. "I can barely wrap my head around it at fourteen."

How the hell is this guy fourteen?! I use all my self-control not to say something stupid about his age. I feel like a flimsy piece of paper compared to him; I'm insanely skinny, no doubt about that, but this guy . . . Beefy doesn't cut it: he's built like a brick shithouse. His upper arms are almost as big as his head; his tight black shirt barely slims down his massive pecs; and his straight-cut jeans strain around his muscular thighs. It's no wonder everyone calls him Teddy.

Matthew frowns, a familiar despair permeating his features. "I would say it gets easier, but . . ." He shakes his head.

Teddy sighs. "Yeah, I don't think I'll ever get used to my metabolism being seasonally out of whack. I had the worst cravings

over the summer and into fall, and now I hardly ever feel hungry."
He stares at his hands, frowning. "Like, I wish we got a manual or
something for this stuff. I just about lost my shit back in July."

"I was pretty confused at first, too," John says, leaning back on
his elbows, "but then we figured, oh, bears hibernate, so no wonder."

"Something similar happened to us when we were eleven."
Matthew looks at me from under his baseball cap, smiling lightly.
"You were only partial for the longest time, so the whole family was
freaking out when you never wanted to eat anything that first winter.
I was worried you'd turn into a skeleton."

"How do you think I felt?!" I rub my arms. "I love good food as
much as the next guy, so suddenly losing my appetite shocked me,
too."

"Actually, what are you?" Teddy squints at me.

"A dragon," I say, which only confuses him more. "Back in the
day they were often called great serpents, so I'm like a snake person,
which includes dealing with the reptile version of hibernation."

"I didn't know snakes hibernate."

"You're forced to learn a lot about animals just to get by when
you're one of us." It's not like we're *exactly* the same as our respective species, but there's enough going on that it's better to know
than be ignorant and confused—it can be fun, too, like learning I
can smell better if I use my tongue.

"I'm just glad my teeth don't grow indefinitely." John suddenly
brightens and hops to his feet. "Oh, actually, guess what?" He faces
Teddy, rocking on his heels.

"What?" Teddy asks.

"I finally got my braces off!" John grins, showing all of his
brace-free teeth; tiny white squares dot the middle of each off-
white tooth, right where the metal brackets used to be.

"Oh, look at you~" Teddy sits up straight and grins back. "Now you can smile all pretty for pictures."

John slumps forward. "Speaking of, my mom's been nagging me about getting a new hall painting done."

"But you gotta cut your hair?"

"But I gotta cut my hair." He crosses his arms and raises his nose. "Which isn't happening. Ever."

"Sounds about right," Teddy says.

John sits back down with a childish pout.

Suddenly, Matthew takes his hat off, perking his ears up out of his hair; his right ear swivels toward the bedroom door, while the left remains pointing toward us. He looks at John. "I think someone's calling for you."

From deep within the bowels of the house, Mrs. Woodcock yells his name.

John crosses his arms. "She might be calling for Dad."

Teddy raises an eyebrow. "You know she never calls for your dad."

John shrugs. "Doesn't mean it couldn't happen."

Matthew puts his hat back on and shuffles, obviously uncomfortable.

Mrs. Woodcock yells much louder than before, "John Eliza Woodcock Jr., come down here right this instant! You do *not* want me walking up those stairs!"

John sighs and stands. "I'll be back." He walks to the door, puts his hand on the knob, and looks over his shoulder. "Just . . . please don't do anything stupid while I'm gone."

"I'll make sure they don't touch Jenny's stuff," Teddy says. "Now hurry along before your mom gets really pissed."

"Thanks." John leaves, slamming the door closed a little too hard behind him.

I say, "Now I understand why all of you call him Jack. He never told us he has a nickname."

Teddy smiles softly. "He never told me, either. Not until I convinced him to let me come over once. It was pulling teeth to get him to hang out after school."

"I'm actually wondering . . . You talk like you've known each other a lot longer than a few months."

"Oh, yeah. We've been friends since seventh grade." Teddy looks up. "So . . . about two and a half years." He grins at me, crossing his arms. "I actually knew he was a bunny boy long before I turned into a bear boy, though I didn't tell him that until it happened."

"How'd you find out?"

"I got him to come over to my place, then I begged him to sleep over just once. I think he had a nightmare or something because he transformed in his sleep. I was pretty shocked, but so much of his behavior suddenly made a lot more sense. I thought I should keep it to myself, but, man, was he mad when I told him while he was helping me out with my first transformation."

I'd be pretty mad, too. If someone secretly knew what I am . . . there's no telling what they could do with that information. "I can't say I blame him. It's definitely better to be up front about that sort of thing, but I also get that it's a hard subject to broach."

Teddy smiles awkwardly. "I understand that now that I am one. I'm scared of what would happen if my dad or mom found out, or my sister, or the football team, or anyone, really. It's a lot to think about." He touches his ear, rubbing the lobe between his thumb and the side of his index finger. "I'm glad most people don't notice my ears, at least. Or my canines, which are way too long. I thought it'd be a little less obvious, but I'm lucky they aren't permanently bear ears."

It does confuse me that his ears are pointed despite being a bear, which, as far as I know, all have round ears. The truth is we only have each other to go off of, so there's a lot none of us can know about our strange biology; there's no manual, as Teddy said earlier. "I'm actually curious . . . If you're comfortable, could we see your active form?" Maybe now isn't the best time, but the door's closed and I'm dying to check out a new variant.

"Active . . ." He turns the term over in his head, then drops his fist in his palm. "Oh! You mean . . . you want to see what I look like transformed?"

"Righto," I say. "I'm a bit of a connoisseur, if you will."

"But don't feel like you have to," Matthew says. "Mark's a weird one, but he won't force you to do anything you don't feel comfortable doing."

Way to make a guy look good, bro . . .

Teddy crosses his arms again, closing his eyes and turning his head away, a tight frown on his face, then leers at me. "I'll do it . . . if you both show me first."

I immediately look at Matthew, locking my hands together and hoping he'll be okay with it.

He stares at me, and I stare at him, practically begging, and he finally sighs after I pout long enough. "Fine. But you first."

"Deal!" I take my socks off, stand up, and part the back of my clothes to make room for my tail; I go active in one flat second, careful not to tear into my clothes with my claws or hit anything with my tail. In all my dragon-boy glory, I sit back down, pushing my tail to drape over the right side of the chair. "Your turn." I cross my arms and proudly lift my chest.

Matthew rolls his eyes and removes his hat. He sits up straight, pulls his tail out from around his torso, and removes his socks; he goes active in one fluid motion, fur rippling across his skin and feet morphing into cat paws. He settles back against the chair, folding his furry hands over his hat in his lap. Although his neutral expression makes him appear calm, his outward-facing ears and low-hanging tail betray his frayed nerves.

Teddy stares at us, wide-eyed and gaping. "Well, damn; you weren't kidding when you said you're a dragon dude."

"Yep. It's pretty cool until you have to deal with the side effects."

"I can imagine." Teddy smiles good-naturedly and takes a deep breath. "I guess it's my turn. Just . . . bear with me a second. I'm not great at this whole thing yet." He takes another, shakier, breath. "Do y'all care if I take my shirt off?"

"Go for it."

Teddy takes his shirt off, displaying the full glory of his well-defined pecs and the faint six-pack on his thick trunk; he drapes his shirt over the arms of the guitar stand and slips his socks off. "Alright . . . Here we go . . ." Grimacing, he closes his eyes, holds his hands away from his body, and slowly goes active: first, his nails sharpen and lengthen millimeter by millimeter; next, dull-brown pads form on his fingertips and about half of his palm, and his arm hair thickens into a layer of fur that goes from light brown on his hands to blond on his biceps. He seethes, his ears growing a covering of fuzzy fur before they shift up to the top of his head; once they're in their new position, perfectly round and fluffy, he plasters his aching bear ears against his skull. He gasps, tears pricking at his eyes and hands shaking; he must've grown his tail—the most painful part. He puts his hands down, breathing heavily, his ears lifting away from his head and facing forward; he wipes his eyes with his thumb pad, careful not to scratch himself with claws far longer than mine. "God, it still hurts like a bitch." He pants, sweat trickling down his face and chest; once he cools off, he pats himself down with his shirt and puts it back on, then smooths down the fur on his arms.

"You good?" I ask.

"Yeah, I'm good." He holds his arms out at his sides. "Anyway, here's how I look." He wiggles his fingers, watching them move. "It still feels weird to see myself like this, though."

I can see it in his face, what he wants to say. *Like it's not my own body, right?* I don't see it that way anymore, but I know someone who does. It's hard to come to terms with, I'm aware of that, but this isn't some curse that can one day be broken; at some point, you have to accept yourself for what you are. "Could you hold your hand out to me? I want to compare our claws."

Teddy holds his right hand out, spreading his fingers.

I pull my chair toward him with my paws, then reach out with my left hand; our fingertips touching, my claw tips land in the middle of the grooves under his. "Jeez, you have a good inch or two on me."

Teddy chuckles. "Grizzly claws are no joke. They get in the way of everything, too; I have to tap my phone like those girls with acrylic nails."

"I have to do the same thing; makes you wish they were retractable."

"I guess I have that one over you both." Matthew lifts his hand and stretches taut the fur-covered webbing that ends right before his digital pads; his claws unsheathe from the thin slits at the tips of his fingers, all the way down to the cuticles.

"Your fingers are webbed," Teddy says stupidly.

"Yeah," Matthew says. "Most cats have webbed feet because they hunt near water."

"Weird."

"Speaking of weird"—I eye Matthew's hand pads—"can I compare your hands?" Truthfully, I want to compare their softness; paw pads are so much fun to touch.

"Sure, I guess . . ." Teddy holds his right hand above my left thigh.

Silently, Matthew pulls his crappy wooden chair up and puts his left hand over my right thigh.

I linger over both hands, holding them from below. Matthew's hand is much smaller than Teddy's; deeply entrenched in his fur, Matthew's pads look tiny in comparison. Both of them have the same number of pads, though Teddy's metacarpal pad covers a larger portion of his palm. Because I can, I squish their metacarpal pads under my thumbs; Teddy's is noticeably tougher, but that's to be expected of a football player, and it's probably hard to compete with someone who grooms as meticulously as Matthew.

I humor myself, pressing each of their digital pads—most of Teddy's are calloused—until I melt into pure paw-pad heaven, and—

The door slams shut. "What. The fuck."

Matthew flinches violently, pulling his hand away and curling into himself, his ears folding tight against his head.

A short girl with a pixie cut stands in front of the door, her face covered in heavy makeup and contorted into a disgusted expression.

Teddy pulls his hand away and I shoot to my feet and—

The girl glares straight into my eyes. "Sit down, lizard boy."

I obediently sit back down like some scolded dog.

"And you." She points at Teddy with her sparkly acrylic-nailed finger. "When the *hell* were you one of them?! You were human last I checked!"

Teddy lifts his hands placatingly. "Damn, girl! Chill! Jack never told you?"

"No, he didn't! So why don't you explain yourself, huh?" Sneering, she crosses her arms.

"Look, it happened back in May. What else do you want from me?" Huffing, Teddy crosses his arms and shrugs.

"Who's she?" I whisper.

Teddy glances at me, then stares at the angry girl. "Why don't you introduce yourself. You're being really rude right now."

She clicks her tongue and lifts her chin. "I'm Jenny, Jack's lovely twin sister. It's nice to meet you." Sarcasm rolls off her tongue. "My brother didn't warn me that three boys would be sitting their furry asses down in my room."

"Hey! My ass isn't furry!" I say.

"Oh, I'm sorry. Your *scaly* ass."

Her correction does *not* make me feel any better.

"What the hell has your panties in a wad?" Teddy says, "And this is Jack's room, too."

Jenny's glare intensifies. "My panties aren't in a wad."

"Clearly." Teddy raises an eyebrow.

She grimaces, opens her mouth and points her finger at him again, then grits her teeth. "You know what? I'm gonna get in my bed and you're all gonna be quiet. Agreed?"

Teddy glances at me and a terrified Matthew. "We're cool with that." He waves her off.

"Great." Jenny stomps to the ladder attached to the bunk bed, climbs up, and crashes onto her mattress, making it squeak obnoxiously. I wait for her to look over the railing and yell at us again, but all she does is lie down and play on her phone, her nails occasionally clicking against the screen.

Teddy and I look away from the top bunk, letting Jenny do what she will in her own space, and turn our attention to Matthew; he's holding his arms and shaking, his tail fur puffed out.

"Hey, are you okay?" Teddy asks.

Matthew glances between me, Teddy, and the floor; he shakes his head, screwing his eyes shut. "I just, um . . . I just need a moment." He breathes slowly, methodically, the way he does when he's feeling particularly out of control, and carefully perks his ears back up; he glances at the top bunk, confirms that Jenny has no interest in staring at him, then slides his hands down to his thighs. "S-Sorry about that."

I put my hand on his shoulder and squeeze lightly, rubbing my thumb over his shirt. "Nothing to be sorry for, Matthew."

He nods weakly. "R-Right."

"Do you think you can go dormant?"

He shakes his head. "I'm too nervous." He takes his right hand off his thigh and places it over the one I have firmly on his left shoulder; he closes his eyes, taking deeper, calmer breaths until his tail fur smooths down. "Okay, I think I'm—"

A sharp gasp pierces our ears.

Matthew whips his head back and stares at the cracked-open bedroom door.

Six girls stand stacked in a three-by-two formation, each one staring at the three of us.

"Oh . . . Oh God . . ." Matthew covers his face, his tail puffing out all over again.

I get up and stand between Matthew's hunched form and the bedroom door, hoping to block him from the girls' view even if that means they can see all of me; one of the girls, a goth type with lots of piercings and a half-shaved head, blatantly stares at my paws, and I'm a little creeped out by her awfully fascinated expression. Three of the girls I recognize—the bleached blond, the girl in the Santa dress, and the Mrs. Woodcock look-alike—while the other three—another bleached blond with braided hair, a mean-looking brunette, and the aforementioned goth—I haven't seen before.

"Ladies." Teddy saunters past my defensive line with all the bravado of a seasoned playboy. "Didn't Jack tell y'all to leave us be?" He blocks the gap between the door and its frame with his wide body, keeping one hand braced against the doorframe and the other on the outside knob.

All the girls start talking to him, most sounding somewhere between condescending and genuinely interested.

"Aw, Teddy, when did you get so fluffy?" one asks with a cheerful lilt.

Teddy crosses one paw behind the other, curling his bear toes over the carpet. "C'mon, I'm not that big."

"Your fur's so soft!" Another says.

"Hey, I'm not a teddy bear." He fails to sound like he's truly scolding her; it doesn't help that he can't move out of their range.

"Are these sharp?" a soft voice asks.

Teddy jerks back, readjusting his hand on the frame. "Don't touch them!"

They go on and on and on while Teddy slowly forces them back until he can finally close the door behind him; as dangerous as it is for him to be out in the hall where anyone can see him, I trust he knows what he's doing.

With the coast clear, I back away to the office chair, sit down, and pull myself directly in front of Matthew, who's freaking the fuck out: he's hunched forward and trembling, his mouth covered by his hands, and clearly close to crying. I gently coax his hands away from his face, holding both between my own.

He sniffles, taking shallow breaths.

"Hey, they're out of the room, okay?" I run my thumbs over his shaking hands. "Nobody's staring at you anymore."

"O-Okay." He dares to squint his eyes open, turning his head just enough to see for himself that the door's closed. He glances at the top bunk again, and I'm glad Jenny has the foresight to keep playing on her phone, her back turned to the railing.

I keep holding Matthew's hands, not sure what else I can do for him other than wait for him to calm down on his own. Even though his tail fur begins to smooth back down, he keeps his ears trained in the direction of the door, surely waiting for the girls to barge back in. He sniffles again, shutting his eyes in a poor attempt to prevent some tears from falling down. He mumbles another apology and tugs against my grip; I let go so he can wipe his own tears.

Surprisingly, he places one hand back in mine. I'm more than happy to let him hold my hand as long as he needs; it's the least I can do after all the times he's given me a shoulder to cry on. We sit in relative silence, long enough for his tail fur to flatten out and his ears to relax, until someone shouts in the hall.

"What the hell are you all doing up here?!" It's John, and he's royally pissed. "I told you not to bother my friends!"

"No harm, no foul, right?" one says.

"No harm?" John scoffs—I doubt Teddy has gone dormant, what with his weak ability to transform, so he knows Matthew and I are also active. "Do I need to remind you how I felt when you all found out about me? Think about it for just a second, or do I need to spell it out?"

It's so quiet I can hear the other guests shuffling around downstairs.

"Ugh, fine. We'll go." The six girls presumably stomp down the hall and around the corner.

Teddy slowly opens the door and backs inside.

John comes in behind him and slams the door shut, fully active and face contorted with a fury I didn't know he was capable of.

Jenny throws an arm over the railing of her bunk and gazes at us with a bored expression.

John looks at her, then looks at me, then lingers on Matthew until his anger morphs into guilt; his ears, long released from their hairpin prison, lie completely parallel to the top of his head. "I am so, so sorry about them. I should've known better than to invite you over like this."

I wave my free hand in the air. "Don't blame yourself, bro; we knew what we were walking into."

Teddy slings an arm around John's shoulders, smiling without a care. "And, granted, I probably should've told our dragon friend no."

John slaps his face with his very fuzzy hand. "Mark."

I half shrug. "What? Did you really expect me to pass up on a golden opportunity?"

"You are so . . ." John grits his teeth. "You know what? Forget it." He puts his hand down, walks to his bed, and crashes ass-first on the mattress; he leans forward, looking at Matthew. "Are you alright?"

His face flushed, Matthew looks away. "Um, yeah, I'm okay." He holds his arm with his free hand, his ears turning outward.

John smiles gently. "You don't have to be embarrassed. If it helps, I totally cried like a baby every time one of my sisters figured out what was up."

"I was there for the first time," Jenny says. "He was crying for a good thirty minutes at least."

"You were crying, too." John crosses his arms childishly.

Jenny pulls more of her body over the railing so she has a better view of her brother. "Of course I cried! I was worried about you! And we were literally twelve!"

He grimaces at her. "You're not helping my point!"

Matthew sniffles, but there's a small smile on his face. "Thanks for trying to cheer me up. I didn't think it'd make me so anxious; like, I knew I was scared of this sort of situation, but I . . . I didn't think it was this bad."

Teddy sits down next to John, the frame creaking under his weight; he's heavy enough to create a clear depression in the mattress. "I feel you there. I knew about Jack's situation so long I thought transforming wouldn't be so rough; boy, was I wrong . . ."

John elbows him. "I think that was the first time I saw you get emotional about something."

Teddy laughs. "To be fair, I didn't realize how painful that first one would be. It felt like I'd done a full-body workout for a week straight."

John leans back on his hands, his eyes landing on Matthew. "And, hey, if you want to sit out the party and hang out in here, that's not a problem with me. The whole thing's just an ego boost for my mom, anyway."

"You don't want to say hi to your cousins?" Teddy asks.

"Not really," John says.

Matthew's ears perk, his smile fully grown. "Unfortunately for you, I think I'll be okay for the festivities." He wipes the remains of tear tracks off his cheeks with his wrist, then moves the hand holding mine up to my elbow. "As for you, Mark"—he tugs me forward, his fist colliding with my shoulder—"that's for being a shameless teratophile"—he lifts his hand, holds his middle finger with his thumb, and flicks my forehead—"and that's for not thinking twice."

I pout and rub my head, pretending it hurts.

"What's a teratophile?" Teddy asks.

John leans over and whispers in his ear, "A monster fucker."

"A *what*?!" Teddy jumps away to the edge of the bottom bunk.

I rub my shoulder a few times and place my hand back in my lap. "Hate to break it to you, but if you ever get laid, that girl would be a monster fucker. It comes with the territory."

Teddy gapes, holding his hands in the air defensively. "You're not serious!"

"Oh, he's serious." Matthew lets go of my elbow, totally calm, and leans back against his chair; he locks his fingers together over his stomach and closes his eyes.

"Oh my God." Eyes wide, Teddy places his claws near his lips. "I think I'm gonna need a moment."

"Want me to rub your ears to help you feel better?" Jenny asks.

Teddy jolts, covering his mouth to suppress a gasp, his ears pressing against his head; he slowly looks up at Jenny. "You're serious?"

"Am I?"

He looks back down, his brow furrowed, then stands up and rests the back of his head against the railing of the top bunk, lifting his ears tentatively, a rosy blush painting his cheeks.

John's jaw hits the floor. "Dude, that's my sister."

"And she wants to pet some bear ears." Jenny reaches her arm over the railing, pinches Teddy's fluffy ear with two fingers and a thumb, and rubs back and forth.

Teddy melts—I bet he's never had his new ears handled yet, and he's getting pet by a cute girl at that. He covers his mouth with his fist, his eyes fluttering closed.

"You've been taking good care of your hair. It's really soft." Jenny scratches closer to his scalp, eliciting a pleasant hum out of Teddy.

John, clearly uncomfortable with his friend and his sister getting freaky in his presence, screws his face up with understandable disgust. "Can you *not* do this right now?"

Jenny smirks, strokes Teddy's ear one last time, and takes her hand off his head.

Teddy sits back down at the edge of John's bunk, keeping his gaze on the wall and holding his hands in his lap; his glowing face says it all.

Jenny peers over the railing. "Do you feel better?"

"Mm-hmm." Teddy barely nods his head.

"I can't believe you two." John crosses his arms with a huff. He looks away, glares at nothing, then points at the present I placed in the corner earlier. "Who's that for?"

"It's for you and Jenny," I say. "You can open it now if you want."

John looks at Jenny. "Well?"

"You have me curious." She crawls over to the ladder, steps down two rungs, then hops off to the floor; she and John walk over to the present together.

Using the claws engulfed in his fur, John easily rips the wrapping open; when the two tear off the split paper, they both gasp. "You didn't." John says.

Teddy finally comes back to his senses. "What'd they get y'all?" He peers over our heads at the big box on the floor and grins. "Well, would you look at that."

"Isn't this, like, five hundred dollars?" John brings the one-tera-byte Xbox One container into his lap. "How'd you two even manage this?"

"Emily and I pitched in with our allowance," I say, "but most of it came from Matthew."

Still resting his eyes, Matthew nods.

"Well, I'm really thankful, but now I kinda feel bad." John puts his hand behind his neck.

"Don't worry about it." Matthew waves a hand dismissively. "We knew you'd never upgrade, so we thought we'd do it for you; it's not every day you find a semi-reliable fourth person to play with. And we know Jenny plays, too, so we got the one with the bigger hard drive so you don't have to worry so much about storage between the two of you."

"We'll just have to worry about getting games for it," Jenny says.

"There's plenty of free-to-play stuff we can try, too," Teddy says, "but I'm just glad y'all can finally catch up with the rest of us. I'm surprised your 360's still kicking, honestly."

"My first one got the red ring of death," I say. "I was devastated for a whole week."

Matthew squints. "I don't think I knew you yet."

I cup my chin. "I can't remember you being around, either."

John places the box back down, rises to his full tiptoe height, and puts his hands on his hips. "We can set it up later. There's food to eat and people to meet."

"Woo, party time." Teddy wears a wide, fake, toothy grin. "Want me to fix your hair up?"

John goes dormant and says, "Sure."

⌒

Teddy strums the top string of his acoustic guitar, then adjusts the tuning peg it's attached to. The party's in full swing, with most everyone—that being a good chunk of John's extended family—already here for the night. People have been filing in and out of the kitchen, grabbing what they want from the buffet of random catering trays and Christmas classics, while John, Teddy, Matthew, and I have been chilling in front of the giant painting of *The Last Supper*; most of the people our age have been designated to stay in the dining area anyway, and for what it's worth, at least two of us don't have the energy for excessive socializing. I don't consider myself much of an introvert, but even I'm feeling like a fish out of water around the sheer number of people, not to mention how wealthy they all dress and act—I've been catching quite a few gazes simply for the crime of existing in the same space.

Teddy keeps strumming his guitar, and I try to eat something despite not feeling particularly hungry; my metabolism slows down during the winter, so I often have to deliberately ignore my nonexistent hunger cues to ensure I don't lose what little weight I have. Teddy said he'd eat later, while Matthew and John help themselves to whatever strikes their fancy. Despite the apparent wealth in the house, most of the dishes on display are the typical Christmas fare: stuffed and roasted turkey; honey-glazed ham; mashed potatoes and gravy; oyster dressing; turkey dressing; green bean casserole; sweet potato casserole; cranberry sauce; deviled eggs; yeast rolls; mincemeat pie; pecan pie; sweet potato pie; sugar cookies; gingerbread cookies; snickerdoodle cookies; an assortment of cheeses, crackers, and cold cuts; eggnog; and an expansive selection of alcoholic beverages. All I know is that the way things are looking, at least one person is going to be wasted by the end of the night.

As soon as Teddy moves on to the next string, Mr. Brown walks into the dining room with Mom; he talks animatedly, his hands flying up and down, this way and that, while Mom nods along. They mosey around the kitchen island, fixing their plates and chatting, randomly stopping here and there, and I'm struck by the smile on Mom's face; I'm sure now, despite the earlier fiasco, that it was a good call to come here. Mom isolated herself for a long time—partly to grieve, partly because everyone tossed us out of their lives the moment Dad was gone—so I'm glad she has a chance to put herself back out there.

After they make their rounds, weaving around the other guests loitering by the island, they spot the four of us hanging out against the wall and decide to stop by.

Teddy lifts his head away from the body of his guitar, gazing at his towering father. "What's up?"

"Just checking in with you." Mr. Brown smiles jovially, glancing at me and Matthew—mostly me, his eyes squinting like he's scrutinizing every pore. "I see you made some new friends."

"I'm Mark."

"I'm Matthew."

I gesture toward Mom. "I see you met my mom."

Mr. Brown's eyebrows raise. "That's your son?"

Mom giggles, her eyes nearly closed she's smiling so hard. "Oh, yes. We don't look much alike." She gazes at the boy on my left. "And you must be . . . Teddy, right?"

"That's right."

"Well, it's nice to meet you."

"Likewise."

They stand there awkwardly, the sound of idle chatter filling the silence. "I suppose we should leave y'all be." Mr. Brown frowns worriedly. "Just holler if you need anything."

"We'll be in the living room with the other adults," Mom says.

They make their leave, going down the hall they came from.

Teddy hangs his head and sighs. "My dad's been such a worrywart lately."

"He's been looking at me weird every time he's seen me," I say. "Like, weirder than most people. Do you think he knows?"

Teddy side-eyes me. "Knows what?"

"You know."

He gapes. "No way! I don't think so."

John leans over to look at us from Matthew's right side. "Isn't your dad's friend Kyle like us?"

"Kyle?" Teddy asks. "You think Kyle's like us?"

"I mean, he does look a little off: his ears are pointed."

"Dad said he said that's a birth defect."

"You ever thought he might've been lying?"

"No, I never considered . . ." Totally distraught, Teddy hovers his fingers over his mouth. "I've known him my whole life, and never once . . ." He shakes his head and stares at the floor. "I've never seen him active before, so . . ."

"He might be good at staying dormant. My mom knew a guy like that a long time ago." Some wolf man she had a brief sexual relationship with, as far as I know; she told me back when I was young and anxious about everything.

"I just . . . I can't believe it . . ."

"Maybe you should ask him," John says. "He probably has his reasons." The truth is, no matter how much you think you know someone, they could still turn on you; there's a reason we only ever find out about these things on accident.

"Yeah." Teddy strums down all six strings, the dissonant chord swallowed up by small talk. "I'll have to do that sometime." He plucks the second string from the top, turning its tuning peg in tiny increments so it doesn't snap.

⁓

"Aw, why the long faces?" The sister in the Santa dress smiles at us, leaning forward with her hands clasped behind her back.

"None of your business, Olive," John says.

She giggles into her hand, her eyes squinting nearly closed from her ridiculous grin, but it doesn't hide her shrewd stare. "Well, I thought I'd pop by to say sorry about earlier! Our little brother is just *so cute* we couldn't help but want to meet his new friends!"

"Knock it off!"

"Oh, fine~ I'll be in the living room if you ever want to say hello~" Olive winks and skips away down the hall, her copper curls bouncing with every step.

John hangs his head as soon as she's out of sight. "I seriously can't with her."

"She's certainly . . . quirky," I say.

"That's rich, coming from you," John says.

"I second that thought," Matthew says.

"I just met you and I can agree," Teddy says.

I don't even know what to say.

⁓

The mean-looking brunette stomps into the room like she has names to take; scowling, she walks clear past us, turns her head enough to catch Teddy in her peripheral, makes an abrupt U-turn, and stops in front of me and Matthew, her arms crossed and feet spread hip width apart. With a glare worth one thousand venomous fangs, she says, "Sorry, I guess," turns back to the hall, and leaves.

We watch her go, and even though she only has socks on, I imagine kitten heels clicking on the linoleum.

John sighs. "At least you tried, Ruth . . ."

The flat-chested bleached blond pulls up a chair, spreads her legs, and squats down on the seat, her arms casually slung across the backrest. "So how're you guys doing?"

"What do you want, Esther?" John asks.

She sags, resting her head over her arms. "They're talking about politics in the living room."

"That's what adults talk about. You shouldn't be surprised."

She lifts her head, holding her cheeks in her hands. "Anyway, I thought I'd come hang out for a bit because I have a question for you guys."

John crosses his arms. "What kind of question could you possibly have for us?"

"Okay, so, hear me out: there's this guy I met at college, and, you know, he's pretty normal and all, but I recently noticed he likes to spread his legs super wide whenever he sits down. He also has gray hair, but I never thought much of it 'cause some people gray in their twenties and whatnot, but then . . ." She pauses, lifting a finger up.

"Uh-huh . . ." John looks at her like she's talking crazy.

"One of his buddies got him to laugh real hard, and I saw he has some gnarly canines on him, so I was thinking, maybe this guy is, you know . . ." She drops to a whisper, cupping her mouth with one hand. "And maybe he has, like, a tail down there. Do you think I should ask him about it?"

"I mean, you could, but he'd probably deny it." I've done it plenty of times to Emily, because even if it's painfully obvious, it's not like she can prove anything.

Esther holds her chin, tilting her head and raising her brow in a classic thinking pose. "So what you're saying is I'll have to catch him with his paws out."

"That's not at all what I was saying!" I groan, knowing full well she doesn't care.

Esther grows a satisfied smile and stops slouching over the back of the chair. "By the way, I kinda started the whole bedroom heist thing." She claps her hands in front of her face and bows her head, her long, straight hair hanging down to the edge of her seat. "My bad!"

John sighs, shaking his head. "We're getting the apology circus tonight, huh?"

Esther lifts her head, grinning. "Yep! We did make a boy cry, after all."

Matthew clenches his hands together in his lap, his cheeks flushing pink.

"Maybe don't rub it in?" I frown.

"Just . . . go back to the politics, would ya?" John shoos her away with his hand.

"Fine. Jeez." Esther rises from her impressive skinny-jean squat, puts the chair back in front of the dining room table, and stalks off down the hall.

The braided bleached blond walks up to us, an unreadable smile on her face; she opens her mouth—

"Zip it." John makes the appropriate gesture in the air with his finger and his thumb. "Just say it and go."

"Aw~ You're no fun~ Anyway, my apologies, boys." She gives us jazz hands for some reason.

"Thank you. Bye." John glares at her as she leaves, and she stares back, all the way until she reaches the corner at the end of the hall.

I lean forward and look at John. "Sheesh, harsh. What's up with her to get you so short?"

He runs a hand down his face. "She will talk, and talk, and talk, and talk about absolutely nothing if you let her. And she's a real blond if you catch my drift."

Teddy sighs. "I got to hear about her day with her crush once. Every. Excruciating. Detail. She remembered everything he ate for breakfast, lunch, *and* dinner, and they weren't even on a date! It was at dinner, too, and nobody gets excused from the table until Mrs. Woodcock says so, so there was no escape."

"Yeah. Mary's something, alright."

Remind me to never stay for dinner . . .

"Ahem." The Mrs. Woodcock look-alike catches our attention, one hand on her hip and the other tugging the goth sister along; neither seems happy to be here. As soon as she confirms she has our attention, she lets go of her sister and bows her head. "I'm sorry for failing to consider your feelings earlier; that was an oversight on my part. I hope this apology is sufficient for you."

"Thanks?" I say, perplexed by her overly formal speech.

She nods again and promptly walks away.

The goth sister reaches out for her and cries, "Hope! Wait!" only to be ignored by the stern sister's rapidly retreating figure. She slumps over, her arms hanging limp, and glances at the four of us. "H-Hi." She looks everywhere but our faces.

Surprisingly, Matthew says, "Hey. Your name's Grace, right? I think we had Honors English II together."

She squints at him, then lightens up. "O-Oh, yes. Matthew, right? You sat two seats in front of me and one to the left. O-Or something like that." She fiddles with the metal claw ring on her right index finger.

"I'm surprised I never realized you're one of John's sisters."

John says, "You can call me Jack."

Matthew scratches his cheek. "Okay . . . one of Jack's sisters."

Grace glances at me before diverting her gaze straight to the floor. "We don't hang around each other much at school. A-And most people don't think we look much alike because of . . ." She rotates one of the bracelets on her arm. "E-Everything, I guess."

"I was just thinking I should've put two and two together with your last name." Matthew puts a hand behind his head. "Though to be fair, I'm pretty awful with names."

"Hmm." Although hunched, Grace tries to maintain eye contact with Matthew. "I remember the teacher would call on you a lot for closing your eyes. Do you get tired often?"

"Mm, sometimes. I try not to fall asleep in class without something covering my head." I'm surprised he's being frank with Grace; then again, her pitiful posture makes it hard to be rude to her.

Grace straightens out and holds her right forearm with her left hand, squinting at the top of his head. "I understand. You must be like Jack." Her eyes flick toward me and Teddy just long enough to catch whatever she wants to see. "It's strange to me that some of you revert further." She glances at me again, an unmistakable blush dusting her cheeks. "Though . . . I see that . . . some of your features are more . . . exotic."

Being more up-front with the subject kills Matthew's momentum, though an awkward smile remains on his face.

She fidgets, shuffling her feet back and forth. "U-Um, I'm sorry, you probably don't want to talk about that stuff." She stares at the floor again. "I-I just wanted to say that I'm r-really sorry for barging in earlier. I-I'm so curious about this stuff that I wasn't thinking." She looks like she could cry.

"It's okay, Grace." Matthew smiles kindly. "I think it's normal to be interested. But it can be a little awkward for us to be seen like that, you know?"

"O-Oh, yes, thank you." She nods profusely, locking her fingers together. "I-I'll try my best to be more mindful of that." She smiles to herself, her gaze flitting between me and the floor a few times. "U-Um, one more thing."

We give her our undivided attention.

She looks straight into my eyes, her own going back and forth between the left and the right, and her face sours with something akin to fear; she covers her face and peeks between her fingers. "M-Mark."

I straighten up, startled she knows my name.

Grace flattens her lips, her legs trembling so hard her knees knock together. "I think your eyes are really pretty!"

Huh?! I-I—

She squeals. "Oh, I said it!" She wiggles strangely, sees my face again, smiles an I'm-stupid-into-you smile, and runs away like a silly schoolgirl.

My mind goes blank for a second, and, oh, I can feel the blood rushing to my face because never once in my life have I been complimented like that by a pretty girl. God, why are all of Jack's sisters pretty?

Teddy leans forward, grinning so wide his canines show. "Dude, what is that face?"

"W-What face?!" I sputter.

Matthew also leans forward, smirking like he's trying to infuriate me. "Looks like somebody has an admirer."

I scowl at him, which only makes him snicker, which makes me cross my arms and huff; I glance over his curly-haired head to see if Jack's going to join in, but he looks absolutely dumbfounded about what happened, his mouth hanging open.

Jack brings a fist to his mouth, furrows his brow, closes his eyes, and sighs. "I don't have the energy for this." He claps his hand on Matthew's shoulder.

Matthew jumps, whipping his head toward Jack.

"I hope you and Emily work out. I don't need all three of you becoming my brother-in-law one day."

I'm exasperated. "Wait, you—"

"Not now, Mark." Jack waves his index finger back and forth. "I'm mourning our friendship." He pretends to sniffle.

"For shame." Teddy shakes his head.

I gape. "Dude! You're part of the problem!"

Teddy slings his arm around my shoulders. "We can be problems together." He sighs wistfully.

I hang my head.

A posse of boys resembling Jack walk up to us; they're nicely cleaned up, sporting short, coifed hair and business casual outfits.

"Hey, Jackie~ How's my favorite cousin?" The one at the front—he happens to be the shortest—grins like he's the best thing since sliced bread.

"Call me that again and see what happens." Jack lifts his head with a nasty glare but remains slouched.

Shorty scoffs. "What're you gonna do? Punch me?"

"You wanna find out?" Jack raises a brow and cracks his knuckles with an audible pop.

Shorty grimaces, glaring at Jack like he's some lowbred scoundrel; then he glances at Matthew, who on his best days looks mean, but the glare on his face right now . . . "Fine, Jack. You and your . . . *friends* . . . win this time." He struts away, his legion of cousins following behind.

His sheer audacity astounds me. "Who was that?"

"Peter Baldwin IV, my uncle's firstborn son. He's a real asshole, as you can tell." Jack massages the bridge of his nose. "I'm surprised it took him this long to come taunt me."

"I got *so close* to ripping him a new one last year"—Teddy huffs—"but when he saw me stand up, ooh, he backed off real quick. How tall is he again?"

"Like, five three or something."

"Sheesh!"

Matthew grumbles. "Even I'm taller than that."

"By like two inches," I say.

"Two very important inches!"

"How tall are you, Teddy?" I ask.

Teddy grins. "Six two. I was a little shorter last year, though."

"Shorter as in six even," Jack says.

"You guys are something else," I say. "I'll be lucky if I hit five ten."

"That's still above average." Teddy shrugs.

"Barely." I grumble.

Matthew puts his hand on my shoulder. "Sometimes, you have to take what you can get."

I guess I shouldn't complain . . .

I stare at the hot-pink nail polish in my hands, truly baffled that Peter had it out for me so bad that I ended up with the most girly white elephant present available; most of the gifts were fairly comical—Matthew ended up with an army-green tie covered in a pattern of tiny stegosaurus; Jack ended up with a questionable apron designed like a Heinz ketchup bottle (it says, *CATCH UP WITH JESUS: LETTUCE PRAISE & RELISH HIM, 'Cuz He loves me from my head to-ma-toes*); and Teddy ended up with a coloring book titled *Life with a Fat Pussy*. Peter must've deemed me the safest target for his petty revenge, if you can even call it that; at least nail polish is useful to someone out there, though it might not be the highest quality considering the budget we were given. All things considered, I recognize that out of the four of us I appear the least threatening; my boyish face and thin frame, along with my unnatural features, make me look like an emo twink. It's clear why he wouldn't want to further agitate the two tall and muscular members of our group, but even Matthew is a force to be reckoned with; I've only seen him get in a fight once, and it wasn't pretty: He fights dirty, using any advantage he can get except kicking a dude in the nuts. He may have come out of that fight bruised and battered, but the rumors that ran afterward were enough to get people to leave us alone—the only hard negative was that people wrongly assumed I was Matthew's boyfriend, so that's why he went batshit crazy on anyone who messed with me.

"Something wrong?" Matthew asks.

I drop out of my stupor. "No. Why?"

"You're making a face."

I realize I've been frowning deeply in the face of hot-pink nail polish. "Just thinking about my . . . good looks."

Matthew gives me a strange look. "Don't tell me you're going to start painting your nails."

I smile, suppressing a laugh. "I don't think that'd work out very well." I wonder what would happen to painted nails once they turn into claws: Would the paint fall off, or would there be a weird patch of polish in the middle of each claw? I'd test it myself, but even I have limits. And no way in hell would I paint my claws: I don't want to know how that would work going dormant. I lift the nail polish in front of our faces. "But this is perfectly good nail polish. I'd rather it not go to waste."

Matthew frowns, his hand cradling his chin. "Hmm . . . You could give it to your mom?"

"She doesn't paint her nails, though."

"I would say Emily, but she doesn't either." He leans back, crossing one leg over the other. "Maybe her friend . . . Oh!" He drops his fist in his hand.

"Oh?"

"Her friend's name is Heather."

"So that's where I heard that name before . . ." Emily moved to our area when she started ninth grade; Heather is her friend from middle school.

"But there's no guarantee she paints her nails, either."

It appears we're at an impasse.

Jack sighs. "Don't take this the wrong way, but Grace would probably use it if you gave it to her."

Chatting with her sisters and female cousins across the room, Grace lifts her hand sporting lilac painted nails; curiously, they match the dyed portion of her hair.

"She changes it up a lot, doesn't she?" Matthew asks. "I think it was yellow orange earlier in the semester."

Jack nods. "It was green before that. She redyes her hair every few months and repaints her nails to match."

Now that I think of it, I vaguely recall a girl with neon-green hair in one of my freshman classes last year; I almost never bother remembering people unless I see them in all of my classes, so a girl who went to a different middle school would've easily slipped my mind. But besides that, there's another problem. "No offense, but I really don't want to give her the wrong idea." She's cute and all, but I'm not so desperate as to jump on the first girl to express an interest in me; I do really appreciate the compliment, but I don't think I could ever get past the nose ring.

"In that case, I'll give it to her for you." Matthew plucks the nail polish out of my grasp, stands, stretches, and tosses his prize on top of my head. "Keep the tie. My parents wouldn't want me wearing something like that to parties anyway." He saunters over to the girls as I pull the tie off my head, quickly catching Grace's attention. He lifts the hot-pink nail polish, holding his free hand behind his head. She opens her mouth, wide-eyed, and shakes her hands in refusal. There's some back-and-forth, but she ultimately offers him her Hello Kitty hairbrush; he swaps with her, they share platitudes, and he returns to us. "Mission accomplished." He sits back down.

"You sure you don't want the tie back?" I ask.

He lifts the brush. "Nah. I've been trying to find a better brush, anyway, so may as well give this one a try. I don't care that it has Hello Kitty on it."

I shrug. "Suit yourself." A good old comb has always worked for me, but I understand my hair is straight as a rail, so I don't have room to talk.

Teddy suddenly stands and throws his interesting coloring book onto his seat. "I'm gonna hit the john." He wanders off without another word.

Strangely, Jenny follows after him.

Teddy comes back toting a box wrapped in red wrapping paper and a big green bow; he drops it into Jack's lap. "Delivery for one John Eliza Woodcock VII." He winks obnoxiously, sits back down with his guitar, and fingers the strings.

"*Thanks*. What's the occasion?" Jack's voice drips with sarcasm; nonetheless, he rips off the wrapping paper, revealing a shoe box. Jack looks pleasantly surprised. "Teddy, you didn't."

"I sure did, though you'll have to thank your sisters, too. Those things are expensive."

"I know. I've gone through four already." Jack opens the box with a wide smile; a pair of black leather dress shoes with two-inch heels rest inside. He pulls them out, looks at the bottoms—oddly enough, the heels and tips of the toes have dozens of silver nails hammered into them—then flips them over and looks at the tops. "Man, no wonder you guys were asking about my shoe size."

"What're the nails in the bottom for?" I ask.

Teddy grins, strumming his guitar as if it answers my question. "I think he might need a demonstration."

Jack turns all sheepish. "Oh, c'mon, I'm not dressed for it."

"I don't think any of us care if you dance in sweats."

"You dance?" I never would've guessed someone as shy as Jack does something that requires a lot of confidence.

Jack laughs nervously. "Oh, it's just a hobby."

Teddy shakes his head. "He's being modest. C'mon, Jack! Dance in your new shoes!"

Jack hesitates, but everybody in the room figures out what's going on, and Jenny returns with their sisters in tow.

"Yeah, Jack! Dance!" Esther grins like he won't.

The rest of the room jumps in, overwhelming us with chanting and clapping. "Jack! Jack! Jack! Jack!"

"Alright, alright!" Jack grins wider than I thought possible. He takes his socks off, slips the shoes on, ties the laces with practiced grace, rises to his feet, unzips his jacket, slides forward, and shouts, "Make some room, would ya?!"

His male cousins, Peter included, surround the long dining room table and heave it to the back left corner of the room; once they clear out to the perimeter, Jack takes his stand in the middle of the space. His sisters clap in a practiced rhythm, and Jack slowly, meticulously lifts his arms into the air, his body almost perfectly straight, and Teddy starts to sing. In Spanish.

Jack snaps to the rhythm, moving his legs slowly as Teddy's unusual singing takes center stage; although I can't understand the words, there's a vicious grief to his tone, like he's ripping each word from his throat raw. His singing peters out into lively chords with all six guitar strings, and the clapping intensifies, and Jack truly, honestly, starts to dance. He stomps his feet along the wooden floors, sometimes with fanciful kicks, sometimes in rapid succession, and he uses the entire available space as his dance floor, and I finally understand that those nails are meant to make noise. Jack uses his entire body as his instrument, from meticulous hand movements to slapping his chest and his legs to elaborate lunges and turns that make his hair whip into his face, and some of his moves cause him to flash his ears and tail, but I'm convinced nobody is capable of registering such an anomaly when this guy is quite literally tearing up the floor with his new shoes.

The whole spectacle lasts less than five minutes, and at the end of the performance, Jack practically moonwalks out into the hall, and when he walks back in, face flushed from the exertion and a wicked grin on his face, the clapping and whistling that erupts is so loud I think I might go deaf.

Jack strides into the kitchen and gets himself a drink.

"That answer your question?" Teddy beams.

Still reeling, I say, "Uh, *yeah*! Just a hobby, my ass! How long have you two been practicing that?"

Teddy places his guitar on the stand next to him. "Jack's been dancing about two years, but I've been singing and playing guitar since I was . . ." He counts on his fingers. "About eight? I'll tell you, learning to sing when your voice starts to crack is a real trip."

"What dance is that?" Matthew asks. "I've never seen it before."

"Oh, it's flamenco," Teddy says. "It's a Spanish folk dance. I'm not surprised you've never heard of it: it's not very popular in the States."

Jack returns to his seat, disposable cup of water in hand, and drinks calmly as if nothing happened at all.

⁓

"Y'all boys staying the night?" Mr. Brown asks, putting his coat, hat, and shoes on at the front door.

I look at Mom. "Is that okay with you?"

"Sure, hon," Mom says. "I can come pick you both up in the morning."

"I'm cool with it, too"—hands in his pockets, Jack leans down between me and Matthew—"but are you sure you want to stay with my sisters hanging around?"

"What's the worst they can do? See us again?" I whisper, "I'm not going to miss an opportunity to stay at a friend's house over that."

Matthew nods.

"Have fun, then." Mr. Brown finishes buttoning up his coat, then addresses Mom. "I'll walk you to your car."

"Oh, thank you." Mom smiles at me. "Just give me a call if anything happens; otherwise, see you in the morning. Love you."

"Love you too." I wave goodbye.

Once the door closes and Jack locks it up, the four of us go back upstairs.

"Yay. We survived the party." There's no hint of emotion in Teddy's grin.

"Good riddance." Jack sighs, shaking his head. "I probably would've lost it if you guys weren't there, so thanks for that."

"Glad to help, I guess." Sometimes good company does wonders for a sour mood, and I'm happy to be that company when I can—though Jack gets tired of me a lot, too. Right as we turn the corner upstairs, I ask, "Hey, do you have a Wii?"

"Yeah. Why?" Jack asks.

I lock my fingers together in front of my chest. "I've always wanted to play Super Smash Bros. with four people."

"Well, damn; y'all have been missing out." Teddy nudges Jack. "You're in luck 'cause this guy has way too many controllers."

"Too many siblings does that for you." Jack opens his bedroom door, lets us in before him, and closes it behind us.

Jenny looks over the railing of the top bunk, obviously annoyed. "Why are you three still here?"

"We're staying the night." Teddy sits back down on the stool.

Matthew and I follow suit with the desk and office chairs.

Jenny sneers. "You're all sleeping in the living room, got it? I'm not dealing with four boys in my room."

"You got it, girl." Teddy salutes with a straight face, then smiles. "So, you gonna play with us?"

"Why would I want to play with you?" She huffs.

"I don't know; it's almost like you play with me all the time."

While Teddy and Jenny bicker, I watch Jack lie on his side so he can pull storage containers out from under his bed. He shuffles a couple around until he finds the ones with his Wii and a bunch of Wii Remotes. He takes the Wii out of its plastic prison and works on hooking it up to his TV.

Teddy smacks my shoulder with the back of his hand. "You know, I just thought of something funny."

"What's that?" I ask.

Matthew perks his ears.

Teddy points at us in turn. "You're Matthew, you're Mark, he's John"—he jerks a thumb at himself—"and my real name is Luke."

"You're kidding." A strange grin splits Matthew's lips.

"No, no. I'm serious." Teddy chuckles.

Shaking his head, Matthew scoffs. "Sometimes I'm convinced my life is a bad joke."

I feel you there, bro . . .

CHAPTER 11

An Annoying Annual Appointment

Matthew

A silver 2014 Lexus RX 350 pulls up to the curb of the car pool lane. I enter the vehicle on the passenger side and toss my book bag on the floorboard between my legs; when I close the door, Mom pulls away without giving me a single second to put my seat belt on—it's par for the course for her, ever the impatient woman.

She chews her gum and pretends I don't exist, so I look out the passenger-side window. It's already March, my birth month, which means it's time for another doctor's appointment. Mom usually sets it shortly after my birthday, which was Thursday last week, on the seventeenth. I don't like to do much for my birthday other than spend time with everyone, which basically meant staying up until ungodly hours playing games together; it's been interesting to have Teddy and Jenny join us in parties, though we don't always play the same stuff at the same time.

Mom stops at a red light and looks into the vanity mirror on the sun visor, fluffing her freshly blow-dried hair—it looks *just* perfect enough that she probably went to the blow-dry bar this morning before picking me up. She starts reapplying some lip gloss, but the light turns green, forcing her to hastily shove the wand back into the bottle and the bottle back into her massive purse.

I turn my head back to the window. Sometimes, I feel like time passes too quickly; we've gone through three birthdays in three months, though Mark and I didn't end up going to Teddy's party back in January—to be fair, we barely knew him, and the prospect of a house full of rowdy jocks wasn't particularly enticing.

I thought about getting Emily something for Valentine's Day back in February but chickened out in the end; there's not much point in investing in a relationship that won't work out.

With the doctor's office less than a mile away, I put my jacket hood over my head and grit my teeth; using extreme mental effort, I slowly, agonizingly reabsorb my tail into my spine, all while my ears crawl millimeter by millimeter down from the top of my head until they rest where human ears belong. I touch my earlobes to distract myself from the cotton fuzz infiltrating my brain, relishing the soft, furless skin.

Mom doesn't notice a thing. She parks her SUV in front of the office, popping a bubble of pink gum as she swings her heels onto the cracked pavement.

I slide out of the car and slam the door shut.

Mom locks it with the press of a button on her key fob, then rushes inside; the sooner we're in the door, the sooner we can leave, which happens to be best for the both of us, else she finds out I'm not the normal son she thinks I am.

After checking in, we sit down in the waiting area where an old box TV plays a random children's show without sound; I don't have the energy to look at the grainy pixels, much less read the closed captions. Mom scrolls through Facebook on her phone, I rest my eyes, and two children screech in the play area; the noise intensifies my headache, the incessant shushing from the parents not helping in the least.

It takes thirty minutes for the nurse to call my name; Mom doesn't bat an eye as I get up and follow the nurse into the back by myself—my parents stopped coming back with me as soon as I was old enough to go alone. I'm weighed and measured and led into my designated room.

Another ten minutes pass before the doctor walks in. He goes through the usual tests and asks the usual questions, then leaves.

Given another few minutes, a different nurse walks in; she carries a tiny plastic tray filled with syringes and related peripherals. I look away and close my eyes as she prepares to give me my meningococcal booster. She wipes down my left shoulder, and I try not to tense up. The burn of the needle piercing my skin is gone almost as soon as it comes, and the nurse swiftly applies a bandage to the tiny puncture wound; it throbs, already sore.

The nurse releases me, and I walk back into the lobby. I glance at a tank of colorful fish, trying to keep ahold of myself; I'm lightheaded, my mouth dry.

Mom gets up when she sees me coming, and we quickly check out. We leave the doctor's office, get back in the car, and ride home; I'm so disoriented I don't realize we arrived until Mom opens the driver-side door to get out of the car. I slowly get out too, staggering behind her, my heavy book bag held over one shoulder; although I can open the door with my own keys, I let Mom open it for me and slip in behind her.

Barely lucid, I walk upstairs to my room, throw my book bag in front of my desk, and stumble across the hall to the bathroom. I slam the door closed, hastily strip off my clothes, and tear the bandage off my arm—there's a dime of blood on the pad, but the wound no longer bleeds. Trembling naked, I pull the shower curtain aside and get the water flowing; I jump in just as the water turns hot.

I clean myself with shaking fingers, from my head down to my feet, and I don't need to protect my ears or wash every square inch of fur on my tail, and the soap rinses so easily down my skin. I grin maniacally because I haven't had a shower so pleasant in months and I'm sad I can only give myself five minutes. By the time I turn off the water, my nails are already growing sharp.

I grab a towel from the towel cabinet and try to dry off, but the pins and needles in my limbs stop me. I leave the cabinet door ajar, too preoccupied with getting to my room before I involuntarily go active. Towel covering my head, my hazy mind pulls me into my bedroom, and I close the door with my ass and collapse ungracefully on my bed, still damp but unable to care.

I pull the towel off my head and bunch it up into a sloppy ball; panting, I bite it to muffle myself. I focus on the taste of wet cotton, the rough texture of old fabric on my equally rough tongue, and push my forehead against my soft pillow. I dig my claws into my comforter and clench my stomach as gray pads form on my hands and feet. I huff through my nose, a wave of searing pain washing over my arms, legs, and ears as my hair thickens into striped fur. My ears morph into thin triangles, each millimeter of their journey to the top of my head a stab to my skull; they plaster themselves back as soon as they reach their destination. Pressure builds down my back, all along the length of my spine, until my tail erupts all at once.

I scream, tears spilling from my eyes in hot streams, and collapse onto my quivering stomach; the towel falls from my mouth, but I can't muster the strength to pull it away from my face.

I feel hot and cold and sweaty, and everything hurts, even my eyes in the dim sunlight filtering through the closed blinds of my bedroom window. I shut down, wishing I had some water for my parched throat, and promptly pass out.

A deeply familiar and fake explosion sound pulls me back to the waking world. Music I've heard before, but can't quite place, flows from somewhere next to me. Sore and loopy, I push myself up on my knees only to feel a blanket fall down my back; I look down and see I'm still naked, but the towel is gone. Lagging mentally and physically, I turn my head toward my occupied computer desk and watch a blocky character model spin violently into the ether of a poorly made sandbox arena. "Why are you playing *Roblox* on my computer?"

Mark spins the chair half a quarter to the right and glances over his shoulder. "I got bored waiting for you to wake up."

I squint, multiple questions popping into my head, but struggle to figure out what to address first. At the very least, I was expecting Mark to come over at some point after school; I made a copy of the house keys for him a long time ago—a copy my parents don't know about—so he can cover for me when I'm too out of it to get chores done. "How are you even on my computer? And you still remember your login?"

"You act like you don't remember yours." Mark turns back to the monitor. "And you haven't changed your password since you were ten."

I face-plant onto my pillow because he's right; even though I haven't played *Roblox* in five years, I do remember both my username and my password; as children do, I used the same two or three passwords everywhere, the kind made up of one word and some numbers, and the username SapphireKing. The only reason I switched it up to Tabby Swain for my Xbox Live account was because the other had already been taken.

Mark continues playing, the quiet SFX drowned out by a somber orchestra accompanied by piano. "Never Forget," my mind supplies.

"How long was I out?" I ask.

"I got here around three, so . . ." He reads the time displayed in the bottom right corner of the monitor. "At least two and a half hours."

Ugh. "Make that five." My mouth feels gross.

"Sheesh. Need anything? I already washed the dishes and took out the trash. I went ahead and swept and mopped the floor, too. Oh, and I cleaned your toilet; it was kinda gross, no offense. If you're hungry, I have dinner in the oven right now; it should be ready in ten minutes. And—"

"Mark." I lift my index finger as a sign for him to shut up. "I could really use some water, but then I want you to tell me what's wrong."

Mark frowns, refusing to look me in the eye. "Nothing's wrong, Matthew." He gets up and grabs a glass of water that he left on my dresser; he puts it on the nightstand next to my bed.

I sit on my knees and take a sip.

Mark sits back down, his back turned to me, but doesn't go back to playing. "I just have a lot on my mind, I guess."

I drink half the glass before placing it back down on my nightstand, then lie back down, pulling the blanket over my body to stave off the cold. "I'm not good for much other than listening right now, so lay it on me." I'm awfully sore and my head is pounding, but that doesn't mean I can't take a much-needed rant.

Mark sighs and stares at his hands in his lap. "I . . . think my mom is seeing someone."

My ears perk up; I wasn't expecting *that* to be the problem.

"And, like, it's not that I have anything against that, but it still scares me a little. I just . . . I don't think I can handle some guy trying to play dad with me, and with what we are . . . I don't want to lose the one place I can be myself, if that makes sense. And, God, what if he's not a good guy, and he's just playing with Mom's feelings, or . . ." His elbows on the desk, Mark puts his head in his hands, his fingers digging into his scalp. "What if he's actually a good guy but he can't handle having a stepson like me? I don't want to get in the way of Mom's happiness."

I close my eyes, digesting all Mark said. "I think she's seeing someone, too. Miss Ashley has seemed . . . different lately."

"She even smells different, like, uh . . ." Mark snaps his fingers, trying to find the words for the complex scent I've caught once or twice on her skin.

"Cabernet Sauvignon," I say. "It's the red wine my mom always drinks. She smells like that, but it's . . . mustier, and as far as I know, Miss Ashley doesn't drink, much less drink wine."

"Yeah, she's always said she prefers rum, whiskey, or beer." He lifts his head and looks at me. "Wait, you don't think . . ."

Knowing her . . . "I don't think she'd get involved with someone that would put us in jeopardy, so, maybe . . ."

He turns away and holds his head again. "Oh my God, she would, wouldn't she? Date a damn monster person."

My ears tilt downward. "She's technically done it before."

Mark shakes his head, his eyebrows drawn up. With a frown,

he closes the window on the game he was playing, logs out of *Roblox*, closes Google Chrome, and signs out of my computer. "I should probably head home soon." He stands up and hunches over the desk to check his phone. "After I clean up in the kitchen, of course." Just as the words leave his lips, his phone jingles out a default alarm, which he swiftly stops with the tap of his finger. "Be right back." Mark leaves the room and gently closes the door behind him.

Loathing the thought of moving my sore limbs but tired of being naked, I struggle out of bed. On shaky paws, I stumble to the door and turn on the light, then teeter over to my dresser; I pull out some pajama pants and a shirt, take them over to my bed, and put them on while sitting down. I close my eyes, panting over something that shouldn't have taken so much effort. My heart rate rises, a wave of heat coursing through my body, so I drink the rest of the water Mark gave me. Fatigue and discomfort are par for the course after being fully dormant for over an hour, but I'm beginning to think I may have come down with something, and it's only Monday.

Mark knocks on the door before coming back inside, precariously holding two plates and another glass of water with one arm. He closes the door with his foot, places one plate and the glass on top of my dresser, and hands the other plate to me.

I stare at the cube of alternating ground meat and pasta slathered in tomato sauce. "Lasagna? We had lasagna in the freezer?"

Mark picks up his plate and brings it to my desk. "Yeah, it was either that or meat loaf. I would've made something fresh, but your fridge was basically barren."

I'm not a fan of most frozen meals, especially since my parents stock up on them so much I've grown increasingly sick of them, but food is food and I'm beyond hungry right now. "I forgot to send them a grocery list since this week is going to be . . . a week for me." I'm dealing with the consequences of going full dormant now, and this coming Wednesday will be the full moon; I'm not going to have the energy for cooking anything. "But thanks anyway." I smile. "I always appreciate you coming by for me."

Mark smiles, too. "Aw, well, I know you'd do the same for me in a heartbeat."

We dig in, taking clean portions with our forks so neither of us make a mess; I'd typically avoid eating in my room, but circumstances demand otherwise.

I struggle to swallow my first bite, a sharp discomfort filling my gut; I stop eating.

Mark places his fork down. "You okay?"

"I'm feeling kinda nauseous." Not the I'm-about-to-vomit sort of nauseous, but enough that eating any more sounds like a bad idea. I place my plate next to the empty glass on my nightstand.

"Do you want me to get you some medicine?"

I nod. "We should have ibuprofen somewhere." It's not meant to relieve nausea, but I could use something for the headache; it's best I do what I can to avoid getting any sicker because I really don't want to miss school tomorrow; I have a test, and I'll be missing enough class on Wednesday.

Mark places his half-eaten food back on my dresser and grabs my empty glass. "I'll get you some more water, too." He leaves the room to root around all the cabinets in the house.

I lie down, my head throbbing incessantly. Mark returns with more water and a pill and promptly puts them in my hands. I sit up long enough to place the pill on my tongue and swallow it with a swig of water. I drink a little more to wash the gross taste of medicine out of my mouth, then get under my covers. "I'm gonna sleep this off. See you tomorrow."

Mark lifts his hand toward me but puts it back down before I can determine what he's thinking. "Don't force yourself." He frowns. "Just text or call, you know, if anything changes."

"I will." I blink slowly, consciousness fading, until my mind drifts away.

CHAPTER 12

Cat Scratch Fever

Emily

Matthew staggers into first-period American History I, Mark right behind him, which is strange because Mark isn't in our class; they appear to be arguing about something in hushed whispers, and Mark thrusts his hands on Matthew's desk as soon as he sits down. He looks genuinely upset, gritting his sharp teeth, but Matthew won't budge. In an effort to convince him, Mark puts his elbows on the desk, lifts his hands together, and begs.

Matthew shakes his head.

The five-minute bell forces Mark to leave, but he jabs his finger at Matthew, totally fuming, before he exits the room. I consider walking up to Matthew before class starts but think better of it when he puts his head down on his desk, his arms draping across its width. I wonder if he's having another one of those days, the ones where he acts all sleepy and fatigued; it's almost funny that it happens once a month, as if he has a period, but unless I'm mistaken about his sex, that's not biologically possible.

I stare at him until a classmate looks at me weirdly, so I put my attention on my desk until the bell rings for the start of class.

Matthew barely sits back up, his posture all hunched.

The teacher hands out a stack of history tests to each first-row student; they pass all but one copy back to the person behind them, all the way until they reach the last row, which includes me—Matthew sits all the way over in the far right second row, very close to the door. I try not to glance at him, instead focusing on starting my test; I write my name in the top right corner of the page, then move on to the first multiple-choice question. I work through each question steadily, marking out answer choices that are absolutely wrong, then make an educated guess; before long, I reach the two long-answer questions, write out a paragraph or two for each, and scan for errant typos. As soon as I'm done, I look over all my questions again and turn in my test at the teacher's desk.

I sit back down and glance at Matthew; surprisingly, he's still working on his test—he's usually done way before me. I frown, watching his painful body language. He holds the side of the desk with a vice grip while his right hand hovers over his paper; he doesn't move for a long time, scribbles a few answers out, then pauses again. His face is pale, and he appears to be panting, like the effort of moving his pencil even an inch is too much to ask. He doesn't finish until five minutes before the end of class, at which time he stumbles out of his seat, staggers to the front desk, places his paper on the stack with a heavy hand, and returns to his seat with as much grace as a fish out of water.

When the bell rings, I speed walk up to him before he can leave. "Are you alright? You don't normally take so long."

Matthew stares at me with dazed eyes, keeping one hand on his desk, the other trembling around the strap of his book bag.

"I'm . . . I'm fine. Just a little tired is all." He shakes his head, his Adam's apple bobbing. "See you in third . . ." He smiles weakly and staggers away.

"Matthew . . ." I watch him go, wishing desperately he'd be honest and tell me what's wrong. I know there's something wrong with him; he has to have a condition or illness that puts him out of commission all the time, but he won't tell me, because I'm—

I grit my teeth. *He's not like that. Matthew's not that kind of guy.* Hardly believing my own thoughts, I trudge to second period.

I stare dumbfounded at the short story on my desk; despite being in Creative Writing I together for two months, I've never had the opportunity to peer edit one of Grace's stories, and she has quite the imagination. Her story is about a serf boy who got transformed into a dragon boy and enslaved by an evil magic princess, so the dragon boy's best friend trains for years to become her bodyguard so he can infiltrate her quarters and release the dragon boy; they manage to escape, but only after the princess transforms the bodyguard into a tiger boy. It's obviously *fujoshi* bait, but I'll admit I sometimes enjoy homoeroticism if it doesn't go too far, and the monster boys are a plus. I'm impressed she has the balls to unabashedly share something like this with the class and have the teacher grade it, too. I'd never have the guts to do the same.

I mark her story with what constructive criticism I can think of, and once she's done with mine, we trade our papers back. My short story is a mess of purple ink, but I try not to take it to heart—just like with art, I'm not the best at writing. Instead of ruminating on her critiques, I decide to strike up a conversation with the hot pink–haired girl next to me. "Hey, Grace? Can I ask you something?"

She looks up from her loose-leaf paper. "Hmm, oh, yes. You're one of Jack's friends, correct?"

"Um, yeah, that's right." I fiddle with a stray thread. "Do you know, um, his other friends? Matthew and Mark?"

She closes her eyes. "Yes, we're acquainted. Matthew is a nice boy, and Mark . . ." She lifts her metal claw ring–wearing index finger to the edge of her lip and bites the tip. "He's . . . also nice . . ." Grace sobers, removing her jewelry from her mouth. "What is it you wanted to ask?"

"Oh, uh . . ." I stumble over the words in my mouth. Grace is super intimidating, what with her piercing good looks; she has her sharp features in common with her brother, who's somehow leagues less frightening to me—maybe because I've always been more comfortable around guys compared to girls, or maybe it's because he's so awkward and shy that I find him harmless. "I was wondering if you've ever noticed anything unusual about them."

"Like what?"

"Like . . . the way they look or . . . act sometimes." Now that I've said it, I feel dirty; isn't it strange to ask other people if they think your friends are weird?

"Hmm . . ." Grace closes her eyes again and sits up, putting her hands in her lap over her lacy black skirt. "They're certainly handsome, much like my brother."

What does Jack have to do with my question?

"Yes, I can admit Teddy has a handsome face too, despite not being my type. But he's very fluffy, which is quite nice. Sometimes, I consider running my hands down his arms and legs."

Is she calling him fat? And that other comment . . .

"Matthew is fluffy too, but he certainly wouldn't want to be pet."

Where did petting come from?! "Um, Grace . . ." I whisper, trying to get her attention without alerting the entire class. In the back of my head, I freak out about how and why she concluded that Matthew is fluffy; does he have a gut or something?

"Oh, but Mark . . . he must be so smooth . . ." She lifts her right hand and curls all her fingers except for her pointer and middle. "And that tongue of his . . ." Her left hand dips between her thighs as she grabs her left earlobe between her two outstretched fingers, rubbing her skin between them.

Without my permission, a despicable image of Mark licking her ear with his bifurcated tongue pops into my head. I feel disgusting, a blush burning my ears, and pray dearly that Grace will stop talking before other people hear her blatant fantasies.

Grace removes her fingers from her ear, and just as she's about to lay the offending digits on her left boob, her eyes snap open— "Ah!"— and she returns both hands to the tops of her thighs. "I've said too much. My apologies."

"Um, no . . . I-It's okay . . ." I squeak.

"Mm. I hope that answers your question."

"Yeah . . ." *Sure it does* . . . I have more questions and absolutely no answers. Honestly, I'm still stuck on whether Matthew is chubby or not. I don't think he is. His lower body might be on the thicker side, but his arms and face are average at worst. But he's always wearing those big shirts, so he could be hiding some fluff. And how the heck would Grace know? Has she seen him shirtless? Matthew? Shirtless?!

Try as I might, I can only imagine the unrealistic slender physique of an anime *bishounen*. Mark might be like that, but I don't want to think about Mark right now with his long, split tongue.

I recall when he licked his nose in front of me, wiggling the two prongs in the open air. It was so gross. Mostly because Mark did it. Forked tongues are otherwise absolutely sexy, so I get where Grace is coming from.

I pause, staring at the mess of lead and purple ink that is my rough draft. *Why am I like this?* If there was ever a time to slam my head on my desk, that time would be now.

Matthew staggers into Marine Ecology with only a second to spare; he barely acknowledges me when he sits down in the neighboring seat, and completely ignores the first half of class by resting upright.

The teacher notices, but doesn't bother correcting him, perfectly happy to keep droning on and on about ocean biomes until the bell rings for B lunch.

Everyone but me and Matthew file out of the room; because Mark and Jack have A lunch this semester, we eat in the classroom instead of the cafeteria.

Matthew immediately lays his head on our desk.

I take my lunch box out of my book bag. It's not until I'm halfway through a PB&J that I realize Matthew has yet to take out his own lunch. "Aren't you going to eat?"

He opens his blue eyes a smidgen, recoils, and covers his face with an arm. "I forgot."

"Forgot to eat? There's still plenty of time."

"No. Forgot lunch."

That's . . . really unlike him; Matthew never skips lunch. I wonder if he skipped breakfast, too. I look into my lunch box, pull out a gra-nola bar, and place it in front of him. "You can have this if you want."

He lifts his arm away from his eyes just enough to see the wrapped bar. "Thanks." He pockets it. "I'll eat it when I'm hungry." He covers his face again, tugging on his hood so it covers as much of his head as possible.

I rest the back of my hand on our desk, still holding the remaining quarter of my sandwich. "Are you sure you're okay? You've been acting strange all day."

"I'm fine." He huffs, sucking in a shaky breath. "Maybe I just need a nap."

"Were you staying up all night again?"

His mouth parts, but he doesn't say anything.

"Matthew?"

Nothing.

I quickly finish my sandwich and lean really close to his arm-covered face; he's breathing softly, the little puffs warm on my cheeks, and I realize he fell asleep. Part of me wants to shake him awake, but another knows he wears himself out all the time and probably needs the rest. I sit back up and start to eat my Goldfish crackers.

Kicking my feet back and forth, I decide I'll do all I can to help him out for the rest of the day.

～⌒

I shake Matthew awake after the bell rings, surprised the piercing noise didn't wake him up on its own.

He groans, burying his head in his arm.

"Class is starting soon," I whisper. "You need to take your hood off."

Matthew removes his arm from his eyes, holds his hood with one hand, and sticks the other inside to fix up his hair—he's super touchy about his hair and won't tolerate so much as grazing the edge of any one strand; as soft as it looks, I'm not going to disrespect his boundaries just to feel it. He pulls his hood off and sits back up, slouching horribly with a dazed look in his eyes; he closes them, his arms tense.

The teacher and our classmates shuffle back into the room, all of them looking like they'd rather be anywhere else, and the bell rings again to signal the start of the second half of third period.

Matthew cringes at the sound, gritting his teeth.

The teacher takes her time pulling up the PowerPoint slides and returns to lecturing us about the terrible effects of pollution on marine ecosystems. Ten minutes later, when she slaps her pointer stick onto an image of bleached coral, Matthew raises his hand. She pauses, expression stern, and asks, "Do you have a question, Matthew?"

"Yes. I'm not feeling well. Can I go to the nurse's office?" His still-raised hand shakes, his nails half a centimeter too long—Matthew usually keeps his nails completely blunt, with only the thinnest strip of white showing at the edges.

The teacher stares at Matthew, squinting her eyes from afar to assess whether he really needs to go or not.

Matthew puts his hand down, trembling all over with his shoulders hunched.

The teacher clicks her tongue. "You may go, but get back to class as soon as you feel better."

With more energy than he's had all day, Matthew pushes himself to his feet and power walks to the door, leaving his chair askew and his book bag on the floor.

"Wait, Matthew!" I shout, "You forgot—"

He opens the door and slams it closed.

Without a second thought, I grab his bag and run after him, the teacher's gasping and sputtering—and our classmates' snickering—quickly forgotten once I leave the room.

Holding Matthew's heavy book bag properly over both my shoulders, I quickly look to the right and see him staggering down the hall; he runs one hand along the lockers on his right, as if he needs the guidance, and stops at the intersection. The hall to the left leads to the nurse's office, the hall to the right leads to the theater and the gym, and straight ahead are doors leading outside to the teacher parking lot; Matthew goes straight.

I bound up behind him, grab his shoulder, and point to the left. "Matthew, the nurse's office is that way."

Matthew jolts, shrugs me off, and trudges to the glass doors leading outside, using his body weight to open one.

Confused, I follow him. "Matthew—"

"Don't follow me, Emmie . . . Please . . ." He keeps walking, but I don't let the distance between us increase.

"But you're going the wrong way. Aren't you sick?"

"Go back to class . . . I'll be okay . . ." He reaches a tree near the theater's emergency exit, huffing as he staggers to a halt against the trunk; he spits in the grass, heaving as if he's about to puke his guts out. Strangely, his nails are long enough to dig into the bark.

"Obviously not!" I get close enough that he can't possibly look away from me. "I just want to help! You never tell me what's wrong! I'm not blind, Matthew! I can see something's wrong!"

"I can't do this right now . . ." He refuses to look me in the eye. "Just go . . ." He scratches the bark.

It's cold outside, but I feel hot all over, absolutely fuming. "Why won't you tell me, huh?! I know Mark and Jack know about whatever's going on with you!" I seethe, only to see a pitiful expression on Matthew's face; the fight leaves my voice entirely. "Am I just not a good-enough friend?"

He stares at me with wild blue eyes. "No, Emily . . . It's not like that . . . It's just . . . It's complicated . . ."

"I don't care if it's complicated. I could understand if you'd just explain it to me."

He looks away. "Trust me, you wouldn't. You can't understand." The rims of his eyes start to turn red, and he trembles all the more, like just being in my presence makes him uncomfortable.

A fresh doubt creeps back into my mind. "Is it . . . Is it because I'm a girl? Is that it? I can't understand because I'm a stupid girl?" I always get treated differently, always . . . What makes Matthew any different? I fooled myself, didn't I? Fooled myself into thinking he's special.

"Emmie, no . . ." he whispers. "It has nothing to do with that . . . I wish I could tell you, I really do, but . . . I can't."

I still don't understand. I don't understand why he can't tell me.

"Please go back to class . . ." He grits his teeth again, screwing his eyes shut. "I'm begging you . . ." The bark cracks.

I shake my head, but I'm starting to feel scared; I'm afraid to look at his hand. I'm afraid because he's starting to purr, because his sharp canines poke out from his open mouth and the moon hangs just shy of full behind the passing clouds. I'm afraid because I don't understand but I know deep down that I've been right all along.

Matthew puts his hands on me, squeezing my biceps because he's too distressed to control his strength. Something pokes my skin at five places on each arm. *His nails . . . His nails are poking me . . .* "Just go . . ." He prepares to push me away, but shudders violently, gripping me harder. And I see them, just as his needle-sharp claws pierce my skin. Through fresh tears I watch cat ears lift up from under his hair, and when I glance down, a tail falls out from under his jacket. And I think about all the times I've felt something move under his shirt, all the times he'd awkwardly shuffle whenever I hugged him, and it's no wonder . . . It's no wonder . . .

Matthew slowly lets go of me and backs away, shaking his head in unbridled horror.

My arms sting, and I think they might bruise as tears trail down my cheeks. "M- . . . Matthew . . ." I say it so weakly, and he looks at his furry, claw-tipped hands, each sharp end decorated by a tiny splotch of red.

"I-I . . ." He gasps, hyperventilating. "Emily . . . I . . ." He covers his face and turns around, his long cat tail puffy and free of its confines, his cat ears plastered back against his head, and runs. He stumbles as fast as he can across the parking lot, until both of his shoes slip off his feet, and he's running on his toes, and he disappears behind the ticket booth of the school's outdoor stadium at the edge of the parking lot.

I stand there, my arms aching, staring at the navy blue tennis shoes in the middle of the parking lot; his book bag feels heavier, the corner of one jostled book digging into my butt. I readjust the bag, wincing from the burn in my biceps, and sniffle. I feel so stupid. I knew it. I knew it! He really isn't human! I was right, so why do I feel so terrible?

A cloud passes over the sun, briefly shading the shoes in the road, the shiny cars next to them no longer glinting in the corner of my irritated eyes. I walk forward, slowly make my way to the shoes, and pick them up; they're well-worn, but not particularly dirty. The clouds pass, and I squint my eyes against the sunlight. I keep walking, passing car after car until I reach the entrance to the outdoor stadium; I don't need inhuman ears to hear him crying and purring behind the booth wall.

Despite my survival instincts screaming at me to leave him alone, I peek around the corner to check on him. He's huddled against the wall behind him, holding his knees up to his chest with his tail curled around his leg. He's sobbing, his eyes shut tight as he trembles with each tear that falls. He digs his hand claws into the fabric over his shins, while four foot claws tear through his socks; I gape at the implication. "Tabby . . ."

Matthew's tail immediately puffs up again; he shoves his face between his legs, shaking his head profusely. "N-No. Go away. Don't look at me."

"Wait, I just—"

He lifts his head, the angriest look I've ever seen on his face. "I mean it, Emily!" And he growls at me—he actually, literally growls at me.

I gasp, flinching.

Matthew's face crumbles all the way down to despair; he hangs his head and weeps. "I can't do this . . . I can't . . ."

My heart pounding in my chest, I back away and return to the parking lot side of the wall. His bag is so heavy I have to put it down; I put his shoes next to it, right against the wall. I sit down next to his bag and pull my shaking knees up to my chest. Birds chirp and cars pass by along the street down the hill, but all I can hear is my own sniffling. And even though Matthew weeps, I feel so afraid.

I spent so many days getting to know him: I remember all the days in Honors Biology trying to knock down his walls; I remember all the nights we stayed up late talking about everything and nothing at all; I remember all the times he'd let me hug him, all the times he'd gingerly reach out and touch my hand whenever he wanted my attention, and all the times he'd blush and clear his throat so I wouldn't catch him purring over me; and I remember all the stories Mark told me about fighting big cats in the wilderness, and even though I want to trust Matthew—even though I don't want to be sad—I'm still so scared.

Knowing I lost something I can never get back, I cover my face and cry alone.

CHAPTER 13

The Sky is Blue

Mark

A foreboding sense of dread invades my gut when I enter German I. Emily's book bag sits on the floor next to her desk, neither her nor Matthew anywhere to be found; they usually get to class long before me since I'm on the other side of campus for third. I approach a girl who shares Marine Ecology with them. "Hey, Rebecca, do you know where Emily and Matthew went?"

She looks up from her notes. "Matthew went to the nurse's office, but he forgot his book bag, so Emily ran after him. They never came back to class, so I brought Emily's book bag with me."

Oh, no; that's not good. I knew this was going to happen. I knew it! But he wouldn't listen to me.

"Uh, Mark? Are you okay?"

I replace the scowl on my face with an awkward grin. "Oh, yeah, um . . . Could you tell the teacher I went home early? Thanks!" I slip out of the room and dash back the way I came, reaching the stairwell as the bell rings for class to start—all while stitching together a plan of action in my frazzled mind. God, I'm beyond worried right now. Anything could've happened, and I can't call either of them because Matthew turns his phone off during class and I don't know what I can and cannot say to Emily without rousing her suspicion. At least I know Matthew wouldn't go to the nurse's office, or anywhere inside for that matter, but there are only so many places to hide on campus.

I find their third-period classroom and face the direction that leads to the nurse's office; there's only one way he could've gone. I run straight outside, but hit a roadblock: Would Matthew have gone left or right? Left leads to the car pool lane, while right leads to the bus lot, staff parking, and outdoor stadium.

I decide to go right. I know I made the right choice when I notice scratch marks on one of the trees near the theater; it looks like he was digging into the bark, but it's not a clean mark.

I scan the parking lot, my gaze falling upon the outdoor stadium entrance; someone's sitting in front of the ticket booth. *Shit.* I know exactly who's sitting there, and I'm already losing my composure; I need to calm down and handle this.

I slowly walk down the sidewalk so she can't see me behind all the cars, and as I get close, I catch soft, tremulous purring. I can't see him, but judging by the sound, Matthew's behind the ticket booth; Emily's in front of it, hunched up next to Matthew's book bag. I quietly place my book bag on the ground, walk over to the one girl I didn't want to see, and squat down next to her sniffling form. "Emily . . ."

She jumps to her feet, stepping away so fast she nearly trips over herself, and raises her arms in front of her chest as if to shield herself; it's clear she's been crying. Trembling, her body clearly screaming at her to run away, she stares at me—truly sees me for what I am—and more tears fall down her face. "I-I . . . Mark, I . . ." She shakes her head, staring at the concrete below her feet. "It's not just Matthew, is it? None of you are human."

I grit my teeth. "Don't say it like that." My hands start to shake. "He can hear you."

Wide-eyed, she brings a hand to her mouth; she points at me, slightly down.

I follow her frightened gaze to my hands: my nails have grown into claws, my skin slowly blotching red; I shove my hands in my pockets, a shameful heat flooding my face.

We remain at a standstill, and I hate how she looks at me like I'm going to hurt her.

"Don't look at me like that . . . I'm not . . ." *Oh, who am I kidding . . .*

"I . . ." She removes her hand from her mouth, guilt in the tilt of her brow. "I'm sorry . . . I just . . . Matthew, um . . . he . . . he got me when he was trying to make me go away. I was just so tired of you guys lying to me about . . . well . . ." She gestures wildly in my direction. "Whatever this is, and I . . . I just . . ." More tears fall down her face; she covers her eyes with her hands, and I finally see the holes torn in the arm of her jacket—five of them on the one I can see.

I raise my arm toward her, muttering her name, but recoil at the sight of my scaly hand. "Look, why don't you go to the nurse's office and get that taken care of. You . . . wouldn't want it to scar."

Emily nods weakly and trudges away, sniffling and wiping away her tears.

I watch her go, hoping that I can trust her to be the friend we've always thought she is, but I can't know. I can't know what she'll do, or what she won't do, or if we're even still friends at all, and it hurts. It hurts to know this might be the end.

When Emily disappears behind the rows of cars and the sparse trees in the distance, I turn around. I put Matthew's heavy-ass book bag on my back, pick up his shoes, and drag my own bag behind the ticket booth.

After I throw his shit on the ground, Matthew looks up at me. "Mark . . ." He shakes his head. "I'm sorry. I should've listened to you." His self-soothing purrs break up his quivering voice.

"It's too late now." I shuffle over and plop down next to him. "And we both knew she was going to find out eventually."

"It didn't have to be like this. I've never seen her look at me like that. She was terrified of me. Terrified!" He stares at his shaking hands, flexing his fingers so his claws emerge. "She used to look at me so sweetly, you know." He smiles, a wan little thing. "But now . . ." His smile falls. "Now she knows I'm just a fucking freak of nature."

"Matthew—"

"Don't bother." His face twists. "I don't care anymore. I don't fucking care. If it wasn't for these fucking claws . . . !" More tears trail down his face. "She's right. I'm not human. I'm not even an animal." He curls his right hand into a fist, letting his arm drop to his side; he looks up and covers his eyes with his other hand, trying and failing to keep his sobs at bay. "I'm just a fucking monster!" He hiccups between his purrs, the two sounds blurring into a mess of noise I wish he didn't have to make.

Sitting hip-to-hip with him, I look up at the sky and stare at the nearly full moon. "You're right. You are a monster, and so am I. And Jack, and Teddy, and that guy my mom is fucking around with, too. But you know what?"

"What?" His voice cracks.

I lift my shaking hand with its rich-red scales and bold-black claws. "We're also people, Matthew. People. And right here"—my hand trembling, I point at my chest, pressing the tip of my claw against my sternum—"we have a soul and a spirit, just like every other person on this planet." My hand falls into my lap. "At least, that's what I think."

Matthew wipes his eyes only for more tears to fall down his face. "I believe you. But it doesn't matter what we think. It never has."

And it never will. I rest the back of my head against the ticket booth behind us and cradle Matthew's head with my left hand. He rests his head on my shoulder, weeping while I stroke his hair and ears. I stare at the blue sky with its fluffy clouds and its lazy sun and the moon that steals its light for itself, and I can't bring myself to cry. I feel so empty, as empty as the atmosphere and the lifeless planets that make up the Milky Way.

Matthew's purrs wane as he drifts to sleep, but I keep my hand on his head. It's cold outside, but it's not so bad when we're together.

CHAPTER 14

You Can Lean on Me

John

Mark's been awfully antsy these last two months. I'm not sure if it's just his brumation getting to him, but I've noticed his mood swing drastically every other day during lunch. Some days he charges ahead with some wild conversation I can barely keep up with, while on others, he barely speaks at all; on his worst days, I've had to remind him to eat his lunch—which worries me a little, if I'm honest—and on new moons, I've let him rest his head against me, one arm wrapped around him because I'm too tall for him to drape his arm over my shoulders.

Today was another one of his moody days. He was ranting about Matthew coming to school even though he obviously wasn't feeling well and completely ignored his lunch again, and between the complaining and the worrying, I never got a single word in—it completely ruined my only peaceful thirty minutes in this godforsaken school, but what are you gonna do? But I'll be real, his concerns have me all worried, too.

My leg bounces up and down under my desk as I impatiently wait for the bell. I don't even know what's going on at this point—I've never cared for Shakespeare—and by the time the bell rings, I'm so wound up that I spring right out of my desk and charge out of the room, teacher hollering about how he releases us, not the bell, but I really don't give a damn. I make large strides down the hall with my long legs, shoving past students that stand in my path as they all start flooding out of the classrooms.

I think about going straight to the busses, but halfway there, I change my mind and go toward the gym; Matthew and Mark usually hang out with Emily there before her soccer practice starts. I figure I should check on them, make sure they're okay and all that. As I shuffle through the cramped halls, I spot a certain girl wearing a dirty-blond ponytail and an old, olive-colored book bag. "Hey, Emily!"

She trudges on, staggering forward at a languid pace.

I call her name again with no results. Since she's going so slow, I easily catch up to her and place a hand on her shoulder.

Emily nearly jumps out of her skin, squeaking with her eyes wide open; they're swollen and bloodshot, like she's been crying. When she realizes it's just me, she becomes . . . scared? "O-Oh, um . . ." She stutters, unable to avert her gaze from mine; her eyes flit to my hand on her shoulder. "P-Please don't touch me . . ."

Confused by her cold attitude, I let go of her shoulder. "Is there something wrong?" I lean my forearm against the nearest locker to shield her from all the students swarming by. "You look like you've been crying." I wonder what it could be; I've never seen her get genuinely upset, much less cry.

She stares intently at my stomach, holding her arm with the opposite hand. "I don't know how, or what, but . . ." She shakes her head minutely, lips quivering. "Y-You, and them, you're not . . . None of you are . . ." She starts crying, closing her eyes and covering her mouth to hide her whimpers. "No, I . . . I need to go!" She dashes away, down the hall and to the right until I can no longer see her, leaving me stunned in her dust.

As much as I want to, I get the feeling there's not much point in following her; despite my reservations, I take a left at the intersection she ran to and push my way outside so I can wait for the bus with my sisters, but as I'm walking down the sidewalk, I notice something off about the area; there's a strange scent in the air, something I vaguely recognize. I follow the scent to a particular tree in front of the theater; oddly enough, the bark is haphazardly cracked at about chest height, but I'm certain the smell is coming from this tree. It smells like pine even though it's not coniferous. *Where have I smelled pine before?*

"What the hell are you doing, Jack?"

I look over my shoulder.

Jenny scowls at me, her hands on her hips.

Always with the attitude . . . "This tree smells weird."

She walks up next to me, crosses her arms, and takes a deep breath. "I don't smell anything."

"Get closer to the scratch marks; you know I have a better sense of smell than you."

She gives me a disgusted frown, crinkling her nose, but steps up to the tree; the scratches are high enough she has to stand on her toes to smell it. "You're right. It smells like some weird cologne." She takes another whiff. "Actually, I think I recognize this smell. Your comb and shears reeked of it a few months back."

Why would my . . . "Oh~ That must be Matthew's scent." I feel pretty good for figuring it out, even if it did take a comment from Jenny. Then it hits me. "Oh, shit. That's Matthew's scent."

Jenny whips around. "Why the hell would he mark a tree?"

I bring a hand to my chin. "I'm not sure, but it can't be good." He must've been going active, but I haven't heard a thing from either him or Mark since lunch, so I have no idea where they might be. I doubt Matthew would be able to make it home by foot, not if Mark's whole rant is anything to go by. Emily's behavior earlier is all the more concerning.

"Why are you two staring at this tree?" Grace tilts her head curiously, her metal claw ring against her chin.

"Hey, Grace," I say, "don't you have a class with Emily? She was acting strange earlier."

Grace's gaze slowly shifts away from the tree as she tilts her head up at me; she's not much taller than Jenny, so she has to crane her neck. "Emily?" She tastes the name on her tongue. "Oh, yes, she did ask me if I thought there was anything strange about Matthew and Mark." She wiggles in place, covering her mouth as a blush blooms on her face. "I may have said too much about my . . . interests."

It's unlikely Emily could've gathered any meaningful information from Grace, as she likes to go on strange tangents full of what basically amounts to gibberish; I mean no offense by that, but she's a special one. Somehow, she's also the sister I can most tolerate being around—mostly because she doesn't make a point of antagonizing me for shits and giggles.

"She's asked me that question, too," I say, completely ignoring Grace's fangirling. "She freaked out when she saw me earlier. I think she may have found out about us."

"Oh, no! I hope it wasn't my fault!" Grace slumps forward, holding her hands together in front of her chest.

I put a hand on her shoulder and squeeze gently. "Trust me,

Grace; there's no way it's your fault. I think these claw marks can attest to that." But Matthew isn't a particularly rough guy, not even to inanimate objects, so there's only one conclusion I can come to.

I scan the parking lot behind the tree: beyond the busses and the students entering them, there's a small expanse of woods; similarly, there are more woods on the other side of the paved hill that leads out of the lot; and there's the outdoor stadium, along with a path adjacent to the school building that leads to the gym locker rooms. If I was thinking rationally, I'd suck it up and hide in the woods, but if I was thinking irrationally, then somewhere moderately more familiar would be more appealing in the moment. Let's hope neither of them got caught by the cameras, not that there's much hope for that these days—I doubt someone is checking them all the time, anyway.

"Could you two watch my six? I think I might know where he is." I can only hope my hunch is correct.

"Sure, I guess?" Jenny doesn't sound particularly convinced.

Grace simply nods.

"Thanks." I step around the tree and onto the nearby sidewalk, then walk past the cars lining the edge all the way to the entrance of the outdoor stadium; I immediately spot part of a book bag past the wall of the ticket booth. "Wait here." I look around the wall.

Matthew and Mark rest against the back side of the wall, both appearing to be asleep. Matthew, fully active, rests his head on Mark's shoulder; Mark's hands are covered in scales, but he still has his shoes on and his ears dormant—I didn't know a partial active form is possible.

When my shadow stretches out in front of them, Mark opens his eyes. "Jack."

"Hey. You good?"

He scowls. "Emily found out. She didn't take it well, but . . . the circumstances weren't great."

"What happened?"

Mark shakes his head, careful not to jostle Matthew. "I wasn't there, but Emily said something about being tired of us lying to her. She must have blocked Matthew somehow, and he scratched her when he was trying to get her to leave."

That's pretty fucking bad; no wonder she was acting so scared earlier. "Where did he scratch her?"

"Her arms, right below the shoulders."

"Oh . . ." I recall how badly she jumped when I put my hand on her shoulder, that look of fear when she saw that I was the one putting hands on her. I must've terrified her.

Mark frowns at me with more concern than upset. "What's wrong?"

"I saw her in the hall not too long ago and couldn't get her attention, so I grabbed her shoulder. She told me not to touch her and started crying after I asked her what was wrong." I look away, feeling ashamed even though there was no way for me to know. "She looked at me like I was some kind of monster."

Mark grimaces. "I'm sorry. This is such a mess." He runs his right hand through his hair, tangling the red strands in his fingers.

I flatten my lips and look back at my sisters diligently watching out for us.

Jenny catches my gaze. "Hey. Our bus is here."

Grace turns her head to listen in.

"Go without me," I say. "Tell Mom I'm going to Mark's house tonight."

"You don't have to do that, Jack," Mark says.

I give him a glare that means business. "I want to."

"Mom will complain about that." Jenny crosses her arms.

"Let her complain," I say. "If she cares so much, she can pick me up herself."

Jenny shrugs and rolls her eyes. "Don't say I didn't warn you."

"We should go," Grace says.

Jenny sighs. "Yeah." They saunter away, Grace looking over her shoulder with a somber expression until straining her neck becomes impractical.

Once they're gone, I take their place in watching out for interference, leaning back against the edge of the side of the ticket booth so I can still speak to Mark without raising my voice. "You should call your mom. I doubt either of you are walking home like this."

"Yeah, I . . ." Mark's face twists up terribly as he pulls his hand out of his messy hair. "I don't know why I haven't thought to do that yet."

Probably because he's not thinking right now, but I won't say anything about that; I know where he's coming from.

Mark pulls his phone out of his right pocket.

I stare at the parking lot; even with my hearing dampened from hiding my ears, I catch Mark's claws tapping against his phone screen.

His phone rings as it tries to connect with Miss Ashley; he puts it on speaker, and considering all the noise from hundreds of students and old-ass busses, I don't blame him—it's not like lizards are known for great hearing, so his is probably no better than average.

The phone clicks. "What's wrong, baby?" Miss Ashley's voice is tinny, but recognizable.

A shaky breath escapes Mark's mouth. "Emily found out. Could you pick us up? We're at that outdoor stadium in the teacher parking lot."

"Of course, but are you all okay?"

"We're fine," he says. "Physically, at least."

"Alright, good. I'll be there as soon as I can. Love you."

"Love you too." He ends the call. "God . . ." He rests his head against the wall behind him, closing his eyes in devastation.

"We'll work this out, Mark," I say.

He grimaces. "I wish I could believe you."

The sky is bathed in yellow by the time a black SUV pulls up next to the outdoor stadium. It stalls, stops, and parks, and Miss Ashley tumbles out of the driver side in her haste to check on us as soon as humanly possible. I can tell she came straight from work, what with the black blazer, white blouse, tight pencil skirt, and little kitten heels clacking against the concrete.

She huffs as she walks up to me, her low-bun updo in disarray, and skirts the edge of the wall to see her son. I stay where I am just in case, but glance over my shoulder to see their current state.

Mark had nodded off again, but Miss Ashley's noisy heels roused him from sleep; spotting his worried mother, he gently slaps Matthew's face.

Matthew groans, his pale face covered in a thin layer of sweat and his hair full of knots.

"C'mon, Matthew. Mom's here."

Matthew opens his eyes but immediately screws them shut against the afternoon sunlight. He lifts his head off Mark's shoulder, crinkling his nose and gritting his teeth as if it takes him immense effort; he puts his hand on Mark's shoulder to keep himself steady, his arm shaking horribly.

Miss Ashley crouches in front of them and places the back of her hand against Matthew's forehead. "Goodness, hon. You feel like you have a fever."

"Yeah . . . not feeling great . . ." Matthew lets go of Mark. "I'm sorry you had to leave work over this . . ." Tears build in his red and swollen eyes; he sniffles, looking down shamefully.

Miss Ashley cups his cheek in her palm and rubs her thumb against the corner of his eye. "Don't worry about that, hon. Let's get you home, okay?"

Matthew nods weakly. With some assistance, he gets his shoes back on and puts his hood over his head to hide his ears, and we get ourselves and our things inside the SUV. I end up in the passenger seat. Mark doesn't say as much, but I have a feeling he doesn't want to be too far from Matthew right now; as much as he was complaining about him today, I know that comes from a place of worry rather than disdain.

Miss Ashley pushes a button to start her car instead of putting a key into the ignition, which surprises me—I'm more familiar with vehicles almost as old as I am, but I figure it's only natural that newer models would have more advanced features than what I'm used to. She pulls away from the stadium and slowly rolls down the hill that leads back to the main road, passing over the two speed bumps a little too fast for comfort.

An awkward ride ahead of us, I try to make some small talk. "How are you liking the new car?"

"I like it so much better than that truck. It's much easier to maneuver; better on gas, too." Miss Ashley makes a sharp left turn, causing the keys in the center console tray to slide to the right. She makes another left across a five-lane road, cutting it close with how small a gap she had between the cars coming from the left and right. I don't know if it's the nerves or if she usually drives so frantically, but considering the reckless driving I've been subjected to from my sisters and mother all my life, I'll be happy as long as we reach our destination in one piece. When we stop at the one major intersection between us and their street, she asks, "How have you been, hon? I feel like I haven't seen you in a while."

"I've been alright. School is boring as usual. My parents keep hounding me about my grades, but it's not like I'm going to college anyway." I wonder when that fact will finally get through their thick skulls, but with Hope on the way to graduating with all of her amazing grades in all those AP classes she took throughout high school, they'll be acting like I have to walk in her footsteps awhile yet.

Miss Ashley seems deep in thought, so much so she doesn't go when the light turns green.

"The light." I point at it.

"Oh, gosh." She presses her foot down on the gas pedal. "Here I am with my head in the clouds again." We cross the intersection safely, but not without someone honking their horn at us. "I was just thinking . . . My advice to you is to follow your passion, but to be smart about it. I was basically on my own at eighteen and racked up tens of thousands in college debt just to end up pushing papers in an office for years. I'm in management now, but I wasn't able to pay everything off until recently, so if you don't want to do something that requires a degree, then don't waste your time or money on it. Maybe they don't see it now, but if you're still serious about beauty school by the time you're eighteen, I hope your parents will respect that." She grins mischievously and winks. "If you're lucky, they'll put up with you long enough to help you get on your feet. I hear it takes a long time to work up a client base in that field."

I huff good-naturedly. "Either way, I'll figure it out." Though if I'm being honest, I don't think I could stomach living in that house beyond eighteen, even if it meant I'd have to put myself in debt.

"You're still young, Jack. You never know what the future might bring, so don't be shy if you ever feel the need to reach out to me or someone else you trust. It's our job as parents to look out for our children." She turns down her street.

I don't know much about Miss Ashley's personal life, but from what little Mark has told me, she never had parents she could truly rely on; it's not lost on me how fortunate I am to have met her. "You're very kind, Miss Ashley."

She smiles, a far-off look in her eyes. "It's the least I can do."

She pulls into her driveway and parks on the right side of the truck; despite being white, it's spotless. The doors automatically unlock, and Mark wastes no time getting out, ushering Matthew along with him; the two head to the door to get inside while I grab two of our book bags, Miss Ashley taking the third. Mark unlocks the door with his keys and we all file inside.

Glenn runs straight to the door as I close it behind everyone, meowing loudly in greeting.

Matthew stumbles past the lithe black cat, stepping straight out of his shoes and throwing his jacket on the coffee table, his ears pointing outward in a clear sign of discomfort. "I'm gonna . . . take a bath . . ." He teeters toward the hall.

Mark tries to follow him, holding a hand out, but cringes and collapses on his knees near the couch. "Shit . . ." With an incredibly shaky hand, he hooks his claws into the knot tying his laces together, pulls it free, removes his shoes, and takes off his socks, revealing partially active feet; he seethes as they morph into dragon paws, and his tail violently snakes out from under his jacket, leaving him winded.

I put my boots on the rack and collect his and Matthew's shoes to do the same.

Miss Ashley lingers next to Mark after picking up Matthew's jacket, looking toward the hall as the bathtub faucet squeaks on, the sound of running water quickly overtaking the heavy silence.

Glenn chirps, winds around Miss Ashley's legs, and hops up to rub his cheek against Mark's face.

"Not now, buddy." Mark pushes the cat away with the back of his hand, but Glenn rubs his face against it. "Oh, alright." Mark chuckles dryly, relaxing enough to sit back on his knees; he scoops the cat up and puts him over his shoulder, supporting Glenn's haunches with one hand and petting his head with the other.

As Mark carefully strokes his fur, Glenn purrs and kneads his back, his little claws pulling up Mark's jacket with each repetition.

Miss Ashley puts Matthew's jacket on the coatrack near the door, then returns to Mark's side; she places her left hand on his head, running her thumb over his tangled hair. "I'll go check on Matthew. You just take a breather for me, okay?"

Mark nods weakly, his elven ear brushing against Glenn; the cat nuzzles and licks him.

Miss Ashley walks down the hall.

I free my ears from my hair, take off my socks, and sit on my knees next to Mark; Glenn sniffs me and trills. Although it embarrasses me to do so around Miss Ashley, I go active as an act of solidarity.

Miss Ashley knocks on the bathroom door. "Matthew? Are you alright in there?"

"I-I'm fine."

"Is there anything you need, hon?"

I perk my ears so I can hear better.

Matthew says, "S-Some water, please."

Miss Ashley goes into the kitchen, pours him a cup of water, and returns to the door.

The lock clicks.

"Do you need me to help you take your temperature?" Miss Ashley asks.

Matthew pauses for a long time. "No. I can . . . do it myself." The door softly thumps closed and a cabinet creaks open.

Miss Ashley walks back into the living room, a flash of surprise crossing her face.

I look down and pull my ears back.

"I think that's all I can do for now," she says. "It may be best to give him some space."

"I'll check on him later," Mark says. "If you need to go back to work or something, you don't need to worry about us."

Miss Ashley cups her cheek. "Of course I'm going to worry."

"I know, but . . . this is our mess to clean up." Glenn struggles, so Mark lets him go; the cat climbs across his shoulders and jumps onto the arm of the couch.

Miss Ashley frowns, but ultimately sighs and picks up her purse. "Alright. I have to make some calls, but please don't hesitate to get me for anything. I'll be in my room until dinnertime."

"Okay. Thanks for bringing us home."

She smiles softly and ruffles Mark's hair. "Of course, baby. I'd do anything for you."

Mark looks down shyly, a hint of pink on his cheeks.

Miss Ashley huffs a heavy breath through her nose and retreats upstairs.

The bathtub faucet squeaks off.

Mark doesn't make any attempt to leave the floor, so I wrap my arm around him. "Why don't we sit on the couch?"

He glances at me briefly. "S-Sure, I guess."

I help him to his feet, watching him tremble all the way up, and sit down next to him on the couch; consciously or not, his tail wraps around my back, the tip curling over my right thigh. I keep my arm across his shoulder, casually crossing my ankle over my knee; his shoulders feel so bony, even under two layers of fabric. "Mark."

"What?" He gazes at my fuzzy foot.

"Can I ask you a question?"

He looks away. "I have nothing to hide from you."

I furrow my brow and flatten my lips. "I was just wondering why you forget to eat so often."

A beat of silence passes. "It's not that I forget. I've just been stressed out lately. Today especially."

"What does stress have to do with it?"

He frowns. "Do you remember . . . when you asked me about my dad back in August?"

Now I frown. "Yes, I do."

"He died of a heart attack when I was twelve, right at the end of sixth grade. He had heart disease but never went out of his way to do anything about it. Still ate like shit most of the time, hardly exercised, that sort of thing. He seemed fine enough most of the time, but one day, he just dropped dead right in front of me, in the kitchen." He says it quietly, without emotion.

I gently squeeze his shoulder.

"Even though I knew both of my parents were unhealthy, I never expected one of them to die like that. No one does. Some people live their whole lives with the shittiest health imaginable and make it to eighty or ninety anyway, so I never thought . . ." He grits his teeth and takes a sharp breath. "After that . . . You know how my mom used to be fat?"

I nod uselessly. "Yeah." The pictures on the wall speak for themselves.

"After Dad died, she stopped eating. She still cooked for me and kept the house stocked with groceries, but every time she sat down for dinner, she just stared at her plate until she broke down crying. At some point she stopped sitting at the table altogether. And I watched her, day by day, melt down into nothing. She lost more than eighty pounds that year.

"At some point, I couldn't bear to eat around her. I think part of it was because I was afraid."

"What were you afraid of?"

"I guess . . . I was afraid of being like my dad. Gaining weight. Something like that. You know, my entire family is overweight or obese. Back then, all they ever wanted to talk about was how skinny I am. That's all I was. The skinny kid. They always said I should eat more, but all I could think was *God, I never want to be as fat and miserable as you.*

"So, at some point, it became impossible for me to eat whenever I was stressed, which was very often that year. I cried every single day. If not for Matthew, I'd be extremely underweight by now.

"He was my emotional support back then. He'd sit with me and eat with me even if it took me an hour just to eat one sandwich; sometimes, he'd eat at my pace on purpose just to help me feel better about it, even if it meant his food got cold. I seriously don't know how he could be patient like that when we were twelve."

He smiles a little, but his eyes are red; he blinks rapidly and sniffles. "So that's why I 'forget' to eat sometimes. It's just . . . at times like this, the thought of eating makes me so nauseous, and a thirty-minute lunch isn't nearly enough time for me to eat when I'm like that. And the brumation thing doesn't help at all.

I force myself sometimes, but, God, it's so hard. It's not that I don't want to eat, I just . . ."

Despite his best efforts, he starts to cry.

"I just can't sometimes. I haven't eaten all day, and now Emily knows and Matthew's depressed and"—he covers his face, his hands shaking so badly his claws clack together—"God, I don't know what the fuck I'm supposed to do! How am I supposed to fix anything if I can't even keep myself together?!" He slumps into his hands, doing everything he can to stifle his sobs.

I move my hand to his quivering back and rub up and down. "It's not just you and Matthew anymore. You've got me, and, hell, Teddy would be here right now if you asked him to come over."

A sob breaks free, teardrops falling onto his thin thighs; his tail grips me harder, but it's not painful.

"So don't be afraid to ask me for help. We can talk to Emily together if she'll let us. I'll even skip class if you want me to; I don't give a shit if I miss a lesson or two."

He sniffles loudly. "Thank you."

I sit with him while he cries it all out, those tears he didn't want to shed, and eventually he leans back and lets me hold him against my chest, just like I did every time it was the new moon and he was feeling a little cold and a little tired. The worst of it only lasts a few long moments, and his sobs die down into stray tears that he wipes away with his scaly fingers.

He relaxes and pulls away.

I sling my arm across his shoulders again.

"I'm sorry. I hate crying like that over something so stupid."

"C'mon, it's not stupid. You and Emily are really close, too."

He pouts, gaze on his wringing hands. "*Were* really close . . ."

I stop myself from smacking him upside the head. "How would you feel about me getting you something to eat? It's hard to think straight when you're hungry."

"I won't be able to eat it very fast."

"I'll wait. What do you want?"

He stares at the space between his knees. "A ham and cheese sandwich. With mayo."

"What cheese do you want?"

"Cheddar is fine. Put the mayo on the meat side."

"Got it." I coax his tail off my leg and go into the kitchen. I make a serviceable ham and cheddar cheese sandwich with plenty of mayo and bring it back to him on a small plate.

When I hand it off to Mark, Glenn decides it's the perfect time to jump into his lap.

"Ah, Glenn! You're so bad." Mark holds his plate away from the cat so he can't put his paw on the sandwich.

I sit back down and take the plate so he can deal with his cat.

Mark puts Glenn on the floor, but he jumps right back up and decides to curl into a ball on his lap.

"How old is he?" I ask, handing the plate back.

"I found him when I was thirteen, so he's about three now."

"You found him?"

Mark nods. "Yeah. It was about a year after my dad died. Matthew and I found him on the side of the road while we were walking home from school." He smiles and strokes Glenn's head. "We heard something mewling, and what do you know, a fuzzy black kitten was in the bushes all alone. He was a tiny little thing. Real scrawny and shaking. We couldn't just leave him there, so I scooped him up and brought him home. Would you believe I could fit him in the palm of my hand?"

It's hard to believe the lanky cat in his lap used to be so tiny.

"Mom was all hesitant at first, but I begged her to let us keep him, so she took him to the vet and bought him kitten formula and stuff. Looking back, that's about when she started eating again. Glenn needed a lot of help because he was so young, so I guess looking after something like that helped her look after herself more. I know she's still underweight, but I was glad she wasn't losing more than she already had.

"Glenn helped me a lot, too. I've always loved cats, so it was the cutest thing ever the first time Glenn wanted to crawl in bed with me! He still sleeps with me pretty frequently, but I'd say he's more Mom's cat than mine. He likes Matthew a lot, too, probably because he was over just about every day back then. But!" Mark taps Glenn's nose.

He lifts his head and meows in protest.

"He can be a naughty little boy, trying to eat my food all the time." As if to make a point, Mark picks his sandwich up and bites a decent chunk out of the corner; he chews for an abnormally long time, but eventually swallows.

Glenn meows and paws at his plate again.

Mark lifts the plate away and puts one finger on the cat's forehead. "No, Glenn. You have cat food. People food isn't good for you."

Glenn rubs his whiskers against Mark's finger.

"You're silly." Mark smiles so lovingly I barely recognize him.

"Why did you name him Glenn?" I ask.

"I didn't name him; Mom did. I would've named him Shadow or something if she left it up to me."

How cliché . . . But I can't say I would've come up with much better.

Mark rubs Glenn's chin; he stretches his neck and purrs. "Glenn means valley. I'm not sure why Mom picked that name, but I think it suits him."

It's the only name I know him by, so I think so, too.

True to his word, it takes nearly half an hour for Mark to eat his entire sandwich. He didn't speak all that much, but he did show me a cool trick; apparently, Glenn will play fetch. So while Mark ate, I threw a feather toy across the room, and Glenn would chase after it, bat it around, and bring it back to me in his mouth, promptly dropping it near the far corner of the coffee table so I'd have to stretch down to pick it back up again. Glenn played fetch the entire time, and when Mark finished his food, Glenn decided that my thigh would be a great place to rest his forelegs.

I rub Glenn's head with my thumb, eliciting a few purrs from the playful pet.

Mark places his empty plate on the coffee table. "Thanks for putting that together for me." He wipes errant crumbs away from the corners of his mouth with his thumb. "Sorry it took me so long. I always feel kinda dumb that I can't do something so simple."

I put my arm across his shoulders again, catching his attention enough that he actually looks at me instead of the floor. "Don't beat yourself up. Disordered eating isn't an easy habit to kick."

His brow furrows. "You talk like you know from personal experience."

I furrow my brow, too. "You could say I know a few people who have their own problems. I have a lot of sisters and a strict family that cares too much about appearances, so I've seen what that does to people's heads." Most of my sisters are able to ignore my mom's comments, but Olive had a hard time before she went to college; she and Ruth shielded all of us from the brunt of it, but I get my own special brand of bullshit for being the only son. "But besides them, you're not the only guy around who's irrationally afraid of getting fat. Do you remember how Teddy mentioned that he almost lost his shit last summer?"

"Teddy?" Mark looks at me like I'm crazy. "Mister beefcake is afraid of getting fat?"

"Yep." I nod, staring at the ceiling. "But it's a little different for him because he's actually been there before. He was still on the chubby side when I met him, but he was pretty big back in elementary school. Got ruthlessly bullied for it, too. So yeah, he really wasn't taking it well when he got hit by hyperphagia in July. I had to help him with that—along with the mess that was hiding the whole bear thing from his dad—all summer."

Mark contemplates for a moment.

I pat his shoulder. "I guess what I'm saying is that it can happen to anyone if the circumstances are right—or maybe wrong is the better word here. And even though I've never had that kind of trouble personally, I can see how easy it is to think that way."

Mark smiles sadly. "I hate that that makes me feel better, knowing we're all a little fucked up somewhere."

"Everybody has problems; it's what you do about them that matters. You can do something or you can stew in it, and sometimes, it's okay if you need a little help along the way."

Mark huffs. "Thanks for being that help for me; I know I needed it, whether I like it or not." He stares at the bathroom door I can't see. "I think Matthew could use some of that right now, too."

I move my hand to his back and give him the push he needs to get up off his ass. "Go give him that help, then. I'll be here with the cat."

Mark smiles lopsidedly, waving me off as he walks toward the hall, his legs and hands no longer trembling. "I'll let you have that excuse this time." And he disappears down the hall.

CHAPTER 15

Misery Loves Company

Matthew

My head throbs as I wallow in shallow, lukewarm bathwater. I don't know how long I've been sitting here, but I cried and ate Emily's granola bar and cried some more. I feel silly and pitiful and I hate myself, but I'm so tired I can barely think.

I didn't fill the tub all the way because it's a very real possibility that I might pass out, and I'd rather not accidentally drown to death right after the girl I'm into found out I'm the cat boy she always thought I was; she'd feel like it was her fault, even though it would've just been my dumbass depressed self being a dumbass. What a way to go, right? I laugh a little thinking about it and keep crying because I'm a sorry excuse for a monster. I must be running out of tears at this point, but my eyes keep leaking like a poorly fitted faucet. I'm so upset I barely care about my heavy, waterlogged fur or the cold on my skin from the chilly air.

I zone out, all tired and groggy and sick, until a sharp knock on the door pulls me out of my head.

"Matthew, you forgot a towel," Mark says.

I wait for him to open the door because it has one of those old, shitty locks you can stick your thumb against and turn to unlock it, but he doesn't do anything.

Mark sighs. "Could you unlock the door for me?"

I groan, using the edge of the tub to pull myself onto my shaky paws, and worry I might trip because I never let myself get accustomed to walking digitigrade, and my paw pads are slick, and with my fucked-up head, I don't trust myself to achieve much of anything right now; breathing too heavy for such little effort, I step safely out of the tub and drip water all over everything. Panting, I unlock the door, step back into the bathtub, and pull my knees up to my chest after I resubmerge my ass in the water.

Mark opens the door holding a gray towel in his scaly arms, his eyes red and puffy; he gently closes the door and sits down on top of the toilet lid. "Did you have a fever?" His tail rests on the edge of the tub, squiggling like a long strand of wavy hair.

I nod, exacerbating my headache. "It said 101 degrees. I took some Tylenol. I think it's from the shot yesterday."

"Makes sense." His tail coils up more; I want to pet it to help soothe him, but that would probably shock him instead.

"I'm sorry I was mean to you earlier." I steal a glance, feeling like my ten-year-old self, all confused and barely knowing anything anymore. Mark was all smiles and bravado back then, proud of the eye scar he'd surely develop out of the lacerations I gave him, which could only be cool when you're young and stupid and mostly normal.

Mark smiles lightly, his eyebrows furrowed. "You don't have to be sorry for that. But I forgive you."

"Thanks." I sniffle. "How are you holding up?"

"I'm holding," he says. "Seen better days, you know?"

Yeah, I think, but I can't bring myself to say it. "My head hurts."

Mark grins, his serrated teeth all shiny and white. "Want me to do something about it?"

Blushing, I lean my head toward him.

Mark plants his right hand between my ears and rubs back and forth, petting my head like I'm an overgrown cat.

I purr, partly because I've conditioned myself to whenever Mark touches me, but mostly because he's insanely good at handling my ears and it feels really nice. I would never, ever let most people put even the tip of their pinky finger on my ears, but Mark's an exception to that—he's an exception to a lot of things. We've known each other so long now that it was bound to happen eventually.

I first let him pet my ears some years ago, back when I still barely knew him. It was the first week of sixth grade, right after the summer he truly awakened. Mark didn't take his eyes and hair permanently changing color, nor his teeth becoming sharp and his tongue forever forked, all that well, and neither did most of the people around him. Mr. Koenigsegg and Miss Ashley argued about what the hell they were going to do come school starting, people at church would stare at him and whisper things we could both hear—I figured it was the kind of gossip meant to be heard, the self-righteous pricks—and the teachers immediately got on his case about it. But all that wasn't all that bad in the grand scheme of things; the real problem was the other kids at school.

Mark already had a reputation after his doctor had to shave his head so his injury could heal, so when he showed up for the first day of middle school with short, cherry-red hair, bright-yellow eyes, and a fading pink scar across the left side of his face that everyone could see in its totality, all the kids were abuzz about him; it didn't help that when he smiled and spoke, everyone could see that his teeth weren't right and his tongue was split in two. One guy thought it'd be real funny to poke and prod at Mark like he was some kind of circus attraction, right in the middle of the hall where I could see him. I was so angry, and I knew I was going to beat his ass if he touched Mark again and told him as much. Mark pleaded with his eyes not to fight this kid, because he was older and taller and all around bigger, and I was none of those things, but I made up for it in sheer spite. The guy touched him again, scoffing like I wouldn't do anything, and I lunged at him. I turned him into my personal scratching post and didn't feel bad about it until it was over and done.

By the time two teachers broke us up, that guy was blue and bloody from how much I'd bitten, scratched, and punched him. That was the first time I ever felt like a wild animal, like I was truly a monstrous person, but I was defending my best friend, so it was justified in my mind.

And I didn't get out unscathed; for every blow I gave him, he returned it twice over. Bruised and sore as I was, I wanted nothing more than comfort and a long nap. Mom had to come to school because I got in trouble for starting a fight, and Miss Ashley came because Mark called her about what happened. Mom let me ride home with them and I immediately collapsed on their couch. Mark felt bad about the whole thing, and I didn't feel good either, so when he asked if he could rub my head, I let him; I knew he always wanted to, because he's weird like that, and I was feeling off enough I didn't care. So he pet my head, and I was so out of it and it felt so good I wondered why I never let him pet me before.

I'm not afraid to admit that Mark has a gentle touch. Yeah, he's a real nerd for monster people and a shameless teratophile, but he treats my ears like they're a sacred relic, handling them with the utmost care, almost with an incomprehensible reverence. And he'd usually do it with human hands, but even with his claws and scales, it feels soothing like nothing else; he may not be able to scratch behind my ears right now, but I don't mind the bumps and ridges of the scales on his palms and fingers.

I remember my stupid wish—that one day, a cute girl would pet me like Mark does—and weep. "I loved her. I still love her." I sob and cover my face with my hands, hating how gross my drenched fur smells and wanting so badly to disappear.

Mark cradles my head, running his thumb over my right ear so slowly and gently and perfectly. He doesn't say anything, but I know he's hurting too because his eyes water and his fingers tremble and his lips wobble with poorly veiled sobs. And I know, just as his gentle petting soothes me, it soothes him, too. So we weep together in his tiny bathroom, weep over the loss of our first human friend, and I know, deep down, it's more a loss for her than it is for us.

CHAPTER 16

Bumps in the Road

Mark

Matthew stumbles into my room sopping wet, the towel I gave him haphazardly wrapped around his hips. He crashes to his knees in front of the couch, flushed and trembling and sniffling.

"Matthew, why didn't you—"

"I don't feel good." He heaves a breath. "I need to lie down."

"Bro, just . . ." I run my hand through my hair. "Let me dry you off first."

Matthew pants, his ears unmoving.

To spare his decency, I grab a second towel out of my dresser and bring it to him. "Did you hear me?"

He nods, albeit weakly.

"Do you want me to do it for you, or do you want me to leave you alone?"

Matthew gasps for air, claws scratching at the leather. "Please, I . . . I can't . . ."

"Hey, hey, hey." I try to stay calm. "I've got you. Don't worry about it."

"Thank you . . ." Tears cut through his wet cheeks.

I plop down behind Matthew and put the towel on his head; gently, I rub his hair and ears dry, then wipe off his face, careful not to stab him with my claws in the process. I get his neck and his shoulders and his back, then pull him against my chest so I can dry him from his collar to his lower belly; his arms get my clothes wet along the way.

I coax him back against the couch cushion and take his right arm; it's a pain in the ass to rub the water out of his damp fur, but I work inch by inch down both arms, one after the other, taking extra care to run the towel over the webbing between each finger.

"Stick your leg out."

Matthew straightens out his right leg.

I do to his thigh and calf what I did to his arms, painstakingly drying every square inch of fur; once I reach his paw, I carefully wipe down his sensitive pads and rub the towel between each toe.

Matthew tucks his dry leg and straightens out the other without me having to ask; I dry it exactly as I did the other.

With the easy part out of the way, I set my sights on his tail. "Do you want me to finish?"

Considerably calmer, Matthew nods.

Despite anticipating it, he jolts when I wrap the towel around the base of his tail. "You good?"

His claws unsheathe. "Yeah."

I gently rub down the length of his tail, vertebra by vertebra, until he's as dry as he's going to get; he jerks less and less the farther I get from the base and settles entirely once I reach the tip. My work done, I wipe down the couch and take the wet towel to the laundry room; by the time I return, Matthew hasn't moved an inch.

"Do you need anything else?" I ask.

"Underwear," he says.

I hand him a pair of gray boxers he keeps in my dresser for nights like these.

He removes his towel, bends over the couch cushion, and uses a marathon of energy to pull them up his legs; he slumps as soon as he's covered.

Someone knocks on the door. "May I come in?" Mom asks.

Matthew's ears fold back and he shakes his head.

"I'll come out." After giving Mom a few moments to step back, I leave the room and close the door behind me. "What's up?"

"I'm going to get started on dinner soon. Jack said he'll help so you can rest." Mom smiles, but she can't take her eyes off the door. "How is he?"

I walk past her to the dining room and stand near the entryway to the kitchen.

Mom follows, her gaze lingering on Jack's active form.

Jack, still sitting on the couch, plays on his phone with one ear pointed toward us.

"He's not doing great right now," I say. "I'm not sure what'll help."

Mom looks down the hall. "Some food and rest should go a long way. I called out of work tomorrow, too, so you won't have to worry about him while you're at school."

"You didn't have to do that."

She smiles. "I hold on to paid time off for these moments; I won't miss a dime."

I pout, but I'm glad she treats Matthew so well.

"You should shower while we cook; dinner should be done by the time you finish."

I nod and glance at the couch.

Jack glances back; he makes a shooing motion with one hand, face completely blank.

I roll my eyes but obey his command. I strip in the bathroom, attempt to go dormant, fail because of course I'm not calm enough, and make my walk of shame into the bathtub; I immediately manage to knock the shampoo off the tub edge with my tail. I sigh, put it back, and start the shower.

It's been so long since I washed myself active that I forgot how nice water feels rolling down my scales. They're just as sensitive as my skin, even more so at the base of my tail. I technically have two tail bases because mine is shaped like the body of a snake; the spot between the anal scale and subcaudal scales feels exactly like the area where my tail meets my lower back. Those scales, including all the ventral scales lining the underside, are the only ones that are beige instead of red.

I stand under the stream for a long time, my mind emptying and body unwinding. I wash myself slowly, taking special care of my tail—and manage to knock the shampoo over again. But I don't worry about it. I can always pick the bottle back up. Plastic doesn't break like glass.

I finish my shower and dry off in my room, the water effortlessly sliding off my scales. I get dressed and check on Matthew; he lies completely passed out on the couch, wrapped tight in his blue blanket.

Jack opens the door. "Dinner's ready." He glances at Matthew. "Should we wake him up?"

I shake my head. "Let him sleep."

Jack nods and backs out of the room.

We eat in silence, Matthew's absence apparent by his empty seat. Mom doesn't comment; she knows he does things on his own time, especially when he's feeling sick.

While I help her clean up, Jack goes dormant and takes a quick shower, then we head to bed. I didn't do much of anything today, but I feel exhausted. I crawl under my comforter in nothing but my underwear, while Jack takes the sleeping bag on the floor.

Matthew remains conked out on the couch.

I face the wall, curling up under my many blankets to stave off the cold. I close my eyes and try to get comfortable on my side, keeping my tail tucked near my legs and my claws from catching on my sheets. I zone in and out of consciousness for at least an hour but struggle to find any real sleep; even so, I stay down and keep my eyes closed, hoping it'll come soon enough and I can get at least a few hours out of this stressful night.

Another hour of sleeplessness passes, and the covers shift behind me. A cold, sticky back presses against mine, and with a great sigh, the covers fall back down; Matthew's tail curls over mine, the tip of it touching my ankle.

"Matthew . . . ?" I mutter, barely lucid.

He begins to purr. "Sorry, Mark," he whispers, "I don't want to be alone right now."

"It's okay. I was kinda cold, anyway."

Matthew continues to purr, shifting and stretching until he finds a comfortable-enough position, his back remaining against mine. His thunderous rumble fades in and out as he nods off again.

My consciousness slipping away, I think about all the nights Matthew used to sleep with me while I was deep in grief, and the first time he ever purred for me, and I know this whole situation is eating him up inside because acting like a cat is the last thing he ever wants to do, and yet . . .

I still remember that day, and the day before it—the day Dad dropped dead on the kitchen floor—like it was just this morning. Matthew wasn't at my house when it happened, and I never called him to let him know because he was busy at some work event with his parents and I hated to bother him, even if I needed his company more than anything else that night. I was alone because Mom rode to the hospital in the ambulance carrying Dad, and I cried myself to sleep, woke up, barely calmed down enough to go dormant, and walked to school. It was Monday, May 28, 2012, the day after Dad was declared dead on the operating table.

Halfway through the day, the lady on the intercom called me to the front office, and when I went there, staggering like a zombie and just as pale and sick, I took Mom's call; she said her piece, and I put the phone down, and I went back to class, and it took everything I had to make it to the end of the day. Matthew kept asking me what was wrong in the few classes we had together, but I couldn't answer him or else my flimsy composure would melt down into nothing.

When class ended, I walked out to the car pool lane with Matthew, but instead of going home, I sat on the wooden bench outside, and although he didn't understand why I was sitting there, he sat beside me and did his homework. I waited in that near-summer heat until everyone was gone and no more cars were coming to get anyone, and I told him what had happened. And Matthew studied my face, put his stuff away, scooted closer until we were hip-to-hip, and held me in his arms. He whispered, "I'm sorry," and wept over my shoulder. And I remember looking up at the clouds, at the two streaks left behind by a plane, and when I heard Matthew purr, I finally broke; I clutched his shirt with my sharp claws and shook and cried and sobbed until there was nothing left.

The bed dips, and I groggily open my eyes. Something furry and fleshy forces its way between me and Matthew, who must've scooched away when he got too hot from our combined body heat; when the invader gets down to my tail, I turn onto my other side and see Jack's chiseled face.

"Jack . . . ?" I mumble, wondering why the hell he got in my bed.

"Lift your heads."

I do because I'm too tired to protest.

He slips his arm under my head. "You too, Matthew."

Matthew grunts.

Jack wiggles to properly nestle himself between us.

"Bro, why are you in my bed?" I ask.

He grins. "What? I can't be part of the fun?"

"This bed can barely handle two of us." It's so cramped my tail falls into the crack between the bed and the wall. "You better not break my bed frame."

"C'mon, I'm not that heavy."

"You're not, but all three of us together are!" My old twin frame isn't built for 450 pounds of monster-boy ass, and I know we all weigh a little more in our active forms on account of the extra features—my tail alone adds about fifteen pounds to my total weight.

Jack hums. "If it breaks, I'll owe you one."

I sigh, burying my forehead in the crook of his fuzzy arm. "Fine, you can stay."

"I wasn't gonna leave anyway." He rests his head on the pillow he brought with him, his hair fanning out in glossy waves; he smiles like he's exactly where he belongs.

I sling my left arm over his stomach, rest my right hand over his bicep, and close my eyes again. Jack's stomach rises and falls in a gentle rhythm, encouraging me to reach the land of dreams, and I drift—

"Hey," Matthew says.

"Mm. What's up?" Jack mumbles.

"Do you think we'd still be friends if we were human?"

In the dredges of half consciousness, I imagine what human Mark would look like. He'd still have my face, but his hair would be black—and have that awful mushroom cut—and his eyes would be dark brown; he wouldn't have a scar people sometimes point and stare at, nor pointy teeth and a split tongue, and, tired as I am, it occurs to me that he may as well be a stranger.

"I doubt it," Jack says. "I don't think I'd be friends with Teddy, either."

"Why do you say that?" Matthew asks.

"We only became friends because he got tired of people making fun of me for looking girly. But the only reason I let those idiots make fun of me in the first place is because I go active too easily when I'm mad. If I was human, I would've defended myself no problem."

"Huh." He goes quiet for a long moment. "I think you're right, and even though Emily might hate us forever, I'm glad I got to meet you guys, even if I had to be a monster for it to happen, because I can't imagine my life without either of you. Especially you, Mark. I don't want to imagine that."

My eyes well up with tears. "God, you're gonna make me cry."

"Sorry. I just couldn't stop thinking about it."

Jack plants his fluffy hand on my back. "This is sweet and all, but I think we should go to bed."

"Yeah . . ." Matthew murmurs, and I'm sure he passed out this time. And as Jack rubs my back and falls asleep, I, too, lose consciousness.

Glenn steps all over my face, meowing up a storm because the sun is up and I'm supposed to be up with it, but I'm groggy and my mouth is dry and it's so awfully hot in this bed. *Why is it so hot . . . ?*

I open my eyes halfway to be immediately greeted by Jack with his mouth hanging open, drool trailing out of the corner of his mouth.

Careful not to squeeze my claws into Jack's stomach, I put down enough pressure to lift myself and look at my alarm clock from over his bare chest; it reads 7:15 a.m. I forgot to set my alarm last night. And school starts in ten minutes.

My head crashes back down onto Jack's bicep. I'm about to get my first tardy slip, aren't I? Why do I even care? I groan, go dormant, and pat Jack's cheek. "C'mon, wake up, we're gonna be late."

He opens his eyes, and I get up so he can wipe his mouth with his hand; he carefully pulls his other arm out from under Matthew's head and sits up. He looks at the clock. "Well, shit."

Before either of us can get out of bed, someone knocks on the door. "Are you both awake?" Mom asks.

"Yeah," I say.

"I made breakfast and two lunches; you can eat in the car. You better hurry so you're not too late."

I slump forward and thank God for Mom.

Jack and I rush to get dressed—I get to hold his very soft ears down so he can fix his hair—grab two containers of warm scrambled eggs, and hightail it to Mom's new Subaru. She drives way too fast and manages to drop us off about fifteen minutes after class started. I gracefully accept a pink slip for being tardy, and as class drones on, I don't miss the way some of the girls on the soccer team sneer at me.

My second class goes much the same: glares from the sporty girls, and one asks me what happened with Emily yesterday; I don't say anything conclusive, and I wager Emily didn't tell them anything concrete either. Rumors spread fast, but that's no surprise—Emily is generally well-liked by most people who know her, and it's no secret that she spends a lot of time with the three of us, and what makes a girl cry more than boys? Probably a lot of things, but this is high school drama at its finest.

At lunch time, I reconvene with Jack, who tells me he's experienced the same passive-aggressive looks, but nobody had the guts to confront him about anything. As we eat, dread slowly pools in my stomach at the thought of confronting Emily, but I know it's better we get it over with; I can only hope she's the friend we always thought she was.

When the bell rings, I say, "I hope you don't mind being late for another class today, because I think we should go find Emily."

Jack smirks. "I don't think my teacher will miss me." He gets up from his shitty cafeteria stool and throws his trash away; I follow close behind.

We enter the hallway and walk slowly toward Emily's third-period classroom, then wait at a distance for everyone to leave the area. As soon as it's empty, I peek into the classroom.

Emily lies face down at her desk, sobbing.

CHAPTER 17

The Eye of the Beholder

Emily

Someone knocks on the door at the front of the classroom. "Hey, Emily . . ."

I lift my head, tears streaming down my cheeks, and see Mark's sad face. I've never, ever seen him get anywhere close to crying, but his eyes are puffy behind his purple frames.

Mark smiles weakly. "We . . . wanted to talk, if you're up for it."

Jack pops his head through the door, looking no worse for wear other than a guilty tilt to his lips and brows.

I burst into tears and wipe at my surely red face. "I-I'm so sorry! I-I was . . . I was so scared, and . . . and I . . . M-Matthew didn't come to school and . . . and . . . and I was so mean to you guys, but . . ." I crash onto the desk, sobbing and shaking and sucking in short breaths. "P-Please don't hate me!"

"Hey, it's okay." Mark's hand lands on my back. "We don't hate you. We would never hate you." He rubs my quivering back as I continue to cry. "Would you like to step outside for a bit? That way we can talk about it, okay?"

"O-Okay . . ."

Mark guides me out of my seat, keeping his hand on my back as we walk out of the classroom; Jack joins us at my other side, my book bag in hand.

I try to stop sniffling and gasping from all my tears, but I feel so terrible about yesterday I can't. We walk outside, right through those doors Matthew stumbled through yesterday, but this time, we take a left. Toward the end of the sidewalk, there's a stone bench; I sit down in the middle, the school at my back; Mark sits on my left and Jack sits on my right.

Mark takes his hand off my back, but the bench is so small both of them are right against my hips, so their presence isn't lost on me. Mark leans forward, his arm brushing against my shoulder. "How are your shoulders?"

"Th-They're fine." I wring my hands in my lap. "I-It didn't take long for the, um, s-scratches to scab over." I wipe my eyes, my waterfall of tears reduced to thin streams. "I-Is Matthew okay?"

Mark smiles. "He's just a little sick is all. You don't need to worry."

"Of course I'm worried! He looked so awful yesterday, and I didn't listen to him at all, and he . . . he must feel so bad because . . ." I can't see it at this angle, but I can envision exactly how Mark's scar looks. "He did that to you, didn't he? That scar?"

Mark stares at his clasped hands, hands made up of blunt nails and beige skin. "Yeah. We were both young, though, and I pretty much cornered him, so it was self-defense on his part."

Assuming the worst, I grimace.

Mark grins awkwardly. "Of course I was trying to help him at the time but went about it the wrong way."

"What were you trying to help him with?"

"His first transformation." His hands suddenly grow sharp black claws and smooth red scales.

I gasp.

"We don't start out being able to change like this." His hands turn back to normal. "I was effectively human the first five years of my life—Matthew the first ten of his life."

"I was human the first twelve," Jack says. "It was just as sudden and shocking for us as it was for you to find out."

My brain is too foggy for me to truly process the implications of their words, but I'm sure they'll explain in greater detail later. "Mark, could you show me your hands again?"

"Sure." They turn all sharp and scaly and red again.

"Can I . . . feel them?"

He holds his right hand out to me, showing me the rugged scales of his palm.

I carefully run my fingertips over the bumpy scales. "Are you a, um, lamia or something?"

Mark snickers. "Hell no. I'm probably some kind of dragon."

"Probably?"

"Hell if I know."

How does he not know?! I sigh, my tears finally drying up. I stop feeling Mark's scales and look at Jack. "What about you, Jack? I could never tell with you."

Jack brings a hand to his chin and ponders the woods. "How about this." He gets up, straddles the bench—it doesn't have a back—and hunches down. "I want you to touch my ears." He closes his eyes, leaving his head at my mercy.

I'm not sure how touching his ears will answer my question, but I slowly slip my fingers under his hair; they glide over his skin until I reach . . . more smooth skin. My eyes bug out as I reach up and down and around where his ears should be, but there's nothing there. "Where are they?!"

Smirking, he opens his eyes. "Can I guide you? I'll be gentle."

He makes me feel all nervous with that haughty expression, but I nod gingerly.

He takes my hands with his bigger ones and slowly pulls them toward the back of his head.

My fingers graze something cool, soft, and furry.

He lets go of my hands. "There you go. Whatever you do, please don't pull."

Don't pull . . . I lightly grip the ends of his ears, feeling incredibly soft fur on the back and something fleshier under my thumbs. I run my fingers along the roundish shape of the bottom, which lie low enough to graze the nape of his neck. *Long, round ears* . . . "Are you one of those floppy-eared bunnies?"

"My ears aren't lopped, I just keep them down to hide them. Jenny thinks I'm a black Havana rabbit."

I don't know anything about bunnies, but that's probably the last animal I would've guessed for Jack; he's more wolflike in my opinion. I explore his ears more, running my fingers from a spot higher up down to the ends a few times. "They're very soft." As I continue to rub his ears, I notice hard, thin, metallic bumps along the edges—hairpins to keep them held down. I pet them a little longer, almost mesmerized by the sensation of his fur, until I hear a strange sound; it's like a muffled motor, and I notice Jack's jaw moving back and forth. Confused by his bizarre reaction, I pull my hands out of his hair. "Um, Jack? Why are you grinding your teeth?"

Jack straightens up, a bright blush on his face; he turns away, coughing awkwardly into his fist. "D-Don't worry about it."

Mark slaps my arm with the back of his hand, wearing a huge grin. "Somebody was enjoying himself."

Grimacing, Jack crosses his arms. "Shut up, Mark."

I'm very confused. "What am I missing here?"

Mark whispers loudly in my ear, "He was purring."

"Oh my God . . ." Jack runs a hand down his face. "Please don't take it the wrong way . . ."

I giggle; even though Jack has become a lot more comfortable with us, he can still be all shy sometimes. "Don't worry, Jack. I guess I got a little carried away there."

He smiles and sits properly next to me. "It felt so nice I didn't think to stop you; I don't usually let anyone touch my ears like that."

"I don't blame you. It *is* a little strange." I stare at my shoes and the dry grass on the hill below them. "Gosh, this is all so strange . . . Here I thought all of this was some sort of fantasy in my head, but . . ." There's a reason Mom has always told me to trust my gut.

Silence hangs in the air, broken only by the wind.

"Now I feel bad because I'm really into monster boys, so it doesn't even bother me all that much. I mean, God, I just touched your hand and pet your ears without thinking twice." I hold my hot face and part my fingers so I can still see my shoes. "I don't want Matthew to think I see him differently because of this."

Mark bends forward far enough for me to see his face; he looks at me sweetly and winks. "Matthew's really only worried you hate him now, so don't think too hard about it."

I frown. "I don't hate him. I could never hate him."

"Make sure you tell him that when you get the chance."

Just the thought of talking to Matthew after everything makes me nervous; he knows very well how I feel about cat boys—even if the real thing is more than just the ears and tail—and the last thing I want is for him to think I see him as nothing more than a sexual object. He's my friend first and foremost, and I better make sure he doesn't forget that. "Of course." I nod, but slump forward. "I just hope he'll forgive me for freaking out on him yesterday. I kinda accused him of being sexist . . ."

"Huh?! Where the hell did that come from?!"

I pout and cross my arms. "Well, he refused to tell me why he got sick once a month, but I knew he told both of you, and I was mad about it because I've known him longer than Jack. So I thought he didn't trust me because I'm a girl."

"I feel like out of all of us he'd be the last one to be sexist."

"What's that supposed to mean?" Jack asks.

"I don't know, bro; you're kinda harsh to your sisters."

"That's because they constantly try to get on my nerves!"

Mark shrugs, holding his palms in the air. "Whatever you say~"

"You're making me want to be sexist toward you."

"That would make you Marxist."

"Oh my God . . . ," I say, "you're both so stupid . . ."

Mark puffs out his chest. "Stupid and proud, Emily. Stupid and proud."

Before I can retort, the bell rings, reminding me that I totally skipped lunch. Then I realize they skipped class just for me.

"Think you're good to go back to class? I'm down if you need to talk a little more about everything."

"Same here," Jack says.

I shake my head, a tiny smile on my face. Yeah, these guys of mine are super stupid, but they're also kind; I couldn't ask for better friends. "I think I'll be alright. But we're all going to have a long conversation later. Like, after spring break because I'll be visiting my grandparents."

Mark grins. "Fine by me."

Fresh out of the shower and lying on my bed, I stare up at the phone in my hand, reading a text I received not too long ago. *Can I call you?* It's from Matthew. He's never once called me before.

I linger over the keyboard, thinking about how I should reply, *if* I should reply; ultimately, I exit the messaging app and go to the phone app, press the favorites tab, and call the contact labeled Tabby.

He picks up immediately. "E-Emily . . . I didn't expect you to call."

"I thought I may as well. How are you doing?"

"I've been better. I just . . . wanted to say sorry about yesterday. I'm sorry you had to see me like that, and for hurting you. Mark told me you're healing alright, but . . ."

"It's okay. It's just a little sore is all." *Nothing worse than a cat scratch*, I almost say; I don't tell him about the yellow-brown bruises from his harsh grip, either. "And I forgive you. I'm also sorry for getting in your face about what was going on; it really wasn't my business to know anything."

"No, it's . . . probably for the best that you know. It was . . . really hard to hide it from you. I hated lying to you, but I was worried you would hate us, or something like that."

I want to say that I wish they'd trusted me more, that they should've known I'd never do anything bad to them over being what they are, but I can imagine how scary it must be to be something so mysterious, and that there are a lot of people that would have bad intentions toward boys like them. "I'd never hate any of you over this. You guys are my best friends, and what you are doesn't change that. So . . . I hope you'll still have me if that's okay."

Matthew sighs heavily. "Of course. I should . . . see you after spring break, I guess."

"Yeah. I'm glad you're feeling better."

"Yeah," he says. "Good night."

"Good night."

He hangs up.

I drop my phone at my side, smiling stupidly. Matthew will probably be nervous for a while, but now that I finally know what's up with him, we can get even closer! And maybe he'll finally . . .

I cover my face, suppressing a stupid lovesick squeal, and start texting Heather about everything, carefully leaving out the monster-boy part.

Matthew doesn't text me much while I'm out of state, but I figure he's still feeling shy.

The Monday after spring break, I anxiously wait outside of our first-period classroom. I try to look nonchalant, leaning against the lockers near the door with my arms crossed, but some classmates and other students give me funny looks as they go about their business.

After a while, Matthew walks down the hall; he notices me and looks away shyly, but still stops next to me. "Hey. Why are you standing out here?" His cheeks are pink, his hands stuffed in his pockets.

I'm so relieved to see him and hear him that I charge forward and wrap my arms around him; he stiffens but lets me rest my chin on his shoulder. "I'm so glad you're okay." I feel his tail move away from my arms, and the quick pitter-patter of his heartbeat against my chest, and his soft stomach from under his clothes.

Matthew rests the side of his head against mine. "I told you I would be." His heart beats faster. "I would hug you back, but . . . I can't show my hands right now."

"Oh!" I step back. "I hope that's not my fault." I smile, hoping he'll take it as a playful statement, but . . .

Matthew looks away, a downplayed grimace on his face; his eyes look a little watery. "I'm just . . . a little nervous . . . is all . . ."

I frown, but the bell stops me from prodding. He walks around me to go into class, and I follow him, but decide to go straight to my desk to give him some space; I shouldn't push his buttons too much right now.

Throughout class, I catch myself staring at Matthew over and over again. I can't stop thinking about him being a cat boy. How does his tail connect to his body? Are his ears soft? Does he really have cat paws when he changes? If he can growl and purr, can he also hiss? Does it hurt to keep his tail around his body and his ears down all day?

Near the end of first period, Matthew glances back my way.

I immediately snap my head to the left, pretending I totally wasn't dissecting him with my eyes; now that I've been caught, I feel pretty awful for looking at him like that. I slowly turn my head forward again and glance at him.

Matthew put his hands back in his pockets, his head down.

Second period passes by in a flash, and so does the first half of third period. It's quiet after everyone leaves; Matthew doesn't look at me and doesn't speak. He was silent throughout class, too, looking sick to his stomach the entire time.

When he doesn't make a move to pull out his lunch, I ask, "Are you okay?"

"No, I'm not okay," he whispers.

A pit forms in my stomach. "What's wrong?"

He grimaces and screws his eyes shut. "I can't calm down, Emily. I can't. You know . . . you know I'm a fucking freak, and I . . . I hate it so much. I don't know how you can stand being around me, when I hurt you, a-and growled at you like a damn animal."

Matthew starts to cry, resolutely leaving his hands in his pockets; his arms tremble, tiny tears dropping onto his desk.

"It's not cute in real life, Emily. I-I'm disgusting and dangerous, and here you are, s-sitting next to me like there's nothing wrong." He shakes his head over and over. "I can't do this . . . I can't pretend that nothing happened, knowing that I could hurt you again."

He weeps, small sobs racking his body, and I don't know what to do.

"That's all I ever do. That's all my hands are good for: hurting the people I care about. Y-You'd be better off without me around . . . without a shitty friend like me."

I don't know how to tell him that I'm not scared because he's one of the sweetest guys I know, that I'd never find him disgusting because I still think he's cute, and how I wish I could wipe all those tears off his handsome face because I can't stand to see him cry over me, over this, over something he's making up in his head. So I reach for the hand in his pocket, grazing the fur on his wrist with my fingertips.

Matthew yelps, launching himself out of his chair. "Don't touch me!" His chest heaves, and his legs tremble, and he looks at me like I'm the most terrifying thing in the world; he stares at the hand I'm cradling, his pupils blown out. "I hurt you again. I-I . . ." He backs away, stumbling hard into another desk, and gasps in pain. His face contorts, and he pulls his brown-furred hand out of his pocket to hold his back, over his hidden tail. "I need to go . . . I can't . . ." He stalks away, using his other furry hand to support himself on each desk as he passes them, his breath coming out labored and short and quick, and when he gets close to the door, he covers his mouth. He stands there for a moment, shaking horribly. Then he leans over and retches into the trash can; he heaves again for round two.

I'm glued to my seat, stunned by his visceral reaction to my touch.

After spitting out whatever vomit was left in his mouth, he straightens up, wipes his mouth with the side of his fist, and licks off whatever got on his fur without a second thought. He licks his hand over and over again, as if grooming himself, until he snaps out of it and shoves both of his hands back into his pockets. He stumbles out of the room, leaving his book bag behind.

And I sit there, watching him go.

⌒⌒

Matthew doesn't come to school on Tuesday, and that afternoon, in the short half hour between the end of fourth period and the beginning of soccer practice, Mark pulls me aside to talk. I had told him what had happened at lunch on Monday, how Matthew had freaked out and puked and probably walked home despite himself, and Mark looked at me with this defeated expression, a half-hearted apology leaving his thin lips.

Mark tells me about the moon and Matthew and the scar on his heart, the one he got when he scratched Mark, and that scratching me ripped that wound right back open. And when he bids me farewell and walks home, I stand there and wonder how to tend to a wound deeply ingrained in your psyche.

That night, as I lie in bed, everything hits me all at once. I cover my face and cry, letting hot tears trail down my cheeks and onto my comforter. But when Mom calls me down for dinner, I wipe my eyes and pretend the red on my face is because I'm tired, not because I've lost my best friend to something I can't hope to fix.

Matthew comes to school on Wednesday, but he doesn't speak to me unless I talk to him, and even then, it's only with short, one-word answers. He goes somewhere else for lunch, and when he comes back for the second half of third period, I don't bother trying to talk to him anymore. Even though he sits right next to me, it feels like he's miles and miles away, and it hurts way more than the scratches and tender bruises he gave me.

Mark doesn't talk to me much in fourth period either. He told me that, even though we're still friends, he has to focus on helping Matthew over me. And I understand where he's coming from, that those two have a history I can't possibly contend with, and I hate that Mark has to pick a side at all; even though he has to abandon me for a little while, I'll still call him my friend, too.

When I trudge to the locker rooms shortly after the final bell rings, I find Jack leaning casually against the wall next to the doors that lead outside; I pause a yard away. "What are you doing here?"

Jack looks down at me listlessly, like nothing could ever bother him. "Mark asked me for a favor; I hope you don't mind me being your buddy for soccer practice for the time being."

"You don't have to do that," I say, but appreciate it nonetheless. "Don't you have to catch the bus to get home?"

Jack grins. "Mark promised to drive me home as long as I don't mind walking to his house after practice is over. His loss on gas, but I guess he owes me one."

I smile sadly—Mark is looking out for me after all. Overcome with emotion, I charge forward, wrap my arms around Jack, grip the back of his jacket in tight fists, and bury my face in his chest. "Thank you."

Jack puts one hand on my shoulder and another on my head. "It's the least I can do." He strokes my hair, from the crown of my head down to the start of my ponytail, and it feels really nice—I guess petting feels good to humans, too. "Hopefully Matthew will get over this, but until then, I'll be here."

I nod against his jacket, a few tears slipping out despite myself, and he strokes my head until I decide I'm ready to get changed for practice.

Jack proves to be a strange and distracting presence during practice. Unlike Matthew and Mark, he chills out on the bleachers in front of the track and doesn't leave until he drops me off with Mom after it's over (and it was such a headache to explain to her that no, I'm not dating or interested in dating Jack, and yes, there is such a thing as girls having platonic male friends), or with Dad on those days I have a game, which last long enough for him to come by after work (he doesn't say much about Jack, only making a backhanded comment about his long, "girly" hair). Jack's a real gentleman, and he becomes familiar enough with the rest of the team that they all start calling him Jack, too.

On Wednesday, Jack does his homework, reads, then sleeps with the book over his face, but on Thursday and Friday, he does body-weight exercises on a mat he places on the ground next to the bleachers. He keeps his back to the playing field while he exercises—I choose to believe it's to help him focus—which isn't usually a problem, except when he does squats, or lunges, or any other exercise that emphasizes his glutes or hamstrings or quads; on more than one occasion, a few girls get distracted by his muscular display, causing more than a couple mishaps here and there. At the very least, no one ends up with a soccer ball to the head.

On the following Monday, I find Jack dressed to the nines in black high-waisted boot-cut trousers, a white dress shirt with loose sleeves and a ruffled chest, and a short black vest; to top it all off, elaborate makeup covers his eyes—the only normal thing, as far as Jack is concerned, are the cowboy boots on his feet. He looks as unflappable as always despite his fanciful appearance, paying no mind to the looks the team gives him as they enter the girls' locker room.

"What's with the new look?" I ask, awfully perplexed.

He smirks. "It's a surprise."

I raise an eyebrow but choose to move on with my life rather than agonize over Jack's seemingly random behavior. As the rest of the girls and I change for practice, a few of them whisper and heckle about Jack, who I expect has already walked out to the bleachers. When we finally walk out to the track, he's sitting normally, his legs spread wide as if he wants to take up as much space as possible; with his eyes closed and arms crossed, the dark makeup covering his eyelids is all the more striking. Practice goes on as it usually does, barring more distracted gazes, until a new figure walks down to the bleachers. From this distance, the most I can make out is his tall, bulky build, short blond hair, and the . . . large slab of wood he's carrying? When the big tall guy gets to the bleachers, he places the slab on the ground and waves. Jack stands up and they hug. They appear to talk for a time, then Jack changes his shoes. The big tall guy pulls a guitar out of the case that was on his back.

Through the wind and the sound of balls being kicked, I hear the big tall guy plucking the strings of his guitar; Jack sits on the lowest level of the same bleacher, tying two things that look like clams to his hands. Our practice stalls for a second, all of us curious about this newcomer, but our coach whistles to get us back on track—I think he's annoyed that Jack's been hanging around lately, but it's not like he has a good enough reason to tell him to leave, especially since he stays off the track and field entirely.

A few minutes later, the big tall guy starts to play a melody, and Jack steps onto the wooden slab, raising his arms high into the air while stretching his body upward; as he spins slowly on the tips of his toes, he plays the instruments tied to his hands. The loud, percussive clacking is impossible to ignore, but we carry on with practice anyway, treating the music as a backdrop to marvel at later. At some points, the big tall guy sings in Spanish, and at others, Jack stomps around on that wooden slab; their performance swells and wanes, at times imperceptible beyond the noise of soccer practice, and at others demanding to be heard—our coach gets very close to telling them off, but they stop shortly before he stomps over.

We have a home game against Workbourne High School, which Jack and his friend watch without any distracting fanfare; even without their music making, the match ends in a tie, each team scoring one goal—not particularly exciting, but soccer is like that sometimes. Sweaty and sore, I change out of my soccer gear in the locker room, then return to the track and field.

Quite the crowd of girls surround the bleacher Jack and his friend have been sitting on, chattering to the two boys. There are so many of them talking at once, the majority of them from the opposing team, but I manage to catch his friend's name.

Given enough time, the crowd clears out as everyone prepares to go home or watch the upcoming varsity game at the outdoor stadium, leaving me alone with two boys and the setting sun. I walk up to them, squinting against the harsh light.

"What's wrong, sweetheart?" Teddy has a bit of a Southern drawl—not as light as Heather's, but not so heavy it's obvious— and medium-brown eyes that remind me of her. His ears are pointed, just like Mark's.

"Dude, that's Emily," Jack says.

"Oh! It's nice to finally meet you, girl. I'm Teddy, but you'd know me best as Lucha." Jack suddenly invited Teddy to a party of ours way back in January—although I knew his name is Teddy, we often call each other by our gamertags whenever Matthew and Mark's one online-only friend is around. His gamertag is LuchaLiberty.

"I didn't expect you to be so buff," I say, recalling Grace's strange description from a few weeks ago.

Teddy says something about me looking different than how he imagined, too, but it suddenly dawns on me exactly what Grace meant when she called Teddy and Matthew fluffy, and it wasn't because of their weight. If Matthew is fluffy because he can grow cat fur, then Teddy must be some kind of mammal, too; those elfish ears are a dead giveaway. But there's still a small possibility he isn't a monster boy, so I shouldn't assume anything yet.

"Hey, Jack," I say.

"What?"

"Two things"—I step onto the bleacher and lean down to his ear—"Is Teddy like you guys, and does Grace know about it?" I back off so I can see his expression.

Jack raises his eyebrows, then leans over and whispers something in Teddy's ear.

Teddy makes a face like he's trying to hold back laughter. "Oh, sure, I don't care!"

Jack leans away, and I sit down one level below them.

Teddy says, "Jack already told me about what happened between y'all, and I figure once you know one it doesn't matter how many more you notice. So yeah, I'm in the same boat as those three."

"As for Grace," Jack says, "she and the rest of my sisters have seen all four of us, so, uh, sorry you have to suffer knowing what Grace was talking about now."

I smile. "Oh, it's okay. I kinda get it."

Teddy and Jack lean away, grimacing.

I immediately regret my words. "Don't look at me like that!"

"Sorry, girl." Teddy raises his hands placatingly. "I still can't get over that some of y'all are into this shit."

I huff, crossing my arms and turning my nose up. "You should be grateful."

"I never said I wasn't, but that doesn't make it any less weird."

Pouting, I glance at Jack. "I forgot; there was a third thing: My dad's not going to be here until seven. If you need to go, that's okay."

"Nah, I can wait. What about you, Teddy? Is Kyle or your dad picking you up?"

"Mm . . . I was honestly going to walk to Mark's house with you. I've never been over so I'm a little curious. I wanted to come see how they're doing."

"I hope Mark won't mind driving you back home; at least he drives a truck, so you can put the slab in the trunk. Let me text him real quick." Jack pulls his phone out of his book bag and quickly sends a text, then puts it back. "We'll be having dinner there; it's nice not having to fight for food, and Miss Ashley isn't half bad at cooking either. She's very nice."

"My dad said as much, but his taste in women is questionable at best. And my track record with moms has been awful so far; yours is a bitch and a half, but mine takes the cake."

"Doesn't your mom treat you well, though?"

"That's precisely the problem! She's a two-faced bitch; she worships the ground I walk on but treats my sister like dirt, which pisses me off. I don't even like my sister much, but she doesn't deserve that kind of treatment from her own mother." He looks genuinely frustrated, his earlier carefree attitude completely wiped away. "But I'm told Mom wants to move back out here this summer, so at least she'll be able to see Dad and Kyle more often."

I piece together that Teddy's parents must be separated, so I ask, "Does your dad not have custody?"

Teddy frowns. "It's complicated. My sister and I fought a lot when the divorce happened, so our parents thought it'd be best to separate us. They didn't want to spend the money fighting for custody either, so it was the cleanest option at the time. Mom wanted me, but Dad played the gender card because my sister wanted to go with her for my sake. She's the toughest girl I know, but living with Mom's mind games can't be easy for her."

"That's rough." I can't say I understand what he's been through, but I can't imagine being separated from my brothers even if they annoy me sometimes. Teddy looks so troubled that I decide to change the subject. "Who's Kyle?"

"Mm . . ." Teddy strokes his chin. "In the strictest sense, he's my dad's childhood friend, but he's kinda like a second dad to me. Can you believe he's been friends with my dad for forty whole years? That's the kind of friendship I want one day."

Jack elbows him. "Are you saying you don't think we could last forty years?"

"That depends, dude. Would it kill you if I end up marrying Jenny?"

"I think you're setting your goals too high, but it wouldn't kill me if you were my brother-in-law. Just never tell me a damn thing about you two if it does happen; I don't want to hear shit like that about my sister. And you better treat her right."

Teddy clasps his fingers together, clearly entering some fantasy world. "I would treat her like a queen . . ."

I decide it'd be best for my health that I don't know what he's imagining.

Jack pretends to gag, rolling his eyes and pointing his finger into his open mouth.

I can tell these two are close, like Matthew and Mark. "Guy friendships make me jealous." I kick my legs a little. "I've never been all that close with other girls." I've tried to be close with Heather, but she hides a lot of herself from me; the physical distance doesn't help much, either. And now my best friends are estranged from me over something I have no control over.

Jack looks down on me with an angelic smile. "Can I show you something?"

"What do you want to show me?"

"You'll see." He gets up off the bleacher and steps onto the wooden slab, the setting sun reflecting off his black dress heels. Teddy picks up his guitar while Jack stretches his body up into the sky, and, without the distraction of soccer practice and the game after, I realize Jack must have dressed up for this dance. And he looks almost ethereal with those smoky eyes and the horizon bleeding orange behind him.

He dances slowly this time, putting emphasis on his arms and hands rather than his legs, while Teddy strums along. The intensity comes from the clam-like instruments held in his hands, which he clamps together so quickly I can't make out his precise movements. It's more shocking and louder up close, but Jack smiles so beautifully I'm swept up in his song. A part of me knows he's just showing off, but another knows this dance must be his favorite thing in the world.

His performance ends after only a few minutes, and he looks at me with his gentle dark-brown eyes. "That smile suits you better, Emily."

My eyes crinkling, I blush and cover my mouth.

Tuesday is full of drizzling rain, which isn't enough to cancel practice, but is enough for Jack to show up in his normal jeans and jacket; Teddy appears as well, this time without his guitar or the slab of wood.

Because there's no musical spectacle today, practice goes on in perfect peace, even if it's all wet and muddy. When practice ends and I change out of my dirty gear, the two boys walk me to the bus lot to wait for Mom. We sit on an old wooden bench without a back, one that's much wider than the stone bench, so I don't have to be cushioned between them.

"I was wondering what got you two into flamenco. It doesn't seem like the kind of thing most people would just stumble into." They told me what the dance was called yesterday, and that Jack was playing castanets.

"Teddy got me into it shortly after we met, but . . ." Jack leans forward and looks at him. "I don't think you ever told me why you got into it."

"My sister got into it first. She liked the dresses the female dancers wear. After watching a few recordings of performances with her, I decided I liked the guitar and wanted to learn. I used to practice with her before she moved away, but now I mostly practice with Jack when we have the time. Of course I play just about every day, but it's nice to have somebody dancing along."

I figure it's like practicing soccer techniques at home: you can go solo just fine, but having somebody to pass to or score against makes it more effective. "What's the singing about?"

Teddy smiles crookedly. "Flamenco is about the struggles of the outsider. Its origins aren't certain, but most people trace it back to the Gitano of Spain, or the Spanish Roma in our language. They were ostracized by society, and some chose to find solace in art, such as flamenco. Some songs are about love and desire, but others are about death and suffering. It attracted me because I could relate to that struggle: not fitting in and feeling like there was no way out."

"Yeah," Jack says, "I felt like that, too."

I look at them both, at their deep frowns born from a recent past, and say, "I think it's beautiful." I stare at the gray cloud cover and squint against the drizzle pitter-pattering over my face. "I'd like to see it again sometime."

"That's not a hard wish to fulfill," Jack says.

Teddy's smile doesn't look quite as strained. "Not at all."

The sky is clear on Wednesday, and when I walk down to the locker rooms, I find Jack wearing a vibrant red outfit with a black-and-white polka-dot shirt, his eyes made up in hues of orange and gold; if Monday's outfit was eye-catching, this one is breathtaking. He gives me a wink and a grin as I walk by, a flabbergasted smile on my face.

So we start practice, and Teddy comes by with the slab, and they practice, and we have another game against another school. And when I come back out to the bleachers after I change into less sweaty clothes, I push through the crowd of girls and sit myself on the row below the two boys just as Jack steps back down onto the wooden slab. Teddy starts to play his guitar and Jack gets into position, this time with most of my team as their audience. When Teddy sings, Jack unfolds a bright-red fan that matches his trousers and vest.

And I watch them and their faces, the way Jack comes alive in the light of the setting sun, waving that fan in complicated flips and spins and tapping his feet in a particular rhythm upon the wood held by fresh grass, and I think I understand why they love flamenco. I can hear it in Teddy's agonized voice, see it on Jack's effervescent face: the passion of people put down by life, people who decide to make something beautiful out of their own suffering.

The setting sun ignites Jack's red clothes as he dances, and with the fiery makeup accenting his eyes, and the fan flowing through the work of his hands, I'm reminded of a reborn phoenix, and I believe for just a moment that all my problems are mere ashes at his feet. He casts them aside with each step, giving me some respite as long as his flame burns.

But the fire dims, and the boys' performance comes to an end. Jack fans himself coquettishly, his silly grin masked by the red fabric as he levels a smoldering gaze at his captivated audience; he definitely thinks he's hot shit right now, but I can't blame him for it after displaying himself for a bunch of cute girls. Jack is undoubtedly gorgeous with his sharp face and rugged demeanor, and the balls he has to have to go to school dressed like that certainly boosts his appeal, but he's almost too beautiful, an unobtainable boy only the finest woman could even think of taking for herself. At least that's how I feel about him; he's too much for a plain girl like me. Not that I like him like that, anyway; I'm not into guys with big egos.

Many of the girls stick around to talk to Teddy and Jack, some of them singing their praises, some of them awkwardly trying to flirt, but Teddy has a crush and Jack's obviously playing around. I wonder how these girls would feel if they knew that the attractive boys in front of them have a fluffy secret.

By the time Thursday ends, the team has had their fill of Jack and Teddy's performances, so at the end of practice on Friday, I'm left alone with them at the bleachers. They both seem tired, the sun lazily warming their backs; I guess practicing as they were for three consecutive days takes a lot out of you, not to mention lugging that slab of wood all the way to Mark's house on foot each time.

Mom texts me that she'll be late, so I tell Jack as much, and he reminds me he doesn't care how late he has to wait. "It's a good excuse to stay away from home a little longer, though I'm spending the weekend at Mark's house, anyway."

"Is that why you hang out so long?" I ask.

"Pretty much." He lies back on the bleacher with his arms behind his head and closes his eyes; his hair cascades over the edges so far back it reveals the smooth skin where his ears should be.

"How have those two been? Mark . . . and Matthew?

"Mark's been himself. He just acts like a busybody when he's stressing. Sometimes I have to force him to calm down a sec." He opens his eyes and looks at the clouds. "He complains about having to drive me home, but I think it's good for him to be away from home and school for a while." He gives me a smile. "He asks me how you're doing, too, if you were wondering."

I smile too, happy that Mark cares enough to ask about me, but that bit of happiness disappears before I can savor it. "What about Matthew?"

Jack closes his eyes again. "He's been fine, I guess. More closed off than usual. He's been sleeping a lot, too. He sleeps more than your average person already, but what he's doing now is a bit much."

Matthew's been looking worse every day. He looks tired. Very tired.

"You know, he pays for Mark's gas. Pumps it himself, too. I don't know if that means anything to you."

I wish I could understand Matthew better. I wish I knew how to make whatever this is better.

"Yo, Teddy!" Jack looks up at Teddy sitting next to his head. "You wanna spend the weekend, too?"

"Mm . . . Let me call my dad real quick." He puts his guitar in its case, walks a few paces away, takes out his phone, and brings it to his ear.

While Teddy's out of earshot, I say, "I wish I could understand what Matthew's thinking."

Jack glances at me, then stares at the cloudy sky, one cloud stretching out toward the setting sun. "You know, back in sixth grade, I almost looked exactly like my twin sister. The kids that knew my sisters' nickname for me would call me Jackie, and they would constantly harass me for looking girly. At some point, I really started to believe I looked like a girl, which fucked with my head because I *am* a boy and I want to look like a boy. It was hard for me to look in the mirror sometimes because I'd see Jenny more than I'd see myself. And when I awakened in the first week of seventh grade, I couldn't even cut my hair anymore.

"Even when I got taller and finally developed some muscle, I always worried I looked too girly or gay or something. And I always felt more comfortable around girls and liked some girly things, so I started to believe that maybe they were right, that I didn't deserve to call myself a man. I couldn't be satisfied, and the bunny stuff didn't help at all."

Jack, who was confident enough to dress up and wear makeup to school and dance with a fan, felt like that not too long ago. "How did you stop feeling that way?"

"I still feel that way sometimes, even though I think I look pretty manly now. I just have to remind myself of that every time I get close to thinking bad about myself. You know what helped me the most?"

"What's that?"

He grins. "Every time I see my reflection, I think to myself, *Goddamn, I'm looking sexy as hell right now.*"

He laughs at me when he sees my face; I seriously can't with that answer, but, for once, I think I totally understand what he means. I school my face in and stare at Teddy's broad back. "I think I get where you're coming from, but the other way around. I've always gotten along better with boys, and I like sports and video games more than I've ever liked makeup and pretty clothes. I used to get made fun of for that; boys would laugh and jeer, and girls would give me mean looks and leave me out of stuff. There were always people that didn't care, but it's easier to remember the bad stuff."

"It always is."

"The stupid part is that I don't want people to treat me like I'm just another girl, but I still want to feel like I'm allowed to do what I like without being less of a girl. I'm sorry if that doesn't make much sense. I'm not always good at explaining myself."

"No, I get it." He bends his knee, stealing a glance. "I think . . . that's kinda what Matthew's feeling like, except it's not about gender for him. What he wants to be and what he sees in the mirror don't match."

I think about what Matthew sees in his reflection as Teddy walks back to us, letting Jack know he can stay the weekend. We chill out awhile longer, and I stare at the clouds until Mom finally comes to pick me up. When I get home, I take a shower and go to my room, but before I put any clothes on, I look at myself in the mirror; I don't feel much about my small chest, but when I look at my backside, I feel a little sexy.

The following Thursday, Matthew doesn't leave the room when our lunch period starts. I don't say anything to him, and we eat quietly next to each other. His nails grow sharp, and his hands shake the entire time, but he never gets up except to throw his trash away. When he returns to his seat, he lifts his hood, puts his hands in his pockets, and lays his head down facing me. I try not to turn my head, letting him simply look at me until he closes his eyes to sleep; he turns his head away, but can't hide the low rumble in his throat.

One Step at a Time

Ashley

My phone rings while I'm in the middle of flipping pancakes on the griddle. I check my phone, see an out-of-state caller ID, and reject the call, assuming it's just another scam; the caller will leave a voicemail if it's important. I hardly get any calls, but it wasn't that long ago that Alex called me without a warning.

I was making chicken noodle soup for Matthew all the way back in January. It was a Saturday night around seven when he called, and although I found it unusual, I picked up because I wanted to be sure he was alright; I knew how he used to get on full-moon nights, and it wasn't like him to not ask in advance.

"Hello?" I said.

He was breathing heavily. "Ashley . . ."

"Hello, Alex. Is there something you wanted to talk about?"

Glass clanked against a surface, and a cork popped out of a bottle. "I need you . . . to tell me to pour it out."

I didn't answer right away because I knew what he was holding. "Please . . ."

I frowned, but said, "Pour it out, Alex."

I heard bubbling; *champagne*, I thought. He turned on his sink and rinsed out the bottle. "I poured it out."

"That's good." I stirred my pot of soup slowly. "Where did you get it?" Alex had texted me a few times about his alcoholism, and I had made him promise to never buy another bottle; I have no time in my life for flirting with a drunkard.

"I got it"—he heaved another breath—"at a work event. New Year's. It was a gift."

"Okay. I'm glad you didn't buy it yourself. You've been very good so far." I felt silly talking to him like he was a puppy who needed positive reinforcement to learn new tricks.

"I've been . . . trying my best . . . It's hard. I want to drink so bad, Ash."

"I know. But you need to be strong," I said, "for me."

"For you . . ." I heard static, then a thump. "I'm sorry. I shouldn't be calling you like this."

Maybe not, I thought, but I'd rather him call than make a mistake. "It's okay. I don't mind at all."

"Ashley, I . . . I think I lo—" He was suddenly quiet except for a low growl. "I need to go."

He ended the call before I could say anything. I put the phone down and decided not to call him back; as worrisome as his behavior was, I knew he'd been taking care of himself on these nights since he was a boy and thought he wouldn't pick up, anyway. He seemed quite frustrated, growling at himself like that; he always said exactly what was on his mind on those nights, and whatever he was about to say was something he didn't want me to hear. I had a feeling I knew what it was, but . . .

The next day, he called me again to apologize for bothering me and invited me to have lunch with him the following Wednesday. I hadn't seen him since that day at the Barnes & Noble, and after months of texts and calls, I felt like it was about time I stopped distancing myself; try as I might, I couldn't convince myself to avoid him.

So on that day, as I got dressed for work, I wondered what Alex saw in me. I stared at my shrunken, drooping breasts, breasts that were once full and round and perky, and their large, dark areolas, and wondered if he'd still wag his tail at the sight of them, if he'd tease them with his padded hands and his wet tongue and run his hands down my side, over my bony, stretch-marked hips, and wander the length of my thin legs with a firm grip. Would I still be beautiful to him, or would I be a shriveled old thing, too lined and scarred from the weight I've had to bear over the years? *It doesn't matter*, I thought, clasping the band of a bra that I filled out better than a few months ago behind my back. I dressed for work, donning my jacket and cardigan for the cold weather.

We met for lunch at a Mexican restaurant near our workplaces. I walked inside and got us a booth because he was running late. When he arrived not five minutes later, he looked like some middle-aged metalhead that had just woken up with the worst hangover of his life: his long, straight hair was unbound and tangled, like he'd made an attempt to comb it but gave up halfway; his lower eyelids were heavily lined from lack of sleep; and he had a faint five-o'clock shadow. To his credit, he was dressed well in dark jeans, a fur-lined coat, and slip-on boots; he always tried to look stylish back when I first met him, so I supposed that hadn't changed.

"You look cozy," I said, trying to break the ice.

"Oh, uh, thanks." He appeared out of his depth. "You look very nice. I feel like I underdressed."

I smiled. "It's nothing special, just what I wear to work every day. Actually, I'm surprised you're dressed so casually; did you not have work today?"

"Uh, no; I took the week off. But even if I didn't, I wouldn't wear scrubs out of the office."

"Oh, I should've thought of that." My gaze lingered on the basket of tortilla chips. "Any special reason you took off?"

Alex seemed hesitant to answer. Our waitress came to ask about our drinks, and after she left, Alex idly ate chips with salsa, like he wanted an excuse to delay any speech.

I chose instead to prod at something else. "Your hair has gotten very long." It flowed down over his chest, likely long enough to cover his nipples if he was shirtless; even though it was tousled, it had a healthy sheen.

He looked down at his chest, pinching the end of one strand. "Oh, yeah, I've been growing it out for a while now. I'm still deciding when I should cut it again."

"What's the longest you've ever had your hair?"

He lit up with a grin. "Down to my butt."

"Goodness gracious." I immediately imagined him with hair that long: those cute wolf ears peaking above a certifiable curtain of hair, a golden-brown river only parted by a stiff tail. "Your hair was short back when I met you. Did you decide you like it long?"

"Kinda." He grew somber again. "I tried growing it out after my mom lost her hair to chemo. She loved doing fancy shit with her hair more than anything, so it was a massive blow when it slowly fell out. So I thought I'd let her play with my hair whenever

I visited her at the hospital." He scratched his cheek. "It was a pretty big change, so I could barely get it past my shoulders before I wanted to cut it off, but Mom was so calm doing braids and stuff that I kept at it until I got used to it being long."

Before I could think of a reply, our waitress came by and took our orders—arroz con pollo for me and diablos tacos for him.

Alex twirled a long strand between his fingers. "I only really cut it when I was job hunting and always donated what I had for wigs."

"That's very sweet of you." I never would've thought Alex could be so selfless.

Alex smiled shyly. "It wasn't that hard of a thing, really."

I smiled, too. "Nonsense."

He blushed, wrapping that strand around his finger. "Enough about me. What have you been up to lately?"

I held my cheek in my hand, resting my elbow on the table. "It's been much of the same, but . . . I went to a Christmas party the other day and met someone interesting."

"Tell me about it."

"My son's new friend had another friend whose father, Bobby, was there. It turns out he knows about people like you."

Alex raised his eyebrows. "Really?"

I nodded and brought my voice to a whisper. "His son turned not too many months ago, but he did a bad job of hiding everything, so Bobby saw him while he was distracted." I flattened my lips. "The only problem is he hasn't told his son that he knows. He doesn't want to upset him, but it's a bit frustrating to watch."

Eyebrows furrowed, Alex covered his mouth. "Yeah, I'd be pretty pissed if my dad knew and didn't tell me. It's such a pain in the ass to hide everything in your own house."

"That's what I was thinking." I tapped my cheek. "Anyway, it was nice to be able to talk to someone about being a parent to children like yourself. It's a unique challenge, I think, not that I'd want my son any other way. It's part of what makes him who he is." I side-eyed him and pushed my limits. "I'm glad I met you all those years ago; it allowed me to be a better person for all of them."

He had his chin down, almost submissive. "You're giving me too much credit, Ash."

Maybe so, but . . .

A runner brought our food to the table: two big plates piled high with rice and meat and soft flour tortillas. We chatted about meaningless things, like work and dinner and TV, and I slowly ate through half my meal. Alex pretended his tacos weren't too spicy, his poker face unable to hide the large amount of water he downed to spare his tongue.

He invited me to meet him again two weeks later. I drove to a small German restaurant in Cary the day before Valentine's Day. It was freezing outside, so I was bundled up and glad to be inside as soon as I got there; he was already waiting for me in a booth so long it could fit two or three families—a quirk of the restaurant, I'd guessed.

It was moderately busy, being a Saturday, but not too loud. Alex looked clean and groomed and well-rested, dressed similarly to his previous attire. His hair was pulled back into a ponytail so I could see his ears, and he couldn't stop smiling. I wondered how he could be so happy to see a woman like me, how I could be so happy to see him when it'd only been a little over two weeks.

After ordering our drinks, Alex glanced at the bar with a far-off gaze. "In another time, I would've tried a beer or two." He flattened his lips. "Those nights, I could drink through a pack of Terrapin if I wanted."

I looked up from the menu. "Did you ever truly want to?"

He looked at me. "Maybe not me. My brain wanted to. My liver, not so much."

"How are you doing, as far as that goes?"

He grinned. "I've been sober since December."

"Two months. That's good progress."

"What about you? With your weight?"

My stomach dropped. "It's been slow, but . . . f-five pounds so far." I felt humiliated. "The holidays helped."

"That's awesome, Ashley." He was positively beaming.

Childishly, I covered my face with the menu.

When I peeked over the top, Alex was looking through his own menu, frowning. "I've been meaning to tell you why I called back in January."

I put my menu back down. "You don't have to."

"I want to." He lifted his menu just as I had. "It was . . . the anniversary of Mom's passing. I was an absolute mess, so I . . . I just . . ."

I mustered my courage and touched his hand. "I'm glad you called, Alex. I was happy to help; I always am."

He put his menu down and held my hand. "Thanks. I just . . . I get so embarrassed when I'm like that."

I rubbed my thumb over his knuckles. "I would never hold it against you. We all have bad days."

That brought his smile back, and after our meal was said and done, we made plans to meet for lunch every other week since.

Today, now that the weather is finally warming up, we're going on a jog at a nearby trail. We're both way out of shape, and even though my eating habits have improved, exercise is just as important for recuperating my physical health.

I turn off the griddle just as the final batch of pancakes cooks through and add them to the pile on a nearby serving plate. If there's one thing I've learned over the past two weeks, it's how much food four teenage boys can eat; my wallet might be crying more than usual, but it makes me happy to see Mark with so many friends. If only girl trouble wasn't the reason for their more frequent visits.

I walk down the hall to Mark's bedroom door, leaving the pancakes and griddle to cool. Just as I'm about to knock, Glenn slips through the gap and winds around my legs, and I'm met with a broad chest.

"G'mornin', Ms. K.!" Luke grins, oddly energetic for a Saturday morning. He has a drowsy Matthew locked in his fur-covered right arm, while a semiconscious Mark wraps his scaly self around Luke's left arm; Jack stands behind his shoulder, his eyes cracked open and his ears held at a forty-five-degree angle.

"Good morning, Luke." I back away from the quartet so I don't have to crane my neck so much to see his face; I can barely believe he's only fifteen, but he does have Bobby's genes in him. "I hope you all slept well."

"Glenn woke us up . . . ," Mark says.

"It seems he woke you up just in time for breakfast. I made pancakes."

"They smell great." Luke drags Matthew and Mark along. "Let's not waste any more time waiting; I'm hungry and we're going to do things today."

"What are we even going to do?" Mark asks, his tail swaying close to Jack's thigh.

"I don't know yet. Maybe you could drive us somewhere."

They keep bickering, and despite being in a headlock, Matthew's tail is raised and curled at the tip; he's the sort to try and isolate himself, so I'm glad his friends are stubborn enough not to leave him alone. I'm still getting used to frequently seeing them in active form; Jack was shy about it for such a long time, and Luke came over for the first time only two weeks ago—Mark's requested payment in bear hugs for a ride home certainly forced his hand. As strange as it is, I think Mark gets some of his openness toward animal people from me; not a day goes by that I don't think about seeing Alex in his active form again.

Because we only have four chairs at the dining room table, I eat my breakfast on the couch. The boys eat faster than I do, so by the time I'm done with my stack of lightly dressed pancakes, they've already washed their plates and gone to get dressed for the day ahead. I take my empty plate into the kitchen, put it in the sink, store the few leftover pancakes for later, and wash my plate, the serving plate, and the griddle. I dry the dishes in the dish rack while listening to the boys' ongoing conversation.

"Maybe we could go ice-skating," Matthew says. "I'd say roller-skating, but I hate the indoor type with the quad wheels."

"God, I haven't done either in years!" Mark says. Their elementary school did discounted ice-skating events one Friday night a month, so I took them both whenever they wanted to go. They learned quickly and are proficient with both ice skates and in-line roller skates; personally, I was always more of a bicycle girl, but I wouldn't mind taking the time to learn how to skate one day. "I honestly don't know what happened to the in-line skates we had."

"Isn't it a little hot for ice-skating?" Jack says.

Mark's beat of silence speaks volumes. "You don't know how to skate, do you?"

"What gave you that idea?" There's a subtle nervousness to Jack's tone.

A smack resounds, and Luke says, "If it makes you feel any better, I only know how to use the quad skates."

"I'd be happy to teach you," Matthew says.

Mark says, "Nah. Let's save him the humiliation for another time."

There's rustling, then the front door creaks open.

"How nice of you," Luke says. "Oh! I think I might have a better idea than skating. How would y'all feel about . . ."

The door thumps closed and the lock clicks.

I finish cleaning up the kitchen shortly after the truck's engine roars to life. I put together a water bottle and take my keys and my wallet out of my purse; it'd be a hassle to jog lugging my purse with me, but I can't exactly go without my license or my insurance cards should anything go awry—I'm also planning to run a few errands afterward, so money is a must. I stick my important purse contents and my phone into my decently deep athletic-shorts pockets, then put on the nice pair of running shoes I purchased for a pretty penny; with everything accounted for, I leave the house and drive to the nearby trail.

I park in the lot at the back side of the trail, glad that it's not too crowded yet. I get out, lock my car, and glance around, hoping to find Alex's old navy blue Honda Civic; just as I spot its bright-red taillights, Alex crosses the lot toward me. He's dressed for the occasion, wearing gym shorts, a loose T-shirt, and a baseball cap, but the most curious thing is his hair; it's neatly tied into a three-strand braid.

We share a hug, then walk down the nearby sidewalk that leads onto the trail. We tell each other about our weeks, mostly exchanging some remarks about work, and around five minutes into the trail, we prepare to jog. We do some warm-up stretches, and Alex pulls out wired earbuds and his phone, inserting the cord into the audio jack. I hadn't thought about listening to music while exercising, and although I could play something directly out of my phone's speakers, I wouldn't want to disturb the other people on the trail.

With his earbuds secured in his ears, he gives me a grin. "Ready?"

I try not to look like I'm dreading it; I've never enjoyed exercise, which is part of why my weight issues have always been out of control. "As ready as I'll ever be."

We start off walking, then pick up our pace into a steady rhythm. I jog behind Alex, but he glances back every so often to make sure I haven't fallen too far back. It felt a little chilly before, but now that we're bounding along the trail, my skin heats up enough for the wind to feel pleasant. The lake to our right sparkles and the trees all around are blooming with leaves and flowers, but my gaze remains firmly on Alex's back side.

I watch his rope of hair bounce against his upper back, the cord attached to his phone swinging back and forth in tandem with his strides. Naturally, my eyes travel down his spine until they reach where his tail would be; with his stomach out of view, it's hard to tell he's a hefty man, but his butt and thighs are noticeably thicker than they were in his youth.

Heavy as he was, George always had nice, shapely legs; it was one of the many things I enjoyed about him. So I watch Alex's calves flex with every step, imagining the soft fur that could cover the length of his sculpted legs like alluring thigh highs.

Alex glances back at me again, lingering long enough that I'm sure he can tell what I've been evaluating; he raises a brow.

I look up and put an awkward smile on my face, and when he refocuses on the trail ahead, I curse my sinful heart for ogling him. I feel like my sense of attraction is broken because I don't give a damn about his beer belly; if he asked me, I'd agree to date him right this second, and if he allowed me, I'd be more than happy to run my fingers through his fur. These feelings of mine feel so right and so wrong and all too soon, my traitorous heart and my lonely mind overshadowing any logical thoughts.

Ashamed, I push myself to pass Alex and jog in front of him. It gets harder to breathe and my legs scream at me, but his delicious lower half is out of my sight. I focus on the nature around us, mostly oaks and pines and geese and ducks, but in one little patch of woods, right near a stream, I spot a young fawn. As common as deer are supposed to be around these parts, I hardly ever see them; the most I usually see are squirrels and small birds. So it feels a little lucky, like a good omen, until my stomach cramps from the effort.

I push through the discomfort for another half mile, and when we reach a bridge that crosses over a muddy river, I slow down to a walk and grip the spot that hurts the most. Panting, I unscrew the cap on my water bottle and take a hearty swig.

Alex catches up, matches my new pace, and pulls out his earbuds.

"I think I need to walk the rest of the way," I say.

Alex pants, a healthy sheen of sweat on his brow. "That's fine by me. We have to work on our stamina before we can run long distances." He takes his cap off, swipes at a few whisps of hair falling over his forehead, and puts it back on. "I was on the cross-country team back in high school; now I can barely jog a mile."

"A sedentary lifestyle does that to you." My legs are sore all over, but as much as I want to sit down, I need to keep moving.

I rub my cramping stomach, keeping my gaze firmly on the trail ahead.

Alex bumps his bicep against my shoulder. "Something on your mind?"

I can't tell him that *he's* on my mind, so I say, "Do you remember Bobby? The father I told you about before?"

His shadow nods. "The bear kid's dad, right?"

"Yes, that's right."

"I still can't believe you know four of them. I've only ever come across, like, one other guy."

I chuckle. "I can't believe it myself sometimes. They've all been staying over on the weekends lately, too."

"So *that's* what I've been smelling on you." Alex casually leans close and sniffs my hair, like it's the most natural thing for a man to do. "Freshly mowed grass and honey."

I assume those scents must be from Jack and Luke, respectively. "Actually, I was curious how you figured out that animal people have a unique scent if you've never been close with any. You would've been mostly nose blind to yourself, so . . ." I look at his face.

Alex dons a deadpan expression. "The one guy I met was a real freak. It was a long time ago, but I came across this guy wearing shades inside with the brightest orange hair I'd ever seen on a man; it was all kinds of unnatural, and when he saw me, he cracked a grin, showing all his razor-sharp teeth, kinda like your kid. I got stuck in an empty hallway with him at some event, and he got up real close and personal." He shudders, frowning with disgust.

"What was he?" I ask.

"An octopus . . ." He rubs his wrist. "The guy smelled like leather and was all slimy after shifting. He grabbed me with his tentacles and shocked me so bad I ended up shifting, too. He had his fun inspecting me, thanked me for my 100 percent–unwilling cooperation, and left. I'll never forget that guy, but I hope I never see him again."

"Oh my . . ." Being tied up by an octopus man would certainly be frightening, but I can imagine there are some people out there who'd enjoy that kind of experience; I'd rather not find out if I'm one of them.

"The smell of leather stuck with me since he wasn't wearing anything made out of it, and a wallet wouldn't have smelled so strong even in my face. So I figured that was just another weird thing about guys like us." He shakes his head, his braid whipping back and forth. "Anyway, what were you saying about Bobby?"

"Bobby called me up the other day to invite me to the beach with him and his friend. I was thinking of taking my boys to help keep their minds off things, but I'm not sure if I should be traveling on my own like that. Bobby's been nothing but kind so far, but a girl's got to be careful, you know?" If George was still around, it wouldn't have been a problem. And Alex isn't an option; there's no way I'm going to spring him on Mark and Matthew anytime soon.

Alex grins. "I'd go with you, but my beach bod isn't ready yet."

Oh my goodness, this man . . . "I don't think mine is ready yet, either."

He looks like he's about to deny my claim, but says, "Well, what does your gut say? I've always been told to trust that whenever I'm not sure about something."

I stare at the sparse clouds in the blue sky and listen to my gut. I don't feel much of anything at all; the only thing in my gut is a cramp. "I think I'll take a chance this time. I haven't been to the beach in a long time, and they'll be down there Mother's Day weekend." I smile in a way that feels funny. "I guess Bobby sends his son off to his mother, so it's a good time for some personal TLC. I'm more nervous about his friend, but he says he usually keeps to himself."

"Then don't sweat it. And if anything happens, you can always call me up, okay?" Alex smiles, his green eyes crinkling in their corners. Why does he have to have such a charming face?

We come across another bridge, and I take a moment to rest against the railing and hydrate. I start to feel a little glum again, so I stare into the water below the bridge, imagining the sparkling ripples are really ocean waves. I wonder if I should buy a new one-piece or finally work up the courage to put on a bikini.

Alex rests his arms on top of the railing. "How are your boys doing?"

I frown and rest my eyes. "Mark is still a little frazzled, but he's fine otherwise. Matthew is doing better than he was that day he came home by himself, but I can tell he's still beating himself up over what happened with that girl he likes."

Alex shifts his weight to his other leg. "I know I'd be a wreck if I ever hurt you."

I open my eyes and look at the side of his face; there's longing in his far-off gaze. "What are you trying to say?" My mouth becomes a desert and my heart pounds; I can barely stay standing, so I rely on the railing below my arms.

Alex steps back and faces me, determination in the line of his brow and the set of his mouth.

Seeing the gravity of his expression, I, too, stand straight, facing him head-on. With the rising sun on his skin, it's as if he's made of gold.

"I don't want to play with my emotions anymore." His gaze wavers. "The truth is . . . I . . ." He grits his teeth, closes his eyes, and huffs a breath out of his nose; when he opens his eyes, he says in the quietest voice, "I love you, Ashley, and I want to know if I have even the slightest chance with you."

My mouth hangs open, but no words find their way through the gap.

He loses his shaky composure and looks down at himself. "I understand if you're not interested."

I look down, too, first at his stomach, then his shins, then his expensive running shoes; I look back up at his clean-shaven face. "Are you sure you want to be with a widow and a mother? And . . . I look a lot worse now . . . than I used to."

The hesitation in his expression makes me feel stupid for worrying about my appearance. "I think it's better to say you look different. That doesn't have to be a bad thing. You can't expect to look exactly how you did when you were eighteen; I wouldn't expect you to look the same." He glances at his stomach. "I definitely don't look the same."

And he doesn't. He isn't toned and firm and free of the wrinkles that come with age, but neither am I. He's heavier, and I'm lighter, and it's not a good thing for either of us, but . . . "I love you, too, Alex."

He smiles, but his eyes are unbelieving. "Are you sure you want to be with a fat-ass and a wolf man?"

I give him a playful, warped smile. "You certainly have a fat ass."

"So you *were* staring at my ass!"

"What can I say; it was hard to miss."

"Dammit, Ashley." His eyes squint hard from his huge grin. "Can I kiss you?" He holds his hands out, palms up.

I put my hands in his. "I think I'd like that." Our position reminds me of the way I held George's hands on our wedding day, and I hear it, the famous last words of our vows. *Until death do us part, right, George?* If he's up there in Heaven, I hope that he's beyond these human needs, beyond jealousy and longing and loneliness, and I know, if I was in his place, I'd never hate him for moving on. So I rise up on my toes, and Alex meets me in the middle, and we lock lips; as I taste his sweat and breathe his heady scent of wine, my weary bones alight with a heat I haven't felt in four years.

CHAPTER 19

Suddenly Sashimi

Mark

Mom stands tall in a lilac bikini, holding the wide brim of the sun hat protecting her serene face from the bright beach sun. I was shocked when she bought her swimsuit; from what little I can remember from before I turned ten, she only ever wore a one-piece that covered as much skin as possible, but here she is, baring her mangled stomach for the world to see. I don't find it repulsive, but it's not a pretty sight either, her skin wrinkled and covered in stretch marks radiating from her navel, the saggy skin making it appear pudgy—no matter how much weight Mom lost, her belly always stuck out, and the loose skin from her excessive starvation only compounded the problem. In the days leading up to our trip, she smelled more strongly of that man she's been seeing, and I wondered if he was the one that gave her this newfound confidence.

Matthew and I follow Mom onto the white sand of a sparse, flat beach; we drove three hours away from home to one of the less popular barrier islands of North Carolina, one I've never heard of nor been to in my sixteen years of life. I already forgot which one it is, but it's toward the border between North and South Carolina, the only way onto the island proper being a curving bridge road; the area is fairly underdeveloped and has a low population, so the only buildings bordering the beachfront are rentals and other beach houses—it's different not having a backdrop of massive hotels and beachside businesses. Considering our often-conspicuous biology, I'm glad there aren't too many people around, especially for a Saturday on a typically popular weekend; if that Kyle guy really is a monster person, I'm not surprised he'd pick a place like this for his beach getaways.

I take my flip-flops off as soon as we hit the sand at the end of the boardwalk entrance—there are plenty of signs warning not to cross the dunes directly and damage the vulnerable vegetation— and immediately spot Mr. Brown's massive form.

He waves at us from his setup of folding chairs, his swimming trunks leaving nothing of his upper body to the imagination; he's a big guy with all the flab of a dad—objectively fat, but reminiscent of a heavyweight wrestler.

"Great to see you again, Bobby." Mom shares a brief embrace with him.

"Great to see you, too, hon." He holds a hand out to me.

Feeling clammy, I shake his hand.

"I believe your name is Mark," he says.

I let go of his hand. "That's right."

Mr. Brown holds his hand out to Matthew. "And you are?"

"Matthew." He gingerly shakes his hand. "I'm Mark's friend."

Mr. Brown smiles kindly. "I think Luke mentioned you once or twice."

Matthew nods.

Mr. Brown puts one hand on his hip. "Kyle and I plan to be on the beach all day, and I'll probably pick up lunch a little later; if y'all don't mind, we'll have a cookout at the campground for dinner."

"That sounds fine by me." Mom readjusts the oversize beach bag on her shoulder and faces the two of us. "I'll probably be hanging out with Bobby and his friend all day, so you two can do what you want. I know dawdling on the beach with us old folks might not be the most exciting thing in the world." The smile on her face says what she really means: even though he knows how to, Matthew can't swim in public due to his tail.

He's wearing swimming trunks, but it's more for show than anything else; he covered his torso with a blue-and-green Hawaiian shirt and his ears with a matching baseball cap. I'm dressed similarly, but without a hat and with slightly different colors; I found a blue shirt with pink flowers that looked classy, and I have my glasses on, their transition lenses allowing them to double as sunglasses.

"Wherever you end up, just keep me posted," Mom says, "and try not to wander too far."

I grin. "No promises, but we'll try our best."

"You have your phone?"

"Yes."

"And your wallet?"

"Of course."

She shifts her attention to Matthew. "What about you, hon?"

He nods. "I have everything. I'll try to keep Mark out of trouble."

"Alright." She nods to herself. "I'll stop worrying. Go have your fun. You know where to find me." Her brow furrowed, she sits back with Mr. Brown and relaxes in the sun, already striking up a conversation.

Matthew and I walk toward the water; he may not be able to swim, but we can get our feet wet. Cold waves roll over our skin, the weather mild and breezy.

"It's a shame there are no caves or coves around here," Matthew says. "I got myself a little excited, but it's pure flat beach."

"I didn't realize you liked swimming so much."

He gazes into the distant horizon. "I try to forget how much I loved it most of the time. Sometimes I wonder if I forgot how to swim entirely."

It's been a little over a third of his life purely on land, but I have a feeling it's like skating; you might not be great right away, but your body remembers the basics. "Let's at least walk a little while."

Matthew nods, and we meander along, the ocean at our right and the parents behind us.

Matthew stares at the lapping waves rolling across the entire ocean, and I wonder what he's thinking. Maybe he isn't.

We walk such a distance that Mom and Mr. Brown become mere specks in the distance, so we stop. Matthew wades knee-deep in the waves; they aren't particularly strong here, so I join him, my legs adjusting to the chill. He looks up at the clear sky, where all kinds of seagulls fly around, crying and diving down for fish, but my eyes follow one that seems pretty big for a gull.

"That's a big bird," I say, tired of being quiet.

Matthew squints. "I don't think that's a bird."

I take my shaded glasses off and stare at it. The undersides of its wings are a blinding white, though slightly discolored at the edges. Long, white-feathered legs trail behind it, ending with three long toes, and they're so thick I can't see its tail, and—

Matthew's right; birds don't have legs that big, and it's wearing a helmet.

"Is that?"

"I think so."

The closer it flies, the more I can make out. He has light-brown skin and well-defined pecs, betraying how frequently he flies. A powerful flap of his massive wings reveals dark-brown feathers topside, and sand-colored scales cover him from the ends of his taloned feet to about halfway up his calves. With greater scrutiny, I realize his groin and thighs aren't covered in feathers at all; he's wearing a white, formfitting swimsuit to give the illusion of feathers, so what he has probably ends at his upper thighs like it does for the rest of us. "His arms are fucking wings."

Matthew nods stupidly, craning his neck to keep looking at him.

I also crane my neck to continue staring at the harpy casually flying overhead; he's not paying a bit of attention to us, riding the wind without a care. "You know, I just thought of something fun we can do."

Matthew glances at me. "What's that?"

I put my glasses back on with a grin. "Let's follow him."

Matthew sighs, shaking his head. "You're lucky I'm bored." Yet he smiles.

So we turn our backs on the ocean and trudge along a fair distance behind the gliding harpy. We cross the beachfront, put our flip-flops back on and cross a boardwalk back to more stable ground, and cross yards and sidewalks and roads all the way to the other side of the island, where the harpy flies past the waterway we have no convenient way to cross.

"Damn," I say, my feet already sore from walking in unsup-portive footwear.

"I wish I wore my tennis shoes over here." Matthew pulls at the collar of his shirt.

The harpy lands at a patch of woods near the mainland side of the waterway and folds his massive wings tight against his sides. Now that he's on the ground, I can actually see his tail; oddly enough, it's rust orange at the base, and has a strip of black at the round edge. He folds and smooths his tail feathers down, covering his ass and the upper half of his thighs, then walks with an intoed gait into the shadows.

I plop down on the grass, brushing the remaining sand off the soles of my feet while giving myself a break.

Matthew copies me but stares at the treetops, like he's waiting for the harpy to suddenly reemerge.

Some specks of sand refuse to fall off my clammy skin, so I give up and deal with it. "Should we walk back to the car?"

Matthew huffs. "I don't feel like getting up. And he might be gone by then."

"I feel you, but we should—"

A shadow passes over my head. "What are y'all kids doing in my yard?" A man with hair so wispy and white he has to be in his eighties or nineties glares at us, obviously miffed we're trespassing on his lawn.

"Oh, uh . . ." I try desperately to think of a good excuse. "We were . . . bird-watching."

"Bird-watching, huh?" The old man crosses his arms, clearly unbelieving. "Where are your binoculars? You aren't gonna see much from the ground around here."

"Oh, jeez." I get up and brush off my knees; I feel more confident when I realize I'm a bit taller than the man, though he's hunched with age. "I'm always such a birdbrain; I completely forgot about them when I saw this huge bird flying over there!" I point at the trees across the waterway. "It's too bad we can't get across on foot."

Matthew shuffles to his feet behind me, ever silent.

"I'm sorry to hear that," the man says with an irritated tone, "but y'all better ske—"

An old woman hobbles up next to the man, regarding us with intrigue. "My, Tom." She must be the old man's wife, if the rings on their fingers are anything to go by. "Who are these two boys you're talking to?"

Tom regards her, then pinches his nose. "Just two rascals that claim to be looking for a bird over yonder." He points toward the trees but can't quite hold his finger out straight. "I was just telling them to leave."

"Oh, nonsense!" She smiles at us, studying my hair and eyes. I want to squirm.

"You were looking for a bird?" she asks. "Was it very big?"

I nod slowly. "Yeah. It was really . . . interesting. We wanted to get a closer look, but it flew off the island."

She smiles wider, shaking like she knows exactly what "bird" we're talking about. "Tom, why don't we take them over there on the boat."

Tom scowls at her. "Margaret, what has gotten into you? We can't just take two strangers on the boat like that."

"C'mon, love." She waves her hand up and down. "Just consider it some Southern hospitality. Don't they remind you of the grandkids? Oh, they haven't come to visit in so long."

Tom rolls his eyes. "I quite like my nest empty." He grumbles but turns around and walks to the boat attached to their dock.

The smile doesn't leave Margaret's face as she regards us again, this time lingering on Matthew, who shies away under the brim of his hat. "Come, come." She beckons with a wave of her hand, hobbling toward the boat; she looks at us over her shoulder. "Would either of you like some water? You're looking rather flushed."

I'm parched, not to mention generally nervous. "Yes, ma'am. That'd be wonderful."

She hums, leading us to the back door of her beach house.

We linger outside, giving each other a look that asks if we should bail while we still can, but remain rooted to the grass at our feet.

When Margaret returns, she hands us unopened plastic bottles of water.

I waste no time opening mine, guzzling half the water in mere seconds.

Margaret leads us to their boat; it's fairly small and without any frills, sporting four bench-like seats and a motor with a handle control on the back side—judging by the mess of gear inside, I imagine its primary purpose is for fishing.

I hesitate; I've never been on a boat before, so I hope I don't get seasick.

"Oh, don't be shy, boys." Margaret sits on the front-end bench. "Get in, get in."

Sharing another look questioning our decisions in life, we get on the wobbly boat and sit on the middle bench.

Margaret smiles while Tom prepares to untie it from their modest dock. "Tom, we can probably dock at Roger's house since he's close to those woods. Maybe we ought to say hello while we're at it."

Tom huffs, and the motor rumbles to life.

My stomach drops at the sudden movement but settles after a few tense moments; I glance at Matthew, relieved he's perfectly fine, though I wouldn't be surprised if he's been on fancier vessels before.

"So what brings you boys out here?" Margaret's short white hair flies about in the wind. "I can tell you're not from these parts."

"We're on vacation for the weekend," I say.

"Where're you from?"

"Raleigh."

Margaret pauses. "Oh, one of our kids lives over there. I haven't been in a long time, though. I'm getting too old for so much traveling!" She laughs, the sound light and airy.

I smile awkwardly, lost on how to engage with her other than how's the weather–level dialogue. Ocean spray coats my glasses, so I take them off and hang them on the collar of my shirt.

Margaret unabashedly stares into my eyes. "You both have marvelous eyes."

My heart skips a beat; our pupils must be contracted into mere slits in this bright sunlight.

"I never thought I'd meet boys like you again after so many years."

Again? My mouth becomes dry, stuck on this boat with a woman who knows more than she should. "I'm . . . not sure what you mean."

"Oh! Forgive me." She cups her cheek, looking out at the woods across the waterway; Tom didn't sail straight across, probably due to boat traffic rules or something like that. "How about I tell you a story. It was many, many years ago. I think it was . . . Yes, it was 1983. I was on a cruise right about this time, celebrating with my lady friends, right in the middle of the Atlantic.

"I was in my fifties back then, and all my kids had moved out. You could say I was having a midlife crisis, wondering what I ought to do with myself now that I had no one to take care of. So me and the girls were partying, drinking and eating and lounging in the pool on the ship, and I was enjoying quite a few margaritas. I always loved margaritas ever since I got my hands on one—they called me Margarita Margaret back in my drinking days!"

I don't find any humor in a woman's drinking problems, but it's her story, not mine.

"So as the day wore on, and I got to be positively drunk, I managed to stumble my way off the side of the ship. I remember thinking, *Oh, I'm going to drown*, but I wasn't afraid because I could barely comprehend what exactly was happening. I closed my eyes, but instead of sinking like a rock, I remained afloat. I could feel a hand at my back and something wrapping around my legs, holding me up above the waves. I turned my head to see a boy, but not just any boy: he was a merman."

"A merman?" I match her secretive tone. "What did he look like?"

She smiles, the sun shining in her eyes. "He was about the same age as you, with bright-orange hair and eyes. But he was a special kind of merman; he wasn't a fish, but an octopus, complete with rectangular pupils. I remember telling him how marvelous they were, but he got mad at me for staring."

If her story is to be believed, I can understand where he was coming from; even if the sentiment is nice, it's pretty uncomfortable to be stared at like a zoo animal.

"He was a funny boy, chastising me for falling overboard; he told me I was lucky I reminded him of his mom because he made it a principle not to reveal himself to humans. He also made me promise not to say anything about him before he would help me get back on the ship. Of course I promised these things, but I couldn't just leave it at that. So while everybody was looking for me and it was too risky for him to guide me back, I asked him all kinds of questions."

"What did you ask him?"

"The first thing I asked was where he comes from; I was thinking there must be a secret mermaid society out there under the ocean that none of us knew about, but you know what he said?" She pauses dramatically. "He said, 'I'm from Atlanta,' and I said, 'Don't you mean Atlantis?' and *my goodness* did he laugh in my face. He said, 'Naw, lady, I'm from Atlanta, Georgia. You know, the capital city of the state.'

"I was right shocked. He went on to tell me he was only there because he got a little turned around on his swim and thought following a boat might help him get back to land because he'd been gone three days and his mom would be very upset with him for disappearing all of a sudden, but he mostly wanted to go back to see his girlfriend. I asked if his mom and his girlfriend were mermaids, too, and he laughed at me again. He had such sharp teeth, just like yours."

I glance away; I know they're hard to miss, but it feels weird that she knows why they're serrated.

"It wasn't too long after that that the people on the ship started searching the other side, so he pushed us over with the tentacles that weren't wrapped around me, all slow and gentle, then shocked me again by fusing his tentacles into two legs before calling out for somebody to get me; the minute I had a life buoy around me, he disappeared back into the depths. I never did get that boy's name, but I have a feeling he wouldn't have given it to me. Goodness, it's been so long he must be fifty by now."

She looks across the water at the island; we've long made the U-turn to the other side of the waterway. "No one ever believed this little story of mine, said I must have hallucinated the whole thing. Sometimes I think it was just the grace of God, but . . ." She glances at me and Matthew out of the corner of her eye. "We live in a mysterious world, don't we?"

I remain speechless, and even though she was inebriated at the time, I'm inclined to believe she really did meet an octopus boy; the description, as little as was given, is in line with the "rules" our strange biology follows, completely unlike your typical depiction of merfolk in popular media—I doubt her drunken mind would've made up something so specific.

Margaret smiles. "My, you boys are shy." She straightens up, though it's more of a hunch, and points a knobby, thick-knuckled finger at the trees. "That big bird you were chasing, I think I've seen him flying around lately. He likes to spread his wings in the morning, then comes back to those woods after a while. I think there's a house tucked inside where he lives, but that's just a guess; I only started seeing him around this past year."

It sounds like he needs to get better at being inconspicuous, but her house is right across the waterway from those woods. I glance at Matthew just to make sure he isn't freaking out or anything, and seeing he's calmly looking out at the water and the houses lining the waterway, I bring my attention back to Margaret. "Sorry about being so quiet, ma'am. We're just a little out of our element is all."

Her smile loses its underlying mischief. "Oh, that's quite alright. I understand most folks wouldn't believe certain things even if it was right under their noses."

I can't say I'd be any different if I was normal. But I'm not, and I'm eager to get a closer look at a harpy, boy or no. "Your story certainly was unbelievable."

"That it was." She looks us over again. "I never did get your names."

"Oh, my bad. It's Mark."

She looks at the side of Matthew's face. "What about you?"

He glances at her, then dips his head down in an effort to cover his eyes. "Matthew."

"It's nice to meet you both."

Just as the words leave her lips, Tom kills the motor and docks the boat at their acquaintance's house. We all shuffle out—the relief I feel at being back on land nearly brings me to my knees—and Tom stalks past us to knock on the door.

"Thank you for helping us across, ma'am," I say as politely as I can.

She cups her face again, positively beaming. "Oh, it was my pleasure. If you're ever in the area again, don't be a stranger; Tom and I won't be moving anywhere anytime soon if I can help it."

I thank her again, not bothering to engage with Tom because he clearly wants nothing to do with us, and we go on our merry way to the woods that the harpy disappeared into. We stare into the midday shadows as I wipe the water droplets off my glasses with my shirt; when I put them back on, we walk into the woods.

"I'm glad we're off that boat." Matthew holds his hand against his chest. "I was so nervous I almost went active."

"You get nervous at the littlest things." I nudge him with my elbow. "But that old lady was pretty intense."

Matthew nods, grimacing.

"At least we got through the hard part; now to find that harpy!"

He looks at me all exasperated, laughing breathlessly. "You and your fetish."

"Like you aren't curious." I elbow him again.

He growls playfully and elbows me back, and we shove each other back and forth for a few dozen feet, leaf litter crunching under our flip-flops and the wind rustling the foliage above.

Suddenly, an owl hoots. We stop in our tracks, Matthew lifting his hat just enough to perk his ears from underneath.

A different owl, much farther away, hoots back.

Matthew puts his hat down. "I'm beginning to think this might be a bad idea."

I gaze at the treetops; there's nothing out of the ordinary. "It's a little late to be backing out now."

He shakes his head, walking on without me. "If I die, I'll kick your ass in the afterlife."

I chuckle breathlessly, knowing he isn't joking; I hope we don't have physical forms in the great beyond, but knowing my luck . . . I shake my head and half jog on sore feet to catch up.

We find an impressive light-blue two-story beach house a ways into the woods; there's a large rectangular in-ground pool with various articles scattered around, including plain black slides, colorful beach towels slung over white pool chairs, and a Bluetooth speaker playing moody alternative rock—so many signs of life, but not a soul in sight.

Matthew steps closer to the pool, lifting his hat to hear better.

I flick my tongue out, relying on my sense of smell to catch anything strange; there's a distinct lack of chlorine, the space permeated by the scent of ocean breeze and garlic powder, both with that telling musky undertone.

Suddenly, Matthew snaps around, and I don't get time to wonder what's got him all bug-eyed; someone grabs me from behind, brandishing a pocketknife at my neck.

Shock silences my entire being, reducing me to a rapid heart-beat, my only thought my impending death.

"Who the fuck are you?" a guttural voice asks, piercing my shoulder with sharp claws and locking me in place with sandpaper skin.

Matthew crouches, kicking his shoes off and effortlessly going active, a low growl emanating from deep within his throat; he brandishes his razor-sharp claws and lets his tail lash out from under his shirt, the appendage swaying wildly with his open aggression. Matthew revealing himself tells me all I need to know.

The man's grip slackens as he gasps at the sight of Matthew, so I immediately go active, maneuver my tail up and around the knife-wielding arm, and constrict as hard as I can.

The man grunts painfully but doesn't drop the knife, his claws digging deeper into my right shoulder.

I seethe, holding back tears, but don't relent in my onslaught against his arm; my ventral scales scrape against his rough skin and bend what feels like a fin on his elbow.

"L-Let go," the man wheezes, desperately resisting the pressure I'm putting on his wrist with the tip of my tail.

"Drop the knife."

He drops the knife, narrowly missing my foot, and gasps for air.

I unwind my tail from his arm and shove him back.

The man stumbles past me on webbed, dinosaur-esque feet, giving me a short-lived view of his massive shark tail, and falls face-first into the pool.

I drop to my knees, trembling all over from the adrenaline spiking my bloodstream. I grip my bleeding shoulder with my left hand, my collar and tail stinging from the sharkskin that was rubbed against them.

Matthew backs away from the pool, puts his paw on the handle of the knife, drags it toward us, and stashes it in his pocket.

Seconds pass, and the shark man fails to resurface from the pool.

As if the whole ordeal wasn't stressful enough, the harpy, now without his helmet, drops down to the edge of the pool from somewhere in the trees. "McGill!" He leans over the water with the wrist parts of his wings propping him up at the edge. He pays us no mind, waiting with bated breath for his homicidal friend to resurface.

Matthew's legs tremble, his tail puffed and flicking back and forth; he takes his hat off because it's better to hear rather than hide his cat ears from fellow monster people. He glances at me, his pupils dilated all to hell, and sinks to his knees with a hand over his hammering heart.

The shark man pops his head above the water, drags his left hand through his wet bangs to get them out of his eyes, and cradles the arm I constricted because my life depended on it. "I'm good, Caldwell. My gills took over for a second is all." He stares at us with calculating eyes, his open mouth revealing jagged shark teeth.

The harpy follows suit.

All four of us regard each other warily, not making another move. I study their features in an effort to calm down, starting with the one who tried to kill me. Both of them look no older than twenty, but the shark man has a meaner face framed by straight brown hair that reaches a little past his chin. He has the telltale pointed ears and light-brown eyes with round pupils, but I can't make out anything else because he's submerged in five feet–deep water.

I move on to the harpy, first regarding his wings now that he isn't hundreds of feet in the air; the topsides have white markings trailing through the middle of each wing, which have dark-brown feathers at the ends and medium-brown feathers from his wrists to his shoulders. When I reach his face, I'm intrigued by his hair and eyes; there's a clear divide in his short haircut—the top half is a dusty brown matching his shoulder feathers, while the bottom half is white—and his eyes are rust red. Much like the shark man, he has pointed ears.

The shark man sighs and grimaces, bringing his webbed, white-clawed hand to his face. "Dammit, they're just kids." He removes his hand and points at me. "Lizard, how old are you?"

I flinch. "Sixteen. We both are."

He mutters, "Not as young as I thought."

I don't verbalize my offense.

"Show me your shoulder, kid."

I take my hand away from my shoulder, the sudden cold on my clammy skin uncomfortable. I unbutton my shirt so I can see the damage myself, and it's not pretty; five bloody holes leak red down to my scales.

He looks at the injury he inflicted on me, clearly conflicted, and faces the harpy. "Why don't you patch him up for me, Caldwell."

The harpy nods, and I watch with poorly veiled fascination as he goes dormant: his wings reduce down to a feathery silhouette of his birdlike bone structure; his fingers slowly become distinct from his previously fused hand; then his feathers disappear altogether. He stands up on human feet and jerks his head at the sliding glass door leading into the back of the house. "C'mon, I'll clean you up, kid." He gives me a grin full of teeth just like mine.

⌒

Freshly patched up with waterproof bandages, I step out of the house and notice Matthew across from the shark man in the pool; his damp furry arms rest on the edge, his curly hair so drenched it hangs down to his chin. The two regard each other with cold gazes, contempt etched into their frowns.

The harpy joins me. "Oh? I see our uninvited guest made himself comfortable."

The shark man nods. "I told him he could." He looks at me. "You can come in, too, kid."

My shirt and shoes are already off, so I empty my pockets and slip in next to Matthew.

"What's your name, kid?"

"Mark."

He looks at my neighbor. "What about you?"

"Matthew."

He nods, then points to himself. "I'm Tyler"—he points at the now-active harpy—"and he's Gideon. Sorry about the knife thing. I thought you two were hunters or some shit."

"What made you think that?" I ask.

Tyler glares at Gideon kicking his legs in the water next to him. "Somebody gave me some bad intel."

Gideon holds a wing behind his head, gesturing as if he still has arms. "My bad. I couldn't tell that your hair is green and missed the ears and stuff."

"His hair is red."

"Oh, really?" Gideon laughs, like it's totally normal he can't tell the difference between polar-opposite colors. "No wonder I had a hard time seeing his blood against his scales."

Tyler notices my weird expression. "Gideon's color-blind. Most colors look greenish or yellowish to him."

That must suck. I don't comment aloud; I'm sure Gideon has received that sentiment many times.

"Anyway," Tyler says, "when did you two get cursed?"

"Cursed?" Matthew asks. "What do you mean?"

Tyler's expression twists. "Okay . . . When were you turned into a . . . uh . . . whatever the fuck we are?"

I slowly process Tyler's words, eventually recognizing the disconnect.

Matthew carefully says, "We were born this way."

Tyler's eyes widen, then he grins, then he laughs like he's gone mad. But he sobers within seconds. "You're serious?"

We nod.

Tyler's face screws up. "So you're saying that my children, and my children's children, will be fucking sharks." He raises his right arm, but flinches from the developing bruise; his fist flops back into the water. "That fucking bitch." He seethes, his face going red.

"Cool it, Tyler." Gideon rests his wrist on Tyler's shoulder. He faces us with his brow furrowed. "We weren't born like this. It's only been about a year now, so we're still coming to terms with what happened."

I say, "We've never met someone who wasn't naturally a monster person. And if it makes you feel any better, everyone we know has human parents and siblings; in theory, your kids would be human, too." I don't know if reproducing with a monster woman would have different results—I don't even know if monster women are real.

Tyler's expression softens.

Gideon rubs his shoulder.

Matthew takes a deep breath, crossing his arms over his hairy chest. "If you don't mind me asking, how did you become monster people?" He stares through the water at his cat paws. "I've always wondered where we come from. Why we exist."

Gideon's wing freezes. "Do you want me to tell them?"

Tyler lightly bites his lip, careful not to pierce his skin with his stalactite-like teeth. "I-I'll tell them." He lets out a shaky breath.

I can only imagine all the awful things that could've stolen their humanity; I wonder if we're the result of mad science or crazy magic, and which possibility is worse.

Tyler clears his throat, avoiding our eyes. "It was last year, in early August, the summer after we graduated high school. I'd been in California since June; I usually go out there every summer to catch some waves and all that, participate in competitions, maybe pick up a chick or two depending on how things go." He glances up long enough to catch my disgusted look. "And no, I don't two-time! I just have short flings."

Gideon blocks the left side of his face with his wing. "This guy will fuck anything that walks." He snickers at Tyler's expense.

"C'mon, I have *some* standards!"

Gideon flaps the end of his wing up and down as if trying to wave his hand nonchalantly. "Okay, okay. He'll fuck anything with tits."

Tyler runs a hand down his face, rolling his eyes up. "Let me make it clear that I only fuck women. Decently attractive women."

"Sure, bro."

"If you keep it up, you'll have to learn to preen with your teeth."

That ruffles Gideon's feathers. "Alright, I'll stop."

Tyler grins, then returns to his resting bitch face. "Anyway, back to the story. So last year, in June, I meet this chick on the beach who's kinda hot and definitely interested in me. She was a *bit* on the chubby side, but her tits were big, so I was ready to hit it if she was ready to put out. So we flirted a little bit and she watched me surf, and I could tell she wanted to get some and I was more than happy to provide. This girl, Courtney . . ." He pauses, as if saying her name leaves a sour taste in his mouth. "Became my summer fling. I was up-front with her that I don't do long-distance relationships, so once I came back to North Carolina for college, that was it. Relationship over.

"I had no idea she thought differently. Apparently she was insanely obsessed with me. Like legit crazy obsessed. I never noticed anything was wrong until Gideon told me I should break up with her."

Gideon says, "Courtney was my childhood friend, so I knew a lot more of her secrets than Tyler ever could. We became friends about the same time he started dating her."

Tyler clears his throat. "I didn't want to cut her off early, because goddamn she gave good head, but I knew Gideon well enough by then that I believed he had my best interests at heart. So about a week before my flight home, I met her at the beach and told her it was best we split a little early.

"It was cloudy that day, and not too hot. I met her early in the morning in a spot that almost nobody went near so we'd have a decent amount of privacy. I didn't plan to surf that day, so it was just me and the clothes on my back; she was dressed normally, and acted as she always did until I told her I was breaking up with her." Tyler stares through us with a smile, but there's no mirth in it, only teeth. "She smiled at me and said, 'We're not breaking up, Tyler. We're going to be together forever.' And she walked up to me and put her hands on my chest and pulled me down by my shirt and whispered in my ear, 'I'm not going to let my merman prince go.'"

Tyler frowns, taking in a ragged breath.

"I don't know how she did it, but those words, those stupid fucking words, forced my body to change into this, like she wanted me to be a merman so fucking bad it actually happened. She wanted me to be a monster no one could love so I couldn't leave her." A grin splits his face, and he hugs himself. "But after I suffered through what she'd done to me, she had the gall to act disappointed at the result! What the fuck did she expect?! That I'd actually look good as a half-shark freak?!" He's wheezing now, his face flushed red. "And while I was prone in the sand, barely conscious and in a lot of pain, she tore my shirt off and tried to . . . tr-tried to . . ."

"Hey, hey, hey!" Gideon puts his wrist back on Tyler's shoulder. "Go take a breather. I'll tell the rest, okay?"

Tyler nods, his hands gripping his arms so hard I'm shocked he hasn't pierced his scales with his claws; he walks to the deep end, submerges ten feet under, and huddles in the corner farthest away from us. His hair floats freely, his two dorsal fins bobbing up and down with every heaving breath he takes, and his oversize tail flops to one side.

"It's probably best I tell this part anyway." Gideon watches Tyler with a somber expression, then lays his eyes upon us. "I was there when everything went down, at about the time Tyler started screaming." He looks up, squeezing his eyes shut. "I don't think I'll ever forget those screams; I still have nightmares about it sometimes." He blinks rapidly before looking back down at us with a sad smile. "The good thing is we both made it out okay, human or not.

"I think I should start with Courtney. She was my neighbor since I was born; we did everything together. She was a typical girl who liked typical girl things. She had a Barbie collection and would rather play house than play sports." Gideon smiles awkwardly. "I'll admit I was pulled into an embarrassing amount of tea parties with stuffed animals back then, but I put up with it because I wasn't a fan of sports or roughhousing, and Courtney was always helping me out with my regular wardrobe malfunctions, so I thought I may as well humor her on her whims.

"Courtney didn't get weird until middle school. It was like a flip was switched in her head or something. It's hard for me to remember, but I recall her telling me about some dream she had once; whatever it was, she suddenly became insanely obsessed with merfolk, particularly mermen. I mean you couldn't step more than an inch into her room without seeing something related to sexy fish men." Gideon scrunches his nose. "I'll save you the dirty details on some of the things I found in there.

"Anyway, Courtney developed this obsession of hers over many, many years, waiting for something that came in the form of a boy named Tyler McGill. He was handsome and fit, good at surfing and swimming, and a real Casanova: the perfect target for her sick, twisted fantasy. Through her, I ended up hitting it off with Tyler, especially since we both enjoy surfing and skateboarding, so I tried to look out for him if Courtney pulled anything strange.

"Over the course of July, she said and asked stranger and stranger things about Tyler, all of them wildly absurd and usually related to how he would make a good merman. It got to the point that she was really freaking me out, so I told Tyler he might want to drop her before she does something insane." He glances at his feathery knees. "You can see I was far too late. I honestly think she was going to do what she did to him no matter the timing by that point. Maybe it was better it happened the way it did; I don't want to know what she would've done to him if she had him somewhere he couldn't escape.

"I made sure Tyler told me where and when he would be breaking up with Courtney because I had a bad feeling about everything going on between them. And I was right. I came to that beach to see him on his hands and knees, a tail bursting out of his back." He glances at it. "I wish I'd stepped in sooner, but I was so utterly shocked to see someone change like that out of nowhere I couldn't make myself move. And the look on Courtney's face . . ." He shudders. "I knew she was batshit crazy, but to watch that happen and smile like a madwoman the entire time . . ." He shakes his head and pulls his wings up against his sides.

"When she pulled his shirt off and hunched over his crotch, I knew I had to intervene; I pulled her away from him just as she pulled the zipper down from under his fly. I was so mad I threw her onto the sand and didn't even feel bad about it!" He winks with a wry grin. "So much for being a pacifist, right?"

The fact he can find any humor in that situation is a testament to his composure, or maybe that's just how he chooses to cope.

"Courtney got back up with nothing more than some sand in her hair, but all I wanted was to get her away from Tyler, and she knew not to test me. But she wasn't about to let me get away with stopping her, either; she told me she would curse me too if I didn't step aside.

"In any other world, I wouldn't believe her, but I'd seen with my own eyes what had happened to Tyler. So even though I was absolutely terrified, I raised my arms and stood my ground. She grinned because she knew I wasn't going to give up, and I think some fucked-up part of her mind wanted to destroy me for getting in her way.

"I asked her if she was going to turn me into a merman too, but she just laughed. She said something else would suit me better and told me I should take my shirt off; we'd known each other so long she gave me that one ounce of pity, a last hurrah to an old friendship. Deep down, I knew she was going to go with a bird because I was absolutely obsessed with learning how to mimic their sounds."

"So that owl earlier *was* you," Matthew says.

"Yep. I taught Tyler how to whistle a few so that we could discreetly communicate in certain situations." He grins, showing all his sharp teeth. "I'll admit it's different to whistle with these crazy teeth, but most of the sound comes from the tongue, so it wasn't impossible to adjust."

Gideon hardens his expression. "Anyway, at Courtney's suggestion, I took off my shirt and placed it on the ground, then waited for her to say the words that would end my human existence. But she never said anything, just looked at me with a hunger in her eye, trailing down my chest and back up to my face. I think she only had to think about it hard enough for whatever kind of sorcery she possessed to work on me. Maybe it was because she knew me that well, or maybe it was because she hated me that much for getting in her way. I can't know, really; I don't think even she knew." He stares into the distance like the answer hangs somewhere in the sky, but there aren't any clouds passing by.

Smiling tenderly, Gideon stretches out his right wing. "I watched in agony as my arm deformed itself into this wing, the pain of a thousand needles piercing my limbs as each feather grew out of my skin." He closes his eyes and stretches out his left wing. "But no matter how much my body wanted to shut down, I was determined to remain standing. I wasn't going to let Courtney win, and I think she was betting on my transformation being too much for me to bear, because when she saw I wasn't going down, she finally snapped. She cussed me out, saying so many things I never knew she thought about me; the racist shit was bad enough, but she even had the audacity to say I owed her for making her deal with my protanopia all those years, as if a few questions about the color of a shirt meant I owed her Tyler's body—I mean, how crazy do you have to be to demand an entire human being over that?!"

Gideon folds his wings and shrugs. "Courtney crazy, right?" He smiles, his gaze distant. "I'll admit that the only thing keeping me up was my hard head and a lot of adrenaline, which I knew would fade before long. We had to get away from her, and when she called fucking animal control on us, that was my last straw. I felt bad, but nudged Tyler to get up. He was in a lot of pain—hell, so was I—but we had no choice; it was either get out of there or be captured.

"Given enough prodding, Tyler got up and limped into the ocean, and once he went under the waves, I made my own escape; letting my adrenaline-fueled brain lead me, I took to the skies and flew for the first time." He leans back, propping himself up with his wrists. "It was the most amazing feeling in the world. I felt so free in that moment, so relieved that I was able to protect Tyler from that batshit crazy bitch I used to call a friend, but I felt so elated that I passed out midair and crashed right into the ocean. I came to some hours later in a sea cave, and when Tyler saw I was awake, he hugged me so hard I thought I was going to break in half; he cried and cried, and I'd never seen him so emotional before, so I felt bad I couldn't hug him back all that well without hands, but I knew he'd never hold that against me. I was just happy to be alive, you know?"

I slowly process their harrowing experience. "I'm sorry you guys had to go through all that. Our first transformation hurt, too, but we usually had an opportunity to get somewhere safe first. Not to mention your terrible circumstances."

Gideon waves me off with his wing. "I adjusted well, all things considered. Sure, I have to live far away from my family, but being able to fly is pretty fucking cool." He gazes at Tyler lazing on his side. "Understandably, Tyler took everything harder than me. He can't socialize like he used to, and he often has gill attacks whenever he gets stressed."

"Can he even stay on land?" Matthew asks.

Gideon raises his brow. "He can. He's fine most of the time as long as he gives himself a few hours to soak at night." He smiles gently. "He only got stressed because we weren't expecting guests today. The house isn't spick-and-span, you know?" He winks.

This guy is way too jovial . . .

"Anyway"—Gideon thrusts his wings out, giving us a good view of his crooked feathers—"would either of you be willing to help me preen?"

Gideon lies stomach down on a fully reclined pool chair wearing nothing but a loincloth; his wings stretched out, he rests his wrists on two other reclined chairs turned longways for his comfort.

"So how are we doing this?" I ask, hands on my hips.

Gideon feels around the base of his tail with his right wing. "There's something called a uropygial gland right around here." He taps it with his wrist. "It's like a nipple, but it secretes preen oil instead of milk. Real birds rub their beaks against it, but since I don't have one of those, your claws will work fine. You rub your fingers against it and rake your claws through my feathers. It's that simple."

The idea of rubbing a man's tail nipple doesn't exactly appeal to me. "Isn't this a little . . . intimate?"

Gideon smiles and stretches his wing back out beside him. "It's not any weirder than combing someone's hair." He shuffles and closes his eyes. "Then again, I've gotten so used to Tyler doing it that I don't think much of it. It's like a massage more than anything else. I won't make you if it makes you uncomfortable."

I remind myself of all the times I've handled Matthew or let other people handle me, from trimming claws to molting snakeskin to drying fur; for Gideon, preening his feathers must be just as vital for maintaining good hygiene. I steel myself and carefully part the orange feathers at the base of his tail until I find the oil-secreting gland; it's just a tiny nub of skin. Nothing to write home about. I take a deep breath and rub the gland between the sides of two of my claws; the oil itself is clear, reflecting a barely noticeable sheen in the sunlight. "Do you want me to start with your tail or your wings?"

Gideon shrugs. "Doesn't matter to me."

I rub oil onto all eight of my finger claws and comb through his tail feathers, easily raking through their length.

Gideon sighs happily.

I run my fingers through his tail until every feather is glossy and straight, then move on to his left wing; I figure it's going to take me a while because of its absurd length, so I ask, "How did you and Tyler get out of California?" He ended his story in a cave, and considering the timing, I wonder if Tyler missed his flight. But clearly they're both here, so they must've figured something out.

Gideon hums, stretching his flight feathers out for me. "Tyler was able to make his flight. We had to get back to his rental in the middle of the night so nobody would see us, and it took a few days for us to figure out how to shift into our human forms. Our phones were busted and our wallets ruined, but at least our credit cards didn't get corroded. Luckily, Courtney didn't bother coming to the rental house—I figure she thought Tyler was a lost cause, not that she was satisfied by what she turned him into, anyway. I think she might've thought I drowned because my parents were shocked when I came back home mostly unharmed a week later; never saw her again, but I knew her schedule so well I could easily avoid her. The real mess was dropping out of college so I could move to the East Coast."

"Damn, you had to drop out?"

His cheek lifts in a grin. "Yeah. I'd applied for a college near home, but with Courtney living right next door and what she'd done to me, I couldn't stay. Tyler had told me he'd put me up in his apartment if I didn't mind sleeping on the couch—but honestly, I use his bed all the time because he tends to sleep in the bathtub—so I figured I'd take a year off to work and apply to his college over here. I'll be starting freshman year this August. The real pain in the ass was explaining everything to my parents except the bird thing, then driving my car all the way across the country. I did some sightseeing though, so it wasn't all bad. It's really convenient being able to fly around sometimes."

Judging by his insanely tan back, Gideon must fly often. "I think you might've taken this whole harpy thing too well," I say, continuing to groom his wing.

He chuckles. "You could say that. I just try to see the bright side. I never really slept around like Tyler either, so it's not like I lost much in that regard—though it's hard to rub one out with wings."

God, I hadn't even thought of that; it's annoying enough with scales and claws, but wings? You got me fucked up with that shit. "What did you and Tyler look like before you were cursed?"

"I'm told I had dark-brown hair and amber eyes. As for Tyler, I personally can't tell any difference other than the shark stuff;

he didn't mention anything, so I wouldn't know." He folds his left wing just as I finish up; when I start on the tip of his right wing, he looks me over with his rust-red eyes. "What about you, kid? Did you always have red hair?"

I shake my head, surprised he's even asking; maybe he doesn't see exactly like I do, but it's nice that he cares enough to ask at all. "Even though we naturally awakened into monster people during puberty, Matthew and I were born human. I used to have black hair and dark-brown eyes like my mom; now I look like some twelve-year-old girl's awful OC."

Gideon grins. "At least you have a normal name. And you aren't some crazy angel-demon-vampire hybrid. And can't forget the obligatory cat ears."

I smile, glancing at Matthew nearby; he decided he didn't want to disturb Tyler's nap, so he's lounging in a pool chair with his eyes closed. I know he's listening because he has one ear trained on us, but he's too tired to conversate or just doesn't care to. "Matthew has enough cat in him for the both of us."

Gideon glances at Matthew's tail, its tip flicking with a moderate amount of agitation; sometimes I can't help making innocent digs at him, and most of his annoyance is in jest, anyway. Matthew scowls at us before turning over onto his side.

I comb through Gideon's right wrist. "I have another question."

"What's that, kid?"

"Why was Courtney disappointed by Tyler's appearance?"

Gideon scrunches his face with a thoughtful frown. "Have you ever heard of ABO?"

"Can't say I have."

Gideon's frown deepens. "Well it's your unlucky day." He clears his throat, looking awkwardly at the ground. "ABO stands for alpha, beta, omega. It's some fan fiction nonsense you wouldn't want to know about. The important part is that the alphas in these fics tend to have dog dicks."

I exhale awkwardly, not sure what Gideon is trying to get at.

He notices my strange expression and blushes. "What I'm trying to say is that there are people out there that are into some freak-ass animal dicks on otherwise normal human men. Courtney was one of those people, except she specifically liked mermen. My guess is she not only wanted Tyler to be a more traditional, both-legs-are-a-fish-tail merman, but also wanted him to have a dolphin dick. When she saw he was a shark, she was probably trying to see if he had claspers down there."

"But you stopped her from checking."

He nods. "Right. Fortunately, this whole monster business didn't give us monster dicks, but I wouldn't have complained about an extra inch or two if you catch my drift." He flashes a grin.

I'm perfectly happy with my completely normal human dick myself; some animals have gnarly members, snakes and cats included. But I gotta say, talking about monster dick while grooming a man's wing isn't my idea of a good time. "I'm glad I don't know any girls like that; our only female friend is mostly normal in that regard." I still consider Emily my friend, but Matthew's outburst definitely damaged our relationship. I hope it isn't too late for him to apologize to her; as much as I want to, I can't force him to say sorry.

Gideon sobers. "Does this girl know what you are?"

I glance at Matthew with his ears folded back. "She found out recently," I whisper. "It went well on her end, but not so much on ours."

Gideon glances at Matthew's paws and closes his eyes. "I think I understand." He stares at the pool. "As much of a player as Tyler was, what Courtney did to him will make him hesitant around girls for a long time. He constantly complains about being single but never tries to date anyone. His confidence took a nosedive after everything was said and done."

I nod solemnly, combing through the last few feathers of his right wing.

When I pull my claws away from his glossy, straightened wing, he asks, "Do you mind getting my leg feathers?"

I hesitate—preening his wings and tail was one thing, his thighs and calves another—but before I can decline, Tyler bursts above water. "I can't believe you'd replace me so easily, Gideon! And with a lizard, no less!"

"C'mon, you were sleeping! And I was getting tired of my feathers being all crooked!"

Tyler pouts. "You could've woken me up."

Gideon grins. "If I interrupted your beauty sleep, you'd never get another girl."

"Hey! You know I'm sensitive about that!" Tyler grimaces, pointing a sharp finger at him; a moment later, he drops his hand and deflates. "Plus, what girl would ever want to get with me looking like this?"

"I can name a few." We have Grace, Esther, Jenny, Emily, my mom, and probably way more girls that don't even know they'd be into guys like us. What sucks for me is that three are Jack's weird sisters, one literally gave birth to me, and one I just don't see that way.

Tyler gapes, then grits his teeth; he crosses his arms and turns his back on us, a pout surely on his face.

Matthew, wearing a pair of goggles I didn't know he had, dives gracefully into the deep end of the pool. Tyler and I watch him from the shallow end, chilling on opposite sides while Gideon roots around in their kitchen for lunch. Just as Matthew surfaces and takes a big breath, Gideon pops his head out from behind the sliding glass door. "Anybody got a problem with oven-baked salmon?"

We shake our heads, and Tyler shouts, "Make sure you use the good seasoning!"

Gideon makes a silly face, his lips quirked up like he wants to make fun of him. "It's just a McCormick mix, bro. You need to teach your folks that there's more to life than salt and pepper."

For what it's worth, salt and pepper is all you need for certain dishes, but others, not so much. And I had extended family that didn't season their food at all; I really don't miss tasteless slabs of overcooked meat with a side of soggy vegetables.

Tyler grunts, revealing his teeth; he tends to leave his mouth open more often than not, like he prefers breathing with his mouth rather than his nose.

While Tyler watches Matthew swim around like he's ten again, I observe his body through the perfectly clear pool water. Just as I felt while I was constricting his arm, Tyler has fins attached to his elbows, which stick out in front of him because he has his arms crossed; he also has fins attached to his ankles, which point toward digitigrade feet sporting four long, widespread toes with sharp white claws, each toe connected to the next by thin webbing. His tail is absurdly long and thick, flopping over far enough that the tip of his elongated upper tail fin touches the pool floor. His dermal denticles are sandpaper brown on top of his tail and white underneath in classic shark countershading; interestingly, there are faint medium-brown spots decorating his legs and tail.

"What're you looking at?" Tyler scowls, which isn't much different from neutral.

I stop staring and consider my options; as much as I'd love to pet his tail, he's pretty prickly and I'd rather not piss him off again. "How do your gills work?"

Tyler uncrosses his arms, revealing five open slits below each pec. He points at his face. "I breathe water through my mouth like air." He points at his gills. "I get my oxygen and the waste comes back out through here."

"Can I watch you breathe underwater?"

"No."

"Can I pet your tail?"

Tyler's face screws up. "Why would you want to pet my tail?"

"Have you ever pet a ray at an aquarium? They're really smooth." Also a little slimy, but I'm not worried about that.

Blushing pink, Tyler huffs and turns his side toward me. "I-I guess I'll allow it." He's being surprisingly cooperative; maybe he's trying to solidify the fact that he isn't as monstrous as he thinks he is.

A stupid smile on my face, I wade through the water and situate myself next to his massive tail. Considering our sensitivities, I place my hand directly in the middle of his tail and stroke toward his tail fin; it's soft, smooth, and squishy to the touch. Tyler accepts my petting quietly, eventually relaxing after he gets used to what I hope are comforting sensations. "What type of shark are you?"

"A sand tiger shark. It's a type of nurse shark. They're docile for the most part; I've seen one or two the few times I've gone exploring the ocean."

Ironic, coming from a guy that attacked me without a second thought. "What about Gideon?"

"He's a killdeer. It's a type of shorebird."

"Weird name."

Tyler shrugs. "Apparently the name comes from its call."

I can't imagine what *killdeer* would sound like in a bird's chirp at all.

After one last stroke, Tyler whips his tail to the side, inadvertently slapping the pool wall; he faces me again, arms crossed. "I think I've had enough." His cheeks are so red I can't take his natural scowl seriously.

I back off to the other side of the pool, giving him his much-needed space.

Matthew pops out of the water next to Tyler.

He jumps.

"I'm surprised you let him pet you at all." Matthew takes his goggles off and pushes his wet bangs out of his eyes.

Tyler grimaces, turning his nose up in the air. "I don't owe anyone an explanation."

Matthew stares at his cheek, his lips flat. "Can *I* pet your tail?"

Tyler glares at him out of the corner of his eye. "Why do *you* want to pet my tail?"

Matthew makes a decidedly catlike expression, drifting off into his own world. "I love sharks."

Tyler slumps, but turns aside anyway, putting his tail within Matthew's reach.

Matthew wades over, having to stand on the tips of his toes to keep his head above the water; supporting the above-average girth from below with one hand, he strokes Tyler's tail around the middle, petting it twice before letting go.

"Thanks." Matthew backs off closer to me.

Tyler faces us again, looking more annoyed than embarrassed. There's an uneasy silence as he regards us, staring ominously at our faces. Out of nowhere, he asks, "Either of you got a girlfriend?"

I stare at him blankly. "What do *you* think?"

Matthew averts his eyes.

Tyler says, "I don't know. You said you know girls that like this kind of stuff, so I figured one of you got lucky."

I leer at the back of Matthew's head, noting his out-turned ears. "Matthew had a chance with one, but he blew it."

"Mark!" Matthew seethes, both furious and terrified.

Tyler grins. "What'd you do? Stare at her boobs too long?"

If only . . . I glare with equal measure back at Matthew. "Why don't you tell him, huh?" I've had enough of this, enough of him ignoring the big picture.

Matthew looks away, his ears plastered to his wet hair, and grabs his elbows. I expect him to refuse, but he says, "Fine. I'll tell you." And he explains what happened back in March, every little detail he can remember, stitching together what Jack and I have told him about Emily along the way. Throughout the entire tale, Tyler stares at him with a blank face, so flawlessly neutral that I have no idea what's going through his head. By the end, Matthew purrs softly, trying to comfort himself after relaying such a stressful story.

"So let me get this straight." Tyler crosses his arms. "This girl liked you, found out what you are in one of the worst ways possible, still liked you anyway, arguably liked you more because she's into this freaky monster shit, and you decided it'd be a grand old idea to let your insecurities get in the way. Have I got that right?"

"Basically," Matthew says, his voice wavering pitifully.

"Kid, I'm not gonna mince my words: you fucked up."

"You think I don't know that?!" He sobs, his anger completely overshadowed by sorrow.

"Look, I get it. I'm scared shitless at the thought of showing some girl how I look now. How many girls out there would want to fuck a glorified fish?"

Neither of us reply because we all know the answer.

"But believe me, I would *never* let that fear push a nice girl away. I don't care how nervous it makes me, or if I have to take it slow with her, or if there are days I want to break down in her arms: I'm not letting a good girl go, not anymore; a guy like me can't play around like that." Tyler looks up into the trees, past the foliage, and regards the clear blue sky. "You know, they say there are plenty of fish in the sea, and that's true, but most of those fish are carp; what you have right under your nose is an ornate sleeper ray, one of the rarest fish in the world; you'd be a fool to let that fish swim away."

Matthew hangs his head, his arms falling to his sides. "It's too late. She already swam away."

Tyler looks at him with a shockingly soft expression. "I don't think so, kid. Like I said, you have a rare one; she's been putting up with your shit for over a month now, and it doesn't sound like she's given up on you yet. So here's my advice to you."

Matthew stares at him, totally and utterly desperate for advice he shouldn't need.

"You need to apologize to her. Get on your hands and knees if you have to. Kiss her ass if you have to. Do whatever she asks you to do. Don't give excuses, don't put a damn thing on her: this was all on you, and you need to own up to it." Tyler raises his brow. "Do you understand?"

Matthew nods vigorously, but I don't miss the tug of a grin on his lips.

"What's got you all smiley?" Tyler asks, quirking an eyebrow.

Matthew says the dumbest thing I've ever heard come out of his mouth. "I'd kiss her ass in a heartbeat. She wouldn't even have to ask."

A wicked grin splits Tyler's lips, revealing two rows of gnarly shark teeth. "So you're an ass-kisser, huh, kid?" He suddenly goes dormant, the only obvious evidence left of his inhumanity the teeth in his mouth and the rows of pale scars that used to be gill slits. He glances at me and jerks his head at Matthew. "Grab him, Mark."

You don't have to tell me twice! Without a second of hesitation, I slide behind Matthew and hook my arms under his armpits, lifting him a few inches off the floor of the pool; unable to plant his paws on the ground, he flails uselessly in the water.

Tyler propels himself across the pool; within a moment, he clears the distance, grabs Matthew's furry legs, and hoists them over his shoulders.

Just as Gideon walks out in a gaudy apron to tell us lunch is ready, Tyler and I throw Matthew into the air; he plops with a pitiful splash into the deep end, and when he resurfaces with his hair all in his face, I laugh so hard I can barely breathe.

CHAPTER 20

Wherever I Am

Ashley

sit down in one of the three foldable chairs Bobby brought to the beach, eagerly placing my heavy beach bag onto the sand right next to it.

Bobby eases himself into the chair on my left, leaning back and resting his ankle over his knee. "I'm glad you came out, Ashley. How've you been?"

"I've been doing better these days, getting out more and all that." I don't want to get into too much detail yet. "How about you, Bobby? Have you told Luke yet?"

Bobby averts his eyes, a guilty grin on his face. "I'm still getting around to it."

"Are you now?" I raise an eyebrow. "I know it's already been a year, but it's better late than never. It'll only get harder the longer you wait."

"I know, I know . . ." He sighs, puts his foot back in the sand, and slumps forward. "It's just . . . how do you even bring something like that up? 'Hey, son, I know you're part bear, but it's all good!'" He covers his face. "Ah, God, it's killing me. He's awkward enough around me already."

"He *is* a fifteen-year-old boy. They're supposed to be a little awkward at that age." Luke isn't especially awkward around me, but there's a massive difference between your friend's mom and your dad who you're trying to keep a huge secret from. Mark has never been terribly awkward with me, but he's a bit atypical; Matthew and Jack are more in line with typical teenage-boy behavior toward parents. "I wish I could give you better advice, but Mark was so young he told me himself, so I can't say I know any better than you." Not to mention I had previous experience with a very sexy wolf man. Who happens to be my boyfriend now. And is going to be in my house later today to take care of Glenn; I hope he doesn't find those old photo albums . . .

Bobby frowns, glancing into the distance; when he turns his head, he lights up with a smile. "Kyle's back."

I look to my right. Not too far away walks a man of average height, his skin strongly tanned into a grayish-brown taupe; secured by a toothed headband, his dark-gray hair hangs down to his shoulders in a combed-back style. He holds a red-and-white cooler in his arm, his other hand shoved into his swimming trunks pocket. As he gets close, he regards me with haunting eyes that are such a dark brown they appear black, his thin lips hard-set into a neutral frown that exacerbates his wrinkles; he looks so much older than Bobby, and . . . his ears are pointed at the tips.

"Finally back, are ya?" Bobby says.

"Yeah. Forgot the cooler back at the camper," Kyle drawls in a shockingly heavy Southern accent; he sounds like he came straight out of the country. "And who's this here?" He gazes at me.

"This is Ashley. You know, the lady I mentioned to ya."

Lifting his chin, Kyle grunts; he takes his hand out of his pocket and holds it out to me. "It's nice to meet ya. My name's Kyle Ratcliffe, but you can just call me Kyle."

I grasp his rough palm.

The veins on his toned arm bulge as he gives me a firm shake.

"I'm Ashley Koenigsegg, but you can just call me Ashley. Bobby has only had good things to say about you."

"Likewise." Kyle lets go of my hand and stares at me and Bobby for a moment, gauging something, then places the cooler down next to the chair on my right. "I'll be in the water. Y'all can get back to your conversating." He stalks off to the shoreline and submerges his wiry legs up to his calves in the rolling waves.

"I hope I didn't offend him somehow." I observe Kyle's firm back; he has the body of a man who spends most of his time doing physical labor.

"Nah, he's just not good with new people," Bobby says. "He probably thinks he might scare you off; he's rough around the edges, but he means well."

"I see." I'll have to let him know I'm not at all bothered if he's a little antisocial; of course, I'm also incredibly curious about his pointed ears, which might be part of why he's so standoffish. "I guess we should get back to conversating."

Bobby smiles good-naturedly. "You know how much I love talking." He always has little stories to tell from his work as a salesman, and his easygoing personality makes it easy to talk about anything I can think of. Bobby thanks me for watching over Luke these past few weekends, which I tell him is never any trouble; those boys are already awfully independent for their ages, and Luke's a real sweetheart, just like his father.

I wish I could say I have as many stories to tell, but being an operations manager is about as dull as one could imagine; it pays, but it's nothing to write home about. "I figure Luke is with his mother this weekend?"

"Yep." Bobby rolls his eyes. "She's one of them women who thinks she ought to be worshipped this time of year. I feel bad for him, but it's part of our deal." He told me about his arrangement with his ex-wife a few months ago. They didn't want to go through a long legal battle or lose a lot of money in court fees, and their twins weren't getting along so well at home, so they agreed on split custody. He told me he hates leaving his daughter with his ex-wife, but she's never come to visit harmed in any way, so he doesn't have a leg to stand on. In three years she'll be eighteen, at which point he hopes she'll move back in with him or live with Kyle because she won't belong to anyone but herself.

I say, "I try not to be too overbearing on my son, but it's hard not to worry about him sometimes." I lean forward and look down the stretch of beach on our left, Matthew and Mark long out of sight. "He's always been an adventurous boy." And reckless at that. I hope he knows better by now not to stick his nose where it doesn't belong, even if it works out in the end; that scar on his face is the worst he ever got, but there's no telling when he might come across a much more dangerous situation than a scared cat boy.

"Mine is the opposite!" Bobby laughs. "My daughter's the one always dragging him toward trouble. She's a wild child, I tell ya."

"She sounds like a handful, but I'd love to meet her sometime."

"You might get your chance here yet; her mother is moving back into the area. Got a new job or something; I only know what Heather's told me." Bobby frowns and glances at the clear sky. "I'm glad she'll be closer, though, so I'm not so far away if she needs me."

I can't imagine being separated from my child; it'd be torture never knowing if Mark is okay and being taken care of. I know a lot of people say moms have a special bond with their child that no dad ever could, but I've also known plenty of neglectful mothers in my time. Plenty of neglectful fathers, too. I've known good people and bad people and everything in-between, and I believe Bobby's on the better side.

As the waves crawl over the shore and the sun beats down on my pale legs, my phone buzzes below me. Bobby watches me reach down into my beach bag and pull it out; I hope it's an update from Mark, but it's a message from Alex. Bobby quirks his brow at the half-sour, half-surprised face I make, and when I open the messaging app and see what Alex sent, I can't help the short burst of laughter that escapes my lips. It's a picture and a text: he's clearly lying on my couch, Glenn loafing across his stomach with his eyes closed, totally content to have his ass on my man's chest; his text says, *I think your cat likes me.* I don't have the heart to tell him that Glenn is an extremely friendly cat, nor that he's partial to animal people because he's around them all the time.

"Did you get a text from your boyfriend?" Bobby jokes.

I smirk. "Actually, I did."

"Shit, really?" He smiles. "When did that happen?"

"A few weeks ago, but I've been seeing him since January."

"What's he like?"

I tell Bobby a little bit about Alex. I tell him about the frat parties where we met, his struggle with alcoholism, my struggle with food, and our chance meeting at a bookstore in October. I tell him that he's a doctor, and has hair long enough to braid, and likes food spicy enough to kill his taste buds. I tell him that he's honest, and lovely, and encouraging, and I can't get enough of his legs. Maybe I said too much, but I love him with a passion I haven't felt in a long time.

Bobby grins, the wrinkles at the corners of his eyes so prominent. "He sounds like a good guy. And whatever he's doing is working out for you; I can tell you've put on a few pounds."

"Bobby!" I cry, wanting to cover my face. "A gentleman doesn't make comments about a lady's weight!"

"Oh, c'mon! It's a good thing in your case!"

I know he's right, but it can be hard to watch the number on the scale rise even a fraction of a pound; I've gained three more since February, and as essential as they are, I don't like a single one. "You're right. I know you're right, but . . ." I rest a hand on my stomach.

He stops grinning. "I know it's hard. Sorry for bringing it up."

I shake my head. "No, it's alright." I glance at Kyle's back, just as he lifts his heavily tanned arms in front of him. I can't see what he's holding, but a familiar sound drifts from him; I think, distantly, that I've heard whatever instrument he's playing before. It's light and airy, if a little shrill, and the melody breaks through the din of waves and crying gulls. I remember a movie from many, many years ago, back when we still had a VHS player and Mark had yet to meet Matthew. We were watching one of those *Pokémon* movies, the one with the legendary birds, and the main theme had something like it. It was—

"I was wondering when he'd start playing that ocarina." Bobby wears a fond expression. "He's always had impeccable timing."

I wonder if Kyle could hear us at that distance, if he played just to break the mood. "What song is he playing?"

Bobby shrugs. "Something he made up. He used to do the same thing with a harmonica back in the day. Well, he still plays the harmonica, but he picked up the ocarina a few years ago. Luke had a game on his Nintendo 64 centered around an ocarina, Kyle decided he liked how it sounded, and here he is playing one like he's been doing it his whole life. It's real impressive if you ask me."

Nintendo 64 . . . It was such a long time ago that we got one of those for Mark secondhand. Then it was the GameCube and the Wii, and now he mostly plays on Xbox One. I tried playing a few party games once or twice way back when but could never get into them like he did; video games simply don't appeal to me.

I listen to the music Kyle plays as the waves wash over his lean legs, letting myself forget about my fears for a long moment; he eventually stops, finishing his first improvised song that sounded perfectly planned. "It *is* impressive. I was never musically inclined growing up. I listened to music plenty, but never played it."

"Same here," Bobby says. "Kyle was a lot more help to Luke when he wanted to pick up guitar than I ever could've been. But you know something funny?"

Kyle starts playing again.

I ask, "What's that, Bobby?"

"Kyle can't read a note of sheet music. He's totally self-taught—all pure instinct. He ain't a professional, but it sounds nice anyway."

"It does."

We listen in a comfortable silence, each soothing melody chipping away the fatigue built up in our lives—even the animals are enraptured, some often-fed gulls wading in the shallows behind Kyle.

"Do you mind if I talk to him for a moment?" I ask. "I don't want him thinking I'm scared of him. And he's your friend, so he can't be all bad."

"Want me to call him over?"

I shake my head. "I don't mind getting my feet wet."

Bobby smiles.

I put my phone away, stand up—it takes more effort than I'd like to admit on account of the angle and the sand—and walk to the line where the sand is soaked through; the waves roll in and out, almost in rhythm with Kyle's ocarina, and I dip my toes into the shockingly cold water. Keeping my hat steady with one hand, I gingerly wade through the ocean to Kyle's side; the ocarina, now that I can see it, is off-white and resembles something like a smoothed-out seashell. Kyle plays with his eyes closed, like shutting out his sight enhances his ability to play.

"That ocarina is beautiful," I say.

Unstartled, he opens those deep dark eyes and stares, abruptly ending his mystical melody; he pulls the ocarina away from his mouth. "Thank ya kindly."

"I was wondering if you might like to join us."

He stares at me a moment longer, then glances back at Bobby.

"She don't bite!" Bobby yells.

"I know she don't bite!" Kyle yells back loud enough that I cover my right ear. He looks at me with a hint of concern. "Sorry 'bout that, sweetheart. Bobby likes to tease me sometimes. Gets on my nerves." He regards me, squinting his eyes like I'm a predator in human skin. "I suppose I'll join y'all. Just had to get my nerves out." He walks toward the shore, pocketing his ocarina.

"Your nerves?" I ask, barely keeping up.

He turns his head, looking me in the eye from the corner of his own. "You were staring at me. Made me nervous."

"Oh, I'm sorry." I must've been homing in on his ears more than I thought.

"Ain't no trouble, darlin'." Kyle reaches the trio of chairs and sits in the one on his left while I return to the middle. He takes a tiny cylindrical container out of his pocket, pulls out a toothpick, and puts it in his mouth like a cigarette.

"Finally decided to join us?" Bobby asks.

Kyle pulls the toothpick out of his mouth, holding it between his index and middle fingers. "I was convinced," he says, unamused, and returns the toothpick to his mouth. He turns his head and stares across the expanse of beach to our right.

Bobby quirks his lip. "You're no fun, you know that?"

Kyle pulls the toothpick out again. "Ain't my problem, Bobby." He plays with the blunt end of the toothpick, swinging it back and forth. "You know, I could go for lunch right about now." He turns back to us, regarding me again. "How 'bout you, honey? Hungry yet?"

"Oh, I . . ." I wouldn't say I'm hungry yet, but I could be, and Kyle's trying hard not to grin like he's up to something. I face Bobby. "I wouldn't be against it."

"Oh, so I'm the gopher today?" Bobby grins.

"That's right," Kyle says. "What're you thinkin'?"

"Hmm . . ." Bobby strokes his nonexistent beard. "Well, you've never been here, so what do you want, Ashley?"

"We *are* at the beach, so seafood? I understand if you've had enough of that, though."

"Nah." Bobby waves his hand in the air, winking. "I haven't had my fill yet, and Kyle could eat shrimp every day and never get sick of it."

"It's true," Kyle says.

"Then I'd love to have oysters," I say. "Cooked oysters; I'm not brave enough to have them raw."

"Cooked oysters." Bobby smiles. "I can work with that." He looks past me at Kyle. "They have shrimp just about anywhere, so I have you covered, too. I'll figure myself out when I get there."

"You do that, Bobby," Kyle says. "I'll keep Miss Ashley company."

Bobby stands up. "You better be nice."

"When am I ever not nice?"

Bobby shakes his head, smirking. "I'm just covering my bases." He quickly checks his swimming trunks for his wallet and makes sure he has his money. "Be back when I'm back." With a wink and a wave, Bobby strolls across the beach and exits to one of the many parking lots.

Kyle sighs, leaning far back in his chair. "My goodness, he's a handful."

I wonder if they're playing it up just because I'm here. "Why'd you send him off, Kyle? I figure you're not really all that hungry yet."

"You're right, I'm not, but I figured you wanted to speak to me without Bobby around."

"What makes you think that?"

A painful smirk crosses Kyle's face. "I know you've been starin' at my ears. And the scent of my kind is strong on you."

I gape, truly shocked he just came out and said it. "Kyle, you . . ."

"It ain't no big deal; you know five of us it ain't too hard to recognize more. And I know Bobby's been talkin' to you 'bout Luke." The troubled look on his face and the way he's trying to melt into his chair says otherwise.

I calm myself, bringing my expression back to neutrality. "May I ask you some questions?"

He nods and straightens up, but his toothpick-holding hand shakes.

I'll start slow. "What animal are you?"

His thin lips disappear into a straight line. "I'm a possum." His face is full of disgust.

A possum . . . I regard his dark-gray hair and his prominent widow's peak, and even though his skin isn't light like an opossum's face, I can see the resemblance to the fur on their backs.

He nervously watches me, fiddling with his toothpick.

I think back to Bobby, wondering why Kyle needed him to leave. "Does Bobby know?"

Kyle shakes his head. "He don't know. I told him a long time ago that it's just a birth defect. He believed me 'cause he had no reason not to."

I frown. "Why don't you tell him now?" I figure since he knows about Luke, his best friend shouldn't be a big deal.

Kyle looks away. "I've been lyin' to him for forty years. I can't . . . What if . . ." He shakes his head again, his eyes glossy. "I can't lose Bobby. I'd die."

"You wouldn't lose him. It's not as big a deal as you think it is." I want to reassure him, but I don't quite believe myself.

He shakes his head again. Plays with the toothpick. "That ain't the only thing."

"What else is there?"

He grits his teeth. "I shouldn't tell you."

"I promise you; I won't tell Bobby anything you tell me. I haven't even told Luke that his father knows. I can keep a secret if that's what it takes to help you."

He stares at me. "Why you wanna help me so bad? I'm just some devil creature. I ain't worth the trouble."

I frown deeply. "Kyle, you aren't a devil creature. You're a person. I won't have you calling yourself that because you're not just insulting yourself. You're insulting my son, Bobby's son, their friends, and my boyfriend. So please, let me help you."

Kyle keeps staring, stares into my eyes and my soul, then looks away. "Bobby's daughter."

I gape. "His daughter?"

Kyle nods. "His daughter ain't human either. I've been helping her fool her family since she turned."

"What . . . What is she?" So girls . . . girls *are* possible.

"She's a grizzly, just like her brother. She's smarter than him. More conniving. She had no trouble keepin' it under wraps." He presses against the middle of the toothpick, bending it, but it doesn't snap. "She was only eight, and scared. I wasn't gonna put her into trouble. Bobby was having a hard enough time with his wife, and I couldn't know how he would react. How that woman would react. I worry for her. I really do. She's like my own daughter."

I can't imagine hiding not only himself, but Bobby's daughter, too. And eight years old is so young. "Is she . . . okay, with her mother?"

"She's survivin'." Kyle sighs. "I'm still the one that buys half her shit, though. Ruby don't like to acknowledge that her little girl is becoming a grown woman. I tell ya, bras ain't cheap."

Oh, I know. I've gone through dozens of cup and band sizes in my time, mostly in part to my inconsistent weight. I don't look forward to outgrowing my current bras, though there's a chance I won't; the way weight distributes itself can be fickle.

"But like Bobby said, I'm glad she's movin' back to our area. She told me her girl friend lives nearby, too, so that gives her options if she needs to get out of the house; she's resilient, but everyone has their limits."

"I'm glad . . . she's not unsafe." I may not know her, but I care about her well-being.

Kyle nods. "They've been living with her maternal grandparents the whole time, so it ain't all bad. They're not as harsh on her as her mother."

"I see." Bobby's family situation gets more complicated the more I'm told. I've only known him a few months, and most of our interactions have been sparse conversations over the phone. I can't give good advice without more context. "Can I ask you something more personal?"

Kyle leans back in his chair, his gaze tired. "What's that, honey?"

"How did you and Bobby meet? Or . . . what's your story? If you don't mind telling me. I'll listen to anything and everything." I pause. "Or nothing, if that's what you want."

Kyle grins, flashing his surprisingly normal-looking teeth; they're slightly crooked but not particularly sharp. "There ain't much to a man like me, but . . ." He stares at the clear sky, eyeing the gulls; his grin turns into a more genuine smile. "I don't mind talking to the air."

I lean back and look away, becoming nothing more than part of the scenery.

"Bobby and I, we come from a small town in the country, near the Appalachian Mountains, the sort of town where everybody knows everybody. Bobby lived in a big house with ten siblings; I lived in the trailer park with my mama. I was an only child, the product of a random tryst with a man I'll never know. Anybody in that town could've been my daddy 'cause my mama was the town prostitute; she'd do any man for enough pay, didn't have much in the way of standards. I figure my daddy wasn't White, though; my skin gets too dark in the summer.

"Anyway, since everybody knew everybody, everyone knew I was the town prostitute's bastard child, and I was badly ostracized for it. I couldn't be at home much 'cause my mama was always workin', and some of them men were right awful, cheatin' on their wives and not hesitating to beat a child if you so much as looked at 'em wrong. So I spent most of my days outside; I was dirty, and awkward, and didn't trust nobody anyhow. It was a religious town, and I'd been dragged to church enough times to have a bit of faith in me; some days, faith was all that kept me going, kept me doing what I had to do to survive.

"Eventually, the day came I turned for the first time, at the tender age of eleven. I was out in the woods on my little hammock that I strung up between some trees. I remember that it hurt a lot, but I dealt with it because I believed it was divine punishment for being born a bastard; it was only natural, I thought, because my existence itself is sinful. Out there, anything they wanted could be a sin, and anything they wanted could be righteous. I was always repenting. Always. I know better now.

"But that day, lyin' sweaty and hurt in my hammock, I had one wish. I was lonely, and now I was a creature, so I prayed to God. I said I'll never ask for anything else in my life if He'd answer that one prayer. I said, 'God, I just want one friend. Just one. I don't even care who it is. I don't care if he's a boy or a girl, White or Black, dumb or smart, or anything under the rainbow. Just one, God. Just one.' I was struck by such a sadness that I cried. I don't cry much over anything. The last I can remember was when I held them twins in my arms for the first time.

"I spent a week gettin' used to myself before I returned to school; most folks thought so little of me it wasn't unexpected for me to skip class, and I was still in elementary school so they didn't care all too much. But I looked a little different even in my human form. My hair wasn't black, and my ears were deformed, but I never got haircuts much so I was able to cover them with my, as the other kids put it, old-man hair. I was already teased a lot to begin with, but now them kids had more fuel for the fire.

"There was only one kid who never really bothered me, but that was because he was too busy botherin' other people. They called him Big Bad Bobby Brown. He was fat and mean, and if you dared to cross him, he'd beat you senseless. I didn't like him much, mostly because he was scary. Nobody disciplined him 'cause he was smart enough to butter up the teachers, especially the ladies. People got tired of dealing with his hotheadedness, so they stopped messing with him. But Bobby had a strong sense of justice, a big heart under all that anger.

"Most kids, they just talked shit to me, never did anything crazy. It was easy to make me the butt of a joke, especially if they were makin' digs at my mama. But there came a day I didn't feel right, and I got tired of all the joking, so when one boy dug at my mama again, I told him his daddy had been hangin' around lately. He didn't like that much, me talkin' 'bout his daddy with the whole class listenin'. They all started laughing at him, which only made him angrier at me for making a fool of him.

"Before I knew it, he grabbed my collar and was gearing up to punch my face, which scared me a whole lot because I hadn't been in a fight since I turned, and I had a feeling a little bit of pain would force me to let the possum out. But nothing happened because Bobby put his hand on that boy's fist. He didn't have to say anything because everybody knew if Bobby put his hands on you, you were in trouble. He'd beat you in a second, anytime, anywhere. The boy dropped his fist, let go of me, and sat back down. They stopped joking after that day, too scared Bobby would step up for me again.

"Bobby approached me after school that day, even walked me home. He told me he was sorry for never defendin' me before; I told him he shouldn't be sorry because I didn't deserve defending. A man defends himself. He didn't like that, but he didn't say nothin' 'bout it.

"He kept walking me home after that. As mean as he was, he had no friends either; I guess he was lonely, too. I gave up and started talkin' to him after a while, even though he scared me as much as he scared the rest of the kids our age. Eventually, I wasn't begrudgingly dealing with his presence, but looked forward to seeing him; you could say we were friends.

"It didn't take long for me to learn why Bobby hung out with me for hours and hours after school. He didn't have the best homelife either: his siblings picked on him and his father was too quick to anger, the kind of man that spouts, 'Spare the rod, spoil the child,' but forgets that you shouldn't provoke your child to anger; it wasn't unusual for his father to beat him with a belt over tiny things. We were eager to grow up and skip town.

"Bobby and I did everything together. We'd laze about and play, even bathe in the river from time to time; Bobby snuck me into his house once or twice so I could use his bath since the one at home was gross and tainted with my mama's lovemaking. I stole my first harmonica from one of her customers, then I started stealing packs of cigarettes. We'd smoke sometimes, contemplating life. I stole a rifle, and we entertained ourselves shootin' cans until we ran out of bullets. We both did wrestling starting in middle school, and even though he was a heavyweight and I was quite a few weight classes below him, I'd still take him on anytime.

"After nearly a decade of knowing each other, we finally graduated high school and had a decision to make. I had some cash from picking pockets, but we were both pretty much broke. But we got a little lucky; my mama, awful as she was, had saved a couple thousand dollars for me. She told me to take it and go somewhere. And Bobby's father had provided him a car, so with my money and the car, we set off together and went to the city. We found a shitty one-bedroom apartment. I started workin' construction contracts, and Bobby made do as a server at a little diner a mile away. We saved up so he could go to college; I wasn't smart like him, so I saw no reason to waste my time or what little money we had. Those were hard years, and we probably spent too much money on cigarettes and booze, but he graduated, and I moved on to janitorial work, which didn't pay any better, but it was more stable and actually had benefits.

"Bobby got a real nice job, and before long, we were able to save enough to buy two houses in the same neighborhood, one for me and one for him; his was bigger than mine, but he planned to start a family one day, and although I always wanted to start one too, I knew my chances of that were pretty low. I still have that same house, but can't say the same for Bobby.

"More years passed and I pursued some of my passions. I got myself a 1991 Nissan 240SX hatchback. She's a beauty; I always take good care of her. I worked on that car all the time, and I got my concealed carry and a couple guns. Bobby and I would go out to the shootin' range together, or go bowling, or even mess around at the local skating rink for the heck of it. I'd say we had a jolly old time of things, but the day came when Bobby finally found the woman of his dreams, or so he thought.

"We were getting older, the both of us already in our thirties, and Bobby had been datin' around a long time by then, but he was a romantic at heart and wanted desperately to find 'The One'; at the ripe old age of thirty-three, he met a young woman at work named Ruby. She was a pretty little thing: tall, long red hair, and hourglass curves that would make any woman jealous. She worked in a different department and knew well how to play the game, but couldn't hide that she had some interest in Bobby, who wasn't bad-looking himself; he and I worked out a lot, and at six foot two with muscles to die for, she'd be kiddin' herself not to consider him a catch. Bobby loved her like she was the finest wine God himself poured from the grapevine, but Ruby . . . I think she saw him as a prize, a trophy in the shape of an Adonis worth little more than a good time.

"Bobby and Ruby dated for two years, during which I had my own short-lived romance with all the time I had to myself, and as Bobby worried about the perfect proposal, I noticed something different 'bout Ruby; we were out on the town together for once, as Bobby and I figured Ruby and I may as well cultivate a friendship if she was bound to be his wife, and I noticed she smelled like she was pregnant. I knew she and Bobby were both using protection, but they aren't 100 percent even with perfect use. I didn't say anything because it'd be a strange thing to claim I knew on account of her smell, but sure enough, she had a positive pregnancy test a month later. Bobby was elated—he loved her with all he had and would've wanted to have a family with her after they married—but Ruby was horrified; I'm sure if her circumstances were different, she would've aborted those babies.

"You see, Ruby came from a family not too unlike Bobby's: real Southern and real traditional, the type of people that believe all women should be child-rearin' and homemakin'. Ruby was a modern, independent sort of woman, but she was held down by the expectations she was raised with; if her parents found out she was pregnant out of wedlock, they'd have her head. So she and Bobby chose to have a shoddy shotgun wedding at a nearby chapel, all before Ruby started showing in hopes her family would be none the wiser; fortunately, Ruby had a long waist on account of her height, so it wasn't cutting it too close even with twins. It was a painful ceremony to watch because I could tell Ruby wasn't happy, and I wondered how long they would last.

"Ruby's pregnancy progressed with no complications whatsoever, and after thirty-six weeks, she gave birth to Luke and Heather, both blond and brown-eyed like their father, though Heather looked just like her mother otherwise. They were fussy and exhausting, as babies are, so I often helped out when they were little and Ruby needed a break—she had quit her job soon after the second trimester and spent the majority of her time at home, but children are their own full-time job at that age and it wasn't like I was all that busy with anything after working hours anyway. I'd help her get her naps in, clean up for her here and there, and sit and talk with her sometimes 'cause I was sure it got lonely being at home by herself so much. Ruby hadn't really prepared herself to be a mother, and I had a feeling she may have been suffering from postpartum depression, but she wouldn't see anybody no matter how often Bobby or I nudged her to. The whole thing had done a lot to her general disposition, making her overall more pessimistic and exhausting to be around, but she was Bobby's wife, so I cared for her just as I cared for Bobby no matter what she said or did.

"After about two years, both babies had been weaned and Ruby started leavin' 'em with Bobby more often than not; the both of them had gotten quite a bit out of shape, being new parents and all, and Ruby was eager to 'get her body back,' as she put it. I'd often accompany Ruby on her gym excursions, even though some of them were majority women: we did yoga, barre fusion, HIIT, Pilates, CrossFit—you name it, she was signing up for a class or two in each. So Ruby lost most of her baby weight, but some stubborn pounds decided to hang on to her no matter what she did, which frustrated her to no end, and, eventually, she gave up on the whole thing. I knew she wasn't satisfied with her new physique, but what she failed to realize is that just because it was different didn't mean it was bad—she had bigger boobs and wider hips and her belly stuck out a little, but she was still mighty beautiful and certainly far from unattractive; Bobby had no complaints for her and loved her just the same as ever, but Ruby didn't love herself no more, hadn't ever since the day she found out she was pregnant.

"Ruby managed to maintain her new normal for the most part, only gaining a few pounds back on account of returning to work and general lack of exercise, and Bobby got closer to how he was pre-baby with a bit of encouragement on my part. Things were stable for a few years, but when the twins turned five and went off to kindergarten, things went downhill again. Ruby was always partial to Luke for the most part, probably because her family valued firstborn sons more than daughters—and as enlightened as she was before she got pregnant, every second she spent with her family dug her deeper into traditional ways of thinking—so she liked Heather less and less the older she got. Heather was always a bit of a wild child, getting into things and nearly killing herself with her recklessness, so it was only a matter of time before she crossed a line and earned her mother's ire; not long after she started public school, she had her first kiss.

"Just like her daddy, she was a little romantic and perfectly curious about her sexuality, which isn't ridiculously unusual I'd say, so long as it don't go too far. She asked what sex was at four and all kinds of other questions about human biology due to a child's natural curiosity, and Bobby and I thought it was best to educate her before she heard and believed strange rumors from her peers or prudish adults—of course we taught Luke these things when he brought them up, too—and it was no surprise to me that she'd explore the more innocent things, like kissing, at her age. In any case, we told her she shouldn't run around kissin' boys like that—to which she asked if it was okay to run around kissin' girls—but we didn't hear about any more kissin' after that and figured she was doing as she was told.

"But Ruby wasn't all that happy her little girl was being so promiscuous and doubled down on her unfair treatment of Heather, refusing to let her wear clothes that were too short—most of what she wanted to wear in the summer was barely above midthigh—and often harassing her about what it means to be a proper lady. It was getting quite ridiculous, and before long, Heather found ways to get away with disobedience without her mother knowing, oftentimes taking refuge in my house when she was particularly upset; as much as I felt for her predicament, I was not her father, so I always let Bobby know when she was with me so he'd know where she'd gone. But that changed when Heather hit puberty.

"As I told you before, little Heather turned for the first time shortly after she turned eight, the youngest age typical for White girls to hit puberty. She was feelin' sick and came over to my house, and thinking back, I'm pretty sure she always had a feeling I wasn't a normal man—young ones have that sixth sense to 'em. I saw that her nails were unusually sharp, and her ears were pointed, so I knew what was happenin' to her; I told Bobby as I usually did that she was with me, but I didn't tell him that she was under the weather. I comforted her while she turned, even showed her what I look like with the possum out so she had an idea what was happenin' to her even if she ended up a different animal entirely. She held my thumb with her little hand, and even when her long claws started digging into my skin, I let her keep holdin' tight. She fell asleep shortly after her first change ended, and I had to resolve myself to help her keep her new secret.

"Her grizzly problems weren't the only issues I helped her with over the years. When she started buddin', she came to me about getting training bras, and later on, proper bras. When she started her period, she came cryin' to me about the pain and the blood in her panties, and I had to teach her what was goin' on with her and buy her pads and pain medicine so her cramps wouldn't force her to let the bear out every month. She talked to me about crushes she was havin' and what feelings were normal to feel about the maturing boys around her. I tell ya, I had to humble myself before a great many women in that time because I would've been absolutely lost otherwise. I read a lot of books, too, and had my patience tested more times than I can count. But I'd do it all over again in a heartbeat.

"During those years, Bobby and Ruby's marriage continued to break down. Ruby became more and more controlling, and subsequently more and more unhappy. She stopped trusting me and didn't want me around her or her children, not that they listened to her much; she felt *I* was the one making them kids hate her, when she was the one doing all the damage herself. At some point, she gave up on it all. She told Bobby she wasn't happy and wanted a divorce. She never said anything else. I don't know if she was cheatin' on him or not because I didn't keep track of her schedule and didn't much care to know anyhow, but I knew she'd been unhappy for over a decade by then.

"Bobby was in disbelief for a time and did all he could to negotiate with her. He begged her not to leave him for weeks and weeks, but she wouldn't budge. She just cried and told him she could never be happy with him. So, his heart shattered to pieces, Bobby signed them divorce papers and let Ruby move in with her parents, taking poor Heather with her. Ruby really wanted to take Luke, but Heather knew he wouldn't be able to take livin' with that bitter woman by himself, so she took that sacrifice; I hated to see her go, but I had prepared her to face the world without me and trusted she had the smarts to keep herself safe. And I was always a phone call away; I'd drive across the whole planet to get 'er if she asked me to.

"There were a lot of bad memories in that house, so Bobby moved in with me temporarily while he worked on selling it and finding a new, smaller place for himself and Luke. That lasted about a year, and once Luke finished sixth grade, they settled about twenty minutes away in a decent neighborhood in a different school district. While they were livin' with me, I made sure Bobby didn't eat himself to death and taught Luke about strength training when he showed interest in getting in shape—he was a big kid, just like Bobby when he was little, but didn't have a mean bone in his body to stop bullies from pesterin' him—and later helped him get football fit so he could join the team at his new school.

"With some newfound confidence, Luke made a lot of friends and was out of the house most weekends, so I spent a lot of quality time with Bobby. Naturally, he was depressed and would waste away if I let him, but I did my best to show him you don't need no woman to love life. Some days he wanted to do nothing but watch TV, and some days he wanted to cry in his room, but no matter what he was feeling, I tried my best to keep Bobby company. He's still sad sometimes, but he's doing so much better these days. It makes me happy that he's made a new friend, too, one who knows what it's like to have a son like me. Life hasn't been kind to either of us, but at least we got support where it matters."

Kyle shifts in his seat, groaning from his stiff posture; he pops that crooked toothpick back in his mouth.

"It sounds like you've both been through a lot," I say, "but I can tell you both care for each other deeply."

Kyle smiles softly. "I love Bobby; he's my best friend in the whole wide world." He squints in the bright sunlight. "God answered my prayer, and I kept my promise to Him."

I gaze across the ocean, the blue sky so clear it hurts.

My phone buzzes again, interrupting the last few minutes of silence between me and Kyle; I lean down and pull it out of my beach bag, relieved to see it's an attachment from Mark. I waste no time opening up my messaging app; he sent a photo of himself and a boy I've never seen. The boy is a few inches shorter than Mark, sporting bicolored hair and serrated teeth. A few moments later, Mark texts, *We're okay.*

"Oh, I've seen that boy before," Kyle says, making me jump. "The one with the red eyes. The yellow-eyed one is yours, right?"

"Goodness, Kyle . . ." I hold my hand over my heart. "Yes, that one is my son, Mark. As for the other one, I can't say."

"I'm not sure where he's from. Saw him myself for the first time last week; he came down from flyin' to hear me playin' my ocarina." Kyle holds his chin. "I think he said his name is Giddy-something-or-other."

"He came down from flying?" I want to be sure I heard that one right.

"Yep. He's a little harpy boy. Got big wings and everything." Kyle points at the skyline on our left. "I saw him flyin' out there with a helmet on real early in the mornin', but he came down and walked over to me while I was mindin' my own business. I don't think he's from around here 'cause I ain't never seen him 'til now."

I slowly breathe out my nose, lightly pinching the bridge. I'm not going to worry about how Mark managed to meet this boy or where he is for that matter because he's clearly in some sort of kitchen or dining room. He's safe, and that's all that matters right now.

"You alright, honey?" Kyle asks.

Just trying not to have a heart attack! "I'm perfectly fine. Thank you for asking." I rest my phone on my thigh and lean back again, adjusting my sun hat so the sun stays out of my eyes and I can still see Kyle's face. "Can I ask you some more questions?" Anything to stop thinking about what the hell Mark got himself into this time.

"I ain't got a problem with it."

"Are there any other people like you that you've met? Other than this Giddy boy and Bobby's twins, of course."

Kyle leans back, squinting at the sky. "I only ever met one other individual, and it was right here on this beach, too. Some old gent washed up to shore in nothing but a square-leg swimsuit; he looked normal for the most part, but he had some interestin' eyes on him."

"Can you tell me about him?"

"I remember he was real annoying: he spoke all fancy-like and didn't know when to shut up—I tell ya, I got real tired of hearin' about his wife and his kid and his kid's fiancée, and felt pretty offended when he said I was lucky he was in no condition to hold me down; he said he was some kind of gene scientist and wanted real bad to 'examine' me with the possum out. I could tell by his eyes that he was some kind of octopus or somethin', but he was a real skinny fella, so I bet I coulda fought him off if he tried anything funny—then again, I suppose it might be hard to pin down that many legs no matter how weak they are.

"Given some patience and some proddin', I figured out the man had gotten himself lost at sea—he was meant to be up in Maryland, not down here at Holden Beach—and since he was starving and pitiful, I gave him some sunglasses to cover his eyes and took him to a fast-food place for breakfast; after all was said and done, I drove him to a spot he could hail a taxi and went on my merry way. I hope I never see that guy again 'cause once was tiring enough for a lifetime."

I wonder . . . "What color were his eyes and hair?"

"His hair was gray and his eyes were orange, but I think he said his hair used to be the same color as his eyes when he was younger. Guess some of us still gray naturally."

"Do you remember what he smelled like?"

"Fish mostly, but I caught a hint of leather in there."

Small world, huh . . .

"What about you, honey? I know you've met more than a few of us creatures."

I smile. "I only know the five you can smell on me." I start counting them on my fingers. "There's my son, Mark; his friend, Matthew; my boyfriend, Alex; Luke, of course; and . . ." I pause.

"You know Jack, right?"

Kyle nods. "Mm-hmm. Smells like mowed grass. I never spotted what he is, though; we haven't interacted much."

I figure it's not my place to tell him what Jack is, so I leave it at that.

"I actually have a question for you." Kyle's neutral expression betrays nothing.

"What's that?"

Kyle holds his arm out. "I've always wondered what I smell like. If you don't mind, could you tell me?"

"I don't mind." I smile, taking hold of his forearm; I pull his wrist under my nose, get as close as I can without brushing against his skin, and sniff deeply. "You smell like . . . peaches."

Kyle takes his hand away as soon as I loosen my grip, but there's an obvious grin on his face. "Heather told me that, too, but I didn't believe her."

⌒

"Bobby sure is taking his time," I say.

"He probably knew I needed a little while to warm up to ya," Kyle says. "We've known each other so long he knew I was up to no good; that, and he's real indecisive 'bout food when he wants to be."

I recall Bobby put a little bit of everything on his plate at Delilah's Christmas party, so that doesn't surprise me. "It amazes me you never once slipped up around Bobby after forty years."

Kyle grunts. "I guess I just got lucky. And I've always been a bit emotionally stilted, so I don't feel the need to let the possum out much. The few times I was sick, I just covered up so he wouldn't see nothin'—a hat and a blanket usually did the trick as long as I was lyin' down. The closest I ever got was when I had to have my canines removed."

"Oh, gosh." I'm shocked he's totally nonplussed. "What happened?"

Kyle grins, his gaze on the ocean. "I used to smoke a pack a day, which wasn't so good for my dental health; my canines got so rotten I had to get them replaced with implants—of course, my old teeth were much longer. I still miss them sometimes, but that's what I got for smokin' like a chimney so long. Probably coulda brushed my teeth more often, too."

I wrinkle my nose.

He wheezes laughter. "I was a gross guy twenty, thirty years ago. My mouth ain't made for kissin'."

"Have you ever kissed someone?"

"I've been kissed twice in my time. The first time was right awful; back before I turned, some little girls were daring each other for popular dolls at the time, and one got dared to kiss me; I had to be held down before she stole my virgin lips, and the experience really put me off from kissin' girls ever again. The second time . . ." Kyle stares up at the clear sky again, closing his eyes and removing the toothpick from his mouth; he opens his eyes, glances at me, and glances away. "I suppose I don't mind tellin' you 'bout Julia."

"You know I'm happy to listen."

Another breathless laugh escapes him. "Hmm. Julia was my brief rendezvous back when Bobby and Ruby just started dating. I used to frequent a bar on their date nights so Bobby wouldn't feel the need to invite me along; I'd order a beer and some wings and smoke for about an hour or two at the bar. I kept my ears covered and had lost my natural canines by then, and I looked old enough by smokin' that my hair wasn't all too unusual to your average barfly. I'd chat on occasion if spoken to, but mostly just sat and thought about life.

"About a month into that routine, a petite little thing started frequenting the bar; she'd sit herself on the stool next to me, order a Scotch on the rocks and some chicken tenders, and smoke her own cigarettes. I thought she was pretty, but never said nothin' to 'er, but all my glances caught her eye eventually; inevitably, we started talking about this and that every time we saw each other. The most I ever learned from her was that she came from a Romani family but left home as soon as she turned eighteen; I could empathize with leaving family behind when they weren't no good for ya, though she never said why she wanted to be on her own. She had black hair and the most beautiful blue eyes I'd ever seen; I'll admit I was smitten with her and all her mysteries, but it didn't last all too long.

"There came a day we were both feelin' hot and bothered 'round each other, and when we were done eating and drinking and smoking, she asked me to come outside with her; she brought me out back behind the bar where nobody was lingerin', and the look on her face told me she was wantin' me. I remember her starin' up at me with half-lidded eyes, this woman who couldn't be much more than five foot even, and I found myself leanin' down to meet her; she kissed me, but it was too fleeting for me to kiss her back. Then she watched my face, waiting for something that wouldn't come.

"I remember it was drizzlin' a bit, but I took my hat off in hopes that it would help her out with her problem, whatever it was. When she saw my ears, she reached up and trailed the edge of my left, and I knew she knew what I was, and I wasn't surprised when she looked away, disappointed. But the reason was not because I was a creature; no, she had planned in that moment to turn me into one, but you can't turn a man twice. I know it sounds crazy, but Julia was a witch of sorts from what little I could get out of her. She admitted that she wanted to force my loyalty to her by that twisted form of blackmail, even though I would've got with her with no such arrangement. I didn't know enough about her life to understand why she would think that way, but the damage had been done. I told her it wasn't right to manipulate a man's body and mind like that; I was honestly disappointed in her, but I still saw her to a taxi before going home alone. I went back to that bar for another month, but never saw her again."

"Witches . . ." I gaze across the sea. "Do you think that's where your kind come from?"

"Maybe," Kyle says. "I figure witchcraft makes more sense than some hodgepodge experimentation; the human body shouldn't be able to change the way mine does, not by normal means. I figure some long, long time ago, one of my ancestors had a spell cast on him in some manner I can't comprehend, and I'm the living proof it ever happened."

"That's unbelievable." It'd have to have been centuries ago, wouldn't it? I can't remember any of George's folks, much less mine, being anything but normal.

"It is, but there's no other way I can explain it. Maybe Julia was talking crazy talk, but I'm inclined to believe she was telling the truth."

I let the silence linger, imagining what Mark's ancestor may have been like. He could have been from anytime, anywhere. That ancestor could've even been a she. "If you saw Julia again, what would you do?"

Without a hint of hesitation, Kyle says, "I'd sit down with her and ask her how she's been, and I wouldn't care whether that leads anywhere or not; I'd just be happy knowing she's alright."

I recall that night in October when I met Alex again. I wonder if that was how he was feeling, putting his phone number in my hands. And I barely hesitated to give him my number, and now I—

"Why're you covering your face, honey?" Kyle frowns with his toothpick in his mouth.

"I need to tell my son about my boyfriend, but I'm worried he's going to be upset about it. It's only been four years."

"Hmm . . ." Kyle pulls his toothpick out and fiddles with it with his thumb, staring at the horizon. "Change is hard, honey; I would know. But how about I make a deal with you."

I pull my hands away from my face. "A deal?"

He nods. "I know I need to talk to Bobby about everything. I promise I'll tell him by the end of Luke's summer break if you tell your son about your boyfriend. But I think I'll leave Heather out of this one; she's old enough to speak for herself."

I look down at my lap, at the phone resting on my thigh. "Okay. I can work with that."

Kyle leans back, puts the toothpick in his mouth, and smiles.

Bobby finally appears over the horizon; it's been so long I'm actually hungry.

When he gets close enough, Kyle asks, "What took you so long?"

"What? Did I worry you?" Bobby grins, his eyes crinkling.

"Hmph." Kyle huffs, lifting his nose in the air. "Like I'd be worried about you, old man."

"You act like you aren't the older one." Bobby shakes his head, grunting as he sits down next to me, and gently places the plastic bags of our takeout next to my beach bag; he bends down to pull out each plastic container. He hands me the first: oysters Rockefeller with a side of roasted potatoes. "I hope that'll satisfy you; I thought you might like something on the fancy side."

It certainly seems healthier than fried oysters, but I'm well aware restaurants love to load food up with salt and butter. Anyhow, I promised myself not to worry too much about calories; I'm on vacation, for crying out loud! "Thank you; it looks wonderful."

Bobby smiles and checks the next container; he hands it to Kyle from behind me. "Here's yours, old man!"

Kyle takes the container, immediately puts it on his lap, and opens it. "Shrimp and grits." He smirks. "My second favorite breakfast food."

"What's your first?" I ask.

Kyle's smirk turns into a full-on grin. "Shit on a shingle."

"Kyle!" I smack his bicep with the back of my hand.

Kyle chuckles and pulls some bottles of water out of the cooler next to him; he passes one each to me and Bobby.

I choose not to engage with Kyle's immaturity and face Bobby. "What did you get?"

"Fish tacos." He shows me the contents of his container: three soft tacos with tortilla chips and salsa. "I took so long because I was deciding how I wanted it cooked. And which fish." He cradles his chin. "I went with blackened mahi-mahi. Slightly healthier than fried, slightly more expensive than tilapia, and the most delicious."

I finally turn my attention to the food in my lap. I take my plastic fork out of its wrapping and begin to eat. I scrape the innards out of the first half shell and relish in its buttery taste; my only complaint is having to use a full-size fork rather than the tiny, three-pronged ones typically offered for oysters.

Lunch passes quietly with little bits of small talk here and there, the lulls of silence full of crying gulls and rolling waves—some of those gulls become incredibly invested in our lunches, to our chagrin—and after we're done eating, Bobby shoves our empty containers into the plastic bags they came in and leaves to dispose of them properly.

Kyle leans down, opens his cooler, and pulls out a rich-blue can with a big white logo; he takes one for himself and holds another out for me. "Want one?"

I shake my head. "No, thank you."

Bobby returns quickly, once again sitting down next to me; Kyle hands him the can of Bud Light by reaching out behind my head.

"We're technically not supposed to drink on this beach," Kyle says, cracking his can open, "but it's not like anybody enforces local ordinances around here."

Bobby cracks his can open, too, the beer froth bubbling through the small opening. "Don't worry; we're responsible drinkers."

"Most of the time." Kyle grins.

Bobby grins, too. "It's been a long time since I got drunk."

Kyle makes a face, like he knows the last time very well, but says, "I've only ever gotten buzzed."

"I hope neither of you want to change that today." I sip my water with a poorly veiled smile.

"Nah. I gotta drive myself back to the camper later; can't be drivin' drunk," Kyle says.

"Same here." Bobby glances at his beer, then across me at Kyle. "Why don't we make a toast."

"To what?" Kyle quirks a brow and smiles, holding his can out behind me.

"To . . ." Bobby furrows his brow, bringing his can close to Kyle's; he looks at me and says, "To new friendships!"

Kyle grins. "I'll drink to that!"

They knock their beers together and take nice, long sips, the sun bearing down on our heads.

CHAPTER 21

Something's Got to Give

Matthew

Gideon leads us out front to his vivid-blue Jeep Wrangler, whistling and spinning his keys on his finger; after lunch and some back-and-forth texts between Mark and Miss Ashley, he agreed to drive us to the campground for dinner. He unlocks his car and we pile inside, our two new acquaintances in the front and me and Mark in the back—fortunately for Mark, Gideon washed the blood out of his shirt in their washing machine, but he's going to have a hard time explaining the holes in the right shoulder to Miss Ashley.

Gideon turns the ignition and takes a moment to hook his phone up to the car stereo; as soon as shockingly girly pop blasts through the speakers, he pulls out of the driveway.

Gideon focuses silently on the road ahead; occasionally, Tyler warns him when an upcoming light is red or green, but Gideon seems more than capable of telling based purely on the position of the brightest light.

I look out the window and watch all the colorful cars pass us by, wondering if there would ever be a good reason to turn someone into a monster person; it's easy to imagine survival scenarios where gills or wings would be lifesaving, but how many sorceresses would curse someone with good intentions? Even so, I hope our ancestors were cursed by a nice sorceress, not some crazy sex fiend with an awful fetish; there's not much harm in having weird interests as long as they don't hurt anyone, but clearly Tyler was deep into the hurting territory. I'm glad that even though Emily is into cat boys, she'd never do something like that to me; I'm certain of that, and it's another reason among many why I need to stop being an asshole to her. I hope she forgives me, but I don't expect her to. Maybe she'll never want to talk to me again.

Mark pats my shoulder, jerking me out of my thoughts. "Chin up, Matthew. It'll all work out." He smiles softly.

Tyler glances back at me from the passenger seat, his hair perfectly windswept. "Have some faith in her, kid. She doesn't hate you."

I look back outside as we near the campground. *Have some faith . . .*

⌒

Gideon parks next to Miss Ashley's black Subaru Forester. There are two other vehicles on the lot: an old white Ford Taurus and a red Ram 3500, which I assume belong to Mr. Brown and Kyle. The strong scent of grilling meat overwhelms me as we exit the vehicle.

We walk around the large white camper and spot Mr. Brown and Miss Ashley sitting under the attached awning. A few yards away, a heavily tanned man stands at a small portable grill; wearing a headband holding his dark-gray hair back, it's easy to spot his pointed ears—he must be Kyle, and it's obvious just looking at him that he's another monster person. I share a look with Mark, confirming that he's noticed, but we previously agreed not to approach him about it out of respect for his privacy; since not even Teddy is sure about him, we figured it's something Kyle prefers to keep to himself.

Gideon lights up and drags Tyler by the hand over to Kyle, saying something about last weekend; Mark and I walk over to Miss Ashley instead.

"There you two are." Mr. Brown grins. "Y'all were worrying your mom sick."

"Bobby . . ." Miss Ashley frowns before standing and wrapping us in a hug.

We immediately reciprocate.

"You *did* worry me sick"—she pulls back and cups our cheeks—"but I'll forgive you if you explain yourselves."

"Sorry, Mom." Mark puts a hand on the back of his neck and glances at Mr. Brown. "Is it alright if we step inside?" He points at the camper.

Mr. Brown nods. "Kyle won't mind; just keep your hands to yourselves."

We head into the camper using a pull-down staircase. It's compact, yet comfortable: there are beds on each end; a tiny couch and a similarly small TV; a minuscule bathroom; a compact kitchen fit with a fridge, stove, and sink; and a dining booth against the opposite wall. A heady peach scent permeates the space.

Miss Ashley sits on the right-side bench, so Mark and I sit and face her from the left.

She requests that we tell her everything, so we do. Throughout the story she develops such a disappointed frown that I feel horribly guilty for going along with the whole thing, and the mortified gasp that escapes her throat when we get to Tyler's unexpected assault makes me feel even worse; even with my sharp claws, Mark's fate was totally in the hands of the man with the knife at his neck, and we were lucky he wasn't expecting us to be monster people—Mark's quick thinking with his tail certainly helped, too.

"Can I see your shoulder?" She stares at the holes in Mark's shirt.

Mark unbuttons his shirt halfway and shrugs his sleeve and collar down to reveal his bandaged shoulder; he runs his fingers over the waterproof bandages, his brow furrowed. "It's not as bad as you think it is, Mom." He smiles unconvincingly. "Gideon changed the bandages before we left, and the cuts already stopped bleeding."

Miss Ashley stares at Mark's shoulder, her eyebrows drawn up and a frown on her face; she pushes her lips into a thin line. "I want to be mad at you both for being so reckless, but I can't say I would've done any differently in your shoes." She rests her elbow on the table, massaging her temple. "Just . . . Please be more careful next time. People can be incredibly dangerous, monster or not."

Mark buttons his shirt back up, then takes Miss Ashley's unoccupied hand. "I promise it won't happen again. Not even if I see a cute girl."

Smirking, I shake my head. "I don't think you'll be seeing any girls anytime soon."

Miss Ashley makes a bemused expression before letting go of Mark's hand. "Can you tell me a little bit about those animal boys you met?"

Mark puts his hands back in his lap. "First of all, I think they'd be classified as monster boys—"

"That's beside the point," I say. "They're both freshly awakened. They said they'd been cursed by a girl they knew almost a year ago. I think they're both nineteen because Tyler said he'd just graduated high school at the time and Gideon said he had to take a gap year due to everything that happened."

"I see." Her lack of shock at the revelation astounds me.

"I should add that Tyler is sensitive about how his appearance has changed, so don't say anything about it, especially his teeth; as for Gideon, he doesn't seem to care all that much."

Miss Ashley smiles. "I know better than to comment on someone's appearance, thank you very much. That goes for everyone."

Having learned our lesson after explaining everything, the three of us return outside; Mr. Brown is sitting where we left him, but now Tyler is sitting at his right side nursing a bottle of water. Miss Ashley returns to her seat at his left, leaving Mark and I to take a seat on a wooden picnic table on the other side of the firepit in the middle of the lot. Between our two groups, and on our left, Gideon helps Kyle plate a bunch of quarter-pound burger patties and thick sausages. He has burger and hot dog makings on a foldable table nearby, including buns, an assortment of condiments, sliced cheeses, onions, tomatoes, and iceberg lettuce; in addition, there are large bags of kettle-cooked potato chips, what appears to be some sort of onion dip, a bottle of Coke and a pitcher full of what I assume is sweet tea, two stacks of red Solo cups, one stack of paper plates, a box of plastic utensils, and a roll of paper towels.

"Food's ready," Kyle says, turning off his grill. "Y'all can serve yourselves."

All of us take turns filling up our plates—I figure out that the sausages are bratwurst, and the tea is in fact sweet—then we manage to cram ourselves onto the picnic table: Gideon, Mr.

Brown, and Miss Ashley sit on one side; Tyler, myself, and Mark sit on the other; and Kyle pulls up one of his foldable chairs and sits at the end adjacent to Tyler and Gideon. The adults at the table bow their heads, and the moment they raise them and pick up their food, we all begin to eat.

After our first few bites, Mr. Brown tries to strike up a conversation. "So, Tyler, was it?" he says, looking at the man in question. "What keeps you busy these days?"

Tyler startles, placing his fork down and straightening up with a wince; he rubs his bruised arm, clears his throat, and pushes some errant hair behind his ear, revealing a gleaming diamond stud earring. "Oh, uh, I'm a college student. Exams were just this past week, so I'm done for the summer. I'm thinking about getting a job until next semester. Maybe retail or something like that."

Mr. Brown smiles. "It's good to get some experience when you can; the extra cash definitely helps, too!" He eats a chip dipped in homemade onion dip. "What are you studying?"

"Marine biology. I'm also taking the marine-conservation option for my degree, though I won't be taking any of those courses until my junior and senior years."

"Yeah, those first two years are usually full of general courses and whatnot. I tell ya, I don't miss it at all. And these days employers are pushing more and more for graduate degrees; I'm glad I'm good at what I do, else they'd be dropping me for a fresh grad in a heartbeat."

"Why do you say that?" Tyler asks.

Mr. Brown grins. "It's 'cause they can pay them less. Us seniors are more expensive."

Tyler picks his fork back up. "I hope I won't have too much trouble finding a job once the time comes."

"Your résumé will be important, but as they always say, it's about who you know, not what you know. Focus on making connections and it'll work itself out."

Tyler nods sheepishly. "I'll keep that in mind." He brings the fraction of burger patty he cut out to his mouth and quickly bites it off his fork, chewing slowly with his mouth closed in an effort to avoid flashing his teeth. He's so adamant about hiding them that he'd rather eat a burger without a bun, but props to him for going through the trouble, I guess.

Mr. Brown takes that as his cue to move on. "How about you, Gideon? Are you also in college?"

Gideon holds up a finger, taking a second to swallow the chunk of bratwurst in his mouth. "Nah. I had to take a gap year because of a family matter last summer. I've been working as a server this past year, but if everything works out, I'll be a freshman come August."

"Do you have any idea what you're going to study yet?"

Gideon eats a chip and crosses his arms. "Hmm . . . I'm not sure yet, but I know I want to travel. I've thought about fashion merchandising once or twice, but I'm not ready to settle yet." He takes another chunk out of his bratwurst dog, his serrated teeth making easy work through the meat and bun; when he finishes chewing, he looks at me and Mark. "Actually, do either of you know what you want to do after high school?"

"I want to be a math teacher," Mark says.

"I want to be a pediatrician," I say.

"Really?!" He looks absolutely flabbergasted. "I didn't peg either of you for the type to work with kids."

I shrug, taking a bite of my moderately dressed burger. I've always thought, if I'm going to make a difference through my work, I'd like to be able to help kids like me one day; there aren't many of us, but even one would be more than enough for me, and there's a chance I'll come across monster parents with human children who'll need support, too. As for Mark, I imagine he wished he could've had another adult in his life when Miss Ashley was grieving too much to truly look after him; those were hard years for us both, but at least we had each other.

"I don't mind kids as long as they're not too young." Mark brings a chip close to his lips. "I'd probably work middle or high school, honestly. Probably middle because nobody wants to work with kids that age. It'd be easier to find a job."

"Sounds like you've got it figured out," Gideon says, then chews on another chip.

Mark shrugs, mimicking him. "We'll see where life takes me."

Dinner goes on with plenty of small talk between Mr. Brown and Gideon, Miss Ashley and Kyle chiming in every now and then while Tyler, Mark, and I mostly enjoy our meals. I've never been much of a conversationalist in large groups, and Mark tends to feel awkward around older folks in familial settings; it doesn't help that Kyle and Mr. Brown remind me of his more backwater relatives, who were often the most critical of his appearance. Despite where they come from, Kyle and Mr. Brown are both nice, if a bit cheeky. As for Tyler, he probably feels out of place, compounded with his new self-consciousness; I'm sure that playboy is still in him somewhere, but it takes time to recover from something as crazy as what he went through.

After we finish dinner and clean up the tables, Kyle brings out marshmallows, milk chocolate bars, graham crackers, and skewers; he lights up the firepit so we can roast the marshmallows the old-fashioned way, which is a first for me—I unintentionally burn mine black, but eat it anyway; Mark manages to set his on fire.

Lounging by the fire as the evening bleeds into night, I think about how lucky I am to know all these people, human and monster alike. Staring at that sliver of a moon, I thank God that I still have a chance to make things right.

I wake up late in the night to a darkness my eyes can't penetrate. Mark has his scaly arm slung over my chest, and Miss Ashley is snoring, and I swam so long yesterday I'm bleary and sore and ready to drift away again. So I close my eyes, but before I lose myself to empty dreams, I pray. I ask for protection on the road home and for strength to face the trials that are surely ahead of me; I ask for guidance and wisdom, and I feel so deeply grateful in that moment I nearly cry. I might cry again tomorrow, and on many more days to come. I know these things, and I know I may not get anything I ask for, but imagining someone is out there looking after us comforts me enough to survive another day.

When we arrive at Mark's house after a long three hours on the road, I say my thanks and bid Miss Ashley a happy Mother's Day before walking the short distance home. I arrive to a driveway empty of everything but a clearwater-blue 2012 Toyota Camry, the car my dad bought me for my sweet sixteen—I didn't want a car yet, but it was either tell him what I want or get some brand new, overpriced luxury vehicle. If things work out with Emily, I'll need to work on getting my provisional license; I should see if my parents can give Miss Ashley legal permission to help me get my hours in.

Looking over the shiny car I haven't driven an inch in yet, I walk to the front door, fish out my keys, and go inside. Once I lock the door behind me, I head up to my room and sit in my old office chair, staring longingly at my flat-screen TV. I haven't played games in this room once since everything went down, and the most recent preorder I picked up mid-April has been collecting dust on my shelf. I turn on my phone and read the date on the lock screen over and over again. Tomorrow, May ninth, I will apologize to Emily. Tomorrow, the day after Mother's Day. Tomorrow, Emily's birthday.

I put my phone down, recline in the chair, and stare at the ceiling fan and the popcorn ceiling above it, the storm in my head so strong it could tear the fan from its housing. I close my eyes, take a deep breath, and let it out slowly. I'll go to a ridiculously fancy Mother's Day dinner with my parents and their uptight friends, then I'll ask them to take me to the grocery store; I actually need to get groceries for the week, but it'll be a good chance to get Emily a card or something. I don't want her to think I'm buying her forgiveness, so I'll give it to her discreetly. I don't know. Maybe that's a bad idea. I want to get her something anyway.

I drift into a hazy sleep only to startle awake from my busybody mom entering the house with her mom friends. I get up and open my closet door so I can get dressed for the upcoming occasion. Hopefully, I can get away with business casual; it's too hot for a stuffy suit jacket and tie. At the bare minimum, I'll be tucking my shirt in and wearing a belt; I wish dressing like a prick is the worst thing I have to worry about.

⌒⟶

The next day, I have a quiet walk to school with Mark, and a quiet first period, and a quiet second, and I sit quietly next to Emily during the first half of third; when the lunch bell rings, my fingers shake from dread and anticipation and the awful amount of effort it's taking me to remain dormant. It's as warm as yesterday, but I'm wearing long sleeves just in case I lose my cool.

Just as she pulls out her lunch, I mutter, "E-Emily . . ."

Her lunch box clatters against our shared desk. "Y-Yes?!" I haven't spoken to her in so long she's surprised.

God, I'm a piece of shit. "I'm sorry I've been ignoring you for so long." I put my hands in my pockets and stare lamely at the glossy black surface of our desk. "It wasn't right to treat you that way." My claws tear through yet another pair of socks. "I don't expect you to forgive me. I just wanted to apologize."

Her gaze burns my cheek, but I don't dare look at her sweet face.

I close my eyes in hopes of damming up my nearing tears. "I hope we can be friends again. It's okay if you don't want to, though." The thought of never again nearly breaks me apart.

Her tennis shoes squeak against the tile floor as she leans forward into my peripheral vision.

An errant tear slips from the corner of my eye. I'm so fucking weak.

"I forgive you, Matthew," she says, her voice wavering. "I'll forgive you a thousand times if that's what it takes."

I should be the one saying sorry a thousand times. "Why?" I ask, choking up.

"Because . . ." She trails off, but a moment later, the tip of her finger grazes the fur on my wrist; I flinch, and she takes her hand away, but when she sees I'm not going anywhere, she slides her hand over my fist. "Because you're my friend."

She runs her thumb over the knuckle of mine, and I want to hold her so badly, want her to hold me, but I'm so fucking scared to be that close. I'm so choked up I can't speak, but my larynx shifts without my consent; I clear my throat to no avail, left a miserable sniveling and purring mess.

Emily lets go of my wretched hand and unzips her book bag; something wrapped in plastic crinkles. "Here, for when you think you're ready for it."

I open my eyes long enough to recognize a pack of travel tissues. "Th- . . . Thank you."

She pops the lid off her lunch box and places it down gently. She sniffles as she opens a sandwich bag, then pushes everything aside. "I wish I could hug you right now." She pouts, her head on her arms over our desk.

"I'm sorry." I cast my eyes down, mopping up some of the tears on my face with the fur on my index finger.

"You don't—" She cuts herself off, making a human's best attempt at a growl deep in her throat as she thrusts her head in her hands. "Did you at least bring your lunch this time?"

"Of course I did."

"Good." She sits back up. "Don't forget to eat it."

"I won't." I sniffle, feeling calm enough to go dormant again. With normal, furless hands, I use the tissues Emily provided to wipe my face clear; when I finish, I get up and dispose of them in the trash can near the door. As soon as I sit back down, I take out my usual lunch to prove I didn't neglect to bring it.

We eat together quietly, the atmosphere peaceful, yet awkward. We finish eating at about the same time, and I offer to throw her trash away; she lets me, careful to keep our fingers from touching. I'm both grateful for and disheartened by the lack of physical contact. I need to take it slow. I know I need to take it slow, but I wish my body didn't have a mind of its own—I wish I could be normal around her again, like nothing happened and nothing will happen.

I plop down in my seat. "I'm sorry I'm still so nervous around you."

She smiles gently. "It's okay. You'll just have to get used to me again." She cups her cheeks, her elbows on the table. "You know I don't give up easily."

"I guess."

"I knew you for six months before you'd give me the time of day."

I cover my face with my hands, but part my fingers so I can see. "Now you know why. You were a big risk. A really, really big risk." My cheeks warm. "I always liked you, but I try to be careful. I didn't want to get attached and have it blow up in my face." Talking about it makes me want to cry again, but I do my best to rein it in; it's already embarrassing enough that I've cried in front of her three times.

"It unfortunately blew up a little bit," Emily says with a half-hearted huff. "But we can rebuild." She places her head down on the table again, her ponytail all I can see. "And, um, I'm glad I wasn't imagining you purring every time it happened. I thought I was, like, some hopeless lunatic. Oh, and Mark . . . He's so obvious it was killing me."

"He'll be happy to know we made up. He got mad at me the other day because I was still being stupid."

Emily turns her head, a tender expression on her face. "Your feelings aren't stupid." She looks down at her elbow, her eyebrows upturned. "I know I can't fully understand what it's like, but I kinda get it, you know? It was scary for me, but it was scary for you, too."

I fold my hands overtop of each other on the table, nodding. "Thank you for being patient. I'll probably need a lot of that going forward. Honestly, I'm still scared, but I don't want that to ruin my life anymore." I don't know the future, but I know that, right now, I want to take care of the relationships within arms' reach while they last.

Her smile returns as she gazes into my eyes. "I hope you don't mind me helping with that. I care about all of you, more than I've ever cared about anyone. You guys keep me going."

I smile at her. "We're more than happy to have you, Emmie."

She blushes, her hazel eyes shining under the heavy fluorescent lights; she brings her right hand out from under her head and covers her mouth and nose. "Can I hold your hand again?"

I raise my brow, my lips parted with obvious surprise; I look away from her adorable face but hold out my left hand. "S-Sure." I put all my mental effort against going active.

Emily grabs my hand, worming her fingers between mine until they're interlocked; she squeezes, and I carefully squeeze back, and even though my nails are closer to claws and my finger pads have emerged, I run my thumb along her soft skin until the bell rings.

CHAPTER 22

New Normal

Emily

"We made up!" I say just as Mark walks into our German I classroom.

"Oh, thank God!" He wraps me in a tight, albeit brief, hug, then sits down, throwing his book bag on the floor next to his chair; he fixes me with an intense stare. "Okay, super important: How far are you in *Dark Souls III*?"

I put a wry grin on my face. "I haven't even taken the wrapping off the case yet."

"Neither have I." He glances at Matthew sitting behind him. "We have to play tonight! It's been forever!"

Although I wholeheartedly agree, I say, "It might be a bit late because my parents are taking me out for dinner after school." Then I remember something equally as important as finally playing *Dark Souls III*; mindful of the other students in the room, I drop down to a whisper. "Also, will you guys finally explain everything to me? You've left me hanging for a month now!"

Matthew pouts.

Mark grins awkwardly. "We'll have to get Jack in on it, but yeah."

"Let him know to meet us at car pool; I had my last match last Wednesday, so I don't have practice anymore."

"I heard." Mark faces the whiteboard. "It's about time he started taking the bus again. Driving him home every day was a pain in the ass." Yet he can't hide his tiny smile.

"I heard somebody finally got over himself," Jack says, putting his hands on my shoulders from behind.

I startle.

Matthew glares at him.

Mark smirks. "Yeah, so our explanation is due tonight."

"Explanation?" Jack moves to my left but keeps his right arm across my shoulders.

I slouch. "Did you seriously forget?"

Jack squeezes my shoulder with a stupid smile. "I just remembered. What time should I get on?"

Mark shrugs. "We'll text you."

Jack nods, letting me go. "Talk to you later." He waves one hand and walks back inside.

Matthew wilts.

Mark watches him until he notices my gaze and smiles all tired-like.

I stare at the car pool lane and try not to worry too much about the awkward atmosphere; it'll take a while for us to get back into the groove of things.

"Hey, Emily." Matthew's fingers graze my hand, but he quickly thrusts his into his pocket, looking away shyly.

"Yeah?" I gaze at his dark lashes.

His eyes flit between me and the grass until he musters the courage to hand me an envelope. "Here. For your birthday."

I take the white envelope and bring my thumb under the corner so I can open it.

"Wait!" Matthew says, startling me; he looks away again. "Open it when you get home." He scuffs his shoe in the dirt.

"Okay, I'll wait." I hold the envelope against my chest. "Thank you."

Matthew purses his lips like he isn't bothered. "N-No problem."

I bump into his shoulder just because I can, and he begrudgingly lets me hang there; miraculously, Mark pretends he didn't hear a thing.

⌒⟶

As soon as I get home, I go to my room, turn on my Xbox One, and open *Dark Souls III*. I take the disc out and check to make sure I haven't left a different disc inside the console; it's empty, so I put the disc inside and begin installing the game.

With that taken care of, I pull Matthew's envelope out of my book bag. I turn it over to the back—it says, *To Emily*, nothing else—then turn it back over to the front; I hook my thumb under the seal flap and tear the letter open. The envelope contains a simple birthday card, the kind you can find in a grocery store or pharmacy, and inside sits a green twenty-five-dollar gift card for the Microsoft store; Matthew's unmistakable pseudocursive handwriting fills the normally blank left side in black pen.

Dear Emily,

I hope you have a nice birthday. If things go well, we'll have made up by the time you read this; if not, I plan to give it to you anyway. Sorry if I continue to act like a pussy around you, both literally and figuratively; I promise to work on it even if it takes forever. I'm still getting over the fact that you know about us.

I'm not good at this whole letter thing . . . Anyway, I thought it'd be nice if I got you something more than a card. I hope you don't mind. You could save it for DLC or something, or waste it on loot boxes for all I care.

Sincerely,

Matthew

I smile as I read, hearing his voice in the words. It's simple and blunt, but I'd rather have that than something flowery and insincere. And I'm happy he's trying; not everyone gets that far in a situation like ours. After reading the letter a second time, I close the card and shuffle over to the box on the shelf of my TV stand where I keep all the cards I've ever received; even though some of them only contain a signature, it feels wrong to throw them away. I gently place the card on top, lingering on the ever-growing pile while I decide what to do next.

My head snaps up to my TV screen when I hear a notification noise: it appears Mark just got online; before he ends up inviting me to a party, I text him that I'm downloading the game.

He shoots back a text that says, *Good idea!* Not too long after, he sends another message in our group chat. *Finally . . . I have been released . . .* He sends an attachment I don't feel like looking at right now.

As I move on to update Heather on the improved status of our friendship, Teddy pops into the chat. *Took y'all long enough.* He also sends an attachment.

And I was just beginning to enjoy some peace and quiet, Jenny says, and she also sends an attachment that I imagine is quite different from what Teddy and Mark sent.

Ugh. Now I need to avoid the group chat again, Jack says.

No one was even using it the past month, bro, Mark says.

For real, Matthew says.

Yeah. I didn't have to avoid it because there was nothing to avoid, Jack says.

Touche . . . Mark says. *Emily! I humbly summon thee with this sacrifice!* Mark sends another attachment.

I roll my eyes and open the group chat. The first two image attachments are sexy anime girls—one with significantly larger boobs than the other—the third is an extremely muscular anime boy, and the fourth is an admittedly hot anime demon dude. I say, *Not bad, not bad. I shall accept this sacrifice*, then send my own attachment: a decent arachne I found the other day. *Here is your reward.*

Your too kind, Mark says. Why he likes the more extreme monster girls, I can't say, nor do I want to know.

**You're*, Matthew says.

Bro. I know where you live.

I know where you live, too.

Don't make me come over there.

Nobody's stopping you.

For lack of a wittier reply, Mark sends an angry red emoji.

To add insult to injury, Matthew sends an emoji with a halo over its head.

With that conversation going nowhere, I back out of the group chat just as Heather replies. Assuming she doesn't mind waiting a second, I go back over to my book bag and pull out my homework for the night; with my history worksheet on top of my binder and a pencil in my hand, I sit on the fabric chair in front of my TV and look over Heather's text.

I'm glad he came back around to you, honey. You have so much more patience than me. If that was my man, I would've been in his business the next day.

He's not mine, I say, *and everybody needs some space every now and then.*

A whole month is a little more than just space, she says. *Anyhoo, how's your birthday going otherwise?*

It's a Monday, you know? But my parents are taking me and my brothers out to dinner after my dad gets back from work. Then I'll probably be up a little late playing games.

I never could get into games. My brother loves them, and my dad plays fighting games sometimes. Like Mortal Kombat or Street Fighter.

Did he go to arcades when they were more common?

Yeah. He and his buddy did long before I was born.

I don't like fighting games much. I'm awful at them.

They seem complicated with all those combos.

It takes a lot of practice to get good at games like that. A lot of the best players play those sorts of games exclusively, and probably only a select few characters at that.

Makes sense. You know, I should visit again sometime. It's been a while since we've seen each other. Maybe in June? I'll be staying with my dad for Father's Day.

Heather and I make plans while I finish up my homework; since Father's Day is well past the end of school, we'll have plenty of time to hang out.

By the time we're set and I've put my complete homework away, *Dark Souls III* has long finished downloading and Dad has come home. I throw my phone in my purse, toss it over my shoulder, and head out of my bedroom, ready to go.

I take a quick shower as soon as I get back home, eager to get online. I'm a bit shaky, maybe from the sugar in the soda and cake, or maybe because I'm that excited to finally get some answers. When I enter my bedroom, I quietly close and lock my door, get dressed in my pajamas, and hop online.

Mark immediately invites me to a party. "Yo, Emily!"

Matthew and Jack say their own greetings.

"I already made the party invite only, so we can talk freely; not like anyone would believe half of what we say anyway."

To be fair, talking about monster people isn't too far out of the ballpark; they're prevalent enough in Japanese media that no one would bat an eye. "Sounds good," I say, "though I'll admit, I'm not sure where to start."

"We'll explain the basics, then you can ask whatever comes to mind."

So they explain what little they know about themselves: their imperfect dormant forms and the active forms I barely got a glimpse of; the moon curse afflicting Matthew, Mark, and some wolf man Mark's mom knew a long time ago; that their families are all perfectly human; and something about sorceresses that likely cursed their ancestors a long time ago. The important thing I learn is that it's some magic nonsense that they have the misfortune of dealing with for the rest of their lives.

"So you said you have two forms," I say.

"Yep," Mark says.

"Are you able to hold a partial form, or transform just one part of your body? I remember you having just your hands changed the other day."

"No," Matthew says. "Holding a partial form is incredibly difficult; we're only there if we're trying to hold back from transforming all the way, but it's either we calm down or end up active."

"As for me," Mark says, "the only reason I can transform just my arms is because they awakened independently from my legs, ears, and tail. So for most of us it isn't possible."

"How did they awaken independently?" I ask.

"I broke my left wrist and my right forearm when I was little. I guess my body activated those parts so I could heal better."

"Would you consider either form to be dominant?" I ask. "Like a true form or something like that?"

The boys are silent at that one. Have they never thought about it like that before?

"Considering I don't have any moon problems, I'll answer for you," Jack says. "I'd say it's complicated. There isn't a limit per se on either form, but I've noticed it's harder to remain dormant the longer I go. Like, if it's been a long time, smaller things will make me go active. For example, my family tends to annoy me more often than not, but I don't get angry enough for it to be a problem in most circumstances; however, if I've stayed dormant for more than a week or so, just being a little ticked might make me go active. So usually I sleep active whenever I can so it doesn't become a problem."

"I spend so much time active at home I've never noticed," Mark says. "You know, I actually can't go active on the new moon at all. Or it's extremely hard to, so I don't bother trying."

"Really?" Jack says. "No wonder you can stay dormant even with all that lizard shit."

"I've noticed the same as you, Jack," Matthew says, "so I also sleep active most of the time. Even the wrong dream can make us go active anyway. And I have the opposite of Mark's problem on the full moon. That's why I usually miss school once a month."

"I guess you could say our active forms are the dominant form," Jack says, "but it's not to a ridiculous degree. There's a pull, but it's gentle."

"Does it hurt?" I can't imagine having to suffer a painful transformation every day for the rest of your life.

"It hurts less with practice," Mark says. "I hardly feel it, personally, but if you resist, it'll hurt more."

"The first year is rough," Jack says, "but like Mark said, it's a pretty painless and natural process afterward. The tail is the worst part."

"Definitely," Matthew says. "It feels like getting your spine ripped out."

"That's awful!" I deal with my own share of monthly pain, but nothing that extreme.

"It's not that bad, Emily," Matthew says. "It lasts a second and then it's just sore. And that's only when I have to force myself into a full dormant form, which I only do once a year. I'd just done that the day before you found out, which was part of why I had less control on that day. I didn't give myself enough time to recuperate."

"Still . . ." I pout even though none of them can see it.

"We never said this would be an easy talk. That's just how it is for us whether we like it or not."

I don't like it one bit, but it's like complaining about having a period; it sucks, but it's part of being a functioning girl, so I just have to live with it. These guys have to live with all the inconveniences of being a monster person, no matter how annoying it is. Though it's strange that Matthew and Jack have pretty much permanent animal ears and tails . . . I gasp.

"Something wrong, Emily?" Matthew asks.

"How do you and Jack wear a headset?!"

Jack chuckles. "We put it around our necks and adjust the mic and ear cups accordingly. Our hearing is good enough that it isn't a problem."

"You know, it'd be nice if they made products with people like us in mind," Matthew says.

"That's a nice thought, Matthew," Jack says, still chuckling to himself. "Maybe it'll happen in your dreams."

"I better dream big, then."

"Speaking of dreams, I should be heading to bed." Jack's headset crackles. "I have a bus to catch tomorrow."

"Good night, Jack," I say.

Matthew and Mark follow suit.

"Night." Jack leaves the party.

After a bout of silence, Mark says, "Maybe we should save *Dark Souls III* for tomorrow. If I start now, I'll be up until two."

"I actually agree with you for once," I say.

"Same," Matthew says.

Mark leaves the party after we say good night, but Matthew hangs around for a second.

"Thank you for the birthday present, Matthew," I say while I have the chance. "I'm really glad that we're okay again."

"Yeah, I'm . . . I'm really sorry it took me so long to get over myself."

"It's okay."

Matthew doesn't try to argue with me, leaving us in an awkward silence.

"I'll see you tomorrow?" I hope I don't sound doubtful.

"Of course, Emmie. I promise I won't run away again."

I smile, knowing deep down that he's being completely honest.

"Yes . . . He's complete . . . ," Mark says.

"Oh my God, what monstrosity did you make this time?" I say, still working on my character.

Mark sends an attachment to the group chat, revealing his deprived character with a face only a mother could love: its skin is a glaring purple, and it has impossibly high cheekbones, a jawline so wide it looks square, and a massively long nose, not to mention the horrible application of discolored eye shadow and lipstick. It's so ugly I have no words.

"He looks amazing, I know," Mark says.

"I feel like you have to try to make them look that bad," Matthew says.

"And I try very hard."

That he does; Mark's characters in *Dark Souls* and *Dark Souls II* are just as terrible. I guess he gets a kick out of making them atrocious. As for me, I try to make my characters look closer to how I look in real life, but the Dark Souls–style character creator is so complicated I usually go for White woman with blond hair; as long as the face looks okay, I'm not complaining.

Mark starts playing while I wrap up creating my character. I pick the knight class, and Matthew picks the warrior class. All three of us tend to use strength builds—part of that is personal preference, another part because certain builds are looked down upon in the community—but I'm the only one that likes to rely on shields to a certain extent; I was awful at the first two games, so that extra bit of insurance helps.

Just as I'm thrust into the tutorial area, Pup1McGee joins the party. "Yo, yo, yo," he says in his typical deep timbre.

"Puppy! Hello," Mark says. "I feel like it's been a while."

"It has," Puppy says. "You guys dropped off the planet for a month."

"We had some personal problems, but nothing too serious," Matthew says. "What's up with you these days?"

"You know, just graduated college. Your boy got his bachelor's."

"OMG, congrats, bro," Mark says.

"Yeah, congrats," Matthew says. "Got any plans for the summer now that you're done?"

"Nah. My dad wants me out of the house ASAP, so I gotta get myself a job."

Mark pretends to sniffle. "Oh, they grow up so fast, Tabby."

"I know. I remember when he was just graduating high school. Now he has to actually contribute to society!" Matthew cries.

"Oh, the horror!" Mark cries.

"Yeah, yeah, ham it up, you two," Puppy says, but there's mirth in his tone. "I remember when you guys were little squeakers back in the *Halo 3* days. You especially, Tao."

"C'mon, we were ten!" Mark says. "My voice hadn't even started cracking yet."

"I can't even remember, really," Matthew says.

"Honestly, scratch that: you're still a squeaker, Tao," Puppy says.

"What?! No way!" Mark screeches, his voice cracking.

"Exactly," Puppy says. "You know how to prove a guy's point."

I imagine Mark pouting in a corner; even though Puppy is exaggerating, it's true that Mark has the highest-pitched voice out of the guys. He's always had a somewhat whiny voice, but it's not so bad it's annoying—unless he's trying to be annoying on purpose.

"Tabby, he's being mean to me!" Mark says.

"There, there, Tao," Matthew says. "It's not your fault you have a squeaky voice."

In lieu of words, Mark groans.

Puppy rarely joins the party because he's quite a bit older and quite a bit busier than us high schoolers; that, and he has some other hobbies outside of video games he spends a lot of time on. I'm pretty sure he's twenty-two, making him six years older than us. I don't know him that well, so I don't usually talk much when he's around, but I'm still entertained by the boys' ridiculous conversations with him. I've always thought it was cool how you can make friends with the most random people through video games. Unfortunately, most guys only want to talk to me because I'm a girl; I remember I always had a full friends list back in the *Halo 3* days, but I've since cleaned all those random guys out; now I exclusively talk with Matthew, Mark, and our various friends, both mutual and otherwise.

Puppy hangs around for the time being; he's also a Dark Souls fan and made considerable progress in the game over the past month since he started playing day one. He spends most of his time invading other players for a covenant to varying levels of success while the three of us work on beating the tutorial boss and entering the dark-fantasy world proper; I can already tell that *Dark Souls III* has a few callbacks to the first game, starting with the familiar hub area.

As I play, which mostly means trying desperately not to die to the various hazards the series is known for, I think of more questions I can ask the boys, some more inappropriate than others; even though I'm curious, I don't think I'll ever ask Mark if the carpet matches the drapes.

After a few hours, I take a shower and dinner break; when I return, Puppy is long gone. "Puppy got off?"

"Yeah. He said he needs to work on his résumé," Mark says.

"I don't look forward to that." I'm sixteen, and there are kids that are already working at my age; fortunately, Dad makes enough that I can enjoy what little childhood I have left. "How far are you guys?"

"I found a tree with a ton of balls."

"Same," Matthew says.

Okay. "I'm going to guess you're talking about a boss?"

"Yes," Mark says. "What else would I be talking about?" I can tell by his tone that he's trying to mess with me.

"You know what? Just for that I'm going to ask you a question." Even though I know what I'm about to ask is a terrible idea.

"Alright. Hit me."

"Mark, is all of your hair red?"

There's an agonizing beat of silence in which I regret my words immensely.

"We're getting personal now, huh?" Mark doesn't sound the least bit bothered. "Yeah, all my hair is red. Some parts are darker though, like my armpit hair. I shave, so you probably never noticed."

So it does go that far; I wonder what else might be different under their clothes. "I have another question. It's less personal this time."

"Ask away."

"Matthew, can you get high off catnip?"

"No," Matthew says immediately.

"How did you find out?"

"Miss Ashley—that's Mark's mom—bought catnip toys for their cat. It's the scent that gets cats going, and I could smell it just fine, but nothing happened. Even though I have cat parts, my brain is still human, so it doesn't process catnip the same way a cat does."

Without thinking, I say, "Then it's a good thing I never tried it on you."

"I think it's always a bad idea to drug someone."

My family has two pet cats, so I got very, very close to making a bad purchase at the pet store on more than one occasion. Let's just say, some things are better left to the imagination.

Given many long nights playing *Dark Souls III* and randomly chatting with whoever joined the party, I came to learn a few more fun facts about life as a monster person; from hibernation instincts to signature scents, I think I know just about everything the boys have to tell—or, as much as they're willing to tell.

We've made considerable progress through the game, albeit I'm going a bit slower than the boys, who have more experience than me with the series; I can tell I'm so much better than before, though. I'm currently working my way through a catacombs full of annoying skeleton enemies, one boss and one area behind Matthew and Mark, as far as I know.

Mark makes a disgruntled noise. "Bro, Pontiff is clapping my whole ass cheeks!"

"You don't even have cheeks to clap," Matthew says like it's a perfectly normal reply to make.

"Not all of us have the whole bakery like you!"

"My ass isn't that fat."

"I don't know, bro. I'd beg to differ. Right, Emily?"

"I'm not part of this conversation." There's no way in hell I'm ever going to admit that I occasionally stare at Matthew's butt. And I *have* noticed it's a fairly nice one. "I think the better question is why you've been staring at another guy's butt, Mark." To be fair, Matthew's reply implies he's also stared at Mark's butt, but I digress.

"Is there something wrong with appreciating another man's beauty? And I highly doubt you've never checked out another woman."

I frown, immediately thinking of Heather—straight as I am, those boobs of hers are so big it's hard not to look; she has to be at least a double D, maybe even an F if I'm being generous. "Fine. You win this time."

Mark doesn't bother having the last word, returning to, in his words, getting his cheeks clapped by Pontiff until he can finally beat the boss; it takes him another hour to win, at which point I reach a skeleton lord you defeat by destroying his fancy bracelets.

Mark lets out a tired sigh. "I gotta pee. Be right back." He mutes his mic, leaving me and Matthew alone.

After I'm thrust into the void by the skeleton lord's arm and die, I take a moment to think. I've pretty much run out of questions to ask, but there's one that keeps nagging at me, one that would make me rethink my feelings for Matthew depending on his answer; there's one thing that would weird me out too much to possibly pursue him. But it's not something I should ask yet. Then again, I did ask Mark about his hair.

"I have a question," I say.

"Okay," Matthew says.

"I'm not sure if I should ask it."

"Just ask, Emily."

"It's really weird, though."

"Everything about us is weird."

"But—"

"Just ask, Emmie."

"Okay, um . . ." I sit up and bite my lip; it's now or never. "Do you have a cat penis?"

Dead silence. Then Mark bursts out laughing.

I melt into my chair, my face burning with the worst embarrassment I've ever felt.

"Oh—" Mark laughs so hard he can't speak. "Oh my God!" He cackles, completely out of breath he's laughing so hard, then mutes his mic until he recovers.

Matthew clears his throat. "No, I have a normal human penis."

Mark chuckles. "But I can tell you who *does* have a cat penis: my cat."

"Unfortunately, he's lacking in the balls department."

"Don't come at Glenn like that! He can't help it!"

"I'll give him extra pets to make up for it." Matthew chuckles, too.

The mental image of a cat boy petting a cat makes me laugh, and I'm infinitely glad they've pulled away from my beyond-personal question; then a crazy idea sparks into a flame. "Oh my gosh, can you talk to cats?!"

Matthew sighs happily. "No, but it'd be cool if I could."

CHAPTER 23

Stepping Stones

Mark

I smelled him as soon as I stepped inside the house on Mother's Day—that pervasive scent of wine, wafting straight from the couch. Glenn was lounging on the cushions, and I realized the man Mom had "hired" to take care of the cat over the weekend was no stranger, not to her. If I was an animal, my hackles would've been raised; that primal part of me was greatly offended that a man I didn't know had not only entered my territory but put his scent in it. But the human part of me, the reasonable part, knew that wasn't his intention. It doesn't take much for us to mark something; a rub of the cheek here, a placing of the palm there, and any one of us can smell each other within a few yards.

I hate that smell. It had grown stronger over the month leading up to the beach trip, and stronger still through the rest of May. It faded from the couch, but it was all over Mom; whatever relationship she has with him has grown more physical. And I hate it. I hate it so much, but I don't want to. I don't want to get in the way of something that's clearly making Mom happy. It's just my instincts. My annoying, unnatural instincts mad about some other man claiming something that's mine. She's my mom, but she doesn't belong to me. Not even the house belongs to me. But in my mind, I have a stake in it. I care about it, and I don't want some other monster man challenging me for it.

Matthew nudges my arm, inadvertently trading our scents; we've been around each other so long I'm nearly nose blind to him. I'm not bothered by Matthew's scent, or Jack's, or even Teddy's. I felt odd in Kyle's camper, but that's because I was the invader in another man's territory.

"What're you thinking about, Mark? You have that thousand-yard stare going on."

I come back to myself at the one crosswalk we have to cross to get home. It's a little cloudy and a little hot, and we don't have school tomorrow because it's summer break as of ten minutes ago. "I wonder if Mom will ever tell me about her boyfriend."

The crosswalk sign changes from the orange hand to the white stick figure; Matthew carefully analyzes the intersection before we cross. "She might not realize we know about him. It's not like she can smell him the way we do."

I look out for anyone making a right at the end of the crosswalk before stepping onto blessed sidewalk. "I don't know. It's starting to get to me, though. If she trusts him enough to date him, I wish she'd say something."

"She's probably just worried. It's a big thing. It takes time to know if someone's going to stick around."

"Maybe." I want to agree with Matthew, but I don't. I don't think it matters; I think I have a right to know. But maybe I don't.

As soon as we make it to my house, I step inside and spot Glenn lounging on the couch—he often lies there because it smells like Mom. Matthew comes in after me. He might think I need his company; he's not wrong, not at all, and after spending a month dealing with him over Emily, I figure I've earned it. But it's not a give-and-take sort of thing. I know that. I know a lot of things, but sometimes my brain thinks otherwise.

Matthew and I lounge around, flip through channels on the TV, and clean out our book bags. I'm tired today—worn out, really. I keep thinking about that man, smelling the wine on Mom's clothes, his scent still faintly wafting from the surface of the couch cushions. Sometimes I wish I could stop thinking.

Mom comes home after work and cooks dinner, and we sit at the dining room table with plates of baked chicken breast, rice and gravy, and green beans. It's oddly tense. Mom eats slowly as she usually does, cutting her chicken into thin strips with a steak knife. She's quiet, her brow deeply furrowed in thought or frustration or I don't know what. "Boys," she says after she finishes half her chicken and a third of everything else, "do you remember that story I told you? About the wolf man?"

Matthew and I glance at each other; I already don't like where this is going.

"Of course," Matthew says.

Mom grips her fork and knife with enough strength to reveal the outline of her veins. "Well, I . . . I met him again, back in October. At the Barnes & Noble."

"You met him again?" I ask. "The same Alex?" I never forgot his name; I'd imagine him sometimes when I was younger, when he was the only other monster person I knew about.

"Yes." Mom stares at the prongs of her fork, then carefully wedges it and the knife onto her plate before placing her empty hands in her lap. "He recognized me, we talked a little bit, and he gave me his number. One thing led to another, and . . ."

I grip my fork with way too much pressure, my nails turning sharp and gray.

"We started dating back in April. I'd like you both to meet him."

In my peripheral, Matthew eyes me carefully; I try to keep the anger out of my voice. "Mom, you're not seriously dating your ex."

Mom frowns deeply. "He's not my ex. We never dated before."

"Then what the hell was he?"

She flattens her lips and closes her eyes. "I think the modern term is friends with benefits." She opens her eyes, and it doesn't take a genius to see she's very upset.

If he'd been any other guy, I wouldn't be so angry about it. Why him? Why the perpetually buzzed frat boy with a libido so high he can't keep his hands to himself? I grit my teeth, red scales forming on my arms. He might have changed, I know that, but I also know most people never change. Most people act the same no matter who or what or how they fuck up.

But Mom . . . She would never *ever* bring someone into this house that would put me or Matthew or any of our friends in danger. I need to stop presuming. I need to calm down and give this a chance. *Think of the fluffy wolf ears, Mark . . . The fluffy wolf ears . . .*

"Okay, fine," I say, clearly irritated, "you're dating Alex. It's not the end of the world." I place my fork down and put my active hands in my lap.

Matthew places his hand over my scaly knuckles.

"But I hope you know I'm not going to like him right away. I don't know if I ever will." My brow furrows. "And . . . I don't know if I'll ever see him as anything other than your boyfriend."

Mom's eyes are red, but she doesn't cry. "I expected that. I'm not trying to replace your dad. That's not what this is. I don't care how you see him. You can see him however you want."

I can deal with that. "Okay. When did you want us to meet him?"

"As soon as possible. Saturday, if you're up for it. I can arrange something with him. How does lunch sound?" She smiles weakly.

We hardly ever go out to eat; maybe once a month at most, the only exception being the occasional vacation. So going out doesn't sound bad, and being in a public place will help me feel more comfortable—and much less territorial. "I can work with that."

Miraculously, nobody blows up at the table and we're all able to finish our plates without the food going cold. I consider that a victory; I'm going to need a lot of positivity to survive meeting Alex.

Long after the sun sets, I lie in bed contemplating. Matthew sleeps on the leather couch, his tail twitching every few minutes. My eyes droop, and I turn over and face the wall, wrapping the covers around me to trap as much warmth as I can. It's that weird time of year when it gets into the eighties during the day but dips into the sixties at night; soon it'll be too hot for my covers but too cold without them, causing a whole new problem, but I have other things to worry about right now.

While I try to sleep, I think about Alex; mostly, I think about what he must look like. Mom never said much about him other than that he was a handsome wolf man. Handsome can mean a lot of things to a lot of different people, so I imagine what I think a handsome wolf man would look like. In my mind's eye, I see pale skin and dark-brown hair—pale because he's a creature of the night, and dark brown because werewolves are brown—and a lean, muscular body because werewolves are ripped. He's closer to Jack's physique than he is to Teddy's—maybe not as tall as them, but taller than me. A perfectly mysterious man. Perfect because I can't imagine Mom stooping so low unless Alex is shaped like a Greek god. But Mom has never cared about looks; I know that.

Alex could be none of those things. He could be tan. He could be short and flabby and bald. Maybe he lost a limb along the way, but it would actually be kind of cool if he had a prosthetic. Like a cyborg. A cyborg boyfriend would be cool.

Now I'm being ridiculous; I know that, too.

My heart beats a mile a minute as we get out of the car at an Asian restaurant in another part of town. It's near one of the more infamously dangerous highways, but Mom knows these roads well enough that it's not too much of a bother.

An older navy blue Honda pulls up next to Mom's Subaru, and a lightly tanned man gets out. He has light-brown hair in a long pony-tail, and when he turns, he pushes his aviator sunglasses up from his eyes, letting the top of his head hold up the frames; he smiles at Mom, his light-green eyes scanning me and Matthew as he walks toward us. He has a confident gait, and he wears a loose T-shirt with an ancient band logo, chino shorts, and nice running shoes; even with the loose shirt, I can tell he isn't particularly thin, but he's not obscenely fat, either. He appears to be built like your typical middle-aged man, the type that eats and drinks too much but does enough yard work to maintain some definition in his arms and legs.

Mom shares a hug with Alex before stepping aside so he can introduce himself.

"It's nice to meet you. I'm Alex, the boyfriend." He holds out his hand, smiling stupidly.

I hesitate, so Matthew takes his hand first. "I'm Matthew, Mark's friend." He lets go and looks at me.

I stare at Alex's hand full of nicks and scars, then take it in mine. It's sweaty, so his steering wheel must've been hot; I can't imagine he's as nervous as me. "I'm Mark. It's . . ." I nearly bite my cheek. "It's nice to meet you, too." I let go of his hand.

He smiles good-naturedly, shoving his hand in his pocket. "Why don't we head inside?"

We follow him to the big double doors; he opens the first set and Matthew opens the second.

It's busy inside, but not busy enough for a wait. We're sat at a booth right next to the bar; Matthew sits on one side next to Alex, while I sit next to Mom on the other. A server quickly comes by to take our drink orders, and I busy myself staring at the giant menu so I don't have to talk. The place we're at is one of those fusion restaurants with dishes inspired from all kinds of Asian countries, from China to Japan to Thailand; I know for a fact none of it is even close to authentic, but what American establishment is? We're called the melting pot of the world for a reason; we take everything from everywhere and meld it into an utterly American slush that better appeals to American sensibilities—despite my Chinese heritage, I can't say my palate would appreciate the type of Chinese cooking my great-great-grandfather served Mom.

When the server returns with our drinks, I glance up long enough to notice Alex eyeing the bar, but he looks away after the server asks if we're ready to order; none of us are.

"Does anyone want to get appetizers?" Alex asks.

I figure if he's offering, I may as well. I look over the appetizers, wondering what's most appealing at the moment, but I'm nervous enough about this whole thing that I don't feel all that hungry, but I also stayed up late and slept in like I usually do during summer, so I haven't eaten yet today. "Could we order crab wontons?" I've always loved the cream cheese filling.

"I was thinking pork pot stickers," Matthew says.

"We could order both," Mom says.

I realize I have no clue which one plans to pay, or if the two adults at the table are splitting. I'd hope they've worked that out beforehand.

When the server returns, Alex orders both appetizers.

I return to looking over the menu; it doesn't take me long to pick something off the cheaper lunch menu, and by then, I'm beginning to get annoyed with the utter silence at the table. It's so awkward. I don't want to talk to this guy at all, but anything's better than silence.

"What do you do for a living, Alex?" I ask, putting down the menu.

He raises his eyebrows, clearly surprised to be addressed by me, and smirks. "I'm a gynecologist. Basically a doctor for women."

Wow, wow, wow. I don't know what I expected, but I'm confident a doctor wasn't it. "Interesting," I say for lack of a better reply. "Do you like it?"

He smiles. "It can be a lot sometimes, but I'd say I do. My schedule is a lot more stable now that I work for a private office, too. I'm closer to forty hours a week for about the same pay, but I *have* been doing it for a long time."

So he has a respectable job. Whatever. Probably makes a lot of money, too. Is that what Mom likes about him? That he has a stable job and good pay?

Before I can grumble in my head any longer, our server delivers our appetizers and takes our orders. Mom, Alex, and I order different chicken dishes, while Matthew orders cooked sushi—there's a lunch roll combo, so he picks a crunchy roll and an eel roll; I think he's perfectly okay with raw sushi, but this isn't the sort of establishment nice enough to bother, and maybe he's simply in the mood for shrimp tempura and eel.

With the server gone and food in front of us, Mom passes out the appetizer plates; while she does, I think about what utensils to use. I'm not a super stickler for table etiquette, but we *are* at an Asian restaurant, and I know both Mom and Matthew can use chopsticks without a problem; as for Alex, well, I don't really care.

I take a packet of disposable wooden chopsticks out of a container at the edge of the table, but before I can open it, Mom says, "Could you pass one my way?"

I give her a packet while Matthew grabs one for himself.

Alex watches, then holds out his hand. "I'll take one, too."

I begrudgingly hand him what he asked for.

"Thanks." He opens the packet, splits the chopsticks evenly, holds them perfectly, and effortlessly takes a pot sticker and a crab wonton onto his plate with them like he's done it five thousand times before.

I'm so stupidly angry he knows how to use them that I split my chopsticks unevenly, leaving a fat piece of wood on the stick in my left hand; I have a feeling this is only the beginning of my bad luck with this guy.

Matthew holds his evenly split chopsticks out to me, careful not to point them directly my way. "Here. I'll just use a fork."

I align my uneven chopsticks, place them gingerly on the table, and take Matthew's gracious offer.

Mom giggles quietly, and I *bet* she knew that Alex was perfectly capable all along. She and her boyfriend share a look, silently making fun of me for being childish, but it takes a moment for Alex to realize what I was trying to do; thankfully, he makes no comment, but his goofy grin is more than enough.

As I glumly stuff my face with a cheesy crab wonton, Alex says, "Do you have any plans for the summer?" I'm not sure who it's directed at because he keeps glancing between me and Mom like even he doesn't know who he's talking to.

"Not really," I say after I swallow. Mom has never been much of a traveler, not to mention we have no one to see; I'd say we don't have the money for it either, but that's not the kind of thing I should be sharing here and now. And we're not even that bad off: Mom makes decent money and Dad's life insurance took care of most of the debt she had—even the mortgage on the house is paid off.

"My parents will probably drag me to a bunch of parties." Matthew takes a bite out of the pork pot sticker speared on his fork.

"What about you, Ash?" Alex asks.

I nearly choke on a pot sticker. Ash? *Ash?!* He already has a gross nickname for her?!

Mom blushes, a half-annoyed smile quirking her lips. "I'm hoping we'll be able to spend more quality time together, Mark willing."

Matthew smirks like he isn't going to have to deal with this guy, too.

And of course she's going to put it on me. And of course I'm going to let her have her way because she's my mom and I love her too much to stop her.

I'm going to die.

Before Alex can reply with something mushy, judging by the light blush on his cheeks, our server delivers our food. Matthew gets his sushi rolls, Mom gets her bourbon chicken, Alex gets his General Tso's chicken, and I get my sweet-and-sour chicken.

Mom bows her head to bless her meal, and as I take a bite of sauce-slathered poultry, I wish I was feeling more sweet than sour.

On the way home, I tell Mom that Alex is welcome to come over whenever she wants him to on two conditions: he uses her bathroom and never enters my bedroom ever; I can barely stand his scent in the living room, so I'd rather it not be in the one place I have to myself.

So he comes over the very next Monday, and every weekday after that, without fail. He rings the doorbell a little after six, and I walk out of my room to watch him greet Mom at the door. They hug and he puts his shoes on the rack, and Glenn trots over to sniff his feet before rubbing his cheeks all over Alex's hairy legs. He sheepishly asks Mom if he can use her shower on the first day because doing doctor stuff is a bit unsanitary and he usually cleans up right away; he even brings his own soaps to keep in her room and always has a change of clothes in a beat-up, heavy-duty book bag.

While he showers, Mom and I cook dinner together; cooking has always been our thing, a little ritual that we use for some quality mother-son time. If we're still busy in the kitchen by the time Alex walks down the stairs, he always offers to help, but Mom insists he be our guest and act like one for the time being. So he waits patiently at the dining room table, watching us work while his long hair dries on a towel he keeps around his shoulders. Sometimes he sits on the couch and pets Glenn, who likes him too much, and other times he plays fetch with him.

We eat dinner together, and Alex doesn't bat an eye while Mom says a prayer over our food; whether he's a believer or not, he respects Mom enough to let her do as she pleases in her own home. Usually he greets me and asks me how my day's been, but I never have much to say because I spend every waking hour gaming with my friends. Once or twice, I have something funny to share, mostly around Emily and Matthew's awkward half flirting or Jenny's *tsundere* attitude whenever she and Teddy grace us with their presence.

After dinner, Alex helps Mom wash the dishes and the pots and the pans, then they settle down on the couch to watch TV for an hour or two. He patiently sits through her daily episode of *General Hospital*, then they watch reruns of random sitcoms or new and exciting old-people shows on Hulu and Netflix. When they think I'm not looking, they cuddle on the couch, his arm around Mom and her hand on his thigh, and before he leaves, he gives her a quick kiss good-night and promises to see her tomorrow.

I'm begrudgingly impressed by Alex's polite mannerisms, how he keeps the PDA down whenever I'm watching and never tries to rile me up; if he ever did manage to step on my toes, I imagine he'd quickly backtrack and apologize. He's very careful, measuring every word that comes out of his mouth long before they can reach my ears. But there's one thing about him that confuses me, so on Saturday, while I'm eating my breakfast at the perfectly normal hour of noon on the couch, I ask Mom to pause her show.

"Yes, Mark?"

I stare at my bright-yellow scrambled eggs. "Why doesn't Alex go active?"

Mom's eyebrows raise, and she looks up, putting a dainty finger against her chin. "I never thought about it, but I think he might be shy. He's trying his best to make a good impression on us, so that might be why he's hesitant to transform around us." Smiling, she cups her cheek. "Unlike you, his tail and ears would make his inner emotions obvious to us; canine body language is easy to read compared to most animals."

Frowning, I furrow my brow.

She regards my screwed-up expression and dons something more somber. "It may also be awkward for him. He's always been a lone wolf, so he's not used to being active around others. I'll admit I'm eager to see it again, but I don't want to pressure him if he feels uncomfortable; it's important that we respect his boundaries, even if we don't fully understand them."

I decide I won't mention it, not unless it comes up naturally in conversation.

While I contemplate, Mom runs her free hand through my hair, the edge of her palm brushing against my ear. "Thank you for being patient with him; it means a lot to me."

I put a forkful of scrambled eggs in my mouth so I don't have to reply.

Alex comes over again on Saturday afternoon, but on Sunday, after Matthew trudges inside as the sun begins to set, he fails to show.

Matthew goes active and collapses on the couch, groaning his displeasure at the impending full moon, while Mom settles her giant soup pot on a stove eye.

"Isn't Alex coming over?" I ask.

She shakes her head, pulling out all the preprepared ingredients for the usual chicken noodle soup. "He and I agreed he should stay home tonight."

"Why?"

Mom purses her lips. "Alex can be unpredictable during the night of the full moon. I'm not sure either of us are ready to deal with that yet."

I lean against the pony wall separating the kitchen from the dining room. "Is he dangerous? Like a real werewolf?" I assume not, but I figure I may as well ask.

Mom shakes her head again. "He's not dangerous at all, just a real pain in the butt. He doesn't think before he acts, so I have no idea what impulsive decisions he might make here."

I grin. "Are you worried he might ask you to pet him for five hours?"

Mom pouts, cocking her hip with a glare. "Mark."

I put my hands up. "What?"

Mom huffs and turns back to her cooking. "It's a delicate thing. I'd appreciate it if you'd keep that in mind."

I cross my arms and slouch. "Sorry."

"It's okay."

It's not.

Smiling weakly, she glances at me. "Can you shred the chicken for me?"

"Sure." I walk over and start pulling the previously cooked chicken apart within its container.

Mom watches the chicken broth come to a boil. "He doesn't want to make a fool of himself, that's all. He knows you don't like him much."

"I don't not like him."

"But you don't like him either."

"I don't know how I feel. It's only been a week." But I don't hate him, no matter how much I wanted to. "Let's not fight about this, okay? I just need time, that's all." As much as I want to, I don't accuse Mom of dropping this on me all of a sudden. I knew it was going to drop eventually; I thought about it for months, but I never thought it'd be Alex.

"You're right. I'm sorry."

I tear up the last piece of chicken. "It's okay."

⌣⟶

It's another cold night, so I curl up under my comforter, hoping my trapped body heat will keep me warm, but I don't feel all that tired; bored but trying to be responsible, I turn over and look at the leather couch. Matthew lies swaddled in his blanket, his ragged breathing clearly audible even across the room; after watching him for a moment, he turns over so I can see his face.

Matthew opens his eyes, his pupils reflecting green in the faint moonlight from my window. He stares at the window, then glances at my face, our eyes meeting. "You're awake," he says, almost breathless; it's shocking how weak the moon makes him, like he's been struck with a terrible fever that clouds his mind and body.

"Yeah," I say. "Can't sleep."

Matthew blinks slowly; he props himself up on the arm of the couch, his blue blanket pooling around his stomach. "What's on your mind?"

I look away and flip over so I'm facing the wall. "I've been thinking about Dad a lot."

Matthew's claws dig into the old leather of the couch, then, after a long beat of silence, the bed dips; he drops like a rock next to me, pushing his clothed back against my bare one.

I move over to make some space, stretching out and adjusting my comforter to cover us both.

"What about him?" he asks. "If you don't mind."

"I don't know." I grip the edge of my mattress with my scaly fingers. "Everything, I guess. When I think about him, I realize how little I remember. The little things are gone."

"I didn't know him very long"—the tip of Matthew's tail tickles my ankle—"but I remember he was always kind to me, and that he had a short fuse."

"Yeah." Dad could be incredibly impatient, and little things could easily frustrate him on his bad days; he suffered from depression, which probably contributed to his death—stress is a hell of a killer. "I never told you, but he didn't actually accept me right away."

Matthew pauses. "He didn't?"

"No. He was shocked and enraged; he couldn't believe his son could be a monster. He and Mom fought a lot, which was scary to me. I was only five, you know? My parents were my whole world.

"Dad tried to come up with all kinds of excuses. He first thought I could've been switched at birth, but I have Mom's nose and otherwise look like my dad. Then he blamed her heritage, like somehow being part Chinese could cause someone to grow scales and claws; that was the most racist thing he ever said. I couldn't tell you which side it comes from, but considering what we do know, I'm far more European dragon than Asian."

"Except for not having wings," Matthew says.

I wonder about that sometimes. Like if my dragon ancestor may have had wings. There's no guarantee we both look exactly the same; it's possible that the monster parts of us manifest differently down the line, like microevolution. He could've had green scales and bird wings for all I know, like the ancient depictions of European dragons. He could've been blue, or purple, or black. Maybe he had multiple colors.

I've always thought of myself as just another guy, so I'm glad I don't have wings; they're far too fancy, and they would've gotten in the way, even more so than my tail. Maybe, somewhere deep inside, I decided I didn't want wings, so I don't have them, or maybe the Chinese part of me stripped that down somehow. Who can know with magic involved?

"But Dad came around eventually, gave up on the whole denial thing, and the blame, and the fighting; none of it was going to make me normal." I snuggle into my pillow, bringing my now-warm hand under my cheek. "It wasn't until I met you that I felt okay showing my scales around the house all the time. Whether he intended to or not, my dad scared it out of me for those few years, and since it was only a partial awakening, I had none of those annoying negatives to worry about yet."

Whether he intends to or not, Matthew starts purring.

"I think you cemented the fact that he was wrong about me; I remember he tried harder to be more mindful of our needs. And when I finally awakened for real, he was there for me." That's the second-clearest day in my mind. I felt so sick that day, all feverish and shaking all over, and scared. I was afraid to become more of a monster, but when Dad found me curled up on the floor of my room, he pulled me into his lap and stroked my hair while the transformation racked my body. I remember how gently he eased my tail out from under my clothes and how soothing his fingers were on my sore ears; when I looked up at him, he smiled and told me how good I was doing, how brave I was for staying calm despite what was happening to me. I knew Dad loved me then.

"I remember that day." Matthew takes a shaky breath through his purrs. "I was too scared to watch, so I left the room and told your dad what was happening to you."

I sniffle. "I miss him. And I feel like I shouldn't be okay with Alex, but he's been nothing but nice to me and Mom."

Matthew stretches obnoxiously, shoving his back against mine, and resettles. "You know, there's nothing wrong with liking him. It's not a betrayal. You can love your dad and still like Alex."

I curl up, silent.

"I like your mom way more than I like mine, and she's alive and well." He suddenly stops purring. "Is that wrong?"

"Of course not."

He starts purring again. "I feel guilty about that too, sometimes."

I scooch until my back is touching his once more, then close my eyes and pretend I haven't shed a few tears onto my pillow.

The next week is much of the same: Alex comes over after work, he and Mom chill out, then he goes on his merry way; but on Sunday, without the full moon to hinder him, he asks me if he can help cook dinner in my place. And I let him because one night a week isn't a big deal.

He hovers near Mom the entire time, often brushing against her or whispering something I have no hopes of hearing—not that I'd want to hear some mushy romantic garbage from him—but he does everything she asks him to do, handles the heavy lifting, and grabs things that are stored on the highest shelves. They smile a lot when they're together, and if he had his tail out, I imagine it'd be wagging constantly.

When the next Sunday comes, I'm glad I let him take over those nights; a little after seven p.m., I feel too fatigued to possibly cook in front of a hot stove. Of course the new moon won't always start on a Sunday, but it's working out in my favor just this once.

The heat isn't too bad this late in the day, not to mention it's all cloudy outside, so the worst of my magically induced cold-bloodedness doesn't come to pass. I'm not sure if Alex knows about my moon problems, and when he asks me if I'm okay, I downplay how sick I feel, but he keeps giving me worried looks while we eat dinner. All his staring makes it hard for me to eat, but I manage to ignore him long enough to finish what little I put on my plate. He kindly takes it and the other dishes to wash in the sink, which I thank him for because I'm way too tired to even think of getting up.

When he and Mom are done in the kitchen, they go to the couch to watch the usual shows they're keeping up with. I rest my head on the dining room table, listening to their imperceptible whispers and canned laughter from the TV. Eventually, Mom goes upstairs to take her shower, and just as the water starts running, my stomach rumbles; I obviously didn't eat enough, so I figure I should do something about that. Despite how weary I feel, I get up and trudge into the kitchen, grab the fridge handle, and exert way too much force to open it. I scan the shelves, looking for the bag of grapes, and of course I can't find them, so I rummage around, hoping they're hidden behind one of the plastic containers of leftovers, but no dice. Someone must've eaten them earlier today because I remember there being some left last night. I didn't have them for lunch, and Mom doesn't usually fancy fruit all that much.

Feeling stilted and confused and so tired I can barely think, it occurs to me that Dad used to always eat my fruit. He loved grapes and strawberries and oranges and all manner of other fruit, just like I do. So, logically, I rest my forehead on the cool surface of the freezer door, the refrigerated air wafting over my body, and say, "Da"—my tongue ties before I can close in on a second d; sick to my stomach, I correct myself—"lex, did you eat the rest of the grapes?"

I can't bear to look, but I hear Alex place the TV remote on the coffee table, get up off his ass, and pad over on his bare feet; when his shadow looms over me, I desperately want to disappear.

In the corner of my eye, I notice his hand reaching out. "Don't!" I slam the refrigerator door closed and try to shove past him, but he blocks the kitchen entryway with his entire body. I stand there uselessly, wanting nothing more than to lie down and sleep. "Leave me alone," I whisper, my eyes burning with unshed tears.

Alex parts his lips and closes them like he's not sure what to say or do, like he's walking on thin ice, and he's right to think that because I'm so fucking mad and frustrated and devastated right now, but all those emotions aren't targeted at him, not at all. "Mark, are you sure you're alright? You're shivering like there's a blizzard in here, and you called me . . ." He doesn't need to finish his thought.

I turn my back toward him and lean heavily against the fridge, which doesn't help my temperature at all. "It's the moon fucking with my head," I say, even though it's only half-true. "Now did you eat the grapes or not?"

"I ate them with lunch. It's my bad."

I expect him to walk away, but he lingers.

Alex clears his throat. "I know what you're going through, kid."

"I have a name."

"Mark, sorry." He shuffles and clears his throat again. "I know how annoying it must be to see some guy in your house all the time."

"How would you know?"

"I lost my mom when I was twenty-five. It wasn't a day after the funeral that my dad was bringing random chicks home."

I turn my back against the fridge and stare resolutely at the floor. In the corner of my eye, Alex stands with his back to the wall, his gut doing most of the blocking; even though I could easily slip past him now, I wait.

"Some of them were pretty young, too. My age, even. I tried to be nice, but I hated all of them. I even hated my dad for bringing them home in the first place, especially since most of them had their fun within two weeks."

I glance at his face; he's also staring at the floor.

"So I understand if you hate me and want nothing to do with me."

"I don't hate you."

He's speechless. "Really?"

"Don't push your luck, wolf man."

He smirks. "I promise I won't be some guy who disappears in a month. If you're willing to give me a chance, maybe we don't have to be at odds."

"We're not at odds."

He raises an eyebrow.

I hang my head, my cheeks flaming with shame. "I'm sorry I gave you that idea. I really wanted to hate you. Mom gave me a bad impression of you a long time ago, so I was mad about it. And your scent pisses me off. Do you still drink like a sailor?"

Now both eyebrows are raised. "I've been sober seven months now." He makes a show of sniffing his own armpit. "Do I really stink that bad?"

I groan, running a shaking hand over my face before plopping down on the floor. "Alex, I meant your monster-person scent! You know how I smell like charcoal? You smell like wine. It's everywhere you touch."

"Oh." He twirls some hair around his finger. "I guess there's nothing I can do about that."

I look up at his stupid smiley face; he's jolly enough to make Santa jealous and has a gut to match. "Are you going to keep avoiding us on the full moon?"

His smile wanes. "I think I should. I'm all over the place those nights."

"Are you dangerous?"

He gapes. "Of course not! I would never hurt you or Ashley or anybody!"

"Then come over. If you're going to date my mom, you better." I stand and walk around his stupefied self. "If you're serious about her, you will."

His gaze pricks my back as I go to my room and slam the door shut. Thoroughly alone, I shed a few frustrated tears, wipe my eyes, sniffle, and crash in my bed; with the warm covers around me, I stop shivering so much and drift into an uneasy sleep.

CHAPTER 24

Mood Swings

Ashley

*A*re you sure about this? Alex has been incredibly nervous these past two weeks. We've texted back and forth, over and over again, only to come to the same conclusion every time.

I'm perfectly positive, Alex. I trust you. Do you trust me?

I trust you, he says. *I'm just nervous. Really nervous.*

I know. But it'll be okay. I promise not to judge. If he still acts the same way he did in the past, then he'll be far from impossible to handle.

Thank you. I'll be there soon. And thanks for lending your couch. He doesn't like driving under the influence of the moon, so I offered to let him stay the night.

Alright. It's no problem. I love you!

I love you too!

I put my phone down on the coffee table, then draw my legs up on the couch. I'd be lying if I said I wasn't nervous, too; I'm anxious to see him active, but not eager to admit it to him. God, I can't wait! But I need to be patient and respectful; Alex is making a big decision, trusting me to see him at his most vulnerable so soon.

Although I can predict how he'll react to me, I wonder what he'll do around Mark and Matthew. They're currently hanging out in Mark's room, Matthew sick as a dog with the usual effects of the full moon; he's probably sleeping right now, as he often does this time of the month. I've already baked chicken for the soup tonight, but I think I'll wait until Alex is comfortable before I cook; Lord knows those boys stay up so late they don't even want dinner until nine anyway.

Just as I resettle on the couch, the doorbell rings; I jump to my feet and open the door.

Alex steps inside, a sheepish smile gracing his face; he gives me a hug after I close the door behind him, puts his shoes on the rack near the doorway, and runs his hand through his tied-back hair, fiddling with his long ponytail. "I'll go ahead and shower." He tugs on the collar of his T-shirt.

"Alright. I'll be waiting on the couch." I take his hanging hand and squeeze it lightly. "Take your time, okay?" I let him go.

Alex nods, swallowing audibly, and tugs his book bag up the stairs and down the hall.

I stand and wait until the shower turns on, then sit back down and distract myself with some TV. As my overly dramatic soap opera drones on, I fidget constantly. Truth be told, I only continue to watch *General Hospital* because I watched so much of it with my mother; it's one of the few things I ever did with her, so keeping up with it makes me feel closer to my estranged family.

I often feel horrible that I can't provide Mark with a good family; it's all I can do to provide a good home, and I'm well aware I've jeopardized that by introducing Alex. But these are the growing pains; if this is meant to last, Mark will have to learn to get along with him. I'm hoping Mark will feel more open if Alex becomes comfortable enough to be active around us.

Distantly, the shower squeaks off.

I scramble to pause the TV, my heart pumping faster and faster in utter anticipation for Alex to appear at the top of those stairs. He lingers in my room awhile longer; I imagine him drying his silky hair, dressing himself in a simple T-shirt and shorts, and going active under the light of the setting sun filtering in through my bedroom window.

Alex turns the corner, placing one furry hand on the staircase railing, his dainty wolf paws visible between the bars. As he slowly descends, I spot his tail hanging down the length of his thighs; he holds the fluffy appendage straight down, nearly curling it between his legs, and his cute triangular ears lie back in a similarly submissive position. Typical of a subservient wolf, he avoids making eye contact.

Alex pads over to the couch, his claws clicking on the linoleum, and sits down on the other end; he grips his fists over his thighs and hunches his head between his shoulders, his long, damp hair hiding his face.

I scooch over onto the middle cushion, careful to keep my hands to myself. "Could you look at me, handsome?"

Alex's tail wags minutely at the tip, and he pushes his hair over his shoulder, whipping it back like a horse's tail. He has the tiniest smile on his face and his brow furrowed, worrying over nothing.

If I had no self-control, I'd drape myself over his lap, but I rein myself in and lift my hand cautiously. "May I?" I glance at his half-collapsed ears.

Alex nods, his tail wagging harder.

Using my left hand, I grip his wolf ear and slide my thumb over the delicate edge. It's soft and warm, the golden-brown fur layered with fuzzy black tips. I've seen the expensive shampoo and conditioner Alex keeps in my shower, so it's no surprise that the texture is immaculate. Oh, he's an excellent man.

As I caress his ear, his tail thumps against the back of the couch, and he leans into my hand, eager for more.

I let go of his right ear, guide his head onto my shoulder, and reach around to stroke his left ear. "You feel wonderful, Alex," I whisper, his tail beating the couch so strongly the vibrations tremble across my back. "So wonderful." With my right hand, I reach into his lap and lock my fingers with his left; I run my thumb along his furry knuckle, my fingers pushing against the partial webbing reaching halfway up his.

Alex runs his dark-brown thumb pad over my knuckle, the charcoal-gray claw at the end ghosting over my skin. He cranes his neck and kisses my own, and I close my eyes, willing myself to remain silent despite my parting lips. He wraps his right arm around me and runs his hand over my hip and along my side, reaching my ribs and the bottom of my breast; he cups it and gently squeezes, sucking against my neck all the while, then runs his hand down until his pinky finger touches the bare flesh below my shorts.

He pulls away from my neck and gazes at my lips; we come together in a kiss, my tongue navigating around those long canines that don't frighten me in the slightest, and part with heavy breaths.

Alex leans back and rests his head on the backrest cushion of the couch; his ears remain lying back, but he smiles. "This is nice, being able to be myself around you." His tail dampens its wagging, merely bending at the tip.

I lean forward and press my forehead against his. "I love this part of you, too. I love all of you."

"I hope you won't eat those words in an hour."

I card my fingers under his hair and hold his cheeks; we kiss again.

After we part, he cups my cheek with his right hand, his calloused pads still soft on my skin. "I love all of you, too."

I place my hand over the one on my cheek, stroking the thick fur. "Thank you."

Alex smiles wider and leans back against the arm of the couch; he brings his knees to his chest. "Are your boys here?"

I place my hand on one of his paws and run my fingers over the bony joints. "They're in Mark's room. Matthew's been sick all day from the moon."

Alex nods, his brow back to worrying. "I think I might try to rest for now. I had a hard time sleeping last night."

"I can imagine." I scooch back over to the other end of the couch to give him some room, then pat the middle cushion. "You can stretch out if you like." A grin overcomes me. "I don't mind you using my lap to rest your feet, either."

Alex pouts but adjusts a throw pillow against the couch arm and rests his head, his ears perking up to a neutral position; he turns to face the back of the couch, then stretches his legs over my thighs; his paws press into the arm next to me, his furry calves and the tip of his tail tickling my skin.

I bend across his legs, grab the TV remote, and resume watching my show.

Within minutes, his ears and face go slack, and he snores softly. The tip of his tail twitches against my thigh; I wonder if he's dreaming.

By the time the episode ends and the sun sets, I decide it's time to prepare a late dinner. Very, very carefully, I extract myself from under Alex's legs, lifting them slowly by his ankles before resting his underdeveloped heels on the cushion I recently occupied.

His tail and two fingers twitch, but he doesn't stir.

I sneak over to the kitchen and quietly pull out the pot, the cutting board, a carrot, a stalk of celery, the plastic container of baked chicken breast, a bag of extra-wide egg noodles, and the chicken broth. With everything out in front of me, I peel the carrot, cut it and the celery into reasonably thin slices, and put them in the pot. I pour the chicken broth over the vegetables, turn on the stove, and clean the knife and the cutting board while the broth comes to a boil.

Just as I finish drying my hands on the kitchen towel hanging above the sink, a warm and heavy weight lands on my back and wraps his arms around my shoulders. "What're you up to, beautiful?" Alex rumbles, taking an audible sniff of my hair.

Here we go. Otherwise frozen, I run my fingers through the thick fur on his forearm and attempt to pull his arms off. "I'm cooking; it's a bit hard to do with you hanging all over me."

He hums. "My bad." He lets me move his arms, freeing my own, but immediately latches onto my stomach. He rubs his cheek behind my temple, his tail wagging so hard his thighs sway back and forth over my butt.

I close my eyes, take a deep breath, and trudge back over to the stove, Alex glued to my back the whole way. There's nothing dangerous about Alex on the night of the full moon, but he's extremely affectionate—annoyingly so—and prone to random outbursts of emotion. He has the attention span of a puppy, and right now, I'm the most interesting thing in the room.

When he tires of rubbing my head with his cheek, he nips my neck and kisses a trail down to the edge of my shoulder, pulling the collar of my shirt aside as he pleases, then trails back up my neck.

He nibbles my earlobe, at which point I've had enough. "Alex, could you please calm down?"

His thighs continue to rub against my butt, but he stops slobbering on my ear. "Sorry." He rests his chin on top of my head and distracts himself by running his hands along my sides, keeping my abdomen locked in a hug.

"Thank you, sweetheart." I reach back and give him a rewarding scratch behind his ear; naturally, he leans into it, which makes me lean over until I remove my hand and he straightens out, wagging away. With Alex clamped around me, I grab a ladle and give the chicken broth plus vegetables a hearty stir, then move on to shredding the chicken breast in its container.

Alex moves his chin to my shoulder, enticed by the scent of cold chicken, but has enough sense not to grab any of it.

I tear the chicken apart through our incessant wiggling, then attempt to back up and reach the sink to wash the little bits out from under my nails.

Alex refuses to budge; he grabs my elbows, runs his hands up to my wrists, and gently pulls my fingers up to his face; he licks them clean with his flexible, wolflike tongue, leaving behind a coat of sticky saliva.

I sigh; the chicken bits are gone, but I still need to wash my hands.

Alex returns to hugging my middle, once again resting his chin on top of my head. I'm not even particularly mad, but his antics can be tiring when I'm busy.

Now that he's satisfied, I can—

"Hey, Mom." Mark pokes his nose through the entryway to the kitchen. "Do you need . . . any . . . help . . . ?"

Alex stops wagging his tail, suddenly dangerously still.

I turn my head, my sticky hands held up in the air, and study Mark's slack-jawed expression. He has his beautiful red scales out, as he often does, and stares unabashedly at the spectacle of his mother and her boyfriend in a strange embrace—a boyfriend who's very much active and unpredictable. I feel like I should be embarrassed, but I'm far more curious to find out what Alex will do.

Alex takes a breath so deep his stomach pushes against the small of my back, then lets go of my belly; he thrusts his arms out wide, shouts, "Kid!" and with all the grace of a newborn foal, stumbles over to Mark and engulfs him in a tight hug; he proceeds to rub his cheek all over Mark's hair.

Mark screeches and struggles to get out of Alex's powerful grasp, but he's much too thin to fight the muscle hiding under Alex's fat.

Alex says, "How are you? Is Matthew okay? I missed you when you went to your friend's house the other day. Will I get to meet them sometime? You smell sweaty," and so on and so forth.

While I have some blessed freedom from his embrace, I totter over to the sink, wash the gunk off my hands, and turn around.

Matthew peers around the entryway, his pupils horribly dilated, his tail puffed to twice its size, and his razor-sharp claws unsheathed; hunched and panting, he gapes at the embarrassing display previously blocked by the pony wall.

It's adorable that Matthew mustered the strength to check on Mark, but now that he's out of off-limits territory, Alex sets his sights on him. Wearing a massive grin, Alex drops Mark—he crashes unceremoniously onto the kitchen floor, hands and knees holding him up while he catches his breath—and tail wagging so hard his big butt wiggles back and forth, he staggers forward and embraces Matthew; the two fall on their knees, and Alex rubs his cheek all over Matthew's hair, too.

After the shock wanes, Matthew's ears relax and his tail fur flattens; he goes slack and closes his eyes like he's perfectly fine with falling asleep in Alex's lap.

Alex doesn't ask Matthew a bunch of questions—he either got them all out with Mark or forgot he had any to ask in the first place—and eventually stops rubbing his cheek all over Matthew's head; he merely holds him, his tail wagging away.

"Goodness." I walk over to the boiling pot and the shredded chicken and the wide egg noodles; I dump the chicken and the noodles in the broth, put the temperature down, and stir.

⌣⟶

I lie in bed under nothing but a thin sheet and my nightgown, the ceiling fan swirling lazily overhead. Bone-tired but jittery, I contemplate the man on the couch downstairs, the boy sleeping in his bed with his friend not far away, and the man who I hope is high in the sky, beyond this world and its vices.

The door opens, startling me from a drowsy reverie, and I swiftly switch on the lamp on my nightstand.

Alex stands in the doorway, his eyes shining green and pale yellow in the dim light.

My heart skips a beat. "Alex," I say, dumbfounded. He's almost naked, wearing nothing but an unflattering pair of white briefs. Silver stretch marks snake around his upper thighs, hips, and lower belly, his chest and abdomen covered with body hair he doesn't bother shaving anymore. His long, straight hair drapes over his shoulders, covering his nipples and ending where the curve of his stomach begins.

Alex closes his eyes as he rests his clammy forehead against the doorframe. "Can I sleep with you?" he asks, nearly panting.

I pull the edge of my sheet up to my neck. "Alex, we agreed—"

His face screws up and he holds out his furry, padded hand.

I close my mouth.

He puts his hand down and holds his elbow. "Sorry. I meant: Can I sleep next to you?"

I look him over again, this man so different from the lean boy I knew so many decades ago, and drop my head on my pillow with a great sigh. I turn off the lamp, slide to the right side of my king-size bed, and hold up the sheet behind me.

Alex thumps his tail against the doorframe before slinking forward; he drops his heavy frame onto the bed and crawls to my side. On hands and knees, his ears pulled back and tail down, he asks, "May I hold you?"

I stare into his moon-reflecting eyes and nod.

His tail lifts and wags, and he collapses on his side and pulls my back against his stomach, his semi-erect penis poking my butt through our clothes.

When he adjusts his half of the sheet, a slight draft wafts under my gown and breezes over my vagina; I almost always sleep without underwear—it's good to let yourself breathe down there—but I wish I had the foresight to put some panties on.

Alex places his hand on my stomach, adjusts himself until he's comfortable, and promptly . . . snores.

My heart ceases its protesting, so I close my eyes and place my hand over his, worry and trust and love all twisting in my pudgy gut. Alex doesn't care about how I look—if anything, he thinks I'm the prettiest woman in the world—and when he holds my stomach, that part of me I loathe most, I feel like it isn't so ugly and saggy and marred. When I feel his breath on my neck, I feel safe. His body is warm, and his fur is soft, and he's so emotionally honest under the full moon that it hurts.

I missed this, being held, being in a man's arms, being loved like I'm so lovely and couldn't hope to be lovelier. And I think of George, how he used to hold me at night, even when I was fat and gravid and snored louder than a fan on full blast, and I miss him. I miss his hairless chest and his gray eyes and his dexterous hands that knew all my secret places, all my hopes and dreams. And I sob because I shouldn't be thinking about another man while Alex holds me so gently, even if that man's been dead for four long years.

"Why are you crying?"

I sob harder, hiding my face in my hands. "I miss him." My shoulders shake with each hiccuping breath. "I miss George. I miss him so much." I cry like the day I was born and didn't know anything more than hunger and tiredness. "I'm sorry, Alex . . . I'm so sorry . . ."

Alex takes his hand off my stomach and slips it under my palm, mopping up my tears with his thick fur. "Shh," he whispers. "It's okay, Ash. It's okay." He holds me as close as he can, soaking up my tears until his fur is damp and warm. "Just let it all out."

And I do, until I'm so worn I fall asleep.

⸺

I wake as soon as the rising sun throws its rays through the blinds; I rise to my knees and gaze at the man I allowed in my bed.

Alex's hairy back rises and falls with each soft breath, his hair tangled around his head and over the spare pillow; without any clothes covering them, his thighs look especially thick encased in layered wolf fur. I'd love to run my fingers all around them, to discover the bands of color decorating each individual guard hair in his mostly brown coat, but now isn't the time.

I crawl out of bed, careful not to disturb him. I strip off my nightgown and place it back in my dresser drawer. I stand there naked, the AC and the ceiling fan chilling my nipples.

Alex doesn't wake.

I put on a pair of cotton hipsters and a nude bra that doesn't match the color of my skin, then kneel in front of my body-length mirror and apply makeup for the workday ahead; distantly, I think I should've taken the day off, but I like to save my PTO for appointments and emergencies.

Using black eyeliner, I remember my great-grandmother, that crotchety old woman full of hate; I didn't like her and she didn't like me, but she taught me how to put makeup on my Chinese eyes because I don't have the same contours as the White girls I grew up with. I have different wrinkles and crevices, different lines to draw and fill to flatter my face. She didn't cry when Grandpa Tao died, but they didn't marry for love—they married to survive in this wild, western world full of hate. There are hateful people on every part of this planet, but I only know what I've had beat into me in this country I call home.

As I run pink lipstick across my lips, Alex stirs, his ears perking as he stretches his arms and back. He opens his peridot-green eyes, the prettiest green eyes I've ever seen, and roams my half naked body; he trails down from my shoulders to my waist to my wide, bony hips, and he smiles, soft and sultry, his tail wagging under the sheet.

Alex staggers down the stairs, active and shirtless and tired, at the reasonable hour of two in the afternoon. Shirt haphazardly tossed over his shoulder, he crashes onto the couch and leans back into the cushions.

"You're up just in time for lunch," I say, preparing myself a sandwich. "Would you like something?"

Alex grunts. "Whatever you're having is fine."

"How was work?"

Alex sighs, slouching like he wants the couch to eat him. "Routine vaginal delivery. Also had to perform an emergency C-section. Nobody died, so that's a plus." He got called in the middle of the night about one of his patients. I didn't catch much on account of my midsleep grogginess, but he was out of the door and didn't return until I woke up at eight. "I'm glad it's Saturday. I need a break."

I'd never thought about death in the context of his job. Doctors must see a lot of terrible things over the course of their lives. "I'm guessing you're off call for the weekend?"

Alex nods. "I'm only on call one night a month."

I hum, placing a piece of bread overtop Alex's sandwich; I bring both plates to the coffee table. "Do you want something to drink?"

"Water's fine." He gazes at the pony wall. "I should bring my coffee machine over here. Or buy a new one."

I trail my finger over his ear before walking back to the kitchen; I return with two glasses of water and sit down next to him. "Caffeine isn't great, but I'll take that over booze."

Alex goes dormant, picks up his sandwich, and smirks. "Like you don't have a weakness for ice cream."

I huff. "That's why I don't keep it in the house, thank you very much." Ice cream was by far my greatest food vice; I could eat a whole tub in a night if I wanted to. Alex found out about that one when he asked if I wanted to get some ice cream after a movie; of course, I declined because I can't control myself around it in the same way he can't around alcohol, so we got cake slices from the grocery store instead. "At least I can be normal around other desserts."

Alex chews thoughtfully. "I might try to lay off the caffeine eventually. One step at a time, though."

I nod, chewing through bread and meat and cheese. "One step at a time."

We finish lunch and I clean the dishes—Alex has earned a break on that front—then we settle next to each other to cuddle and watch TV. Glenn crawls over us and curls up between Alex's thighs while I play an episode of *Stranger Things*, a new Netflix series we decided to give a go. It's possible I watch too much TV, but I choose not to worry about it.

Halfway through our second episode of the day, both Glenn and Alex turn their heads and perk their ears at the front door; Alex goes dormant right before the lock clicks.

I pause the show.

Mark opens the door and says, "We're home!"

Matthew, Jack, and Luke walk in behind him.

Alex's arm stiffens around me.

Mark and Matthew kick off their shoes and go down the hall; Jack and Luke linger around the doorway.

"Ms. K.," Luke says, "is that your boyfriend?"

I smile. "Yes. I'm sure Mark told you about him."

Jack wrinkles his nose. "They both reek of wine; kinda hard to keep him a secret." Without a second thought, he removes his hat and pulls the pins out of his hair; his bunny ears rise up, unapologetically perked at Alex.

"Oh," Alex says, "these are the friends."

"That's right," Luke says, his expression oddly calculating; he saunters over to the dining room table, drags a chair in front of the coffee table, and sits down with his arms crossed. He squints at Alex, sizing him up and flexing his biceps.

Alex casually gauges him, propping his head in his hand; he goes active and quietly adjusts his tail.

Glenn doesn't appreciate the modicum of movement, so he leaves.

Luke also goes active, sneers, and . . .

Is he growling?

Alex sneers back. "You tryna fight, kid?" And now *he's* growling.

Jack places his hat on the coffee table and sits down on my right, merely watching the spectacle with an impassive face.

Luke removes his shirt and bares his teeth, his growl far more audible to my ears.

Alex drapes his shirt over the arm of the couch, removes the hair tie keeping his ponytail together, and rearranges his hair into a large, sloppy bun.

They stand at the same time, both growling loudly, but Alex's sneer morphs into a grin and his tail wags.

Luke grins, too. "Don't wag your tail!" He tries not to laugh.

Alex says, "We're fighting. Put the chair away."

"What's going on out here?" Mark asks from the end of the hall.

"Teddy's fighting for dominance," Jack says.

"Over what?"

"Your mom."

"Huh?!" Mark gapes.

I try not to giggle. "Oh, let them fight."

Matthew puts the chair back at the table while everyone is distracted.

Alex and Teddy posture in front of the TV, both wearing nothing but pants and a belt. They keep growling, but it's clearly playful, if their grins and Alex's ever-wagging tail are anything to go by. They bear down into wide squats, and after an intense stare down, they collide; their shoulders crash together and they grab each other's belts, straining to push in opposite directions.

I'm not sure what the goal is, but I'll let them have their fun.

As big as Alex is, Luke is no slouch; despite his age, he's both taller and potentially heavier, not to mention the amount of physical activity he does on a day-to-day basis. With no small amount of strain, Luke slowly pushes Alex back.

Alex digs his claws into the linoleum—I gave up on scratch-free flooring a long time ago—and bears down with all his might; knowing he can't beat a kid like Luke with raw strength, Alex attempts to interrupt his balance by circling right.

"He has a lot of energy this time of year," Jack says.

Mark slinks behind the couch and drops his chin between our couch cushions. "Is he always this territorial?"

Jack holds his chin and closes his eyes. "Hmm . . . Only where his sister is concerned." He opens his eyes and peers at the ceiling. "But now that I think of it, he was like that with Jenny sometimes, even before he awakened. He's usually more passive-aggressive, though."

"You were being territorial too, Mark," Matthew says.

Mark jumps but pretends he noticed Matthew sneak up on us. "I was not."

"You were," I say.

Mark blanches. "You noticed?!"

"Of course I did. You kept scowling at the couch, not to mention all the times you hug—"

Mark laughs awkwardly. "Ah! We get it! I was territorial!"

Jack smirks and returns his attention to the match; it seems Alex and Luke have been going around in circles. They're both sweaty, and Alex's bun is falling apart.

During a lull, Alex says, "Let's call it a truce, kid."

Luke pants. "Fine."

They let go of each other and sit on the floor.

Alex pulls his hair tie out and detangles his hair with his fingers.

Luke looks at me. "He's not bad."

Alex drops his hand on Luke's head and rubs between his bear ears. "Thanks, kid."

Luke blushes, scowls, and swats Alex's hand away.

Alex chuckles, hefts himself to his paws, and drops next to me on the couch.

When I walk down the stairs after my shower, I find Jack combing Alex's hair in front of the full-length mirror; tiny tufts of golden-brown hair lie scattered at Jack's feet and around the stool that Alex barely fits on.

I sit on the couch and peer over the arm. "You asked for a trim?"

Alex glances at me. "He offered."

There's so much hair Jack has to hold it up as he combs its length. "It's not every day I meet a guy with hair longer than mine."

"I kept meaning to ask how long you were going to grow it out," I say.

Alex smirks. "Do you have a preference?"

I quirk an eyebrow. "It's *your* hair."

Alex crosses his arms and tilts his head back and forth. "Then . . . I want to grow it out to my hips again."

I rest my head over my arms and smile. "I'll look forward to seeing it."

Jack makes a strange face. "I think that's my cue to leave." He puts his comb down next to the shears on the table and stalks off to the broom closet.

Alex ruffles his hair, stands, and stretches out his back. "I'll wait for the water to warm up again before I shower."

I nod, watching him migrate to the bookshelf against the wall behind the couch.

"I've noticed you have a lot of animal books."

"I buy one every time I meet a new animal person."

Hand on one hip, he scans the selection. "When did you meet a shark?"

"At the beach. I also met a bird and a possum there."

When he finds the one on octopuses, he snorts. "I can't believe you bought this."

I smile. "You never know: I might meet that guy one day."

Alex exaggerates a shiver. "I hope not." He moves on to the third shelf down and pulls out a big blue binder.

"Oh, that's . . ." I bite my tongue.

Alex reads the cover page and glances at me with a soft expression. "I won't look at it unless you're okay with it."

I frown, but say, "You can look at it, but I won't be pretty."

He smirks, rounds the couch, and sits down next to me. "It'd take a lot to turn me off, Ash. I've seen women of all shapes and sizes over the years, and how you looked before doesn't define you now. I'd be a hypocrite if I thought otherwise." He leans over and kisses my cheek. "No matter what I see in here, you'll still be the prettiest woman I've ever laid eyes on."

I hold his chin and kiss his cheek back. "Now you're just trying to butter me up."

Alex hums with a coy smile and opens the binder: the first page is filled with old photo prints from my junior year of college. George and I were both business majors and started dating that year; neither of us were fat yet, but we were obviously chubby. "What year was this?"

It feels like a lifetime ago. "It was . . . 1990, I believe."

He grips the edge of the page. "And the guy next to you in these photos is . . . ?"

"My late husband, yes."

"I thought so." He flips the page and looks at more college photos. There are parties and games in each other's dorm rooms and college events we attended. Holidays and walks across campus and late-night dinners downtown. I'd stopped drinking by then, but George would have a social beer or two.

Alex scans each page, flipping through our graduation, random family gatherings, and the wedding, until he reaches the photos from 1999. He looks very closely at them, at the photos of George or myself putting our hands on my stomach. It was an exciting and terrifying time. "I almost died, back then."

Alex turns the page: a photo of Mark in the NICU rests in the center. "How many weeks?"

"Thirty-five. I was in bad condition, so George convinced me to go through with a C-section." There are no photos of me in that hospital bed. "He was able to breathe and feed fine, so they only kept him in the NICU about a week."

Alex lingers over a few photos taken after I'd recovered enough to hold Mark. I was a very fat woman with a thankfully average baby; if I'd made it to full term, he probably would've been overweight. Alex brushes stray cat hairs off the sheet protector. "You look really happy to have him."

I smile softly. "It was easy to forget the pain with him in my arms. I messed up a lot, but I was determined to love him the way my parents never loved me."

Alex bumps his shoulder against mine. "I think you've done a good job so far."

"I know . . . I could've done so much better after George passed. I . . ."

"You tried your best, Ashley." He turns the page. "It wasn't perfect, but . . . loss is hard for everyone. And you were alone."

I watch those precious years pass with every flipped page. Mark's first steps. His first day of school. Those days getting to know Matthew. "They grow up so fast."

Alex smiles at the first photos depicting Mark post-awakening; he liked to pout back then. But the next page is blank. Alex doesn't say anything, merely turning to the next page. "Oh my gosh!" He beams at a picture of baby Glenn. "He was so cute!"

"I had to feed him with a little bottle, he was so small." Looking back, that little kitten saved my life. "Once he got stronger, Mark and Matthew used to compete to see which of their tails he would swat at more."

Alex makes a silly grin. "Who won?"

I smirk. "Matthew won every time. Glenn likes fuzzy, feathery things much better than slippery scales."

"That's a bummer for Mark." The next page is mostly cat photos; Glenn went from a palm-size fuzz ball to a full-grown tomcat over the course of a year.

"The silver lining is that Matthew's tail gets mistaken for a cat toy if he isn't careful. If he flicks it the wrong way, Glenn will wiggle his butt and pounce."

Alex snorts, but his mirth is cut short by the final page; he traces his fingers over a photo dated 1988. "Where did you get this?"

"I was cleaning out my closet and found it at the bottom of a box. I forgot I kept it all these years."

It's a photo from one of the many parties I attended with Alex. We were loose and drunk and having a good time, and somebody shot a picture of us smiling with red Solo cups in hand. I was healthy, with cute bangs and long hair hanging past my shoulders. Alex looked similar to his business card photo: chiseled jawline; short, boyish hair; and a flat stomach. "God," he says, "I looked so good back then."

"We both did."

He frowns. "Sometimes I feel so blindsided by everything."

"Like you said, we did what we could with our lot in life."

"I feel like . . . I didn't even notice for so long. I started gaining five or so pounds a year, and all of a sudden, I'm fifty pounds overweight."

I place my hand on his forearm. "These things . . . they creep up on you sometimes. You know there's something wrong but you think you can fix it later." I rub his bicep. "I think . . . you've been improving a lot lately. I've noticed your pants are looser than they were a few months ago."

A small smile graces his lips. "They have been. That's why I've had to wear a belt."

"I might have to buy new undergarments soon, too," I whisper in his ear.

He turns his head so we're nose to nose. "Are you trying to tempt me?"

We kiss gently, the prelude to something more. "I'm very happy. I hope we'll be able to put more photos in there. With you and me."

We kiss again, deeper this time. "God, Ash . . ."

I hum, probing his lips with my tongue.

Alex opens up, sliding his tongue around mine, then pulls back. "I'll go take care of myself in the shower."

I fondle his thick thigh and take the binder from him. "Take your time, handsome."

He stands and stretches, a lascivious smirk on his face. "I will, beautiful." He saunters upstairs before the boys have a chance to see anything inappropriate.

Jack vacated the room a while ago. The floor is clear and clean, and the dining room table is spotless. I study that ancient Polaroid from a defining moment in my life. We've changed, but I think we're better off than we were back then; for the first time in many years, my head is finally above the waves.

Alex holds me in the night, exploring everywhere but my most precious parts with careful hands. He gropes and caresses and trails endlessly, making up for the previous night lost to work. And when he tires, I turn around and do the same. I run my fingers through his hair, down his back, and into the thick fur of his tail. I pet him, squeeze his ass and his thighs, and explore the curve of his stomach. We celebrate these bodies of ours that grow stronger by the day.

I missed loving someone so wholeheartedly. And I will always miss George; we became one time and time again, created life together, and left parts of ourselves behind—he's a part of me and I was a part of him, now buried deep within the Earth, returned to dust. But a part of Alex lingers within me, and a part of me within him, and I love him differently, but equally, to George. I don't love him more or less, but the same, and I hope that can last as long as we live.

CHAPTER 25

———————

Honeydew

John

I stagger into ninety-degree heat wearing flip-flops, long pants, and a dress shirt with most of the buttons undone because, God, is it hot out today. It's the last Saturday before school starts, almost two p.m., and the clouds are doing nothing to cool the sweat on my back crawling down from my neck; I'm extra sweaty because I just finished another hour-long flamenco lesson with Sr. Hernandez and Sra. Rubio, a nice couple that moved here from Spain and teach personal lessons out of their house for a pretty penny—you can't go to any old dance studio to learn what they teach—and I'm ready to get in an air-conditioned house and drink a nice, ice-cold glass of water.

The sun beating down on my dark hair, it's times like these I wish I could shave my head bald. I trudge down the sidewalk on sore feet and burning calves toward the banged-up hand-me-down Volkswagen Passat Grace now drives because nearly all our other sisters are moved out or off at some college hours and hours away; Esther moved back in for the time being, but it won't be long before our parents drive her crazy and she finds some guy to shack her up while she's strapped for cash.

Grace always parks far away, nervous and paranoid because she's still fresh behind the wheel, but she drives safe, like a little old lady, always going exactly the speed limit and making full stops at stop signs like all drivers should. The sun glints off the cream exterior, Grace's now-neon-blue hair barely visible behind the windshield because her head is tucked, likely staring at her phone, and a flash of blond and denim strides past, oncoming on the same sidewalk.

I'm still trudging, slow and hobbling like a sunbaked zombie, my mouth open and panting, and she gets close enough I can truly see her, the most gorgeous girl I've ever seen. Maybe my brain is fried and I'm thinking with my dick more than anything else, but damn, is she smoking hot. Beautiful honey-blond hair cascades halfway down her back, framing her face with the barest hint of a wave, a section of strands hanging over the kind of rack you'd expect on a fat chick but without the belly to match. She wears a white graphic tee thin enough that the hot pink of her sports bra bleeds through; they barely contain her enormous tits, the shirt fabric tucked into washed-out jean shorts that hug the curves of her hips—they aren't wide like Emily's, but they have that womanly quality that's beyond good enough for me—and open up to long, muscular legs, the tight legs of a dancer because I know she's walking to the house I just left with that duffel bag over her shoulder that probably holds her shoes and her practice attire. Her nails are painted robin-egg blue, but only her fingernails; her toenails are bare, refined feet making deliberate steps in flat gladiator sandals. And when she passes me, and I get a whiff of her,

I realize she's tall, almost-as-tall-as-me kind of tall; she has to be at least five eleven, maybe even six feet tall. A big girl. I like that.

I stop, dazed, smelling the distinct scent of honey mixed with feminine must; something clicks in my head, and I turn back, and she's looking at me, a seductive grin on her face, and she looks away and continues striding with those long, sexy legs, and I swear she's swaying her hips at me, like she wants me to stare at her ass, and she stops at the fence bordering the Hernandez Rubio property. "My, they must've just mowed the lawn," she says, loud enough for me to hear, like she wants me to hear. And she strides inside and closes the door behind her like she was never there.

I look at the yard. It's overgrown with clover and dandelions and tall, tall grass that hasn't been mowed in months.

I turn away, the sun beating down on my head, and hobble to the car, too tired to process whatever the hell that was, even though I have an idea and I'm not sure how to feel.

I really need some water; it's too hot out here.

"Ugh, I don't wanna go to school tomorrow!" Mark rests his chin on the edge of the square table in Mr. Brown's dining room, his hand of cards strategically face down against the wooden surface.

We all stare at him, Matthew, Teddy, and I, agreeing but not saying as much. Teddy draws a card, ending his turn, and returns to eating his second bowl of chicken salad. The iceberg lettuce crunches as he chews.

Mark lies there bemoaning the inevitable, so Matthew says, "Mark, it's your turn."

"Oh, sorry." Mark lifts his head, looks at the draw pile, squints, and considers the cards in his hand; he places down a see-the-future card, looks at the top three cards on the draw pile, places them back down in the original order, and draws a card. He betrays nothing on his face, so I have no idea whether to anticipate an exploding kitten or not.

Matthew draws a card, then looks at me.

I study my meager early-game hand, then also draw a card, which is nothing more than a tacocat.

We keep playing and passing and drawing in that order, waiting for the perfect time to save our own skins or backstab someone else; sometimes, when we're feeling extra murderous, we might dogpile one of us with cards that can be played outside of our turns. Mark is a favorite for dogpiling, Matthew not too far behind, because they're older than me and Teddy and it's fun to get under their skin.

I think about the girl I saw yesterday, the one I call Gorgeous in my head, that feminine honey scent and the long legs and the big tits. It was like Teddy's scent, but without the stench of artificial turf and sweaty jockstraps.

Her eyes were beautiful, too: medium brown, decorated by light, smoky makeup that made her lashes long and dark and mysterious. And thick, glossy lips, forming that seductive grin. I really liked that. It was almost predatory. Animal. And I was the prey.

Distracted and dumb, I say, "I think I saw your sister yesterday."

Teddy glares at me, holding up a speared stack of greens and meat on his stainless steel fork. "There's no way in hell you saw my sister."

"I don't know, bro. She was tall, had the same blond hair, and she had big ones." I sit up straight and cup the air in front of my chest.

He drops his fork into his bowl, scowling with a tired sigh. "There are plenty of tall blonds with big ones, Jack."

"But this one . . ." I try not to grin like a boy in love because it's just plain lust here; I don't know Gorgeous like that. "She smelled like you. Like honey."

Dread fills his eyes, something clicking in his head, too, but instead of asking more, he bares his teeth and growls low. "If you say one more word about my sister, I'll rearrange your face."

Kyle coughs in the adjacent living room, that lingering smoker's cough he'll probably have the rest of his life.

I'm not surprised by Teddy's outburst. He's irritable in the summer because of the hunger and insomnia caused by his luke-warm version of hyperphagia, and his sister is his least favorite subject. If he could help it, we would never ever meet his sister because, even though he doesn't like her much, he has that brotherly instinct to protect her from the kind of guys that would see her as nothing but a walking pair of tits. He knows a lot of those guys, the jocks and punks that see girls as fun little sex dolls to stick their dicks in, nothing more than playthings. It's a wonder people can dehumanize the other gender like that, but they're out there, and those crimes are committed every day; us brothers have to look out for our sisters whenever we can.

"Yeah, yeah," I say. "I'll drop it."

Mark and Matthew stare, surprise and concern contorting their brows, but they don't comment. They've become familiar with Teddy's moods over the summer, for better or for worse. He has to eat a lot just for maintenance, and even more to make up for all the working out and tryouts and the fact he's still growing taller by the day, but the extra impulse to stuff his face scares the hell out of him. He desperately doesn't want to be the fat kid again, even though he'd probably have to literally eat the way a real bear does to get that bad. His hyperphagia isn't on that level, not even close, but it's enough to scare him.

Teddy sighs again, cradling his forehead in his palm. "Sorry. I'm just tired. Everything's been getting to me lately."

"I know." His mom and sister happen to live on my street, so I've had him burst into my house so many times over the summer I'd need three hands to count them all; that woman has been all over him, wanting to see him constantly now that she's not more than twenty minutes away. Fortunately, she hasn't introduced herself to my mom yet, as I have a feeling they'd get along swimmingly; both of them are caught up in appearances and wealth and secondhand success more than anything else.

Jenny gave him more than a few "scalp" massages to help him wind down on his most frustrating days; I'm amazed they aren't officially dating yet, but Jenny likes to play hard to get and Teddy doesn't have enough of a spine to catch her yet. It's a precarious thing, their little dance, their beating around the bush. Maybe they're just not ready for that next step, not while Teddy is still reeling from the loss of his humanity and Jenny is finding her place in the grand order of this world. The expectations of our family make it hard to choose something as monumental as a lover for ourselves; our parents' marriage was arranged, for status and shared wealth and perfect male heirs. I just know they'll shove a girl on me, some dainty thing from a rich family I don't give a fuck about, but I won't want her. I won't.

Gorgeous enters my mind's eye again, her swaying hips and long strides. A powerful girl, one who doesn't need a man to find purpose in her life. She knows what she wants, and she gets it eventually. She'll work for it if she wants it bad enough. She's almost a fantasy, Gorgeous in my mind.

"It's your turn, Jack," Matthew says, organizing his hand.

I haven't been paying attention at all, so I play a shuffle, put my hand face down, and shuffle the deck. Instead of playing it safe, I draw the top card, and of course it's an exploding kitten; there goes my one defuse. I pull the deck under the table and put the exploding kitten under the top card hoping Mark will end up pulling it, then place the deck back in the middle where everyone can reach it.

Teddy plays a see the future, looks at the top three cards, his grumpy face unchanging, and draws the top card.

We all grin when Mark draws the exploding kitten, and he doesn't have a defuse. "Aw, what?!" He throws his hand, including the exploding kitten, in the discard pile. He grumbles and we continue the round without him.

We keep taking our turns, throwing attacks and skips and nopes, along with the occasional favor or combo—I snag a defuse from Matthew—until it's just me and Teddy left. Teddy has always had uncanny luck in card and board games, but he's such a massive nerd for the most obscure shit I've never heard of that it doesn't surprise me. Maybe his love for games gives him that sixth sense, that intuition, to remain king.

The draw pile stands only five cards tall, and one of those cards is an exploding kitten; it's do or die now, and I'm all out of defuses. I push my luck, all out of options, and place two fingers on the top card, but just as I'm about to draw, the TV suddenly shuts off, taking away the white noise my mind had been filtering out.

"Why'd you turn off the TV?" Mr. Brown asks.

I expect Kyle to say—no, hope he'll say—he has to use the bathroom, but he says, "Bobby, I've been lyin' to you for forty years."

Mr. Brown goes utterly silent.

Teddy drops his fork in his salad bowl with a metallic clang, his face stricken with fear. We didn't realize it when it was just us, but after learning the scents and the signs and getting confirmation from Matthew and Mark, we all know Kyle's lie, a secret he's held so long he won't even reveal it to us.

I don't know what else to do, so I put my hand down, take my fingers off the top card, and place one hand in my lap and the other over Teddy's tense forearm; his nails are already growing sharp.

"What?" Mr. Brown says. "Kyle, what are you talking about? What could you possibly be lying about?"

"My ears ain't a birth defect. Not in the general sense of the word. I'm a . . . a . . ." Kyle's words fail him; he doesn't have a name for our kind, not like we do. Or maybe he does, but it's not a nice one.

Mr. Brown pauses. "Kyle, I . . . I was starting to figure for about a year now. But I trust you, so I didn't want to say anything. Figured you'd tell me yourself."

Teddy trembles under my fingers; he puts his cards down and his hands in his lap because he knows the implication.

Kyle huffs shakily. "I'm tellin' you now, ain't I?"

"You are." Mr. Brown lets the statement hang in the air. "Can I see?"

"It ain't pretty." There's so much certainty there—so much defeat.

"Dang it, Kyle." Mr. Brown's voice is gentle in a way I've never heard it before. "I've seen you every which way there is; it can't be that bad."

"Close your eyes," Kyle says. "I don't want you watchin'."

Silence.

Clothing shuffles, the couch creaks, and Kyle grunts. The couch groans when he sits back down, and I wish I could see him, see

Mr. Brown's reaction: his friend of forty years isn't human, hasn't been since the beginning. "You can open your eyes."

It's quiet, and we all hold our breath. He's studying Kyle, taking it all in. He could be anything: scales, feathers, or fur. But there's an exhalation of surprise, someone gripping a shirt. "You aren't ugly." Mr. Brown sounds choked up. "I think it suits you."

Kyle sniffles. "Look at you, makin' an old man cry." He doesn't burst into tears, but there's a tremor in his voice.

They quiet down, sharing something that can't be heard.

"But you got your own secret, don't you, Bobby?"

Teddy's fur grows between my fingers.

"You need to tell those boys. All four of 'em."

"Fuck," Teddy whispers, and the chair squeals against the linoleum when he slams his active hands on the table and rises to his full, towering height. I let him go, but he stands there, fists at his sides, his face red and watery.

The couch decompresses, and Mr. Brown enters the angle of my view, standing a few paces back from the doorway. His face is drawn, guilty as he faces Teddy.

Seeing him there, Teddy yells, "You knew?! All this time?! Dad, you . . ." He trembles, trying desperately to hold back a deluge of emotion. "Did you know how hard it was to hide this? I tried so hard to keep it from you and you knew all along." He's crying now, hot angry tears trailing down his cheeks and dropping off his chin. "You could've just told me. You could've saved me all this trouble and stress and . . . and . . ." He breaks and drops back into his seat, head in his hands, his bear ears pulled back against his head; a few strands of hair hang over his forehead, between his lengthy claws. "I hate this . . ." He sobs into his hands, all hiccups and shaking, his stomach trembling under his shirt.

Mr. Brown looks over us, the three of us who remain dormant and his sobbing son, and I know we need to give them space. I look at Mark and Matthew in turn, and once I've made eye contact with them both, I jerk my head toward the doorway. We get up and they follow me past Mr. Brown, who enters the dining room and takes the chair Mark had occupied just a moment before, pulling it forward until he's knee to furry knee with Teddy. "I'm sorry, Luke." He pulls Teddy into an embrace. "I should've told you sooner, but I didn't want to make you cry."

I look away, see that Matthew and Mark have perched themselves cross-legged in front of the couch, and join them where I can't look into the dining room; Mr. Brown goes so quiet I can't hear anything other than Teddy's sobs.

Kyle looks down on us with half-lidded eyes, chewing a toothpick in his mouth; it only takes a glance to see he's an opossum man. He has round, black, furless ears peeking through his hair and tilted toward us. He grips the toothpick between his index and middle fingers and pulls it out of his mouth; the black fur covering his arms and most of his hands resembles fingerless gloves, the furless portion of his fingers pale-pink flesh tipped with sharp yellowed claws. "Y'all boys don't need to be hidin' nothin' if you don't want to no more. Bobby's done known a long while now."

We glance at each other, and I remove the ties and pins from my ears, relishing the release of their sore muscles; Matthew lets his cat ears rise out from under his curls and pulls his tail out from under his shirt. By the time we go active, Teddy's sobs have died down into sniffles.

I bow my head, ever embarrassed to be seen by anyone in active form, and gaze at Kyle's widespread paws; they, too, have that fingerless-glove look, each opposable toe curled up under its respective sole, the other four fingerlike toes pointing straight forward, with similar pink skin and yellowed claws. I glance up and notice his long, prehensile tail draped across the arm of the couch, furless and textured like snakeskin; it's not pink like his fingers and toes, but closer to a pale beige.

Kyle grins. "Well, ain't y'all cute." The crinkle in his eye tells me he means it as a compliment.

I blush anyway, my ears lowering toward my head subconsciously.

Kyle coughs into his fist and clears his throat. "I'm sorry it took me so long to handle this. I made a deal with your mama, Red, and today was the deadline."

"A deal?" Mark's wide eyes roam all over Kyle.

"Yeah, boy. I gave her some courage to reveal that boyfriend of hers to ya. I needed to give myself an excuse to stop this whole charade, anyway"—he fiddles with the toothpick in his hand—"and I was gettin' tired of Bobby pussyfootin' around. I want y'all boys to have another place you can be comfortable in your own skin; I never had nothin' like that at your age."

Mr. Brown appears in the doorway a little worse for wear; when he spots us sitting in a row on the carpet, his eyebrows draw up more and he puts on a gentle smile. "I guess I'll have to get used to seeing y'all like this, huh?" He puts a hand on the back of his neck.

Matthew's tail gets puffy, but he doesn't fall into hysterics, so that's progress on his end; Mark isn't particularly bothered, but he almost never is, and I've known Mr. Brown long enough that I only feel a little embarrassed.

"Bobby, have some tact," Kyle says. "Come sit." After Mr. Brown returns to his spot on the couch, Kyle regards us and jerks his head toward the dining room. "Y'all boys can get back to business."

We get up and return to the dining room, taking the seats we left only ten minutes ago.

Teddy glances at us, holding his arms and sniffling, and stares at the floor right where it meets the wall.

Kyle turns the TV back on.

Teddy looks back up, his ears lifting slightly. "Can y'all stay for dinner?"

"Sure, bro," I say. "Mark, you think you could give me a ride home? Grace likes to turn in early."

"I gotcha." Mark smiles genuinely. "Shall we play another round?" He lifts his scaly hand and gestures all fancy-like.

"Let me see what I was going to draw first." I flip the card at the top of the draw pile for everyone to see, then show my useless hand.

"Looks like I was the winner there, huh?" Teddy forms a pinched smile.

"How many does that make? Five?"

"Four. But I can make it five." His posture loosens up, and he pulls his chair forward so it's back up against the table.

"We'll see about that." I growl playfully.

The mood brought back up, Matthew and I organize and reshuffle the various cards according to the rules—Teddy's the best at shuffling, but his claws are way too long to get a good grip—then we play yet another round of Exploding Kittens.

"Thanks for staying late, y'all." Teddy holds his elbow, long dormant.

"Anytime, Teddy." Mark holds his arms out. "Now give us a hug before we go."

Teddy obliges, giving a hug first to Mark, then to Matthew—he has to bend down because Matthew's so short compared to him—and after the two head outside to start up the truck, he shares a longer hug with me. He holds me close, chest to chest, squeezing as hard as he can without hurting. "I guess I understand why you were so mad I knew way back when," he whispers. "Thanks for putting up with me again. I know I'm real neurotic this time of year."

"Hey, don't mention it." I pat him on the back. "Friends support each other, right?"

"That's right." Teddy gives me another squeeze, then lets go. He looks off to the side, still sheepish about what happened after lunch, but manages to reestablish eye contact. "I know you're real self-conscious about the bunny thing, but please don't be a stranger. Now that my dad's in the know, y'all can come here, too. I'm sure Ms. K. needs a break from all of us every now and then, anyway."

I *am* self-conscious, but as soon as somebody sees me once, it isn't that big of a deal anymore. "Sure, bro. I'm glad we'll get to see more of each other, and maybe . . ." I hold my tongue; no need to rile him up mentioning his elusive sister.

Teddy raises an eyebrow. "And maybe . . . ?"

I pat his shoulder. "Don't worry about it. Get your sleep; we have a big day tomorrow."

Teddy rolls his eyes, but smiles; his eyes are still red, but I'm sure he'll look and feel much better in the morning. Messy as it was, I'm glad Kyle worked up the courage to reveal his and Mr. Brown's secrets.

With one final farewell, I walk outside and enter the back seat of Mark's truck, hoping my parents won't be too pissed I stayed out late on a school night.

Late in the night, I wake up from a dream I can't remember. I don't remember most of my dreams, but I do remember the series of dreams I had the week before I awakened. I'd dream of a black bunny being hunted mercilessly, running and running and running, until it was caught, and I'd wake up before the hunter dealt the fatal blow; but the night before I awakened, I was the bunny, and I was running and running and running, and I was caught, and the hunter cut off my feet—a sign of good luck. I woke up feverish and chilled and spent half the school day transforming, going in and out of sleep. Jenny saw the beginning and had the foresight to tell everyone I was sick and needed to stay home, and my parents happily let her be responsible for my care because they were too busy working; that was a good thing for once, that they'd leave caretaking up to a child, because I doubt they'd be happy to know their little male heir is a bunny boy on top of everything else.

In the dead of night, impossibly dark because few stars shine through in the city and our bedroom window doesn't face the street, I think about the anger I felt when I learned Teddy knew the truth for an entire year, and I think of Teddy's anger at Mr. Brown. I think, as angry as I was, Teddy must've been angrier; hiding from someone you see for a limited amount of time during the school day—a setting in which you're hiding from every other kid anyway—is far different from hiding from someone you live with. And to add the stress of the season on top of that . . .

I turn over onto my chest, readjust my head on my pillow, and settle, hoping to sleep. I remember when Teddy came to me last year, toward the end of May, right in the middle of the school day. It was just after lunch, and he pulled me into the boys' bathroom and showed me his hands slowly growing claws and paw pads, discoloring his normally fair skin. "I know you know what's happening to me." He was shaking, on the verge of tears. "I saw your, uh . . ." He swallowed, putting his hands in his pockets, his knees nearly buckling. "Your bunny ears, when you slept over at my house that first time."

I was pissed. I was so fucking pissed when I heard him say that, and I know it was on my face; I nearly went active right there in the bathroom. But Teddy was my friend, the only friend I had in that godforsaken middle school, the only guy who never called me girly or asked if I was gay, and he needed my help. So I sucked it up and pulled him out into the middle of the woods nearby because we'd be seen anywhere else, then told him to lie down and let me handle it. That was the first time I saw Teddy cry; today was the second.

Thinking of Teddy, even that moment that made me madder than hell, puts a smile on my face; I'm happy for him, knowing he has his dad and Kyle by his side, and that good feeling lulls me back into a silent sleep.

A dull-yellow school bus lurches to a stop, and my two sisters and I step inside. We take different rows, our friend groups utterly divided, at least publicly: Grace sits next to a chubby girl wearing baggy, unflattering clothes and oversize glasses; Jenny sits in the back with dark-skinned girls wearing makeup as outrageous as her own; and I sit by myself, right next to the window so I can watch the same sights I saw all last year.

The bus crawls down the street, sputtering to a stop at the next bus stop with waiting high schoolers. A few kids get on, some dragging their feet, clearly dead tired like me. My eyes drooping, I barely notice someone sit next to me and cross her legs, old white Converse on her feet; I turn my head just enough to spot that long blond hair falling over her generous chest: she's Gorgeous. She's dressed more modestly for school, wearing Bermuda shorts and an oversize T-shirt tucked into the waistband, Guns N' Roses emblazoned on the front. I turn away, my heart pumping too fast, but her reflection taunts me in the window as she studies the back of my head.

She lives on my street, I think, swallowing; she watches my Adam's apple bob up and down with a coy smile, but turns her gaze forward when the bus stops once again. She doesn't speak to me the whole ride to school, and I can't bring myself to talk to her. When we arrive, she saunters off with the rest of the crowd, leaving me in her dust, and I begin my trek to class, watching her hips sway before she disappears inside.

I place my tray on the cafeteria table and promptly sit down next to Matthew, Mark on his left; Emily sits in front of Matthew, centering her between the three of us on the other side. She's in an awfully good mood for a Monday *and* the first day of school, but I imagine she's happy to see us in person again for the first time in almost three months; Mark and Matthew, on the other hand, look like they're ready to drop dead.

I take a bite of whole-grain chicken sandwich, chew, and swallow, but before I can take another dreadful bite, Gorgeous strides up to our table, right behind Emily, and covers her eyes with her hands. "Guess who?" she says, smiling.

Emily gasps and gropes at Gorgeous's hands with the hand that isn't currently occupied by a PB&J. She pushes one hand to her forehead, carefully slides her half-eaten sandwich back into its plastic bag, then grabs them both from her face so she can inspect Gorgeous's robin egg–blue fingernails. "Heather!" Emily cranes her neck back until her head nestles in Heather's covered cleavage. "What are you doing here?"

Heather places her long fingers around Emily's shoulders, some of her hair falling into Emily's face. "I moved, honey. Thought I'd surprise you." She glances up, studying us boys one by one, until she lands on me and lingers; her smile becomes a sinister grin. "So these are your mysterious boy friends, hmm?" She speaks slowly enough I can hear the space between *boy* and *friends*.

Emily splutters. "Oh my God, Heather, shut up!"

Mark chuckles.

Matthew blushes and shoves more of his sandwich in his mouth.

I'm still getting over the fact that Gorgeous is 100 percent Teddy's little twin sister; she looks so dominating, standing there while I'm sitting down.

"Anyway, come sit down!" Emily grins wide. "I can't believe we all have the same lunch period."

Heather surprisingly sits down in front of Mark, places her book bag on the ground next to her stool, and fishes out a hard plastic lunch box and a sandwich bag holding a stainless steel fork. She places her lunch on the table, cradles her head with her right hand, and surveys her prey; she licks her lips, her eyes on mine, and tucks her hair behind her left ear. "Well, aren't y'all cute." The glint in her eye begs for a challenge.

No one says anything because all four of us are busy staring at Heather's exposed ear; it's pointed at the tip, though I focus on the blue marble stud piercing her lobe.

Emily gapes. "Heather, you are not." She puts her head in her hands and groans.

Heather's eyes open wide. "Not what?"

Emily frowns, giving Heather the stink eye. "Show me your biggest smile."

Heather raises one blond eyebrow. "Why?"

"Just do it!"

Heather grins wide, showing off some gnarly canines not too different from Teddy's.

"Oh my God . . ." Emily despairs. "All my friends are monster people . . ."

That awkward, toothy grin plastered to her face, Heather turns her gaze toward us boys. "Oh dear. I didn't realize she knows about y'all."

Emily says, "That's what we fought about!"

"Oh. You never told me that part."

"Of course I didn't tell you that part! I thought you were—" Emily stops herself from saying human.

"I'm sorry, honey. That's something I usually keep under lock and key."

Emily sighs. "I know. I get it. But you're coming to my house as soon as possible."

"Huh?"

Emily rounds on her, a snarl begging to escape. "You are *not* going to drop this on me and expect me not to ask questions. And what was up with that, anyway? How'd you even know so fast?"

Heather taps her nose. "I've been smelling them on you for a long time now."

"Smelling them?" Emily squeaks, a blush blooming on her cheeks.

Mark seems like he's still processing the fact that monster girls exist, and Matthew is far too embarrassed to speak, so I have to break the ice. "Remember, Emily? We told you we rub off on things easily, which includes other people. You've hugged and held hands with us many times, so it's only natural."

Emily conspicuously sniffs her palm. "I can't tell."

Heather smiles gently. "It's hard even for me to pick it up directly from the source, and bears are known to have a strong sense of smell."

"You're a bear girl?" Emily whispers.

Heather nods, biting her lip before scanning her male audience once more.

I'm not surprised she's a bear; knowing Teddy, I can imagine how she must look active.

"You have to show me next time you come over." Emily gushes.

"Hmm . . ." Heather cocks her head. "I'll allow it, but only for you."

"Yes!" Emily pumps a fist, then looks over our bewildered faces. "Oh! I should introduce everyone. So this is my friend, Heather."

We nod stupidly.

"And Heather, these are my *guy* friends." She points at the literal redhead in front of Heather—"That's Mark"—she points at the sheepish cat boy in front of her—"that's Matthew"—she points at me, furrowing her brow—"and that's . . ."

"Jack," I say.

"Mark, Matthew, and *Jack*." The way Heather says my name sends a shiver down my spine. "It's nice to meet you."

"Yeah, sure," Mark says, suddenly out of his funk. "Anyway, what was up with you calling us cute earlier?" He sounds miffed for some reason.

"You got a problem with me stating the obvious?" She smiles like she's toying with him.

"I am *not* cute!" Mark huffs, puffing his chest out and crossing his arms.

"You're very cute. You have a baby face." She covers her mouth like she's trying not to laugh.

Mark scowls. "Just because you're pretty doesn't mean you can say whatever you want."

"So you think I'm pretty?"

He narrows his eyes. "You got a problem with me stating the obvious?"

Her eyes squint with a hidden smile. "I think I like this one, Emily."

"Well, I'll stop you right there." Mark holds his hand out. "You're not my type."

"What even is your type?" Emily asks.

Her words give him pause; he screws his face up, hand cupping his chin. "You know what? I'm not sure. I can tell what I don't like but not what I'm looking for." He nods to himself. "I think all girls can be beautiful, but there's a secret sauce that makes some special."

"All girls?" I ask.

"I know what I said."

"Don't get him philosophizing about female beauty," Matthew says, "or male beauty, for that matter."

"I could be a professor of beauty," Mark says.

I'm not sure if Mark has low standards or if he genuinely believes anyone can be beautiful. But beauty *is* more than skin deep; as extra as Mark is, he does have a brain in his head.

Emily and Matthew bicker with Mark about the many strange things he's professed in party chats over the summer, and Heather focuses on her lunch. She opens her lunch box to reveal an elaborate fried-chicken salad full of colorful vegetables and covered in a light vinaigrette, though there's far more chicken than salad, probably to up the calories; now that I think of it, Heather must also deal with hyperphagia throughout the summer and early fall, yet she seems so calm compared to her brother.

When she leans down to eat a forkful of salad, her tits touch the table; they're visually the same size and shape as what I saw on Saturday, so I imagine she's wearing another sports bra under her shirt, making me even more curious how big those things really are. Heather pulls her hair away from her chest and out of her face so she doesn't end up with something other than food in her mouth; as she slowly chews, mouth perfectly closed, her eyes flit up to mine.

I hastily avert my gaze and return to eating my pitiful lunch. Another bite of subpar chicken sandwich distracts me from Heather's gorgeous body, but as soon as she isn't paying attention, I look at her chest again. Sports bras tend to make boobs look more compact, so hers must be—

"Eyes up here, big boy." Heather smirks, two fingers guiding my gaze from her boobs to her face.

The rest of the table stops bickering as I try and fail to hide my embarrassment.

"Bro." Mark puts a stupid grin on his face.

"For shame." Matthew shakes his head with a smile.

Emily looks disappointed in me.

God dammit . . .

"I don't mind if you stare." Heather leans over her desk, her tits covering half the tiny surface, roaming my body with her smoky eyes.

We have third period together. Personal finance. I'm sitting in the back right corner, and of course Heather took the desk on my left.

"That wasn't my intention." I pretend to pay attention to the boring introductory PowerPoint presentation.

"We both know that's not true." She smirks seductively.

I have nothing to say for myself; I wanted to stare but didn't want to get caught. I close my eyes for a long moment. *Be strong, Jack; be strong—this is Teddy's sister we're talking about.* "Stop talking to me. We're supposed to be paying attention."

"Ooh~ Cold, are we?" She props her chin up on her hands, her tits resting an inch past her elbows; I'm beginning to think she's doing this on purpose.

I grit my teeth, adamantly ignoring her, big boobs be damned.

"Alright. I'll play your game, *Jack*."

There's something about the way she says my name that drives me crazy, but I stubbornly stare straight ahead.

Heather leans back so her tits are no longer on the desk's surface and stares ahead with the rest of us, but I don't miss the glances she gives me out of the corner of her eye, nibbling at her full bottom lip.

This semester is going to be hell.

⁓

I lean against the brick wall near the theater's emergency exit, waiting impatiently for my bus to show up. Fortunately, I don't have fourth period with Heather; unfortunately, she rides the same bus as me.

I spot her rack round the corner before I see her face, and before I have a chance to do so much as blink, Heather sidles up next to me and leans against the brick wall, keeping a respectable one-foot distance between our shoulders. God is she tall; I have maybe an inch and a half on her, but that's it.

She's awfully quiet, her face so neutral it's almost grumpy, and I wonder if she's waiting for me to tell her to get bent. Girls like Heather make me nervous; I can't help but wonder if she's playing with me so she can break my heart for a cheap laugh. It's happened before, back when I was bullied all the time due to my looks. Thinking about it makes me feel stupidly self-conscious.

"Hey." I run my thumb over my funny bone.

Heather's eyes light up with restrained surprise. "Hey."

We stare at each other for a moment, until I need to look away. "What's your angle, Heather? Am I just a game to you?" I glance back, wanting to see her face.

She smiles gently, her usual flirtatious overtone tamped down. "You're not a game, Jack. I know I must be coming on strong, but I've been waiting to meet you for a long time; you're better than I thought you'd be."

I furrow my brow. "What do you mean, you've been waiting a long time?"

"You're my brother's best friend, aren't you?" She taps her nose. "I've been smelling you on him for a long time now, but he'd never mention you to me."

"Teddy never mentions me?"

Heather shakes her head, nibbling her lip again. "Luke and I keep our favorite things to ourselves. I was excited to know there was another person like me around, and one my age at that. It was just Kyle for a long time."

I glance at her beautiful brown eyes. "You know about Kyle?"

"Of course I do. He's the one that protected me from my family when I turned for the first time."

"Did Kyle tell you what he did yesterday?"

Heather tilts her head, clearly confused. "No? I haven't had a chance to talk to him since last week, and he doesn't like calling or texting about important things. He's real paranoid about someone listening in."

I'm not sure if I should tell her, but I figure it's important for her to know. "He told your dad what he is."

Heather gapes. "What? That's . . ."

"Apparently Mr. Brown caught Teddy after he turned last summer but was too afraid to say something to him, so Kyle took matters into his own hands."

Heather grips her arm, her hair falling into her face. "What did my dad say?"

Hesitant as I am, I edge closer to Heather until our shoulders touch. "He took it well. He even gave Kyle a compliment."

"What about me? Did Kyle say something about me?"

I shake my head. "Not a word. Kyle rarely mentions you when I'm around."

"Okay," she says. "Okay."

"I think you might want to tell your dad. He knows about all of us now, even Matthew and Mark. He wants to help as best he can."

"Gosh, Jack, I haven't even told my brother, and he was so bad at hiding it I caught him rooting in the fridge at midnight with the bear out." She brings a finger to her lips, but carefully refrains from biting her nail. "That's probably how Dad found out. Luke kept resisting his instincts all summer, but you can only go hungry for so long before it drives you mad."

"I understand." It's always hard to reveal everything, even knowing someone will take it well.

Heather seems incredibly distressed, so I decide I should change the subject.

"How do you deal with your hibernation instincts? You're mostly laid-back compared to Teddy."

Mirth returns to Heather's face; she lifts her head, sliding her finger down her chin. "Oh, that's simple: I eat when I'm hungry and keep eating until I'm full. Sure, I gain five or ten pounds every summer, but that's not much of anything at my height, and most of it goes to my hips or thighs, then I lose it all in the winter, anyway. But I've never been as big as my brother, so I have a better relationship with the scale than he ever will. Whether I'm 160 or 170 doesn't matter as long as I think I look good and feel good."

And she does look good. She has plenty of womanly curves, and she's toned from dancing flamenco to boot; her biceps are well-defined, and so are her calves.

She chews her lip again, perfectly aware I'm looking her over. "I should thank you for helping Luke out with his paranoia. Kyle helped him where he could, but I think your support was what he really needed. I would've done more, but we don't get along like that; he'd just get mad at me if I told him how to eat."

Yeah, I'd be pretty mad if Jenny told me how to eat, too, and we get along reasonably well for siblings who have to share a room; we're not head over heels for each other, but neither are we at each other's throats. "I've heard you get along as well as oil and water."

She has the self-awareness to look guilty. "I may have pushed his buttons really hard when we were younger, before Ruby divorced Dad."

Ruby? Her relationship with her mom must be next-level bad if she's calling her by her first name. "What's the worst you did?"

Heather makes a silly grin, showing her canines. "When I hit puberty and my boobs were growing, I got really excited when mine finally got bigger than Luke's. Of course I told him as much, which was really mean of me."

I gawk. "That's awful." No wonder Teddy is so sensitive about his weight.

"I know. Our relationship has never recovered since." She shakes her head, quivering like she's trying not to laugh; her shoulder bumps against mine.

"Why're you laughing?"

"Because his pecs are still bigger than most girls' tits, but he'd destroy me if I told him that!" She grins so wide her upper canines slip over her bottom lip.

And she's right; Teddy has some massive pecs that put all seven of my sisters to shame. "C'mon, you shouldn't laugh!" But here I am chuckling, too.

She elbows me playfully. "Says you!"

I lean against her arm, swept up in her energy. When our giggling dies down, I say, "You're pretty cool, Heather."

She smiles sheepishly. "You think so? And here I thought you didn't like me."

"Oh, I like you just fine." The words rumble in my throat. After all these years, my voice is something deep and gravelly; I need to remember I'm not the girly boy I used to be.

"I like you a lot myself, *Jack*." She bites her lip, her eyes hooded by those dark lashes.

The way she says my name, it brings out something primal in me. I want to plant my lips on hers, but I can't—she's my best friend's sister.

Suddenly self-aware, I look past her beautiful face to see our bus in the bus lot. "Our ride's here." I trudge past her, her footsteps on the pavement the only indication she's following. We step into the bus, and I sit where I usually do next to the window on the right side; Heather slides in next to me until her hip touches mine, and I let her rest her head on my shoulder.

About halfway home, she asks, "What are you, Jack?"

The streets pass us by, and when we stop once again, I watch tired kids shamble back to their homes. "I'm just another guy."

She looks at my reflection in the window and smiles softly. Nothing flirty, nothing mischievous—just a smile. She remains silent all the way up to her street; when the bus lurches to a stop, she stands and waits for the kids behind her to clear the middle lane. Before she makes her leave, she looks over her shoulder and says, "See you tomorrow, *Jack*."

I watch her go, her hips swaying, and hide my smitten smile.

CHAPTER 26

Fuzzy Friends

Emily

When the doorbell rings and Geoff starts barking up a storm, I dash downstairs and open the front door for Heather.

"Hey, honey," she says as she walks into the foyer.

Geoff, tail wagging so hard his butt sways back and forth, scrambles past me and immediately jumps on Heather.

"Hi, Geoffrey!" Heather catches his paws and lets him lick her face. "You're always a happy boy, aren't you?"

The yellow Lab barks, tongue lolling.

Heather allows Geoff to give all the kisses he wants, then guides him back to the floor and pets his head. "Good boy, Geoff. Good boy."

Geoff wags harder and charges through the kitchen to the door that leads to our large, fenced backyard.

Heather saunters behind him, lets him outside, and closes the door on him—he'll be outside awhile yet. Because dogs are gross, she washes her hands in the kitchen sink and wipes the slobber off her chin and cheeks.

While she dries her hands off with paper towels, Cream waddles into the room. Heather smiles at the overweight cat, squats down, and holds out a hand. "Are you gonna be nice today, Cream?" She waggles her finger in hopes of attracting the cat.

Cream arches her back, her black tail going all puffy, and hisses.

"Boo, you're no fun." Heather pouts and stands back up. "At least your sister is nice."

Cream hates strangers and is vile enough to let every guest know how she feels; fortunately, she doesn't scratch unless you get too close to her while she stands her ground—not even my family and I are safe from her wrath when she's agitated.

"Why don't we go to my room and leave Cream alone," I say. "We have a lot to talk about."

Heather grins all sly. "That we do." She brings her long fingers to her lips like she wants to nibble on them. "I have some questions of my own, too." She has that mischievous look in her eye like she's ready to talk about something scandalous.

I guess talking about a bunch of monster boys is a little scandalous, especially if she brings up Jack; Heather was looking at him like he's the finest piece of meat she's ever seen. Thinking back, I should've figured she'd like Jack; he's just her type, what with the lean, tall figure and the long, dark hair. Heather prefers guys taller than her already towering figure, and she likes them mysterious and brooding, which Jack fits to a T.

Heather takes her sandals off and we walk upstairs, Heather taking two steps at a time, but before I join her in my room, I knock on Connor's bedroom door. "Hey, Connor!"

"What?!"

"Could you let Geoff back in when he starts barking at the door?"

Connor grumbles. "Yeah, sure, whatever."

"Thanks." I try not to sound too sarcastic.

Heather smiles but saves my brother the trouble of her meddling. I wouldn't say she has a bad relationship with my brothers, but Connor recently reached his edgy-teenager phase: older sisters and their girly friends are the height of uncool right now.

As for Noah and my parents, they're out shopping or something; they were already gone by the time I woke up late in the afternoon, so I assume they drove off for lunch and weekend errands. I recall Noah needed a haircut and a better calculator for middle school math.

Heather saunters into my room ahead of me, so I close the door behind us and swiftly lock it; the locks are so crappy my brothers could find their way inside if they were determined enough, but the jangling of the knob will give us enough precious seconds to hide anything crazy. My anticipation for our upcoming conversation makes my heart hammer way too fast.

After slinging her purse on a hook next to the door, Heather sits on my flowery comforter and leans back on the dark-green backrest pillow against the daffodil-yellow wall behind my bed—my favorite color is yellow, rich greens a close second, so those colors are all over my room. She adjusts until she's cross-legged and cozy.

I turn my olive chair to face her and sit down. "So."

Heather raises one smooth eyebrow. "So?"

"You're a bear girl," I say.

"Yes," she says.

"For how long?"

Her smile turns genuine. "Since I was eight."

"Oh my gosh." I gape.

She grins, revealing her sharp canines. "Wanna see?"

I nod vigorously.

"Is it okay if I strip down to my underwear?"

I have no clue why she needs to do that, but we're both girls and we're both very straight—late nights texting about hot boys, both fictional and unattainable, can attest to that—so I nod again and close my mouth. "Can I watch?"

Heather's grin turns sly. "Watch me take off my clothes or watch me let the bear out?"

"Girl, you know what I mean."

An airy laugh escapes her as she pulls down her high-waisted jeans and tugs off her shirt, which she folds and places next to her on the bed, leaving her in nothing but bikini-cut panties and a magenta sports bra that perfectly contains her enormous tits— no quad boob in sight. She resettles against the backrest pillow, this time keeping her legs straight out in front of her. She takes a deep breath and closes her eyes, her expression contorting into something more vulnerable than I've ever seen on her.

The transformation starts in her nails, just as it did for Matthew when I saw him; they slowly grow longer, the nail polish painted on their surfaces cracking apart into three ragged sections as the nail becomes more cylindrical and clawlike. Then the pads form on the soles of her feet, her palms, and her fingertips, a muddy-brown color unlike the dark gray of Matthew's pads, and bigger, too. The barely there blond body hair on her arms and legs thickens into fur, transitioning into a light brown at her extremities, and her ears, still pierced by blue studs, grow blond fur matching her hair. Her feet shift into bear paws, the process less grotesque on account of the fur masking the shifting structure, and her ears climb to the top of her head, all the while becoming the round, all-fluff ears of a grizzly bear; a tiny dot of blue remains visible at the outer corners, the earrings swamped by fur but otherwise perfectly snug. She sighs, opens her eyes, and turns to reveal her tiny vestigial tail hanging over the band of her low-rise underwear.

"Can you move it?" I ask.

"A little bit." Her tail swipes left and right in a pendulum arc, then hangs straight down again before she lifts it up once; it flops back down over her underwear silently. Unlike the way they're represented on teddy bears, her tail is cylindrical rather than a perfect sphere.

I study her tail until she settles back down against the backrest pillow, once again crossing her legs; her ears point directly at me, so I assume she isn't uncomfortable with me looking. Her arms and legs look so much bigger and much less defined with all the fur, her feet merely claw-tipped slippers from this angle. She must be so cozy to lie with like that; no wonder Mark likes getting bear hugs from Teddy.

I hold my cheeks in my hands, kicking my legs like a little girl. "You look like you could cuddle me and maul me to death at the same time."

Heather's face transitions through at least five expressions. "Was that supposed to be a compliment?" She raises an eyebrow with a strange grin.

I nod vigorously. "Oh my God, you have no idea how much I love this stuff. Like, I literally can't right now."

Her grin loosens into a somber smile. "If I knew you were such a fan of my kind, I would've told you sooner."

I've kept my own secrets, too; I can't come out and tell just anyone that I love monster boys and want to pet Matthew's ears until he purrs like a motorcycle! "I don't blame you for keeping it a secret from me. I didn't even know monster people are real until Matthew messed up and it blew up in my face."

"He's the short one, right? Curly brunette hair?"

I nod, blushing. "He's the one I told you about all the time."

Heather brings the tip of one finger next to her eye, her long claw reaching her temple. "I suppose it makes more sense now that it took him a month to make up with you. What animal is he?"

"A cat." I hope he doesn't mind me telling her, but he'd probably give himself away on his own because of his eyes in the sun or from unintentionally purring around one of us.

"Okay, I thought so." She smirks. "How do you feel about him being a kitty cat?"

I cover my eyes with my hands, only peeking out between my spread fingers. "I love it." But I liked him plenty before I knew he was a cat boy. "I haven't had a chance to pet his ears, but his paw pads and fur are super soft."

Heather's claw slides closer to her lips. "I can imagine. He does seem very pettable."

At the mention of petting, I slump forward. "He hasn't been comfortable with much after what happened back in March. He'll let me hold his hands and stuff, but there's no way he'll let me touch his ears or tail. He's really nervous about physical contact because he scratched me—"

"He scratched you?!" Heather gapes.

I hold out my hands. "It was an accident! I was getting in his face and he really, really didn't want me to know he isn't human, then his claws came out all of a sudden because he couldn't resist going active any longer, and he had his hands on my arms because he was trying to get me to leave him alone, but of course I didn't because I was mad he wouldn't tell me why he got sick all the time but I knew he told Jack even though I was his friend first, and—"

"Calm down, honey. I think I get it." Her claw slides back up to her temple.

I hang my head. "We're pretty much good now, anyway. It just sucks I can't hug him like I used to."

"He used to let you hug him? He seems more like a stay-at-least-six-feet-away-from-me-at-all-times kind of guy."

I squint. "I think Mark beat that out of him a long time ago."

Heather smiles knowingly. "Maybe he just has a crush on you."

My brow furrows. "You think so?"

"Honey, you've got to be blind not to tell."

I sigh. "It's not like that crush is going anywhere."

"You know, you could always ask *him* out."

My eyes widen. "No way!"

Heather cocks her head. "Why not?"

"Because!"

She smiles. "Because?"

I cover my face again. "I want him to ask *me* out."

"Ever the traditional one, aren't you?"

I look down, distraught. "That's part of it, but . . . I think rushing him into a relationship is the last thing I should be doing. It wasn't that long ago he had a total breakdown because I touched his hand when he wasn't expecting it."

Heather suddenly looks skeptical. "I don't mean to judge, but are you sure this is the guy for you?" So she totally means to judge.

"Sure, he has some baggage, but everything else is great." I start counting out his best qualities on my fingers. "He's smart and compassionate, we have a similar sense of humor, we have the same hobbies, same religion, pretty close political opinions, I get along with his friends . . ." That last one could be a hard negative if we ever break up, but the goal is for that to never become a problem in the first place. "He treats me like an equal, and he's cute and handsome and it's a total bonus that he's also a cat boy, but none of that will matter if I can't get him to open up again."

"Well, I bid you good luck with that. I certainly wouldn't have the patience."

I glare at her. "Yeah. You were flirting with Jack the moment you saw him. You don't even know him yet!"

Her claw slides back to her lips. "Can you blame me? He's hot as hell, girl. It's a shame he's friends with my brother, though, because I'm sure he was going to kiss me on Monday but now he's playing hard to get."

My third eye cracks open. Jack is friends with her brother. Heather is tall and blond and well-endowed. Teddy, Jack's best friend, is also tall and blond and well-endowed. I've been friends with both this whole time and none the wiser. "Who's your brother?"

"Luke."

I frown; was I wrong?

Heather's eyebrows shoot up. "Oh, sorry. You know him as Teddy. His real name is Luke, but no one calls him that but me, Kyle, and our parents."

"I still think it's funny he got that nickname before he knew he was a bear boy."

"Oh? He told you?"

I nod. "He's surprisingly open about it as long as you already know about monster people. I've never seen him active, though."

Heather seems confused; it's annoying that all monster people don't automatically use the same terms, but they're so scattered it can't be helped.

"I've never seen him in bear form. Mark and Matthew came up with a few terms for everything. Don't worry about it."

"I figure Jack knows these terms?"

"Yeah."

She smiles. "Then I'll ask him to explain it to me. Maybe with some examples." The tip of her claw dips into her mouth. "I'm a visual learner, after all."

Lord help you, Jack: Heather will stop at nothing to get what she wants.

"What animal is he?"

I squint. "What animal is who?"

She grins. "Jack, of course."

I have a gut feeling I shouldn't give Heather too much ammo; I love her and support her, but I'd rather not disclose information that Jack only shared with me due to the circumstances. If he didn't already tell her after a week, maybe he doesn't want her to know yet—then again, I told her what Matthew is, so I already messed up, but there's no need to dig my grave further. "I think he should tell you himself."

"I already asked, but he wouldn't say."

All the more reason to keep it to myself.

Heather grins. "If you give me a hint, I'll let you pet my ears."

Dang it, my one weakness! *Emily, stay strong!*

"You're missing out, honey. You know I take good care of my hair. My fur could be the softest you ever feel in your whole life."

Emily isn't strong enough. "He's an herbivore."

"An herbivore . . . How curious . . ." She pats my bed. "Come get your reward."

"You are so manipulative." I make my walk of shame to my bed, climb on top, and drop on my knees next to her.

She turns her back to me to give me better access to both ears; the silvery backs of her studs shine from deep within the thick layer of fur. "You know you love me." She glances over her shoulder. "Just be careful around the earrings; I'd rather not get them caught in my fur."

"Hmph." I bring my hands up to her ears. "It's pretty weird your piercings shifted with everything else."

"It's uncanny." She smirks. "Like magic."

I freeze. "You know about that?"

"Oh, sure. I have my sources."

I grip the tips of her ears between my respective index fingers and thumbs. "Who's your source?"

She holds her index finger up to her lips with a wink. "It's a secret."

"Always with the secrets."

"A girl has to keep some mystery about her."

I flatten my lips and rub the backs of her ears with my thumbs; her fur is undeniably soft, but not as soft as Matthew's—not even close.

"So back to Jack." She looks straight ahead. "Is he . . . a horse?"

I snort. "No, but he could pull it off."

"He has that black-stallion vibe."

I wonder how a hooved animal would work in the hands. Obviously, their feet would become hooves, and they'd have whatever tail and ears, but what would become of their fingernails? Would they stay mostly human, if a little discolored, or become some kind of mini hoof at the end of each finger? The only way to find out would be to meet one, but the chances of that are pretty slim.

"Okay, so if he's not a horse, then . . ." Her head cocks back and forth. "Is he a flying fox?"

I freeze. "What's a flying fox?"

"It's a big fruit bat. They can be entirely black, so . . ."

I run my thumbs down to the bases of her ears. "No, he's not a bat. That'd be cool, though. Imagine the wings."

"Imagine the hugs you could get with those wings." Heather relaxes into the fantasy—and my consistent petting—then sobers. "But I like the ears on a vampire bat better, anyway; those're probably the closest we could get to a real-life vampire."

As I scratch at the bases of her ears—and Heather hunches over and leans into my working fingers—I say, "I've never been a fan of the undead. I don't see what's so hot about getting your blood sucked."

Heather, totally absorbed in my amazing petting skills, fails to reply right away. "I think it's more . . . the primalness of it. This deadly creature that fights his bloodlust to love you in the night. A little to the right, honey."

"Which ear?"

"Left."

I rub closer to the right edge of her left ear.

"Yeah . . . Right there . . ."

She leans into my hands so hard I have to put extra effort into keeping her afloat, and I imagine if she was a dog, her leg would be kicking like crazy.

"Gosh . . . I have to get Jack to do this someday . . ." She sighs, all content.

I almost roll my eyes. "Believe me, I wish you were Matthew right about now."

Heather glances at me, mockingly covering her mouth with her long fingers, her claws easily clearing her nose. "Oh my~ How scandalous~ Emily petting her own little cat boy~"

Like she wouldn't want to pet Jack the moment she figures out he has bunny ears. "That's enough petting for you." I take my hands away from her now-drooping bear ears.

"Boo . . ." She pouts and gives me a withering look; and to think, it was supposed to be *my* prize not but a few minutes ago.

After I slide off the bed and return to my chair, I notice Heather's ears perk up and focus on the door. "Something there?"

"I think Cookie's at the door."

Sure enough, a light scratching sound reaches my ears from behind my bedroom door. I get up off my chair, unlock the door, and crack it open just enough for Cookie to push her head through; the admittedly chunky tuxedo cat squeezes through the gap and immediately jumps onto my bed to see her favorite stranger. I close the door, lock it again, and sit back down.

Cookie meows, sniffs Heather's furry knee, and rubs her face against it; she does this in a lot of places, including her claws, which she happily scents with the glands in her kitty cat cheeks. After Cookie completes her rounds, she crawls into Heather's lap.

Heather can't resist; before the cat can process anything, she hooks her deadly fingers under Cookie's chest and lifts her up until her hind paws are resting on her boobs. "Hi, Cookie." Heather touches noses with the cat, and after Cookie squirms, she puts her back down on the comfy comforter.

Despite the surprise Cookie endured, she returns to Heather's lap and purrs, happily accepting pets from her head down to her rump.

"Do you have any pets?" I've never once been to Heather's house; she's always coming over to mine.

Heather shakes her head. "My dad doesn't. Kyle has a fish, but you can't do much with those."

Kyle again. I remember Teddy saying something about him being like a second dad. "Are you close with Kyle?"

Heather looks surprised for a moment, then almost sheepish; she nods, pushing her hair back as if she has a human ear to hold the long strands. "He's very important to me." She stares far off at nothing. "He kept me sane. I would've been alone without him. I love my dad, but . . . he's human. He couldn't . . ." Heather's eyes grow glossy.

So Kyle isn't human, either. Oh, this is all so complicated!

"Hey, Emily; I have a favor to ask."

I study Heather's uncertain face. "What's that?"

"Um, I need to tell my dad what I am. Jack told me that Kyle told him about himself and my brother. I figure I've been hiding this long enough, but I think I'll feel better if you're there with me." She covers her mouth again, this time to hide her frown. "I understand if you're not comfortable with that, though."

I can't believe Heather is actually relying on me for something for once; I smile despite the heavy atmosphere. I'm so happy I get up off my chair, thrust myself over my bed, and give Heather a hug, all without crushing poor Cookie. "Of course I'll help!" I release her from my embrace and notice her pleasantly surprised expression. "But when did you want to do this?"

Heather sticks a claw in her mouth and gnaws on the tip. "Tomorrow? No, I'll chicken out if I wait too long, so it has to be tonight."

"I hate to disappoint, but there's no way my parents are taking us anywhere after dinner." Mom hates driving at night, and Dad won't feel like it.

She worries her claw. "Kyle will take us."

"I'd rather not trouble him."

Heather smiles. "He won't be bothered. Kyle will drive any hour of the night. He loves driving. He ought to meet you and your parents anyway; he's basically my mom."

"Huh?!" First Kyle's like a dad; now he's like a mom?

Heather holds back laughter. "He cooks and he cleans and he buys lady things for me all the time. I'd be wearing terribly ill-fitting bras if not for him."

"Isn't your actual mom supposed to do those things for you?"

Still smiling, she says, "Ruby's barely worth calling a mother, much less a mom. That woman likes to pretend my boobs don't exist. She'd die if I told her my bra size."

I glance down at her boobs providing a decent amount of shade for the cat on her lap. "What *is* your bra size?"

Her smile turns into a grin. "What do you *think* my bra size is?"

I back up from the bed, sit back down, and put on my thinking face. "An F cup."

Heather bursts out laughing. "Honey, you're closer to an F cup than I am!"

I'm taken aback. "What do you mean, I'm closer?! I'm, like, an A cup at best!"

Her giggles die down, and she totally checks me out. "Girl, you're at least a C cup."

In what world am I a C cup?! My boobs barely project off my chest at all! I couldn't even fill double-A bras the one time I tried!

Her lips quiver. "How many letters are in the alphabet?"

I raise an eyebrow. "Twenty-six."

"And how many letters do people usually use for bras? Only six, if you're lucky. Boobs are way more varied than *A* through *F*."

"Okay, then what *is* your cup size?"

She forms a steady grin. "I'll let you guess 'til you get it right."

I stare at her boobs again; clearly, whatever perception of boobs and their letters I have is far different than Heather's, so I venture, "*H*?"

She shakes her head, still grinning.

I squint; maybe I should skip some more. "*K*?"

She shakes her head again.

"*P*?!"

"You're really close now." Her eyes gleam with mischief.

My mouth falls open. "Okay. *S* is my final guess."

"Bingo!" She winks and shoots a finger gun. "I usually wear 32S bras, but it depends on the brand."

"It depends on the brand." I slump, entirely incredulous; there's a reason I stick to sports bras in standard sizes.

"Oh, yeah: the fashion industry is a mess." She nods to herself before regarding me again. "But I can tell you're still skeptical."

"Of course I am! You literally told me I'm a C cup, which is just wrong! C cups are, like, bigger than average!"

She grins again and points to her purse hanging over the hook on the wall. "Take my measuring tape out and I'll show you why you're wrong."

I squint and frown. "Fine. Prove me wrong." I get up, grab her purse, and toss it on top of her clothes so she can get the tape measure for herself; why she keeps a measuring tape in there, I don't know, but I'm about to find out.

Heather goes dormant in one second flat, a blink-and-you'll-miss-it transformation that nearly startles me; using her now-human hand, she rummages through her purse and pulls out a yellow measuring tape with black lettering. "Take off your shirt and your bra and I'll measure you. Then I'll tell you your cup size. I'll measure myself, too."

My blinds are closed as they always are, so I take off my shirt and my bra. I feel embarrassed baring my chest to her until she takes her own bra off, leaving her in nothing but her underwear; without the support of her sports bra, her boobs hang lower on her chest, forming a clear teardrop shape.

Heather unravels the measuring tape—it hits the floor it's so long—and ensures she's reading the side in inches rather than centimeters. "I'm going to take your bust and your band measurement."

"Go ahead."

Heather wraps the measuring tape behind my back and takes a measurement around the area directly under my boobs. "Twenty-eight band." She takes another measurement at the fullest part of my boobs. "Thirty-one bust." She removes the measuring tape and puts her empty hand on her hip. "What's the difference between your bust and your band?"

That's basic math; no need for a calculator. "Three inches."

"So in theory you're a C cup."

I cross my arms, covering my chilly nipples. "Explain."

Heather grins and lifts her chin. "The difference between bust and band is your cup size. Under one inch is double A, one inch is A, two inches is B, three inches is C, and so on and so forth."

I stare at her face, then her boobs. I sing the alphabet song in my head, all while counting on my fingers, until I get to S. "That would mean . . . You have a nineteen-inch difference."

She beams. "Look at you; you're learning."

I hold out my hand. "Let me prove it to myself."

She hands me the measuring tape.

I measure her band and her bust: thirty-two inches and fifty-one inches, respectively.

"Well?" She raises an eyebrow.

I sigh. "Fine. You're an S cup." I take the measuring tape out from behind her back, hand it back to her, and put my bra and shirt back on, thankful to have my titties out of the cold AC.

Heather also puts her clothes back on, then rolls up her measuring tape; she returns it to her purse and her purse to the hook on the wall. She sits back down on my bed and Cookie returns to her lap for more pets. "So? How do you feel knowing you're a 28C?"

I cross my legs in my chair and give her a withering look. "You said in theory."

Her grin returns. "I can give you a crash course in titty science if you'd like."

"You know what? Why not."

So Heather gives me an insanely long lecture about bands, busts, shapes, sizes, roots, projection, separation, fullness, firmness, rib cages, and asinine rules that the fashion industry made up to reduce the variety of bras available to most women. My brain starts melting by the end, and I'm convinced I'll never truly understand the intricacies of boobs, but it's nice to know that I technically have C cups.

By the time my parents and littlest brother get home, it's already five o'clock, so Mom gets started on dinner while Dad watches TV and Noah does whatever he does in his room; once dinner is ready, it'll be our time to strike.

About forty minutes later, Mom yells to the whole house that dinner's ready, so Heather and I exit my bedroom and make our way downstairs.

Noah, whose bedroom is downstairs near the master bedroom, peeks his head into the kitchen, completely oblivious to Heather behind him.

Seeing this golden opportunity, she bounds up and wraps her arms around his shoulders.

Noah squeaks, his big hazel eyes blown wide.

"Hi, little Noah. I see you got yourself a fresh cut, huh?" Heather grins, her eyes twinkling.

Noah relaxes, pouts, and tries to remove Heather's long limbs from over his collarbone. "I'm not little anymore, Big Sis!"

Heather lets him go just so he can turn around and pout directly at her; she rubs the top of his head with her whole hand, messing up his much-shorter blond hair. "I heard. Here you are, a big middle schooler, and almost taller than your sister to boot."

Noah's pout lifts into a beaming smile. "I know! I hope I'll get even taller than Connor someday!"

"Good luck with that one, Noah." Connor walks up behind us, but before he can pass us by, Heather grabs his head and pulls him against her chest.

"Hi, Con-Con!" she says, the embarrassing nickname tumbling out of her mouth like it's second nature. "How come I haven't seen you roaming around Gibson yet?"

Connor's ears turn red as he fixes his best glare at Heather. "Maybe because you're utterly embarrassing!"

"Aw . . ." Heather pouts, crinkling her eyes like she's going to cry. "That's no way to treat a lady, Con-Con."

Connor's hands flail about, but he's too reluctant to possibly touch Heather somewhere inappropriate to do anything about the booby trap he's caught in. "I don't think ladies shove random boys into their fun bags!"

"What did you just say?" Mom stares at him, pasta ladle in one hand and the other on her meaty hip.

"Nothing, Mom!" Connor puts on his most charming smile. "I was just remarking how Heather's such a refined lady. Isn't she?" His utterly fake smile twitches.

Mom frowns, an eyebrow raised because she 100 percent knows Connor said no such thing, but she cuts him some slack because he's Mommy's little boy. "Heather is a wonderful young lady. Now let go of Connor so we can all eat dinner before it gets cold."

Having had her fun, Heather gladly obliges.

Connor rubs his ear and face like that'll remove the memory of having half of his head smothered by Heather's chest pillows—though to be fair, this is far from the first time Heather's smothered Connor's face for her own amusement; her tits have only gotten better at the job every year I've known her.

Noah looks on with wide eyes; girls are no longer strange creatures with major cooties, not that he ever believed that, considering he has an older sister like me. But he's becoming more aware of the things girls have that boys don't, and Heather's are hard to miss.

The four of us file into the kitchen where a spread of spaghetti, meat sauce, Texas toast garlic bread, and canned sweet peas awaits us. All of us serve our own plates—I don't take any peas—move into the dining room, and sit down to eat; Mom and Dad join us soon after, taking their respective seats at the heads of the table.

"Who wants to say the blessing?" Mom asks.

Noah already has a forkful of spaghetti in his mouth, but immediately stops chewing.

Heather raises her hand. "I'll say it!" She smiles like a good Christian girl; this must be part of her plan to butter up my parents.

After throwing a pointed glare at Noah, Mom bows her head, and we all follow suit.

Heather recites our typical blessing, giving gratitude for the food and our families and our friends. As soon as she ends her prayer, we lift our heads and our forks.

Noah finishes chewing and swallows the food in his mouth before continuing to eat; the rest of us take our first bites. Heather, in usual Heather fashion, puts her spaghetti on her garlic bread and eats it together, all without splattering errant noodles on her shirt; in an effort to avoid too much of a mess, she holds her hair behind her head, revealing her usually covered pointed ears. I don't miss the furrow of Connor's brow, nor the return of Noah's wide eyes.

"Big Sis," Noah says, stabbing his fork into a mass of sauce-covered noodles, "your earrings are pretty." He stuffs his face again.

"Thank you." Heather gives him a genuine smile.

Connor studies her ears, taking a bite of garlic bread and chewing slowly.

Dinner goes on quietly until all the boys at the table finish their plates. "I'm getting seconds," Connor mutters, leaving the table with his plate; Noah and Dad follow him.

"I think I'll have another slice of garlic bread." Heather joins them in the kitchen.

I'm honestly full, mostly because I'm in the offseason and I filled my plate with all I could stomach, and Mom is trying to watch her weight, even though I know she'll have dessert after she cleans up the kitchen. All my family members are big eaters, which is awful for my parents' waistlines but expected as far as my brothers are concerned; Noah does gymnastics and Connor plays soccer in the fall and baseball in the spring, so they expend a lot of energy year-round. Suffice to say, with her hibernation instincts and general needs on account of her excessive height, Heather fits right in with the rest of us.

Heather returns to the table with her lukewarm slice of Texas toast, the boys returning immediately after her. "So, Mr. and Mrs. Thompson." She grins, ready to make a deal. "Can Emily sleep over at my dad's house tonight?"

"Why can't you sleep over here, darling?" Mom asks.

"I *love* your house and all, but I *always* come over here, so I was thinking it's about time Emily visits my house for once."

"That's nice, dear, but who do you expect to take you? It's getting late and I think Mr. Thompson and I are tuckered out for the day."

Dad makes no comment, slowly chewing another forkful of spaghetti.

Heather smiles the greatest smile she has in her arsenal. "My dad's friend can pick us up in thirty minutes, so y'all won't need to worry about driving anywhere else tonight."

Mom raises one finely plucked brow. "And this friend is a man or a woman?"

"A man. His name is Kyle and I've known him since I was born."

Mom crosses her arms. "I don't think I can trust some man to take you girls anywhere, especially at night."

While Connor and Noah pretend this conversation is happening in another room, Dad clears his throat.

Mom shoots him a glare that says, *You better agree with me!*

Dad clears his throat again. "While I agree," he says, placating Mom enough, "we can at least meet the man. You trust him, Heather?"

Heather nods. "With my whole heart."

Mom says, "You shouldn't trust your—"

"Semantics," Dad says, shutting up what could've been an annoying lecture about how people have sinful hearts. "You're a good girl, Heather; I can't imagine you'd put yourself in the company of bad men, nor put our daughter at risk."

"Oh, thank you, Mr. Thompson!" Heather springs from her chair and gives Dad a short hug. "I'll call him right away!" And she's gone, her stomps echoing from the staircase.

Dad adjusts his collar, wipes the crumbs off his well-groomed facial hair, and takes another bite of garlic bread.

"Can I meet Kyle, too?" Noah asks, his plate perfectly clear.

Mom massages her brow. "Sure, dear. We can all meet some strange man after dinner together."

"Count me out." Connor gets up, dumps his empty plate in the sink, and stalks off.

I stand. "I'll go check on Heather."

Mom glares at me from beneath her brow-worrying fingers. "Sit down, young lady."

I sit back down, and Mom proceeds to give me a very long, very tiring, very much already-heard-a-thousand-times-before lecture on the horrifying risks of being a girl in today's society.

I check out after the first few sentences leave her lips.

Geoff starts barking up a storm when someone slams a car door shut in our driveway. Heather looks behind the curtains at the front of the house, beams, and dashes to the front door before Kyle has a chance to ring the doorbell. Mom, Noah, and I come up behind her, all while Dad hooks his fingers under Geoff's collar and drags him to the back door so he won't have a chance to jump on our surprise guest; as soon as Geoff is barking outside, Dad joins us at Mom's side.

Heather opens the door to reveal a man who's half a head shorter than her—a little taller than Connor and a little shorter than Dad—with sunbaked skin and long, combed-back dark-gray hair. He removes a brown cowboy hat from his head and holds it in front of his chest; the wrinkles on his forehead and around his mouth give me the impression he's significantly older than my parents, who haven't hit forty.

Heather grabs Kyle's right arm. "Thanks for driving over, Kyle. This is my girl friend's family."

Kyle grunts and holds out his left hand. "It's nice to meet y'all; I'm Kyle Ratcliffe, but you can just call me Kyle. I hear Heather wants to have her friend over tonight." He has an insanely thick Southern accent.

"That'd be me." I step around my parents and shake his hand. "I'm Emily; Heather and I have been friends since she started middle school."

He smiles at me. "I've heard all kinds of things about you, Miss Emily. You've been a good friend to my girl, haven't you?"

Feeling awkward, I let go of his hand. "I'd like to think so."

Dad gently guides me aside, taking my place in front of Kyle. "It's nice to meet you, Kyle. I'm Ron Thompson, Emily's father." He grabs his hand and gives it a firm shake.

Mom tentatively steps forward. "And I'm Georgia Thompson, her mother." She doesn't shake Kyle's hand, giving it a poorly masked sneer.

Noah pushes between them, oddly excited. "Hi! I'm Noah, Emily's littlest brother, but that doesn't mean I'm actually little."

He grabs Kyle's hand with both of his and shakes it vigorously.

Kyle smiles at him with something fonder than what he gave me. "I can tell you ain't little. How old are you, then?"

"I'm eleven!" Noah shouts.

"That *is* pretty old. Won't be long before you're as old as me."

"How old are you?" Noah stares at him with unabashed wonder.

Kyle grins. "I'm fifty-one; I'll be fifty-two in eight days."

Noah gasps, but before he can fire off for another hour, Mom shoos him away. "Why don't you go back to your room, Noah? Us grown-ups need to talk for a little while."

"Aw . . ." Noah pouts but does his walk of shame downstairs.

Heather lets go of Kyle so he can move freely.

Kyle slips out of his flip-flops, places his hat on Heather's head, and follows my parents into the living room; they proceed to sit on the couch while Kyle takes the matching accent chair.

Heather and I sit at the bottom of the staircase; Geoff's barking makes it hard to hear, but we're out of sight, out of mind. I have a decent view of Kyle but not of my parents; before anyone says anything, Kyle takes a container out of his pocket, pulls out a toothpick, and puts it in his mouth.

Mom latches onto his bizarre action. "What's with the toothpick?"

Kyle pulls it out of his mouth like a cigarette. "It's a tic of mine. I used to smoke a pack a day, so I like having something between my lips."

"Do you still smoke?"

"Naw. I've been tobacco-free for over sixteen years; I quit cold turkey when I found out Heather's mother was pregnant. Couldn't be smokin' around no babies like that." He puts the toothpick back in his mouth. "But the withdrawal I endured was something awful. Probably should've done it more gradually, but I'm still here and ain't smoked a cigarette since." His speech remains remarkably clear even with the toothpick between his teeth.

"What about her father, then? I'm told you're friends."

"He quit two years before I did." He crosses his ankle over his knee. "We've known each other our whole lives, pretty much."

"And it's normal for you to tote his daughter around?"

Kyle nods. "It's typical. I take her shopping and stuff, too. I'm the one that brings her here most of the time."

"I just find it strange that she wouldn't ask her father first."

Kyle smirks. "She asks me because I've got more availability. I live a bit closer to her mother's house, too."

"What do you do for a living?"

"I'm a janitor. I clean bathrooms in office buildings. It pays the bills."

"No college?"

Kyle shakes his head. "No, ma'am. I got my high school diploma, moved out, and started workin' straight away. I used to work rough hours doing construction contracts but switched to janitorial work for the stability."

Mom goes quiet, probably thinking about what else she can dig up; our extended family includes plenty of uneducated and/or self-employed people, so she'd be a hypocrite to judge him for being blue-collar.

While they sit there awkwardly, Cream waddles into the living room and stops right in front of the accent chair.

Kyle notices her, bends over, and holds his hand out at a reasonable distance, fingers curled in a nonthreatening manner; he clicks his tongue to get her attention.

Cream's head lifts as she sniffs the air, and I wait for her to arch her back and hiss; shockingly, she waddles forward until her nose nearly bumps into Kyle's index finger, then turns so her flank is parallel with his fist.

Kyle strokes her from her head all the way to the base of her tail. "You're a sweet girl, ain't ya."

Not only does Cream allow herself to be pet, she turns around for another stroke!

"I'm impressed," Dad says. "Cream usually hates strangers."

Kyle lets Cream pass back and forth under his hand as much as she likes. "Does she now?" He sits back up after Cream waddles away.

"Would you call yourself an animal person?" Dad asks.

Kyle grins. "I'd say so, but I don't have anything but a fish at home; I ain't too interested in cleanin' litter boxes or walkin' dogs every day."

"It's not for everyone. They're a lot of work but worth every penny."

"Mm-hmm." Kyle peruses the walls. "I see y'all are people of faith."

Heather grins; she and I both know my parents are more likely to trust a fellow Christian, even if that's a naive way of thinking.

"That we are," Mom says, calculating. "What about you? Do you go to church?"

"I ain't been to a church since Heather's parents' wedding, but I still count myself a believer. I've read the Bible three times, currently on my fourth."

The silence tells me Mom isn't happy about him not going to church.

Dad asks, "What versions have you read?"

"I've read . . ." He counts on his fingers. "KJV, NRSV, and ESV. I'm currently working through the NASB."

"Do you read a lot?"

Kyle nods. "I spend a fair amount of time readin'. Mostly non-fiction, but I've read a couple novels here and there."

The couch cushions squeak as Dad stands. "You seem like a good-enough guy."

Kyle also gets up and shakes Dad's hand again. "It's my pleasure to give you some peace of mind. I'll get them girls to Bobby's house safe and sound, no sweat off your back." After they let go, Kyle asks, "You got a pen and some paper? I'd like to leave my contact info for y'all just in case anything comes up."

"Oh, sure." Dad stomps to his room to get his office supplies, then returns and hands the articles to Kyle.

Kyle writes down his contact info. "You've got my phone number, my address, and the same for Bobby—that's Heather's father, just so you know." He hands the pen and paper back to Dad. "Give either of us a call if you feel the need; I'll let Bobby know you got his contact info so he won't be shocked or nothin'."

"Thank you. I'll send a text later so you both will have my number as well."

"Sounds good." Kyle smiles and looks past Dad's shoulder at us. "Y'all girls get your things; we'll leave as soon as you're ready."

We happily oblige.

My eyes immediately gravitate toward the old deep-green car in our driveway. It's a car I've never seen before, one that sits low to the ground and only has two doors, but it's not a convertible. There are two square outlines on the hood where the headlights probably pop out. It's so old Kyle has to unlock the car manually, and it's so cramped Heather has to lift her seat so I can climb onto the bench-like seats in the back.

Once we're all strapped in, Kyle puts his key in the ignition and starts the engine. "It'll be about twenty, thirty minutes to Bobby's house." He flips his sun visor down, revealing a CD sleeve. "I know this is a drifting car, but I promise you I'm a safe driver and I always follow the speed limit when I have lovely ladies in my vehicle."

"You're a bit too old for us, don't you think?" Heather says, smiling.

Kyle grins. "I never said nothin' about that, sweetheart." He pulls a silver CD boldly emblazoned with *America's Greatest Hits* from the sleeve and inserts it into the CD player lodged in the dash; he adjusts the volume until it's high enough to hear the music and low enough we can hear each other, then puts the car in reverse and rolls back onto the street.

When we reach the road proper, Heather says, "I heard you told Dad about yourself."

Kyle adjusts his grip on the steering wheel. "I did."

"I'm going to tell him about me tonight. That's why I wanted to have Emily over."

Kyle glances at me through the rearview mirror. "I thought you might know about us, Miss Emily. I can smell one of them boys on ya."

Oh, not with the smelling again! I flush and say, "Yes. I'm friends with them, including Teddy."

Kyle narrows his eyes. "Luke ain't gonna be happy about this. He was real mad about your daddy."

"He'll get over it." Heather crosses her arms and huffs. "I'm more worried about Dad."

"If he's gonna be mad, it'll be at me, not you."

Heather drops her arms into her lap. "I'd rather not hear you two fighting over me."

"It'll be alright, sweetheart," Kyle says. "Bobby and I know not to yell around y'all."

Something unspoken lingers; I wonder if Heather's parents fought a lot before they separated. Maybe they still fight now.

Heather looks over her shoulder at me. "Sorry to be dragging you into this."

I smile at her. "It's no trouble. I'm glad you trust me to support you."

Heather smiles back.

We pull up to a house visibly smaller than mine with a bare wooden porch at the front; the porch light buzzes and flickers, a few mosquitoes stubbornly enduring the chilly weather in hopes of a bite. Kyle parks his cramped car behind a large black truck; the only other vehicle in the driveway is an aged white sedan—both are Fords, as stated by their logos.

Kyle removes his keys from the ignition and unlocks the doors so we can file outside; I'm glad to have room to stretch my legs and back again. We walk to the porch, swatting mosquitoes away for the short seconds it takes Kyle to turn his keys in the dead bolt of the front door.

I breathe a sigh of relief once we're out of the elements and in a tiny foyer. We kick off our shoes. There's a kitchen directly to our right, and deeper still is a dining room currently occupied by a broad-backed man with silver-streaked blond hair; Teddy sits directly across from him, furrowing his brow as he concentrates on a game of chess on the dining room table.

"We're home," Kyle says.

The man turns his head and slings his arm over the back of his dining chair, revealing a face eerily similar to Teddy's if he was a few decades older.

Before he can say anything, Heather grabs my arm and drags me into the kitchen. "Hi, Dad! This is my friend, Emily; she'll be staying the night."

Teddy looks up and gawks. "Emily?! When were you Heather's friend?!"

I give him a wry smile. "Since four years ago; I wasn't aware you're the brother she mentions on occasion."

"We have the same skin tone and hair color and stuff, but our faces are pretty different"—Heather suddenly hugs me from behind—"so it wasn't that hard to leave that little detail out."

Mr. Brown quirks one eyebrow up. "All of you know each other?"

Teddy says, "She goes to school with Jack and our friends. I met her in person back in April."

Realization dawns on Mr. Brown's face and he gets up out of his chair; he's just as towering as his kids, so I have to crane my neck to meet his gaze. "I'm their father, Mr. Brown. I've heard a little bit here and there, so it's nice to finally have a face to a name." He holds out his hand.

I tentatively shake it.

Kyle walks up to us. "By the way, I gave her folks our contact info, so don't be ignorin' no phone calls."

Mr. Brown nods. "Good to know." He puts his hand on his hip. "Feel free to make yourself at home. You should probably show her to your room, Heather."

"I'll do that right now!" And she whisks me away, leaving the men of the house in our dust. Heather pulls me by the hand back into the foyer and pulls down an attic ladder from the ceiling. "I get the whole attic to myself; I hope you aren't scared."

"What do you take me for?"

Heather grins. "Attagirl. You first."

Steeling my resolve, I climb up the steep ladder into a large attic space with a vaulted ceiling. The walls are covered by a woodsy brown wallpaper, the floor made of cheap laminate, and the space furnished with only the essentials: a full-size bed in front of the lone window, covered with a surprisingly masculine green-and-blue plaid comforter; a large expresso dresser; a nightstand with a plain lamp; a vanity set fit with a mirror and a cute stool; and a regal armoire—there're plenty of pillows on the bed and a matching patterned rug at its feet. I crawl inside, put my purse and pajamas on the dresser, then sit at the foot of the bed; the nice foam mattress sinks under my weight.

Heather climbs up after me, then Kyle pops his head through the attic door. "May I come in?"

Heather pushes her hair behind her ear, strangely demure. "Sure. We need to talk about, um, the reveal."

Kyle grunts as he pulls himself into the room; he sits cross-legged next to the door, leaving it open. "It ain't that complicated, honey. I think I'll go down there with the possum out and surprise 'em, then you'll join me with the bear out."

"When?"

Kyle pulls a fresh toothpick out and slides it between his lips. "Right now; rip the bandage off and all that. They're busy playing chess, so they won't know what hit 'em."

Heather frowns, dangerously close to tears.

Kyle smiles at her, doubt in the line of his brow. "Don't worry, babygirl. It'll all be okay."

Heather nods, her lips parted but unspeaking; she sits down next to me and goes active, her tail hidden under the waistband of her jeans.

Kyle looks at me. "Would you close your eyes, Miss Emily?"

"Huh? Why?"

He jerks his head at Heather. "I prefer not to be watched, sweetheart."

"Oh." I bow my head and close my eyes, my fists held firmly against my thighs.

Kyle sighs softly, then the floors creak. "You can open your eyes, honey."

I do as I'm told only to see Kyle shoulders up in the attic doorway, his long bald possum tail hanging onto the edge. I try not to look too shocked and amazed.

Kyle grins. "Y'all come down when you're ready, alright?"

Heather and I nod, speechless for completely different reasons.

Kyle climbs down the ladder, his tail trailing after him until he's gone.

In the distant dining room, Mr. Brown says, "Kyle, what are you doing? The girls don't know about this!"

Oh, but we do; Heather especially. Her ears perk at her father's distress, and she stands.

I get up and put a hand on her shoulder; she gives me a strained smile, and I let go.

Heather totters to the attic door and climbs down; I follow.

Kyle watches us approach through the sparse living room furnished with nothing more than a couch, a giant TV, and a large bookshelf filled with random knickknacks, a few dozen books, and a hefty movie collection. What few pictures there are of Mr. Brown, Teddy, Heather, and Kyle decorate the walls; Teddy is overweight in the oldest ones, Heather flat-chested, both a brighter blond. Mr. Brown went through multiple physiques in his lifetime, while Kyle stayed perfectly consistent: always lean, always toned, but always developing deeper wrinkles and thinner skin.

Heather walks up to the doorway Kyle's leaning against with her hands held together, one over the other, like a prim and proper princess; her head tilts down, her ears lie back, and she doesn't turn to face her father and brother once she's in view.

Kyle cradles his toothpick between his fingers and wiggles it with his thumb. "This was my other secret. She had to show you for herself."

Heather turns her head just enough to look at Mr. Brown's face.

Standing a ways back, I can only rely on my hearing to gauge his reaction; there's nothing but silence.

"I'm sorry . . . I couldn't . . ." Heather chokes up, gritting her teeth and screwing her eyes shut. She's scared, and all I can do is witness her.

Mr. Brown leaves the dining room and wraps her in his arms. "You don't need to say anything, Heather. It's not your fault. None of you asked for this."

Heather leans into his hold, shaking and sniffling with restrained emotion; she grips her forearm like her life depends on it.

I sit quietly on the couch and look at the TV, letting the moment pass me blind.

"A lot of things make more sense to me now," Mr. Brown says. "Why you hardly ever rely on me. Why you're so close to Kyle." In the corner of my eye, he backs up and rests his big hands on Heather's shoulders. "I think I need to have a conversation with Kyle. Outside."

"Don't be mad at him, Daddy."

"I'm not mad, not even close. I just want to talk about things in private."

She sniffles and steps aside, her face distraught.

"I figure you knew all about this, Emily?"

I startle, glance at Mr. Brown's gentle expression, and nod vigorously.

His smile grows and he turns away. "C'mon, Kyle. We'll talk on the porch."

Kyle grunts, and when he walks past me from behind Mr. Brown, he's dormant.

The closing screen door clattering leaves us in a tenuous silence.

"Heather." Teddy leans against the doorframe; he's active, his old white socks torn by his claws. He glances at me awkwardly, his ears turned outward.

Heather perks her ears.

"How long?" he asks.

"Seven years," she says.

Teddy's lips part; he pushes off the doorframe and embraces her. She hugs him, clutching the back of his shirt.

"You've met my friends, haven't you?"

She nods. "We have lunch together. I have one class with Jack."

"I guess I can't keep them to myself anymore, can I?"

Heather smiles. "Nope. We'll have to share." She pulls away from Teddy, and he ends their embrace; now free, she has the gall to bring one devious claw to her lips. "Especially that boyfriend of yours." There's no space between *boy* and *friend* this time.

Teddy gives her a look eerily similar to the face Connor makes when I annoy him. "I have zero interest in getting into Jack's pants, thank you very much."

Heather grins. "I have the utmost interest in getting into Jack's pants."

Teddy grits his teeth. "I will fight you, Heather. I don't care if you're a girl."

She grins so wide that her canines pop out. "What are you, his bodyguard?"

Teddy lifts his chin and snarls, flashing his barely bigger canines. "If he goes after you, I'll fight him too."

"So he *is* interested in me."

"Alright, that's it!" Teddy gets into some kind of wrestling position, and despite his apparent anger, goes dormant; with his claws gone, he pulls his socks off. "Come at me!" He growls low.

Heather lifts her chin with her own snarl, and she, too, goes dormant; she pulls a hair tie out of her tight jeans pocket, secures her hair in a bun, and enters her own wrestler's stance.

They circle each other, footsteps soft and silent on the old sandy carpet, growling like wild animals—like siblings that really want to beat some sense into each other. They go round and round, bodies tense, calculating, then, in a flash, they crash into each other. They grapple and push and pull in hopes of throwing the other on the floor where they belong: one's will toppling the other, proving triumphant.

I'm shocked how well Heather keeps up with her beast of a brother, though it's possible he's going easy on her—I've never wrestled anyone, so I can't say. The truth is, they're both genetic monstrosities in their own right, bear people or not.

A few tense minutes into their fight, Mr. Brown and Kyle appear in the entryway from the hall; Mr. Brown's eyes are suspiciously red, while Kyle looks nonplussed. Eyebrow raised at his tussling children, Mr. Brown asks, "What are they fighting about this time?"

So this isn't such an unusual event. "Jack," I say, also watching them go at it.

Kyle's eyebrows shoot up but just as soon return to a perfect facade of neutrality. "I'm not too surprised; Jack's her type."

Mr. Brown opens his mouth slightly, then shuts it. I feel for him; Heather's good at keeping anyone at arm's length, even her own family. Today is the first time I've seen Heather's true self: all her manipulations, all her emotions, all her passions and desires; a girl who analyzes, a girl who calculates, a girl who lusts and loves and lingers in your mind.

Teddy sweats bullets and Heather heaves her chest up and down, veins popping in their hands and feet. Heather gets a hold on Teddy and throws him to the floor with a massive thump, then pins his shoulders with her entire body weight until the two seconds are up; she ends her pin and parks her butt on his belly like he's a flesh cushion. "I win!" She smiles like a little girl on Christmas Day. Her hair is everywhere and her meticulous makeup is smudged with sweat, but she looks so open and so honest I wonder where this girl was when I met her four years ago.

Teddy groans but makes no attempt to move.

Heather looks at me, that smile ever present. "How's that for girl power?"

I snort and smile back.

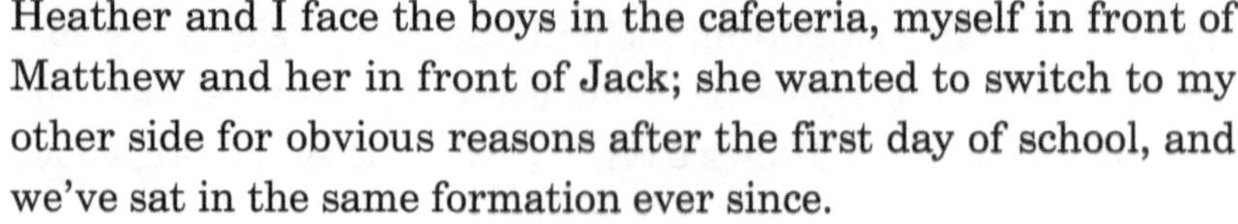

Heather and I face the boys in the cafeteria, myself in front of Matthew and her in front of Jack; she wanted to switch to my other side for obvious reasons after the first day of school, and we've sat in the same formation ever since.

Heather leans close to my ear, clearly studying an exhausted Matthew. "What's wrong with Short Stuff?"

Matthew opens his eyes and glares at her; he understandably hates that nickname but quickly gave up on asking Heather not to use it.

"Remember how Mark was tired two weeks ago?" I whisper.

Heather nods.

"He and Matthew both have a moon curse during different phases."

Heather places a finger on her chin. "How strange."

Matthew returns to resting his eyes, his face much paler than usual. I always wonder why he bothers coming to school when he's not feeling well, but now that we're juniors, even missing one day gives us a whole stack of lessons and homework to catch up on, especially in Honors Chemistry; we have that together for third period, so I'll keep an eye on him just in case he needs to leave early.

Before long, the five of us finish our lunches and the bell rings, giving us a grand total of five minutes to get to our next class; the campus isn't all that big, but it can be a struggle to go all the way from one side to the other in that amount of time; fortunately, Honors Chemistry is fairly close to the cafeteria.

Mark, Jack, and Heather bid their farewells and dash off to class on their longer legs while I gather my things and wait for Matthew to do the same; the cafeteria is mostly clear by the time he stands with his book bag on his back, so we trudge into the hall without too much trouble. Although I could easily make it to class without him, I keep a snail's pace with him, the two of us walking near the edges of each hallway to avoid running into too many people; our school is insanely overpopulated, but we manage to make it to class with seconds to spare.

Matthew eases into his chair next to me, dropping his book bag at his side from high enough that the books inside thump against the floor. Our teacher starts her confusing and boring lecture, Matthew nodding off the longer she drones on; I'm worried he'll fall asleep, which will make it impossible for him to keep holding his ears back against his head.

I elbow him awake before his head can crash against the lab table that doubles as our desk. "Matthew, are you sure you can make it through class?"

He stares at me for a few precious seconds, the gears in his head grinding just to process my simple question. "Maybe not." His eyes flutter closed again.

I return my attention to the PowerPoint and wait for a decent opportunity to get us out of here, which comes when our teacher finally walks around and passes out unit-conversions worksheets. When she reaches our desk, I quietly ask if I can take Matthew to the nurse's office; it only takes one look at his clammy face for her to agree.

I take our worksheets and encourage him to get up. It takes him longer than it should, but he puts his book bag on and trudges out of the room with me; instead of guiding him to the nurse's office, I take him outside.

"I need to hide somewhere." Matthew pants shallowly, his hands shaking and his nails growing into claws.

I grab his hand. "Let's go to the stadium."

Without any better ideas, he nods.

I pull him all the way around the side of the school, past the gym locker rooms and the theater and all the cars parked against the curb, until we reach the ticket booth Matthew hid behind all those months ago. I help him put his book bag down in the corner, which he immediately uses as an awful pillow after he sits down under the counter. I sit with my knees to my chest next to him, my book bag nestled in the other corner.

Matthew doesn't go active, sweat trickling down his brow with the effort to remain dormant; his ears and tail stay hidden, too.

"Aren't you going to go active?" I ask.

He looks pained, his cheeks turning pink. "It's . . . embarrassing . . ."

"You don't need to be embarrassed. Doesn't it hurt to hold it back?"

He nods, tears pricking the corners of his eyes, but still he refuses.

"I won't look, okay? Will that help?"

He opens his blue eyes.

I cover my face and turn my body away until his gaze is on my back.

He shuffles, pierces my ears with a sharp gasp, and pants heavily.

I assume he just didn't want me watching, so I ask, "Can I look now?"

"No!" He says it so fast it's nearly a shout. "You can go back to class without me. Just don't look. Please."

I don't understand why he's so adamantly against me looking at him. I've seen it before, if only briefly, but I keep my face covered and my back turned; if I'm ever going to be in a relationship with him, I need to respect his boundaries. "Why don't you want me to look?" There's no way I'm going back to class right now, not while he's being stubborn.

"Because . . ." He pauses like he doesn't know the answer. "It's unnatural."

"Isn't it natural for you?"

"I wish it wasn't."

Mr. Brown's words linger in my mind. *None of you asked for this.* Jack's words, too. *What he wants to be and what he sees in the mirror don't match.* "I wish I could understand you better. It'd be so much easier if I was a monster girl like Heather."

He doesn't say anything.

"I don't think you're embarrassing or less of a person because of how you look. I want to help. I want you to understand I won't judge you like that. You're not scary or freaky or animal. You're Matthew, my friend."

He sniffles; it sounds wet and sloppy. His claws scrape against concrete, against the fabric of his book bag. "I'm sorry, Emmie. I'm just not ready. I want to get over it, but I just can't."

Will he ever be ready? Are we better off being no more than friends? Should I just confess here and now? Would it change anything at all? "Do you want me to text Mark? I don't want to leave you by yourself like this."

He sniffles and pants and scrapes against the concrete. "Look at me."

I gape, pulling my hands away from my eyes; I nearly turn my head, but stop myself at the last second. "But you said—"

"I'll never be ready." He sounds hysterical. "You have to look or I'll never get over it."

"I don't want to make you uncomfortable."

"I'm tired of being scared. So fucking tired."

I feel awful, but I'm tired too. "Close your eyes."

He tears into the canvas with his sharp claws. "I'm ready."

I turn around.

Matthew lies haphazardly across the ground, his upper body clinging to his book bag, his lower splayed across the rough concrete. His T-shirt and cargo shorts can't hide the brown tabby fur covering his arms and legs. The cat paws replacing his feet stretch out so his claws scrape against the ground, and his puffy tail curls over his thighs, his ears pulled back against his curly hair. He trembles, his eyes screwed shut.

I want to touch him. I want to pet his ears and feel his paw pads and tell him it's okay, but I don't do those things. I settle back against the ticket booth, pull my knees back up to my chest, and rest the side of my head on top. "I looked."

Matthew lets go of his book bag and furiously wipes his face; little droplets of his tears cling to his fur. He sits up and rests against the ticket booth, his head still turned away, but his ears aren't down anymore. He works up the courage to look at me, those ocean eyes watery and red. He looks absolutely awful, the flush on his face making his skin look paper white.

"How're you feeling?"

He pulls his knees to his chest, his toes contracting into fuzzy mittens, the claws barely poking out of their sheaths. "Shitty," he says, "and shy."

"Are you embarrassed?"

He nods.

"You don't need to be."

"It's just . . ." He looks ahead, mumbling into his knees. "Intimate, to show you my active form."

"Intimate?"

"It's like . . . being seen in my underwear. Even if you were a monster girl, I'd be shy."

I never realized that's how he felt about it. Mark and Jack were fairly open, but I need to remember Matthew goes by his own rules. "I'm sorry. I feel like I pressured you too much."

He shakes his head. "You didn't pressure me. I'm trying to face my fears, but I'm not very good at it."

I'm afraid of things, too: afraid of losing him; afraid I'm barking up the wrong tree. "At least you're trying. Not everyone gets that far."

His ear flicks, and he pouts. "Still, I must be the least cool guy you know."

I want to be cheeky and lighten up the mood. "You did say you'd probably act like a pussy around me." I smile despite myself.

Matthew groans into his hands. "God, I did write that . . ."

"I like that you're honest; I don't like guys that try too hard."

"I try really hard"—he removes his hands from his face and spreads his webbed fingers around his knees—"to be normal around you."

I bump my shoulder against his. "You know what I mean."

That gets a smile out of him. "Do I?"

"I mean you're down to earth. You're not some big shot who thinks he's better than everyone else."

He loses his smile. "I think I'm worse."

"Why do you think that?" I have an idea, but I want to hear it from him.

He rests his head over his hands on his knees, mirroring me. "I'm short, for one."

"I like being around the same height; I feel more like equals that way."

He's so pale from the full moon that his blush becomes obvious; he starts to purr.

I must be blushing, too.

He clears his throat but achieves nothing. "I'm a cat, of all things. That's not as cool as a wolf, a dragon, or a bear."

"You know I've always been more of a cat person."

"Not literally, though."

I shake my head playfully. "Not literally."

He frowns. "And I keep crying around you."

"I think you've had good reasons to be sad. Guys have emotions, too."

He smiles again, his purrs louder than I've ever heard them. "You're too nice to me."

I carefully place my hand on his back. "I think I'm nice enough."

He closes his eyes as I rub his back, his face sickly but much more relaxed.

As much as I want to touch and feel other parts of him, I stay within my lane; Matthew allowing me to look at him in active form is progress enough. So my hand lingers on his back, rubbing up and down and back and forth, and I marvel at the rolling purrs vibrating against my fingers. Even when he's sick and shy, he manages to be adorable.

After a few minutes pass, the school bell rings in the distance.

Matthew opens his eyes. "You should probably go to class. No need to miss fourth over me."

I don't want to leave him here alone, but he's right; he was handling himself long before I knew anything. "You're right." I pull away, trailing my fingers across his shoulder before letting go. I put my book bag on and walk away but turn around at the corner. "Hey, Matthew." I ensure the front of my body is facing him.

He looks at me and blinks slowly. His ear flicks again.

"Heather told me I'm a C cup."

He immediately stares at my chest, his mouth gaping open.

I bite my lower lip, turn away, and hop back to class.

CHAPTER 27

The Whirlwind

John

Heather is quieter than usual at lunch. It's not obvious, but she's not as animated, not as aware of every minute change in our emotions. She doesn't instigate weird conversations or poke fun at anyone, and she doesn't give me looks. She usually gazes at me, steals little glances, waits for me to blunder so she can point out my social mistakes. And she only eats half her lunch, grimacing at her final swallow; it's only the first week of October, so her hyperphagia should still be in full swing. Something's clearly bothering her, but it's possible she doesn't want us worrying about something as minor as a stomach bug.

I wait until third period to ask her about it. It's quiet and dark in the room because we're watching some out-of-touch video about various online messaging scams—basically, don't give your credit card information to some guy claiming you have an inheritance from a long-lost relative in Dubai. The video has the slowest narration imaginable and nobody's paying attention to it except for the teacher, so now's as good a time as any to check on her.

"Heather," I whisper. "Are you okay?"

Heather turns her head and opens her eyes, her long lashes fluttering low. She gazes at me for a long time, gauging something; finally, she says, "I think I started my period."

Oh.

She smiles wearily. "What did you think was wrong?"

"A stomachache or something. You didn't finish your lunch."

"My cramps snuck up on me; I'd usually have some medicine, but my cycle's been off since the move." Her smile wanes as she adjusts her position in her seat.

I have no idea how bad her cramps are, but her behavior reminds me of Grace; hers are so bad she has to lie down for two days, sometimes even with medicine. "What do you usually take?"

"Ibuprofen. Why?"

I make sure no one is looking, reach into my book bag, and slowly open the pill bottle I keep on me for situations like these; as soon as the child-resistant cap comes off, I pull one tablet out, close the bottle, and remove my hand from my bag. I gently take Heather's hand in mine, place the tablet in her palm, and close her fingers overtop.

She peeks under her fingers. "What's this?"

"Ibuprofen."

She closes her fist and raises an eyebrow. "Why do you have ibuprofen in your bag?"

"One of my older sisters gets bad cramps and always forgets her medicine, so I carry it on me."

She smiles at her fist. "You're a strange one, Jack." She grabs the water bottle in her book bag's mesh pocket, places the pill on her tongue, swallows it with a swig of water, and drinks some more to get rid of its sour aftertaste. "Thanks. Now I should be able to make it through the rest of the day."

I cradle my cheek in one hand, my elbow on top of my desk. "I'm glad I could help."

Heather remains rigid in her seat; it'll take a while for the ibuprofen to kick in, if at all. "How many sisters do you have?"

"Seven."

"Wow. Are they all older?"

"Almost. One is my little twin sister."

She smiles weakly, glancing at me through the corner of her eye. "You're a big twin brother, just like Luke."

"Yep. Part of why we get along so well."

"Is he the one that got you into flamenco?"

I nod. "I hear you were the first to get into it."

Her fingers find their way to her chin. "That I was, back when things were simple. Pretty clothes and makeup: that's all I cared about."

"What do you care about now?"

She closes her eyes briefly, taking an unsteady breath. "It's a secret." She dips her index nail between her lips.

"Give me a hint."

She gazes at me, hunger in her eyes. "You'll have to bargain something."

I smirk. "I believe I already have."

She raises an eyebrow and grins. "Hmm . . ." She pulls her finger away from her mouth and cups her cheek, mirroring my position. "It's a boy."

"That doesn't narrow it down much."

She leans forward, her boobs resting on her desk. "Not at all."

The credits roll, and the teacher leaves her seat. We both pull back, and by the time the lights turn on, the class is none the wiser to our little conversation.

Heather rests her head on my shoulder during the bus ride home. It's quiet, but a comfortable quiet. Even with some medicine in her system, she's exhausted.

When the bus lurches to a stop on her end of the street, I stand up with her. She glances at me, questioning, so I give her a smile; she smiles back, and we get off the bus together.

"Following me home?" she asks, the sun shining on her pale face.

"Just making sure you get back alright. I live close, so it won't kill me to walk."

She exhales audibly and slowly walks ahead.

I keep pace with her, just a little behind. She doesn't need me walking with her, but I can't leave a girl in pain by her lonesome.

Her house is stupidly close to the bus stop; we only had to cross one intersection. It's a nice house, if small—probably enough for two bedrooms and a guest room, if I had to guess. It looks brand new and barely lived in, crammed between two other houses on what was once a single lot.

"Thanks for walking me home."

My hand lands behind my neck. "Sure. No biggie."

Heather smiles.

We stare at each other; I'm unsure what to say.

"I guess I should head inside."

"Yeah. You should rest."

She looks into my eyes, then turns away.

I grab her shoulder.

Her head whips back, her eyes open wide. "Jack?"

I rub my neck. "I never gave you my number."

She gazes at me softly. "Hand me your phone. I'll give you mine."

I pull my phone out of my pocket, unlock it, and open up my contacts app.

She takes it in her hands, types in her name and number, then locks my phone.

I place my phone back in my pocket.

"Call me." She winks, gesturing a phone next to her ear, and walks to her front door.

I wait for her to disappear inside, then leave. I walk home within twenty minutes, enter my oversize house, and go to the living room; Jenny is probably in our room, and I want to be alone for a moment.

I sit on the couch, placing my book bag on the carpet in front of the arm. I pull my phone out, unlock it, and open my messaging app; I search Heather only to see she added a sparkling pink heart emoji to the end. I grin, roll my eyes, and type, *Hey. This is Jack.*

It doesn't take long for her to reply. *Hey. Just got out of the shower.*

My mind wanders. Heather naked. Wet.

I thought I told you to call.

I wanted you to save my number first.

Fair enough, but why don't you call me now.

I stretch my body out across the couch. *Why do you want me to call so bad?*

Three dots linger on my screen. *I want to hear your voice.*

Blood rushes to my face; I swallow, go to my phone app, and call her.

She picks up after a few agonizing seconds. "Hey."

"Hey. How are you feeling?"

"Better, now that I'm in bed. My flow is light for now, so it's not as bad as it could be."

That's right. Shark week. It slipped my mind. "That's good." Silence lingers; I'm not good at talking to girls I like.

"I actually wanted to ask you something."

"Ask me what?"

"I think our school is doing a talent show at the end of the semester. I'd like to sign up together."

A talent show? "Why would you want to do that?"

"I want to dance with you. It could be fun."

"Dance with me? You mean flamenco?" It's mostly a solo act, so . . .

"It's not common, but it's not unprecedented to dance as a pair. We could figure something out with Sr. Hernandez and Sra. Rubio, maybe have Luke sing while Sr. Hernandez plays the guitar."

"Wouldn't the talent show only be for people at our school?"

"We can make a recording for the music. That way it won't be a problem."

"You've thought of everything, haven't you?"

She sighs longingly. "I like to cover my bases. So how about it?"

A talent show. Dancing with Heather on a stage in front of a bunch of students, parents, and teachers. If I was younger, the idea alone would embarrass me to death, but that old John is long gone. I dance in front of my family and friends without a care; strangers are actually easier to perform for because you don't ever have to interact with them again. "I'll dance with you."

"I'll look forward to it, *Jack*."

The way she says my name . . . How I'd love to hear her whisper it into my ears . . .

Blood rushes below my core. I shouldn't think about her that way, but she makes it so easy.

⌒

The next day, on the bus ride to school, during lunch, in the middle of third, and on the bus ride home, we talk details. I'll dance anything, so it's mostly about her: the dress she wants to wear; the hair, the accessories, and the makeup; and most importantly, what exactly we plan to perform. She wants a big train with all the ruffles, an eye-catching but difficult garb to master. I tell her we should ask Jenny about makeup; I know how to apply it myself, and Heather clearly does too, but Jenny wants to do makeup professionally, so she has a lot more precision than we do. We're not too concerned about what Teddy and Sr. Hernandez can sing and play respectively; like myself, they'll do just about anything as long as it has enough soul.

We find a few performances we could emulate; I'm a big fan of the one where the woman uses castanets. What can I say? There's something sexy about them, and Heather seems to agree, but we have to consider Teddy and Sr. Hernandez's opinions as well.

Emily is pleasantly surprised to learn Heather dances, too, while Mark and Matthew leer at me for agreeing to a talent show in the first place; I figure I'm in for a lot of teasing in the future.

We plan to talk everything out on Saturday, when we usually have our weekly practice sessions with Sr. Hernandez and Sra. Rubio; of course, Teddy will be tagging along.

⌒

I enter the Hernandez Rubio home and shake out my umbrella; rain beats against the roof as I place it to dry on a mat, unzip my jacket, and put aside my boots and socks. With my dancing shoes in hand, I walk down to their retrofitted dance-studio basement. Teddy and Sr. Hernandez sit on stools, both with their guitars and their stands where their instruments sit patiently, waiting to be played. Heather speaks to Sra. Rubio, both in flamenco skirts with long tails, their hair pulled back into tight buns. Heather's fitted black top does the impossible job of downplaying her excellent chest.

Heather turns around. "There you are." She scans my outfit. "We were waiting for you before making a final decision."

"You know I'm good with anything." I place my shoes on the wooden floor and slip them on.

"I know, but it's better not to get ahead of myself."

Teddy gives her a flat look. "Like how you decided to participate in a talent show without even asking me first?"

Heather looks back at him, fingers on her chin. "I knew you'd say yes. It's a good opportunity to practice more of your singing."

Teddy crosses his arms; his silence proves her point.

"Come now, no need to argue." Sra. Rubio snaps her tan fingers. "We haven't helped with a dual performance in a long time, so we'll need every second to practice together." She says something else to Sr. Hernandez in Spanish.

He replies to her, then says something to Teddy.

Teddy replies, his Spanish smooth and effortless; seven years practicing the language has made him fairly proficient. After a bit of back-and-forth and a clap on the back, Teddy looks at Heather. "Apparently I'm the final decision-maker, so show me which performances you were thinking about."

We spend thirty minutes on Teddy's decision; fortunately, he picks the dance with the castanets. We spend the next thirty minutes on the basic choreography and timing; it begins with guitar and singing, then I enter, then Heather enters another minute in. There are parts where I have to be very close to her; I'll have to learn not to step on her train and mirror her stance even without looking at her. It's a different kind of dance, one where I can't rely on my instincts the way I usually do: one where I have to fight my senses when she gets so close I can smell her.

And she's beautiful, working her powerful arms and kicking that train out of her way with unmatched fluidity. And the way she puffs out her chest, her boobs barely bouncing against her perfectly fit clothes, gazing down on me like her prize . . .

It's only because we have an audience that I keep my cool.

Week by week by week, we play the same song and dance. In that time, I slowly learn the contours of Heather's body, the feel of her bicep in my hand, of her arm on my shoulder, of the curve of the small of her back. We move as one being, in rhythm and rotation, syncing up like the stars and their planets and their moons. The stomp of her shoes reverberates through my body, the click of her castanets invading my mind. I dream of her sound and her gaze and her body until she's the only thing I can bear to think about. It's too much all at once, yet not enough.

So I sit in the cold of night on a freezing metal bleacher at a high school football game Heather would never want anything to do with, Matthew on my right and Mark on my left. A gaggle of cheerleaders hype up the football players entering the field in their heavy gear and hard helmets, most of them thick and tall and mean. Teddy stands among them, playing for the home team, the Workbourne Bobcats; on the other side is the away team, the Gibson Gladiators, in all their yellow-and-green glory—they look garish under the stadium lights.

My eyes wander back to the cheerleaders doing their stunts and their chants, bouncing and jumping and thrusting their arms up and down. There are short girls and tall girls, chubby girls and skinny girls, Black and White and Hispanic girls, all with their pros and their cons, their beauties and their blunders, yet all I can think about is Heather. If Heather was the one bouncing there in a short skirt, her boobs jiggling from the force of her jumping, her long, muscular arms shaking those pom-poms to death. She'd make a pretty cheerleader, but she's a much-prettier flamenco dancer.

"Earth to Jack. I repeat, Earth to Jack," Mark says, waving his hand in front of my face.

His annoying fingers pull me out of my fantasy.

"Somebody's head has been in the clouds lately." He grins obnoxiously.

I glower at the cheery cheerleaders. "You don't say." The level of sarcasm in my voice is denser than a jar of honey. *Dammit.* Heather, Heather, Heather. She's all over me, a parasite of the mind.

"Oh, he's lovesick!" Mark puts the back of his hand on his forehead and pretends to faint against my side.

"Heather has him hook, line, and sinker!" Matthew collapses against my other side and fans his face with one hand.

"You know what? I expected this from Mark, but you have no room to talk, Matthew."

Matthew knocks the brim of his baseball cap aside so I can see his goofy grin; he's been in an awfully good mood this past month. "Exactly; I know girl crazy firsthand, bro."

"I'm still wondering why you haven't asked her out." Mark strokes his chin wisely. "She literally drools over you every single day, bro."

"It's not that simple." I huff, my breath condensing white in the dark.

Mark cocks his head. "It's not? Seems pretty simple to me."

At least Matthew looks more sympathetic to my plight.

"First of all." I scowl at Mark, then point at the field where Teddy squares up in his orange-and-black uniform; I only know it's him because of the number on his jersey. "She's Teddy's sister; that's hardcore dodgy territory."

Mark frowns at me like I'm stupid. "Bro, Teddy literally has the hots for *your* twin sister; if Matthew has no room to talk, Teddy definitely doesn't."

"Okay, fine!" A few heads turn back at us; I grit my teeth and cool off. "Fine, the sister thing doesn't matter, but that's not the real problem."

"Okay, then what's the real problem?"

"I . . ." My fingers travel to my neck, grazing the hidden tips of my ears.

A whistle blows, temporarily taking our attention away to the first play of the game.

Matthew gazes at my face, his eyes lingering on the back of my head. "You're worried she won't like you because you're a bunny." It's a statement, not a question; he says it quietly so no one but us can hear.

My hand glides into my lap; I nod, trying to keep my face hard and unforgiving.

Mark sits up, giving me some much-needed space; I feel emasculated and embarrassed by such a stupid concern.

Heather has become more than an object of lust; she's the first girl I've truly liked romantically, the first girl that plays to her own tune and easily pulls me along; it'd crush me if she stopped liking me over the bunny thing. I'm too scared to get hurt, but it's getting harder and harder to remain dormant every time I get close to her during our damned dance.

We watch the first quarter in silence; neither team manages to score.

Mark elbows me after the second quarter starts, sporting a mischievous smile. "I'll be honest, Heather seems like the type to prefer something cuter. She has that dominatrix vibe going on."

I scoff. "What the fuck are you on about?"

Mark puts his hands up. "Just saying, bro. You're letting your insecurities get the better of you."

"He's right," Matthew says. "Either way, Heather seems to like you for more than just your looks. And I bet she'd enjoy petting your ears."

"How would you know?" I ask.

Matthew smiles, gaze distant. "Emily tells me things sometimes."

My heart drops. "Don't tell me she told Heather."

Matthew shakes his head. "She only told Heather you're an herbivore. Her first guess was a horse."

"A horse?!" Mark giggles. "What was the second?"

Matthew grins. "A fruit bat."

Mark smacks my back multiple times. "Oh my God, a fucking bat! She'd take you without hands!"

"I need these hands." How else am I supposed to appreciate all she has to offer?

Mark and Matthew stare at me like Cheshire cats; they definitely know what I want to hold in my hands.

Even so, I hang my head. "But that doesn't mean anything. Maybe she'd be happier with a horse if that's the first thing she thought of."

Mark gives me his best impression of a disappointed mom. "Bro, do you hear yourself?"

"I don't think he does," Matthew says.

I sigh. "None of us can know for sure."

"Not without asking her yourself." Matthew puts his left arm behind my back in a side hug.

Mark does the same with his right arm, patting my chest with his left hand. "Do you honestly think Heather's that shallow?"

The Gladiators stomp the Bobcats by the end of the second quarter.

"No," I say.

Mark grins. "There's your answer, Jack. There's your answer."

They let go of me, their body heat dissipating from my sides, but no matter how deep the cold pierces my skin, my heart remains warm.

⌒

The next day, I dance with Heather to Teddy's passionate singing and Sr. Hernandez's vibrant guitar. Sra. Rubio corrects us and demonstrates as she sees fit, but her interruptions have grown farther apart with each session. I have confidence we'll be ready for auditions later this coming week.

After our hour of practice, we wrap up and prepare to go home, though Teddy's staying behind to make a recording for us with

Sr. Hernandez. "I'll have it ready for you tonight," he says, "so come over and stay the night. We haven't hung out in a while."

"Sure thing. Want me to have Mark and Matthew come over, too?" I'd rather have Mark take me so I can give Grace a break from being my chauffeur.

Teddy nods. "I'll text him about it, so hang tight until then."

I nod, then turn to Heather; sweat covers her face, making it shine in the harsh light of the basement. "Are you still good to ride home with me and Grace?" She started riding with us some time ago to save Kyle the trouble and the gas.

"Of course." She smiles, running her fingers behind her ear as if she has hair to push back, but it's safely tucked away in the usual tight bun.

She lets her hair down and changes into casual clothes—there's a changing closet and a storage room connected to the studio— then we walk upstairs together, put on our socks and shoes, and exit into the chilly outdoors. The weather likes to be fickle in Raleigh, but November promises more cold than warm, so I've made the switch back to my cowboy boots; because her feet get cold, Heather wears shearling boots with fur-lined cuffs.

We get into the back seat of Grace's car together, and she pulls away from the curb. Grace doesn't speak much, partly because she and Heather don't have much in common, but mostly because driving makes her nervous; the classical music droning from the radio helps with her nerves and makes the ride feel more regal than it is.

Heather and I don't talk to each other, instead stealing glances every now and then; when I prop my hand on the middle seat, Heather places her hand on top, fingering my wrist and the bones leading down to my knuckles.

Grace parks at our house and I walk Heather home, our twenty cherished minutes alone together; sometimes we speak, sometimes we don't, and today, she grabs my hand. She has such long fingers, her skin perfectly soft to the touch; there's something new to love about her every day.

When we make it to her house, I remember my conversation with Matthew and Mark last night; I need to swallow my nerves and bare my heart to her if I want this to go anywhere real.

"Heather," I say, interrupting her long strides up the walkway.

She turns around. "Yes?" She pushes her hair back with her fingers, revealing her left ear.

"Do you remember when you asked me what I am?"

She smiles softly. "I do."

"I'm . . ." My throat closes up; I can't bring myself to say it. "Come here."

Without a word, Heather walks up to me, close enough I can reach her.

I hold my hands out. "I'd like to show you something. Can I guide you?"

She puts her hands in mine. "You may."

I appreciate her big, slender hands, grip under the meat of her palm, and slowly bring them up to the sides of my head; her fingers slide across my cheeks, under my tangled hair, and touch the tips of my ears. I let go.

Gently, she pinches the ends, feels up their length, glides over the hairpin bumps, and strokes back down so slowly it takes everything I have not to grind my teeth. "I was right: You *are* a bunny."

My heart drops into my stomach. "You knew? How?"

Her smile remains soft as she brings her hands to my cheeks, cupping them and stroking my cheekbones. "You underestimate me, Jack. I pay attention to the things I like; it was only a matter of time before someone slipped."

"Who slipped?"

Her smile morphs into a grin. "You did, sweetheart."

My eyes nearly pop out of my skull. "But—"

"Shh." She puts a finger against my lips. "The clothes you wear to dance are formfitting; I noticed a little lump on your lower back and eventually guessed it was a tail, one the size and shape of a bunny's."

"How long have you known?"

She puts her silencing finger against her lips. "About a month. I decided to wait for you to tell me yourself."

"Then . . ." I bite my lip, brow furrowed. "How do you feel about it?"

"I would've liked you even if you were a pig"—she steps back, her long fingers trailing down to my chin—"so I'm happy I got something good."

Good, she says. A bunny is good to her. My body badly wants to go active, so I bite my cheek and rein it in.

She pulls her fingers away. "See you later, *Jack*." And she leaves me behind, sauntering up to her front door and disappearing inside.

I can't stop smiling. I'm looking at the most convoluted board game in the universe with rules that need two people to decipher, and I can't stop smiling. Heather likes bunnies. I'm a bunny boy. That's pretty cool. So I look at Teddy, his nose wedged in the rule book, a green die rolling around in his palm, and say, "I love your sister."

The die clatters on the surface of the table and rolls; when it stops, six dots are on top. Teddy gingerly places the rule book on the table, stands so abruptly that the chair legs screech across the linoleum, and throws his shirt on the seat. He points at me. "You. Me. The living room. Now."

He doesn't have to tell me twice; I stand and throw my shirt on the seat behind me, the poorly heated air cool on my spine and tail. I straighten my posture, my muscles tense, and stride into the living room, Teddy by my side. My ears are out and my tail is showing and Mr. Brown and Kyle can clearly see it all from their place on the couch, but I don't care; they can stare all they want because this is happening right now.

Kyle pauses the TV, Matthew and Mark watch us from the doorway to the dining room, and Mr. Brown asks, "What are y'all up to?" There's a smile on his face because he knows; we've done this song and dance before.

I say, "I love your daughter."

Kyle grunts.

Mr. Brown crosses his arms and raises one eyebrow.

Teddy and I get into position and circle each other between the TV and the couch. He growls, and I growl, and as soon as his muscles tense, we slam into each other with everything we have. We grapple, tug, hold, and attempt to throw each other off balance; Teddy's a monster, so it takes all my willpower and stamina to weather his storm. He's strong, stronger than I remember two years ago, but I've gotten stronger, too, and I'm riding a love high. God, Heather likes that I'm a bunny boy!

Teddy takes advantage of my distracted mind: he easily kicks my legs out from under me and tosses me on the floor.

I crash, and over 250 pounds of muscle and fat crush my shoulders. I give up, knowing there's no way in hell I'm lifting him off my chest, and let the two seconds pass.

Teddy gets up, huffing and puffing, his face flushed and covered in sweat. "I don't give a shit if you love my sister"—he wheezes—"but you better treat her right."

I nod, closing my eyes and catching my breath with my open mouth.

"And if you ever break her heart, I'll kiss you on the mouth and tear your tongue out with my teeth."

"That's a gay way to go, bro." I open my eyes and look into his.

"Exactly." He puts his hands on his knees. "I know your weaknesses, bro."

"Bro."

He pants. "Don't try me. I'll do it. No hesitation."

I salute weakly. "Message heard loud and clear."

Teddy closes his eyes, struggling to catch his breath. "Goddamn, you've gotten strong."

I already feel sore all over. "Speak for yourself." I take unsteady breath after unsteady breath; eventually, I recover enough to prop myself up on my elbows. I look at the men on the couch. "Mr. Brown, do I have permission to date your daughter?"

Mr. Brown raises one eyebrow and smirks. "Son, I trust my daughter to make her own decisions about her love life; she's old enough she doesn't need Daddy's permission anymore."

I nod, flattered he called me son.

Mr. Brown leans back and throws his arm across the back of the couch. "And I'll be honest, she could do a hell of a lot worse than you." He relaxes, but side-eyes me. "I trust she'll be in good hands?"

"Absolutely. Thank you, sir." I collapse onto my back again, smiling stupidly.

Teddy collapses next to me, and a second later, dramatic dialogue spills from the TV speakers.

Mark and Matthew walk over to my side and stand above me, looking down. "What was that all about?" Mark asks.

"Big brother things," I say. "You wouldn't understand."

Mark grins. "You fought over Jenny once, didn't you?"

I grin back. "We did. And I won."

"That's because I was stupid in the head," Teddy says, "like you are right now."

Matthew taps his temple. "Girl crazy. Makes you weak."

If I'm stupid to love her, then so be it. I'll be weak. I'll bare my soul to her, let her take all of me until there's nothing left, because I'm in love.

Late in the night, something warm, soft, and calloused shakes me by my shoulder, five points of pressure tickling my skin.

I open my eyes but can't see shit in the dark.

Teddy says, "Can we talk?"

I rub my face with my furry hands, head bleary and mind tired. "Sure." I stand, using Teddy's muscular arm for support.

Teddy carefully guides me around Matthew and Mark, the large pads on his bear paws muffling his movement. He leads me down the hall and into the living room, then sits down on the couch; he pats the seat next to him.

I take it and perk my ears.

He doesn't speak.

"What did you want to talk about?"

"My sister," he says. "You're serious about her?"

"Yeah." She's the hottest girl I've ever seen, but she's more than her body; it's her mind that captured me.

Teddy shuffles. "I worry about her. I've always worried about her. When I found out she's a bear person like me, had been a long time, it gave me new things to worry about."

I know what he means, but I ask, "Like what?"

He sighs long and low. "Somebody taking advantage of her, you know? If the wrong guy found out what she is, he could blackmail her. Force her to do things I don't want to think about."

Sexual things, no doubt. Even us boys have those risks, but it's more likely for a girl.

Teddy puts his hand on my shoulder and squeezes softly. "So I'm trusting you to take care of her. I won't hold it against you if things don't work out, but as long as you love her, I want you to look out for her. She puts up a brave face, but I know she has as many fears as I do. Probably more."

Because she sees it firsthand. The way strange men must look at her, the way she has to always hide in plain sight like the rest of us, hoping bad people won't notice. I run my hand across his back and pull him close. "You have my word. As long as it's within my power, I'll do what I can to protect her."

My word doesn't mean much, but it's enough; Teddy pulls me in and gives me a powerful hug that I return with equal strength. We hold each other for a long time, longer than I'd normally be okay with, but I let the moment be. He needs it, and maybe I do, too.

The doorbell rings, so I open the door.

Carrying a duffel with all her dance gear, Heather smiles at me with a plain face; without makeup, her eyes seem smaller, and there's a smattering of faint freckles across her nose and cheekbones. Her eyebrows are less defined and her lips are a paler pink, but she's still beautiful. Her appearance is so shockingly different that blood rushes to my head—both of them.

I avert my eyes, put on my best smile, and let her inside.

Heather looks around the two-story foyer. "So this is your house. It's very big."

"Too big."

Heather walks past me down the hall with all the portrait paintings of my namesakes. She looks at the first painting, mutters, "John Eliza Woodcock I," and continues on her merry way, checking out each and every painting as she goes.

I hurry to catch up to her, but not before she finds mine; I really didn't want her to see it because I look so girly, but I need to remember that I was only ten at the time.

She looks at my face and back at the painting. "Is that you?"

I nod.

She smiles. "The seventh, huh?"

I place my hand on the back of my neck. "Yeah."

"You really are like a prince."

"It's not as cool as you'd think."

There's something soft about her expression. "Your parents kept having kids until they had a boy, didn't they?"

I step closer to her, my right shoulder behind her left, and stare at that loathsome painting. "Yeah. I'm expected to inherit my dad's business and marry into another rich family."

"Do you want to do that?"

"No."

She glances at me over her shoulder. "What do you want to do?"

I gaze at the short hair I used to have. "I want to go to beauty school and be a hairdresser. And I want to marry who I choose."

She glances at the painting. "You have gorgeous hair. It was the second thing I noticed."

I blush. "What was the first?"

She grins. "Your hot, sweaty chest."

I take a deep breath; it doesn't do much. "What do you want to be?"

Her grin softens to a smile. "I want to be a car mechanic."

I'm not surprised because she grew up around Kyle, a guy who regularly services his vehicles; I've watched him work on Mr. Brown's old-ass Ford Taurus and F-150 on more than one occasion. "Do you like cars?" It's a stupid question, but that's been my MO as of late.

"I do, but I prefer American ones in particular. I want to get a Mustang someday. Kyle is already teaching me how to drive manual, too."

"He drives manual?"

She nods. "That Nissan 240SX of his is a manual drive. It has over 200,000 miles on it, but it rides like a dream. He's put a lot of money into that thing."

"That's cool. I'm not much of a car guy, personally."

She grins again. "I'll happily be the car guy between the two of us."

"Guy, huh?"

Her grin widens, showing her canines, her brown eyes squinting with mirth.

I roll my eyes and match her grin with my own. "C'mon, let's go to my room."

"Your room, huh? What for?"

I raise an eyebrow. "You know what for. Jenny's waiting for us."

She saunters ahead of me like she knows the way to my shared room; I trot over, grab her hand, and lead her upstairs. A barely perceptible laugh leaves her lips at the sight of the old sign I put up on my door when I was little.

Jenny waits inside, spreading out all the makeup and related tools she owns on our desk. "What took you so long?"

"He was giving me a tour," Heather says.

Jenny squints and sneers, as she does. "Whatever. Which face am I painting first?"

Heather raises her hand. "Me! I want to see what you can do. Jack spoke highly of your skills."

Jenny smirks. "He better. Take a seat; time is wasting as we speak."

Heather sits down on the stool Jenny dragged over and pulls her hair behind her ears and shoulders.

I pull the old office chair behind her and sit down. "Do you mind if I do your hair?"

Her cheeks raise with her smile. "Go ahead, *Jack*."

Jenny scowls and gets to work on Heather's face, first asking what sort of look she's going for; in the meantime, I comb her hair into a proper updo, starting with a hard middle part. Women's styles are typically tight and perfectly shaped; sometimes, everything but the earlobes are covered by the shell of a female dancer's hair. As for makeup, dark eye shadow and bright-red lips are commonplace, both features that are easily seen from a distance.

Because men usually have shorter hair, they leave it down, though I've seen videos of women doing the same with longer styles; due to my ears, I plan to put my hair into a low, secure ponytail so I'll have less risk of flashing them onstage.

Within twenty minutes, Heather's hair and makeup are done, and while Jenny gracefully paints my face, Heather switches her studs for massive red-and-gold dangle earrings and sets large red flowers in her hair. She's absolutely stunning, and she hasn't even put her dress on yet.

When Jenny finishes working on me, I step outside the room so Heather can get changed. She emerges in a glorious pure-white dress fitted down to her thighs before opening into two big layers of ruffles; she has to hold the train up so she can walk freely in her golden-yellow flamenco heels, the color of betrayal and hope we thought fit the song we've been dancing to.

I reenter the room after it's vacated and change into my outfit. It's much more understated, comprised of black slacks, a white dress shirt with rows of small ruffles on the chest, and a long-sleeve black vest with gold buttons down the right side; I accent it with a red sash around my waist. After I finish getting everything on as perfectly as possible, I give myself one last once-over in the mirror nestled on the wall next to our bunk bed; I look sharp, if I say so myself.

I walk out of the room.

Heather scans my body from head to toe, nearly biting her lip, but stops herself from ruining her matte lipstick.

With the ruffled train trailing out behind her, I give her a once-over; she's radiant, but I have to keep control of myself.

"You clean up nice," she says.

"So do you," I say.

She picks up her train. "We should get going; wouldn't want to be late."

I nod.

Grace waits for us downstairs; her face lights up as soon as she sees us. "You look so pretty." I think she means it for the both of us.

"Thank you," Heather says, "but you ought to give credit to the artists."

Grace smiles at me and Jenny behind me; she frequently requests our services, so we know how much she appreciates us. After acknowledging us, she checks her phone. "Oh no, it's getting late." She rushes outside.

We follow.

⁓

"John Woodcock and Heather Brown: to the stage, please."

We rise from our seats in the auditorium, walk down the corridor, and step onstage; Heather disappears backstage from stage right to wait for her cue.

The theater tech starts the recording.

Hearing it for the first time, I can tell it's far from professional grade, but it's damn good for a high school performance; Teddy's voice is clear and undistorted, as is Sr. Hernandez's guitar. After the introductory seconds pass, I start my dance. I follow the ebb and flow, listen to the words Teddy translated for me, and interpret them with the movement of my body.

The two minutes pass, and Heather snaps those castanets together, the wooden instruments hanging on to her thumbs by the rope she pulled tight with her teeth. She's beautiful, walking under the harsh stage lights. Her eyes are dark, mysterious, unforgiving. Each step resounds toward me, resonating with my form, and we revolve around each other with the throes of music. I'm so enamored with her I barely notice the time passing, and next thing I know, we're gliding backstage from stage right.

The song ends. The audience claps. We stand there behind the curtains, panting, out of breath. I look at those red lips, that stoic face, that chest held aloft, and reach out, pulling her up to my chest by the small of her back; and she looks at me, at my nude lips, and we kiss fervently.

We pull apart before we lose control of our forms, and I immediately miss the soft pressure of her chest against mine.

We walk offstage and return to our seats like nothing happened.

In the weeks leading up to the talent show, after every rehearsal, we make out briefly behind the curtains, hidden in plain sight. I want to go further, roll around on the floor like animals until she's all I can taste, but we don't have enough time or enough privacy. So I cherish every stolen touch of her, the feel of her fingers gliding over my ears, the thrill of her massive canines every time I invade her mouth with my tongue. And each time, we part with a promise to kiss again.

The day has come. Friday, December ninth. It's freezing cold outside, and the auditorium is full of students, parents, family, and friends. A chunk of them are our people: Teddy, Mr. Brown, and Kyle; Matthew, Mark, Miss Ashley, and Alex; Mom, Dad, Jenny, Grace, and Esther; Emily, her two younger brothers, and her parents; Sr. Hernandez and Sra. Rubio; and Ruby, Heather's mother. I wonder if they're greeting each other, the ones that haven't become acquainted yet—I assume Mr. Brown is as far away from Ruby as he can get.

Heather and I stand backstage in line behind all the other individuals and groups displaying their various talents for the show. We wait announcement after announcement, applause after applause, until we part to opposite sides of backstage; she approaches stage right while I approach stage left.

Finally, they call our names. The music starts, and I glide across stage left until I land in the center. I hear the crowd, the whistles and the shouts, but it all bleeds away until it's only the hot stage lights, the wood beneath my feet, Teddy's sorrowful voice, and Sr. Hernandez's fluid guitar. And I dance like it will be my last.

I'm fast when I must be fast, and I'm slow when I must be slow. I wait when I must wait, stretch when I must stretch, step when I must step, and stomp when I must stomp. I ride out those two minutes, heart pacing, wanting, needing, and it leaps when she steps onstage.

Clacking castanets hail Heather's approach, and she stands iridescently, dragging that train, staring at me with a perfectly stoic expression.

She reaches me, step by agonizing step, and circles me, sizing me up with the glare of a slighted lover.

I watch her the whole way around, then mirror her stance, and we dance an intense conversation until we must walk away, angry at a distance.

But we come together once more, mirroring as before, and she puts her back to me, and I hold her shoulder, those castanets crying out, and we turn our backs on each other, and she turns and puts her arm across my shoulder.

Then we face each other again and dance in perfect unison like our bodies are one interconnected being, finally on the same page.

Yet we part, tempers too strong, each wanting to come out on top, but the pull is stronger still, and we dance like mirror images, and she snaps those castanets, and I lead her backstage with one arm on her shoulder, but I have to step in front of her and see her gorgeous face, then back away until we're behind the curtain once again.

"Come over tonight, *Jack*." She has her hand on my chest, her boobs pushed up against me in the dark of the backstage; we don't kiss, not tonight, not when so many are watching and waiting.

"Your house?" I whisper, breathless.

She bites her lip, not caring now that the dance is done. "We have a guest room. You can stay the night."

"I'll need to get changed. Take all this makeup off."

"You can walk over after you drop by your house."

"In the cold?"

"I'll warm you up." Her finger trails down my chest and my stomach, but no farther.

She's too much; I grab her and steal her lips, and we stumble into the shadows where we won't be seen.

I stare at a plate of fried chicken and Southern sides. Ruby sits at the head of the table, gauging me like I'll be her next meal. She's a big woman, with heavy boobs and short red hair. She stares with dark-brown eyes, her makeup laid on thick to hide the wear and tear of age.

Heather sits across from me, face bare and wearing an oversize T-shirt that hides the true volume of her tits; she stares resolutely at the takeout on her plate.

"I've heard stories about you, *Jack*," Ruby says.

Something in me cowers at the way she says my name. "I hope they were good stories." I scoop mashed potatoes and gravy with my spoon.

Ruby watches me eat, her expression dangerously reserved; I have no idea what she's thinking. "Heather mentioned you once. Your dancing tonight was wonderful." She smiles, but it doesn't reach her eyes.

I smile back. "Thank you. We practiced hard to make it the best it could be."

"You're friends with my son, yes? I recognized his singing; he's quite beautiful, isn't he?"

I nod slowly, awkwardly. "Yes. He got me into flamenco a few years ago."

"He's always been one to pull people under his wing; I expect you're of good character since he likes you so much."

I glance at Heather; she looks like she wants to disappear. "My parents have raised me well," I say, hoping to placate Ruby; I don't know enough about her to know what she's getting at, nor why Heather is acting so uncomfortable, so I need to tread lightly.

Ruby tears meat out of a fried chicken thigh with her perfectly manicured sapphire-blue nails. "You're welcome to stay the night, but I hope you'll remember your manners."

Heather's eyes bug out.

I think I'm starting to understand. "Of course. Straight to bed, in the guest room."

Ruby's smile becomes a frightening grin. "That's right. I cleaned the sheets and the comforter just the other day, so it should be to your liking."

"Thank you." I pat myself on the back for having the foresight to shower before coming here because I have a feeling Ruby would be unhappy to have a naked boy in the same house as her daughter.

Ruby finally looks away from me and focuses on her dinner. Heather and I do the same.

I take off all my clothes except for my charcoal-gray boxer briefs and place them on top of the dresser in the guest room. I came in and locked the door right after we finished dinner because Ruby scares me and I'm not about to step on her toes right after she allowed me to stay.

I sigh, crawl into the massive king-size bed that takes up nearly the entire room, and turn off the nearby lamp. I know exactly why Heather wanted me to come over tonight, but I don't have the guts to pull through with it; honestly, I'm absolutely unprepared, so it's probably for the better. There'll be other opportunities at better times and in better places.

But I won't deny I was looking forward to her warming me up tonight; in lieu of her body heat, I snuggle under the silky sheets, hoping it won't be long before my body heat gets trapped under the layers.

I have two minutes of peace before I start to doubt myself. Will Heather be upset with me if I don't take the initiative? And heeling to her mom so fast might not be such a good look. But Heather isn't a shallow girl, and she anticipates everything; with that thought, I calm down enough to relax into the plush mattress beneath my back. All my muscles unwind, and I nearly fall asleep.

But someone knocks on the door.

I sit up and turn on the lamp. "Heather?"

"That's right," she says. "Could you let me in?"

My heart rate jumps; it looks like she's taking the initiative tonight. I crawl out of bed and stand half naked next to the dresser. I glance at my folded-up clothes but turn away and unlock the door, then dive back into bed, sit against the headboard, and pull the covers up to my neck. "Come in."

She does. She opens the door, steps inside, and closes and locks it behind her.

I take in her figure. She's wearing lingerie: a pretty pink push-up bra and matching bikini panties. The bra is way too small on her; over half the flesh of her tits spills out from the top, her pale-pink areolas peeking out of the cups.

"Hey," she says. "Sorry for the wait."

I tear my eyes away from her body and look at her face; she put on new makeup, a subtle blue shadow accenting her eyes. "Um, that's okay." My heart pounds against my ribs.

She bites her lower lip, eyes trailing down to my raging hard-on that's thankfully concealed by layers of fancy fabric. "Do you still need me to warm you up?"

My mouth goes dry. "I might be a little cold."

She smiles and brings a trembling claw-tipped finger to her lips. She crawls onto the end of the bed, her boobs jiggling freely, her cleavage a deep abyss I'd love to shove my face into; she covers the distance between us and rests her hands on my knees.

I have to ask her. "Are you sure you want to do this?"

She sits on top of my thighs, her hands traveling to my stomach. "Yes. Are you?"

It's an easy answer; I nod.

Heather grins and goes active before my eyes.

I go active in turn, my ears pulling free from the pins I left in my hair.

She lingers over my long ears while I take in all her fur and claws. She backs up, pulling the sheets away from my body; she goes slowly, first uncovering my torso, then my tented underwear, then the entirety of my long fur-covered legs. "You look good."

"So do you."

She returns to my lap, sitting millimeters away from where I want her. She licks her glossy lips like she's ready to devour me whole, but dips two claws deep into her cleavage and pulls out a tiny square package; she puts it in my hand. "You'll have to open it; my claws are too long, and I'm worried I'll rip it."

I place the condom on the nightstand; I'll have to fight to go dormant so I can put it on, but we'll have to get there first. I stare at her cleavage, wishing she would smother me already. "What size is that bra?"

"Thirty-six triple *D*."

The biggest bra I've seen in my house was a double *D*, so I know she's way, way bigger than that.

"It's a little tight. I should probably take it off."

"I can help with that." Smirking, I lean forward and wrap my arms around her back, crushing her tits against my chest.

She puts her entire weight against me, reaches behind my back, and strokes my tail from base to tip.

Moaning, I grip the band of her bra, pull it tight, and unlatch the hooks.

CHAPTER 28

Downtime

Ashley

A giant Christmas tree covered in tinsel and baubles glitters in the corner of the Woodcocks' lavish living room. Ruby and Delilah hit it up across the room, both holding tiny glasses of bubbling poinsettia; I'd never heard of such a thing until John Sr. mixed and explained the cocktail in front of us in the kitchen. Alex, Bobby, and I declined any drinks, but Kyle, oddly somber, requested a glass of mulled wine.

With the noise of John Sr. and Delilah's extended family filling the room, I observe Ruby from between Bobby and Alex. I know very little about her, and considering the only opinions I have are from two men who share a rocky history, I want to reserve any judgements until I get a more rounded picture. And I must say, Ruby is certainly round—not ridiculously so, but with Kyle's years-old description in mind, it's obvious she's put on more than a few pounds since she and Bobby divorced. She's a tall woman teetering on the edge of fat, but retains a curvy hourglass figure emphasized under a tight dark-blue cocktail dress with a danger-ously low neckline; heavy sapphire earrings hang below her chin and a matching necklace with five large jewels arcs above her massive breasts. Her deep cleavage on full display, more than a few men in the room ogle her, and when she notices their gazes, she flirts back; Peter Sr., Delilah's brother, keeps staring at her even though his wife is in the room.

"I'm gonna get another drink," Kyle says, and he's gone in a flash.

"Is he alright?" I ask.

Bobby shrugs. "You never know with Kyle. I won't let him get drunk, if that's what you're worried about."

Fair enough; he's old enough he should know better. "How about you, Alex?"

"I'm fine." Alex smiles awkwardly. "It's just weird being around all these drinks."

I blanch. "Oh my goodness, I'm sorry; I really should've thought of that before inviting you."

He wraps his arm around my shoulders. "Relax, Ash. I'll be fine if you keep an eye on me." He grins hard enough that his canines show.

Relieved, I place my hand over his.

"And I wanted a chance to get to know your friends better, anyway. That talent show was a bit too crazy for much more than a hello."

He's right. Last week, at Jack and Heather's performance, I met more than a handful of people. Of course there was Ruby, but I also got to meet Emily, along with her brothers and her parents; the youngest one—Noah, if I'm remembering correctly—sat next to Kyle and interrogated him the entire time. The older brother, who I believe is Connor, kept his distance, but I caught him stealing glances at Kyle and Alex a few times; as for the parents, Ron and Georgia, they mostly spoke to Bobby about his daughter. Emily herself was fairly shy and stayed with Matthew, Mark, and Luke after we introduced ourselves.

Kyle slinks back into the room, a fresh glass of mulled wine in hand; he returns to leaning against the wall on Bobby's left.

Alex leans forward, keeping me held against his side. "Bobby, right? I heard you and Ashley met at this party last year."

Bobby smiles. "That's right. Kyle didn't come last year, so I had to find some new company."

"Kyle, why *did* you come this year?" I ask.

Kyle leans forward and peers at me; his wine glass is already nearly empty. "I came"—he points at Ruby—"because of that one and her daughter." He squints and downs the vestiges of wine in his cup. "Just in case."

I'm not sure what he thinks might happen, but I almost never know what Kyle's thinking.

"I take it there's some bad blood?" Alex asks.

Bobby gives him a strained smile. "Nothing too crazy. I can be in the same room as her, but she's not someone I like to talk to more than absolutely necessary."

"Yeah, we're civil." Kyle spins the last drop of wine around in the bottom of his glass. "Don't mean we gotta like her, though."

"Enough about that," Bobby says. "How about you, Alex? Tell us about yourself."

"Let me get another drink first," Kyle says.

Bobby rounds on him. "Kyle, you've already blown through two and it hasn't even been an hour yet."

Kyle rests his head against Bobby's arm. "God, I don't wanna tell ya, Bobby."

"Drinking ain't gonna help with your problem, so just tell me."
Kyle yanks him down by his arm and whispers in his ear.

Bobby gapes.

Kyle lets him go and buries his face in Bobby's bicep. "Don't tell her I told you anything. Our baby girl is growing up too fast."

Bobby stands there with a blank face.

⌒

"OMG, is that you, Mister Kyle?" Olive, wearing the same Santa dress from last year, saunters up to our little group with a boy I've never seen.

Kyle squints at her, his processing speed slowed down by an abundance of wine. "That's right, Miss Olive. Now, who's this here fella you brought with ya?"

"Oh, let me introduce you." She pulls the boy along and holds his arm up to her chest. "This is Craig, my fiancé."

Craig, wearing regular winter clothes and a Santa hat covering the tips of his ears, waves at us; he has a gold band on his ring finger. Teal bangs curl down toward his right eye, and . . . his pupils are slit like a lizard's.

Olive charges on while I stare at the boy's eyes. "And these people are Mister Kyle, Mr. Brown, Miss Ashley, and . . ." She cocks her head and puts a finger on her chin. "I don't believe we've met, Mister . . ."

"Alex. I'm Ashley's boyfriend."

"It's nice to meet you all." Craig gently pushes Olive off his arm and holds out his right hand. He has warm beige skin and abstract tattoos trailing from his fingers up his right arm, along with a silver metal bracelet; looking more closely at his moss-colored eyes, he has a thin layer of eyeliner around the edges of his eyelids.

We all shake his hand in turn.

"How long have y'all been engaged?" Kyle asks.

"Three months!" Olive says.

Craig smiles, tight-lipped.

"Well, congratulations," Kyle says. "I bet you gotta introduce him to your folks now, don't ya?"

Olive frowns, her index finger returning to her chin. "I do, but . . . Oh!" She lifts her finger straight in the air. "Let's go meet my brother!"

"Shouldn't I meet your parents first?" Craig says, "And you told me the other day your brother isn't much a fan of boyfriends."

"Mm . . . You're right . . ." Olive sighs. "You remember what I told you about my parents, right?"

Craig nods. "Don't worry; they won't scare me away."

Olive smiles and wraps herself around his arm again. "I suppose we should get that over with." She drags him away.

Once they're across the room talking to Delilah and Ruby, I whisper, "Was he . . . ?"

Alex furrows his brow. "I think so." He leans forward. "What do you think, Kyle?"

Kyle squints and sips more wine. "Definitely. He got them lizard eyes."

Alex rubs his chin. "The real question is what lizard he is."

We may never know.

⁓

The longer the night goes on, the drunker people get. John Sr., Peter Sr., and a bunch of other men lounge, drink, and argue about the recent election on the large sectional couch; Peter Sr. is particularly wasted, his words barely registering as the English language.

Kyle isn't doing much better. Bobby gave up on stopping him from drinking, so he's somewhere between buzzed and drunk.

"How many drinks have you had at this point?" Bobby asks.

Kyle contemplates his empty wine glass. "Two too many." He slumps against Bobby's side. "Ay! Fiancé boy! C'mere." He points at Craig.

Craig walks away from Olive, Ruth, and Mary, clearly nervous. "Yes?"

Kyle leans forward, scrutinizing him. "What are you?"

Craig flinches. "Excuse me?"

"You know what I mean."

Craig smiles. "I don't think I do, sir."

Kyle grins. "Yeah, keep smilin', boy."

Craig matches him with an awkward grin, revealing blunt-tipped conical teeth and visibly longer canines. "Maybe you should lay off the drinks."

Alex leans forward, taking hold of me once again. "You've got some teeth on you, kid."

Craig covers his mouth, face paling.

Alex grins, showing off his sharp canines. "Don't let Kyle bother you; we were just curious. It's rare to see someone like us." His eyes roll up to the ceiling for a second. "Actually, it *should* be rare, but we know more than a handful at this point."

Color returns to Craig's face. "Olive mentioned her brother, but—"

Kyle chuckles. "He admits it!" He slaps Craig's shoulder roughly.

Craig sidesteps closer to Alex's end of our group, obviously flustered.

Alex gives him a gentle smile. "I'm a wolf. What about you?"

Craig looks back and forth nervously, then whispers, "A mugger."

"A what now?" Kyle asks.

"It's a crocodile," Craig says.

"That explains them lizard eyes." Kyle slouches against Bobby again, satisfied.

Craig frowns and inches farther away from the pacified drunk.

"You can go now, kid," Alex says.

"Thanks." Craig returns to Olive's side.

Olive latches onto him, a knowing smile crossing her face.

The drunk men on the couch move on to greener pastures after they get too wasted to possibly discuss important political matters any longer—in front of the large hearth, swaying bodies slur off-tune Christmas songs with the karaoke machine.

Most of the women have taken to the couch, some similarly drunk, and all encouraging the spectacle. There are claps and cheers and overall noise; Ruby quietly peruses the menu of men from the center of the sectional.

Alex keeps glancing at the machine.

"Do you like karaoke?" I ask.

Alex smiles. "I do, but I was usually as wasted as those guys when I did it. It takes me back to those parties I'd go to with my folks or with work buddies." His eyebrows furrow and he scratches his cheek. "I might be too shy to go for it now, though."

"I'll sing with ya, Wolfy," Kyle says, leaning past Bobby.

"Kyle, when have *you* done karaoke?" Bobby asks.

"I sing in my car *all* the time," Kyle says, "but not with anybody in it."

"He's definitely drunk," Bobby says.

"You're just now noticing?" Alex says.

Bobby grins. "Oh, I noticed." He wraps his arm around Kyle's back and pushes him forward; Kyle stumbles, but Bobby keeps a firm grip on his shoulder so he won't face-plant on the carpet. "He's gonna have a hell of a hangover in the morning, ain't ya, Kyle?"

Kyle waves him off; he looks like he'll pass out on his feet. "I've been through worse and you know it."

"You're one prickly drunk." Bobby smiles at Kyle for a moment, then thrusts him away; Alex catches him before he falls. "Have fun, you two."

Alex grins. "Oh, we'll have fun alright." He drags Kyle away to wait in line at the machine.

"What do you think they'll sing?" I ask.

Bobby shrugs. "Hell if I know. It's not like we blast Christmas music ever."

"That's fair." It gets annoying after hearing the same twelve songs at every store you go to starting November first; I like my Christmas contained in December, where it belongs.

The drunks ahead of Alex and Kyle eventually finish their ballads, and the two take their places at the machine; Kyle leaning against his arm, Alex makes a selection on the connected tablet, then a familiar song starts to play. Alex wraps his arm behind Kyle to keep him afloat, and they both watch the TV over the fireplace, holding the mics up to their mouths; within a few familiar seconds, they belt out a Christmas song about giving away your heart. It sounds awful, especially with Kyle's drunken Southern twang.

I laugh, watching them sway back and forth to the music, the two of them somehow staying on beat despite Kyle's inebriation and Alex's self-proclaimed shyness; I guess he was so used to being drunk all the time that he forgot how much confidence he has sober.

By the time they're done, they have the other men laughing and clapping and whistling; full of Christmas spirit, Alex says, "Let's all sing a song!"

John Sr., one of the few who has remained perfectly sober, saunters up next to him, and all the other men swarm them in a mass of business casual and dark coifed hair. A certain series of high-pitched bells ring, then the multitude of men sing in drunken unison, swaying so much I'm surprised none of them have fallen over.

"They sound awful." Bobby grins.

I focus on Alex's firm cadence through the howling. "They seem to be fitting in just fine."

Bobby's grin eases into a smile. "Kyle was real jittery when he came here two years ago. He spent most of his time chatting with Jack's sisters. Olive was a real fan; I figure she must've realized what he is long before I pieced it together."

"I've noticed all his sisters are smarter than they seem."

Bobby's smile wanes. "They live around people that regularly underestimate them. Sometimes playing dumb keeps you safe."

I get the idea he isn't talking about Jack's sisters. "How have you been now that Luke knows you know?"

Bobby leans back and crosses his arms; his smile returns. "He was upset with me at first, but I'm glad he and his friends can look however they want in my house. I was honestly more shocked seeing Kyle like that." He peers at the swaying men engulfing our singing friends. "He doesn't change often in front of me, but I can tell he's much more comfortable with himself in my house now."

I smile, too. "I'm glad it worked itself out."

"Me, too."

CHAPTER 29

Leap of Faith

Matthew

J ack's been acting awfully strange tonight. We came to his parents' Christmas party again, but unlike last year, Jack has actually been in a good mood—an insanely good mood. He smiled at everyone, happily helped his mom set up the living room equipment and his dad set up the bar, and when all his cousins arrived, he thanked them for coming.

Even stranger was his reaction to Heather: he barely acknowledged her existence, merely nodding his head and letting her guide herself down the hall. Oddly enough, she didn't seem bothered by his behavior, merely mimicking his standoffishness as if they were no more than classmates that saw each other on occasion.

Now we sit in front of *The Last Supper*, Teddy, Mark, Jack, and I in a row, chilling out and eating Christmas favorites without much of a word between us. Teddy brought his guitar again, his light strumming adding a calm ambience to the otherwise busy dining room. Heather, wearing a crisp baby blue pantsuit and tailored white blouse, towers over Jenny, Grace, and Hope as they talk about whatever it is girls like them talk about. Quite a few of Jack's cousins have glanced her way, so I'm expecting Peter to pull something again.

"Hey, Jack," I say, looking at his dopey face.

"What?" His eyes don't leave Heather's back for a second.

"What's up with you tonight? Did something happen with Heather?"

Jack glances at me for a single moment, giving me an insanely wide smile. "Nothing happened. And I'm perfectly fine."

I shrug and glance at Mark and Teddy on my left; they both look suspicious of him, but neither bothers to protest. We'll have to grill him for details later.

I return to eating and observing Heather across the room. She's been a strange addition to our social circle and the last girl I expected to be Emily's closest female friend; whereas Emily is reserved and considerate, Heather has no problem breaking barriers and stepping over boundaries. She also scares me a little.

Back in September, the day after Labor Day, Heather approached me while I was on my way to car pool. My guard down, she yanked me into an empty hallway, pushed me against the wall, and slammed her arm next to my head, the other on her cocked hip. If Emily was wearing heels and did that to me, it'd be hot, but Heather was anything but flirtatious; she had her chin lifted so she could glare down at me, and our height and build difference—along with knowing she's not only a bear girl, but Teddy's sister—had my tail puffing up under my shirt. "Emily told me everything that happened back in March," she said, nostrils flaring. "If you *ever* hurt her like that again, I'll end you personally." She grinned, baring her massive canines. "And I'll start with tickle torture." Having said her piece, she smiled and left; my legs gave out then and there, and I've been careful around her ever since.

Frankly exhausted from the memory, I almost miss Peter tapping her shoulder.

Heather turns around, a glass of water in hand, and looks down at him; she shares a nearly imperceptible glance with Jack and exclaims, "Oh my gosh, you're tiny!"

Peter nearly drops his plate, mortified.

Heather cups her cheek with her free hand, wiggles, and walks around Peter like he's an exotic display. "Wow, wow, wow. What did you want from me, small one?"

Peter clears his throat and stands ramrod straight, puffing out his skinny chest like it'll give him a few extra inches. "I . . . couldn't help but notice a lovely new lady." He looks at Heather's chest, smirks, and bows obnoxiously. "I'm Peter Baldwin IV; and you are . . . ?"

A dangerous grin splits Heather's face. "You can call me Lady Anastasia, little Peter."

Jack nearly spits out his drink.

Peter's cheeks flare pink as he glares at his much-taller cousin. He adjusts his tie and cranes his neck to look at Heather's face. "Lady Anastasia, I'd appreciate it if you'd use my name."

She smiles stupidly. "I did use your name, little Peter."

He gives up quickly. "A-Alright. Well, I hope we can be . . . friends."

Heather frowns and places an index finger near her lips. "Mm . . . You'll have to pass a trial first."

Peter blusters. "A trial? Why would I need to pass a trial?"

She grins again. "I only have room for one small boy friend in my life." She glances at me. "Short Stuff."

I stand and place my plate on my chair.

Peter watches me saunter up to her, his mouth gaping open when she wraps her arms around me from behind. "You can't mean . . ."

"Oh, I do. You'll have to compete with Short Stuff for a spot on my boy-friend list."

For added effect, I crack my neck, my face perfectly neutral.

Peter pulls at his tie. "You know what? I think I'll be alright with remaining acquaintances." He backs away, half-heartedly adds, "For the time being," and slinks into the kitchen to sulk.

"Aw, what a shame." There's a pout in her voice. "And here I was, looking forward to a short-boy brawl." She backs away from me, giving a friendly pat to my shoulder. "Thanks, Short Stuff; now I might feel bad about beating you up one day."

I turn around wearing a strained smile. "I hope you never feel the need to beat me up one day."

Heather smirks. "You and me both." She returns her attention to Jack's sisters.

I sit back down and immediately slouch from another dose of Heather exhaustion.

Teddy, Mark, and Jack use every ounce of restraint they have not to burst out laughing, and I can't help but grin.

⁓

Esther trudges into the dining room, pulls up a chair, and slings her arms over the back.

"Politics?" Jack asks.

Esther sighs. "Politics. All our uncles got drunk and started arguing about the election. Hillary this, Trump that, the injustice of the Electoral College versus the popular vote!" She holds up her fist, accenting her point.

"That sounds about right. It probably doesn't help that Dad encourages it."

"He doesn't encourage it; he just mixes drinks."

Jack flattens his lips and raises an eyebrow. "It's implied."

Esther smiles like she's done with his shit. "Enough about that. I have a question for you guys."

"What's that?" Mark asks. "Did you catch that one guy you told us about or something?"

Esther grins and pulls her phone out of her back pocket, unlocks it, and given a few seconds of lightning-speed tapping, shows us a picture.

All four of us lean in and regard the photo. It's a graduation picture of Esther and some guy in a cap and gown; their tassels are swept to the side by a gust of wind, both smiling and holding out peace signs. The guy next to her is slightly taller and just as thin, wearing gray bangs so long they cover half his nose; one blue eye barely peeks out between the windswept strands. Overall, he has a shaggy look that rivals Esther's laid-back aesthetic.

Esther zooms in close to his face and points at a spot right under his cap; it's too pixelated to see anything. "Call me crazy, but I think Dustin has a floppy dog ear under his hair here."

No matter how hard I squint, I can't see it.

Mark holds his hand out and gestures for the phone.

Esther hands it over.

Mark puts his glasses on and inspects the image closely, tilting the phone this way and that to get the clearest image possible. "You might be right, but it's impossible to tell." He holds it out to her, pointing at the same place. "There *is* an odd shadow here, but that could just be his hair; it's pretty wavy, so it's clumping together into overlapping sections." Dustin's hair is so wavy it borders on curly, though that could be the wind tousling it to hell and back.

Esther takes her phone back and hangs her head. "Ugh. And I thought I finally had some evidence."

"Maybe you do, maybe you don't, but at least you tried." Mark shrugs with his hands up.

Esther rolls her eyes and pockets her phone; she turns back to Jack. "Anyway, did you hear that Olive got herself a fiancé? He seems pretty cool so far." Her grin tells me she's leaving out some pertinent information.

Jack shakes his head and shrugs. "I haven't heard a word. Not that I care." He squints. "How did Mom and Dad take it?"

"He has tattoos and dyed hair, so you tell me."

Jack cradles his chin. "You know, I'm inclined to believe our parents want grandkids too much to care at this point."

Olive is already twenty-six, so that wouldn't surprise me; with a family as big as theirs, they obviously put a lot of emphasis on having as many children as possible, mostly for the worst—I'd struggle to handle two, much less eight kids.

"Oh man, I don't look forward to that," Esther says. "Honestly, I don't think I want any kids."

"That's fair." Jack glances at Heather. "I'm not sure if I want kids, either."

Esther smiles softly. "You're too young to be worrying about that, anyway."

"Maybe," he says. "It's still something worth thinking about, though."

"I'm surprised you're not arguing with me."

Jack smirks. "I may have had a pick-me-up recently."

Esther leans forward, grinning. "I take it Olive's not the only one with a secret relationship, hmm?"

Jack mimes zipping his mouth shut and throwing away the key.

"I see you, Jack." Esther gets up off the chair, thrusts it under the dining room table, and glances back at Heather as she leaves.

A man in a Santa hat wanders into the kitchen, Olive directly on his heels. He has teal bangs, a ring on his finger, and abstract black tattoos on his right hand and forearm; he must be Olive's fiancé, and he looks absolutely exhausted.

Some inhuman caterwauling drifts in from the distant living room; the old men are having a blast singing Christmas songs, which likely chased him away.

After he gathers some leftover food and heats it in the microwave, Olive drags him over to the four of us. "Hello, boys!" She hangs off his arm. "I thought I should introduce you to my fiancé! This is Craig." She snuggles closer.

He regards us coolly until he realizes what's wrong with all of us.

And we can tell what's wrong with him: he has slit pupils, and his lips part enough to reveal conical teeth.

Olive chugs along, pointing at all of us in turn. "That's Teddy, Jack's bestie; that's Mark; that's Matthew; and that's my cutest little brother, Jack."

Jack smiles and waves. "It's nice to meet you. I hope Olive hasn't scared you off yet."

Olive pretends to be mad. "Oh, Jack, I'm not scary!" She looks at Craig's dumbfounded face. "Right, Craig?"

"That's right," he says, "but, um, you never told me there were four of them."

"Make that five, mister fiancé." Heather comes up behind him—he nearly jumps out of his skin—and proceeds to look closely at his face. "Ooh, another reptile."

Craig is too shocked to speak.

Olive says, "He's a crocodile. I found him while volunteering at the food bank."

"You talk like you picked him up off the street," Jack says.

Olive waves him off. "Nonsense; he was volunteering, too. And we hit it off right away. Right, Craig?"

Craig nods stupidly. "Uh-huh."

"Have you seen him yet?" Heather asks.

Olive nods vigorously. "His tail is huge!"

"I'm right here, Olive!" Craig says.

Olive frowns. "I'm sorry, Craig. Tell you what: Heather and I will have a chat about things, and you can hang out with the boys for a while." She giggles, all excited, and runs off to the other side of the room with Heather.

Craig looks back, running a hand down his face.

Jack smiles at him, finding everything hilarious, I'm sure. "Why don't you pull up a seat? Let's get to know each other."

Craig, full of annoyance and a dash of disbelief, sighs, drags a chair over from the dining room table, and places it between me and Jack; he sits down, places his plate in his lap, and leans back like he just ran an entire marathon.

"So . . . ," Jack says.

Craig glares at him. "What?"

Jack grins. "Did she blackmail you?"

Craig blusters, nearly shouting, "Not at all!"

Jack looks surprised. "You actually like her?"

Craig settles down, back to being annoyed but also flustered. "Yes. I wouldn't have proposed to her otherwise."

"You proposed? And here I thought Olive jumped the gun."

Craig chews some turkey. "She thought about it, but I was quicker."

After a moment, Jack asks, "How long have you known her?"

Craig blushes. "A little under a year."

Jack whistles. "That's a little soon, don't you think?" But his face screws up, and he leans back with his hands behind his head. "Then again, I'm just as impatient."

Craig purses his lips. "I don't know. I don't think the timeline matters as long as it works out. Some people are slow, some people are fast." He smiles lightly. "I guess I'm more of the fast type."

Jack snorts but doesn't comment.

Mark leans forward so he can see Craig. "Yo, is that your natural hair color?"

Craig turns his head and regards Mark's outrageous hair; he shakes his head. "I dye it; my natural color is olive green." He smiles. "Is yours natural?"

Mark grins. "Unfortunately. I could probably dye it purple or black, but the roots would stand out too much."

Craig nods. "At least olive is more muted, so most people don't think about it."

Mark gazes at Craig's tattooed arm. "Are your tattoos visible when you're active?"

I know he's going to be confused, so I quickly whisper what Mark means.

"Oh." Craig gazes at his inked skin. "Surprisingly, they are. I wasn't expecting them to be, honestly."

"I'm surprised you have any at all," Mark says. "Wouldn't the pain be too much?"

Craig grins. "I had enough willpower to tough it out for a short session. I don't think I could handle a whole sleeve, though."

Jack sighs. "Tattoos are one of the many things I would've eventually done if not for being what we are."

"What else have you thought about?" Mark asks.

Jack crosses his arms. "Definitely piercing my ears and trying a Caesar cut."

"Really?" Mark squints at him, then nods to himself. "I can see it."

Craig cocks his head, causing the pom-pom on the end of his hat to hang near his shoulder. "Couldn't you do those things anyway?"

Jack shakes his head, then discreetly uncovers his bunny ears. "I can't exactly get these pierced or cut my hair short." He lets his hair back down.

"Damn. That sucks."

Jack glances at Heather again. "It's not so bad." And he smiles the fondest smile I've ever seen.

⁓

Teddy thrusts his entire massive self on top of Jack's bottom bunk. "Jenny . . ."

Jenny looks over the railing of her top bunk. "What?" She glares at the back of his head.

Teddy whimpers and goes active in one flat second—now that it's been over a year and a half, he can transform as easily as the rest of us.

Jenny huffs and rolls her eyes, crawls down the ladder, and climbs over Teddy's legs before situating herself next to his shoulder; after glaring at the three of us, she rubs his bear ear.

With Teddy preoccupied, Mark gives me a look and nods his head toward Jack, who's still in la-la land even after helping his parents clean up the messy remains of the party.

I nod back a silent go-ahead.

Mark saunters up to Jack, puts his hand on his shoulder, and walks him out into the hall.

I follow them.

As soon as we're out of earshot, Mark says, "So what's the deal with you and Heather tonight? You never spoke to her once."

Jack blushes. "Nothing big. We just had some fun the other night."

Mark gapes. "You mean to tell me you . . ." He makes a circle with his finger and thumb, then pokes his index finger through the middle.

Jack bites his lip and nods.

"Well, how was it? You gotta give us the details, bro!"

Jack shrugs. "Nothing crazy. I mean, it was our first time, so it was a little awkward." He puts a hand behind his neck, smiling stupidly. "But it was awesome; I mean, God, have you seen Heather?"

Mark shuffles close and whispers, "What positions?"

Jack quickly glances left and right. "Cowgirl, then missionary."

Mark holds his chin, nodding solemnly. "Vanilla, but wholesome." Then he frowns. "But I'm very disappointed in you."

Jack's screwed-up face says, *What the fuck are you on about?*

Mark's expression twists into clear agony, his nostrils flared, teeth grit, and brow drawn up. "I can't believe you had premarital sex! How could you?! You were supposed to be a good Christian boy!"

Jack gapes. "I never said I was a good Christian anything! There's no way in hell I was gonna turn her down!"

Mark pretends to sniffle. "That was some real virgin behavior, bro."

Jack fumes. "You're just jealous because I got laid before you!"

"Of course I'm jealous! I don't have a big-titty dommy mommy to ravage me every night!"

Jack's face turns to stone. "I'm going to pretend you didn't just say that."

I step next to Mark and pat his shoulder. "There, there. You'll get your dommy mommy one day, bro."

Mark sniffles. "Thanks, bro. You're a real homie."

Jack sighs and rolls his eyes exactly like his twin sister.

I turn to Jack. "If everything went well, then why were you and Heather trying to ignore each other all night?"

Jack sobers, leans against the wall, and crosses his arms. "Her mom's a real prude, at least as far as Heather's concerned, so we're keeping our relationship a secret from her. I told her I should keep it from my parents, too, since her mom hit it off with mine, so don't go around telling anyone."

I think about Emily, how her parents don't want her dating until she's eighteen—perhaps she and Heather have more in common than I realized.

"My disappointment aside," Mark says, "we'll keep it between us."

"Yeah," I say. "We're all good at keeping secrets, anyway."

"Thanks." Jack's brow furrows. "I'm worried her mom will punish her over it. I won't go into details, but there's a reason Heather calls her mom by her first name."

Mark and I nod; we've known plenty of holier-than-thou people in our time, so we can imagine what that punishment might look like—the real question is just how spiteful Heather's mom is. I only saw her briefly during the talent show and while she was in the kitchen tonight, and she didn't so much as acknowledge our existence, so I don't have much more than a physical impression of her; she seemed nice enough, but most people are able to fake it 'til they make it no matter how awful they are inside.

With the Heather situation cleared up, we return to Jack's bedroom door, open it, and file inside.

Their eyes blissfully closed, Teddy engulfs Jenny in an intimate embrace.

Jenny cracks an eye open and glares. "Get. Out."

Eyebrows raised across the board, we back out and close the door.

Jack decides we should let Jenny and Teddy have their moment, so while he and Mark watch YouTube videos on the TV in the living room, I draw a bath in the upstairs master bathroom. I'm more of a shower kind of guy, but their bathtub is so ridiculously nice that I indulge myself every time I stay the night.

Once the pure-white porcelain tub is full of warm water, I disrobe, step inside, and duck my head under the water. Thoroughly soaked, I bring my head above the surface, rest my neck on the little bath pillow attached to the edge, and melt into heavenly bliss. I feel so good, my muscles unwinding and my head clearing, that I purr.

So Jack and Heather are a thing now, and they ran through all the bases as fast as they could. A part of me is jealous, but another knows that I'm a very different person from Jack, with different priorities and different problems; what's natural for him doesn't have to be natural for me. And I already knew a long time ago that I wouldn't be getting any action right away with Emily; she wants to wait until marriage, which I'm fine with. I won't say that I'd absolutely never have sex before marriage—if the opportunity arose, I'd probably take it—but I don't mind waiting for the right girl. I think Emily's that girl, and it's about time I do something about it.

I survey the pristine bathroom, its beachy blue wallpaper and decor, the marble countertops and the clean cabinets and the shiny silver faucets, and close my eyes. It's taken months and months of stolen afternoons, but I almost have all my hours to get my provisional license; once that's in my hands, I'll have no more excuses. I'll make a plan and I'll execute it; I can wait forever for the perfect moment, or I can make it with my own hands.

I lift my flesh-and-bone fingers out of the water and look at my perfectly trimmed fingernails, the same nails that can turn into claws at a moment's notice, the same claws that have hurt people I love. But they can protect, too, in the right situation. They can even be used as a sharp-edged tool; maybe that's dumb, but seeing them as box cutters feels more innocent, more human.

With my hands full of potential, I grab the pricey organic vegan shampoo and wash my hair and tail; when I finish lathering, I submerge and run my fingers through my hair and fur until the water becomes soapy with suds. Sopping wet, I rise and pour the matching liquid bodywash into my hands, rub it into every nook and cranny, and submerge all over again. Sufficiently clean by the work of my hands, I rest my head on the pillow again and lie in the soapy water as long as it remains warm, dreaming about the future.

*　　⁓*

I make it to school carrying a box of chocolates deep within the largest pocket of my book bag. I go through the motions as if it's any other day: I try not to fall asleep in the bleary hour of first period, then I try not to die in the boredom of second, then I try not to combust from anticipation in the first half of third. As soon as the bell rings for B lunch, I leave the classroom, trudge through the halls, and walk outside into the cold February air; clouds stretch across the otherwise sunny sky, and Emily sits on the stone bench near the stairs leading to the car pool lane, right where I asked her to be through text last night.

My heart rate spikes and my knees tremble, but I swallow my nerves and sit down next to her.

"Hey." Emily smiles.

"Hey." I don't.

Emily catches on. "What did you ask me out here for? You look like you just got in trouble or something."

"Um, well . . ." I might be in trouble: the end of my best friendship kind of trouble. "I have a question for you. A really personal question."

She grimaces, visibly clenching her teeth. "Don't tell me I said something offensive again."

That gets a laugh out of me. "Nothing like that." Emily has asked some outright bizarre questions about us monster people—her worst by far was when she asked Heather if she goes into heat; awkward as it was, she confirmed that monster girls have menstrual cycles, not estrus cycles like some animals—but I'd rather her ask and learn than make a bunch of crazy assumptions about us. She's naturally curious, and that's totally fine; her desire to learn and understand is part of why I like her so much.

That thought brings me back to the present.

"It's something I've been waiting a long time to ask you," I say.

Her grimace becomes a curious frown, her lips parted and eyes questioning.

I stare at my lap, clenching the fabric of my pants in my fists; I close my eyes, take a deep breath, and look straight into Emily's eyes. "Emily, I love you. I've loved you for a long, long time." My ears burn and my eyes waver, but I have to finish. "Will you go out with me?" I search her beautiful hazel eyes with bated breath.

Emily covers her mouth with her hands, and even though her eyes grow watery, a smile stretches her cheeks. "Oh my God, yes!" She throws her arms around me and squeezes like her life depends on it. "I thought you'd never ask." She sniffles. "I love you, too. Since forever."

I hug her back and purr, forgetting everything but her sweet scent and the warmth of her skin on my cheek.

We let go of each other, but Emily grabs my cheeks before I get too far away. She sheds a few stray tears and smiles and sniffles as she looks into my eyes. "Aren't we supposed to kiss or something?"

I'm shocked. "I mean, uh, if you want, I guess—"

Emily bites her lip and pulls me forward so fast I accidentally grab her hips, then her lips are on mine, and it's dry and sloppy and I can barely feel it at all, but her plush hips are in my hands, and my fingers sink into her soft curves, and—

She pulls back, licking her lips.

I lick mine, hoping she won't notice how close I am to going active.

"I'm not very good at kissing," she says.

"Neither am I."

"I guess we need to practice."

I nod.

We kiss again, our lips locking with more grace, wet with saliva, and our mouths moving at a slow pace, testing the waters.

We part once more.

Her nose and ears burn red. "That was better."

"Yeah."

She lets go of my face and grabs my hands, sliding her fingers under my palms so she can pull my hands off her hips. "I'm fine, but your nails were poking me."

"I'm sorry."

She brings my knuckles to her lips. "It's okay. That's why I took your hands." She kisses between my index knuckles, blushing pink. "I like them. You have pretty fingers."

I blush, too, my ears red-hot despite the cold. "You're not hurt? Or scared?"

She shakes her head. "You were being careful. I know you'll keep me safe."

I hug her and shed a few tears. "Thank you."

She rubs my back, her fingers running over the middle of my hidden tail.

When I feel ready, I let her go; we share a smile, one wet with happy tears. "I actually got you something. For Valentine's Day."

Emily grins. "I got you something, too."

"Really?"

She reaches into her bag and pulls out a bar of dark chocolate. "I remember you said you prefer stuff that isn't too sweet."

I'm flattered she remembered something so random; before taking it from her, I reach into my bag and take out the heart-shaped box of assorted chocolates. "I didn't know what you like, so I got this. I know it's kinda lame, but—"

"I love those," she says. "Everything except the orange cream."

"Then I'll eat it for you." I give her the box and she gives me the chocolate bar.

Even though we have proper lunches, we eat the chocolates,

Emily kicking her feet like she does when she's thinking. After she nibbles the corner of the orange-cream chocolate, she hands it to me; I pop it in my mouth, savoring the tangy taste of citrus on my tongue.

CHAPTER 30

A Fish Named Killer

John

Heather leans against me in the bath, her big boobs floating free in the water. We usually shower together whenever she stays over, but she wanted a change of pace tonight, and I wasn't about to argue. The water feels weird on my thick fur, but it's pleasantly warm next to my favorite girl.

"Do you think I could stay over for spring break?" she asks.

"I don't see why not," I say, "but you might get dragged to church on Easter Sunday."

Heather furrows her brow. "Your family goes to church?"

"Not really. Only Christmas and Easter service. They're too busy working. Or just don't feel like it." I prefer not to go anyway; it's not something I care about.

Heather looks around the bathroom bigger than my bedroom. "I guess you'd have to work a lot to own a house this big."

"Yeah." My parents usually work between sixty and eighty hours per week—between food and clothes and school, eight kids are a huge expense. "Doesn't your mom work a lot, too?"

"She claims as much. She works high up in the HR department, but I think she goes to dinner with rich guys almost every night; sometimes she doesn't get home until eleven." Heather puts her hand on my thigh and gives me a sweet smile. "That's why I can get away with you in the guest room so easily."

I wrap my arm around her and grab her hip. "That's a blessing in disguise, if there ever was one."

Heather pulls me in for a chaste kiss; when we part, she strokes my right ear. "You're my blessing."

This gorgeous girl . . . "You're more than a blessing." I cup her cheek and kiss her again.

Heather eagerly reciprocates, wrapping her furry arms around my shoulders.

I hold her by her waist and press her boobs against my chest; there's nothing better than her weight all over me.

We make out until we tire, then settle down side by side. My arms around her soft belly, I lean my head against her left tit.

Heather strokes my ears until I start grinding my teeth.

"I really hope all this purring won't destroy my enamel."

Heather slides her hand down my back, her pinky claw poking the base of my downturned tail. "Hopefully being a bunny boy prevents that from becoming a problem."

I sigh. "Wouldn't that be nice."

"I'll pet you less if you're that worried about it."

I shake my head. "I'll take the risk."

Smirking, she runs her pinky finger down my tail, gropes my left butt cheek, and returns to stroking my ears.

I resume purring, my teeth grinding lightly against each other. I reach across her chest and knead her right tit, my other hand sliding down to her thigh.

We caress each other for a long while, so much so the water becomes cool. I unplug the drain, and we continue our petting, even as the cold indoor air makes our nipples hard; once the tub is empty, I turn the faucet on to refill it with hot water.

"Maybe we should actually bathe," Heather says, her soft hand pads gliding over my damp fur.

"I don't mind hanging out awhile longer," I say, palming her boobs.

"Someone might notice we've been gone too long at the same time."

"My sisters will cover for us. And my parents couldn't keep track of all of us even if they tried."

Heather smiles. "You're right. That's why I like it here."

Once the water is nice and hot and submerging our bodies, I turn the faucet off and guide Heather to place her back against the narrow end of the tub. I rest the back of my head between her pillowy boobs, my tail touching her crotch.

Heather locks her long legs around my hips and plays with my ears, her claws barely grazing their delicate flesh. "I think Ruby's been looking through my stuff."

I tilt my head back into her cleavage. "What makes you think that?"

Heather cards my hair out of my face. "The junk in my night-stand was out of order." She frowns, a furrow in her brow. "I keep the condoms in there, buried under everything."

I copy her expression. "Do you think she found them?"

"I don't know, but it might be best not to use them." She pushes her hair back like she has a human ear to hold the strands. "We were getting low, anyway. I'll hide the new ones somewhere else. Or just give them to you."

I run my hands up and down her legs. "That's probably for the best if she's snooping around."

Heather hums and reaches away from me; she pours shampoo in her hand and starts lathering my hair. My head rocks back and forth over her chest as she skillfully winds her long fingers in and out of the easily tangled strands. As soon as she's satisfied, she eases me into the water, rinses all the soap out, and pulls me up to do it all again with conditioner. My hair thoroughly cleaned, she gets me to stand and washes my body by hand.

I enjoy each and every caress like it was the first, then reciprocate in kind.

I stretch out my legs and get comfortable on the large sectional couch in the living room; upstairs, Heather sleeps in my bed, pretending she's here as Jenny's friend and not my girlfriend. It's a convincing excuse; she and Jenny get along well and have a few classes together, so Heather came over a few times previously to work on various projects.

I'm glad she's been able to fit in with my family, though part of that's because she's an excellent actor; Heather can play the part of a delicate, well-adjusted lady at the drop of a hat, and exudes a richness even my most obedient cousins struggle to portray. But the Heather I like best is the one she shows me late in the night, when we're alone, our bodies and hearts naked to each other.

I turn my face toward the backrest cushions and adjust the throw pillow under my head. I snuggle into my blanket, close my eyes, and hope sleep will take me soon.

A large, soft body presses into my back; she wraps herself around me, her arms pinning mine against my chest.

"Heather?" I ask.

"Hey," she says.

"What're you doing here?"

She holds me closer, her boobs compressed against my upper back. "I was feeling lonely."

I hum.

"I wish we could sleep together."

"Me too, but we'll have to hold out until we're older."

Heather lets go, turns me onto my back, and gets on top of me; she squeezes me, her hair all over my face.

I pull one arm out from under her, gather her hair, and push it over her shoulders. It's too dark for me to see her face, so I brush her brow, her cheek, and the edge of her chin with my fingertips.

She copies me, and we kiss. "Good night, Jack."

"Good night."

She removes her warmth and walks away.

Heather and I enjoy a long spring break together, suffer through the Easter sermon on Sunday, and stomach a long dinner with my parents and sisters. By the time the sun sets and I walk her home, I don't feel like leaving her for the night, so I linger outside her house.

Ruby walks into the dining room, a chocolate cream pie in hand, and looks out the window; she spots me and stares.

I avert my gaze and walk away in the direction of home, not looking back until I reach the first intersection and make a left turn onto the street. I keep walking until I reach another intersection and make another left. I circle the entire block until I come up to Heather's house from the opposite side I left from; I cut through the bushes, reach the window of the guest room, knock on the glass, and crouch under the sill.

Moments later, the window slides open and Heather pokes her head out, her long blond hair cascading downward. "Missed me already?" She smiles, her brown eyes crinkling.

I rise to my full height, appreciating the way the light behind her outlines her scantily clad figure. "You know I can't get enough of you."

Heather grins, goes active, brings one long claw to the edge of her lips, and backs away from the window.

I climb inside and quickly undress while Heather closes the window and draws the curtains, leaving us in total privacy; in nothing but my boxer briefs, I go active and sit on the edge of the bed.

Biting her lip, Heather saunters over, pushes me back a foot, and crawls into my lap.

I wrap my arms around her, unlatch her pale-blue bra—a newer one that actually fits her—toss it aside, and take her heavy tits into both hands. I work on one nipple with my mouth and the other with my fingers.

Heather nibbles on my ear and strokes my tail.

We slowly make our way across the bed until my back is cushioned by fluffy pillows against the headboard, and I've switched tits, and she's pulling down my underwear, and—

The door slams open.

We freeze.

Ruby glares at us nearly naked and fully active and in the middle of foreplay under her roof. "You bitch." She fumes.

Heather scrambles away from me, covering as much of her chest as she can with her arms. "Mom, I—"

"Zip it, Heather." She looks her daughter up and down, then me, her scowl growing deeper. "I always knew you were a whore, but this is a new low"—she sneers at the sight of us—"dressing up like animals and fucking in my house."

Heather's lips part. "We're not . . ." Wide-eyed, she goes silent.

"I didn't raise you like this."

Heather looks away and whispers, "You didn't raise me."

Ruby's nostrils flare. "What did you just say?!"

Heather glares at her. "You didn't raise me!"

Ruby grins. "That's right." She takes a deep breath. "That bastard Kyle did this, didn't he? Corrupted you just like that prostitute mother of his." Her nose scrunches. "The apple doesn't fall far from the tree."

Heather scoffs. "What does that say about you, Mother? I'm the apple to your tree, aren't I?"

Ruby jabs a finger at her. "You will *not* speak to me that way, girl."

Heather sneers. "I'll speak to you however I want. Now get out." She points at the wall, her finger trembling.

Ruby screams, "You're in *my* house, you whore! *You* get out, and take your toy with you!"

"Fine!" Heather's shrill voice stings my sensitive ears. She scrambles off the bed, moving so fast her toe claws tear up the comforter, and grabs her bra; she fumbles to reclasp the back, all while stumbling over to the window; just as she gets the hooks secure, she trips over my boots.

I slip off the bed, charge across the room, and catch Heather, my back slamming into the corner of the dresser and my shoulder hitting the wall.

Heather grabs me, managing not to pierce my skin with her claws. "Jack—"

"I'm fine." I wince and glance at Ruby.

Her arms are crossed and her scowl is rough, but she's remarkably calm.

Heather draped over me, I rotate us until my back is to Ruby, carefully holding my ears and tail erect to keep up the illusion that I'm wearing a bunny costume. I shove the window open with my uninjured arm and gently push Heather toward it.

She climbs out into the cold.

I gather my clothes and boots, climb out the window, and slam it shut.

⌒

Heather stomps ahead of me for two streets, cutting through yards and bushes and patches of trees in her haste to get as far away from Ruby's house as possible. I struggle to keep up with her, forcing myself to awkwardly walk plantigrade until we're far out of Ruby's line of sight.

Heather falls to her knees next to a dogwood obscured by overgrown gardenias; she grips the trunk with one hand, digging her claws deep into the bark.

I crouch down next to her and place my jacket across her shoulders; it's too small for her to zip it up over her chest, but it's better than nothing.

Heather gazes at me, tears gathering in her eyes; she pulls the sleeves on and hugs her cold chest. "Dammit. I should've known this would happen."

I wrap my arm around her and pull her against my chest. "You couldn't have—"

She shakes her head, her bear ears plastered to her scalp. "Ruby is just as smart as I am. She knew as soon as she looked through my nightstand." She covers her face with her hands. "And I forgot to lock the door. I'm so stupid."

I pet her head. "It'll be okay. We'll figure something out."

Heather sniffles. "I-I need to call my dad, or . . ." She removes her hands from her face, clearly distraught. "I left my phone in my room. What're we gonna do?"

"Hey, it's okay." I fish my phone out of my pants pocket. "You can use mine."

Tears fall from her eyes. "I don't know my dad's number, or Kyle's, or . . ." Her eyes widen. "I know his home phone. He still has one."

I unlock my phone for her, and with shaky hands, she fumbles around her claws to press the correct numbers on the keypad; as soon as it starts ringing, she holds the phone up to her ear.

After four agonizing rings, the call connects. "Who's calling me at nine o'clock at night?" Kyle asks.

Heather moves the phone closer to her mouth. "Kyle, it's Heather. Ruby caught us and kicked us out of the house. Could you pick us up?" She moves the phone back up to her ear.

Kyle stays silent for a long moment. "Did she see y'all with the animals out?"

Shakily, Heather says, "She thought we were role-playing."

"Good. Better she don't know any different. Where are y'all?"

Heather hands me my phone; I stand up, spot the closest street sign and mailbox, and relay the address to Kyle.

"Hang tight; I'll be there soon, and hopefully without any speedin' tickets." He hangs up.

Relieved and chilled, I pull my pants on, pocket my phone, and crouch back down, but before I can shrug my shirt on, Heather touches my back.

"You're hurt."

"I hit the corner of the dresser when I caught you. It's not a big deal."

Her lips part and her brow furrows.

I put my shirt on and grab her hand. "It's not your fault. I'm just as guilty for coming over and leaving my boots in the middle of the floor."

Heather hangs her head, tears dripping to the dirt beneath our knees.

I cradle her head in my arms, and she cries deep into the fabric covering my chest, her claws gripping my back like I'll fall apart any second.

I hold her together until our ride comes.

Kyle's green Nissan pulls up to the curb in front of the gardenias; after checking our perimeter for unwanted eyes, we climb into the back seat and buckle up.

Once we're on the road and stopped at a red light, Kyle looks at us through the rearview mirror. "Are y'all alright?" He worries a toothpick in his mouth.

Heather says, "Jack hurt his back because I tripped on his boots."

"And my left shoulder," I say. "I didn't want Heather to hit her head on the dresser."

Kyle grunts. "Good on ya, kid. I'll check you out once we get back to my place."

"Thank you." I keep hold of Heather's hand in the middle of the seat.

Kyle still looks worried. "She didn't hurt ya, did she?"

Heather shakes her head, but her face screws up all over again. "She only said some stuff."

"What kind of stuff?"

Heather closes her eyes tight. "I don't want to talk about it."

The light turns green, so Kyle pulls through the intersection. The ride remains shrouded in silence, the darkness broken up by intermittent streetlights and brightly lit buildings still open in the dead of night.

Kyle drives road after road, street after street, carefully teetering between five and fifteen miles per hour above the speed limit, until we reach a quaint house with a camper and a big red truck parked in the driveway. Kyle eases his car into the garage, closes the garage door with a remote, parks, and turns off the ignition.

He helps us both out of the back and unlocks the side door into the kitchen; Heather rushes in ahead of us, bolting out of the room to who knows where.

Seeing my worried face, Kyle says, "Give her a moment; she's probably rooting in my room for something to wear. I would've brought something myself if I knew she wasn't dressed."

"She keeps clothes in your house?"

Kyle shrugs. "She and Bobby are bad about leavin' stuff lyin' around, and she stole half her shirts from her father, anyway."

That explains all the oversize band T-shirts.

Kyle jerks his head. "C'mon to the livin' room and let me look ya over. Wouldn't want Heather's boy in disarray."

I blush—mostly from the sudden warmth inside—and follow him into a sparse living space with a couch, a coffee table, a TV stand covered in old DVD players and movie cases, two large bookshelves littered with books, and an aquarium with a single fish hiding inside a decorative cave. Thrift-store art pieces decorate the walls, creating a homey atmosphere. I perch on the couch, remove my shirt, and fold it up on the coffee table.

Kyle grabs his first aid kit from the kitchen, opens it up on the coffee table, and inspects my wounds. "Looks like it's mostly bruised, but I'll put a bandage on the cut for ya."

"Thanks."

Kyle disinfects it with a wipe and smooths a bandage over my skin.

I put my shirt back on and sink into the couch cushions.

Heather enters the room wearing a baggy T-shirt and soft pajama shorts; evidently, she took both her bra and her makeup off. She gives Kyle a tight hug before joining me on the couch.

"I fixed him up for ya." Kyle strains a smile. "There wasn't much to fix, though."

Heather nods, holding my hand tight in hers; she looks like she could cry again any second now.

Something buzzes in Kyle's pocket; he pulls his phone out, sighs at the caller ID, and answers it.

"You bastard!" Ruby screeches.

Kyle puts the sound down and shoulders his phone, rolling his eyes. "That ain't no way to greet nobody." He pulls a pistol out from under his shirt—a sobering sight. With the phone hooked between his shoulder and ear, Kyle casually inspects his firearm; once he's satisfied, he places it on the coffee table, barrel pointed at the TV, and crosses his ankle over his knee.

Despite the volume being down, I catch a number of expletives clearly meant for Heather; she grips my hand harder and turns her face into my shoulder.

Kyle notices out of the corner of his eye, returns his pistol to its hidden holster, and walks down the hall to his bedroom; he closes the door quietly and lets loose a torrent of muffled curses I wish I could make out.

I want to distract Heather from everything going on, so I look at the fish that swam out of its cave; it's a big gray fish speckled with a metallic sheen of turquoise, green, and blue spots. "What kind of fish is that?"

Heather gazes at the fish. "Oh, he's a Jack Dempsey. Kyle named him Killer."

"Why Killer?"

"Because he killed everything in the tank."

"Oh."

"He's seven years old now." She manages to smile. "Kyle got him to liven up the place after I started hanging around all the time."

Killer floats lazily, staring with one big eye.

"He's pretty, isn't he?"

"Yeah. Deadly, too."

Heather's smile barely reaches her eyes. "It's part of his charm."

I hold her close.

She returns my embrace, holding one hand over my heart. "Jack?"

I run my hand over her ears. "Yeah?"

She grips my shirt. "Do you think I'm a whore?"

I search her face for a joke; there isn't one. "Have you been having sex with anyone other than me?"

She shakes her head. "No. Only you."

I smile weakly. "If that makes you a whore, I must be the biggest man whore on the planet."

Heather smiles through her tears; she cups my cheek in her softly padded hand.

I lean down and kiss her, a gentle kiss full of something more profound than passion.

Kyle slinks out of his room in active form, his jaw tight. "Ruby's having a cow. She changed her mind and wants you back home alone."

"I'm not going back there." Heather shakes her head against my chest, her ears held back.

"I know, honey; I don't intend to bring you back." Kyle rubs his eyes. "I'm going to call your father. I'm thinking we've got to change the custody agreement; it's ridiculous to keep you with your mother at your age."

Heather looks at him, wide-eyed and tearful. "But what if you can't change it?"

Kyle sits on the other end of the couch, his tail draping over the arm. "Ruby might fight, but we'll fight harder; I promise you, we'll make this right."

"Why would she even bother? She clearly hates me."

Kyle shakes his head. "I wish I knew." He dials Mr. Brown and brings the phone to his left ear, putting the volume back up. "Maybe she won't want to pay child support. And she'd lose access to Luke because he'd pick your father in a heartbeat."

The call doesn't go through.

Kyle grumbles and dials Mr. Brown again.

In the meantime, I try to soothe Heather by petting her head and ears, careful not to jostle her studs.

Mr. Brown misses the second call, but finally picks up the third. "Kyle?" He sounds drowsy.

"We've got a situation, Bobby. Ruby kicked Heather out the house and called her a few choice words. I got her and Jack at my house right now."

A long, heavy sigh crackles through the speakers. "Looks like Ruby called me fifty billion times."

Kyle grins. "I guess she gave up 'cause she called me. Chewed me right out."

"What'd she say?"

He glances at us. "I'll tell ya later. I may have said a few things myself."

After a long beat, Mr. Brown asks, "Are they okay? Did she find out about y'all?"

"They're fine; physically, at least." Kyle fiddles with his toothpick. "Ruby thought they were wearing elaborate costumes." He laughs. "She thought I bought the damn things!"

Mr. Brown groans. "Okay. Is Heather next to you? I want to talk to her."

"Yeah. I'll hand her my phone."

Heather takes it into her trembling hand. "Daddy, I'm sorry. I messed up."

"No, your mother blew everything out of proportion. Kicking you out of the house in the middle of the night on a school night is absolutely irresponsible. Do you even have your things?"

Heather bites her lip. "Only the clothes on my back. She kicked me out in my underwear."

Another sigh, like he's forcing away what he really wants to say. "Alright. I want you to stay home from school tomorrow and cool off. We'll get all your stuff out of there in the afternoon, then you'll start living with me again. I'll drive you to school for the rest of the semester—"

"Are you sure? What about—"

"Heather, taking you to school is the least I can do. Ruby messed up and I'm tired of letting her walk all over you."

Heather's eyes waver.

"I should've put my foot down a long time ago. I'm sorry for failing you all this time."

"Dad . . ."

"Get some rest, okay? Kyle and I will handle this."

"Okay."

"I love you."

Heather sniffles. "I love you too." On the verge of tears, she hands the phone back to Kyle.

He presses the screen against his shoulder. "You and Jack clean up and go to bed. I've got to talk business with your father for a little while longer." He looks at me. "I can take you to school in the morning, or you can skip—don't matter to me."

"I'll stay with Heather," I say, squeezing her hand.

Kyle nods. "Y'all can have my bed; I'll sleep on the couch."

"Thank you." I guide Heather to her feet, and we stumble down the hall.

I hold Heather close under the spray of a compact shower. She cries into my shoulder, eaten up by Ruby's words.

The next day, starting at the crack of dawn, I get multiple calls. First, it's Teddy, frantically checking in on us both, but mostly the sister he claims to barely stand. She talks to him quietly while lying in bed with me, and when she tells him what Ruby said, a growl erupts through the speakers—I won't repeat the series of names he curses out, but they put a silly smile on Heather's face.

Next, around noon, it's Mom. Lounging on the couch and watching Heather cook lunch in a cute apron, I fish out my phone and take her call. "What?" I ask, not in the mood for scathing dialogue.

"Don't 'what' me. I heard about your little escapade last night. I'm told that Heather girl has been seducing you."

I scoff. "Seducing me? She's not a succubus." Not that I'd complain if she was.

Mom prattles on, ignoring me. "I understand you're at that age when hormones take control of basic mental function, but you have to think more about your future. You're almost sixteen, and it's about time you start focusing on your grades and preparing for college."

I almost throw my phone across the room. "Mom, how many times do I have to tell you I'm not going to college?"

"You'll change your mind, John; you're not the first and certainly not the last who thought he knew what he wanted. It's just a phase. I know you'll come around."

"I hope you're ready for this phase to last the rest of your life, Mother."

"Hmph. Perhaps I'll get your father to knock some sense into you."

"I'll wait for his call with bated breath."

She hangs up.

I wait, but Dad never calls.

⁓

After lunch, I get a call from Mark.

With my arm around Heather and a random sitcom on the TV, I tell him everything that happened.

"That's crazy, bro." The noise of the cafeteria drowns out his voice. "Say, do you guys need a hand getting all of Heather's furniture out of her room? I can bring my truck. And Alex. He likes lifting things. And I can lift stuff, too."

I grin. "Are you sure about that, bro? Your arms put twigs to shame."

"Bro! I might be skinny as shit, but that doesn't mean I'm weak!"

I chuckle. "I'm just messing with you. Do you mind relaying everything to Matthew and Emily? They probably won't notice we didn't go to school."

"Sure thing!" The bell rings. "Oof, gotta run. Send Heather hugs and kisses!" With an obnoxious mwah, Mark hangs up.

Heather grins. "You heard the man."

More than happy to provide, I give her a hug and a kiss that turns into a make-out session.

Only a few seconds in, Heather places her hand on my chest and pushes me away.

"What's wrong?" I ask, cupping her cheek.

She closes her eyes and leans into my palm. "I can't stop thinking about what she said. I know it's not true, but . . ."

I run my thumb under her eye, catching a tear. "You've been told all your life to ignore your feelings. It's normal to be intimate with your boyfriend, and we've been responsible about everything, too." I remember all the vile things I've been told about myself in the past. "But I know lies hurt just as much as the truth, so we'll go at your pace, whatever you need."

She smiles. "Thank you. I'm a lucky girl, aren't I?"

I press my forehead against hers. "And I'm a lucky boy."

She touches her nose to mine; we rub the tips against each other, at ease.

⸻⟩

After school ends, Emily calls. "Hey, Jack; Mark told us everything. I wanted to check in before practice starts. Could you put Heather on the phone?"

I press a button. "You're on speaker; Heather's right next to me."

"Oh, that works; I'll put you on speaker, too. Mark went home, but Matthew's with me."

Figures; those two have been attached at the hip ever since Matthew finally confessed, though I'm not any better with Heather.

"How're you doing, honey?" Heather asks.

"I'm doing okay," Emily says, "but the better question is how you're doing."

"I could be better, honestly, but it was only a matter of time before Ruby and I blew up on each other." Heather places a finger on her chin, eyes half-lidded. "We never got along, not since the day I was born."

"That's harsh," Emily says. "Even I'm not that bad with my mom. I still haven't told her about Matthew, though."

"We'll get there," Matthew says; I imagine he's no more excited to introduce Emily to *his* parents, who I've yet to meet myself.

"Anyway," Emily says, "can I come help move your stuff tonight? I know you have a lot of clothes and jewelry and stuff."

Heather glances at me. "Sounds like this whole event is becoming a party. Are your folks okay with you riding out with us?"

Emily laughs. "I may have told my parents that Kyle is picking us up after practice."

Heather grins. "You sly dog. This is why we're friends."

"I learned from the best."

"How did you two even become friends?" I ask.

Heather smiles. "Two lonely girls played dodgeball together in a mixed gym class."

"And the rest is history." Emily sighs longingly.

"I still remember making fun of that one girl who twerked against the door every time we went to change."

"That girl was weird."

"Where did that come from?" Matthew asks.

Heather says, "Don't question a woman's mind, Short Stuff."

Matthew sighs. "Forget I asked."

"Anyway, I should probably get changed for practice," Emily says. "See you tonight!"

"See you." Heather ends the call.

Kyle comes home after a long day of work, uses the bathroom, conceals his pistol under his shirt, and piles us into his big red truck.

Curious, I ask Kyle why he's carrying a gun.

He puts his key in the ignition. "I don't expect to need it, but I'm not one to tempt fate."

I hope he won't need it and try to remain perfectly calm as the diesel engine roars to life. The drive over feels impossibly long and insanely short at the same time; I see the same sights I've seen a million times before, the same city I was born and raised in, but there's a finality to our destination.

We pull up to the curb across from Mr. Brown's Ford. Mark's Chevy sits across the intersection from us, its driver leaning casually behind the trunk.

Mark waves at us after we get out, grinning madly despite the situation at hand.

Kyle looks both ways and crosses the street, meeting up with Mr. Brown and Teddy, who's scowling so hard it might give him permanent wrinkles.

Heather and I join Mark behind his white truck; the other four occupants get out.

Mark holds out a hand. "Bad weather, huh?" It's cold, cloudy, and drizzling on and off; I hope it doesn't start pouring down rain because not everyone has a tonneau cover over the bed of their truck.

"I think the forecast only called for light rain," Matthew says.

Emily trots over and gives Heather a big hug.

Heather reciprocates, swamping Emily's shoulders with her jugs.

Miss Ashley and Alex stand close by. "Hopefully we'll be in and out quickly," Miss Ashley says, a roll of trash bags hooked under her arm. "Your father told me that there may be some . . . disagreements."

Heather looks across the street.

Mr. Brown, Kyle, and Teddy crowd Ruby's front door.

Ruby throws it open, face full of unbridled rage. "What are you doing here? Get off my property!"

"I'm not here to play games," Mr. Brown says, his voice barely raised. "We're coming in to get Heather's stuff whether you like it or not."

"I will call the cops, Bobby."

Mr. Brown crosses his arms. "Go ahead. See if I care."

Ruby doesn't budge.

"We can do this the easy way or the hard way, your choice."

Ruby notices the rest of us across the street; angry as ever, she retreats into her house, leaving the front door open.

Mr. Brown and Kyle shoulder their way inside, Teddy close behind.

"That's our cue." Alex saunters across the street with a fabric tool bag in hand, his hair in a tight braid.

The rest of us follow.

Inside, Ruby screams profanities at her ex-husband and former friend, the two keeping her blocked out of the way of Heather's room.

Teddy waits next to her bedroom door, his collected facade already cracking.

The girls and Miss Ashley go in ahead of us.

"Jack," Alex says, "why don't you help with getting everything off the furniture? I think the rest of us will be enough to tote everything out."

I nod and join the girls in Heather's room; they're already ransacking her pastel blue dresser, stuffing shirts and pants and underwear into trash bags with abandon. I get to work clearing all the random knickknacks off the top.

"Heather, how old are these bras?" Emily holds up the lacy pink one she wore for our first time.

Holding a pair of faded jeans, Heather says, "Middle school."

"Middle school?!"

Heather wilts. "I'm sentimental, okay? That was part of my first lingerie set."

"Girl—"

Miss Ashley snaps her fingers. "Let's focus, ladies. No time to waste."

"Sorry." Emily frowns.

Miss Ashley gives her a smile.

I reach behind the dresser, pull out the plug connected to Heather's frilly pink lamp, and carefully set it aside in the corner near the closet.

As soon as the dresser is emptied, Miss Ashley and I pull the drawers out while Emily and Heather work on packing up her beauty supplies.

I step into the hall. "Dresser's clear!"

"Put anything she don't want in my truck first!" Kyle shouts over Ruby's cursing.

Alex yells, "Got it!"

"We can use my truck for anything she definitely wants to keep," Mark says. "Mr. Brown's truck will be for everything else."

Alex and the boys squeeze into the room, ask Heather what she wants to keep, and haul drawers out of the house; when everyone returns, Alex orders Mark and Matthew to lift the gutted particleboard dresser out.

Teddy and I strip the bed, remove the twin mattress and the box spring, and stand them against the wall so Alex can disassemble the bed frame for easier transport. While he works, we lug out the vanity, the desk, the nightstand, a tiny chair, and a stool; once Alex separates the headboard from the railing, we haul every part of the frame, the mattress, and the box spring out to the trucks.

Alex puts his tools away and wipes his hands on his pants. "Looks like that's everything."

"We have all my things packed away, too," Heather says, a hand on her hip; her room is nothing more than an empty box littered with full trash bags and a single suitcase. She slings her purse over her shoulder and grabs a bag and her suitcase.

The rest of us grab everything else.

We clear the house, bags in hand, and throw everything into the bed of Mark's truck; Mr. Brown and Kyle retreat, and Ruby slams the door behind them.

Teddy sinks into his twin XL bed, active and exhausted.

Mark, Matthew, and I sit on the floor of his bedroom, also active.

With the door cracked open, I can hear what's going on in the rest of the house.

From Heather's attic bedroom, Emily says, "Oh my God, you do not need to keep these tiny bras, Heather! And do you really need three lamps?"

"Maybe I want them," Heather says. "They're pretty."

I have to perk my ears to catch Emily's frustrated sigh.

From the living room, the adults quietly discuss next steps.

Mark leans back and closes the door.

Teddy groans.

"You good, bro?" Mark asks.

Teddy turns his head, all frowny. "I feel like shit."

Mark smiles. "You wanna talk about it?"

Teddy glares at him. "Not really." But he turns on his back and crosses his arms. "I feel like a shitty son because my shitty mom got what she fucking deserved and I'm happy about it." He blinks rapidly, turns his back on us, and sniffles. "I'm, like, so relieved I never have to see her again"—he wipes his eyes out of view—"and that Heather doesn't have to live with her anymore."

I say, "I'd be pretty happy if I never had to see my mom again, too."

Matthew's tail curls back and forth. "Sometimes I think my mom would forget I exist if I stopped going home."

Mark says, "Damn; now I feel left out."

"Be happy you're not part of the shitty-mom club," Teddy says.

Mark fake sobs. "I get to be part of the dead-dad club instead!"

"Damn, bro," Matthew says.

"That sucks, bro," I say.

Mark opens his big mouth, but Alex opens the door. "We're ordering pizza. Got any requests?"

Mark pouts. "I want Hawaiian."

Teddy rolls over. "Bro, you like that shit?"

"I like it, too," Alex says.

Teddy frowns and rolls back over. "I want a supreme pizza."

"Barbecue chicken," I say.

Matthew says, "Philly cheesesteak if they have it."

Alex nods, smiles, and closes the door.

Mark crawls across the carpet to Teddy's cluttered TV stand. "Wanna play something?"

Teddy clumsily slides off his bed and joins Mark. He looks at his games and his absurd collection of multicolored controllers. "I want to shoot something." He turns on his Xbox One, removes *Resident Evil 7: Biohazard* from the disc slot and puts it in its case, then holds up two other games. "*Three* or *Reach*?"

I leave myself out of the equation: Mark and Teddy could talk for hours about which Halo game is better.

"*Three* for nostalgia," Matthew says.

Teddy shrugs and puts *Halo 3* in the disc slot.

He starts a custom games lobby and we all log in for a good hour of four-player split screen slayer. We play free-for-all, so I mostly get destroyed, but it's worth it to put a smile on Teddy's face.

The girls come down after three matches, and I happily let Emily take my place in the fray. Heather sits on Teddy's bed and watches.

I join her and wrap my arm around her waist.

She leans on me without a word.

CHAPTER 31

Takoyaki Takedown

Matthew

Emily slumps against her desk and groans.

"I'm going to take that as a no?" I say.

"I really want to go, but there's no way I can get away with being out of town with a bunch of guys my parents barely know." Despite the unfortunate news, Emily smiles sweetly. "But definitely next year, when I'm eighteen; Mom and Dad can't stop me once I'm an adult."

I love seeing her smile. "I'll look forward to it."

"I bet you just want to see me in a bikini." Emily grins as bright as the sun.

I scratch my cheek. "I wouldn't be against it."

She cups her cheeks in her hands. "It's a tragedy I won't be able to see you shirtless."

I blush. "I'm not much to look at."

Emily reaches over and hugs my middle. "You're too hard on yourself."

I pat her head, thinking I'd love to groom her hair one day. She has soft hair. With her squeezing me, her chest against my hip, I can't help but purr. "Probably, but you help me believe that I look okay."

"You look handsome," she says.

"And you look beautiful," I say.

She lets me go and gives me a kiss.

I toss my luggage into the bed of Mark's truck, close the tailgate, and secure the tonneau cover on top. It's a warm eighty degrees and the sun shines through the breaks in the clouds. The last day of school was a week ago and we're about to be on our way to Holden Beach with Mark as our trusty ride; Miss Ashley and Alex already rode off in her Subaru, leaving us to pet Glenn goodbye and lock up for the weekend.

Mr. Brown and Kyle postponed their usual Mother's Day retreat to include Teddy and Heather, which was for the better; apparently, the weather was cold and rainy on the beach last month, so there wouldn't have been much fun in the sun. Teddy and Heather are with us now, and even Jack—it took some convincing, but he got his parents to agree after a lot of complaints and post–sweet sixteen guilt trips.

"I call shotgun!" Heather raises her hand like a schoolgirl.

"Damn, she beat everybody to it." Mark grins. "I guess you guys are squeezing in the back."

We pile into the truck: Mark in the driver's seat; Heather in the passenger seat; and myself crammed in the middle back seat between Teddy and Jack. Mark puts his glasses on, turns the ignition, and backs out of the driveway.

⌒

Mark's playlist abruptly stops about an hour into the drive. "Mm, I should've prepared a longer playlist. I have Spotify, if anyone else wants to play whatever."

"I can find something." Heather takes his phone out of the holder on the dash; we're going straight down the highway, so he won't miss the GPS yet. Unlike myself, she's familiar with Android phones and effortlessly finds the aforementioned music app. She looks at his piss-poor personal playlists, presses the search button, and looks for whatever pleases her; classic rock flows through the speakers, and she returns to the GPS app before clamping the phone into its dashboard cradle.

After a few songs, Mark says, "You have the taste of an old man."

Heather pouts. "I can find something else."

Mark waves her off. "I don't mind it; my dad liked this kind of music. It makes me feel nostalgic."

Heather's lips briefly part and her brow furrows, but she smiles.

⌒

Mark stretches his arms high into the air, his hair shining cherry red in the bright sun. After one night crammed in a two-bed hotel room with Miss Ashley, Alex, and Jack, we're ready to hit the beach. Mark, Jack, and I walk across the boardwalk to the sand and remove our flip-flops to walk barefoot across the beach. We reach a cluster of foldable chairs occupied by the four adults who came ahead of us; not far away, Heather and Teddy stand knee-deep in the ocean.

Those of us who came last year are dressed the same. As for the rest: Alex and Jack are in swimming trunks and Hawaiian shirts, plus a straw cowboy hat on the latter; Teddy wears nothing but plain swimming trunks; and Heather has a green halter-top bikini with a matching side skirt over her bottoms—the top is modest enough to hide most of her cleavage, but that doesn't stop Jack from staring.

She and Teddy walk away from the water and join us; I never noticed it before, but they both have a smattering of freckles across their shoulders—likely a genetic holdover from their fair-skinned mother.

Jack walks up to Heather and puts one arm around her waist, but refrains from flirting with her around her brother; he looks like he's using every ounce of willpower to contain himself. If Emily was here, I'd probably be feeling the same way.

"Hey, boys!" Miss Ashley calls.

We walk over to her.

"And Heather." She smiles. "Try not to go on any crazy adventures this year, okay?"

Mark grins. "No promises!"

"What happened last year?" Alex lifts his sunglasses up.

Miss Ashley cups one cheek. "They got into a fight with a shark man."

"We became friends," Mark says. "I can tell you all about it later."

Alex smiles awkwardly. "Alright, then."

"That's all I wanted to say," Miss Ashley says. "You can run along and have fun while us adults catch up."

"Will do!" Mark trots off.

The rest of us follow.

Once we're a fair distance away, Jack says, "I remember you saying something about that last year. There was another one, wasn't there?"

Mark nods. "There was also a harpy. A killdeer, if I remember correctly. The shark was a sand tiger." Thinking dangerously, Mark squints into the sky.

I look, too. There's a big bird up there, and he has a helmet on.

Mark puts his hand up, stopping the rest of us; he points at the oversize "bird." "I think that's him. I didn't know they'd be in town."

Jack, flabbergasted, holds his cowboy hat with one hand and peers into the sky.

"Yo, Gideon!" Mark waves his hands in the air frantically. Fortunately, there aren't too many people around; it's early enough the beach crowd has yet to arrive.

Gideon's helmet-covered head adjusts minutely; he banks left and flies toward us.

"Oh, damn; is he actually going to land out in the open?"

Gideon dives down and flaps his massive wings to slow his descent; his bird feet hit the edge of the rolling tide, and he stumbles, but manages not to fall. He goes dormant and removes his helmet with freshly reformed hands. "What's up, dude? I'm surprised to see you, and . . ." He surveys our quintet.

"You know Matthew already"—Mark points the rest of our group out—"and this is Jack, Heather, and Teddy. We're all monster people, as you may have guessed."

"I figured since you called me out right next to them. I'm surprised to see a lady. Guess we aren't all dudes after all!" Gideon laughs. "So what brings you out here? Another vacation?"

"Pretty much. I think it might be a new yearly thing for us. Anyway, do you think we could drop by your beach house again? Some of us can't swim in public."

"Oh, sure; I don't see why not. Tyler's been chilling in his pool like he usually does. We took the weekend off, too."

"Still working as a server?"

Gideon grins. "Yep! Tyler's working too, but he does retail; he's the one who wanted a break from all the crazy old ladies he deals with on the daily."

"I guess that worked out for us." Mark asks for their address and types it into the notes app on his phone; while he's at it, he records Gideon's phone number, too. "We'll see you in a bit!"

Gideon salutes. "I'll be flying back now!" He puts his helmet back on, goes active, and takes off.

⁓

Mark pulls the truck into Tyler's driveway, conveniently nestled beyond a trail cloaked by tall trees. Gideon's blue Jeep Wrangler sits in the same spot as last year, but there's a dull-sea-green Toyota Prius parked next to it. I assume it's Tyler's car, but it's the last vehicle I'd expect him to own.

"Looks like Gideon's not here yet," Mark says.

"I guess we can walk around the side." I slip out of the back seat behind Jack.

The five of us cut through the yard to reach the pool, but stop in our tracks when Tyler says, "Would you go home already, old man?!"

"I just got here, Tyler dear," the man says. "Is it so wrong to want to spend time with a fellow mutant?"

Tyler huffs. "At least stop climbing on me, would ya?"

Mark and I share a look, then peer around the corner of the house.

Tyler stands in the shallow end of the pool in active form, his wet hair sticking to his head and face contorted into a scowl.

A middle-aged man clings to his shoulders with his arms—specifically, his eight orange octopus arms. The appendages replacing the man's legs stick out of a black square-leg swimsuit, four thin limbs crammed into each leg hole. His arms are the same rusty orange, his webbed hands tipped by hooked black claws, and he has short gray hair and orange eyes fit with rectangular pupils.

The octopus man takes a deep breath and gazes in our direction. "Oh, my, my, my." He grins, revealing serrated teeth. "You didn't tell me you had friends."

Mark grimaces and steps out of hiding.

I take my hat off, perk my ears, and tell Jack, Heather, and Teddy to stay hidden before standing by Mark out in the open.

Tyler gapes at us. "What the hell are you guys doing here?!"

Mark scratches his cheek. "Gideon invited us. We . . . also brought some other friends."

"What?!"

Mark holds his hands out. "We're all monster people, so it's no big deal."

"It would be less of a big deal if I didn't have this idiot around!" Tyler points at the man gripping his shoulders.

"You're so mean, Tyler dear." The man sounds oddly fond. He lifts the tips of his legs and takes another deep breath. "How many of you are there?" Oddly, his intense gaze lingers over my head.

Tyler immediately grabs the man's narrow waist. "Don't you dare think about it."

"Hmm . . . You with the red hair." He points at Mark with a webbed finger. "How old are you?"

"Seventeen. Why?"

The man sneers. "That's a real shame."

Tyler sighs and glances at the corner we were hiding behind. "You three, just come out already."

Caught peering around the house, Jack, Heather, and Teddy awkwardly join us; Jack removes his hat and perks his ears.

The man stares at Jack's ears, eyebrows raised, then looks between me and him repeatedly. "How curious; your ears are transformed, but the rest of you is not."

Suddenly, Gideon crashes through the trees, lands at the edge of the pool, goes dormant, and throws his helmet off. "Dr. Rausch!" He scrunches his nose and bares his teeth. "Why the hell are you over here?!"

"No need for the dramatics, Gideon dear. I was simply dropping by. Wonderful weather we're having, yes?" The man faces us again. "I suppose I ought to introduce myself. I'm Dr. Jacob Amsted Rausch, a geneticist at UNCW." He bows, one arm locked in front and the other behind. "It's a pleasure to meet you."

We're all speechless.

Gideon slumps dramatically and groans. "I would've told you guys to stay at the beach if I knew Dr. Rausch came over again."

Dr. Rausch completely ignores Gideon. "May I have your names? I'm always quite excited to meet more of our kind."

Reluctantly, we give him our first names.

Tyler sighs. "I'm sorry you guys get the displeasure of meeting him. I promise I'll stop him from inspecting any of you; his legs are slippery, but there's nothing he can do if I hold his waist."

Dr. Rausch looks down on him. "I'll have you know I only inspect adults." He glances at Heather. "And I only get rough with the boys."

"What do you mean by inspect?" Mark sits at the edge of the pool, his legs dangling in the shallow end.

I take off my shirt, toss it and my hat on one of the lounge chairs, and sit next to Mark so I can get in at a moment's notice. I trust Tyler to watch out for us, but I don't miss Dr. Rausch's pondering eyes on my tail.

Jack, Heather, Teddy, and Gideon sit in a row next to me.

Tyler grimaces. "By inspect he means violating your personal space and touching things he shouldn't. Legally, it's assault." He glares at Dr. Rausch. "You're lucky you've never been sued, or, you know, arrested."

"Perhaps I'm too eager," Dr. Rausch says, "but I only got really handsy back when I met my first fellow mutant. I was young and excited, and my, he was a handsome subject."

"What was he?" Mark asks.

"A wolf. He had golden-brown fur, dark-brown paw pads, gray claws, a doglike tongue, lengthy canines, and smelled like a fine wine."

Mark gapes.

"What's wrong, Mark dear?"

"You just described my mom's boyfriend."

"Small world." Dr. Rausch grins. "What's his name?"

Mark hesitates. "Alex."

His grin widens. "Yes, that's the one. Alexander Delgado, a medical student. Oh, I could never forget him, not even if I tried. Did he ever finish school?"

"Um, yeah," Mark says. "He's an ob-gyn."

"Wonderful. I suppose I should call him Dr. Delgado now." Dr. Rausch lights up. "Is he here at the beach?"

Mark doesn't answer.

His grin turns diabolical.

Cringing, Mark asks, "Who else have you met?"

Dr. Rausch frowns thoughtfully. "I never got to inspect him, but I met a man named Kyle Ratcliffe a few years ago."

Heather and Teddy dawn stony expressions.

"I was incapacitated at the time, so he bought me breakfast at a Hardee's and called a cab. He was quite eager to get me out of his hair."

"I don't blame him," Tyler says. "You're insufferable."

Dr. Rausch wiggles his legs. "I think it's about time you let go of me, Tyler dear; I have no plans to inspect anyone."

"I'll let you go if you promise to stay in human form while they're here."

"Your wish is my command." Dr. Rausch's slimy legs slide behind Tyler's back and merge into two legs; his orange octopus skin smooths into pale human skin, his black claws shorten into blunt nails, and his gills close, leaving him a middle-aged man with octopus eyes and one long scar under each pec.

Tyler lets him go.

Dr. Rausch drops into the pool; standing next to Tyler, he's surprisingly short. He wades closer to us, obviously studying me and Jack.

Jack holds Heather close, his ears lying low. "What're you staring at?" He growls.

Dr. Rausch grins. "I'm simply curious about you and your cat-eared friend. It's highly unusual to have an incomplete human form."

"You said you're a geneticist." I keep my ears perked and voice level. "I was wondering if you might have some answers about us."

Dr. Rausch grimaces. "Unfortunately, I know very little. It's a mystery where we come from and how we can function—I study genes for a living, yet no amount of combing my DNA has given me any answers."

Tyler joins him. "I've told you a hundred times that Gideon and I were cursed. It's plain magic."

Dr. Rausch scowls. "Magic, he says."

"You've got a better explanation?!"

Heather smiles. "My dad's friend met a witch once upon a time."

"He did?" Teddy asks, shocked.

She glances at Teddy. "She tried to curse him, but it couldn't be done."

"It couldn't?" Tyler asks.

"Of course not. He was already a monster person when she tried."

Dr. Rausch sneers. "Loath as I am to admit it, magic is the most likely cause; what frustrates me is that we're left with an infinite-regress dilemma: sorceresses themselves have no known origin." He shakes his head. "It's not worth thinking about."

"But the old man's right." Tyler crosses his arms. "It's weird that you have permanent ears and tails, unlike the rest of us."

"Hmm." Dr. Rausch cradles his chin. "Perhaps whoever cursed your ancestors simply messed up."

"What do you mean, messed up?" Jack asks.

"I recall Gideon mentioned a dream Courtney had before she started behaving strangely." He looks at Gideon. "Am I correct?"

Gideon nods.

"As for the rest of you, did you develop your mutant features during puberty?"

We all nod.

Dr. Rausch nods to himself. "So as we all know, our kind emerge naturally during puberty; perhaps the same can be said of sorceresses." He waits a beat. "If a sorceress uses her magic before her abilities properly develop, that could be the cause of your incomplete forms. It's unfortunate such a defect was passed on so far down the line."

As strange as it is, that's the best theory we might ever get.

"I have another question." Mark raises his hand. "Alex, Matthew, and I suffer from a moon curse, but they're all different. Nobody else experiences something like it that we know of."

Dr. Rausch raises his eyebrows. "Might you describe these conditions to me?"

Mark and I share what we know about ourselves and Alex.

His brow furrows. "The only possible explanation I can think of is that each sorceress behind your heritage used the moon as a catalyst. We have next to nothing to go off of: Courtney channeled extreme emotions toward her target, but that might not be true of all sorceresses. Or maybe it is, but using a specific environmental circumstance could enhance their abilities." Dr. Rausch frowns deeply, his forehead wrinkling. "Oh, this is why I hate magic; it's too uncertain."

"It's only uncertain because we can't talk to one," Tyler says, "and there's no way in hell I'm ever going to be within one hundred miles of Courtney ever again."

"I avoid visiting my family because of her," Gideon says.

Dr. Rausch looks at Heather. "Does your father's friend still know that sorceress?"

Heather shakes her head. "No. She disappeared after attempting to curse him."

"How unfortunate." Dr. Rausch turns away, goes active, and climbs onto Tyler's back again, his eight legs anchoring him to Tyler's shoulders.

"What the fuck are you doing?" Tyler asks.

Dr. Rausch crosses his arms and turns his nose up. "I hate being in human form in the water. I figure you won't mind as long as I'm where you can stop me."

Tyler slumps forward and sighs.

I swim over to Tyler and Dr. Rausch in the deep end, the webbing between my fingers and toes efficiently pushing me through the water despite all the fur weighing me down.

"You're surprisingly comfortable in the water, Matthew dear," Dr. Rausch says.

"I've been swimming since I was a baby," I say, treading water, "though I wasn't able to swim much after I awakened." Behind me, the rest of our friends toss a beach ball around.

Dr. Rausch doesn't bat an eye. "It must be troubling to always have cat ears and a tail."

"I'll be honest, it is, but I've been living with it for so long it feels weird without them."

"Are you and Jack able to go into a full human form?"

"Yes, but not for more than a few hours. It's physically taxing."

"I see." He cups his chin, his eight legs splayed against the wall of the pool, the front two lifting out and up enough for his torso to stand upright; it must be challenging to control six extra limbs, but Dr. Rausch makes it look easy.

Tyler gazes at me from his spot nearby; he's sideways, one arm holding the perimeter of the pool, because his dorsal fins and thick tail prevent him from keeping his back to the wall.

I say, "I was wondering how you met each other."

Tyler sighs. "I found him half dead in the middle of the ocean."

My eyebrows raise. "Tell me about it."

Glaring, he says, "It was last year, shortly after you and Mark went home for the summer. I was going for a long swim because, as much as being a fucking shark man sucks ass, it's pretty awesome that I can breathe underwater. So I was chilling in the Atlantic, as a shark man does, seeing the sights, and I spot some dumbass octopus man floating in the middle of nowhere. I swim up to him because, you know, there's a damn octopus man just sitting there, and lo and behold, he's not only unconscious, but also feverish; even his gross octopus skin was a ghostly white. So I did the sensible thing: I hooked his slimy arms over my shoulders and dragged his sorry ass back here. It took me the entire damn day.

"I get here from the waterway in the middle of the night and carry him all the way to the front door, get him inside, and lay him down in the bathtub because he's aquatic and I wasn't about to dry him out—that slime layer is more important than you'd think—and nurse him back to health. And what does he do to thank me? He 'inspects' me."

"He tried to inspect me, too!" Gideon shouts. "But I flew away!"

"I couldn't help myself," Dr. Rausch says, "and it was quite the coincidence that I work at the same university they go to."

"And in my major at that," Tyler says, "so I get to see his ugly mug almost every day I'm there."

"You're so spunky, Tyler dear." Dr. Rausch regards me. "What do you think, Matthew dear? Do I have an 'ugly mug'?"

I grin awkwardly. "I don't think I've ever met an ugly monster person."

Dr. Rausch smiles. "That is certainly one perk of ours; I'm still looking good even in my old age."

"Speaking of looking good." Tyler grins at me. "Did you apologize to that girl of yours?"

Heat fills my ears. "Yes. We've been dating since Valentine's Day."

Tyler pats my shoulder, his dermal denticles rough on my skin. "Good on ya, kid. You better cherish her."

I nod. "I plan on it."

"Oh, young love~" Dr. Rausch swoons, his hands folded over his chest. "How long have you known your girlfriend, Matthew dear?"

I pause to think. "Almost three years. We met in our freshman year."

"And high school sweethearts!" Dr. Rausch exclaims way too enthusiastically. "I'll be rooting for you both, my dear."

Tyler shakes his head. "This guy is hopeless. Don't ever ask him about his love life."

I recall a story I heard last year. "Do you have someone, Dr. Rausch?"

"Certainly," he says. "I'm married to my middle school sweetheart. We even have a child together, though he's grown now. Recently married, too."

"Are they both human?"

"Yes, though they're well aware that I'm an octopus man. I hope my grandchildren will be spared the same; I imagine our kind rarely appear because my particular heritage was lost over the generations. What of you?"

I shake my head. "My parents have no idea, and my extended family are all human, as far as I know, so I think you're right. It's the same for all of us."

"Though I figure, considering Alex, Mark's mother must know?"

I nod. "She actually met Alex before you did, though only briefly at the time."

Dr. Rausch grins. "It's such a small world."

Speaking of . . . "Mark and I were actually told a story about you last year by an old couple . . . Er, by an old woman. Does Margaret ring a bell?"

He looks pleasantly surprised. "Now that you mention it, yes, I met a Margaret once upon a time. I was only eighteen, but I remember I saved her from drowning after she fell off a cruise ship in her drunken stupor. She reminded me of my mother."

"That's exactly what she told us."

His brow furrows, yet a smile remains. "I'm surprised she remembered me after all these years. My, she must be in her eighties by now."

"She remembered you so well she could tell Mark and I are monster people right away. She freaked me out, but it was nice of her to get her husband to sail us down the waterway on his boat."

His eyebrows shoot up. "Margaret lives here?"

"Yeah. She lives on the island right across from the edge of the woods."

Dr. Rausch eases his expression. "I really ought to say hello to her."

"I don't know the address, but we could point her house out to you. I'm sure she'd love to see you."

He smiles. "I'll take you up on that offer."

"And I'll chaperone." Tyler grins.

Dr. Rausch frowns. "I don't need a babysitter, Tyler dear."

"Sure you don't."

Dr. Rausch shakes his head and huffs.

⌒⟶

I rub myself dry with a towel, throw my shirt on, and cover my ears with my baseball cap. Mark also puts his shirt on, but Tyler and Dr. Rausch merely slip sandals on, perfectly happy to stay shirtless.

"Alright, we're off," Tyler says. "Watch the kids for me."

Gideon smiles, the beach ball hooked under his arm and his hand on his hip. "I'll make sure they don't burn the house down. We'll probably make lunch while you're gone."

Tyler gives a thumbs-up, and we walk away into the woods.

Mark and I lead them to the waterway in silence, a pleasant wind cutting through the summer heat. The leaves shake, the shade dancing at our feet.

The trees break, revealing the glistening waterway occupied by an abundance of vessels of different shapes and sizes; they float languidly on the water, their motors propelling them either left or right. I gaze at the houses on the island, most of them small and painted bright, beachy colors; I point out Margaret's house. "She lives right there, but it looks like the boat is gone."

"It's docked at their friend's house," Mark says, pointing his thumb to our right.

Sure enough, their fishing boat floats next to the tiny dock of the nearest house.

"Perhaps I shall return at a later time," Dr. Rausch says.

"I mean, we could always knock and ask if she's there." Mark shrugs.

Dr. Rausch stares at the back door. "Alright, but it would be best if the both of you knock; you're less threatening." He looks at Tyler. "And you should stay back; your face is frightening on a good day."

"Hey!" Tyler scowls, his two rows of shark teeth clear as day.

Dr. Rausch shakes his head. "My point exactly."

Mark and I walk up to the back door and knock, Dr. Rausch behind us while Tyler keeps his distance.

An angry old man opens the door. "What do ya want?" He scowls as mean as Tyler.

"We were wondering if Margaret is here," Mark says with his nicest smile.

The old man cranes his neck back. "Margaret! There're some boys here after you!"

Given a few moments, Margaret shuffles to the door, as cheerful as I remember her. "Oh, it's you marvelous boys from last summer." She's hunched and shaky in her old age, but full of energy. "What brings you out here?"

Mark says, "We met an old friend of yours," and steps aside.

Dr. Rausch stands before her, an oddly gentle expression taming his features. "It's been a while, hasn't it, Margaret dear?"

Her face lights up. "Oh, look at you." She steps outside. "You've gotten old, haven't you?" She holds up her hand.

Dr. Rausch leans down.

She touches his cheek. "Your eyes are as beautiful as I remember."

Dr. Rausch smiles. "It's not nice to stare."

"Oh, shush." She beams. "I never got your name, mister merman."

"My name is Jacob."

"Jacob . . ." Margaret lets go of his cheek. "Would you humor an old woman for a few minutes? We just made lunch."

"I have more than enough time on my hands."

Throwing a wink back at us, Dr. Rausch wraps his arm around her shoulders and walks inside; he closes the door behind him, the water-damaged wood peeling under the hot sun.

CHAPTER 32

Olive Branch

John

After we enjoy a lunch lovingly crafted by Gideon and Heather, along with a few more hours in the pool, the five of us drive straight to the RV campground for dinner. Kyle does his thing on the grill while I sit back with the boys and my favorite girl in the world.

"You look content," Heather says.

"And you aren't?" I ask.

She surveys Kyle's rented campsite: Mr. Brown speaking to Miss Ashley and Alex under the camper's awning; Luke talking animatedly about something nerdy with Mark and Matthew; and Kyle in his own world. "I'm happy I got to come here, but sad about the cost."

"What do you mean?"

She leans against me, her hair flowing over my shoulder. "I never liked Ruby, but it hurt to know what she really thought of me. She's my mother; I wouldn't exist without her."

I wrap my arm around her and squeeze her waist.

She smiles. "But the important thing is that I have all of you."

I press my head against hers, taking her hand into mine. "I'm glad we can be here for you."

She closes her eyes. A pleasant wind wafts through our hair, the burger patties on the grill sizzling hot.

A blue Jeep rolls up beside Mark's truck, then Gideon and Tyler step out; fortunately, no one else exits the vehicle. "We're here!" Gideon trots across the lot to the grill.

"Good timing, y'all," Kyle says. "I just finished cooking."

Instead of joining them, Tyler stalks over to the picnic table Heather and I are occupying. He sits down with a sigh, the metal earrings dangling from his ears glinting in the sun.

I say, "I never noticed your ears are pierced." They're shaped like spearheads, sharp and gray.

"Oh." Tyler fingers one earring. "I wear clear plastic studs in the water; they're hard to see."

"Wouldn't want to damage the good stuff," Heather says.

Tyler winks. "Exactly."

Mark walks over. "What happened to Dr. Rausch?"

Tyler scowls. "I told him to go the fuck home."

"Jeez, harsh much?"

Tyler sneers. "You're either harsh or he yanks your chain; fortunately, his sense of direction is abysmal, so he couldn't find his way here even if he tried." He jerks his head back at Kyle. "Thought I'd save the adults the trouble, too; that guy has an uncanny memory, and he definitely would've tried something if he got Kyle alone in his camper."

Matthew and Teddy join us. "I'm glad we happen to be seventeen," Matthew says.

Tyler smirks. "Yeah, he would've jumped you both in a heart-beat at eighteen."

"Scary," Mark says.

"Enough talking!" Kyle calls from the grill. "Come fix your plates!"

We happily oblige.

"So how was the pool?" Alex asks, burger in hand. We managed to cram ourselves together at the picnic table, though Kyle, Gideon, and Tyler are seated in foldable chairs.

"Mm . . ." Mark chews slowly. "It was good, but we met some weirdo octopus guy."

Alex nearly drops his burger, his face so pale he looks off-white. "He didn't happen to know me, did he?"

"Oh, he did. He remembered everything about your active form; it was creepy as hell."

"Is he still here?"

Mark shakes his head. "He went home. And I made sure not to reveal your location; you know I wouldn't do you like that, Da—" Mark blushes and clears his throat. "Alex." He stuffs his face to shut himself up.

"I could take him anyway, Wolfy," Kyle says. "He wouldn't last a second."

Tyler scoffs. "No offense, but his legs are no joke."

Kyle waves him off. "I'd chop 'em off if I had to."

"You sound like you want to fight him," Gideon says.

Kyle squints. "I think he needs to be taken down a peg."

"Amputating his limbs seems a bit much, don't you think?" Tyler says.

"They grow back, don't they?"

Tyler gapes. "I mean, they do, but . . . he'd be out of commission for months."

Kyle smirks. "Good."

Jeez, remind me not to get on Kyle's bad side . . .

The rest of our Saturday goes by peacefully. We have s'mores and talk around the campfire, enjoying each other's company; no matter how many family vacations I've been on and events I've been to, tonight is the first time I've ever felt like I fit in. There's no need to pretend with these people, no need to act perfectly prim and proper because I'm *totally* going to go to college and become some stuffy businessman.

Heather feels the same. She smiles wide and laughs boisterously and teases relentlessly, totally free to be herself around us; there was a cost, but I think the ultimate outcome was worth every broken tie.

We drive home Sunday morning; Mark drops me off at home around noon. My parents get home from work at five, and once dinner is ready at six, my sisters and I gather at the lengthy dining room table; I sit in the middle, my back to *The Last Supper*.

"How was your trip?" Mom spears a stalk of oven-roasted asparagus.

"It was nice." I stare at my plate. "I'm glad Heather had fun, too. And her family seems to like me, so that's a plus."

"I'm surprised you're still with that harlot." Mom dabs her lips with a napkin. "I understand she has great"—she presses her lips together—"assets, but there are more important qualities to look for in a life partner."

I wish I could throw my plate at her face. "What am I supposed to look for, huh? Daddy's bank account? Unwavering submission?"

Mom sneers. "Do *not* raise your voice at me, young man."

My nostrils flare, the handle of my fork held tight in my fist.

Jenny looks like she might maul her meat loaf; Grace looks like she wants to shrink into oblivion; and Esther looks like this is any other day of the week.

I slam my fork onto the perfectly folded cloth napkin next to my plate and stand up, shoving my chair back with my legs. "You know what? Fuck this. I'm leaving." I turn away and take long strides down the hall.

Mom yells, "Get back here *right this instant!*" but I don't care. I keep moving, digging my sharp nails into my palms. I reach the coatrack, grab my cowboy hat off the top peg, slip my flip-flops on, and charge outside, slamming the door behind me.

I leave our yard, take a sharp left, and walk. I walk until my feet are sore, then I walk some more. Clouds pass on a gentle breeze, the warm sun sinking toward the horizon; a pleasant wind passes through the trees and bushes and flowers lining every manicured lawn, through my hair and against the insides of my hidden ears. My head hurts, but my nails are blunt again. I sit on the curb, find out where I am, and take my phone out of my jeans pocket. I scroll through the few phone calls recorded in the past two months, find the one listed on April sixteenth after nine o'clock, and call.

Kyle's deep-green ride rolls to a stop, flush with the curb; I get in the passenger seat, and we drive away.

"I ought to give you my mobile number," Kyle says, "and get rid of that damn home phone."

I nod sheepishly, looking out the window at all the houses flying by. Soothing folk rock rolls out of the speakers. "Thanks for picking me up."

"It ain't no big deal. It was better for you to leave rather than say something you'd regret."

Yeah, I think, staring out; the houses disappear as he turns, leaving only trees.

I sit on the couch with Kyle, watching Killer drift from one side of his tank to the other, my knees up to my chest.

Kyle flips the page of the large paperback Bible in his hands—his usual Sunday reading. He clears his throat. "Jack."

I rest the side of my head on my knees. "Yeah?"

"I've been thinkin' awhile. About how you have trouble at home."

"I don't have trouble." I glance at the edge of the coffee table. "We just don't get along most of the time."

Kyle snorts. "That's its own kinda trouble."

"Yeah."

Kyle places his Bible down. "I want you to know that when you turn eighteen, you're welcome to come live here. I've got an unused bedroom and there's always space in the driveway for another car."

I look at him, at his nonplussed face, like what he said isn't totally unearned. "You'd just give me a place to stay?"

He smiles genuinely. "Of course I'd expect you to be in school or workin'." He places his hand on top of my head. "But I've been considerin' you one of my own for a long time now. I may not have any biological kids, but you're all my children in spirit."

I feel stupid and childish and immature, but I reach across the couch and hug Kyle. He pets my head slowly with his rough hand, and I don't tear up, and nothing falls on his shoulder. Nothing at all.

His phone buzzes in his pants pocket.

I let him go and shuffle back to my side of the couch, furiously wiping my irritated eyes.

Kyle takes his phone out, looks at the caller ID, and stands up. "I gotta take this."

I nod, returning my gaze to his sparkling fish.

He walks down the hall, enters his bedroom, and softly closes the door.

The doorbell rings, startling me out of my tired daze.

Kyle puts his book down and stands. He opens the front door.

A short man with coifed black hair walks in; he looks at me with a sour face.

I jump to my feet. "Dad."

He stares. "Son."

I grab my elbow and glance aside. "What're you doing here?"

Dad smiles. "Kyle texted me earlier. I'd like to go on an outing, just father and son."

"Go on, Jack," Kyle says. "You only got one daddy."

I frown but walk to the front door, put my shoes and hat on, and follow Dad outside to his Mercedes-Benz.

We get in and drive silently—Dad's never been one for words. We travel half an hour in light nighttime traffic, smooth jazz flowing from the radio.

Dad parks in front of a burger bar, a place Mom wouldn't be caught dead in. We get out of the car and walk inside.

"Table for two?" the hostess asks.

Dad smiles, pointing up. "We'll be going to the bar."

We walk up a flight of stairs to the second floor and sit on hard stools at the empty bar nestled in the back left corner.

"It's good to see you, Barbara," Dad says.

A heavyset woman drying glasses behind the counter smiles. "I haven't seen your face in a while. The usual?"

Dad nods.

She looks at me. "What about you, big guy?"

"He's not of age," Dad says.

Barbara laughs. "Could've fooled me!" She works on his drink.

Dad drags a menu in front of me. "Would you like to order something? You didn't finish dinner."

My stomach sucks sharply inward. I look over the menu, eyeing the options with barbecue sauce.

Barbara places a coaster and a peach-colored cocktail topped with a sliver of orange and a black cherry in front of Dad. "Need a few minutes, or are y'all ready to order?"

Dad takes a sip of his drink, glancing at my menu. "I'm ready if you are."

She looks at me again.

I say, "I'll have the smokehouse burger, medium rare, no onions or tomato, and a sweet tea."

"Fries alright?" she asks.

"Yeah."

She looks at Dad. "What about you, honey?"

"Fried pickles," he says, "and a glass of water."

She takes the menu and whips around to the POS machine so fast her ponytail flies sideways.

Dad sips his drink, squinting in the dim light; ancient rock and roll fills the silence. He takes a long pull and swallows deeply. "When I was your age, I wanted to be a bartender."

I look at him, at those deeply hooded eyes Olive inherited to a T.

"I loved the science of it, mixing drinks and ice and syrups to make enchanting cocktails. I thought for sure I'd work my way up as soon as I was eighteen and start serving drinks as a barback, but my parents thought otherwise. I was the oldest son, the heir to their corporation. It always went to the oldest son. Always.

"But I held onto my dream for as long as I could; it wasn't until your mother came along that I stopped dreaming. She was a sweet girl and I wanted to take care of her—bartending couldn't do that, not for certain. So I gave up, got an education, trained under my father, and started a family. I'd done everything right, but . . ."

He picks up the toothpick spearing the fruit and twirls it around. Barbara places a tall glass of tea in front of me.

"After all of my siblings had successfully had boys, Delilah had only had girls. There was a lot of pressure from both of our families to have a boy, so we kept trying, but by the time Mary came along, I was thinking we ought to stop. We could afford to have more, but pregnancies take their toll on a woman's body, your mother no exception. But not having a son was unheard of; our parents blamed her for failing to produce an heir, so we continued.

"Hope and Grace came one after the other, and your mother was in hysterics. 'One more try,' she said. 'Lucky number seven.'

And we had you and Jenny. Your mother was overjoyed: Finally, she had done something right; finally, everyone could be happy."

He scrutinizes the orange and the cherry, then drags them off the toothpick with his teeth.

"But we forgot that you're your own individual. All of you are. Not one of you ever let us tell you what you could do with your lives." He glances at me and smiles. "And I'm proud I had the privilege to father those children."

I stare at the counter.

He picks his drink up and takes a long sip. "I wish now that I had had the strength to disregard our families. For a long time, we tried so hard to change you, when we should've been changing the very foundation we'd built on.

"I know that now, but I also know I can't take back everything we did wrong throughout your lives; perhaps it will be better for all of us if you make your own way after you graduate high school."

"What are you implying?" I ask.

His gaze grows soft. "I plan to pay for you to go to beauty school; I've paid for your sisters to go to college, so it's only fair."

"You're serious?" I whisper.

He looks at his drink and nods, a smile on his face. "I've realized how ridiculous it is to insist on a male heir in this day and age. Ruth has wanted to take over the business for years, so I'm going to start training her immediately; she already got her master's and everything. The only thing that needs work are her social skills, but plenty of billionaires are eccentric on their best days."

Barbara places our orders in front of us. "Anything else I can get y'all?"

"No," I say, "we're good."

She returns to shining glasses, watching a basketball game on the flat-screen TV hanging overhead.

Dad dips a fried pickle in the ranch dressing that came with his order.

I stare at my food. "Kyle said I could move in with him when I turn eighteen."

Dad eats the pickle. "Will you?"

Barbecue sauce dribbles over my patty and the bun and pools on the paper covering the tray. "Yeah."

"I'll keep you on the insurance." He sips at his drink; it's half-full. "Will you still visit?"

I pick up a fry and nibble on the end. "Only if Mom stops insulting my girlfriend."

"I have a feeling Heather will be around a long time."

"I hope so."

"She's a beautiful girl." He dips another pickle and eats it. "Wild, too, just like you."

"You think so?"

Dad picks up his drink and twirls it around; the ice clinks. "You've found yourself good company over the years. I'm proud of you for standing up for yourself."

I definitely don't cry. "Thanks."

"Eat your burger, Jack: you earned it."

I do.

CHAPTER 33

Precious Metal

Ashley

We're cooking when he pops the question.

"What's your favorite gemstone?" Alex asks, stirring noodles in boiling water.

I think for a long moment over the frying chicken. "Peridot."

"Silver or gold?"

I flip the chicken. "Gold."

Alex stirs carefully, putting the heat down a smidgen so the water doesn't boil over.

The chicken sizzles.

〜

Alex holds me close under the sheets and nuzzles my neck, his tail thumping repeatedly against the mattress.

"We need to sleep, Alex." I flip to my other side and face him.

Alex pulls our chests together, smiling wide with his ears pulled back. "I'm excited."

I pet his ear. "What about?"

His tail wags even harder. "I'm not supposed to tell you yet."

I hum, snuggle against his warm chest, and slide my hand across his side until my fingers meet fur. "That's a little ominous, don't you think?"

His tail thumps to a stop as he pouts. "It's not ominous."

"So it's a surprise for me? A good one?"

His tail wags all over again. "I won't let you trick me tonight." He's determined enough to hold his tongue against his full-moon haze.

"Will you tell me in the morning?"

Alex flips over.

I pull myself higher up his back and clamp his tail between my thighs, barely containing its force; the tip wiggles back and forth, but it's no longer beating the mattress. I throw my arm over his side and run my fingers through his coarse chest hair.

His ears and tail relax, and he snores softly.

I close my eyes and sleep.

⌒⟶

I open my eyes at the crack of dawn. Sunlight filters through the blinds, illuminating the dust particles hanging in the air; I turn my head away.

"Morning, beautiful." Alex lies languidly on his side with his head propped up, the elbow beneath cushioned by his pillow.

I prop myself up and reach for his head. "Morning, handsome." I pet his right ear.

Alex hums, his eyes half-lidded. "I have that surprise ready for you, but you need to close your eyes first."

I place my hand on the bed, right in front of my stomach, and close my eyes.

The sheets swish. Something velveteen grazes my fingers; he wraps them around the hinge. "You can open your eyes."

My eyes slowly open, and I gaze at the object pressed against my palm: a blue ring box holding a dainty gold ring with a peridot center stone.

Alex stares at me with an impossibly hard expression. "Ashley Koenigsegg, will you marry me?"

I smile softly, take the ring out of the box, slip it onto my naked ring finger, and take his hand in mine. "Alexander Delgado, I'd love to marry you."

Without a second thought, Alex sweeps me up in a tight hug, his tail thumping against the mattress faster than it ever has before.

⌒⟶

Mark, Alex, and I sit down for dinner late in the afternoon. We tried our hands at making Japanese sticky rice on the stovetop with limited success, but it's edible, especially with the beef stir-fry mitigating the subpar texture and taste.

I watch Mark chew up beef and vegetables with his serrated teeth and catch a flash of his forked tongue when he scoops up another mouthful. He's deep in the throes of his midsummer gaming sessions, so he's mostly tired and going through the motions. After he finishes chewing, I say, "Mark."

He stalls. "Yeah?"

"Alex proposed to me this morning. We plan to marry."

He blinks. "Okay." He scoops up another forkful of rice, beef, and veggies.

"Okay?" I ask, flabbergasted.

"I mean"—Mark makes a face like he's been asked to sequence the human genome—"congrats? I was honestly wondering when Alex would propose."

"Saw right through me, huh?" Alex says, oddly bashful.

Mark rolls his eyes but smiles. "All I ask is that you don't give me any siblings—seriously, I'm too old for that."

I grin awkwardly. "I think I'm a bit too old myself."

"And besides," Alex says, "I've had a vasectomy."

Mark nearly drops his fork. "When did *that* happen?"

"When I was twenty-five. I never wanted kids in the first place, so I figured if I ever got lucky again, I didn't want any chance of leaving a baby behind."

Mark pouts. "You don't want me?" His round eyes fake tears.

Alex gapes. "Kid, I mean I didn't want *biological* kids."

Mark grins. "I know, Dalex." He chews his next forkful with a smile.

Alex and I share our own smiles, our opposing hands finding each other under the table; he squeezes once, and I squeeze back, feeling like the luckiest woman in the world.

CHAPTER 34

Nothing but the Truth

Emily

park on the curb near a large, unassuming house with a single light-blue car in the driveway. The yard has a few bushes and an oak tree, and the grass is perfectly mowed. It's warm bordering on hot, the sky dotted with wispy white clouds. I'm not wearing anything crazy: just a graphic tee, five-inch shorts, and tawny sandals I picked out with Heather the last time we went to the mall. I thought about painting my toenails, but decided I didn't want to set any precedents I have no intention of keeping up.

I get out of my car and walk up the driveway—Matthew's driveway. When I get to the door, it takes all I have to ring the doorbell. I stand there forever in the summer heat, the band of my thick sports bra sticking to my rib cage, until Matthew finally opens the door.

He smiles at me, his eyelids drooping like he just woke up from a nap. "Hey."

My heart pounds into my lungs for no good reason. "H-Hey."

He backs up and holds the door open. "Come on in."

I shuffle inside, immediately relieved by a blast of cool AC.

Matthew closes the door, takes off his hat, and places it on a rack with eleven other baseball caps. He runs his hand through his hair, pulling a few knots free, and lets his ears out, all while his tail slides out from under his shirt, curves upward, and curls at the tip. "You look cute today." He glances up and down so fast I'd have missed it if I wasn't overly focused on everything about him.

"Thank you." A blush heats my face. "You too." Embarrassed, I bend down and unstrap my sandals.

"You don't have to be so nervous, Emmie. It's just my house."

I slip my sandals off and glance at his feet; I've never seen him barefoot. Before I end up staring, I stand up straight and look around. "It's a boy's house. My boyfriend's house."

Matthew grins. "Scandalous, I know."

"My mom would have a stroke."

His grin softens to a smile. "I can show you around if you'd like. Demystify it and all that."

I nod shyly, ashamed I feel so antsy being home alone with Matthew; this is one of those scenarios Mom has warned me about for years. But I had to take a chance and drive over as soon as Dad got me a car because we're dating and I want to hang out alone more. In private. So we can do mostly appropriate things.

Matthew takes my hand, locks our fingers together, and shows me around the house: first, a posh living room with a large glass-top cocktail table and two plush white couches facing each other, decorated with soft hues of pearl and cream; second, a quaint kitchen and dining room with sparkling white granite counters and beautiful black leather chairs, all accented with flashes of red; and third, Matthew's bedroom and bathroom, which have blue, brown, and black decor—perfectly boyish and totally Matthew. There's nothing out of the ordinary in his room except for a shredded scratching pad lying innocuously on his nightstand.

Matthew blushes. "Oh, sorry; I sharpened my claws last night." He walks over and hides it behind his nightstand.

"Oh, no, that's okay. I leave stuff lying around, too, but my cats are quick to remind me." Cream has a habit of knocking things over, both on purpose and because she's too pudgy to squeeze through some of her chosen obstacles.

Matthew hums and wanders over to his bed; he sits on the edge, his big butt depressing the plain blue comforter. "I'm glad my cat instincts don't include knocking glasses off the table." He pats next to him.

I swallow, holding my hands over my collar. Mom has said a lot of things about sitting on a boy's bed, but Matthew isn't the kind of boy she's always warning me about, and we both believe in waiting, so he won't do anything; I huff and plop down next to him. "God, I'm so nervous." I cover my mouth with my fists.

Matthew wraps his arm around me, resting his hand over my right hip. He left the door open, and there's nothing in the way if I ever feel like I need to leave, and his grip is loose, and the rumble of his purrs through his rib cage soothes my frantic everything. "Just . . . let me know if there's anything I can do to help you feel safe. I know this is a big deal for you."

I nod and let my hands fall into my lap. I lean against his shoulder and try to forget all the horror stories twisting my gut. "I trust you. I wouldn't be here if I didn't." I look around the room, at the closed closet door and the old PC and the little flat-screen he plays on. "This is a nice bedroom. I didn't know you have your own computer."

"It's getting pretty old now. My dad gave it to me when he upgraded his. The monitor is newer, but the computer is on its last legs; you should hear the fan when it heats up."

I smile. "I probably wouldn't hear it as good as you."

He snorts. "Fair enough. I tend to forget my hearing is better than it should be. It's actually worse when I hide my ears."

I glance at his cute brown ears with their fluffy furnishings peeking so perfectly out of his curly hair. I want to pet them, but don't dare ask.

Matthew notices my staring; his ears swivel outward and his face sours, his tail puffing up behind him.

"Ah, sorry." I wring my hands in my lap.

Matthew shakes his head. "No, I get it." He puts on a wobbly smile. "I'm nervous, too."

"Can I, um . . ." I don't want to say it.

Matthew presses his lips together; his hand departs my hip so he can twiddle his thumbs. "Yeah, uh . . . I'd like that."

I tentatively reach up and brush my fingertips against the furry back of his right ear; it flicks, then perks up. More confident now, I lightly stroke it from base to tip, relishing its utter softness.

Matthew closes his eyes and purrs louder, his hands firmly fisted on his thick thighs.

Bolder than ever, I scooch back and settle behind him, gently shoo his tail away from my knees, and pet both ears with my thumbs, scratching where ear meets scalp; to my delight, his curly hair is nearly as soft as his fur.

Matthew gives up and goes active within seconds, gripping his thighs so hard his claws poke his cargo shorts. "God, Emmie . . . This feels amazing . . ."

I beam. "It's a treat for me, too. Your hair is so soft I might be jealous."

Matthew is too busy melting into my touch to reply; he leans back and back and back against my hands until his weight topples us over. His head lands on my chest, my legs bent oddly under his waist. We both blush and smile and laugh awkwardly, and he lifts his torso off of me and twists around. He gives me his hand, pulls me up, and wraps me in a hug. "I feel like the luckiest boyfriend ever." His voice rumbles with his purrs.

I wrap my arms around him and slowly rub his back; it shocks me how firm it is, his shoulders so much broader than my own. "I feel lucky, too." How many girls get to say their boyfriend is a cat boy? The cutest, sweetest, and kindest one at that?

We part and gaze at each other, quiet and satisfied. "What do you want to do for the rest of your time here? I remember you have to be home before dinner."

I bring a finger to my cheek; as much as I'd love to pet him for five hours, we'd both get tired of that fast. "We could cuddle and watch videos for a while. Maybe go on a walk around the neighborhood?"

Matthew smiles. "That works for me."

We watch videos on YouTube for two hours, then go on a walk. Matthew shows me around his neighborhood—we even walk past Mark's house—which isn't all that different from mine. There are lots of different houses painted different colors at different sizes, each with different cars and yards and people; it's eclectic, a neighborhood that's been updated randomly year by year and attracted both young and old to build their lives in this ever-growing city of ours.

By the time we get back to his house, there's a silver SUV sitting in the driveway next to Matthew's car. He stops and stares. "Mom's home."

"That's okay," I say. "I should meet her."

"She's a little vain, so don't take anything she says to heart."

I run my thumb over his knuckles. "I won't." My parents will have a lot to say about him, too.

Matthew nods and leads me back inside.

As if waiting for us, a short and stout woman with pristine hair and makeup walks out of the kitchen holding a glass of red wine; ornamental rings with massive jewels decorate her thick fingers. She looks me over, takes a hearty swig, and asks, "Who's this, Matty?"

Matthew frowns, his eyes bold and fiery. "This is my girlfriend, Emily."

Mrs. Stroud puts on a strained smile. "Your girlfriend?" She tastes it on her tongue—sour and bitter. "She's very . . . homely."

I try not to grimace.

Matthew squeezes my hand. "We've been dating for a few months. I met her when we started high school."

Mrs. Stroud keeps her disgusted smile up. "That's good for you, Matty." Nose crinkled, she walks into the living room, lounges on the couch, and grabs the remote off the cocktail table.

Matthew sighs and pulls me back upstairs.

"Matty?" I ask the minute we enter his room.

He grits his teeth. "I hate that nickname, so don't ever use it." He's actually, genuinely angry about it.

I pull his arm against my chest. "I prefer Tabby anyway."

He relaxes, his ears lifting away from his scalp, and turns me to face him; we stare into each other's eyes, his beautiful blue into my humble hazel, and press our lips together in a kiss.

I chomp into a crunchy ground beef taco, the grease dribbling down my chin as I chew; I quickly wipe my mouth with a napkin. "So . . ."

Mom raises an eyebrow, my brothers pay a fraction of their attention, and Dad looks on solemnly.

I purse my lips; some sour cream curdles on my finger. "I have a boyfriend."

Mom stabs her fork into her giant taco salad. "Thank goodness!"

I gape. "Thank goodness?! I thought—"

"I was beginning to think you were a lesbian, sweetheart."

Connor hacks, Noah goes wide-eyed, and Dad coughs.

"Where did you get that idea?!"

Mom puts a hand over her heart, smiling matronly. "Well, you've always been a tomboy, and you never had any interest in those handsome boys you're always hanging around, and you're so close with Heather—"

"How many times do I have to tell you we're just friends?"

"Apparently a lot," Noah says.

Mom glares at him.

He shrinks and nibbles on a tortilla chip.

I sigh, hovering my taco over my plate. "And Heather has a boyfriend."

Mom lights up. "Oh, it's that boy she danced with, right? The girly one with the long hair? You know, I thought he and that tall blond boy had something going on back when they stayed with you for soccer practice. I mean, what normal boy wears makeup—"

"Mom."

Mom goes wide-eyed and clears her throat. "Sorry, dear. Which one is your boyfriend? I hope it's not that red-haired boy."

"Oh my God, I am *not* dating Mark!" That would be gross! And weird! "I'm dating his friend, Matthew."

Mom furrows her brow. "Which one was that?"

I grit my teeth. "The one with curly brown hair. Blue eyes?"

"Hmm . . ." Mom ponders, eats a forkful of overdressed salad, and ponders some more. "Oh! The short one."

I want to bang my head on the table. "Yes, the short one, Mom."

"I suppose it could be worse," Mom says. "Are you sure you don't like the tall one?"

"He's taken!"

"I meant the blond, honey."

"He's taken, too!"

Mom frowns. "Well, isn't that a shame."

I want to bang my head so hard against the table that it shatters into a million pieces—if only someone shared the sentiment.

CHAPTER 35

Playing the Part

Matthew

I park in the massive parking lot of the megachurch a few miles from my house. The sun shines bright on the rainbow of cars lining every square inch of the lot, the brim of my cap saving my eyes the displeasure of their glare.

After a lot of back-and-forth over the last three weeks, I agreed to come to Sunday service with Emily's family in an effort to impress them at least a little bit; I haven't gone to church in a very long time, but I have nothing against it if it'll assuage some of her mom's irrational fears.

I get out of my Camry, shut the door, and lock it with my key fob; take a long, deep breath of fresh air; and walk lonesome up the ramp. The entrance—one of three—has a long row of four double doors, each one being used by multiple streams of couples and families and the occasional loner; I join them, entering behind a hobbling old couple and their grandchild. Once inside, I lean against one gigantic wall and take everything in. Calling it a megachurch is no exaggeration: it used to be a warehouse, so it has insanely high ceilings and massive decorations wrapping around the various support beams—it must look amazing during the Christmas season with all this space to work with.

While I'm preoccupied with the architecture, Emily nearly sneaks up on me, but I catch her happy hazel eyes in my peripheral at the last second.

"Nearly had you," she says, a cute smile gracing her face.

I smile back. "I was just about to ask where you were. This place is huge."

"We just got here. My brothers were dragging their butts this morning."

I don't blame them: church is never fun.

Mr. and Mrs. Thompson, Connor, and Noah walk up to us. Mr. Thompson seems disinterested, Mrs. Thompson looks constipated, Connor shambles, and Noah buzzes with energy.

Mrs. Thompson clears her throat. "It's nice to meet you, um . . ."

"Matthew," Emily says. "His name is Matthew." It appears her fuse is short today.

Before Mrs. Thompson can share any pleasantries, Noah charges up to me. "Hi! Do you remember me?"

I smile and nod. "We went trick-or-treating two years ago. Are you in middle school now?"

Noah grins. "Seventh grade tomorrow! And look!" He flexes his surprisingly muscular arm. "I joined the cheerleading squad and started lifting! You should feel it."

Mostly to humor him, I squeeze his bicep, then brandish mine. "You're better than me, and I'll be eighteen next year."

Noah squeezes my bicep. "It's squishy," he says, his smile ever present.

"Noah . . ." Emily mutters.

I smile at her and shrug, hoping she'll understand that it doesn't bother me; I'm glad Noah has come out of his shell since that time he was a shy swashbuckler. And I'd like to get along with her brothers—they may be mine one day, too.

Connor squints at me, crosses his arms, and lifts his chin; unlike me, he's grown a few inches taller.

Instead of matching his stance like I did two years ago, I simply smile and nod—I exist; you exist; we're on the same team.

Connor deflates and looks away. "I'm going to service. C'mon, Noah." He stalks down the nearby hall.

Noah waves and bounces after him.

Emily clears her throat. "I think Matthew and I should go to service, too!"

Mrs. Thompson doesn't question her. "Have fun, honey. We'll come get you after our service ends." They wait for us to walk away, and once we're a few paces down the same hall the brothers went through, they're swallowed up by the crowds.

Emily pulls me along by the hand, her face tight; we traverse hall after hall, making this right and that left, until we get to a sign for the youth center. Emily stops and stares. "I don't feel like service today."

I squeeze her hand. "It doesn't make a difference to me, but I can't say I'm eager to be lectured on the Gospels again."

Emily smiles. "I'll give you a different lecture." She pulls me along to a door that leads outside.

I push the door open for her.

She steps outside and takes a deep breath of fresh air.

I join her, and we cross a little roadway separating the parking lot from the sidewalk.

Grinning, Emily grabs my hand again. "I think I'll show you around."

"Lead the way."

Emily walks me around the perimeter of the warehouse turned church, following the road so we're facing any oncoming vehicles. She shows me the one-way service road where you can donate to the church thrift store; the front entrance that's as big as the side entrance, fit with a visitor lot full of colorful cars; and the little playground at the corner on the way back to the side entrance.

We walk back inside, the massive room utterly empty now that service started. Emily continues her little tour, taking me past the children's area and nursery; the tiny café that serves coffee and muffins early in the morning; the two general service rooms where the gospel choir belts out contemporary Christian music; the little library nestled in an office space; and the chapel room for adults that want a deeper dive into the Bible.

By the time we sit down on a bench near the hallway we started in, I'm left feeling overwhelmed; a megachurch is leagues beyond the little chapel I used to go to with the Koenigseggs. "This place is so much bigger than I expected." I settle close enough to Emily that our hips touch.

"Yeah, it was a big learning curve for me when we moved here. We used to go to a much-smaller church."

"I used to go to a Baptist chapel so small it was just one big room full of pews. They had hymnals slotted on the backs, and an organ player."

"I've never heard an organ before."

I reminisce. "They sound beautiful. That pipe organ was the only thing I missed when we stopped going every Sunday."

"Why did you stop?"

I grin. "Classic holier-than-thou behavior. It was always there because of Mark's heritage, but then the whole red-hair, yellow-eyes, sharp-teeth thing happened and the devout legion couldn't take it anymore."

Emily snorts. "I hate that. We're taught to treat people how we want to be treated, yet so many go around judging people for stupid things." Emily cranes her neck and rolls her eyes. "My mom is so bad about that. Can you believe she stopped caring about the no-dating thing just because she thought I might be a lesbian? Like, come on, I never showed interest in boys because you told me not to! Then she has the gall to dismiss you because you're not as tall as Jack and Teddy. She can't even remember your name, for crying out loud."

I scratch my cheek. "I can tell it's a sore spot for you." Emily ranted about that exact sentiment constantly over the past three weeks.

"Of course it is!" She lifts an angry fist in the air. "I was always *so* careful to keep you guys off her radar, but I guess she had more important things to worry about than me potentially sleeping around. And don't even get me started on her opinion about Noah on the cheer team."

I lean back against the wall, cushioning my head with my arms. "What's not to like about making gains while lifting pretty girls, right?"

"Matthew . . ." Emily collapses against my side, and as much as I'd love her to, she doesn't drape across my lap—we're in a church, after all; God forbid two teenagers show any affection beyond holding hands in public.

I wrap my arm around her shoulders and hold her close.

She smiles, her hand daring to rub my knee.

We chill against each other for the rest of service, whispering over the faint preaching in the distance.

Emily smiles sweetly at her mother. "Can I ride with Matthew?" She bats her eyelashes.

Mrs. Thompson scrunches her nose. "Honey, I barely know him; I'm not going to trust him with you alone in a car."

Although I'm disappointed, I can't fault her for worrying: boys can be real bastards if you trust the wrong guy.

Emily huffs, her arms hanging limp.

Mrs. Thompson crosses her arms. "Don't give me that look."

Emily frowns harder anyway.

Mr. Thompson looks at me. "We'll meet you at the restaurant. Do you need the address?"

I shake my head. "I know where it is." We're going to an Applebee's at the edge of the closest shopping center.

Emily waves her hand, keeping her distance for the sake of her family. "We'll see you there!"

I wave back and walk away.

I sit sandwiched between Noah and Emily in a large family booth that's lost its cushion. Connor glares at his menu from the other side, Mr. and Mrs. Thompson gazing at me like strangers.

Mr. Thompson clears his throat, holding up a menu between himself and his wife. "Do you want to do the two for twenty?"

Mrs. Thompson regards the menu with serious consideration.

I look over the menu, too. Applebee's sells typical American fare: burgers; sandwiches; chicken; steak; pasta; and salads packing as many calories as everything else.

The waiter comes by to take our drink orders; feeling saccharine, I order a sweet tea.

Mr. Thompson places his menu on the laminate table.

Mrs. Thompson smiles too brightly. "So, Matthew. What do you do in your spare time? Any sports?"

Glancing between the chicken and ribs, I say, "I mostly play video games with friends, but I used to swim all the time." I'm leaning toward chicken: it's less of a mess.

"Oh? Do you not swim anymore?"

I shake my head. "I had a . . . medical complication. In fifth grade."

"Medical complication?" She tastes it, pondering too deeply. "Did you get injured?"

I furrow my brow, hoping she'll think I'm having trouble deciding on my lunch. "Not an injury. I developed a condition."

"What sort of condition?"

"Mom," Emily says, "that's private information."

Mrs. Thompson glares at her. "Well, I'd hope you're aware of this condition because it could be contagious or pass on to your children." She has the gall to look offended. "Goodness, you have to think of these things."

"She knows," I say politely. "And it's not contagious." But it is, unfortunately, genetic.

Mrs. Thompson huffs but leaves that conversation behind.

Mr. Thompson takes up her mantle. "Do you have any plans for the future?" His voice is gruff, yet gentle.

I place my menu down and lift my head. "I want to go into pediatrics."

"Pediatrics? That'll require medical school, won't it?"

"Yes. I know it's a big commitment. At least twelve years after we graduate."

Mrs. Thompson worries her lip. "So you won't be able to start a family until you're thirty?" Her gaze on Emily says it all. *Are you sure about this?*

Emily frowns, her gaze cold hard steel. "Plenty of women start families in their thirties and are perfectly fine."

I wait for Mrs. Thompson to go on a tirade about fertility, Down syndrome, and making her wait for grandchildren, but our waiter comes to take our orders in the nick of time; she gets distracted enough ordering fried shrimp, fries, and a side salad that she loses her opportunity.

The rest of us make our orders, too: grilled chicken and shrimp for me and Mr. Thompson; three-cheese chicken penne for Emily; and the brothers go two for twenty—cheeseburgers and a mozzarella sticks appetizer to share.

While I pretend the previous sentiment was never made, Mr. Thompson strokes his short salt-and-pepper beard. "I can't believe you're about to be seniors." He smiles. "You kids grow up so fast."

Emily pouts. "Dad, why are you being so sentimental?"

He grins. "My little girl got herself a boyfriend. Let an old man grieve."

"You're barely over forty!"

He smiles so wide his mustache fans out, a laugh escaping his lips.

CHAPTER 36

The Little Things

Mark

plant my dragon paw on my carpet and swing my gaming chair back and forth. "Puppy, you should, like, totally come to our graduation next year."

"Bro," Puppy says, "I'm a broke bitch right now."

"I know, bro; that's why I'm telling you now, so you have time to stop being a broke bitch."

"Ugh . . ." He mouth breathes noisily into the mic. "Don't you guys live in North Carolina?"

"Yessir."

"That's six hours away!"

"It's not my problem you live in Maryland!"

Emily giggles, as she does when Puppy gets into petty arguments with us.

I swear Puppy growls playfully, but it's there and gone so fast I assume it's a trick of technology. "Maybe I'll get my dad in on it. I don't want to drive that long alone, and he keeps calling me all the time to hang out, anyway."

"Didn't he want you out of the house?" Matthew asks.

"He did"—I imagine Puppy shrugging nonchalantly—"but he's a lonely old man. I keep telling him to go find a girlfriend, but he won't hear it."

Whereas I had a single mother, Puppy has a single father. He was around before my dad died, and it took me a long time to tell him what had happened, but when it managed to come up, he told me he'd lost his mom at a young age, too. It was a strange conversation, but I was relieved that someone else, no matter how far away or how much older, understood that pain. I've never met Puppy in real life, but he's as good a friend as the rest of them.

"I imagine it takes a long time to move on," Emily says. "Sometimes I think I could only love someone at that level once."

"My mom kept her wedding ring on for three years," I say, "and I think her finding another good guy was a stroke of luck."

Puppy sighs. "I hear you. Maybe I just don't get it yet because I've never been in love."

"Not even a crush?" Emily asks.

"I mean, I've seen plenty of hot chicks. Thought about plenty of hot chicks." He pauses. "There was one girl I met in college that piqued my interest, but she was a bit too nosy for my taste. And she was flat as a board. Pretty face, though. Good taste in music, too."

Emily says, "Shallow, much?" The small-tits comment hit too close to home.

"Look, Emmie," he says, "we all have preferences. Nothing wrong with that."

"Lucha likes small tits," I say.

Emily breathes noisily into her mic. "I'm well aware, Tao."

"I've always been more of an ass man," Matthew says.

Puppy laughs. "She had no ass, either!"

"Damn, bro," I say, "cut her some slack."

"Alright, alright." He chuckles. "She had pretty hair. Long, bleached blond. Very flexible, too. Yeah, she had nice legs."

A girl I know comes to mind. Someone older who would've graduated at the same time as Puppy. "What was her name?"

Puppy grunts. "Wouldn't you like to know."

He never does tell us her name.

I go outside into the chilly October air, carrying mail that I need to deliver to the pods. I stride to the first outdoor trailer and interrupt the first of two classes in my capacity as a Student Services assistant. I already delivered to all the indoor classrooms, so as soon as I'm done here, I'll return to the office and totally do my homework early with the time I have left.

When I enter the second classroom—it's a history class, judging by the PowerPoint on suffrage—I notice Connor scowling in the corner; I give the teacher the mail and wave at him, earning a personal glare from Emily's sourpuss brother. I grin and make my leave, a pep in my step despite the cold; it's nice to have a break in my classes—one of the few perks of being a senior.

I follow the sidewalk from the gym locker rooms to the theater exit and trail the winding concrete toward the front of the school. As I get closer to the doors just outside Student Services, I spot Jack on the stone bench; shockingly, he has a lunch box in his lap and a stainless steel fork in his hand instead of the usual foam tray and plastic utensils.

Figuring the front desk lady won't miss me for a few more minutes, I approach him. "How's it going, Jack?"

His back goes ramrod straight, but as soon as he realizes it's just his good old friend Mark, he huffs and says, "Going good. You?"

"Living the life!" I smile. "Care if I join you?"

Jack scooches over to the right.

I sit on his left, staring down at the woods at the bottom of the hill.

"Aren't you supposed to be in class?"

I flick the lanyard hanging from my neck. "I'm an assistant this period. I just finished delivering mail."

He looks at my plastic ID card and nods, a smile gracing his lips. "Must be nice, being a senior and all."

I grin. "It would've been nicer if my dumb ass didn't take AP Calculus."

Jack grins, too. "My dumb ass stays put in the normal classes where it belongs."

"I don't blame you. All I get out of it are headaches and pretty printed paper." In the end, there are skills Jack has that I'd have a hard time cultivating, and the same can be said for him and my skills.

Jack spears a chunk of familiar-looking salad with his fork, lifts it to his lips, and eats it.

"I'm surprised you brought a lunch."

Jack finishes chewing and gathers another forkful. "Heather insisted on preparing some for me last night. She thinks it's a crime to eat cafeteria food." He smiles boyishly.

I'm happy for him. "How has she been, with the move and all?"

"She's been alright." He eats more of Heather's chicken salad. "Teddy's been complaining about going to school with her after all these years. She gets hit on a lot, so he has to go out of his way to scare guys off." He grins at me, a strip of lettuce sticking to his recently grown chinstrap beard. "He has his work cut out for him."

"That sounds about right." I laugh and point at my chin.

Jack's eyebrows shoot up, and he thumbs the food scrap off his neat black hairs. "It's too bad I can't see her every day anymore, but I'm glad she has a better relationship with Teddy now. And she doesn't have to spend so much energy hiding herself away."

I look at my wrist and my forearm, the ones I broke when I was little. "I can't imagine how hard that was on her."

A weak smile on his face, Jack stares at the food she prepared for him. "I know it all too well."

"Is your mom still having a problem with you two?"

He shakes his head, his long hair swaying back and forth. "Not out loud; my dad got her to keep it to herself." He gathers another forkful. "Actually, I've been meaning to tell y'all that Jenny and I won't be attending my parents' Christmas party this year."

I lean forward so I can see his face better. "Oh? Where're you gonna go?"

He beams. "Mr. Brown and Kyle want to have a celebration as a family." He scratches his cheek. "I guess that includes us now."

I grin and pat his back. "That's awesome, bro."

"It is." He looks up at the gray-blue sky; the clouds break, sending a stream of light onto his glistening hair, and he smiles, soaking in the ray.

⌣⟶

After a long day of Christmas-birthday festivities, we settle down at the table for dinner, Alex and Mom on one side, Matthew and I on the other. We're having twice-baked potatoes stuffed with all manner of cheese, sour cream, chopped bacon, and chives. Mom says a blessing and we eat quietly, too focused on enjoying good food to talk.

When we finish our meal, Mom gets up and brings over her homemade apple pie that we eat every year instead of a birthday cake. She puts in a big one candle and an eight, lights the wicks, and they sing "Happy Birthday" to me.

I grin, make a wish, and blow out the candles.

Mom cuts the pie into eight even slices.

"So," Alex says, sliding a slice onto his cleared plate. "Your mom and I have a big question to ask you both."

Mom reaches for his hand under the table. "And a surprise gift."

Matthew and I perk up, giving them our utmost attention.

Alex twirls his hair around his finger. "We're thinking we might get married in July, at the courthouse."

"And we'll need witnesses to sign the marriage certificate," Mom says. "Two of them."

"You want us to be your witnesses?" I ask, knowing full well that's what she's saying.

Mom nods. "Only if you're willing, of course. It would mean a lot to me."

I smile, but I feel like I could cry. "Of course I will, Mom."

"Me, too," Matthew says. "I'm honored you want me there."

Mom tears up. "Of course I do, Matthew. I've always thought of you as my own, ever since that day Mark brought you home."

Matthew tears up, too. "Thank you."

After a few tears are shed and we calm down, Alex clears his throat. "I'm glad we got that settled." He glances everywhere but at us. "So. The gift."

Mom nudges him. "Go on, Alex."

His brow furrows. "Um, so, I'm going to move in with Ashley soon, and that'll free up some money on my end since I won't need to pay for the lease on my apartment anymore. But I thought, I know exactly how hard it is to hide what we are in a dorm room with a random roommate, and it's not like I'm strapped for cash, so . . . I want to rent an apartment for you both near whatever college you get into. I know you're hoping for NC State, so if everything works out, it'll be perfect."

My jaw nearly hits the floor. "Alex, you don't have to do that!"

"I know, but I want to. You'll be my kid—God, I already consider you my kid—so that's what I think a good dad would do."

Speechless, I shoot to my feet, round the table, and hug Alex. He gets up and hugs me back, and Matthew squeezes himself in there under our arms, all fuzz and purrs and disbelief. And Mom watches us, tears rolling down her cheeks as she smiles brighter than the sun on the clearest summer day.

CHAPTER 37

You Only Live Once

Emily

Vast clouds pass heavy under the setting sun, casting Matthew's front door in shadows. I drove here immediately after soccer practice because Matthew had his annual doctor's appointment today. I hesitate for a second, then knock.

Loud footsteps thump down the staircase and the door swings open, revealing Mark's gleeful face. "Joining us for dinner, Emily?" He grins obnoxiously.

I puff a strand of hair out of my face and walk past him. "How's Matthew feeling?"

Mark closes the door behind us. "He's alright. Tired and grumpy as usual, but he'll cheer up knowing his lovely girlfriend is visiting."

I huff, blush, kick my tennis shoes off, and walk upstairs.

Mark trails close behind; when we reach the second floor, he strides ahead and knocks on the door. "Oh, Tabby~ Emmie's here to see you~"

A low groan flows through the door. "Shut up, Mark . . ."

Mark smiles, cracks the door open, and shoves his head inside. "Can she come in?"

Silence lingers. "Yeah."

Mark opens the door the rest of the way, and I step inside.

Matthew lies in his bed, his blue blanket covering everything but his pale face; he looks at me, his eyes half-lidded and cheeks pink.

Mark clears his throat. "I'll get started on dinner." He leaves.

When the door clicks shut, I realize how alone we are, but I don't let that perturb me; I put on a brave face, sit in Matthew's office chair, and roll over to the side of his bed. I card my fingers through his bangs; his forehead is warm. "How're you feeling?"

He nods into my hand, a soft purr rolling out of his throat. "I'm sore all over, but I'll live."

"Is there anything I can do to help?"

He looks at me, at my hair and my lips and what little skin shows over the neckline of my shirt. He lifts his upper body with furry, shaky arms, and the blanket pools around his hips; he's shirtless, wearing nothing but plaid pajama pants.

I can't tear my eyes away from his torso. "Um, Matthew, what happened to your shirt?"

His ears perk up and he looks down at himself blankly. "I didn't put one on." He looks back up at me, his tail lifting out from under the blanket, the tip curling back and forth. "Does it bother you?"

"No, I'm not bothered. I'm just . . . surprised, is all."

Matthew watches me watch him, his elbows trembling and his claws unsheathing from the pressure against his mattress. "Good surprise or bad surprise?" He suddenly looks embarrassed, his ears drooping and tail falling flat behind him.

I take his shirtless self in. Matthew isn't slender like Mark, but he isn't chubby, either; there's a curve to his stomach and the hint of love handles curling over his hips. And he's hairy, a shocking amount of coarse brown hair covering his chest and belly, including a distinct happy trail leading from his navel down to something I try not to think about. He has pink nipples much smaller and less developed than my own, a difference between the sexes I hadn't ever thought about. And he's cute, and handsome, and perfect because he's Matthew and that's all I need to know to like what I see. "Good surprise."

Matthew smiles and drops on his side, totally spent. "Can I hold you?"

I go wide-eyed. "In your bed?"

He nods. "I promise to be appropriate." He grins. "I'm a good cat boy."

"Mm . . ." I fidget, wondering if I should be a bad girl. Mom would kill me if I got in his bed, but Mom won't have to know. "Okay." I get out of his chair and climb into his bed.

Matthew accepts me with open arms and holds me by my stomach against his chest. I feel safer knowing his unmentionables are covered by both pants and a blanket, though I can still feel him when my butt presses against his crotch. He buries his nose at the back of my neck, breathing deeply and purring loudly. "Thank you. I love you."

I card my fingers through the soft fur on his forearms, taking a deep, content breath. "I love you, too."

"Emily."

"Hmm?"

"I have a really embarrassing request."

I turn my head in a fruitless attempt to see his face. "What's your really embarrassing request?"

He holds me closer, idly kneading my stomach, his claws poking out but not piercing. "Can I . . . groom your hair?"

I crane my neck. "Groom my hair?"

He nuzzles closer. "With my tongue."

I swallow slowly. "With your tongue."

"I don't know." He's embarrassed. "I'm having stupid cat-boy thoughts right now."

"I . . ." With all my willpower, I conjure my stupid bad-girl thoughts. "Yeah. You can, um, groom my hair. With your tongue."

He holds me even closer. "Really?" His voice is low, husky with sleep.

I nod; my hair must be tickling his nose. "Yeah."

Matthew's hot breath crawls around my neck, and he licks a long, sandpaper drag up from my nape to the lowest strands of my dirty-blond hair. It scrapes my skin all the way down to my scalp, and I enjoy the burn and the pull of the papillae on his tongue.

But when he combs my hair, he gags, takes his hand off my stomach, and pulls my hair out of his mouth. "Ugh. That was better in my head."

I giggle. "Hair in your mouth is no fun."

"I don't know how cats do it."

"It's probably because my hair is longer than a buzz cut."

"That's true." He returns to kneading my stomach. "I'm not as bothered on the rare occasion I lick my fur."

I wonder, briefly, if he can reach the fur on his thighs, but I doubt Matthew is flexible enough; nonetheless, the image worms its way through my brain, him casually hiking his leg and dragging his sandpaper tongue throngh the fur covering his inner thigh. I feel some feelings I don't usually feel, but I'm not daring enough to act on them; I let desire pass me by, acknowledging and appreciating that no amount of religious sexual repression has broken my ability to become horny. It's a strange feeling, like a powerful pressure down there, uncomfortable and pleasant at the same time.

Matthew hums, face buried in the curve of my neck. "Emmie."

"Yeah?"

"Do you want to go to prom together?"

I consider it. "I figured you guys don't care about that sort of thing." They're all sorely lacking in school spirit, not that I'm much better outside of the varsity soccer team.

"I'm kinda like 'why not' about it. It's a good excuse to dress up and hang out."

I grin. "So you wanna see me in a pretty dress is what you're saying?"

Matthew hums, holding me close. "And you wouldn't want to see me in a suit?"

I pet his arms and hands more. "You have me there. We should get everybody in on it. It'll be more fun that way."

"Mm. But I'd feel bad for Mark."

"Now why would you feel bad for me?" Mark barges into the room, holding a ladle like a mom with an attitude, but when he sees our precarious position, he grins. "Oh, do I love to see the fruits of my labor!"

"Your labor?!" I'm glad we're presentable.

Mark cocks his hip and an eyebrow. "Who do you think supported your boyfriend all these years?" He puffs his chest and jabs himself with a thumb. "That would be me, baby."

Matthew chuckles, his purrs crackling. "We're thinking about going to prom, but you wouldn't have a date."

Mark frowns, regarding Matthew with a shockingly cold gaze, but he cracks quickly, his eyes squinting and lips quirking up. "You know I don't need a date. I'm an independent dragon man who don't need no woman!"

Matthew huffs a laugh. "Keep telling yourself that."

He whips around and wiggles his narrow hips. "Oh, we have to go shopping!" he says in a poor posh accent. "Suits and ties. And fancy shoes."

"Dinner first," Matthew says, "then we can worry about shopping."

Mark looks over his shoulder, lips pursed. "It'll be ready soon, honey." He winks, blows a kiss, and sashays out, that ladle poised to whip a man.

Lying there in Matthew's arms, I say, "You two are ridiculous."

Matthew rumbles deep in his throat. "I wouldn't have it any other way."

I stare at the racks of sparkly dresses littering one corner of one department store at the mall. "These are kinda . . ." I squint, searching for one word that encapsulates my feelings perfectly.

"Kinda . . .?" Heather prods.

"A lot."

Jenny steps in front of us, chewing gum and regarding the dresses far too long to fit her short frame. "You know, you don't have to get a prom-dress prom dress. It can be any dress." She glances at me, long fake eyelashes giving her a calculating look. "All I know is sequins aren't your thing."

"Not all prom dresses have sequins," Heather says, "and there's nothing wrong with experimenting." She runs her hair behind her ear, a smile playing on her lips. "Sometimes all you have to do is try it on to fall in love."

"We're not shopping for wedding dresses," I grumble.

"You can fall in love with any kind of dress, honey."

And I can't argue; I should try to be positive and embrace my girly side. I want to feel pretty; I know that. And it's for myself as much as it is for anybody else.

Heather grins. "What're you thinking?"

I swear she can read my mind. "I'm thinking . . . green."

"Lime or what?"

"A deep green, but it'll depend on the dress."

She smiles. "Of course."

Jenny huffs. "I know exactly what I'm looking for." She saunters between the racks, losing us in a split second.

"C'mon, honey!" Heather grabs my arm and whisks me away, using her superior height to spot Jenny's petite self.

As she pulls me along, I take passing glances at all the different dresses; they're in all the colors of the rainbow, in different lengths and cuts and levels of glitter coverage, but none of them scream at me to try them on. But I won't lose hope; if nothing else, Heather will scour the whole mall until we find what I'm looking for.

Jenny stops in front of a rack of risqué navy blue dresses; they're floor-length, sparkly, and have a thigh-high leg slit. She rifles through the dresses and pulls out her size, then holds it in front of her. "What do you think?"

Heather taps her cheek. "It'll need to be hemmed, but I love the plunge neckline."

Jenny smirks, admiring her pick. "Could you go get Kyle? I want to get it in a bag before Teddy sees it."

Heather salutes. "Will do!" And she drags me away all over again.

Kyle pays for Jenny's dress with a sleek credit card, gently folds the receipt, and slips it in the pocket of his wallet for safekeeping. He took us to the mall in lieu of our parents under an agreement that they'd pay him back for each of our outfits—basically adult stuff I'm trying not to worry about; Heather already stopped me from agonizing over sales tags three times so far.

Since Heather and I didn't like anything at this store, we leave.

Jenny struts ahead of us, her opaque shopping bag swinging side to side.

Teddy and Kyle follow along, both obviously bored but cooperative.

"Hey, Heather," I say.

"Hmm?" She looks down at me, slowing her stride.

"Why is Teddy here, anyway?"

She gazes forward, eyebrows pinched. "He's security detail."

"Security? Why would we need that?"

Heather smiles like I'm silly for asking. "Certain individuals are less likely to bother me when my hulking brother is around to scare them off."

"Oh." I've never had strangers look at me that way, but I've always had an adult around whenever I've gone shopping. I glance down, walking as fast as I can to keep up with her long legs. "That must be scary."

She whips her long hair back. "It unfortunately comes with the territory." She squints, her voice a near whisper. "It makes me glad I have claws whenever I need them."

Scary . . . I look over my shoulder at Teddy; he's so big he stands more than a head taller than Kyle, and his tight black shirt emphasizes his overgrown pecs, massive biceps, and thick trunk—yeah, I wouldn't want to mess with him, either.

Teddy notices my gaze and gives me a suave smile.

I quickly face forward just as we make it to the next store.

Teddy and Kyle remain outside while we girls peruse our options. We look around for ten minutes, find nothing, and go on our way.

I groan as I sit down at a table in the food court; after two more hours of searching and trying on dresses, Heather and I found our picks: hers, a lacy red halter-top mermaid dress; and mine, a short dark-green A-line dress with floral-patterned lace over the bodice.

Heather eases next to me with a large Chick-fil-A bag; she divvies out bags of chicken sandwiches, boxes of nuggets and tenders, and containers full of waffle-cut fries to each of us. Once she's done, she picks out a fry and says, "So."

I pop a warm nugget in my mouth and chew. "So?"

Heather dips her fry in a tiny container of honey. "We have our dresses; now we need accessories."

I stifle another groan. "We're going to be here another two hours, aren't we?"

Heather pats me on the back. "Cheer up; you're not the only one suffering."

I glance at the two across the table. Kyle seems perfectly fine, but he's probably used to Heather's long shopping sprees by now; Teddy, on the other hand, looks exhausted.

Jenny comes back from the bathroom, sits next to Teddy, and rubs his muscular arm.

He wraps his arm around her shoulders. "I'm suffering, Jenny."

"You'll live," she says. "I might need you to reach for things at the shoe store; they put some stuff way too high."

Teddy smiles stupidly; I imagine he enjoys grabbing things Jenny can't reach. "Are you gonna get heels?"

Jenny closes her smoky eyes. "I'm thinking at least four inches."

"Mm . . ." He rubs her shoulder. "Sounds good."

I wonder if I should try heels, but if I wear something even as short as two inches, I'll end up taller than Matthew. Would that bother him?

Heather blinks at me. "Why the sour face, honey?"

I flatten my lips. "Do you think I should wear flats?"

Heather's eyes narrow. "Did Short Stuff say something?"

I shake my head vigorously. "Not at all. I just don't want to . . . offend him."

Heather grins, looking haughty. "Who knows? Maybe he'd like it."

I consider the possibility, agonize over more chicken nuggets, then say, "I'll ask him." As much as I want to surprise him, some things are better known than possibly reviled, so I take out my phone and ask, *How would you feel about me wearing heels to prom?* I wait impatiently for his reply, eating and staring at the messaging app with my phone on my thigh.

After way too long, he says, *I think you should wear what you want to wear.*

I glare at my phone; that was the most unhelpful answer ever. *Let me rephrase: How would you feel if I was taller than you?*

Matthew immediately says, *That'd be hot, ngl.*

Heather snoops over my shoulder. "Sometimes you have to appreciate a man's simplicity."

I sigh. *Don't I know it.*

Another hour passes searching for shoes. We go store after store until we find the perfect pairs: sparkly silver lace-ups for Jenny; elegant black stiletto sandals with overlapping ankle straps for Heather; and strappy gold block heels for me, because there's no way in hell I'd be able to walk with the teeny-tiny heels my girl friends are accustomed to. And I don't want to talk about the price.

Bags in hand and a spring in her step, Heather says, "Now we need bras."

Jenny nods along. "And accessories."

"Oh, Emily!" Heather grins, a gleam in her eye. "You'd look so cute with something in your hair."

Jenny glances back. "I could do your makeup for you, too."

"No makeup, but I'm not against jewelry." My ears aren't pierced, but a necklace or bracelet could go a long way.

Kyle coughs over Teddy's massive sigh; Jenny's going to owe him so many pets later.

My boobs feel so naked right now. Never in my life have I worn a bra lower than a scoop neck, but here I am, fitted with a hook-back bralette that barely covers my nipples, all in the name of keeping it out of sight under the V-shaped neckline of my pretty green prom dress.

Heather ties the back tight behind me, adjusting the strings into a secure, double-knotted bow. She cards her long fingers over my hair, pulling a few strands out of my low, twisted-bun updo to frame my face; she spent half an hour putting it together and secured the style with a green-and-gold fern-leaf hair comb. "You look beautiful."

"I don't think I've ever looked so pretty in my entire life." I smile like an idiot in the mirror, fiddle with the gold chain bracelet adorning my right wrist, and adjust the matching necklace resting on my collar.

Heather touches up her elaborate updo and puts a fresh layer of lipstick on her red lips.

Jenny hangs massive silver dangle earrings in her ears, her fresh pixie cut allowing them maximum display.

I twirl in front of the mirror, enjoying every angle of myself.

The doorbell rings.

Grace calls, "Coming!" and charges down the stairs, her stomps resounding with each step.

Heather, Jenny, and I finalize any last-minute details, grab our respective heels, and join Grace downstairs; like the rest of us, she's dressed to impress with a fresh marigold dye job, a short purple off-the-shoulder prom dress, black knee-high gladiator sandals, and a ton of ornate jewelry fitting her pastel-goth aesthetic. Timid as ever, she carefully opens the front door.

"O~M~G~!" Mark enters the foyer in a classy burgundy suit. "I've never seen so many lovely ladies in one room!"

"Speak for yourself, Mark." Heather steps close and inspects his fit; along with the red-brown jacket and trousers, he wears a purple tie, brown oxfords, and two gold clips holding the long portion of his hair out of his face, making his pale scar obvious on his lightly tanned skin. "You look surprisingly masculine in a suit."

"Jeez, Heather." He grins. "You have a way with words."

She pats his cheek. "I appreciate the sarcasm, little lizard." Wearing her heels, Heather stands a good five inches over Mark.

He makes a silly face. "Only next to you, Heather . . ." He adjusts his tie and clears his throat. "Anyway"—he bows and winks—"your carriages have arrived."

He leads us outside; the late afternoon sunlight breaks through the clouds, illuminating a row of familiar cars and the boys waiting beside them. Each has on a similar suit: Teddy's is gray with a blue tie; Jack's is black with a red tie; and Matthew's is blue with a green tie. Teddy has a fresh fade and styled his hair with gel; Jack blow-dried his hair, his loose black waves styled in a left-side part; and Matthew . . . Matthew's hair is unlike anything I've seen on him before. His bangs are combed back to reveal his entire face, the rest of his hair pulled behind his head in undulating curls; it must've taken a lot of work to tame his hair so handsomely. Matthew stares at me in awe, and I know my expression mirrors his own.

I try my best to cross the street to his car with womanly grace, and when I make it to his side—I notice he has a small, curled ponytail at the nape of his neck—we remain starstruck. "Did Jack do your hair?" I ask, hoping to clear the air.

Matthew clears his throat, a beautiful blush on his cheeks. "Oh. Yeah. I told him to do whatever he wanted." He nervously touches the hair covering his missing ears. "Do you like it?"

"It looks really nice on you."

He smiles sheepishly. "Your hair looks nice, too." He looks me over, all the way down to my shiny shoes. "You look amazing."

I blush. "Thank you." I glance at his clean oxfords. "You, too."

He tilts my chin up with the tips of his fingers; we smile at each other, nervous and flattered and excited, and share a quick kiss. Matthew leads me around his car and opens the passenger-side door. "Shall we?"

I grin, a giggle bubbling to the surface, and bow inside.

Matthew's car rolls to a stop in the teacher parking lot. He waits for the chaotic electronic song on his playlist to end, then turns off the ignition. He takes a deep breath, glances at me, and reaches over my lap to open the glove compartment; he pulls out a clear container holding a tiny white-flower arrangement with overwhelming green foliage.

I gape. "Oh my God, the boutonniere!" I scramble to open my purse, then let out a resounding sigh of relief when I see it firmly crammed inside the pouch. I take it out and thrust it toward Matthew's chest. "I thought I forgot it."

Matthew chuckles breathlessly, trading my corsage for his boutonniere; he pins the matching arrangement to his left lapel. "Do you want me to put yours on?"

I nod, holding out the open container.

Matthew removes the corsage and carefully slips the elastic around my left wrist. I adjust it after he lets go, and we get out of the car, leaving both of the empty containers inside.

A few parking spots down, Mark climbs out of his truck, a purple boutonniere pinned to his lapel; Grace walks around from the other side, wearing a yellow corsage that matches her hair. She bows nervously, gives him a hug, and trots away, leaving him scratching the back of his head.

We walk up to him. "You gave her a corsage?" I ask.

"Oh, nah." He grins. "My mom got her one as thanks for watching our cat last summer. She thinks every girl should get to feel special on prom night."

Grace came to hang out with her friends from the anime club—Mark agreed to drive her over so she wouldn't have to feel like a third wheel in Jack's car. Her crush on Mark has waned over the years, but she still finds him amazingly attractive.

"Your mom has the right idea." I'm not one to worry about the little details at events like these, but I did feel special when Matthew slipped my corsage on; I bet Grace appreciates the sentiment.

"She has the right idea about a lot of things," Mark says, hands on his hips.

Jack and Teddy pull up as the sun makes its descent; they park and exit their vehicles with Heather and Jenny, respectively. Much like us, the two couples have matching boutonnieres and corsages—red and blue to compliment their ties and dresses. With everyone accounted for, we walk up to the school together, flash our tickets, and wade inside. We're early, so the hallway between the gym and the outdoor courtyard is sparsely populated by a few students and teachers.

Mark walks backward in front of us with his hands behind his head. "We *have* to take a bunch of terrible pictures. Like, the cringiest shit you can imagine."

Jack grins. "For once, I agree with you."

With nobody around to get in our way, we enter the courtyard to take awful photos. We get the expected photos out of the way first: everyone together in a row; each couple side by side; Jack holding Heather in a dip, her long leg held aloft as they gaze at each other; Heather dipping Jack just the same; Teddy carrying Jenny bridal style; Heather bear-hugging me and Jenny from behind; and the boys standing stiff and straight with easy smiles—as soon as they take that last picture, I know by the gleam in their eyes that they're about to act all kinds of extra.

Mark turns to his side, and the rest follow suit; they're laterally stacked in order of height, with Matthew on the far left and Teddy on the far right. A devilish smirk on his face, Mark juts his left knee forward and suggestively pulls his trouser leg up to reveal a colorful patterned sock covering his ankle. "I thought I'd . . . give a little show for the ladies."

"Oh~ How scandalous~" Heather fans her face with her hand. "I haven't seen a good ankle in ages~"

The rest of the boys copy Mark's position, each one wearing silly socks: Matthew has blue socks with green frogs; Mark has black socks with pink flamingos; Jack has salmon socks with red lobsters; and Teddy has gray socks with blue butterflies.

Jenny snorts and snaps a picture of their incredibly sexy ankles.

They move on to bigger and better things. Teddy holds Jack who holds Mark who holds Matthew by his stomach, wearing loving gazes as if each boy before them is their luscious lover. Then Jack, Matthew, and Teddy—in that order—hold Mark up together, the dragon boy himself propping his head up with one hand and holding his hip with the other.

They go on and on and on, pairing off randomly and without discrimination. Matthew and Mark take a picture with their fingers interlocked between their chests, staring into each other's eyes. Teddy and Jack stand back-to-back with their arms crossed in an attempt to look suave. Jack carries Matthew bridal style next to Teddy holding Mark the same way.

We humor them, occasionally joining in or requesting our own silly or romantic pictures, laughing and cheering with abandon; by the time they get tired of it, there are too many people wading around between clusters of cliques and clubs and close friends to take simple pictures without interference.

Mark sighs happily. "Make sure you send everything to everybody. Anyway, I'm off to the gym!" He struts away.

Jenny latches onto Teddy's muscular arm, locking her small fingers between his big ones. "I ought to show you off to my friends."

Teddy grins. "You know I'll be doing the same when you come to my prom next year."

Jenny smiles and tugs him away.

Heather sits down on the short brick retaining wall next to us. "I'll have to do the same with you, Jack."

He sits down next to her, easily wrapping his arm around her waist. "I'll bet." He looks up at me and Matthew. "I figure we'll chill here awhile; I don't have any other friends around here."

"I might want to join Jenny's circle a little later," Heather says. "What about y'all?"

I look at Matthew. "I don't think I ever made you official business with the soccer team."

Matthew glances up and frowns. "Honestly, it was never much of a secret."

"True, but we should mingle anyway; I probably won't see them again once we're off to college." The girls on the soccer team aren't forever friends, but I've played with many of them for years; one last goodbye never hurt.

I lead Matthew away from the courtyard and back into the hall. We do our rounds across the school, talking to acquaintances here and there, snapping photos with classmates and teammates as they come and go, and making small talk with beloved—and not so beloved—teachers and staff we've come to know over the years. I feel sentimental knowing I'll leave this campus in a month, only to return for my brothers on occasion.

Matthew and I step outside for some fresh air. "I'm glad we made it into the same college," I say, watching my step on the worn sidewalk that leads to the car pool lane, "though I hear I'll be the only one living on campus."

Matthew smiles, his eyes reflecting moonlight in beautiful shades of green. "I still can't believe Alex is getting us an apartment."

Feeling more confident in my balance, I dare to look straight ahead. "That's really nice of him. I don't know what you'd do about your moon curse otherwise."

Matthew snorts playfully. "I'd try to get Mark as a permanent roommate, that's what. Or just deal with commuting because NC State is only, what, twenty minutes away?"

I purse my lips. "We drove out there and traffic is kinda crazy. Apparently finding a parking spot is hard, too. And I want to live away from my parents, anyway."

Matthew gazes ahead. "I get that. For me, it's lonely at my house; my parents would only notice I'm gone because the dishes don't wash themselves."

"I still haven't met your dad."

"He works weird hours and holes away downstairs when he's home." Matthew stares at the dark sky. "Maybe he'll show up at our graduation ceremony."

"Maybe?" We stop in front of the stairs.

Matthew shrugs. "I never know if he'll find the time."

I look at my heels. "I hope he does."

Matthew grabs my hand. "Me, too."

We walk back the way we came hand in hand, the trees shivering in the breeze. "Cha-Cha Slide" flows out faintly from the gym, and Matthew leads me to the tree I cornered him against all those years ago.

He whips around to face me, holding my hands in his. "You're so beautiful tonight," he says, his pupils glowing.

"Thank you." I tear my gaze away and lay it on his knuckles; I bring them to my lips, gracing them with a kiss. "I've never known a man as handsome as you."

He grins, a purr rumbling deep within his throat. Swift as a cat, he pulls me close and rearranges our hands, putting my left hand on his right shoulder and his right hand below my left shoulder blade; his left hand grasps my right, our fingers interlocked. "Shall we dance?"

"Here? I don't know how."

He smiles. "Just follow my lead."

I nod, resolutely staring at our feet and the dark dirt below.

Matthew gently pushes my right hand back and moves his left foot forward; it's choreographed enough I instinctively move my right foot back. He swings his right foot forward diagonally; I sweep my left foot back in tandem. Then his left foot joins his right, and I mirror him; and his right foot steps back, and I jerk forward; and his left foot swings back diagonally, and I follow; and his right rejoins his left, back where we started. "It's the box step. Easy, right?"

My heart beats against my ribs. "Uh, yeah."

He pulls me close, our chests touching. "Do you want to keep going?"

I nod.

He smiles and pulls away, giving us a mere foot of distance. And we dance.

Matthew pushes and pulls in that invisible box, guiding me with the faintest pressure of his hands and the confident swing of his feet. We dance in that square of ground until I'm as smooth as I'm going to be.

All of a sudden, he moves the box with me in it.

"Matthew!" I squeal.

He laughs, grinning so wide his canines stick out over his bottom lip. "I've got you."

And he does. He has my everything—my mind, my soul, my spirit—all of it in the palms of his hands.

We twirl at Matthew's inner tempo, forgetting our place in the world until it's just us, the ground, and the tree. He mutters a tune that I vaguely recognize as a famous waltz, each step like a heartbeat. "Da-dum . . . Da-dum . . . Da-dum . . ." In tandem, we revolve around the tree, disturbing the ground with light footwork, the moon our only witness; I lose track of time, caught up in his energy, the ethereal shine of his eyes, and that breathtaking smile on his face.

We dance and dance and dance, long after we flow as one, anticipating each second into eternity.

CHAPTER 38

Together

Matthew

Mark and I scrutinize the image at the bottom of our group chat with Puppy, mouths gaping.

"I knew it," Mark says. "He's that dude Esther kept pestering."

Puppy's selfie has the same shoulder-length gray hair and absurdly long bangs; one blue eye peers out from behind his shaggy curtain. "Does that mean . . . ?"

"I think so . . ."

Sharing a look, we sit back on Mark's leather couch, clear our throats, and grin. Mark takes a selfie of us together, his serrated teeth obvious between his lips, and sends it to the group chat.

Which one's which? Puppy asks.

I'm on the right, Mark says. *Tabby is on the left.*

After a few moments, Puppy says, *I didn't expect you to look so alternative, Tao.*

Obviously annoyed, Mark says, *I didn't expect you to have hentai-protagonist hair.*

I try not to grin. "You didn't have to come at him like that."

Mark flattens his lips. "He was asking for it."

Puppy reacts to Mark's message with a laughing-and-crying emoji. *Wicked scar btw.*

I take out my phone and say, *Don't ask him where he got it. He'll bore you to death.*

Do ask me where I got it, Mark says. *I love telling boring stories.*

Maybe in person, Puppy says, *if I remember to ask.*

Are you still coming down tomorrow? I ask.

Yep, he says. *Hopefully we'll get down there by dinnertime. We could meet up somewhere if you like. Bring Emmie along if she's up to it, though I understand meeting some random dude might be a bit much. Stranger danger and all that.*

She might be busy with her folks, I say. *She has a lot of family coming down for graduation.*

I always forget she has a normal functioning family, Puppy says.

Same, Mark says.

I'm not allowed to forget anymore, I say.

Imagine having a girlfriend, Puppy says.

Couldn't be me, Mark says.

For lack of a better comeback, I send a rolling-eyes emoji.

Mark chuckles and elbows me; I elbow him back.

⁓

Puppy stands next to a slightly taller man near the entrance of a steak house, his excessive bangs pulled back over his head. He's taller than me, which isn't much of a feat, and about the same height as Mark. The other man has a resemblance to him, all long, skinny limbs, short graying hair, and wrinkles born from frowns and smiles—he must be Puppy's dad.

Puppy smiles and waves as we approach. "Hey."

"Hey, bro." Mark saunters up with a grin. "Glad you made it."

"Same. Traffic was pretty bad." He nudges his dad. "Though my old man slept through most of the drive."

Said old man closes his eyes, briefly annoyed. "Dustin, how about you introduce me to your friends."

Puppy's eyebrows shoot up and he laughs awkwardly. "I completely forgot to ask for your real names." He scratches his neck.

"I'm Matthew."

"And I'm Mark." He holds out his hand to Puppy's dad. "And you are?"

The man smiles and shakes his hand. "You can call me Dallas."

Mark says, "Dallas and Dustin, huh?"

Puppy grins. "Like you're much better with Matthew and Mark. Even your gamertags are both *T*s."

Mark shakes his head, holding a hand up in a half shrug. "And it wasn't even intentional." Peering at Puppy, he licks his lips, the prongs of his tongue slipping apart.

Dallas shifts, his bony arms crossed over his slight chest; he stares at Mark's mouth, then glances at me. His phone buzzes in his hand. "Our table's ready."

Puppy perks up, his hair moving oddly, like something shifted up beneath it for a split second. "Good timing; I'm hungry."

We walk inside together, and a host leads us to a freestanding table with four chairs; Mark and I sit across from Dallas and Puppy.

Dallas picks up the drink menu. "Do you mind?"

"Do what you want, Dad," Puppy says. "I'm driving anyway."

Dallas squints at the menu in the faint indoor lighting. With a frown that exaggerates his wrinkles, he pulls out a pair of rimless reading glasses and puts them on. When he finds the drink he wants, Dallas folds the menu and peers over his lens. "Mark, yes?"

Mark looks up from the dinner menu. "Yeah?"

"I was wondering . . . Your hair: Is it natural?"

Mark tries not to gape.

Puppy stiffens.

Wary, Mark says, "Why do you ask?"

Dallas smiles. "I've seen a boy like you before. And no dye job is so thorough."

Mark furrows his red eyebrows, stealing glances at Puppy; silence pervades our slice of the noisy room.

Puppy clears his throat. "Dad, why don't you give us a moment?"

Dallas nods and pushes his chair back. "Order me a Coke." After sliding his bony fingers across the table, he exits our field of view.

Puppy sighs, massaging his brow.

Before he can open his mouth, Mark asks, "Bro, do you know a chick named Esther Woodcock?"

Puppy snaps to attention. "How do you know her?"

Mark leans in. "She's Jack's sister, and she's been suspecting you're a dog person for years." He squints, scrutinizing our long-time friend. "Are you?"

"What the fuck." Puppy also leans in. "Yes. How the fuck are you both also monster people?"

"Don't ask me, bro."

"When you sent that picture, I just about lost my shit."

"You think we didn't feel the same way when we saw you? Esther showed us your graduation photo a year and a half ago thinking she finally had you."

Puppy groans. "Please tell me you didn't tell her anything."

Mark shakes his head. "I didn't plan on it. Jack's sisters are a menace."

Puppy takes a deep breath. "What *are* you guys, anyway?"

"Cat," I say.

"Dragon," Mark says.

"What the fuck, Tao," Puppy says.

Mark squints, his arms held tight across his chest. "Just don't think too hard. Your dad knows?"

Puppy sneers. "Kinda hard to miss your blond kid going gray at nine years old."

"Goddamn, bro."

Our server walks into view and makes a strange face.

All of us smile awkwardly and sit back.

The server introduces himself, takes our drink orders, and leaves.

Dallas returns and eases himself into his chair. "I figure we're all on the same page?"

Sheepishly, Mark says, "Yes, sir."

Dallas smiles. "Please, no need for formalities. Forgive me for prying; I've never met more boys like Dustin before."

Mark scratches his cheek. "You might be meeting a few more of us at our graduation."

"Oh?" Dallas says.

Puppy glowers. "You're shitting me."

Mark shakes his head. "Jack and Lucha are like us."

Puppy sighs. "You know, when I agreed to this whole thing, this isn't what I had in mind."

"I should probably mention Esther will be there, too."

Puppy smacks his face. "Of course she will."

"I've met her before, haven't I?" Dallas asks. "That tall bottle blond?"

"Yeah. We graduated together." Suddenly angry, Puppy jabs a finger at us. "You two better not sell me out to her."

Mark lifts his hands placatingly. "That's on you, bro."

I smile. "Those sisters are stupidly perceptive."

"I keep forgetting he has a million of them," Puppy says.

Dallas smiles, the corners of his eyes crinkling. "You all talk like you've known each other for years."

"That's because we have," Puppy says.

Mark slings his arms behind his head with a big grin. "Distance doesn't make us strangers!"

"Back in my day, all we had were letters." Dallas picks up his dinner menu. "You only knew the people you met at school, church, and work. Maybe a family friend once in a while. And I suppose there were always bar hookups." His eyes stare distantly through his rectangular lenses. "I'm happy I got the opportunity to travel a little. It's hard to find the time."

Puppy elbows him with a smile. "Don't be sappy, Dad."

Dallas grins. "It's my job to embarrass you in front of your friends, is it not?"

Puppy rolls his eyes but doesn't argue.

⟿

Puppy peers around Mark's room from his spot on the leather couch, legs and arms spread wide. "Nice room you got here, Tao."

Mark grins from his gaming chair. "It won't be my room much longer."

Puppy appears to raise an eyebrow from beneath his bangs.

"My mom's fiancé is getting us an apartment."

Puppy grins. "Lucky you; I actually have to pay for mine."

"Damn, bro. I can't believe you actually pay your bills."

"It's not as fun as it sounds."

Mark props his chin up in his hands. "So are you one of those permanent-ears-and-tail types?"

Puppy crosses his ankle over his knee. "That's a type?"

Perched on Mark's desk chair, I let my ears out of my hair.

Puppy gazes at them, lips parted, then smirks; he grabs the tip of and pulls out one floppy dog ear covered in wavy gray fur. "Mine blend in easy, but it's tough to stop them from perking at every little sound." He lets the appendage go, and it flops against the side of his head; he doesn't try to hide it, but the texture matches so well with his hair that it's difficult to make out.

"I wish I could keep my ears relaxed all day; mine get sore." I pull my tail out from around my torso. "Same with my tail."

Puppy nods. "I have to keep my tail tucked between my legs all day. It puts me in a mood, honestly."

"You can take it out if you want," Mark says. "Everybody here knows, and Alex is one of us."

Puppy's ears perk up out of his hair, displaying a rounded tri-angular shape. He stands, unbuckles the fabric belt holding up his loose cargo shorts, and drops his pants to his knees; the tip of his tail covers the crotch of his boxers. Once it uncurls from between his legs, he pulls his pants back up, buckles his belt, and sits back down. He visibly relaxes, sinking into the worn cushions of the couch. "If I didn't have this thing to worry about, I'd wear skinny jeans more often."

Mark makes a funny face. "Skinny jeans? Really?"

Puppy grins. "I'd look like an emo boy straight out of Hot Topic."

Mark leans back in his chair, his hands behind his head. "You'd fit right in with your crazy bangs."

"Like you're any better." He chuckles.

Suddenly, the doorbell rings; Puppy and I perk our ears and turn our heads toward the source. The front door creaks open, and Miss Ashley says, "Oh, hello, Emily."

"Hi, Miss Ashley! Are Matthew and Mark home?"

"They're in his room, first door down the hall on the right."

"Thank you!" She stomps across the floor and bursts into Mark's room before we have time to react.

Puppy stares, his perked ears obvious.

Emily stares back, blinks, looks at me with my ears and tail out, looks back at Puppy, and slaps her face. "Of course he's a monster boy. Why wouldn't he be?"

Mark crosses his arms, smiling. "Did your mother never teach you how to knock, Emmie?"

"Hmph." Emily puffs out her chest and crosses her arms with a glower. "Maybe I'm just excited to meet Puppy in person." She withers, returning her attention to Puppy. "I'm so sorry I couldn't make it to dinner last night. I had lots of aunts and uncles and cousins over yesterday."

"Oh, uh . . ." Puppy straightens out, carefully relaxing his ears. "It's no big deal, Emmie." He glances at me and Mark. "I didn't expect you knew everything already."

"Do you remember how we disappeared for a month when *Dark Souls III* came out?"

Puppy's ears perk again. "Well, yeah."

"Long story short, we had a fight about the whole monster-people thing." Emily smiles beautifully. "We got over it, though."

Puppy scratches his ear. "That explains a lot."

Emily rounds on us again. "Anyway, what are your plans for today? I'm totally free now that church is over."

Mark and I share a look and shrug.

"That's really up to Puppy," Mark says.

We look at him.

Puppy smiles awkwardly, as much at a loss as the rest of us.

I hold Emily's hand as we wade through the Sunday lunch crowd at the mall. Puppy and Mark saunter ahead of us, long and lanky and lithe, talking each other's heads off about things I'll hear about later. I don't worry about keeping up with them, instead enjoying Emily's presence at my side. We're on our way to the food court for an early lunch before we hit up the few hobby shops dotting the building.

As we round the bend, I survey the jewelry stores displaying cases of luxury watches and wedding rings, glance at Emily's cute face, and lengthen my stride to catch up with our friends.

Standing in a long line full of students in dark-green caps and gowns, I look for Dad's face. Our friends and families watch from the mass of foldable chairs in the Raleigh Convention Center: Miss Ashley, Alex, Mr. Brown, Kyle, Gideon, and Tyler surround Dallas, talking in hushed voices; Puppy tries to ignore Esther leaning so close to him her shoulder brushes his; Heather, Jack, Teddy, and Jenny sit nearby, the Woodcocks and Craig taking up the row behind them; and Emily's family sits toward the front, Noah kicking his feet while Connor glowers at the unfairness of it all.

I sweep the other side, my gaze gliding over thousands of unimportant faces, through all the family and friends waiting for their precious senior to walk the stage, and find his unassuming face; far in the back, next to my overdressed mom, sits Dad. He watches with calculating blue eyes, his red tie loose over his mostly buttoned dress shirt.

The valedictorian finishes her speech, and the principal takes the stage; he calls the first name, and the line shuffles forward. Each exchange is short: the student walks up, accepts their diploma holder, shakes the principal's hand, and walks offstage, hoping not to trip on their heels. After half the alphabet spills out, Mark takes the stage, earning some shouts from random acquaintances he's made over the years; he exits with snakelike grace, and the line shuffles on.

After another long stretch of endless moments, the principal calls my name. I step up on the stage, accept my reward for surviving four meaningless years of schooling, and stride to the stairs leading down. I find my father's face graced with a rare smile and join those before me backstage.

The ceremony over, I find Mark and Emily inside the huge crowds swarming the massive room. In the distance, Grace celebrates with her friends while she waits for her family to find her.

"Phew; glad that's over with." Mark pulls his cap off, fixes his hair, and unzips his gown.

Emily does the same, revealing a cute yellow sundress underneath.

"Tao!"

Mark turns around.

Puppy speed walks toward us, Esther hot on his heels.

"Bro—"

Puppy runs behind Mark, holds his shoulders, and uses him as a blockade between him and his bleached blond nemesis. "Save me!"

"Esther . . ." Mark gives her a withering glare.

Esther puts her hands behind her back and whistles.

"C'mon, Esther." Craig saunters up behind her. "Give him a break."

Esther grimaces. "Ugh, fine . . ." She walks away.

"I swear . . ." Craig shakes his head. "She never learns."

"Thanks, dude," Puppy says.

"No problem, man," Craig says. "I don't blame you one bit for wanting to stay out of that mess."

Mark grins. "Enjoying the family you might marry into?"

Craig slumps. "I have to tell myself every day that Olive is worth the trouble. It's not her fault her family is obnoxious." He shakes his head. "Anyway, future-son-in-law business calls." He leaves in Grace's direction.

Mom finds us next. She places a large gift bag on the floor, then rifles through her purse.

"Where's Dad?" I ask.

She pulls lipstick and a pocket mirror out. "He went to work. You know how he is about taking time off."

"So he woke up, came, and left?"

Mom shrugs and reapplies lipstick while looking through her tiny mirror.

I'm disappointed even though I expected him to do what he always does.

Mom flattens her lips to rub her lipstick in, then puts both items back in her purse. She picks up the gift bag and hands it to me. "He got this for you. He said it's a graduation present."

I take the bag from her but don't look inside.

Miss Ashley, Alex, and Dallas join us. "Lisa! I haven't seen you in ages!" Miss Ashley notices my glum expression and puts on a saccharine smile.

Mom suppresses her surprise and turns around. "Ashley! It's been too long!" She looks Alex up and down. "And, goodness, who's this you've brought with you?"

Alex smiles awkwardly and holds out a hand. "I'm Ashley's fiancé. You must be Matthew's mother."

Mom shakes his hand with both of hers, perhaps a little too reverently. "Oh, we do have a resemblance." She slowly lets go of his hand. "David would've been with me, but he had to run off to the hospital."

Alex gapes. "Is he okay?"

Mom laughs. "He's a surgeon, dear. A heart surgeon. He's a bit of a workaholic, but you can't blame a doctor for wanting to save lives."

Alex pinches his expression.

Miss Ashley maintains her smile. "It's such a shame he couldn't make some time today. Do you have any plans this afternoon?"

"Oh, sure. I'm going to meet up with some friends for a glass of wine and some fine dining. May as well since we're already downtown for the evening." Mom checks the time on her phone. "Speaking of, I'm supposed to meet them in a few minutes. It was nice talking to you again." She smiles at Alex in an unsavory way. "And meeting you, dear." Then she disappears between the crowds.

Miss Ashley watches her go, her smile growing on her face until she bursts out laughing. "Oh my gosh, I'm sorry, I shouldn't laugh." But she keeps giggling.

Mark smiles awkwardly. "It was the doctor comment, wasn't it?"

Miss Ashley nods.

"She was looking at me weird," Alex says.

"I'll refrain from commenting," Dallas says.

Emily grabs my hand, catching my attention. "I'm sorry your dad went to work."

I lock my fingers between hers and squeeze softly. "Yeah. I wanted him to meet you."

She pulls close so we're shoulder to shoulder. "Next time."

I smile. "You've met all the important people, anyway."

She smiles back.

Tyler chugs an entire glass of water without taking a single breath.

I pop a loaded Tater Tot in my mouth, totally amazed by the spectacle.

"You good, dude?" Gideon asks.

Tyler leans back, eyes half-lidded. "Being landlocked sucks."

"How long are you guys staying down, again?" Mark asks, grabbing another Tot.

"Three days," Tyler says, "so we're heading back on Wednesday."

Gideon looks at Puppy. "What about you, dude?"

"My dad and I are also leaving on Wednesday."

Mark, Puppy, Tyler, Gideon, and I went to a sports bar after everybody figured out postgraduation plans. Most of our other friends had family responsibilities to attend to, considering Emily and Grace were fellow graduates, and Miss Ashley took her friends, including Dallas, out to dinner, leaving us to our devices.

Mark groans. "Man, we'll have to find shit to do."

Puppy massages his brow from under his bangs. "I'm too exhausted to think."

Mark grimaces. "Esther really put you through it, huh?"

Puppy sinks into the booth. "It's all your fault, bro."

"Don't blame me!"

Gideon chuckles. "You really weren't kidding with those sisters, but the one with the half-shaved head seemed nice enough."

"She's going to our college, too," Tyler says.

"Good luck," Puppy says. "I'm taking my happy ass back to Maryland and never coming back."

I snort. "We'll visit you next time, so you won't have to worry."

Puppy gives a thumbs-up.

"Are you two coming back to the beach this year?" Tyler asks.

"Probably," Mark says, "but maybe not until August because we have a lot going on this summer."

"Fair enough. Just text us and we'll be around."

Gideon grins. "He likes any excuse to be in that beach house."

"How do you even afford that thing?" Mark asks.

"My parents are rich as fuck," Tyler says. "I don't pay for shit."

"Makes me lucky to be his friend, right?" Gideon says.

"You should appreciate me more. I gave you a whole-ass apartment, dude."

"Don't forget I do the cleaning." Gideon smiles. "And the cooking."

"At least I clean the bathroom." Tyler grabs his empty glass. "I need more water."

As if waiting for that very moment, our waitress flies by, refills our drinks, and takes our orders. She looks like your average college girl working hard for extra cash to get through her years of schooling. Although my parents take care of everything for me and will continue to do so, I want to try working for once in my life.

While everyone is busy ordering dinner, I look inside Dad's gift bag; there's a large gift-wrapped box inside.

"I'm curious," Mark says. "What's in there?"

I shrug, pull it out, and tear off the wrapping. "It's a laptop."

"Damn, I gotta get one of those."

"You'll need it," Tyler says. "Lots of classes require them."

"Not to mention ebooks are cheaper," Gideon says.

"Man, I'm glad I'm done with all that shit," Puppy says.

"One more year to go," Tyler says.

"Two for me," Gideon says.

"Make that twelve . . . ," I say.

Mark pats my back. "You did it to yourself, bro."

I sigh because he's right.

Alex, Teddy, Jack, and Mr. Brown drop a used chocolate-brown couch in front of our apartment living room wall.

"There we go." Alex stretches his back. "Everything's accounted for." He turns to Mr. Brown. "Thanks for helping us move everything, Bobby."

"Hey, it was no problem," Mr. Brown says. "Especially after y'all helped with Heather's stuff last year."

Jack and Teddy collapse on the couch.

"Are y'all gonna hang out for a bit?" Mr. Brown asks.

"Probably," Teddy says.

"We'll drive you guys home later," Mark says.

"I'll leave y'all to it." Mr. Brown waves goodbye and leaves the apartment.

Alex looks everything over one last time. "Call me if you have any problems. Have fun!" He also leaves.

Mark locks the door behind him, then crashes on the couch between Jack and Teddy. "Man, this is great." Smiling wide, he goes active.

Jack puts his feet up on Alex's old coffee table. "I might crash here all the time if you let me."

"I don't blame you, bro."

I look at the empty balcony attached to our second-floor apartment; it's made of concrete, has a black metal railing, and lacks a cover. There's a good view of the center gazebo between our building and the one across from us, and the sun shines perfectly overhead.

I grab my laptop, squeeze between Mark and Jack, and pull out my wallet.

"Already online shopping?" Mark asks.

"I want to furnish the balcony," I say. "We both like sunning."

Mark melts into the couch. "True . . ." He watches me shop over my shoulder.

The entire time, half my brain is on a different purchase entirely.

Facing the mirror hanging over my bedroom door, I tighten my green tie around my neck, straighten out my blue jacket, and smile, ready to drive to the courthouse in half an hour. Since I have time to spare, I grab the black ring box off my desk, open the balcony door behind the dining room table, and step out into the summer heat; I place the box on a tall round table and kick back in a cheap patio chair I bought a month ago.

I close my eyes and soak in the sun, then gaze at the perfect blue sky and its lazy white clouds; in the distance, the first-quarter moon hangs beyond the trees.

I take the ring box into my hands, gently snap it open, and carefully remove the precious cargo nestled in the fabric folds within. I hold up the thin gold ring between my index finger and thumb, the tiny emeralds set flush inside glinting green in the sun.

Mark steps outside in his burgundy suit and settles in the chair on the other side of the table. "That's the ring?"

"Yeah."

He smirks, closing his eyes. "When are you gonna give it to her?"

I rotate the ring encasing the moon. "Maybe . . . at the beach."

"That's so sappy." Mark stretches his legs out, crossing one foot over the other, and gazes at the moon. "But I bet she'll love it."

I hold the ring in my lap. "I hope so."

We sun in a comfortable silence, waiting for the bell to toll.

His phone finally rings. "Time to go."

I put the ring back in its box, place the box back on my desk, and rejoin Mark in the living room.

"I hope I don't cry." He unlocks the door, and we step outside.

"I think I will cry."

Mark stares at the sky as we walk to my car.

With one last glance at the moon, I get in the driver's seat and wait for Mark to buckle up. A slow beat drones out of the speakers, something ambient and quiet to prepare me for the future. I take a deep breath, pull out of the parking lot, and drive down the road.

Characters

Matthew David Stroud – born March 17, 2000; male; 5'5"; blue eyes; brown hair; cat person (domestic short-hair); White

Mark Tao Koenigsegg – born December 25, 1999; male; 5'10"; yellow eyes; red hair; dragon person (medieval European drake); White (⅛ Chinese)

John Eliza Woodcock VII – born June 9, 2001; male; 6'3"; brown eyes; black hair; rabbit person (Havana rabbit); White

Emily Clementine Thompson – born May 9, 2000; female; 5'4"; hazel eyes; blond hair; human; White

Ashley Eris Koenigsegg – born November 21, 1969; female; 5'6"; brown eyes; black hair; human; ¾ White, ¼ Chinese

Chen Tao – born March 13, 1896; died August 9, 1988; male; 5'4"; brown eyes; black hair; human; Chinese

George William Koenigsegg – born October 19, 1968; died May 27, 2012; male; 5'9"; gray eyes; brown hair; human; White

Connor Jeremiah Thompson – born August 12, 2002; male; 5'9"; brown eyes; brown hair; human; White

Noah Blake Thompson – born April 5, 2005; male; 5'7"; hazel eyes; blond hair; human; White

Alexander Nathaniel Delgado – born August 8, 1970; male; 6'0"; green eyes; brown hair; wolf person (Eurasian wolf); ½ White, ½ Mexican American

Esther Harrison Woodcock – born April 20, 1994; female; 5'8"; brown eyes; black hair; human; White

Delilah Patricia Woodcock – born April 28, 1967; female; 5'8"; brown eyes; black hair; human; White

John Eliza Woodcock VI – born July 14, 1962; male; 5'6"; brown eyes; black hair; human; White

Bobby Oscar Brown – born January 6, 1965; male; 6'2"; brown eyes; blond hair; human; White

Luke Oscar Brown – born January 15, 2001; male; 6'5"; brown eyes; blond hair; bear person (grizzly); White

Jennifer Abigail Woodcock – born June 9, 2001; female; 5'2"; brown eyes; black hair; human; White

Olive Bianca Woodcock – born October 27, 1990; female; 5'4"; brown eyes; brown hair; human; White

Ruth Petunia Woodcock – born July 7, 1992; female; 5'6"; brown eyes; brown hair; human; White

Mary Annabelle Woodcock – born February 22, 1996; female; 5'7"; brown eyes; black hair; human; White

Hope Veronica Woodcock – born November 3, 1997; female; 5'4"; brown eyes; black hair; human; White

Grace Alice Woodcock – born September 30, 1999; female; 5'3"; brown eyes; black hair; human; White

Peter Quincy Baldwin IV – born June 12, 2001; male; 5'3"; brown eyes; black hair; human; White

Lisa Holly Stroud – born December 29, 1975; female; 5'0"; blue eyes; brown hair; human; White

Thomas Harley Harrison – born May 17, 1927; male; 5'7"; blue eyes; white hair; human; White

Margaret Jolene Harrison – born September 24, 1928; female; 4'10"; blue eyes; white hair; human, White

Tyler Ludwig McGill – born February 11, 1997; male; 5'11"; brown eyes; brown hair; shark person (sand tiger shark); White

Gideon del Rosario Caldwell – born November 18, 1996; male; 5'7"; red eyes; half-brown, half-white hair; plover person (killdeer); ½ White, ½ Filipino American

Courtney Ulysses Taylor – born May 4, 1997; female; 5'5"; hazel eyes; brown hair; sorceress; White

Kyle Adrian Ratcliffe – born September 11, 1964; male; 5'8"; brown eyes; gray hair; opossum person (Virginia opossum); ½ White

Julia Rivers – born July 31, 1968; female; 5'1"; blue eyes; black hair; sorceress; Roma

Dustin Carter Williams – born August 1, 1994; male; 5'10"; blue eyes; gray hair; dog person (Weimardoodle); White

Heather Anastasia Brown – born January 15, 2001; female; 6'0"; brown eyes; blond hair; bear person (grizzly); White

Georgia Hannah Thompson – born June 2, 1979; female; 5'4"; brown eyes; brown hair; human; White

Ronald Timothy Thompson – born October 10, 1976; male; 5'9"; hazel eyes; blond hair; human; White

Jose Hernandez Ramos – born March 26, 1947; male; 5'7"; brown eyes; gray hair; human; Spanish

Ana Maria Rubio Castillo – born July 23, 1950; female; 5'9"; brown eyes; gray hair; human; Spanish

Ruby Anastasia Brown – born October 16, 1973; female; 5'10"; brown eyes; red hair; human; White

Craig Rock Smith – born February 2, 1988; male; 5'11"; green eyes; green hair; crocodile person (mugger); White

Jacob Amsted Rausch – born April 23, 1965; male; 5'6"; orange eyes; gray hair; octopus person (giant Pacific octopus); White

Barbara Katherine Shelby – born December 3, 1967; female; 5'6"; brown eyes; brown hair; human; White

Charles Dallas Williams – born September 27, 1964; male; 5'11"; blue eyes; gray hair; human; White

David Gregory Stroud – born December 13, 1964; male; 5'5"; blue eyes; brown hair; human; White

About the Author

Sithia Queen is an author, artist, and businesswoman. Her writing primarily revolves around middle-class monster people and their day-to-day struggles with body image, mental health, and interpersonal relationships. When she isn't writing, she spends her time reading, playing video games, and roaming the internet. She lives in West Virginia with her husband and her cats.

Website: https://sithiaqueen.com
Instagram: @sithiaqueen

www.ingramcontent.com/pod-product-compliance
Lightning Source LLC
Chambersburg PA
CBHW032058310726
48972CB00001B/11